The Salem Frigate

BOOKS BY JOHN JENNINGS

The Salem Frigate

The Shadow and the Glory

Gentleman Ranker

Call the New World

Next to Valour

THE

Salem *Frigate.*

TAKE NOTICE!

YE Sons of Freedom ! all true lovers of the Liberty of your Country! ſtep forth, and give your aſſiſtance in building the Frigate, to oppoſe French inſolence and piracy. Let every man in poſſeſſion of a *White Oak Tree*, be ambitious to be foremoſt in hurrying down the timber to Salem, and fill the complement wanting, where the noble ſtructure is to be fabricated, to maintain your rights upon the Seas, and make the name of America reſpected among the nations of the world. Your largeſt and longeſt trees are wanted, and the arms of them for Knees and Riſing Timber. Four trees are wanted for the Keel, which all together will meaſure 146 feet in length, and hew 16 inches ſquare. Pleaſe to call on the Subſcriber, who wants to make contracts for large or ſmall quantities, as may ſuit beſt, and will pay the READY CASH.

ENOS BRIGGS.

SALEM, NOV. 23, 1798.

Facsimile of the first appeal for *Essex* timber

THE

Salem Frigate

A NOVEL

BY

JOHN JENNINGS

DOUBLEDAY & COMPANY, INC.

Garden City, New York, 1946

For
NANA
With Love

FOREWORD

SOME REASON, it seems to me, should be given for the telling of this tale—lest I be accused of having roused the dead past to no purpose. What is done is done, it may be said, and nothing is served by reopening old wounds. However, granted that after the event it is often easy to see how a thing might have been better done, I submit that this is not the cause of my writing.

In part I have undertaken the tale in order that those who are now close about me may have a clear understanding of all that took place. Of a small part each of them knows something. But of the entire story there is but one who knows all—and even she may yet be bewildered by its ramifications. In part, too, I have undertaken to set it all down so that I myself might see the whole sequence of events in true perspective; that I might not judge too harshly what others have done, and that I might not, in my own mind, take too much credit to myself. Finally, I think, I have written it by way of some small penance for the wrongs that I myself may have done—for I have long since come to the realization that there is no one of us who is wholly good or wholly bad.

Had I had any notion, at the time, that I would one day come to write it, no doubt I would have kept a journal. But the plain truth is that I am not the sort who does such things, save under the stress of official duty, and then the entries are like to make poor reading. During each of my voyages, of course, as well as during my tours of duty ashore, I was required by the Regulations for the Government of the Navy to keep an official record, and these logs—with the exception of that kept on board the *Philadelphia* during her ill-starred cruise to the Mediterranean and that of the *Essex* on her last voyage, which no longer exist —are in the custody of the Navy Department at Washington.

I have used them only to refresh my memory on certain points, for they are musty going.

But even had I kept a journal of the entire period, I doubt it would have served; for what I have here attempted is not my own story alone, but actually several. My tale, of course, runs through the whole as a connecting thread. It is little more. Overshadowing it, it seems to me, is the story of the *Essex* through its brief career. And paralleling this is the story of Ben Price. Interwoven are the stories of Patience Nowell and Selina Hackett, while snatches of the tales of others—of Porter and Preble and Bainbridge, of Hamet, the dragomen, and Jorah, the little Arab wench to whom I owe so much—all lend color to the pattern.

All of this I have attempted to tell with justice to others as well as to myself. It is my hope that what I have set down will be looked upon as fair to them, in all the circumstances, and not be judged to have been written too greatly in the light of "Poor Tom!"

> T. TISDALL
> Surgeon, USN.
> Late of the **UNITED STATES FRIGATE** *ESSEX*

Salem, Massachusetts,
1 December, 1816

CONTENTS

			PAGE
I.	SALEM		3
II.	THE FRIGATE		149
III.	TRIPOLI		221
IV.	FREE TRADE AND SAILORS' RIGHTS		387

I

Salem

IT BEGAN, for me at least, on a blustering April night, now seventeen years and more ago, in the year 1799, when, making my way homeward in the darkness, with my fists crammed deep in my pockets and my collar turned up about my ears, my coat-tails whipped in between my buttocks in a way that is still uncomfortable to remember, I stumbled upon him lying half frozen and unconscious in the icy gutter, as naked as the day his mother bore him, albeit a great deal greater grown.

It was a foul night; not such as you might expect of the season. By rights the touch of spring should have been in the air. It was the time of year when the lilacs should be coming into bud and the violets and the trillium should begin to show in the woods. Instead it was bitter cold. The wind came in off the Atlantic laden with snow and with a bite that struck through fur and cloth to nip at the cringing flesh underneath. Winter had returned and was doing its spiteful worst to wreak vengeance on a world long since grown weary of it. It blanketed the land in white, and blew a shroud of misty flakes across the harbor like a ghostly veil. It drove the sea spume and sleet in from the open ocean, and piled the seas like foamy mountains upon the grim headlands of the Cape. Sailors ashore that night gave thanks for a snug berth and a warm hearth. In town the streets were filled from gutter to gutter with rushing, trickling, freezing, ankle-deep slush, and the storm had laid a coating of ice, like a sheath of glass, upon every surface, making a death-trap of each cobble and curb and doorstep in Salem.

It was not a night to be abroad, even clothed and in one's right mind. That I was out in it was due not to inclination but rather to the fact that I had stayed late, working, at the ship-yard when all other than myself had long since gone. Inside the yard office, which was my post of duty, there was no interference with the day's routine. With a little, round potbellied stove to keep the room warm, a high stool on which to perch, and a desk at which to work, there was no reason for me to give over. Consequently I stayed my time, and something over, for upon one point I was bound: if I could not be at least a poor physician I could most certainly be a good clerk, and Enos Briggs's account books were in a state to need my best attention.

So it happened that it was dark when I turned the key in the door and set my back to the wind and my face toward home.

The first warning I had of him was when the toe of my boot came up with something solid lying athwart my path. I tripped and went down upon hands and knees in the darkness, with my sleeves in slush up to the elbows and the tails of my coat and the knees of my breeches all sopped in muck in a manner to make a saint swear.

It was as well that none of the elders of Salem could hear my remarks as I groped, on all fours, for the thing that had tumbled me. I had some notion that it was a branch, overburdened with ice and torn from a near-by tree by the storm; and it was my intention to take it up and hurl it into the harbor when I found it. Imagine my astonishment, then, when my searching hands came in contact not with any branch at all, but a knee; bare and cold and clammy, but unmistakably a knee. My left hand, then feeling downward in haste, discovered cold calf and bony, hairy shin, while my right, groping in the opposite direction, found first a thigh, smooth and muscular and of a length to indicate that its owner was at least tall, and above that came upon more private parts which left no doubt in my mind that what I had stumbled upon was a man, lying there as bare as Adam and as cold and wet as any halibut ever fished up from off the Newfoundland Bank.

The shock of my discovery was so great that I must have squatted beside him for a full minute, my hands rooted to his chill flesh, utterly without thought. It is a startling thing to come suddenly upon a naked body in the dark of a stormy night. Then gradually, as my senses returned to me, I remember thinking that he must be dead, for he lay with his legs athwart the walkway and his body in the gutter, in such a way that the water and slush and ice backed up behind him as if he were a dam, while the overflow gurgled and sucked about his hinder parts like a millrace and made a miniature spillway across his throat. But then, of a sudden, I called to mind a saying of Dr. Leeds's, that a man wasn't dead till you'd proved

him so, and at that I made haste to fish him out of the gutter
and fell to making an examination.

An ear to his chest proved wholly unsatisfactory. Such was
my excitement that I could not tell whether the bumping I
heard came from his heart or my own. As to whether or not he
was breathing, it was all but impossible in that howling gale to
tell. But it seemed to me that his pulse showed some faint
flutter of life, and with this encouragement I made haste to
strip off my greatcoat and wrap it about him. What protection
the coat was to him, I must say, I am now uncertain, for it was
already wet from my tumble, and he, being limp as a rag, was
scarcely co-operative. By the time I had him wound in it both
he and the coat were as soggy and slush-soaked as the gutter
from which I had taken him.

My next problem was to lift him like a meal sack, across my
shoulder, for he was too heavy to manage in any other way.
Relaxed as he was, this was no easy task. No sooner would I
get his arms up over my shoulder than his head would loll back
with a snap that was fit to crack his neck. And then, when I had
placed his chin upon my neck in precarious balance, and prepared to lift his torso up across my shoulder, his heels would
slide down between my feet, and we would go down together
all of a heap; or my own foot would slip off into the gutter and
I would go down on one knee, to fill my boots and breeches
fair to the crotch with water that icy it caught the breath in my
throat. In the end, I managed to get him up across one shoulder,
with his feet dangling down before me and his head behind.
Had he been conscious, I doubt he would have thought it the
most comfortable mode of carriage possible, but luckily for
me, he was in no case to protest at the moment. In this fashion
we made the short remaining journey from the spot where I
had come upon him, in lower Derby Street, to my lodgings on
Daniels Street.

Now, it may seem strange that I should choose to carry this
stranger, whom I had found lying naked in the gutter, into my
own lodgings rather than to any one of the brightly lighted,
beer-scented little water-front ordinaries that stood as nigh if
not nigher to the place where I had come upon him. But I was
acting purely upon instinct.

In the first place, I was little more than a stranger in town,

having come there but a scant six weeks since, and in strange
surroundings a man turns naturally in an emergency to that
which is most familiar to him. In the second place, what little I
knew of them led me to view these Derby Street ordinaries only
with suspicion. Even staid Salem has its share of crimps, and it
seemed to me better than an even possibility that it was out of
one of these very dens that he had come upon his present misfortune. Doubtless, I told myself, he was also a stranger in the
town, who had unwittingly fallen among thieves. They, after
robbing and stripping him, had in all likelihood been in the very
act of spiriting him on board one of the ships in the harbor
when my approach had interrupted them.

As a theory this had its weaknesses. Still, as a newcomer, I
was scarcely in a position to judge, and the obvious fact remained that, whatever the cause, he needed my help, and that
help could be best given in my own quarters. When I came to
the door I thundered upon it, hoping that my landlord, Samuel
Nowell, a carpenter at the shipyard, might be well home before
me and would give me a hand. As luck would have it, however,
it was not he but his daughter, Patience, who let me in.

"You are late," she began, teasing me and no doubt meaning
to chide me that I had kept supper waiting, though her smile
belied her severity. Then all at once she caught sight of my
burden, and her eyes flew wide in alarm.

"Oh!" she cried. "Good Lord defend us! What———"

At any other time I might have been tempted to linger on the
doorstep and admire the picture, for, standing there with the
candlelight behind her making a red-gold halo of her hair and
outlining her figure, she was a sight to quicken the pulse of any
man not altogether senile. But for the moment I was too preoccupied to have eyes for such matters. I glanced down at the
feet and hairy calves that protruded from beneath my great-
coat, aware that lying in the street had left them none too clean.
Neither was my coat adequate covering. With my free hand I
adjusted the coattails to cover thighs and bottom and at the
same time slipped past her into the hall.

"Some poor devil," I said, "come by ill use in Derby Street.
I stumbled on him in the darkness. He'll die if we do not care
for him."

She shrank back in natural horror. It occurred to me that
she was prettier than ever in her concern.

"What will you do, Tom?" she asked. "How——"

I paused with one foot on the stair.

"I'll put him in my bed," I said shortly. "Be a good child, Pat, and fetch hot water and brandy. We'll see if we can revive him. Where's your grandfather?"

"He's supped and gone off to the Ship and Anchor," she told me.

I was glad to see that a fire had been lit and that my room was cheerful and warm. I managed to get my coat off my limp friend and stretched him out on the bed, covering him with warm blankets. A hasty examination then revealed that, wonderfully enough, despite his exposure, there was nowhere upon him any spot of the telltale white of frozen flesh. I judged that the running water had prevented downright freezing. At the same time I was aware that it was not necessary that his outer parts be frozen in order for him to die of the cold. For the moment the best I could do for him was to dry him thoroughly and see that he was warmly covered.

Having seen to these details, I made a further more thorough examination, which revealed upon his head, close behind his right ear, an ugly black-and-blue lump and a jagged white-edged cut from which seeped a thin trickle of blood. Plainly it was the work of some sort of bludgeon, and it left no doubt as to the cause of his unconsciousness. I felt for indications that the bone beneath was cracked or broken, but could discover none. It took but a moment to wash and bind the cut, and only then did I feel free to stand back and allow myself a good look at him.

I would not have said, from the look of him, that he was the sort one would ordinarily find brawling in sailors' taverns. He was fairly tall, perhaps an inch or two above my own height, which is not too inconsiderable. He was well made, with broad shoulders and a slim, tapering waist, flat hips and groin, and long, muscular thighs. His hands and feet were well shaped and slender; his features dark and aristocratically narrow. His age I guessed to be in the neighborhood of twenty-two or -three. His dark brown hair clung in rain-soaked ringlets about his well-shaped skull, emphasizing the angularity of his face, the prominence of his arching nose, the high, wide cheekbones, and the lean length of his jaw. Seen in repose, it was a strong face;

a handsome, even guileless face, save for a slightly crooked eyebrow that gave it a somewhat quizzical expression. There was no hint in it now of the slightly mocking expression that I was later to find characterized its hours of animation.

It seemed to me that Patience was a long time fetching the brandy and water I had called for. In the meantime I was physician enough to relieve him of an ounce or two of blood, and I was thus engaged when she entered.

"I had to bring the kettle to a boil," she began, then broke off abruptly. "What are you doing?"

"Bleeding him," I told her over my shoulder.

"As if he hadn't lost enough blood already!" she cried scornfully. "See how pale he looks, the poor creature!"

"He'll look better when I finish this," I said. "A man's color has naught to do with the amount of blood in him. Reach me yon noggin and bottle."

I closed the lancet wound and checked the flow of blood. Next I poured out a generous potion of brandy. For the moment I thought it best not to water it. Instead I raised his head in one arm and with my other hand lifted the mug to his lips.

"Don't choke him," she warned me.

I looked for results, but scarcely such as I achieved. Doubtless he was in the very nick of coming round when I poured the drink between his teeth, for even as I did so his hand fluttered on the counterpane and at the same time he coughed, spraying me well with brandy, sputtered, gagged, and opened his eyes.

For a moment he was unable to speak, but could only lie clutching and gasping, his face purple, his eyes watering. But after an instant he found his voice and glared at me.

"In God's name," he sputtered, "what do you mean to do, drown me?"

I stood back and let him fall amid the pillows, as much piqued, I must confess, by Patience's half-stifled laughter as by his ungracious reception of my efforts.

"Happy the man," I said, "can drown in good brandy. Most folk I know would relish the opportunity. But perhaps you'd rather I kicked you back into the street to drown in the ice water I found you in?"

He rolled an eye at me that was at once both baleful and sardonic.

"That's a matter of opinion," said he between fits of coughing, "both as regards the quality of that stuff you call brandy and the desirability of the end. Your question I make neither head nor tail of. Am I a tomcod to wallow in ice water? What is this talk of ice water, anyway?"

I made him a leg, as mocking, I hoped, as his stare.

"I know naught of your ancestry," I said, "never having clapped eyes on you before. But tomcod or plain mud puppy, I'll give you the same answer. 'Twas in a gutter of ice water I found you, and to the same I'll return you, say the word."

He had raised himself upon one elbow, the better to clear his throat after his fit of coughing, but this brought him up sitting in anger, for despite his own sharp tongue he was in no mood for Teddy-my-Godson. The movement dropped the covers about his loins, leaving him naked to the hips. At the same time it fetched the blood to his head in such wise that he clutched at his skull in a spasm of pain and cried out an oath, flinging himself back among the pillows.

"Lord God and his angels!" he moaned. "My head!"

I made haste to cover him, less for his own benefit than out of regard for Patience's modesty.

"You took a nasty rap on it," I told him.

"What happened?" he asked faintly.

"You take the words out of my mouth," I said.

His own reply was a long groan. Nor did he open his eyes, but rather lay with his face screwed up in pain. Patience, whose gentle heart could not but be wrung at sight of such suffering, made a sympathetic sound.

I doubt if he had been aware of her presence until that moment. At this, however, he opened one eye cautiously, in a tentative way, and turned it in her direction. For a moment he eyed her, as if trying to make certain that he saw aright. Under his scrutiny Patience flushed and edged in my direction. The movement appeared to convince him, for he opened his other eye and stared at her openly.

"Who are you?" he said. Then, before she could answer, he turned his eye in my direction. "And who are you?"

"I had it in mind to ask you that," I replied, disgruntled at his attitude and the bluntness of his questions.

But he was not listening. Instead he was glancing about him, at the room, at the frosted windows, and the bright fire dancing on the hearth.

"Where am I?" he demanded, and all at once appeared to become aware of his own nakedness beneath the covers. "Where are my clothes? How did I come here? Who are you?"

I saw that he was becoming panic-stricken, and realized that I had him at an unfair advantage. I made haste to reassure him.

"Gently! Gently! You're safe here. My name is Tom Tisdall, and this is Mistress Nowell, whose grandfather owns this house. I was coming home from work, when I stumbled upon you in the gutter on Derby Street."

He fixed me with a puzzled stare.

"Gutter—Derby Street?" he repeated, frowning as if trying to reconcile the words with something half remembered.

Something like comprehension flashed in his eyes, and he broke off abruptly. His face took on a sullen look.

"How do you feel?" I asked.

He seemed to turn his mind to that with an effort.

"I'm cold," he said almost querulously.

Patience looked sympathetic.

"I shouldn't wonder," I grinned. "In another ten minutes I believe you'd have been frozen to the cobbles."

I poured out a generous portion of brandy and filled the rest of the cup with hot water from the earthen jug.

"Drink this," I ordered. " 'Twill help warm you."

He took it eagerly, and as he drank I turned to Patience.

"Is there aught on the fire, Pat?" I asked.

"There's mutton broth and potatoes," she replied, "and half of the joint left. I was saving them for your supper——"

"Broth!" I exclaimed. "The very thing. Run and fetch up a bowl. 'Twill do him more good than a dozen fires and a gallon of brandy!"

No sooner was she gone than the stranger leaped from the bed and rushed to the fireplace, where he crouched before the blaze, reaching out his arms and hands toward the flames, so close that I wondered that his arms were not singed.

"Get back into bed," I told him, "unless you hanker to be one big chilblain."

"I'm freezing!" he protested. "I itch and tingle all over from the cold. I've got to get warm!"

He shuddered violently and let his teeth chatter.

"You'll itch and tingle a thousand times worse if you don't get away from that fire," I told him.

I took him by the arm and steered him reluctantly toward the bed. As he climbed back in between the covers I found a flannel nightshirt in my wardrobe and tossed it to him.

"Put this on," I said, "before Patience comes back. You're no fit sight for a young girl's eyes."

He did my bidding meekly enough, and I rewarded him with a dram of brandy.

"How do you feel now?" I said as he tossed it off.

He gave me a grin which lighted his Mephistophelean features remarkably.

"More human," he admitted, "something less like a corpse."

"That's gratifying," I told him. "Has your memory thawed with your body?"

He looked puzzled.

"Don't you remember anything?" I prompted.

He frowned, and his face resumed its saturnine cast.

"I don't understand," he said musingly.

I shook my head with impatience, for I mistook his meaning. At the time I applied his remark to my own question. It was not until later that it dawned upon me that his words referred to something beyond my own ken.

"Think, man!" I said. "Have you no recollection of anything? You were unconscious when I found you. No doubt you were unconscious when you came there. What is the last thing you remember?"

He puckered his brows in a frown.

"Perhaps if you can't remember specifically where you were during the evening," I put in, trying to be helpful, "there may be some place to which you are accustomed to go?"

He looked at me blankly.

"The Three Fishermen, perhaps?" I suggested, naming one of the most notorious of the water-front dives. "The Frigate, the General Hancock?"

He shook his head.

"I was never in Salem before in my life," he said.

"Is that true?" I cried. "That's something! You remember the town you are in. Perhaps we can go on from there."

It was not my intention to pry, but if we were to recover that which had been stolen from him and lodge a complaint, it was evident that we must know more. At my words, however, the veiled look that I had previously noted crept into his eyes. He stared at me coolly.

"I remember no more than that," he said flatly.

I was sure the man was lying, but before I could pursue it further we were interrupted by Patience, bearing a bowl of hot soup and a loaf of crisp bread.

At her entry my patient eyed her with new appreciation. The dour, almost sullen look with which he had greeted my questioning vanished, and in its place came a quizzical, half-teasing glance, brightened by a flashing smile that revealed the white evenness of his teeth sharply contrasting with his somewhat swarthy complexion.

"Hot soup!" he breathed. "Darling, I shall love you forever!"

Patience blushed in startled confusion, but I thought she made an excellent recovery.

"You had better taste it first, sir," she replied.

"My dear," he teased, "any food that you prepared could not help but be delicious!"

He made an effort to capture her hand, but she evaded him with a dexterity that amazed me.

"Tush, sir!" she exclaimed. "Eat your soup before it cools."

He sulked, thrusting out his lower lip.

"Stop sirring me," he said.

"You have the advantage—sir," I told him.

"Eh?" He glanced at me.

"We don't know your name," I said.

He blinked and then smiled again.

"So you don't!" he said. "Stupid of me! Forgive me if I seem sluggish. My brain has been affected by the cold."

"Rather by the brandy," I retorted.

He gave me a twisted grin.

"And who's to blame for that?"

I shrugged and made no answer. He glanced at Patience.

"Ben Price is my name," he said. "Eben Eleazer, my parents

christened me, but I prefer plain Ben. Will you call me Ben, Patience, my sweet?"

She bobbed him a pert curtsey and gave him a saucy smile to match his own.

" 'Tis a pleasure, Mister Price," she said.

"Ben!"

"Oh, eat your soup," I put in, "while it's hot."

"Not until she calls me Ben," he grinned at me.

Patience gave me a helpless glance, and I nodded.

"All right—Ben," she said. "Now eat your soup!"

"With the greatest of pleasure," he beamed, and fell to.

I caught Patience's eye and signaled with my head toward the door. She turned away. Price looked up.

"Where are you going?"

"She's going to set out my supper," I told him. "I haven't had it yet, you know."

"Because of me, you mean?" he asked. *"Touché,* Thomas! Forgive me! You may go, Patience, my love, and feed the brute, but I shall expect you to come back and soothe my fevered brow with your lovely cool fingers!"

"If your brow were any cooler," I said, "it would be a block of ice! Go along, Pat!"

"Tut, Tom," he grumbled, his mouth full of soup and bread, "do you imply that I am a blockhead?"

"If the shoe fits, wear it!" I retorted.

Patience laughed as I shut the door behind her. I could hear her footsteps going away. When she was out of earshot, I turned about and stood with my back to the door eying him in the bed. He glowered back at me, not smiling now.

"You certainly played the skeleton at that feast."

"In the circumstances," I replied, "it was my privilege."

He made no reply to that. I went on.

"Let us have one thing clearly understood from the start. Leave Patience Nowell alone!"

"So that's the way it is!" he said.

"It isn't any way at all," I told him, though I could feel myself coloring. "It's just that I like and respect the girl and her grandfather. They've been friends to me in a place where friends are hard come by, and I've no mind to see her lot made harder through any act of mine."

"She has a hard lot?" He looked surprised.

"She does!"

"Perhaps you'll tell me?"

"Perhaps I will—one day," I told him.

I opened the door.

"I'm going down for my own supper," I said. "If you want anything knock on the floor."

I found Patience setting a place for me at the table.

"I'm sorry, Pat," I said. "I should have taken him into one of the ordinaries and washed my hands of him."

She looked at me in amazement.

"Why, Tom Tisdall," she exclaimed, "whatever makes you say a thing like that! Just because he teased me? I think he's nice!"

For some reason this made me angry.

"You do?" I said. "Well, don't be too hasty. Remember, we know nothing about him."

"Pooh!" she scoffed. " 'Tis plain to see he's a gentleman."

"That word's very loosely used these days," I said.

"I think you're mean!" she told me, and I did not trouble to deny it. I felt mean, though not in the sense she intended.

I ate my supper in silence, speculating on the events of the evening. Perhaps an hour later I went upstairs again to find that the warmth of the fire, the brandy, and the hot soup had done their work. He had turned over on his side and gone to sleep. Carefully I banked the fire and went back downstairs once more, leaving him to enjoy his rest in peace.

2

PATIENCE was still working in the kitchen.

"How is he?" she asked.

"He's asleep."

"Poor lad!" she exclaimed. "He must have been hardly used."

"No worse than many an honest sailor at sea this very moment," I said dryly. "As you saw, 'twas naught he could not recover from in jig time."

She gave no sign that she was listening.

"He seems so young, too," she mused.

I laughed outright at that.

"He was old enough to be involved in a low tavern brawl or worse!"

She stamped her foot.

"How can you say that?" she demanded. "He said he could not remember what happened."

I shrugged. She turned on me savagely.

"Why would he lie?" she demanded.

"Because," I grinned, "he's probably ashamed."

"Oh, you, Tom Tisdall!" she exclaimed angrily. "You're like everyone else—always ready to believe the worst about anybody!"

I could not accept that.

"That's not fair, Pat! And it's not true!"

She made no reply, but merely shrugged, and fell to scrubbing the table vigorously.

Watching her, I could not but be struck again with her untouched charm. Nor could I fail to be saddened by it. The arm with which she swept the table top was slender and supple, the hand with which she steadied herself was small and shapely. Under the coarse stuff of her dress, as she bent across the table, her figure was revealed subtly: slim, tapering waist and gently rounded hips, long, shapely legs. Beneath her bodice the young breasts swelled, firm and tempting. Her face, framed in a mass of curls the color of birch leaves in the autumn, was fresh and appealing without being syrupy sweet or prettily empty. Such a person, I told myself, should have friends everywhere, not be shunned. When she went out into the market kind words and cheerful greetings should be her portion, not the sly whispers that followed her wherever she went. She should have friends of her own age. She ought not to be left out of things. If people could only know her, I felt certain they would forget the stigma that they had placed upon her. It was not fair to hold her responsible.

I had not been long in Salem, it is true, but I had been quick to learn the story of Patience Nowell. Neither she nor her grandfather, of course, mentioned it. But there are always those who take pleasure in talebearing.

It was not a pretty story. Samuel Nowell had had one son,

Rufus, a handsome lad, by all accounts, part owner and master
of a ketch-rigged pink which he used for fishing and trading on
the coast. In the course of his trading he met and fell in love
with Elizabeth Lake, the daughter of a West India merchant
of Ipswich. She returned his sentiment, and doubtless they
would have been married without delay but for her parents'
opposition.

They, according to rumor, were not all they might have
been. Unlike many another merchant of the day, Tobias Lake
appeared to have been little touched by the Revolution, and
there were dark hints that he maintained his business by trading with the enemy. They were wealthy, though, and proud, and
the trader-fisherman, son of a lowly carpenter, was not their
notion of a proper match for their daughter. Tobias Lake
forbade Rufus Nowell his house.

Rufus and Elizabeth, like other lovers, however, found
ways to avoid the command. Throughout the summer, and into
the fall, they met among the dunes or in the woods around
Ipswich.

The gossips' stories did not describe those meetings, nor
did they tell what plans they laid, though there is no doubt
they laid them. It was to carry out those plans that Rufus
Nowell put out from Salem on a day in November. It was late
when he weighed anchor, and the weather was not promising.
There was a growing wind from the north and the sky had the
metallic color of lead. But Rufus Nowell did not fear the
weather, and perhaps he might have reached his goal and carried out his plan if weather had been his only obstacle. What he
did not know, however, was that a British sloop of war, less
daring than he, had run in under the lee of Plum Island to ride
out the coming storm. When Nowell's pink hove into view,
having taken all night to beat about Cape Ann and make westing, it looked like fair game to the Englishman. He hoisted sail
and drove out from his sheltered bay in hot pursuit.

Nowell now found himself trapped between the Englishman
and Two Penny Loaf, with no choice but to run for it to south
and east, along the shore, in the hope that he might be able to
outdistance pursuit sufficiently to bear northeast from the
mouth of the Annisquam and clear the Cape. But as luck would
have it, the gale chose this instant to break in all its fury from

the northward and drove the little ship aground on Essex Bar. It is cold consolation to know that the British sloop was likewise driven aground. Both vessels broke up in the storm, with the loss of all hands.

Elizabeth Lake's situation was tragic. She had lost her lover and she was with child. Upon learning of his daughter's condition, Tobias Lake, with the righteousness of the Pharisee, turned her out of his home, and she had no choice but to make her way to Salem and cast herself upon the mercy of Samuel Nowell.

Whatever his origin, the old carpenter had a heart as great as Tobias Lake's was small. The loss of his son was a bitter blow to him, but it never occurred to him to blame the girl. It was enough that Rufus had loved her, and that she carried within her his son's child. He cared not a snap for convention. He took her in and cared for her. Patience was born in his house, and her mother had named her in a moment of bitterness.

Elizabeth Lake died within three months after the baby's birth, and the old carpenter had been both father and mother to the child. The rest of Salem had not been so kindly. The taunts and gibes of more fortunate children had followed her as she grew up. And as she came into womanhood, her lot became even less enviable. Those who thought themselves better folk shunned her. A few looked on her with pity, which was as galling. And there was a third class who, evil themselves, could not credit one born in her circumstances with a shred of purity.

I believe it was on this account largely that Samuel Nowell opened his house to me and took me in as a lodger. As an evidently sober and respectable person, a stranger in the town, he perhaps hoped that I might offer the girl something of the friendship and association her life had hitherto lacked.

"Do you know, Pat," I said abruptly after a long silence, thinking back to the way in which she had championed the stranger, "you are a very sweet and very understanding person."

She stopped her work in midsweep and stared at me.

"Why——" she said, obviously taken very much off guard. "Why, Tom, that's the kindest thing anyone ever said to me."

I do not know where this conversation might have led had not at that moment the front door burst open, letting in a great gust of wind that licked across the floor and set the ashes on the hearth to dancing up the chimney. Sam Nowell, home from the Crown and Anchor, came in with it, wiping the snow from his beard and shaking his shoulders as a dog shakes water from its shaggy coat. He tossed his worn hat upon the table, and his sharp gray eyes flicked from me to Patience and back again shrewdly but at the same time jovially.

"Eh, now," he said, "what's afoot?"

He moved to the hearth and spread his gnarled hands to the warmth of the blaze, looking over his shoulder for the answer to his question. He was a man in his late sixties, weather-beaten as an old oak, and with a beard and white hair that were in startling contrast to the leathery texture of his skin. In his younger days he had sailed as a ship's carpenter, and during the Revolution he had served the young Navy until wounds had retired him. Then he had been content to come ashore to work as a shipwright in the Salem yard, a life that had none of the hazards and all of the profits of seafaring. But sometimes I would surprise him gazing seaward with a look in his eyes that suggested that he occasionally longed to be abroad again upon the ocean. Although he was not an old man, as age goes, lately he had begun to complain of rheumatism and to doze of an evening before the fire; signs that I took to mean that he was aging.

Patience answered his question.

"Tom's fetched in a young lad he found lying in Derby Street," she said.

"Eh?" barked the old man, squaring round on me. "Have ye fetched a drunken brawler into my house?"

I made haste to explain. The old man eyed me narrowly a long instant before he nodded.

"Aye," he said finally. "Ye could scarce leave him to freeze." I made no reply to that.

"Where is he now?" he asked.

"Upstairs in my bed," I told him, "asleep."

"He'll recover then, ye think?"

"He'll be good as ever by morning," I laughed.

He stared at me.

"And where will ye sleep?"

I nodded toward the settle on the far side of the room. He chuckled and thumped me on the back.

"Ye're a softhearted looby, Tom," said he, "but I love ye for it."

<h1 style="text-align:center">3</h1>

I DOUBT NOT that my guest spent a more comfortable night than I. The settle was hard and unyielding as a rock, and toward morning, when the fire died, it was colder than I like to remember. However, the dawn came at last, and I was happy to see it. At the first light I rose and uncovered the coals of the fire and rekindled the blaze, after which I dressed before its warmth. When I had finished I put on the kettle to boil and went upstairs to renew the fire in my bedroom.

I found that my patient was before me. He had rescued a few live coals from the ashes of last night's fire and had a cheerful blaze crackling on the hearth, while he himself sat propped up amid the pillows with his nose buried in a copy of Culpeper's *Herbal* which I kept among my small library of professional books. He looked up at my entrance, and his face brightened in that peculiar saturnine smile.

"You wake early," I said.

"It's a habit of mine," he replied. "Where did you sleep?"

"On the settle in the kitchen," I told him shortly.

He cocked a quizzical eyebrow in my direction. "I hoped you'd found a softer bed."

"What I said last night," I said, "was meant to cover thoughts as well as acts. I still mean it."

"Honi soit qui mal y pense," he said dryly.

"What?"

"Evil to him who evil thinks."

I made no answer, but crossed to the fireplace and emptied my pan of smoking coals. He waved the book.

"So you're a sawbones?" he said.

I was forced to smile at his effrontery.

"Many would not be so complimentary," I said. "As a matter of fact, I am a clerk at the shipyard, though I'll not deny I've had some notion of practicing medicine."

"You'll never reach it by reading in books," said he.

"Not by books alone," I agreed, "though they help. But

I've six years' apprenticeship behind me, and but for a stroke of ill luck——"

I broke off abruptly. He waited a moment.

"Well?" he said at length, curiously.

"Why should I tell you my troubles?" I demanded.

He shrugged.

"Turn about's fair play," he said. "Tell me your story, and I'll tell you mine. Is it a bargain?"

"There's not much to tell," I said. "I was born and raised in Portsmouth. My father was a sawyer, who was killed in an accident when I was six years old. My mother was a sempstress. She saw me through the Free School but had not the means to send me to college. When I finished schooling she found me a place as assistant to old Dr. Leeds."

"You mean you were apprenticed to him?" he asked.

"I suppose that's what it should be called," I grinned. "Isn't that what I called it just a moment ago? Actually I mowed the doctor's meadow. I fed and milked his cow. I harnessed his horse and saw that he was shod and the leathers were in shape. I cut wood and filled the wood box. I even tended the garden in the summer. When there was opportunity, I was allowed the run of the doctor's library and sometimes went out with him to be of what help I might."

He eyed me curiously.

"It sounds more as though you were a general handy man," he said, "than an apprentice."

"I suppose I was," I replied. "The doctor paid me three dollars and fifty cents a week. I gave three dollars of that to my mother. I had to work that out some way."

"I see," he said. "Go on."

"In the evenings the doctor would lecture me on medical subjects. I learned a good deal that way, of pharmacopoeia and physic and anatomy and physiology. Later he taught me what he knew of surgery. Toward the end he even turned some of his cases over to me."

I stopped talking abruptly, my mind running back over the turn of events that had brought me where he found me.

"With all that behind you," he said at length, "how does it happen you are a clerk in Salem rather than a physician in Portsmouth?"

"Do you recall," I asked, "the bilious yellow-fever epidemic?"

"Last winter?" He nodded. "It struck Boston all of a heap. Folk couldn't get out of town fast enough."

"That may be," I replied. "I only know what it was in Portsmouth. It was complicated there by an outbreak of dysentery."

"What started it?"

"Does anyone know?" I shrugged. "It is not a familiar disease in these parts. In Boston 'twas thought that it was caused by a cargo of rotted beef jettisoned in the harbor. My own notion is that it was brought in ships from the Indies."

"But you treated it."

"Aye," I said dully, remembering. "I treated it. But I had no patients that recovered. I treated it as I would any fever, by cupping and purging and salt baths and dosing. But once the fever had taken hold, nothing seemed to help."

"You saved none?" he asked. "None at all?"

"Not one! Others had little better luck than I, but folk were used to them. For my case it was 'Tom Tisdall's a fine young fellow, but no great shakes as a physician.'"

"What about Dr. Leeds? Didn't he help?"

"Dr. Leeds died," I said, "before the fever struck."

I hesitated.

"Yes?" he encouraged.

"My mother died, too, of the fever."

"Oh," he cried. "I'm sorry!"

I shook my head.

"After that I had no wish to stay in Portsmouth. I came away and took the first thing that offered."

"And have you given up doctoring?" he asked.

"Someday, perhaps," I said, "I may have opportunity to go back to it. But I see no chance of it at this moment."

He stared at me, moodily, for a time.

"You put me to shame," he said at length. "I have no such tale to tell."

I had been so engrossed in my own woes that I had almost forgotten our bargain.

"I'm only interested in how you came to be where I found you," I told him shortly.

"As to that," he chuckled, "I'm afraid I won't be able to enlighten you, for you see, I don't know myself."

"Well," I said, "tell me the rest of it. Perhaps in the telling you'll come on something that will remind you."

"I doubt it," he shrugged. "But if you insist—— I come from Sudbury, where my father is a designer and maker of fine furniture."

He eyed me to see if I were impressed. I said nothing.

"You know," he said, "not just an ordinary cabinetmaker, but a cut or two above. Somewhat in the nature of your master builders, I should say."

"Yes, I know," I said dryly. "Go on."

"There's not much to go on to," he replied. "My father would have me follow in his footsteps, but I had no stomach for that. He then insisted upon my going to Harvard, for, he said, 'if a man will not work with his hands, he must work with his head.' But that was as dismal as cabinetmaking in Sudbury, so I wrote to him, after two years, that I would have no more of it, and he replied that, having tried to make a silk purse of a sow's ear, he had now to acknowledge that it could not be done; that he had done everything in his power for me, and that henceforth I was to consider myself my own master and make my own way in the world. And so I came to Salem."

He beamed as though he had said something very clever.

"Why?" I said.

He blinked.

"What?"

"Why Salem?"

He seemed taken aback.

"Well," he said, "why not? Salem ships go out all over the world. Everyone knows there are better fortunes to be made on the coast or at sea, these days, than at such places as Sudbury or Worcester."

I had to smile at that.

"You certainly are starting from scratch," I said, "if you mean to make your fortune! All right, you reached Salem. What did you do? Come! let us see if we can't pick up some thread to help you remember."

He looked out of patience.

"Are you still worrying about that?" he demanded.

"Naturally!" I said.

"Well," he said, "you recall the sort of a day it was?"

"Of course," I assured him.

"Well, I went into a place——"

"What sort of a place?"

He gestured impatiently.

"Oh, an ordinary."

"And what happened?" I pressed him.

"Why——" he began, and then looked away and broke off. "I—I don't seem to remember."

"Oh, come now!" I cried in exasperation. "You can do better than that. You must remember."

He turned about to face me impatiently.

"Look here!" he exclaimed. "What difference does it make? I tell you I don't remember! What's more, I'm not much concerned. If I don't care, why should you?"

"As you say," I shrugged, "it doesn't really matter to me. I thought it might to you."

"Why?" he challenged.

"Well," I said, "here you are in a stranger's bed and a stranger's nightshirt, without so much as a pocket handkerchief to your name. I should be concerned in your place, if only to get my clothes back."

He smiled in a sort of reminiscent fashion.

"Do you think you could get them back for me if I chanced to remember where I'd lost them?"

"I might. At least I could try."

"I doubt it," he said cryptically.

"Well, have it your own way," I shrugged. "But what do you propose to do? Do you mind my asking?"

"Not at all!" he chuckled, eying me up and down. "I'll tell you. We're about of a size. I thought you might be persuaded to lend me a suit of clothes until I could find work and earn a suit of my own."

"Oh, you did?" I demanded, completely taken aback by the calm effrontery of the man. I turned sarcastic. "And what sort of work do you think you might do?"

He grinned at me, refusing to take offense at my tone. "I'm not a bad carpenter," he said.

"Oh," I growled, "so you'd come down to your father's level after all, if it were a matter of necessity."

He gave me a sharp look, which came as near resentment as anything he had yet shown.

"Don't misunderstand me," he said. "I've naught against cabinetmaking or any other work you care to name. It's simply that I find the prospect of a lifetime of it in Sudbury singularly dull. My father is a good man, and I hold nothing against him. But he has grown accustomed to Sudbury. I never could."

I had to admit he was frank about it.

"How do I know——" I began doubtfully.

"Try me!" said he, interrupting.

"What do you mean?" I said.

"Oh, come now," said he, "didn't you tell me that you worked at a shipyard? You could arrange it if you would."

I tossed up my hands in complete surrender.

"Very well," I said. "I'll do what I can. But, mind you, I'll have an eye on you."

He grinned engagingly.

"Naturally!" he agreed.

4

As soon as he was dressed and shaved, we went downstairs and found Patience and Sam before us. The old gentleman had not bothered to wait, but was already engaged with an immense bowl of porridge. Patience was bending over the skillet, tending the eggs and ham that popped and sputtered over the hot fire.

"Good morning," I said. "You've breakfast enough for all, Patience? Sam, this is Ben Price, of whom I spoke last night."

Nowell rose and held out his hand in greeting. His gray eyes were alert and watchful, but not unfriendly.

"Price," I said, "this is Sam Nowell, our host."

I half turned in Ben's direction, to find him staring at Patience in frank admiration. The sound of my voice, directly addressing him, however, recalled his attention, and he started round to face us, smiling his apologies.

"Eh? Oh—er—yes, Mr. Nowell. A pleasure, sir! Forgive

me if I seemed rude, but your daughter, sir—er—if you will pardon my saying so, such charm, such grace, and such beauty are seldom combined in a single person!"

Sam Nowell's mouth twitched slightly at the corners, but he remained grave. Patience flushed. But I am afraid I looked none too pleased. Sam, however, was equal to the situation.

"I am sure my granddaughter is flattered, Mr. Price," he said as he shook hands. "Pat, meet Mr. Price."

Patience curtseyed.

"We've already met, Grandpa," she said. "Good morning, Mr. Price."

"Your granddaughter, you say, sir?" Ben demanded incredulously. "Why, then you're an older man than I took you for!"

He made an elegant bow in Patience's direction.

"Your servant, ma'am! A bit of ill fortune turns out to be a stroke of sheer luck!"

Patience looked confused. Sam chuckled.

"You were lucky enough, at any rate," said he, "to have Tom come along when he did. Ye'd be eating breakfast with St. Peter otherwise."

"Mr. Price tells me that his father is a cabinetmaker," I put in, "and that he's by way of being a carpenter and woodworker himself. I've agreed to speak to Mr. Briggs about him."

Sam Nowell regarded his guest with fresh interest.

"Would ye be related to Jonathan Price, the furniture maker of Sudbury, by any chance?" he said.

The glance Ben gave me before he replied was triumphant.

"He is my father."

Sam Nowell's eyebrows rose in surprise.

"Do ye say so?" he exclaimed. "Has he taught ye well? Can ye use your hands?"

"Try me!" Ben's smile was assured.

I thought a shade more modesty would be more becoming, but evidently the same idea did not occur to Sam Nowell. I knew nothing of Jonathan Price, though the old man obviously did. He looked at me.

"Why didn't ye tell me?" he demanded. "I'll speak to Enos Briggs myself."

Patience slipped a hot platter of ham and eggs upon the table.

"I can arrange quarters in the old barracks," I said.

Patience turned on me.

"You'll do no such thing, Tom Tisdall!" she cried. "We've plenty of room."

Ben leaned across the table. The smile he gave me as he did so was almost derisive.

"I hoped you would say that!" he cried. "I can think of no better companions than the three of you. I hope you may be as well pleased with me!"

Sam Nowell snorted.

"Hah!" he exclaimed good-naturedly. "Well, we'll see!"

The storm had blown itself out, leaving the morning sky high washed and pale. In the course of the night the temperature had risen. The snow had changed first to rain and then had ceased entirely. Most of the slush and snow had been washed away, leaving the curbs and cobbles and flagged walks gleaming and clean. Only in the hollows under the evergreens, and on the shady side of the houses, beneath the shrubbery, was any snow left, and there it was old and pitted and gray-speckled, like the weary foam left high on the beach by the receding tide.

At Briggs's Yard the warmth of the morning sun brought out the pleasant odor of fresh-sawn timber to mingle with the scent of pitch being applied to a new-finished brig in the ways. In the number-one berth the massive keel and thick rising timbers of the new frigate, all that had thus far been completed, rose like the mighty skeleton of some prehistoric monster, reaching skyward amid the web of the scaffolding upon which the shipwrights swarmed like so many ants. From all over the yard came the sound of hammers, filling the air with pleasant thunder, so that only occasionally, in the brief intervals of silence, was it possible to hear the chanting of the ropemakers in the ropewalk across the cove. I saw Ben's eyes gleam with interest as we entered the enclosure. It was plain that he was impressed.

Enos Briggs was supervising the stacking of some new timber, not far from the yard office. I explained our delay, and as he listened he looked critically at my companion.

"So you're a carpenter?" he asked.

Ben nodded, smiling with that candor that I was to learn never failed to win him what he wanted.

"I am."

"Build ships?"

Ben shook his head.

"I can't say that I have," he replied, "but I've helped build houses, besides having some experience as a turner and a joiner. I've played some at cabinetmaking. I'm at home with tools, and I daresay, working with others, I'll soon catch on to the tricks of the trade. 'Tis not difficult, is it?"

Briggs shrugged.

"No," he said. " 'Tis not difficult."

He glanced at Sam Nowell.

"Have you a place for him in your crew, Sam?"

"Aye," the old man nodded, "I've a place for him."

"All right," Briggs said, "he's yours."

The day passed quietly and, as far as I was concerned, swiftly, for I became engrossed in my work and scarce noticed the passing of time. As a result I was surprised and more than a little pleased when, shortly before sundown, Ben appeared in the office doorway in search of me.

"Do you work all night?" he grinned banteringly.

"It's as well for you I work later some nights than others," I told him.

"True for you!" he laughed. "I'll look upon it always as evidence of the virtue of industry."

"How did you do?" I asked.

"How did you expect?" he shrugged. "I did well enough, of course. Any good carpenter can do it, and if I were not better than most I'd have had no trouble still."

It may have been the plain truth for all I knew, but it occurred me that he might be a shade more modest. It was perfectly clear, however, that he was not troubled by such thoughts.

Our route homeward lay along the same way I had gone the night before: over the Causeway, and so on up into Derby Street, past a row of fishermen's shacks and rickety, ramshackle wharves and a handful of boozy taverns, which in turn gave way to the long wharves and moss-grown warehouses of the town's wealthier merchants, whose proud residences crouched upon the townward side of the street and stared with watchful caution through bright glazed window-eyes at the activities of the harbor below.

I had an ulterior motive in following this route, for I wished to see if Ben would betray recognition of any part of it. But I might have spared myself the trouble. As we left the countryside and rounded the shoulder of the hill, the tang of the sea dropped behind and our nostrils were assailed by that peculiar redolence that is Salem's. Coming upon it for the first time, Ben stopped in his tracks and sniffed.

"Aaahhh!" he breathed. "That smell. What is it?"

"Mostly fish," I grinned wryly, "though there's a hint of cinnamon and clove from the warehouses yonder, with some smell of green coffee and muscovado mingled. Then there's rank tallow and green hides, pitch and bare tidal mud."

He stared at me curiously.

"Have you never felt the urge to see the lands where such things come from?"

I shook my head.

"I've watched too many fishermen come in covered with ice and frozen guts and gills over decks and rigging to feel any curiosity about the Grand Banks. Tallow and pitch I have seen made in my own yard. I can see a green hide in a farmer's barn any year. And as for cloves and cinnamon and coffee and all the spices of the East—thank you! I'll be satisfied just to have them on my table. There's too much wide ocean 'twixt me and the Indies. I was not cut out for the sea!"

Which only serves to show what an ill judge I was, even of my own future!

We went on past the rows of lesser warehouses, and the fishermen's wharves, with the twisted, rickety pilings and the slack-rigged little pinks and luggers and shallops snug alongside; past the little clutter of ordinaries, where the mingled smell of rum and stale beer was strong on the evening air; past the first of the great warehouses, where the tall masts and spars of the ships beyond showed clean cut against the sunset sky. Opposite these the brief row of stately houses, though still aloof, seemed somehow relaxed, as if in repose at the conclusion of the day's business.

There was a carriage standing before the Hacketts' door,

and as we approached, a man and a girl came out of the house and paused upon the doorstep. At my elbow I heard my companion utter a low exclamation and sensed an instant's hesitation in his step. I glanced at him curiously and saw that he was staring at the couple with an expression almost of consternation. Even as I looked, however, the startled look vanished, to be replaced by one of sharp anticipation. When I glanced back I saw that Eli Hackett himself had joined the couple on the doorstep.

Although the street was all but deserted, they did not appear to notice our approach. The merchant closed his door firmly behind him, and together they moved toward the waiting carriage. It was evident that our paths would cross just as they reached the gate, and as our ways converged I had a momentary opportunity to study them.

The girl was small and dainty, but almost voluptuously full of figure, with high, firm breasts and a slim waist. She was darkly lovely, with bright, radiant coloring, a small straight nose, and a little provocative mouth. Black, lustrous hair showed beneath her bonnet, and although at that distance I could not make out the color of her eyes, I could at least tell that they were dark and brightly vivacious. She was laughing gaily at some remark of one of her companions, and her face was lighted remarkably at the moment.

Both of her companions were tall. Eli Hackett was close on six feet and spare in proportion. He was a man in his late fifties or early sixties, with shrewd features and agate-hard eyes and a shock of snow-white hair. The other was tall enough to dwarf even Captain Hackett, and his face looked as if it might have been chiseled out of granite and covered with fine leather. I took him to be in his early thirties, and his dress was modern: fawn trousers, well cut and looped under the instep, with a bottle-green coat and a ponderous gray shaggy beaver hat. From his rolling gait he was a seaman; probably master of one of the Hackett ships.

Only when we came abreast of them did they become aware of our presence. At that moment my eyes were upon the girl's face, so that I did not see the expression with which the others sighted us. But the effect upon her was immediate and remarkable. Her laughter died in mid-swing, and a startled look replaced her gaiety. Behind her surprise I thought I detected a hint of consternation; a flash almost of panic, that flickered across her eyes, to be replaced by an expression of curious, watchful alertness. As I watched her I heard the merchant's exclamation of astonishment.

"God bless me! 'Tis Eben Price!"

My companion halted abruptly.

"Good evening, Captain Hackett," he said, nodding gravely. To the girl he bowed.

"Selina! Your servant still!"

I have said before that there was about him, on occasion, an expression of sardonic raillery, but not before had I seen it so pronounced. His greeting was almost mocking.

Her only response was a brief, almost fearful nod. Hackett, however, was booming on, quite engrossed in his own surprise.

"By heaven, boy, what brings you to Salem?"

Ben faced him, smiling.

"I am finished with Harvard, sir," he said. "I came here to learn something of shipbuilding."

I had the impression that in some way the words were meant for the girl as much as the man. Hackett himself appeared to take the statement as entirely natural.

"You could not have chosen better," he said. "You must come and see me. I can help you."

"Thank you, sir," Ben nodded, "but I have already found a place. I am working for Mr. Briggs, upon the frigate."

"Ah?" Hackett's voice was almost disappointed. "Starting at the very bottom, eh? Why did you not let us know?"

Ben's smile was wolfish, but his reply was conciliatory.

"You'll forgive me, sir," he said, "if I preferred to make my own way?"

The merchant nodded.

"That's commendable. But where are you staying? Why not give us the pleasure of your company?"

Ben's eyes flickered in the direction of the girl, but momentarily. Toward the older man he was utterly correct.

"Thank you for your thought of me," he said. "For the moment I am lodging with my friend, Dr. Tisdall, here. We board with Samuel Nowell, on Daniels Street."

"Nowell?" Hackett's surprise was evident. "Nowell!"

Abruptly he appeared to remember and glanced at me.

"Dr. Tisdall?" he said, offering his hand. "I don't believe I have had the pleasure, sir."

It was both an acknowledgment and a challenge.

"I am but lately come from Portsmouth, sir," I said.

I offered no further explanation. He turned.

"Forgive me," he said. "My astonishment at seeing Eben has robbed me of my manners. This is my daughter Selina, Dr. Tisdall. Selina, you are acquainted with Eben Price. Doctor— Eben—may I make you acquainted with Captain Webb, of the *Exchange,* brig?"

I shook hands with Captain Webb and bowed to Selina.

"Your servant, ma'am," I said.

She tilted her head in acknowledgment, with a smile and provocative flash of eyes as black as her hair.

"Welcome to Salem, Dr. Tisdall," she said.

I must have gaped at her like any bumpkin, for my next recollection is of Eli Hackett saying they must be on their way. Only then did I realize that Ben had no more than nodded to the girl. Captain Webb he ignored entirely.

The trio swept on to the carriage, and Selina, as her escorts handed her in, flashed a smile over her shoulder which could only have been meant for me.

I must admit that I stared after them.

"There's a charming person," I said almost to myself.

"Yes, isn't she?" said Ben dryly.

I stared at him sharply.

"I thought you didn't know anyone in Salem?"

He cocked one eyebrow in my direction.

"Not at all," he said. "I told you that I was a stranger here."

"Well?" I said testily, for to me it seemed that he was being deliberately contradictory.

"My dear man," he exclaimed, "the Hacketts spend a good deal of time in Boston! It happens that I met them there."

5

IT MAY BE HINTED, in the light of all that followed, that I would have done better to take a different route home, that stormy night in April. Perhaps! Had matters not fallen out as they did, who can tell how they might have gone? Certainly nothing is so bad that it might not be worse! On that night I think some trick of destiny had the guiding of my footsteps, so that I would stumble upon Ben Price. Once I had stumbled, the rest followed logically. To have left him there would have been inhuman. To have denied him shelter, once I had brought him in, would have been inhospitable. To have withheld friendship would have been unmannerly.

Nor, I daresay, was anyone meeting him for the first time inclined to withhold friendship. Even seeing him in his true colors, as I was afterward to do, impatience and annoyance were tempered by admiration. It was impossible not to marvel at his superb self-assurance, just as it was impossible not to be irritated by it. Black he may have been in many respects, yet there is no denying his charm. When it was his pleasure, he could appear as genuine as gold itself. Among men he was convivial. Among women he was courtly. In a word, he was ingratiating, and so long as he was that, his faults were not likely to be too closely examined.

Proof enough of this, I believe, was his popularity at the yard. He made no secret of the fact that he considered himself a better carpenter than any employed there, and yet it was not resented even by men old enough to have built his cradle. Perhaps this was in part due to the fact that he was perfectly good-natured about it, simply stating it as the truth and letting it stand as that, neither quarreling with those who would dispute him nor becoming ruffled at the chaffing of others.

He was born with an instinctive feel for the use of tools, and his father had done much to foster it. In short, he was good and he knew it. His comrades knew it too.

I was amazed at the way in which he fell in with the work. At the outset I was willing to grant he might have some skill but I doubted his tenacity. It was my guess that he would stay with us a few weeks, perhaps, until the novelty of the situation wore off. Then, I believed, he would disappear, as suddenly as he had come; perhaps to return to Harvard, or perhaps to his people.

I could not have shot wider of that mark. Instead of slackening, his enjoyment of life among us and his interest in the vessel he was helping to build seemed to increase. In the first weeks he was there I formed the habit of stepping down to the ways at noontime, to find out how he was getting along. Invariably I found him part of a group, sometimes pitching horse-shoes, but more often simply sitting in the sun with his shirt off—for he was always a great one for "soaking up sunlight," as he called it—whittling and carving at a block of softwood and taking his part in the talk around him, whether it was of ships or women or politics or cattle or hunting or fishing. It was all of a piece.

He took, I found also, a great interest in ships and the sea. If he could get some of the old hands in the yard to talking of the ships they had sailed in or helped to build, he was content to listen, speaking only as often as might be necessary to keep their tongues rolling. Often in the evenings, if I were not yet ready to go home, he would roam about the yard, after the others had left, examining the brig in the number-two stocks and comparing the manner of her construction with that of the frigate.

As we went home, he would insist on passing by the wharves to look at the tall ships moored there or would pause at the top of the road to look out across the harbor and count the vessels at anchor.

"We have nothing like this in Sudbury," he would say to me, half joking and half in earnest.

Toward the end of his first month with us, as I recall, I ventured to ask him what he thought of shipbuilding by now. It was an idle question, tossed up to make conversation at supper, but the answer he gave me was one I was to remember.

"I don't know," he said slowly. "If you mean building this ship, I like it. For another——" He shrugged.

"What do you mean by that?" I demanded, for I made neither head nor tail of his reply.

He ignored me and turned instead to Sam Nowell.

"Will you tell me, Sam," he said, "how is it with you? Do you form an attachment for the ships you work on? Do you feel the same for each one of them?"

"I know what you mean," the old man nodded. "Aye! There's a feeling you have for the ships you build. 'Tis a fine thing to see them take shape in the stocks. 'Tis finer yet to see them slide down the ways and float proud upon the water."

Ben shook his head.

"Yes, but," he said a shade impatiently, "isn't there some one ship above all the others that's your favorite?"

Samuel Nowell chuckled.

"Large and small," he replied, "I've helped build and launch nigh on a hundred ships. I've had a hand in so many of 'em that I couldn't tell you one from the other."

He shook his head slowly.

"I can't say I've a favorite," he went on. "But I take your meaning. There are those for whom each ship as it takes shape is a favorite. Those men make shipwrights. Young Thatcher Magoun down at the yard's one such. Mark my words, he'll make a master builder to top 'em all before he's through, that lad. You'll be another, Ben."

"No"—Ben was dubious—"no, Sam, I think not. I think I will build one ship, and that will be my ship."

I laughed.

"Do you plan to sail in her?" I scoffed. "You talk as if you'd like to marry the ship!"

Ben did not even smile. Instead he gave me a blank stare and then looked away with a little shake, as if to tear himself away from something in his mind.

Ben had not been a week in the house before he came upon my guilty secret. Hitherto diffidence had kept my flute packed in my chest. It did not occur to me that anyone other than myself could enjoy the plaintive tootlings with which I had long amused myself in Portsmouth. But Ben came upon the instrument one evening while rummaging through my chest in search of a clean shirt—he had no reticence whatever in the matter of borrowing—and egged me into playing for him. Once I had shown myself no fumbling amateur, nothing would do but I must take the pipe downstairs and play for Patience and her grandfather. They greeted my rendition of "Fair Aurora, Pray Thee Stay" and "Queen Mary's Lament" with gratifying applause, and I went on to give them "In Infancy Our Hopes and Fears" and "Bess of Bedlam."

After I had played five or six pieces, Sam Nowell, with a sheepish air, arose and went up into the attic, where he rummaged about for some time, reappearing presently with a battered old guitar, which he said he used to play in his younger days. I gave him the tune upon my pipe, and in a few minutes we were away with "Water Parted from the Sea," followed by "The World Turned Upside Down" and "Anacreon in Heaven." The evening closed with "I Love Them All" and "Harkaway to the Downs," in which Ben and Patience joined, Patience singing in a warm and tender soprano and Ben in a throaty baritone.

After that there was scarcely an evening when we did not gather round the fire to sing and play, and each of us racked his brain for new songs, or old ones that might have long lain forgotten. It was enough for me that it gave Patience and her grandfather a good deal of pleasure. It was something new for them, and I believe they enjoyed every moment of it.

I also enjoyed it. It gave me a warm and friendly feeling, and between times, while I paused for breath, Ben would take the floor and entertain us with stories and recitations, such as would keep us all a-laughing, for there was no denying that when he wished he could be as charming and accomplished a conversationalist as ever entered a drawing room. He could keep us in stitches with a funny story, or quote a verse, or mimic, or sing a ballad. I was not quite so intrigued, however, when, one evening, he bowed to Patience and proposed they dance a figure to our accompaniment.

I saw Sam Nowell scowl suddenly, and I myself stopped playing in mid-measure. Patience flushed.

"I—I don't know how to dance," she said.

Ben blinked at her in amazement.

"You don't know how?"

"I've never been asked before," Patience explained.

"The devil!" Ben exclaimed. "Why, then 'tis high time someone asked you! And if you don't know how, why, my dear, I will teach you!"

He held out his hand to her.

"Come!" he cried. "Let me show you!" Then, whirling to us: "Play! Music!"

I glanced at Nowell, and after an instant's hesitation he nodded and we played, now quickly that he might show her the tempo, now slowly while he taught her the steps.

Like any beginner, she was shy at first and awkward through

self-consciousness. But it was apparent that she was eager to learn and that she enjoyed learning. Later, however, in the privacy of our room, I ventured to remonstrate with Ben, for it seemed to me cruel to teach her the pleasures of companionship when it could not be hoped that she would ever, in Salem at least, benefit by it. He turned upon me.

"Nonsense!" he cried. "Why shouldn't she learn? What are you and the old man trying to do? Would you make a nun of her? She's too lovely a creature for that."

"Aye! She's lovely! She's too lovely to be hurt."

"In God's name, then, what are you prattling about?" he demanded. "Who wants to hurt the girl?"

"It isn't your intention I question," I said. "It's the hurt you might do to her unwittingly. She hasn't an easy life of it, Ben."

"Look here!" he exclaimed savagely. "That's twice now you've thrown out dark hints of the hardship of her life. What's behind it?"

I stared at him, half tempted to tell, yet realizing that the story was not mine to divulge.

"Forget it," I said. "I only meant to warn you. A hint should be sufficient."

There it rested for the moment, though I had the uncomfortable feeling that this was not an end to it. In the meantime the dancing lessons went on, nevertheless, and despite me it was a pleasure to see how quickly she learned.

6

IT WAS NOT LONG after this that, toward the end of a day, I had an unexpected caller at the office. I had no warning of his presence until his foot scraped upon the lintel and I heard his apologetic cough. Startled, I whirled about to see an enormous blackamoor framed in the doorway. In my surprise I may have been a little curt.

"Yes?" I said.

The black man rolled his eyes, looking in each corner of the room timidly, before answering.

"Tell me, suh, please wheah kin ah fin' Doctah Tisdall?"

"I'm Dr. Tisdall," I said.

"Yo' is?" The black face split in a wide grin. "Ah ahsk'e lady in Dan'l Street 'n 'e say fin' 'e in shipyahd, but ah don' think 'e be so easy."

"What can I do for you?" I said.

"Please, ma'an"—I had not heard the broad West Indian address before, and it startled me—"please, ma'an, my lady say 'e don' feel good. 'E say please yo' come."

I was puzzled. I had made no effort to set up in practice in Salem. Indeed, at the moment I could think of no one except Ben and the Nowells who even knew my interest in medicine.

"Who is your lady?" I asked.

" 'E Mis'tess Hackett. 'E say please yo' come soon."

I remembered then that Ben had introduced me as "Dr." Tisdall on the day that we had met, but this did not serve to lessen my puzzlement. I had not seen Miss Hackett since, and I had no reason to believe that our meeting had made the least impression upon her. Yet, here, of a sudden she was sending for me as a physician, as though I had been prescribing for her all her life. Surely the Hacketts had a family physician. Why had she not sent for him?

All these thoughts raced through my mind together and left me more bewildered than ever. At the same time my curiosity was aroused, and I told myself there was no point in looking a gift horse in the mouth. Who could tell? This might be a reopening of the door of medicine to me. I would be foolish if I did not snatch at every opportunity. Accordingly, I left a message for Ben that I would meet him at dinner and followed the black to the Hacketts'.

I was ushered into a high-ceilinged drawing room, whose tall windows were draped with luxurious brocades and whose walls were painted in soft tones with scenes depicting the glories of ancient Greece. A bright fire crackled on gleaming andirons in a fireplace framed by delicately worked pillars. Above the mantel a dour Hackett ancestor stared gloomily out of a dark portrait. The floor was covered with a handsome, deep-piled carpet into which one sank as one walked, as in a feather bed. In one corner I noted a glass cabinet which housed a number of pieces of delicate chinaware and pottery, evidently fetched from abroad.

This much I observed as I entered. But I saw little else, for my patient lounged upon a sofa before the fire, propped up amid a mass of pillows, with a luxurious down comforter thrown negligently across her lap. As I entered she reached out a hand and greeted me with a wan little smile.

"Doctor!" she said. "It was good of you to come."

If I had thought her lovely before, it was evident now that I had underestimated her. At our previous meeting she had been dressed for the street. Now her head was uncovered, and her hair was freshly brushed and combed and carefully dressed in a narrow golden ribbon admirably calculated to set off its luxuriant glory. About her shoulders she wore a filmy sacque, decked with lace and ribbons, over what seemed to me an equally filmy nightdress. If her previous garb had hinted at the rounded firmness and gentle perfection of her young breasts, her present attire left no doubt of it. I looked at her face in search of any trace of illness, but aside from the wan smile which she affected I could find none.

"I'm afraid Ben gave you the wrong impression," I said. "You see, I work as a clerk at Enos Briggs's shipyard."

Her smile died abruptly.

"You're not a doctor, then?"

I smiled.

"Oh yes," I said, "I am a doctor. But I have not practiced since coming to Salem."

"I don't understand." She looked even more puzzled.

I shrugged, and explained briefly, as I had to Ben.

"But everyone died who took the fever," she protested. "Here in Salem they did."

"That's true," I told her. "Few who took it survived it, but I found it impossible to convince Portsmouth of that."

"Well!" she exclaimed. "They may be that stupid in Portsmouth, but in Salem we're not so unfair. I still have faith in you!"

It might have occurred to me that her use of the word "still" was redundant, since she had no reason to believe in my skill in the first place. However, I have never pretended to be other than human. I was both touched and flattered by her declaration, as she undoubtedly intended that I should be.

I bowed.

"Thank you," I said. "You are very kind."

She waved her hand negligently.

"Nonsense! I liked you the moment I saw you! If you say you are a doctor, I think you must be a good one."

I smiled at that.

"It does not necessarily follow. Nor does it explain why you should send for me."

She looked annoyed, as if I had no right to question her. "I said I liked you," she replied.

"Surely you have a family physician?"

"Dr. Binney!" she exclaimed scornfully. "He's so stuffy! And besides, he smells. I don't like *him*. I always say that if a doctor's to do you any good you must like him first and have confidence in him. Don't you think so?"

"I never saw it mentioned in any medical text that I ever read," I chuckled. "But I see no reason why it should not help. Suppose you tell me what's the trouble?"

She smiled brightly, forgetting, for the moment, to look wan.

"Then you will be my doctor?" she cried.

"If you are sure you want me to be," I answered.

She edged toward the back of the sofa and patted the small space beside her.

"Of course I do!" she said. "Do sit down."

I followed her suggestion and reached for her wrist.

"Tell me," I said, "what seems to be the trouble?"

"I feel simply awful," she replied.

I snorted.

"You'll have to give me other symptoms than that," I said, "before I can prescribe for you."

"Well," she said, "I just seem to have the megrims. Sometimes I'm just dreadfully depressed, and at others I feel unnaturally gay, for no reason at all. But mostly I just feel listless."

"Those aren't symptoms," I said.

"I feel dreadfully nervous," she said.

"Nausea?"

She shook her head.

"Headaches?"

"Nooooo."

I felt her head. It was perfectly cool. I took her pulse. It was steady. I asked to see her tongue, and she showed it to me. It was quite clear. As a matter of form I peered into her throat and saw nothing to cause alarm. I thumped her back and chest and found them sound. Having exhausted these possibilities, I sat back and looked at her. She met my eyes steadily, almost mischievously.

"Well, Doctor?" she asked.

"Miss Hackett——" I began.

"My name is Selina," she put in.

"Miss Selina," I began again, "I would diagnose your trouble as a mild case of spring fever and would prescribe a dose of sulphur and molasses for it."

"I hate it!" she exclaimed, making a wry face.

"I have no doubt you will survive without it," I said. "Perhaps a sound spanking would serve as well."

Her eyes widened.

"You wouldn't dare!" she exclaimed.

For a moment I toyed with the notion of accepting the challenge, but then thought better of it. A third and still more effective cure for her ailment occurred to me, but I was not so indelicate as to mention it.

" 'Tis not for lack of daring, my dear," I told her, "that I don't. I am your physician, not your parent."

I rose.

"If that is all . . ." I said.

She was all smiles again and caught at my hand.

"Don't go!" she begged. "I want to talk to you."

I sat down again with some amusement.

"Do we come to the truth now?" I asked.

She nodded, smiling.

"What's your name?" she asked.

"Tom," I said.

"Tom!" she repeated. "Well, Tom, I was lonely. I wanted someone to talk to."

"But why me?"

"I've already told you I liked you as soon as I saw you."

"But why all this nonsense about being ill?" I demanded. "Do you think that was fair?"

"I—I wasn't sure you'd come if I just asked you," she said. "I had to give some reason. And besides, I wasn't lying when I said I would want you for my doctor. I meant that."

I reached out and took her hand. She made no effort to withdraw it.

"My dear," I said, "I'd be happy to serve you. But don't you think this is a bit indiscreet? What would your father say?"

"Oh," she said gaily, "he's gone to Boston."

I made no answer. Indeed, I could think of none.

"I thought Ben might bring you around," she said, "after we met. When he didn't, I thought of this."

"I can't say that I'm sorry," I laughed.

"Why didn't he?" she demanded. "He hasn't been near us."

"He hasn't?" I said, although I knew he had not.

"Is he angry about something?" she asked.

She seemed quite intent on my answer.

"He never spoke of it if he is," I replied.

"He must be!" she said positively. She sat back with a small sigh. Then: "Oh well, what does it matter?" she asked gaily. "You're here now!"

She leaned forward until her hair was fairly brushing my cheek.

"You will come back again," she said, "won't you, Tom?"

"Whenever you like," I replied.

I must have looked startled, for she fell back and snuggled down amid the pillows.

"I have it!" she cried. "Tom! There's to be a ball at the Assembly next week. Will you take me? It isn't right that you should live here and have no friends. I'll sponsor you!"

"Oh, I have friends," I assured her.

I don't know what reply she might have made, for at that moment there was a knock at the outer door. We heard the houseboy's steps go past in the hallway.

"Who in the world——" Selina said, and her tone was a shade apprehensive.

There was a mumble of voices and then a step. I was already standing, facing the door, yet even so I was unprepared to come face to face with Ben Price.

Evidently he was equally startled to see me. He was already scowling when he appeared, but at sight of me he stopped short and his scowl deepened.

"What——" he began.

"Why, Ben!" I heard Selina say. "We were just talking about you."

I glanced at her and saw that she had worked herself lower amid the pillows and drawn the comforter up beneath her chin. I chuckled inwardly at that as I turned back to Ben. Her words had done nothing to calm him. He looked enraged and suspicious. Had he been the lady's husband I could not have expected him to look more upset. He glared at me.

"What the devil are you doing here?" he demanded.

I balked at that. I thought at first that he must have followed me from the yard, but an instant's reflection showed me the folly of that. I had left no indication of where I was going. No, it was purely coincidence, and its corollary was evident. It was the first night I had not been on hand to accompany him home from work; therefore it was the first opportunity he had had to come here without me. I found myself more amused than irritated by that. I bowed to Selina.

"Shall I tell him?" I asked.

She smiled at me, as though we had some secret together between us. I had a momentary impression that Ben was on the verge of fainting, so stricken did he appear.

"I came at Miss Hackett's request," I said, "as a physician."

"That's likely!" Ben snarled.

"Don't be a boor!" Selina snapped. "I sent for Tom because I felt ill, and he came and prescribed for me. I don't know why I trouble to explain it to you!"

He glanced from one to the other of us once more, and the doubt upon his face was so plain that I laughed.

"It's true," I said. "I found her suffering from spring megrims and prescribed a tonic. I was leaving when she asked why you never came to see her, and—pouf! There you were!"

He turned to stare at her, and slowly his expression changed. The mocking smile touched his lips and he bowed in her direction.

"Forgive me," he said. "I didn't understand."

To me he said, "I had not expected to see you."

"Nor I you," I replied.

There was an awkward pause.

"Well!" he said with mock brightness, breaking the silence, "isn't someone going to say something?"

"I'm going to say good-by," I said. "I think Selina should rest now. I prescribe it for her."

Selina gave me a half-smile and a lifted eyebrow, but it was to Ben that she spoke.

"Tom has promised to take me to the Assembly Ball next week, Ben," she said. "You'll come with us, won't you?"

"And be the third wheel? No, thank you."

I picked up my hat. Selina extended her hand.

"Next week, then," she said. "Wednesday?"

"Wednesday it is," I replied.

At the door I paused and glanced at Ben.

"Coming?" I asked.

He hesitated an instant and then followed sulkily, giving Selina no more than a curt good-by.

It was dark when we reached the street, and Ben fell in beside me, walking furiously.

"Why did you go there?" he demanded.

"I told you," I replied. "She said she was ill."

"Was she?"

"No, she's no more ill than you or I."

"What did you tell her?"

"I prescribed sulphur and molasses or a good spanking. We got along famously."

He stopped abruptly and turned to face me.

"Is that all?"

"What more did you expect?" I said.

"I mean is that all that happened? Did you tell her anything about me?" he persisted.

"Why should I?" I snapped.

"Did she tell you anything about me?" he demanded.

"She didn't mention your name," I said, "except to wonder why you hadn't called."

"Hah!" he snorted.

"Look here," I said, "you seem mighty touchy tonight. Is there something she should have told me?"

He looked away.

"Nothing," he said, "except that once we imagined ourselves in love."

"But now you don't, is that it?" I chuckled.

"No, we don't," he snapped.

"Well, if you ask me," I grinned, "you're well out of it. She's handsome, but she's selfish and flighty. She might be amusing—so long as you're not serious about her. Why don't you come to the ball?"

He shot me a sardonic glance.

"No!" he said.

For a few paces we walked in silence. Then all at once he stopped abruptly.

"Wait a minute," he exclaimed, "wait a minute! I believe I will! By God, I will!"

He looked at me and grinned. Then all at once he burst out laughing.

7

The dinner which Patience served and the music which followed seemed even gayer than usual that evening. Both Ben and I danced with Patience, and it was only when Sam Nowell put his guitar firmly upon the table and announced that he was too tired to play more that Ben dropped the little bombshell, which I suspect he had been nursing throughout the evening. As the last strains of the music floated away up the chimney, he turned to Patience and bowed elegantly.

"My dear," he said, "there is no more we can teach you. You dance perfectly, and it seems a shame and a selfish crime to keep you all to ourselves. There's to be a ball at the Assembly next week. Will you honor me as my partner?"

Sam Nowell frowned abruptly. Patience gasped.

"A ball? Me? You want me to go to a ball?"

"Why not?" Ben nodded. "Anyone as lovely as yourself, Pat, was not meant to hide forever!"

Patience gave him a rapturous look.

"Oh, Grandpa, may I?" she cried.

"We'll see!" the old man mumbled evasively.

I felt as though I had suddenly swallowed a cake of ice. Not

until we were in our room, however, did I feel free to protest.
As I shut the door and leaned against it, Ben tossed his jacket
upon the bed and turned about, spreading his hands in a
triumphant gesture, his face wreathed in a grin so smugly
self-satisfied that I could cheerfully have punched it.

"You fool!" I exclaimed. "You poor damned fool!"

If I had hit him in the face with a cold, wet rag I could not
more effectively have wiped away his expression of complacency. He stared at me in blank astonishment.

"What's the matter with you?" he demanded.

"If it were not so cruel to Pat," I replied hotly, "I ought to
let you find out for yourself. Which will give you the most
pleasure—the hurt you hope to do Selina or the enjoyment you
suppose Pat will take from it?"

"What the devil are you babbling about?" he growled.

"Has it ever occurred to you to wonder that Pat has no
friends outside this house?" I said.

"Come to the point, man!" he replied hotly.

I told him what I knew of Patience's background with con-
siderable reluctance, for I did not relish the role of gossip. Yet
I saw no way of avoiding it now. The fat was in the fire. When
I had finished he stared at me hopelessly.

"What am I to do?"

"It's your problem!" I taunted.

"The dogs!" he muttered. "Why must they persecute her?"

"That is my own feeling," I assured him dryly. "I'd rather
take smallpox than risk hurting her more."

He glanced at me hopefully.

"Do you think it could be arranged?"

"Don't talk nonsense," I replied.

"She didn't have to accept so eagerly," he said presently.
"If it's true, I should think she'd have said no."

"Did you never hear of a thing called hope?" I demanded.
"You can't blame the child for hoping that things may be different. She'll go as your guest. You've taught her to dance—to
play a part. Small wonder she lets herself believe that will make
everything right. She's pinned her faith in you. God forgive
you if you disappoint her!"

"Oh Lord!" he groaned. If the situation had not been so
serious in my own sight, I could have been amused.

I will say for Ben that, for all his faults, I believe he was never willful in the harm he did. When he was impelled to some act of knavery it was through self-indulgence, and rarely from viciousness. It only happened that the consequences fell most heavily upon those closest to him. When he perceived that a wrong had been done, no one could be more contrite. The mood might not last long, but while it did it was real enough and he was likely to go to the greatest lengths to make amends; lengths that sometimes brought in their train still greater miseries than those for which he sought to atone.

That such a mood was upon him was plentifully evident during those next few days. He had such an air of preoccupation, such a look of worriment, that it was sometimes painful to break in upon his thoughts. Twenty times a day he asked me what to do, and I could see that several times he was on the verge of telling Patience that he could not take her, only to find her so happy that after a few feeble attempts he had not the heart to go through with it. These occasions served only to increase her excitement and to that extent made matters worse.

Nor did I fall in with his suggestion that I protest to Sam Nowell. In the first place, I objected because Nowell had never mentioned Patience's origin to me, and I was not at all sure that he would relish the fact of our knowledge. In the second, it was Ben's own predicament, and I felt that the solution was up to him. I did, however, manage a word with Patience. The manner in which I fared in that was warning enough to keep hands off and stay on my own side of the fence.

I came home alone and early on Saturday evening; alone because Ben was still busy at the yard, and early because I had finished my own work. As I entered the gate I spied Patience in the garden, weeding, and squatted down beside her. She gave me a gay smile of welcome.

"You're home early, Tom!" she greeted me.

"Yes," I agreed.

She gave me a shy glance, which I pretended not to see.

"You're setting a lot of store by this ball next week, aren't you?" I said.

"Isn't it wonderful?" she cried. "I can't wait! I'm making a new gown for it."

I tried to keep from showing anything of my thoughts.

"You never offered to take me to a ball," she said, and I presume she meant it as a sly dig.

"No," I replied. "They're not really much fun. I don't think you'll like it."

She straightened up slowly and stared at me.

"What makes you say that?"

I found it hard to meet her eyes.

"Well," I said, "I just don't—that's all."

She rose abruptly.

"Oh!" she said. "I know what you're thinking."

There are moments, I suppose, when it is better to be cruel; when a little deeper hurt should be inflicted that the wound may be the better cleansed. As a doctor, perhaps, I should have known that. But it is easier far to thrust in the knife with a steady hand and cut away the offending flesh than it is to perform a like surgery with words. In this moment my courage failed me.

"Pat!" I cried weakly. "I didn't mean that at all! Those affairs are awfully dull sometimes."

It did not occur to me then that with those words I had told her just how much I knew. She looked at me very seriously.

"I don't think *I* will find it dull, Tom," she said.

It seemed to me that I must, somehow, repair the damage I had done.

"Pat!" I said earnestly. "I'm very fond of you."

"Are you, Tom?" she asked.

"If you were my own sister," I assured her, "I could not be more so!"

She looked as if I had slapped her.

"Oh!" she exclaimed. "Oh!"

And then, abruptly, she turned and ran into the house, leaving me staring after her, bewildered at the ways of women.

It was evident that in some way I had upset her. I followed her and found her standing before the fireplace, her arm flung up along the mantelpiece as a rest for her forehead.

"What's the matter?" I asked. "Why did you fling off?"

She straightened with a little shaking movement and turned about toward me.

"I thought I heard the kettle boil over," she said.

"But the kettle isn't on," I pointed out stupidly.

She smiled wanly.

"Yes, I know. Wasn't I silly?"

"Look, Pat," I said, "I was only trying to tell you that I love you——"

"Like a sister," she put in.

"Exactly!" I agreed.

She threw her hands out in a little helpless sort of gesture, and I caught one of them in my own.

"And I don't want anything to hurt you," I finished.

"What's going to hurt me?" she said. "What could hurt me now?"

"The dance——" I began.

"But you'll be there, Tom, won't you?" she said. "You won't let anyone hurt me."

It was plain that we were getting nowhere. I tossed up my hands in defeat.

"Oh, forget it!" I exclaimed angrily. "I'm sorry I spoke of it!"

That evening Patience seemed even more brightly gay than ever, while both Ben and I were so glum that it must have been noticeable to Sam Nowell. For my part, I felt as though she were taunting me for what I had tried to say during the afternoon, and when she danced with Ben it seemed to me that she was more tender and attentive than she had any need to be. In a way, I think, it made me a little jealous.

8

THERE WERE a few small occurrences between then and the ball which might have served to show me which way the wind was setting.

In the first place, I recall clearly that when we retired that evening Ben was no longer gloomy and morose, as he had been. On the contrary, he was once again cocksure, swaggering, full of insolent good-fellowship and amiable conceit. It irritated me and I growled at him.

"If you think a smile or two from Pat has solved the problem, you're a greater fool than I took you for!"

Far from being cast down by my nagging, however, he seemed amused. He gave me a superior laugh and waved me aside.

"You are a dull fellow at times, Tom," he sneered, "and you've a bad habit of prying. Suppose you leave my problems to me and tend to your own knitting for a change."

The following day was bright and fresh and clear as only a Sunday in June can be. The morning was given to worship, but there remained the better part of the day to fill. Sundays and evenings were all the time left to me to pursue my medical studies these days, and such was the conscience of Salem that I dared not let my habit be widely known. Ordinarily I would shut myself in my room with my books, but this day was too fine to spend indoors. Accordingly I made my selection—the final volume of Rush's *Medical Inquiries and Observations*—and borrowed a shallop from the yard. In this I sailed to North Gooseberry, where I felt reasonably sure of being unmolested, and settled myself in the sunlight among the rocks and went about my studies.

I have always been a follower of Rush, whatever may be said of him, and I have perhaps been the more inclined to his views from the persecution of his enemies during the yellow-fever epidemics. Perhaps this is because he, like myself, advocated bleeding and purging to check the fever and hot baths to relax the patient. No doubt I took his success as, in some measure, a vindication of my own theories. But that is neither here nor there so far as this story goes. What matters is that I became so absorbed in my study that it was close to sunset before I laid the book aside and sailed back to Briggs's Yard, where the frigate lay in the stocks, half planked, like a partially decomposed whale.

At the house I found Sam Nowell alone. He told me that Ben and Patience had gone off to walk to Marblehead. At six they reappeared, happy as children, though no more so, it seemed to me, than usual. Patience prepared supper, and so the day ended, pleasantly for all, and yet with no real solution that I could see for the problem.

The next two days added nothing out of the ordinary to the routine of our lives. But on Wednesday, the day of the ball,

Ben did not go to work. When I called him in the morning he put me off with an excuse about not feeling up to it.

When I came home there was no sign of Ben or Patience or Sam Nowell, though there was a cold supper laid out and a note to say I was not to wait. This struck me as odd, but since there was nothing else to do I ate and went up to dress. I was nearly ready when Ben came in.

"Well," I exclaimed, "where the devil have you been?"

He gave me a smile that was almost a sneer.

"Sam had a family matter to attend to, and I went along with him and Patience to see to it."

"You seem to be deep in their confidence," I growled.

He chuckled, rather nastily, I thought.

"I told you you were a dull fellow."

I swallowed that one merely because I had no wish to fight with him at this moment.

"You'd better hurry," I said, "if you expect to be ready on time."

He examined his fingernails with some elaborateness.

"Oh," he said, "forget about that. Patience and I won't be going with you tonight."

I turned and stared at him.

"Have you dissuaded her, then?"

"I merely put my cards upon the table."

"If you said anything to hurt her——" I began furiously.

"My dear innocent!" he laughed. "If you doubt me, you are at liberty to ask Patience how she feels about it. I think you will find she is delighted."

I saw that he was in his most obnoxious mood, and I said no more. As I went out I encountered Patience in the hallway, and she stopped me.

"I hope you're not upset, Tom," she said.

"I think it was a very wise decision," I replied.

She looked at me in the dim light in such a way that I could not be sure whether I had hurt or pleased her. When she spoke at last it was in a voice that trembled.

"God bless you, Tom! You are a true friend!"

Before I realized what she was doing, then, she kissed me on the cheek and fled up the hall, leaving me standing completely bewildered and amazed.

I was admitted to the Hacketts' house by the same blackamoor who had summoned me from the yard a week previously.
He smiled a bright-toothed welcome and took my hat, bowing
me toward the drawing room in which Selina had received me.
I passed on into the room and was startled to find Captain
Hackett. He was enjoying a solitary brandy, topped off with
a fine Havana cigar. At my entry he rose.

"Ah, Tisdall!" he exclaimed. "Selina's not quite ready. She'll
be down in a moment. You know these women!"

He let his glance slide over my shoulder.

"Ben didn't come with you, then?" he asked.

"No sir," I replied, "at the last minute he told me that he
would not be able to join us."

"Ah!" he remarked sapiently. "He's unpredictable, but on
the whole quite a fellow. May I offer you brandy and coffee,
a cigar?"

"Thank you, sir," I said.

"You've been long acquainted with Ben?" he asked.

"As a matter of fact," I replied, "I've known him little over
a month."

"Indeed?" he said. "You say you are from Portsmouth?
You will be acquainted with Dr. Hall Jackson, no doubt?"

I assured him that I was acquainted with the doctor, though
I did not think it fit to add that my acquaintance was mainly
hearsay, having seen his windows broken by the mob in '95 for
having the temerity to sign the letter to the President in support of Mr. Jay's Treaty.

"A great man, Jackson," he commented. "And so you've
made up your mind to take up your practice in Salem, eh?"

"As a matter of fact, sir," I made haste to explain, "I hadn't
gone so far as that."

He chuckled heavily.

"Just looking around, eh?" he asked. "Have you ever
thought of going to sea? As a ship's surgeon, say?"

I confessed that I had not.

"Ah," he said, "that's it! It's amazingly difficult to find
good men willing to ship as surgeons, and the demand is in-
creasing—bound to! It's war, my lad! Inevitable! We can't
continue to lie down under insults as we have in the past. We'll
never be able to hold our own at sea if we do. Thank the Lord

the Government is taking a firm stand at last! These frigates they're building will go a long way toward teaching respect for our flag, but, mark my words, we'll have a fight on our hands before we're through!"

I clucked sympathetically, to hide my ignorance.

"The frigates will help," he said. "But we'll need privateers as well. Both will need surgeons. A point you might think over, Doctor. Prize money, you know. Many a young surgeon has made his start that way."

I murmured that I was sure it was worth considering.

"I cannot understand," he said petulantly, "how Mr. Adams can make such a fool of himself. To dream of treating again with the French!"

I was relieved that Selina chose that moment to put in her appearance.

"Father!" she exclaimed. "Talking politics again!"

We turned to see her silhouetted in the doorway, regarding us in a way that was at once mischievous and mildly reproving. I must say that she made an appealing picture. The light in the hallway beyond her cast a nimbus about her dark hair, bringing out its inky sheen, and brought into relief the swelling curve of her high breasts and rounded hips beneath the dress of heavy yellow silk that she wore. She obviously had an eye for color, and tonight her costume had been chosen with a deliberate eye to setting off her own dark beauty.

I must have gaped at her in open admiration, for she laughed gaily.

"Am I so frightening, Doctor?"

I felt my face grow red with embarrassment, and to me it seemed as though I stammered my reply.

"Not frightening," I said, "but beautiful beyond belief!"

She came toward me with both hands outstretched.

"How sweet of you to say that!" she exclaimed.

I turned to her father as I took her hands in mine.

"I call on you to witness, sir," I said, "if I speak any but the plain truth!"

His flinty face brightened in a rare smile.

"I might be accused of prejudice," he replied. "But I think you have not exaggerated. You do look unusually charming, my dear!"

"That's very pretty, Father dear," she laughed, "but you have a long way to go before you can do as well as Tom!"

She gave my hands a little affectionate squeeze.

"Ben wouldn't come, I take it?" she said.

"He begged off at the last minute," I replied.

"Pouf!" she exclaimed. "We'll have much more fun without him! Are you ready? Shall we go?"

We went—in the Hacketts' coach, dropping Captain Hackett off at the East India Society on the way.

"He does it to escape his social duties," Selina explained to me as he stepped down from the carriage.

He turned at that and thrust his head in at the window.

"You know why I do it," he retorted. " 'Tis to escape having to talk all evening to that blithering bore Bentley."

"Mr. Bentley's no worse than several you'll meet at the Society," she told him.

"Stuff!" he replied. "Get along with you now. Good night to you, Doctor. Take good care of my girl."

"Good night, sir," I replied. "I'll do my best."

Selina settled back beside me, and in the intimate darkness of the carriage I became suddenly acutely aware of her nearness. The faint hint of the delicate perfume that she used, the more tantalizing woman smell of her hair as it brushed close to my cheek when she laid her head back, the touch of her body—shoulder, arm, hip, and thigh—against mine as the carriage jolted slightly, all combined to remind me that she was desirable and set my pulses to throbbing faster. When she reached out a hand and placed it on my knee I started as though I had been touched by fire, and made haste to cover it with my own. No word of invitation passed between us, yet the impulse to take her in my arms and crush her lips against my own was well-nigh overpowering. Nor, I believe, would she have resisted me had I done so. But at that moment the carriage drew up before the Assembly Hall, and there was naught to do but alight.

I must say I did so with a sense of disappointment. I felt hot and flushed, and I found myself wishing that we had not arrived so soon. That she sensed this was evidenced in the look she gave me and the gentle squeeze of her fingers as I handed her down. As we turned to enter the building she accepted my arm with affectionate gaiety, taking it in both hands and hugging it to her so that her cheek brushed my shoulder and I could feel the warm swelling of her breast against my elbow. At the same time she glanced up at me mischievously.

"We'll take a longer way home," she whispered.

We found the Assembly Hall already crowded, and a blaze of light from the hundreds of candles that burned in the chandeliers and in sconces along the walls. For myself I should have been happy to have less light and more air, for all those tiny flames burning at once scarcely made the big room cooler and the smell of tallow was noticeable.

As we entered a black lackey, splendid in white gloves and white knee breeches and a swallow-tailed blue coat with huge brass buttons, announced our names to the receiving line.

"Miss Selinah Hackett and Doctah Thomas Tisdall!"

He spoke in booming tones that must have carried to the very bowels of the building, and for an instant it seemed to me that everyone in the room was eying us curiously, appraisingly. A few followed Selina with their eyes. Others eyed me curiously, as if wondering what I might be doing there. Selina moved toward the line, and I fell quickly in behind her. She went smoothly, gracefully, not lingering except to present me to each member of the line in turn.

"Good evening, Mrs. Derby. So nice to see you out again! May I present Dr. Tisdall? Captain Derby! You had a successful voyage, I am told. You are going out again soon in the *Mount Vernon?* Mrs. Crowninshield! How nice! Captain Crowninshield"—she pronounced it "Grunsell"—"this is Dr. Tisdall. Mr. Bentley! This is Dr. Tisdall."

I had not been through a receiving line before, and I was agreeably surprised to find it not such an ordeal as I had anticipated at first sight. They smiled vaguely and shook hands, repeating my name pleasantly enough.

"Good evening, Doctor. Welcome to Salem, Dr. Tisdall! So nice of you to come."

Only the Reverend Mr. Bentley had more than that to say. He was a rotund little man, not much above my shoulder, with a rounded head and ruddy complexion. He fixed me with an inquisitive bright eye and lingered over his handshake.

"Tisdall?" he said. "One of the Swampscott Tisdalls?"

"No sir," I replied. "I'm from Portsmouth."

"Portsmouth?" he said, and shook his head. "I don't recall any Tisdalls in Portsmouth."

It was not intended to be insulting. I smiled.

"It is not likely you would, sir," I replied. "There were never many of us, nor were we ever prominent."

"Of course!" He beamed apologetically. "Score one for you, my boy! You know Dr. Hall Jackson, of course."

I assured him that I was acquainted with Dr. Jackson, whose fame appeared to have spread farther than I had realized.

"And Dr. Matthew Thornton?"

"I'm afraid I did not move in the same circle with Dr. Thornton," I replied.

"Ah well!" He coughed discreetly. "I'm sure Portsmouth's loss is our gain. I'm delighted to see you with us."

We passed on and joined a knot of guests who had been beckoning to Selina. She presented me to them.

"This is Dr. Tisdall—Tom, everyone." She repeated their names to me.

I bowed to the ladies. Mercy Hawks was tall and rangy, with sharp features and prominent teeth, but intelligent, contemplative eyes. Sally Pierce, who seemed attached to Captain Nichols, was small and rather pretty. Ann Hodges, Martha Harrod, Lydia Dodge were plain, while Susanna Nichols and Betsey Gray were willowy beauties.

Each of the men offered his hand, and I was startled to see how young these "captains" were. Nichols and Delano and Woolridge were my own age, or younger, while the others, I was sure, were none of them over thirty. Bowditch, who was still a supercargo and had not yet attained the fame that was presently to be his, was tall and thin, with a round head, already a little bald, with a sharp peaked nose and studious eyes, and was less reserved than the others.

"You're new to Salem, Doctor?" he said.

"Comparatively so," I replied.

"Do you plan to settle here, Doctor?"

I glanced at Selina.

"I have not yet made up my mind," I said.

Captain Delano laughed.

"Do you mean you have difficulty?"

"Joshua!" Martha Harrod exclaimed.

"Have you thought of going to sea, Dr. Tisdall?" the elder Crowninshield asked. "In the ordinary run of things a ship hasn't much use for a sawbones. But in these times, with letters of marque and reprisal being issued and war in the offing, you'll find yourself in brisk demand."

"Nonsense, Jacob!" Lydia Dodge exclaimed. "There'll be no war."

"That's not what most people think," Captain Nichols put in.

"I understand Retire Beckett's building a privateer brig for Gray and Orne," Captain Derby said.

Ann Hodges gasped, and Captain Derby glanced at her in surprise. But she was not looking at him. Instead she was staring over my shoulder at something beyond my back.

At almost the same instant I heard, behind me, the deep tones of the Negro lackey announcing:

"Mr. and Mrs. Eben E. Price!"

"Selina!" Ann Hodges whispered vehemently. "Selina! Isn't that that Nowell girl?"

9

A STARTLED SILENCE swept across the room. The ladies in the receiving line looked panic-stricken. Captain Derby and Captain Crowninshield appeared uncertain whether to accept or resent them. Behind me I heard a sharp hiss of intaken breath and, half turning, I saw that Selina was quite livid.

"How could he?" she breathed. "Oh, how could he?"

I will confess that I was caught between wind and water myself. The words coming from Selina, however, jarred me, and spurred me instinctively to their defense.

"She's really a very sweet person," I whispered.

The glance that Selina gave me was hot, angry.

At the same moment the Reverend Mr. Bentley stepped forward, beaming welcome to the couple. There was no trace of resentment upon his features, and as he moved we could hear his jovial voice explaining to the rest of the patrons.

"Married 'em myself this afternoon. It's by way of being a wedding party for them, you see, so I asked 'em to come as my guests. Mrs. Derby, ma'am, Mrs. Price and Mr. Price. You'll be acquainted, Mrs. D., with the work of Mr. Price's father. He's Jonathan Price, of Sudbury——"

"The trollop!" I heard Martha Harrod say.

I turned.

"Do you know her?" I asked in a low tone.

Her sharp face turned toward me disdainfully.

"Of course not! But everyone knows——"

"That her parents were not married?" I interrupted her fiercely." Why do you blame her for that? What had she to say in the matter?"

Their faces around me looked shocked and startled, all except Selina, who glanced intently from me to the little group at the upper end of the room. Her eyes narrowed.

"I happen to board at the Nowell house," I was saying, paying scant heed to Selina. "I can tell you that never by so much as word or gesture has she shown herself to be other than decent and respectable and good!"

"You know her reputation!"

"I know the reputation she has inherited, if that's what you mean," I replied. "But of my own knowledge of the girl, I tell you I could not ask better of my own mother."

Selina brought me unexpected reinforcement.

"He's right!" she exclaimed, still looking at me oddly. "It isn't fair to blame *her*."

She turned quickly and started across the floor, walking toward where Ben and Patience still stood facing the sponsors. As she caught Ben's eye she smiled and held out both hands in welcome. Behind me I heard one of the ladies of the group we had just left speak in tones of outraged resignation.

"Well! Since she's honestly married, I suppose——"

Ben and Patience watched our approach; Ben with a look of puzzled doubt, Patience with an expression of surprise. Selina went directly to Ben.

"You never told us!" she exclaimed chidingly. "Why, Ben Price! Surely we're old enough friends!"

It seemed to me that the shadow of a scowl flicked across

Ben's eyes. One eyebrow went up slightly, and an almost mocking expression spread across his dark features.

"I didn't know you cared, Seel," he replied.

He said it casually, and in such a low tone that I am sure no one but myself heard the words. Before Selina could reply Ben continued.

"You know my wife, of course. Pat, my sweet, here's Selina Hackett, come to offer congratulations."

Patience smiled shyly, though a little uncertainly. Selina caught her hands and stood on tiptoe to kiss her cheek.

"My dear!" she exclaimed. "This is wonderful! I'm sure you'll be very happy."

Patience blushed and cast a quick, almost adoring glance at Ben. Over Selina's head I could see that Ben was frowning slightly, staring at her with a puzzled look.

"Oh, thank you, Miss Hackett!" Patience said.

Selina turned abruptly to me.

"Why, Tom darling! You're pale as a ghost!"

If I had been, I knew that I was no longer, for I could feel myself blushing furiously.

"It must be surprise," I said lamely.

"Didn't you know?" Selina demanded.

I shook my head.

"Never suspected!" I replied.

Patience stared at me. Selina laughed gaily.

"Why, this is priceless!" she exclaimed. "Aren't you going to kiss the bride?"

I gave Pat my hand and bent to kiss her lightly.

"The best of everything, Pat!" I said, and for some reason I had trouble with my voice.

"Oh, Tom!" was her only reply.

I turned to Ben and offered my hand.

"Congratulations," I said.

He shook hands with a dry grin.

"Thanks, Tom," he said.

Behind me I heard the Reverend Mr. Bentley call out: "Let's all kiss the bride!"

Others came forward at that, crowding around to offer congratulations and follow the little minister's suggestion. The women, I noticed, remained stiffly formal. The men, on the other hand, were willing to make an occasion of it. Little by little Selina and I were elbowed aside, and presently we found ourselves standing alone on the outskirts of the crowd. It was there that she turned upon me fiercely, almost angrily.

"Why didn't you tell me?" she demanded.

I looked at her in blank surprise.

"I had no more idea of it than yourself," I told her.

She gazed at me intently, then appeared to soften.

"She's hurt you dreadfully, hasn't she?" she said.

"Why—I—— Why, that's nonsense!" I said.

She looked down at her hands.

"I've been hurt too, Tom," she said, "a little."

She lifted her eyes to mine.

"But, in a way," she whispered, "I think it may be a good thing."

This left me completely bewildered. At that instant the Reverend Mr. Bentley bustled up.

"Isn't it magnificent?" he demanded. "After all these years that poor, sweet child—— Well! It's time for music!"

He turned and made a signal to the orchestra.

At once the strains of "Hail Columbia" crashed out. The Reverend Mr. Bentley turned away from us, shouting: "Fall in, everybody, for the Grand March!"

We watched him bustle away to join Captain and Mrs. Derby, who were to lead the march. Selina gave her arm to me.

To my eyes it was a gay party, and yet even I was aware of a certain air of restraint. That reluctance of the ladies to meet with Patience on equal terms was sometimes evident in pursed lips and down-cornered mouths, stiff backs and an attitude of primness in a figure in which she was dancing. But the men of the assembly were persistent in ignoring these signals. It was the sort of an evening that goes off smoothly enough but leaves one with the feeling that feminine tongues would wag in the darkness long after the last note had been played. Once I found myself paired with Patience.

"How do you like it?" I asked.

She smiled up at me radiantly.

"It's even more wonderful than I imagined it would be!"

It occurred to me that she was unaware of the stir she was creating.

"It is pleasant," I agreed.

"You looked startled when we were announced."

"You took me completely by surprise," I told her.

She looked up at me blankly.

"But you said you thought it was a wise decision."

"*I* thought it was a wise decision?" I gasped. "What do you mean? I wasn't consulted."

She looked utterly nonplused.

"You told me," she said, "in the hall, just before you came here, that you thought I'd made a wise decision. Don't you remember?"

I did remember, suddenly, my own words.

"My God!" I exclaimed involuntarily.

"Tom Tisdall!" she rebuked me. "You swore."

"I'm sorry!" I said. "I just remembered. But I didn't know! Ben told me you weren't coming. That's what I was talking about."

"Oh!" she exclaimed. "Then——"

"Pat," I said, "if you love him, it's right, and God bless you both. It's just a little sudden, that's all."

In that instant she was whisked away by another partner, so that I had no further chance to talk to her.

At the punch bowl Ben gave me a triumphant grin.

"Did I solve it?" he said.

"I told you once that if you ever hurt Pat I'd have your hide," I replied. "I meant it, and I still mean it!"

"What do you mean?" he demanded, staring at me as if he did not know.

"Tonight you have succeeded," I said. "Patience is accepted as your wife. Don't ever let her down!"

"If I didn't have my hands full of punch glasses——" he began furiously.

"You know what I'm talking about," I said. "Don't forget it!"

I went back to Selina, and the dance went on.

It was midnight when the ball ended. I did not see Ben and Patience leave. Selina and I said our due good-bys, not with the first, nor yet with the last. The Hackett carriage was waiting. I handed Selina in, and as we rolled away from the door she sat stiffly beside me, her fists clenched tightly on her knees.

"How could he!" she exclaimed, speaking in the darkness. "How could he do this to me?"

I stared at her in the gloom of the carriage, shocked and in a vague way disturbed.

"I don't believe he knew it himself," I said. "He only did it when I told him how difficult it was for her."

She turned on me.

"Then you're behind it!"

"I don't know what you're talking about," I said. "Pat's a fine girl. It wasn't her idea, I'm sure."

"A fine trollop——" she began to retort.

"See here," I exclaimed, "I won't——"

"Stuff!" she interrupted angrily. "You won't hear a word against her! I know! You're as blind as the rest of them! Blinder!"

"If you'll pardon me," I said stiffly, "I'll get down here. I've no mind to quarrel with you."

I thrust my head out the window to call to the driver, but she caught me by the coattails and drew me back.

"I—I'm sorry," she said. "I—I didn't mean to offend you."

"It's not I who am offended," I said.

"Nor Patience, either," she muttered. "It's just that—can't you see? You've been disappointed too!"

"I?" I echoed, surprised.

"Don't try to pretend," she said impatiently. "Anyone with half an eye could see!"

"Hold on!" I said. "There never was anything between Pat and me."

"Well, there was between me and Ben," she replied. "Oh, don't think I care! It's just that—he never said boo, I guess."

I grinned in the darkness.

"You mean your—feelings are hurt?"

I started to say "pride," but thought better of it.

She leaned against me and nodded.

"I suppose so," she said.

She sniffed.

"There now," I said, "Ben's not the only man."

"Oh, Tom!" she said.

The carriage drew up before her door before I could say anything further. At the front door she gave me both hands.

"You've been sweet," she said. "Good night."

"Good night, Selina," I replied.

"We must stick together," she said. "Come and see me—often?"

"I will," I promised, not knowing what else to say.

10

WHETHER it was as a result of the evening's excitement or of my own troubled thoughts, I spent a sleepless night. I tossed and I turned. I counted the hours as the clock downstairs boomed them out. Small noises disturbed me. I lay wide-eyed in the darkness. What time I slept I dreamed wild dreams in which Patience and Selina quarreled violently over matters I could not understand, while Ben stood near by, wearing a darkly Mephisphelean look. When dawn came I was broad awake, and rose and went down to light the fire and draw the water for breakfast. Not many moments later Patience appeared, looking blushingly radiant. Ben and Sam Nowell followed soon after, seeming both refreshed and in good spirits. Only I was haggard.

I greeted them, I think, correctly, though to tell the truth I was somewhat at a loss for the proper form. I felt vaguely that a greater degree of formality should doubtless exist between Patience and myself, now that she was a married woman, yet I had no wish to terminate what, for me at least, had been the most lighthearted of friendships. Patience seemed puzzled at first and then a degree reserved. Ben cocked a quizzical eyebrow at me as he gave me good morning. But Sam Nowell would not let matters rest.

"You don't seem yourself this morning, Tom," he said.

"I feel all right," I replied. "Why shouldn't I?"

He shrugged.

"I was only sayin'."

He peered at Ben and Patience.

"I can see by lookin' at the two of you," he said, "that 'twas a success!"

For some reason this innocent remark annoyed me.

"Oh, it was a great success," I said before the others could speak. "Even I was taken by surprise!"

Patience looked at me in startled amazement.

"Why, Tom Tisdall! We wanted to surprise everybody."

"You did," I assured her.

Sam Nowell fell to chuckling jovially.

"Well!" he exclaimed. "I guess you did! Tell us about it, eh?"

Patience launched into a description of the ball. Her grandfather was serious at the beginning and sharply attentive, but as the story went on his spirits rose with the corresponding rise in Pat's own excitement.

"And Miss Hackett!" Pat cried, turning to me. "Wasn't she sweet, Tom?"

She looked down at her plate, evidently quite moved with Selina's kindness. I felt bitter.

"Oh yes," I agreed, "Selina was sweet all right."

Ben chuckled. Patience looked up soberly.

"She's a dear person, Tom," she said seriously.

"No doubt!" I said dryly.

I went about my work that morning with a sense of loneliness and resentment that I found difficult to explain; a feeling that a change had come to the Nowell house. The evening meal, eaten in glum silence, only confirmed the impression. Nor did the days that followed produce anything to alter it.

I do not mean to imply that we were hostile to one another, or surly. Nothing would be further from the mark. We were all very friendly and considerate, polite, courteous. But something that had been there before was gone. The old spirit of gay give-and-take, of laughter and affectionate raillery, was missing. In its place had come stiffness and formality, a brittleness, as if we were forever walking on eggs and feared to speak to one another lest our remarks be misunderstood and resented. There was no more dancing of an evening when the dishes had been washed and the day's work done. No one called upon me any longer for a tune on the flute. Sam Nowell spent more and more of his time at the Ship and Anchor. Ben's attitude was almost one of smirking exultation at having become master of the house. He was the host now. I was the guest. To me his attitude seemed patronizing, and I think if it had not been for Patience I would have picked up my gear and sought lodgings elsewhere.

I know now that it was on her account that I stayed on. At the time I was only aware that of them all she was the greatest changed, and that I was disturbed by this. I tried to tell myself that marriage made the difference; that she felt that she no longer had the right to continue our former relationship, innocent as it was. Toward me she was especially quiet, rarely speaking unless I addressed her first. Of an evening, as soon as the work was done, she and Ben would retire, leaving me to my own devices. At first I welcomed this opportunity to devote myself to my studies, which had been too much interrupted of late. But as the weeks passed I found myself less and less inclined to reading and more and more driven to seek other diversion.

In these circumstances it was not extraordinary that I should accept Selina Hackett's invitation. There was nothing stiff or formal about Selina. She was gay, vivacious, provocative. There was a laughing challenge in her dark eyes and invitation in her smile. I found her charming and desirable and faintly bewitching, and if I always left her presence with an odd sense of impatience, I found that by the following morning I was looking forward to seeing her again at tea, perhaps, or to going driving with her in the cool of the evening, or even to just sitting with her in the shadows of the veranda overlooking the garden, feeling her close to me though not so much as our hands were touching, deliciously aware of her presence.

At the outset I was diffident about the frequency of these visits, having no wish to wear out my welcome. But when both Selina and her father appeared to relish my coming, I cast my timidity aside and turned to them with greater regularity. As the spring drew into summer and summer passed on toward fall, we became more and more steady companions. I took her to the Fourth of July Ball, at the Assembly. I took her driving. When the summer picnics were held on Baker's and Great Misery islands, it was I who escorted her, and I was touched when, after I had hinted at the loneliness of Ben and Patience, she insisted upon inviting them to join us and thereafter included them in our party. When finally the frigate was launched, it was I, quite as a matter of course, who took her to see the great event, for by then—— But I run ahead of myself. There is more to be told before I come to that!

Other matters of equal importance were also shaping in that time. Work on the frigate went forward steadily. The gaunt, thick ribs and timbers that had given such a skeletal appearance to the early structure were sheathed gradually in a stout hide of oaken timbers, and the tapping of the hammers took on a hollower sound as decks were laid and bulkheads raised. Ben, chosen because of his skill to assist Samuel McIntire with the figurehead and quickwork, became more and more the aristocrat of the yard, with less and less regular hours. Some days he would appear only for a few moments to fit some piece of carved work at the rail or about her stern, or to take measurements or supervise the placing of the figurehead's platform. Then he would be away again to McIntire's studio to work upon more carving. But there was no doubt that more and more he was wrapped up in the work. Indeed, when he came to the yard he would spend a good part of his time admiring the vessel.

It occurred to none of us that of all the green hands about the yard he was the greenest. He made it a point to study ships and their construction, and he begged or borrowed everything he could find that might tell him more about it. He ate and slept shipbuilding. Indeed, the way he talked about it sometimes at the table, I often wondered that Patience was not jealous of the ship that took so much of his time!

I cannot say that I shared Ben's infatuation with the ship we were helping to build. Indeed, I scarcely had the opportunity, for all at once, by a series of accidents, I suddenly found myself plummeted into medical practice willy-nilly, with such force that I had neither time nor energy to spare.

The first of these came shortly after Ben's wedding. They were stepping the mast in the brig that was nearing completion on the ways next over beyond the frigate. The shears were rigged, and the heavy timber was being raised into place, when one of the blocks became tangled, and Noahdiah Hethcote climbed up to free it. Perhaps the jiggling set up by him in climbing the pole loosened it. Perhaps it was not firmly set in the first place. Whatever the cause, he had scarcely reached the entangled block when the shears slipped and down came the timber and Hethcote, shears, tackle, and all, the timber falling squarely athwart Noahdiah's legs, crushing one beyond all saving and breaking the other in three places above and below the knee.

I was in the office, poring over my ledgers, when the accident occurred. I heard the crash, the quick, thick silence that for an instant followed it, and then the blood-chilling squalling that told us that someone was injured. I started through the door, and had not gone ten paces beyond it when I met Ben, who grasped me by the wrist and cried:

"Tom! In God's name come!"

Have you ever heard a man screaming with every breath he drew, throwing his soul out upon the wind for every man to see? It isn't a thing you like to hear. When we reached the scene we found the man laid out upon the ground in a puddle of his own blood, his back arched in agony, his teeth bared and clenched, the cords of neck and face standing out like sinews, and his fists beating the ground beside him in futile pain. There were those who would have held me back as I thrust forward to kneel beside him. But Ben turned on them.

"Let him pass. He's a doctor."

"We've sent for Doc Cutter," someone said.

"This man will be dead before he can arrive," I said over my shoulder. I stood up and peeled off my coat.

"Let me have your saw, Ben," I said. "Sam, I'll borrow your drawknife and a hatchet."

I turned to Thatcher Magoun.

"Fetch me down one of those braziers and a pair of big chisels," I ordered, "and then find a plumb line that's never been used. When you've done that find me some clean lath, planed smooth, and if anyone's got a bottle, in God's name, let's have it!"

The things I called for appeared almost before I had time to turn and drop on my knees by the man's side. I passed the bottle to someone, with the order to let him drink as much of it as he would, and turned my attention to the crushed leg. With a borrowed kerchief I made a tourniquet to stanch the flow of blood, and then, as quickly as I could, I cut deep with the razor-sharp drawknife, slicing to the bone midway between knee

and hip, all around the leg, until the bone was bare and ready
for the saw. With the fresh plumb line I tied off the blood vessels and finally sawed through the bone until the useless,
mangled limb fell away. Next I cauterized the stump with the
red-hot chisels to end the bleeding, and then drew the flap of
skin that I had left dangling from mid-thigh to knee back across
the stump and sewed it to the back of the thigh.

I was as well pleased that Noahdiah had fainted by this time,
for I still had his other leg to treat, and though an amputation
might have been as easy, I determined to try and save it. I
directed three men to sit upon his chest and hold the leg at the
groin, while three more pulled with all their strength at the
foot. As the leg was drawn straight, I manipulated the broken
ends of the bones into place and bade them hold them there.
This done, I bound the strips of clean lath along his leg and
body, fetching the outer strip well up and fastening it securely
beneath the armpit.

I had scarcely finished this when the crowd opened for Dr.
Cutter, an elderly and wizened little man. He took one quick
glance at me, then looked at the man on the ground.

"Hummmmph!" he sniffed. " I don't see much left for me to
do. You've had good training, young man, whoever you might
be."

I stood up.

"Tisdall's the name, Doctor," I said. "From Portsmouth."

"Hummmmph!" he snorted. "Glad to know ye, Tisdall.
Didn't know ye were in the neighborhood. Where'd ye learn to
do a flap amputation like that, hey?"

"From Dr. Leeds," I replied.

"Eh? Old Leeds, of Portsmouth?" he cackled. "He never
did an operation like that in his life."

"No," I replied, "but he used to dream about it, and he told
me often enough how he would do it."

"Well, ye turned into an apt pupil, I'll say that for ye. But
now, let's get this lad home, eh?"

It was a forlorn hope that I had when I set to work upon
Noahdiah, for he had bled a good deal and was weak when I
reached him. But he was a stout fellow, and after a week he
came round out of his delirium and began to recover. To be
sure, it was long before he was able to hobble about on crutches,

but the fact was evident before a fortnight was out that he would recover, and overnight I found myself a man with a reputation.

I began to find myself in demand as a physician, first among families with connections in the yard, and then with others to whom they spoke. If I was fit to amputate a man's leg, it was reasoned, I could cure the worms and the tissick, the rash and the rheumatism, St. Anthony's fire and the king's evil. Then on the Fourth of July a cannon burst upon the green among the men and boys who were firing it in celebration, blowing away a pair of hands, an eye, an ear, a lower jaw, and nigh scalping another man, to say nothing of minor wounds caused by chunks of brass lodged in various portions of the anatomy. It took Dr. Cutter and myself two hours and a half to tend the more severely wounded and pick the pieces from those less seriously damaged. And when the task was done, I found myself a marked man in the town. The very next day Eli Hackett consulted me about a carbuncle he had long been carrying on his back. This he said he had been treating with Dr. Perkins's Famous Metallic Tractors without results. I applied hot cloths and then lanced it. In a day or two it was gone. Within three days I had a dozen such requests from other merchants of the town as well as the Reverend Mr. Bentley. I recommended that they abstain from the rich canary to which they were all addicted, and take a lighter wine. But this I could not prevail upon them to do, and in consequence I continued to do a profitable business in carbuncles.

I soon discovered, however, that I could not serve two masters. More and more the demands for my time as a physician impinged upon my position at the yard, until, at last, I was forced to lay the situation before Mr. Briggs. He was concerned.

"Will you stay, lad," he said, "until we've launched the frigate? You're the only one knows all the details of her business."

"You flatter me, sir," I said. "Anyone with a passing knowledge of figures could go on from where I leave off."

We left it in the end that I would continue to carry the account of the frigate, but the rest of the business of the yard would be another affair.

II

LIFE in Salem during that summer was not altogether made
up of work, however. Evenings and the long summer Saturdays
and Sundays offered moments of pleasure and recreation and
relaxation. I have already told how Selina insisted upon including the Prices in the island picnics.

The first of these came in mid-July, when the summer's heat
was at its peak. George Crowninshield, Richard Derby, and
Eli Hackett provided transportation in their sloops, from Derby Wharf to Great Misery, where the fires were laid and great
baskets of clams and lobsters prepared and a cask or two of beer
broached. There was some reserve toward Patience, until she
volunteered to superintend the cooking, which was a task no one
cared about. I elected to stay with Patience and help her, while
the others went off to roam the island in search of firewood, or
to gather armfuls of grass to sit upon, to dabble their feet in
the cool water, or to chase one another across the rocks in
whooping delight.

This was my first opportunity to be alone with Patience since
the day she was married, and I must confess I felt a certain
pleasure in it. Not that we were anything but entirely correct,
or even that we exchanged many words. But there was a sense
of comfort merely in being with her there alone on the beach,
tending the fires and minding the cooking, that I felt nowhere
else. She went about her tasks quietly, occasionally directing
me to some chore that would help, but for the most letting me
take my own pace and talking pleasantly the while. The rest of
the party was in and out of the picnic spot with wood and grass
and loads of seaweed. I admit to being aware of their coming
and going, but I was not interested to identify them in my own
mind, so that half an hour later I could not have told you which
ones had returned and which had not.

Our conversation, in the main, was impersonal. Only once
did our talk touch upon ourselves, and then it was but briefly.

"You've been a stranger lately, Pat," I chided her. "I haven't
seen much of you."

I meant to joke, of course, but she did not smile.

" 'Tis you are the stranger, Tom," she replied. "You're rarely home these days."

"There's work to be done," I said.

She turned a smiling face to me.

"Oh, I know!" she exclaimed. " 'Tis wonderful how things have turned out for you!"

"Thank you, Pat," I said gravely.

"But you don't work all the time," she said accusingly.

I grinned sheepishly.

"Hardly, but I have to pass the time in some way, now that my old friends seem to have left me to my own devices."

She tossed her head.

"Tom Tisdall, that's not true! 'Tis you have left us."

This accusation both surprised and annoyed me.

"That's nonsense!" I told her somewhat gruffly.

For a long time she said no more but studiously attended the lobsters on the fire.

"You like her, don't you, Tom?" she said at length.

"Who?" I demanded defensively, startled by this turn.

"Miss Hackett, of course," she retorted. "Who else?"

"Of course I like her," I replied. "Don't you?"

She made no reply to that, but jabbed viciously at the fire with her long stick.

"She's very charming," I told her.

She appeared to sniff slightly.

"I can see that."

It may have been her tone, or it may have been her attitude, or both. At any rate, I was angered.

"She's been very kind to you!" I said, and could have bitten out my tongue the next second.

She turned and stared at me.

"You really think so, don't you?"

I believe she would have gone on to say something more, but several of the party came in at that moment, laughing and shouting, their arms laden with driftwood for the fire.

"How are the lobsters?"

"I'm starved!"

"Let us tend them for a while. You two go and have some fun."

Pat turned about toward them, smiling.

"We're almost ready," she replied. "It wouldn't do for me to leave now. You call the others."

They needed no second invitation, but scattered. Only when they were gone did Patience speak to me again.

"Are you going to marry her, Tom?" she asked.

"You mean Selina?" I laughed, aghast, and then scoffed: "She wouldn't have me."

"Don't be too sure of that," she retorted. "You're getting to be a man to watch in Salem, you know."

"Pooh!" I snorted. "But you do give me ideas!"

She attacked the fire almost bitterly.

"You could do much worse," she said tartly. "After all, she's very wealthy."

The rest of the party began drifting in. I noticed absently that Ben and Selina came in together and that they were laughing, as at some private joke. But by then I was too busy passing out the food to pay much attention, and before I had finished that chore I had forgotten it.

I confess the thought planted in my mind by Patience stuck. To be sure, I told myself in those moments when I stopped to think about it that the idea was ridiculous. I had nothing to offer Selina except myself and what I could make of myself. And yet, when I permitted myself to dream, I could see no reason why it should not be so. My practice was growing. With luck and hard work I could make a place for myself of some importance in the town. Marriage with Selina Hackett would certainly do me no harm in that respect. And there was no doubt that she was desirable.

As I lay abed at night I would sometimes think about it, and it would become almost a physical thing. The thought of her, warm and fragrant and tantalizing, would set me off in a hot sweat, and I would have to get up and read half of Sir Kenelm Digby's *Receipts in Physick and Chirurgey,* or *Religio Medico,* or Webster's *Brief History of Epidemic and Pestilential Diseases,* before I could sleep in peace.

I would make up my mind then that at our next meeting I would lay my heart at her feet. But somehow, when that time came, I found myself unable to proceed with my resolution; why, I do not know. It was not for lack of opportunity. Of an evening on the veranda our hands would meet, our shoulders touch. Sometimes, returning from a picnic in the dusk, she would lean against me, and I would let my arm slip about her shoulders. Twice, in the carriage, where there were none to see, I seized her in my arms and kissed her passionately, and she did not resist. Yet I could not seem to bring myself to say the words that were on the tip of my tongue. As the summer wore on I wanted her, in a desperate sort of physical way. But yet some inner caution seemed to withhold me.

In this wise the summer passed while I blew now hot and now cold. In early August a Hackett ship arrived one hundred and thirty-three days out of Capetown, having encountered flat calms for seventy days in the neighborhood of the equator. In all that time she had seen neither land nor other vessels, and the state of her crew was pitiful. Half of them were so far gone with the scurvy that they were unable to get about to tend their personal needs, let alone wear ship. A half a dozen others had raging fevers, and the captain himself was puffed and swollen with beriberi.

The ship carried no surgeon. Eli Hackett asked that I go aboard and see what I could do—partly, I suspect, because he could get no one else to undertake the task, the question of what was aboard her being not yet determined.

At any rate, I went, and, finding nothing that seemed deadly, treated the men and had them brought ashore and quartered in one of the Hackett warehouses, where I could more conveniently care for them. Those that suffered from scurvy I placed on a diet of fresh meat and vegetables, and since there were neither lemons, limes, nor oranges to be had in Salem, I sent to Boston for a load of them. In the meantime I fed them such fresh fruits as were available—raspberries, blackberries, cherries, and the like. By the time the sloop was returned from Boston, they were beginning to show signs of improvement, and I felt ready to let some of them go home.

Of the other men—those with the fever—however, two died, being too far gone before I could treat them. The rest proved stubborn cases. The disease was not one that I could recognize, though it seemed to have elements of both a paludal ague and a remittent fever, with additional symptoms which might have indicated any of a dozen different ailments. There was the quick, hard pulse and chills and violent trembling of the ague.

There were the rose spots and high fever, the bloody flux and griping bowels of the remittent fever. There were severe pains in the joints and bones and muscles, accompanied by violent headache and general lassitude. Whether it was a pestilence of some peculiar African type or whether it was a combination of complaints of a more familiar sort, I was unable to tell. It occurred to me to wonder whether the ship had not, perhaps, taken a side shot at blackbirding. Certainly she was foul enough, from the smell of her, and that might also account for the length of her passage. But if it were so, none aboard would admit it, nor was it any of my affair if they had. My duty was to treat the suffering men and try my best to ease their pain.

This was no easy task. However, I put together a number of specifics and treatments, calculated to attack the malady from every angle. Bleeding, jalap, and Peruvian bark I gave for the ague. I rubbed the men with vinegar to cool the fever and boiled vinegar in the room to dispel the vapors caused by it. An electuary of bayberries was intended to soothe the twisting of the bowels; a decoction of senna to purge, and an anodyne was added to ease the pains in the joints. Whether it was my treatment or not, I could not say, but the fact remains that all, save the two mentioned, recovered, and were none the worse for their illness.

This would have been the end of the matter had not the fever proven epidemic. Fortunately its form, here in these milder climes, was less virulent than that of my patients from the ship. Nevertheless it was yet sufficiently severe to cause us some unease.

The first to give warning of what was in store was Eli Hackett himself. Despite my every plea, he persisted in visiting the warehouse in which I had lodged the men, for he was a man, rare in his day, who took a personal interest in those who served him. I warned him that the disease might be communicable, but he merely scoffed at me and came visiting just the same. One evening I noticed that he dragged rather than walked about the warehouse, and looking more closely, I saw that his face was flushed and his eyes were dull and heavy. I ventured to protest once more.

"You should not be here, sir. You're ill yourself."

"Nonsense!" he scoffed. "I was never better!"

Nevertheless he did not move with his customary vigor, and when he came halfway about the great room he was taken suddenly with an ague and a trembling, and his face drained white, while he was forced to lean upon a post for support.

"Let me take you home," I said.

He made an effort to rouse himself but could not.

"Thank you, Tom," he said in a rough whisper. "Perhaps you're—right. Perhaps you'd best—get me to my bed."

When we reached the house Selina herself met us at the door. At sight of her father she fell back.

"What is it?" she cried. "What's wrong? Is he———"

"Aye," I told her gruffly. "He's caught it. Stand back! There's no need for you to take it too."

Under her guidance I half carried him up the stairs to the bedroom he occupied. There I helped him out of his clothes and into bed.

"Is it serious, lad?" he asked. "In one my age?"

"Don't worry about it, sir," I told him, with more assurance than I felt. "Try to sleep. I'll fetch my things from the warehouse and see that you've everything you need."

Selina met me in the hall below with a worried frown and her eyes swimming in ready-to-shed tears.

"Is he bad?" she asked breathlessly, clinging to me.

"I don't know yet," I said absently, for the moment in my preoccupation forgetting to pretend. "It's only begun. I can't tell for a little while whether 'twill be good or bad."

"You'll do all you can, won't you?" she cried.

"Of course I will!" I said, patting her head.

She looked up at me gratefully.

"I knew you would!" she said, then hesitated. "Tom," she said at length, "Tom—would you think it bold of me—that is, you might stay here. Then you'd be near him. And I'd feel ever so reassured!"

"Well . . ." I said hesitantly.

"Please. It would mean so much to me!"

It occurred to me that there would be an added advantage. I would no longer risk carrying the disease into the Nowell household. There was no need to expose them.

"If it will ease things for you, my dear," I said.

"I'll run right up and see to your room!" she cried happily.

"Don't go in his room," I warned.

It was nigh dark when I was finally able to return from my various errands, which took me from the Hacketts' to the wharf to the apothecary's to the Nowells' and return. Even in this short circuit I was stopped by Abbie Prince, who was wife to Isaac Prince, one of the seamen of the lately arrived vessel, hitherto unafflicted by any of the ailments of his mates. She told me that he was acting strangely and that she feared that he was "coming down ill." I promised that I would come and see him that evening and went on my way. I found Selina waiting with ill-concealed anxiety.

"I thought you would never come," she greeted me.

I made the best explanation I could. She cut me short.

"He's worse," she said, "much worse."

I looked at her sharply in the gloom of the hallway.

"You've been in there with him?" I demanded.

"Naturally!" Her tone was defiant.

"You little fool!" I exclaimed angrily. "I told you to keep out of that room."

"In this house, Dr. Tisdall," she said, "I am not accustomed to taking orders."

"Can't you understand the danger?" I began hotly, but again she interrupted me.

"I am not afraid," she said. "He is my father. I have the right——"

"I'll dispute that point with you," I broke in. "It may seem to you that you have the right to risk your own health to help your father. But I'll remind you that you have not the right to risk the health of others. By placing yourself in danger, you increase the possibility of passing on the disease."

"My health is my own affair," she retorted angrily. "I don't care a fig for others!"

I was fatigued, else I would not have quarreled.

"That is where we differ," I told her. " *I* don't give a fig for *your* health. 'Tis others I am thinking of!"

She recoiled as though I had slapped her, and the color rose sharply in her face and neck. Even in my annoyance I could not help admiring her dark beauty.

"Oh!" she gasped. "How dare you?"

I bowed with what I intended for a mocking smile.

"As your physician," I said, "I dare nothing less."

"There are other doctors," she reminded me.

"As you wish!" I clapped on my hat.

As I turned to the door, however, she caught at me.

"Tom! Please!" she begged. "I—I'm sorry! I am distrait. I didn't mean to offend you."

My anger vanished as a puff of smoke before the wind, and in its place I felt a surge of tenderness for her. I put down my bag and took off my hat again and put an arm about her shoulders.

"My dear," I exclaimed, "forgive me!"

She did not resist my protective embrace, but rather leaned against me, resting her head upon my breast.

"Oh, Tom! I am so tired!"

"There now!" I said foolishly.

"You—you didn't mean it, did you, Tom?" she sniffled.

"Mean what?" I asked.

"That—you didn't care a fig for me!"

I was quite too bemused to see, at this point, that this was something altogether different from what I had said.

"Darling," I exclaimed, "don't you see it was anxiety for you that drove me? I've no wish to see you ill too."

She gazed up at me from the shelter of my arm.

"You can't—I won't let you take all the risk."

If I kissed her then, was I a fool?

She did not resist. Rather, her arms crept about my neck and clung to me. For a moment my thoughts were far away from the sick man in the room upstairs. When she broke away from me it was with a small push of her hands.

"Tom!" she exclaimed, blushing. "We're forgetting! Come! I'll show you your room. Then you must go to Father."

The room she showed me was elegant indeed. In my fondest dreams I had never pictured myself living in such luxury. It was as large as an entire floor of the Nowell house, with tall windows on two sides and a small fireplace against one wall. A great four-poster bed occupied the central space against the fourth wall, and there were comfortable chairs, a great chest of drawers, a writing desk, and a night table scattered about in various positions. Most intriguing of all was a dressing room, opening off the main bedroom, in which there was an elaborate commode and an immense closet. Pictures of Hackett ships, in various stages of sail, decorated the wall, and a small glassed cabinet in one corner contained mementos of various Hackett voyages.

Selina indicated a door in the wall by the fireplace.

"My room is there. Father's is across the hall."

I unpacked such things as I needed for the immediate medical emergency, and together we crossed the hall.

"You should not come in," I remonstrated.

"Please, Tom!" she said, and I was weak enough to surrender.

I found that he was indeed worse. His fever had increased, and he did not recognize either myself or Selina. His mind was wandering. I set up my spirit lamp and put the vinegar on to boil. After that I bled him, which seemed to relieve the fever, and gave him a light dose of calomel. More than this I could not, for the moment, do. He seemed relieved and somewhat easier, and so we left him and went down to dinner.

What we ate that night I have not the least recollection, but I drank in her beauty as if it were wine, and its effect was not much different. Black servants waited upon us silently with self-effacing deference. She talked of what I do not recall except that, at the moment, it was amusing or important, as her own expression might require. That she was there and that she was smiling at me was sufficient.

After dinner there was coffee in the long, high-ceilinged drawing room, where the stately draperies framing the tall, open windows stirred gently in the night air. In that room it seemed strangely cool, in comparison with the night outside, which was thick and oppressive. I was weary and was unhappy to put an end to this comfortable dream. Nor was Selina pleased when I told her that I must go and see Isaac Prince. But, at least, it required none of the quarreling of earlier in the evening to convince her that it must be done. I left her instructions as to what was to be done for her father, should he take a turn for the worse while I was gone, and went out into the stifling night to a house that could have been put entire into the drawing room of the Hacketts'.

I found Isaac Prince in a state much resembling Eli Hackett's, and I knew then what was coming. On my way back I stopped at the warehouse on the wharf and took some comfort from the fact that all of my patients there were resting easily. For them, at least, the crisis seemed past.

Back at the Hackett house I found Selina sitting at her father's bedside, applying cold cloths to his brow. I said nothing, having learned the futility of remonstrance, but I must have looked my disapproval. She made haste to explain.

"He was so restless."

I patted her shoulder gently.

"We must expect him to be," I told her, "until the fever breaks. I wish you would not expose yourself so."

She smiled.

"I am already exposed," she said simply.

I was too weary to argue with her.

"Go and get some rest," I said. "I'll stay with him."

"You'll call me if you need me—if he gets worse?"

"I'll call you," I promised.

She hesitated an instant, her dark eyes fixed on mine with a little troubled frown. Then abruptly she smiled.

"Good night, Tom!" she whispered.

"Good night, Seel," I replied.

She went out, closing the door behind her gently, leaving me feeling vaguely restless and disturbed.

I turned my attention to the man on the bed. There was no doubt that his fever had risen during my absence, but I had yet no fear for his safety. It was my feeling that the fever, though violent at first, was not essentially dangerous. There was no denying, however, the fact that he was delirious. He looked at me with vacant eyes, and when I drew near he called me Abiel and inquired whether he had yet made a landfall.

I told him that we had not yet come in sight of land and bled him once more, after which I bathed him again in vinegar and with some difficulty persuaded him to swallow an electuary of bayberries.

I waited an hour or so for this to take its soothing effect and after that bathed him again in vinegar and, with somewhat similar difficulty, gave him a decoction of Peruvian bark. For a time he seemed griped, and I feared I had been too hasty with him, but presently he fell into a troubled sleep and I dared to leave him.

As I crossed the hall I noticed that a light still showed beneath Selina's door. I paused and then tapped diffidently, hoping that I would not awaken her if she were asleep, and at the same time afraid to risk leaving her candle burning.

At my first scratch I heard her scramble from her bed. An instant later she opened the door and stood gazing up at me in her nightdress.

"He—he's asleep, Seel," I gulped. "I'll leave my door open so I can hear him, should he awake. You go to sleep."

"Yes, Tom!" she whispered, but she made no move.

"Good night!" I said, and fled.

It seemed to me that I had barely closed my eyes when I was awakened by a touch on my shoulder. Nor could I tell what hour it was from the flood of moonlight that streamed in the window. It was still hot, breathlessly hot, and as I opened my eyes I saw that Selina was standing by my bedside, bending over me, her dressing gown caught close about her and the moonlight gleaming on the black sheen of her hair. I was suddenly alarmed and sat up.

"What is it?" I asked.

"He's waked," she said. "Tom, I'm afraid."

"Don't fear," I remember saying. And then, barefooted, and with my nightshirt flapping about my calves, I hastened across the hall.

He was awake and trembling, with a fit of the ague more violent than I had yet seen. At the same time he was feverish beyond recognizing us. Selina stood at my elbow as, by the light of the bright full moon, I gave him a quick vinegar sponge and a new sedative. Within a few moments he was breathing quietly once more, sleeping, if not soundly, at least drowsily and beyond waking. Selina caught my elbow as I rose.

"Is he all right?" she asked.

"He's asleep," I said. "He won't wake till morning."

I turned her toward the door.

"Leave him alone now," I said. "He'll have no further need of us tonight."

I led her from the room, but even as I closed the door she swayed against me, half stumbling. I believe if I had not caught her she might have fallen.

"See!" I exclaimed in a whisper. "What is it?"

"I'm tired," she whispered, "so tired!"

Scarcely thinking, I bent and lifted her in my arms. It was but a step across the hallway to her room, where her bed lay rumpled in the pool of moonlight. She did not protest as I carried her there, but rather clung to me, and as I laid her down her whisper was breathless, passionate:

"Tom! Tom darling!"

Involuntarily our lips met. Her arms crept about my neck, drawing me gently down beside her, then clasping me eagerly, hungrily. For an instant our lips parted, and I felt her breath warm and tremulous upon my cheek, her sigh a whispered invitation in my ear, and my impulse to resistance vanished. For the space of a whispered word—"Ah, sweet!"—we lay thus pinioned, lip to lip. Then the faint, heady perfume of her engulfed us both on the hot night.

12

When I awoke in the morning, in the hot summer dawn, the first rays of the sun were just reaching out above the rim of the world. I felt rested, relaxed for the first time in many months, and for an instant the night's adventures seemed no more than a distant, ecstatic dream until I moved to stretch and found my right arm pinioned. When I turned my head upon the pillow the reality of it struck me with full force.

She lay cuddled in the hollow of my arm, her head pillowed on my shoulder, her lustrous black hair spread all about us on the fresh linen of the pillow slip. Her lips were half parted, in a gentle, slumberous smile, and her long, dark lashes lay peacefully against the rosy tint of her cheeks.

The realization that I had not dreamed brought panic and a gush of shame. I tried to withdraw my arm gently, but even as I did so her eyes opened and she gazed sleepily up at me.

I half expected her to spring from the bed, outraged and shocked. But instead she lifted her hand tenderly and drew it across my cheek and lips.

"Darling!" she whispered.

As if she had wiped them away with the gesture, all of my

sensations of guilt and shame and panic vanished, and I took her in my arms and kissed her hungrily, while she clung to me.

"Seel! Seel! What are we doing?" I burst out.

She gave a little, low, throaty laugh, and once again her fingers brushed my lips.

"Do you mind so much?" she asked.

"Mind?" I cried. "Seel, I love you. I would not harm you for the world. Yet what have I done to you but harm?"

I feel yet that there is some grace in the fact that I believed it; that I meant it with all my heart.

"I do not feel harmed, Tom," she said.

"That is your sweet innocence," I said. "Seel, we must be married!"

"Oh, Tom!" She looked away from me shyly. "When?"

"Soon!" I cried urgently. "As soon as ever may be!"

"When Father is well again?"

"Before that if we can," I said.

"Oh, I couldn't," she protested. " 'Twould kill him if I married without his consent."

"As soon as we can get his consent, then."

She nodded vigorously and snuggled against me.

I should have been happy, but it was scarcely a happy day. Neither Eli Hackett nor Isaac Prince showed any improvement. My patients at the warehouse seemed to have reached a period in which they neither grew better nor worse. Four more cases of fever appeared in the town. My conscience troubled me, and it was hot, stifling hot. There were moments when I wondered whether I were catching the disease myself.

Evening, however, brought a breath of air and an end to the bitter heat. Frayed tempers relaxed, and at dinner Selina was gracious and lovely to look upon, and with a new something in her eyes as she looked at me across the table. My conscience was no better, but at least I found consolation in the thought that she seemed truly to love me. I made my evening rounds with a lighter heart.

The weeks that followed were in many ways grim. Eli Hackett's recovery seemed to my impatient soul unconscionably slow, though actually it was little more than a fortnight before he was able to leave his bed and take to pampered convalescence. In the meantime the epidemic spread alarmingly. In one night there were seventeen new cases, in another thirty-six, and at the peak the count of those brought down with the fever reached seventy-eight in a single night. This increase kept me occupied fully from dawn till long past dusk, and there were nights when it kept me out until nigh on the following dawn. At such times I was often as not too fatigued to do more than give Selina a weary kiss and a well-meant embrace before I tumbled into bed and was asleep.

However, this was not invariably so. I make no excuse for my own weakness in that, nor will I cast blame upon her. I, at least, was no more than a mortal animal unable to resist temptation, and who am I to say that she was worse? Nor will I deny that I found our meetings enjoyable. In my life I had had little of either moral teaching or feminine companionship. The lack of the one, coupled with the discovery of the delights of the other, I suppose, was responsible in some measure for my inability to resist.

Yet I was not wholly without conscience, and I longed for Captain Hackett's recovery, for it seemed to me that he, if he would but say the word, could make honest people of us. To me, then, his recovery seemed longer than need be. Actually it was no more than normal. In two weeks from the time I had led him home to bed he was up and tottering about upon a cane, and the first evening when he came down to supper, close on the end of August, I seized my opportunity.

My chance came after Selina had left us to our brandy and cigars. It had been a long day, and it had seemed a longer evening. Impatient as I was for the opportunity to speak, I counted each moment lost that passed in his presence without bringing forth that chance, and now that Selina had withdrawn I was determined to put it off no longer. As we resumed our places at the table the yellow candles wavered smokily in the draft from the open windows. The unused table silver glistened in the tawny light, and when he held his glass up to the candle I could see the amber gleam of the flame through the liquor like a topaz cased in a transparent ball. Captain Hackett, too, appeared to have something on his mind, for he studied the liquid with more concentration than it appeared to warrant.

"I owe you a debt of gratitude, Tom," he said.

"Nonsense, sir!" I protested.

"Nonsense, my eye!" he exclaimed. "D'you think I do not know what I'm talking about? Your service to me cannot be reckoned in terms of money. As a merchant, sir, it upsets me to have my books uneven!"

"You owe me nothing, Captain," I replied. "On the contrary, it is I who owe both you and Selina for your hospitality and generosity!"

"That's twaddle!"

"But there is one thing I would like to ask of you, sir," I went on. "And I'd be glad if you'd not regard it in any way as a request for compensation."

"Why, of course, Tom!" he agreed.

I took my courage in both hands and spoke up.

"I love Selina, sir," I said. "I'd like to marry her."

He choked in the midst of a swallow of brandy.

"Eh, what's that? Goddamme, did I hear you right?"

"You did, sir," I said stiffly.

He stared at me in frank amazement for a moment, his glass poised. Then, slowly, he spoke musingly, as if half to himself.

"Why not?" he said. "Indeed, why not? 'Tis not just what I had in mind for her. You've no fortune, Tom, and no family that I know of. But I believe you have a future, and it might be a good thing for Selina to be tied to a man with his own way to make in the world, and the stomach to make it. Yes, I think it would be a very good thing. D'you think you could handle her?"

"I think so, sir," I replied.

"Mind," he admonished, "I did not say 'Keep her in the way in which she is accustomed.' I have enough for that, and I long since gave up the thought the man she married would have to be able to match my means. But she's headstrong, Tom. She's willful and spoiled, and she can be mean as a bitch in heat when she's a mind to it. You see, I've no illusions as to my daughter's nature, and I'd have you fair forewarned."

"I've noticed no such tendency," I said stiffly.

"Hah!" he croaked dryly. "You will if you marry her."

"I think I can deal with any problem that might arise."

He chuckled.

"Ah," he said, "just so you're aware of it. I take it you've talked this over with her?"

"I took the liberty, sir," I admitted.

He nodded.

"I thought you had," he said, and I started guiltily.

He did not appear to notice.

"And have you talked about the date?" he asked.

"No sir," I said. "I thought that had best be left until we had your consent."

He smiled at me and, reaching over, decanted another tot of brandy into my glass.

"And now you have it," he replied. "Shall we drink to success and then tell Selina that she may set the day?"

We found her curled up in an easy chair before the fire—for the nights were beginning to sharpen. I thought her a little pale and tired seeming, with a hint of darkness beneath her eyes, though this detracted none from her beauty.

"My dear," I said, "I have spoken to your father."

She glanced quickly, almost apprehensively, at him.

"I am delighted, my dear," he beamed, "truly delighted. I had not expected you to make so sound a choice."

She rose and came to me, both hands outstretched.

"You don't credit me with much sense, Father."

"There was a time," her father said teasingly, "when I feared you'd marry Ben Price."

Her smile wiped away as if she had been slapped.

"How can you say such a thing?" she demanded.

"Tut-tut!" he soothed. "There's no need to fly out so, since you've got the man of your choice. I am but telling you you'll look far before you find a better."

I felt myself flush in confusion.

"Who are you to tell me that?" Selina demanded, giving me a melting glance.

Eli Hackett chuckled.

"Aye," he said. "No doubt you know better than I. But we've left it for you to set the day. When's it to be?"

She did not take her eyes from mine.

"Tomorrow!" she said. "Tonight, if may be!"

"Oh, come!" he laughed. "I know you are impatient. You always were. But let us be serious."

"I am serious," she told him.

"My dear child!" her father protested. "Be reasonable!"

"You've always said I was unreasonable," she said sweetly. "Why should you expect me to be reasonable now?"

He tossed up his hands in a helpless gesture and looked at me with an expression which said plainly: "See?"

To her he said: "Yes, yes, I know! But this isn't a thing you rush into. It's not like a picnic."

She leaned against me.

"Very well, then," she said, "next week. Is that reasonable?"

He stared at her.

"What's the hurry?" he demanded, and glanced sharply at me. "Is there some reason behind all this?"

Selina shrugged and turned her face to my breast.

"Think what you like," she told him.

I put an arm about her shoulders, looking at him over the top of her head.

"Sir," I said, "I am as anxious as she to have it done, I think because I am afraid she might change her mind or I might lose her otherwise, but mostly because I love her very much!"

That softened his mood somewhat, and I could feel Selina's hand at my back tapping me in congratulatory fashion. At length he shrugged.

"Well," he said, "I see you will be wed as soon as may be. But mark this, both of you, the name Hackett is one I'll not have bandied about by every wharf rat in Salem, and whatever you may think, I wish to have it published from the pulpit, by the Reverend Bentley, as decent folk should. 'Twill take three weeks for that, and we should allow another week for preparation. What do you say to the twenty-sixth of September?"

I felt Selina draw quick breath for a hot answer and spoke quickly to forestall her, at the same time giving a warning pressure of my arm.

"What day is that, sir?" I asked.

"Why—ah—'tis a Saturday, I think, isn't it?" he replied. "Or is it Sunday?"

I calculated rapidly.

" 'Tis a Thursday."

"That's no day to be married!" Selina protested.

He chuckled, his good humor apparently restored.

"Shall we make it the twenty-eighth, then?" he asked.

Selina shrugged and went back to her seat by the fire.

"You seem to have decided for me," she retorted.

"Come, come, child!" her father coaxed. "You know 'twill take all of that time to prepare for it. Why, you'll have a gown to order from Boston, and invitations to send——"

"But I don't want all that!" she protested.

But there was no turning him.

"I do!" he replied. "I'll never have it said that I married my only daughter off without proper notice."

There was a finality about the way he said it that meant "This way or not at all." Apparently Selina felt it too. She glanced at me helplessly and shrugged with an apologetic smile.

I glanced at my watch.

"I must be going," I said. "I have patients to see."

Selina pouted petulantly.

"Oh! Your old patients!"

I looked at her in surprise.

"I am a doctor, my dear," I said. "When folk are ill I am bound to attend them."

Eli Hackett beamed.

"Well said, lad!" he applauded. "Let that be a lesson to you, Selina. Don't interfere with your husband's work. Go along, Tom. We'll leave the latchstring out."

"And you, sir," I said, "I'll remind you that you are also my patient. Get you off to bed now, before you lapse."

This occurred toward the end of August. On the following Sunday the Reverend Bentley announced our betrothal from the pulpit, according to custom, and I cannot deny that I heard the faint rustle of surprise which swept the congregation with some satisfaction.

When the service was ended we were besieged with good wishes. People I had never seen before shook my hand and wished us happiness; some because they meant it, some because the thought of a wedding made them sentimental, but most out of plain curiosity to see what manner of young fellow Selina Hackett had got. One or two I heard wondering somewhat openly about my background. All they knew was that I was not from Salem, and I did not enlighten them. I observed, too, that the Reverend Mr. Bentley kept discreetly silent.

The only well-wishers that touched me at all within were

Ben and Patience and old Sam Nowell. Sam was hearty and full of genuine pleasure for me.

"Congratulations, Tom lad!" he cried, taking my hand in a grip of iron. "Ye'll be fair one of us now, and glad I am!"

He turned to Selina earnestly.

" 'Tis a fine young man ye've got yourself, ma'am," he said. "I hope ye'll cherish him as he deserves."

I could see that Selina had not the faintest notion who he might be, and yet she carried it well, smiling graciously that that was her intention.

Behind Sam came Patience, looking somewhat peaked.

"You'll be happy, I'm sure, Tom!" she said with a little catch in her throat.

"Thank you, Pat," I said gravely.

Before I could say anything further she had turned to Selina, and I perforce turned to Ben, who brought up the rear. As I turned I surprised a somber, thoughtful expression upon his face which immediately upon my turning vanished behind his twisted smile.

"I see you didn't let any grass grow under you," he said as our hands met.

I must have looked puzzled, for he followed that hastily with congratulations.

"Thanks, Ben," I told him. "As a matter of fact, I'd like to have you stand as best man."

He looked startled, and I thought I heard either Patience or Selina, or perhaps both, say, "Oh!" Then abruptly one of Ben's eyebrows went up.

"Why not?" he said. "I'd be happy to, Tom."

He made his most elegant leg to Selina.

"Your servant, Seel," he said. "I knew you could be counted on to make a good choice."

On the Saturday following there was a final picnic on Great Misery. It seemed to me that with the fever raging it was hardly a time for picnics, and the night before I ventured to speak my mind on the matter, with results that were more than I had bargained for.

"All you want to do is work!" Selina pouted.

"I don't!" I told her. "But people are ill. I can't refuse them."

"I wouldn't be surprised to see you walk right out of our wedding to go and see some old patient!" she grumbled.

"Don't talk nonsense," I retorted.

"I'm not talking nonsense," she replied. "You just don't want to take me to the picnic!"

"I do want to take you," I said.

"You don't love me!" she sniffed.

"Oh, for God's sake!" I cried, exasperated beyond endurance. "I do love you and I will take you."

"Darling!" she cried, all bright and teary-eyed.

I can't say that the picnic was a great success. Selina seemed nervous and unlike herself. Patience seemed to me even paler than she had been the previous Sunday, and Ben for some reason was acting like a sulky brat.

On reaching the island I went off with Selina in search of firewood, but as the afternoon wore on she seemed to grow more fidgety and flushed and out of sorts, and always, just at the wrong moments, when I seemed to be getting her soothed, we would be found and teased. At length, when one particularly noisy quintet, of which Ben was one, set upon us, I gave it up and we joined them and took to searching for wood in earnest. Between us we gathered a considerable pile, which I volunteered to take in to the fire. This necessitated several trips, and while I was about it the others drifted away over the island. By the time it was all in, I found myself left once again with Patience at the fireside.

I soon found that this day was not to be like others. During those earlier picnics we had gotten back somewhat to our old footing of friendship. Today, however, the barrier of reserve was up again, and nothing I could say or do would seem to lower it. On the contrary, everything I said only seemed to build it higher.

"You're not very happy today, Pat," I said at length.

"Is there any reason why I should be dancing for joy?"

"There's no reason that I can see why you should be glum as an owl, either," I told her. "What's got into you?"

"Nothing's got into me!" she retorted irritably. "I can see that you are very happy, having made such a fine catch."

"Pat!" I exclaimed. "That wasn't worthy of you!"

She made no reply, and I looked up to find her staring over

my head at something beyond me. Instinctively I turned and saw that the others were coming in. What struck me was that Ben and Selina were together. As I turned he was helping her down over a steep spot, holding both her hands, and both were laughing gaily. Selina seemed unusually flushed.

It was a small matter, and one I would never have noticed but for Selina's late vehemence when Ben's name was mentioned. Nothing else of interest occurred. We sat about the fire in the dusk and sang somewhat halfheartedly and ate our clams and lobsters, and sometime after nightfall, when the moon had risen, we re-embarked for home.

With the coming of darkness the night turned chilly, and as we skimmed over the water it seemed to me downright cold. I put my coat about Selina's shoulders, but after a moment she shrugged it off. I replaced it, and again she shook it aside impatiently.

"Oh, don't!" she said petulantly. "It's so hot!"

"Hot!" I exclaimed.

"Yes, hot!" she replied, and almost at once fell into a violent fit of trembling.

I clapped my hand to her forehead and found it burning. I cursed myself for not having read the signs earlier. As soon as we reached the wharf I bundled her in my coat once more and, scarcely waiting to say good night, hurried her off home, where I rang for her maid and ordered her to bed.

"See that she's well covered," I commanded, "and light the spirit lamp. Put on the vinegar to boil!"

Eli Hackett, attracted by the hubbub, thrust his head out the door of his room.

"Oh, you're back, Tom," he said. "What's the matter?"

"Matter enough," I told him. "Selina's got the fever!"

13

IT WAS APPARENT to me from the outset that there would be no wedding on the twenty-eighth. Captain Hackett, I believe, held out hope through the first week, but in the course of time it became apparent even to him that the event would have to be postponed. As for Selina, she was beyond caring.

Never, it seemed to me, had I seen such a virulent case. Elsewhere in the town it seemed the cooler weather put the quietus on the epidemic. Old cases recovered, while new cases became fewer. But Selina's case was such that I was grateful for the Providence that enabled me to devote myself more and more to her care. Day after day and night after night I sat at her bedside, watching the course of the fever, seeking some way to check it. At times I feared that this was one patient I would be unable to save. However, by midmonth she had passed the crisis, though it was a full week beyond that before she was able to leave her bed, and almost another fortnight before I felt it safe to allow her to set foot outside the house.

In the meantime, in Salem, the question of whether or not the Hackett-Tisdall nuptials ever came to pass was overshadowed by the approaching completion of the frigate. The masts were ready to be stepped. The rigging was walked on the shoulders of the ropemakers in a long line from the ropewalks. Any day that month it was possible to go out by Briggs's Yard and see the vessel, standing, finished but for the few final touches needed to complete her upper works, while the tap of carpenters' hammers came hollowly from within and the thump of caulkers' mauls echoed without. On the day after the crisis in Selina's fever passed I walked up that way and found them painting the vessel, black above the waterline, and green below, with a broad yellow band about her gun ports. The smell of pitch and paint hung over the yard, and much of the tumult of the earlier months had died away. Great sheets of copper were being laid out, preparatory to coppering her before she was launched. I walked around her, admiring the quickwork about the transom and along the rails. It seemed to me she had a more graceful sheer than most men-o'-war, but that may have been because she was in the stocks and I was on the ground beneath her.

At the office I encountered Enos Briggs, who seemed in high good humor.

"You appear to have done right well," he said. "I hear you're to marry the Hackett girl."

I could not but chuckle at this backhanded compliment.

"I'd say rather that Salem has done well for me."

"It's all one," he grinned. "I was speaking of you the other day to Captain Waters. The Committee's planning on offering him command o' the frigate. He spoke of you for ship's surgeon."

He looked at me inquiringly and waited. I laughed.

"I've begun to build up a good practice here and earn a place for myself. I'd be a fool to throw that away to go to sea."

He shrugged.

"That's what Cap'n Waters seemed to think you'd say."

I walked home with a feeling of constraint and a slight prickling of conscience, as if in following my own ends and planning to secure my place in Salem I were being unpatriotic. I mentioned the incident to Selina when I got back. To my amazement she burst into tears.

"Great God!" I exclaimed. "What's the matter now?"

"You don't love me any more!" she sobbed.

"What gives you that notion?" I cried.

"You're planning to leave me, even before we're married!"

"I'm not!" I said.

"You are too! You're going into the Navy."

"See here, my dear," I said as patiently as I could, "I am not going into the Navy. I meant only to tell you what Briggs said. I'm sorry I spoke of it."

"A-and," she snuffled, ignoring the explanation, "just when I need you most."

"What do you mean?" I halted my pacing of the room in mid-stride. I knew well enough, but I must hear it from her own lips. "What are you talking about?"

"I should have known!" she said stubbornly.

"Stop babbling," I cried, "and tell me!"

She assumed an air of courage-in-the-face-of-injury, lifting her chin, though her lip trembled.

"I am going to have a baby, Tom," she said.

I went to her and, putting an arm about her shoulders, turned her tear-streaked face to mine.

"My sweet!" I exclaimed. "You must not think such things of me. I would not leave you."

"But——" she began, resting against my shoulder.

"Don't worry," I comforted her. "We will be married!"

She clung to me.

"How soon, Tom?"

"As soon as you are strong enough," I replied.

"I am strong enough now."

"No, no," I said. "I am your physician as well as your be-trothed. Were I to rush you from the sickbed to the altar you know there would be almost more talk than if we did not marry at all."

"Don't put it off!" she begged.

"Not an hour beyond what it must be," I promised her.

The last day of September 1799 came clear and crisp, with a nip of frost. As the sun climbed above the eastern rim of the world the harbor sparkled blue-green beneath its rays. Dabs of color showed here and there amid the green of the trees on the neighboring hillsides.

Salem was already crowded, packed to the last spare bed in the meanest house, with spectators who had swarmed in on the Saturday previous from all the countryside around, for this was the day on which the frigate was to be launched. Naturally none traveled upon the Sabbath. But on the morning of the launching the roads for miles around were black with people; some on foot, some on horseback, others in wagons and car-riages and gigs, coming by whatever means they could com-mand to celebrate the occasion.

All these folk funneled into Salem by different routes. From the center of town they followed a single way to Briggs's Yard: down from the Square to Derby Street, and out along past the Hackett house, toward the Neck.

It seemed to me that I had never seen so many all together at one time before. They began passing at breakfast time, and before the meal was finished they filled the road in both direc-tions as far as it could be seen from an upstairs window. All morning they passed, creeping at snail's pace, and so dense packed that even from the clean-swept cobbles before the house they raised a pall of dust like a light fog. Selina spent hours putting on her best bib and tucker and arranging her hair, just so, for it was her first time abroad since her illness, and I will confess that Eli Hackett and myself had two or three for the road and one for the launching and one for the success of the ship before the carriage was called.

The drive to the yard was slow, by reason of the throngs

that packed the roadway. Far and away the bulk of those we passed were strangers, but every now and again we passed a knot of familiar faces, smiling and bowing and nodding in the holiday spirit. About midway of the road we came upon Ben and Patience and old Sam Nowell, elbowing their way along. At the sound of our carriage rattling behind they glanced over their shoulders, and I noticed that Patience walked heavily and seemed drawn and tired, while her grandfather was limping noticeably. On the spur of the moment I prodded our black driver, Titus, in the back and said: "Wait!"

Selina looked prim and disapproving, but I thought I caught a hint of a twinkle in Mr. Hackett's eye as he nodded.

"By all means!" he said.

I slipped down beside the trio in the road.

"Here!" I cried. "Climb in! You look worn out."

Patience hung back.

"Oh no," she said. "We'll crowd you. It isn't far!"

Unexpectedly Selina leaned forward.

"Nonsense!" she smiled. "There's lots of room."

Sam Nowell bowed elegantly.

"Thank you, ma'am," he said. "Mr. Hackett, sir, with your permission?"

Eli Hackett nodded.

"Climb in, Sam," he said.

We found the yard already packed. People crowded in against the ropes that had been stretched about the lower ways. Others climbed up on the lumber piles and the roof of the yard office or blackened the framework of the neighboring stocks. Even outside the yard the hillside was black with them, and a good crowd had gathered on Naugus Head, across the harbor, where a view might be had, although the speeches could scarcely be heard. Within the harbor itself half a dozen ships had warped into viewing range and were anchored a cable's length offshore, their rigging aswarm with spectators. The newspapers later placed the numbers who came that day to see the launching as high as fifteen thousand.

Patience gasped in dismay.

"Oh," she cried, "we'll never get near enough to see!"

Eli Hackett cast a quick, inquiring glance at me and then turned to her.

"Sit with us," he said. "There's plenty of room."

The box which I held in the special grandstand was not large, but we managed to squeeze ourselves in. Nor was I sorry for the slight discomfort when I saw what pleasure this one small gesture appeared to give Patience. Her eyes were bright with excitement, her color high. Indeed, I found it hard to believe that she was the same girl we had picked up on the road, so animated was she.

"Oh!" she cried, clapping her hands. "Oh, isn't this wonderful? See how close we are! Oh, Ben! Isn't she lovely!"

She referred, of course, to the frigate, whose flank towered sheer above our heads, and well she might exclaim, for it was an impressive sight. The stands had been built in the shape of a U about the bows of the vessel, with a square platform, draped with flags and bunting, in the bend of the U, directly beneath the bowsprit. The spectators ranged in tiers on either side of this platform, the stands extending perhaps a third of the vessel's length. The upper seats of these tiers were almost flush with the frigate's deck. But the lower rows and the boxes, which formed the bottom tiers, were tucked in, well under the vessel's overhang, so that to see the rails and rigging above it was necessary to crane one's neck back and look straight up at the sky.

The impression of immensity which this position lent the ship was unbelievable. The sleek flank, copper-sheathed to a point well above our heads, rose like a blank wall before us and then swept outward in a graceful curve to meet the deck line. From where we sat we could just see the trestle trees and foretop and the upper portion of the lower shrouds which spindled up to them. Fore and aft the stays had been dressed with flags, from bow to stern and over the mastheads. The stout masts and bowsprit looked chunky, more like stubs, and Patience remarked on this with some puzzlement.

"What you see is only the base of the mast," Eli Hackett explained, smiling. "If you will look at yonder ship out in the stream"—indicating a tall vessel lying close offshore—"you will see that her structure is the same, except that now, as she lies, other sections have been fished on to extend the reach of her masts. All of those can be sent up or down as necessary, and they are never rigged before launching because they would tend to make the ship top-heavy on the ways and perhaps cause her to roll over before she could be got into the water."

"I see," Patience said dubiously. Eli Hackett chuckled.

"There's no need to worry," he assured her. "This ship won't roll off the ways. Enos has a reputation as a careful launcher, and he guards it jealously. You'll see."

Patience let her eyes wander down along the ways, where the workmen were busy greasing the timbers with mutton tallow, while others stood by with mauls, ready to knock the blocks out that kept her from sliding down into the water. From the ways her eyes traveled up along the ship's flank once more to the mast above.

"I still think she looks squat and stumpy," she said. "I suppose all warships are like that."

Her husband turned on her.

"She's not squat and stumpy!" he said belligerently. "She's beautiful. Wait till you see her in the water."

The members of the committee were already seated on the platform, where they were being joined by a number of other dignitaries: Captain Waters, representing the Navy, Colonel Hackett (no relation, by the way, to my Captain Hackett), the superintendent of construction, Enos Briggs, the builder, and Samuel McIntire. As they mounted the platform Mr. Gray, the chairman, leaned over and made a signal. At once the band struck up "Hail Columbia" with great vigor and a blast which reverberated from the ship's bottom.

This, however, was almost immediately drowned out by the cheer that went up, first throughout the yard and then taken up by those spectators beyond the enclosure, who took this, and rightly, for the signal that things were about to begin. Patience gasped and took tight hold of Ben's arm. Selina's fingers sought my own. The band played three stanzas and stopped abruptly. Mr. Gray held up his hands, and gradually the cheering died away and a great hush settled.

"Ladies!—Gentlemen!—My good neighbors and friends of Essex County," Mr. Gray shouted, "we are met here today— to launch a ship! Nothing unusual in that. We've all seen ships launched. But there is something unusual about this ship; for this ship will represent *us,* in the service of our nation, upon the seven seas, gallantly, we hope, and certainly with honor!"

A ripple of a cheer passed through his audience.

"Because she represents us," he continued, "carrying to whatever nation would dispute it, our argument that the sea is a free highway to any man, we have deemed it appropriate to name her the *Essex!*"

The cheer that went up at this shook the stands and the ship above us and spread out through the yard and beyond like ripples upon the water. Once again the band, with more enthusiasm than harmony, struck up "Hail Columbia."

After a little, however, the tumult subsided, and the speeches proceeded.

I would not, if I could, repeat all that was said on the occasion. There were speeches by Colonel Hackett, Enos Briggs, Captain Derby, and Deacon Gould, who was building the gun carriages. There was a benediction by the Reverend Bentley that was as long as a sermon. I, for one, was growing numb about the buttocks, and I thought Selina was beginning to show signs of fatigue, when, at length, it seemed they all talked themselves out and William Gray rose once more.

"There remains but one thing to do," he said.

He made a quick signal. The band once more began to play. Out of the corner of my eye I saw the mauls swing and chunk against the blocks. Once! Twice! Three times! The blocks splayed sidewise and then burst clear. Above us the great hull shivered gently as it settled onto the ways. Slowly at first, and then with gathering speed, she began to slide.

At the first movement Ben leaped up and leaned to watch. Behind us a cheer more tremendous than any went up, punctuated by a thumping salute from the cannon in the fort upon the hill. The ship's keel struck the water, and she began to lift off the rails as she slid backward. In the harbor the ship which Eli Hackett had pointed out to us fired an answering broadside to the salute from the fort. The white gun smoke drifted on the wind among her shrouds, and in the next instant the *Essex* was floating free.

There was an instant's hush, almost of expectancy, as she took the water. Then the cheering broke out with redoubled vigor. Ben danced up and down excitedly, pounding me on the back, turning to Patience and shaking her arm, digging Eli Hackett in the ribs.

"She floats!" he shouted. "Did you ever see a finer ship? Tell me now she's squat and ugly! See how she rides beside that other vessel! That's my ship!"

Eli Hackett chuckled.

"Will you sail in her?"

"By God," cried Ben, "I might at that!"

In the spacious coolness of the high-ceilinged living room, upon our return, Selina sank down with a sigh of relief.

"Thank heaven that's over!" she exclaimed.

Her father, standing by the sideboard pouring out brandy, turned and gazed at her in surprise.

"Didn't you enjoy it?"

"I did not!"

Mr. Hackett gave me a sidewise glance and a slight lift of his shoulders.

"You are tired, sweet," I said. "Why don't you rest?"

She smiled up at me and gave me her hand.

"I think I will, Tom," she said, "if you don't mind."

Eli Hackett turned quickly as she rose.

"One toast to the *Essex*," he said, "before you go!"

She looked at him steadily and unsmiling.

"Will we have done with it then?"

"Entirely!" He smiled and gave her a slight bow.

"By all means, then!" she said curtly. "Let us drink! I'm tired of the whole thing!"

On that uncomplimentary note we drank, and Selina put down her glass with a snap on the table beside her. Without further words she turned and walked to the door, but there she stopped and turned again to face her father.

"Now that we have finished that," she said, "perhaps we can give some thought to so unimportant a matter as a wedding!"

Without waiting for a reply, then, she passed on up the stairs. Eli Hackett looked at me with raised eyebrows and an expression of bewildered amazement.

"What the devil ails her?"

"She's tired," I said. "You must remember, 'tis the first time she has been out since she was ill."

"Women!" he exclaimed. "Her mother was the same. Headstrong! How in time's a man to understand them?"

I kept discreet silence on that point.

"What d'you think?" he asked. "Is she up to marrying?"

"You're asking me as her physician, rather than as her impatient fiancé?" I asked.

"Naturally!"

"I can answer the same for both, fortunately," I replied. "I think the sooner 'tis done the better."

He poured me out a fresh pony of brandy and jabbed me knowingly in the ribs with a playful thumb.

"Ah!" He winked. "'Tis wonderful to have a physician's knowledge!"

"'Tis a grave responsibility," I told him seriously. I had no thought that he should have the wrong impression.

"Oh, aye! Aye!" he agreed earnestly. "But do you think she's up to it? See how easily she tired today!"

"Stuff!" I said. "She's young. In a week or so she'll be stronger than ever."

"Ah!" he said, unable to resist a smirk. "As a physician, eh? Well, well! No doubt you're right."

14

WE WERE MARRIED on October 7.

I presume every wedding is, in a sense, an ordeal. Certainly mine was for me. Three days beforehand the guests began to arrive, crowding the house and the near-by taverns. A few of them—Mr. Pickering, Mr. Adams, Mr. Otis—I was able to fix in my mind and remember because of their fame. But the bulk of the rest were mere relatives, most of them distant, and these I could not for my life keep straight in my mind. On the day of the ceremony itself Selina seemed pale and nervous, and at one point during the wedding I thought I saw a flicker of pain cross her face. For an instant I feared she was about to faint. However, she pulled herself together by an effort and repeated the words of her pledge after the bumbling Reverend Bentley, in clear round tones. In the end it was a relief to me when I slipped the ring upon her finger and we were able to escape to the fresh air.

We spent the better part of a month in Boston upon our

wedding journey, and I think no more need be said of it than that we were thoroughly accustomed to one another by the time we returned. I had hoped that this would be an idyllic period. Fond hope! Either I was too eager and annoyed her with my attentions or I was indifferent and neglected her. My attitude toward her friends, of whom we saw much, I was told was insulting, although it seemed to me I made a determined effort to be cordial and affable. My dress was wrong, my haircut vulgar. In short she grew querulous and faultfinding until my patience was tried and I flew out at her, whereupon she would burst into a fit of weeping and say I was cruel to her. Had she been reasonable and shown signs of affection, I could have overlooked her picking and nagging. But now that we were married, she appeared indifferent to me, and I felt only bewildered and resentful and hurt, and knew not what to do about it. In less than a week I found myself wearied of helping to pick and choose frills and furbelows, or of cooling my heels in some dressmaker's anteroom while she tried on a new gown, and heartily wished myself back in Salem, where I had something better to do with my time.

. "In God's name," I would cry out, "what have I done? Have I offended you? Why do you act this way?"

"Oh, don't be so silly!" she would reply querulously. "I can't be forever hugging and kissing."

Yet when I replied that I only asked affection once in a while she would respond with a halfhearted peck. If, after we had retired for the night, my hand chanced to rest for an instant on her breast, she would shrug and turn away from me.

"Great God, madam," I would cry in exasperation, "is this a way to treat a husband? What would you have of me? Should I leave you? Should I move into other quarters?"

At that she would burst into tears, nor would she allow me the satisfaction of comforting her. I found myself completely at a loss to explain it. I knew that she was with child, yet it seemed to me that this was early to begin with pettishness. Still, I could think of no other cause to lay it to. Some women, I supposed, were affected earlier than others.

We came back to Salem through a world turned bare again with winter's chill. The golden flame of autumn, so brilliant on our wedding day, had—almost symbolically, it seemed to

me—burned itself out. The leaves were gone from the trees
and lay now in red-brown heaps by the roadside, while the
trees themselves stretched gaunt black arms against a slate-
gray sky. Salem itself had put on winter dress. Storm windows
were hung upon the more pretentious houses. Lesser homes
were banked with earth and leaves and sawdust, all about their
foundations, against the creeping cold. Few ships lay in the
harbor, but those that were there reared their masts and spars,
bright yellow and bare against the threatening sky. I noticed
that the *Essex* was still there, moored where she had been when
I last saw her, about a half a league from the town and only a
matter of three cable's lengths from the fort on the point. As
we skirted the harbor and turned into Derby Street I saw that
she had been fully rigged in our absence.

"She looks a different ship, doesn't she?"

Selina looked at the ship apathetically.

"I wish I'd bought that blue taffeta with the pink sprigging,"
she said.

"Stuff!" I told her. "It wasn't becoming."

She rolled her eyes heavenward in weary resignation.

"La! How little you men know of such things!"

I did not trouble to reply, knowing that anything I might
say would only lead to further bickering. Instead I glanced
away. A boat was coming in across the water from the frigate,
its oars flashing yellow in rhythm to the coxswain's nod. It
seemed to me that there was a discipline and precision in the
stroke that was lacking ordinarily in the boats we regularly saw
in the harbor. I wondered idly if that meant that she was
manned and ready and preparing to sail.

Captain Hackett seemed happy to see us back again. He
shook hands with me cordially and embraced his daughter.

"Marriage agrees with you, my dear," he said, holding her
out at arm's length. "You've taken on flesh."

"I have not!" she retorted petulantly, and turned and fled
up the stairs.

He stared after her.

"What ails the girl?"

I shrugged.

"You'd a good time in Boston?" he asked.

"Oh, fine," I said dryly.

He looked at me with a surprised grin.

"Like that, eh?" he said. "Well, she's her mother's daughter. You can't say I didn't warn you."

"No," I agreed. "I can't."

He dug me in the ribs with a horny thumb.

"But you'd not change, eh?" he said.

"No sir," I assured him. "I would not."

The strange part is that I meant it.

"Ah!" he said. "There's the lad! Come and have a drink before you dress for dinner."

The evening meal was pleasant. It was like old times to sit down, the three of us together, and talk of what was going on. Captain Hackett had a way of taking hold of a situation and making everyone in it feel at ease, and this he did now, talking of what had happened in Salem in our absence with such cheerful relish that we quickly fell into his mood and listened, prompting him with questions whenever it seemed that his fund of information was likely to exhaust itself. Our wedding, so he told us, had evidently started an epidemic of nuptials. Joshua Delano and Mercy Hawks had been married within a fortnight of us. Jethrameel Woolridge and Susanna Nichols, Peleg Thorndike and Ann Hodges, Amasa Washburn and Martha Harrod, and George Nichols and Sally Pierce had announced their betrothals. Apart from the marriage market, there appeared to have been little social activity other than the first Assembly Ball of the season, which had been a great success. In matters of trade, one small brig, a Wait & Pierce vessel, was long overdue and was presumed lost, though the news of other Salem ships was good.

Talk of ships reminded me of the boat I had glimpsed coming in from the *Essex*. I remarked upon it.

"I suppose that means Captain Waters has shipped his crew and is getting ready to sail," I said.

Captain Hackett laughed.

"You've touched a sore subject there. You've not kept abreast of the situation as regards the frigate?"

I admitted that I had not. He nodded.

"Our local quarrels rarely echo as far as Boston."

"There's been a quarrel, then?" I asked, surprised.

"Well, quarrel's a strong word, no doubt," he admitted. "Captain Waters declined the command."

"I thought he wanted it!" I exclaimed.

Captain Hackett shrugged.

"He may have," he said. "But there was some doubt as to her crew, and so he refused it. The Committee offered her to Richard Derby. But he is away in the West Indies and seems unlikely to return in time to take her out this winter. Secretary Stoddert has declared that the Navy can delay no longer, and has appointed Captain Preble to command her."

"Preble?" I said. "Of the *Pickering?*"

"Aye."

"He should be a good man," I ventured.

"No doubt," he agreed. "At least he is active. But his position here is unenviable. The Committee is not happy about it, and was only mollified by the promise to put Captain Derby in command later, should he care to accept."

"That seems hardly fair to Preble," I protested.

"What would you?" he asked. "It was the understanding the Committee would have the naming of her commander. 'Tis what happens when you mix politics with policy."

"At least she's ready to sail," I said. "He'll have one cruise out of her."

He laughed outright at that.

"Ready to sail!" he exclaimed. "Bless you, boy, she's far from it. Captain Preble arrived in town only the day before yesterday and found no more than seventeen hands and a midshipman on board. Her guns are all to be mounted, and there's still a good deal of carpentry and joining and ironwork to be done, I'm told. She's taken on a deal of kentledge as ballast and some water and provisions. But 'twill be a month yet before she's ready for sea. Preble will have his recruiting parties out among us, and there's all manner of stores to come from Boston. I'd not be surprised if winter caught her before she was ready, and she were forced to lie here until spring."

It was a relief in more ways than one to be back in Salem. For one thing, in familiar surroundings with familiar duties to perform in keeping the house running smoothly for her father and myself, Selina seemed less picking and somewhat more content. For my own part, it was a relief to find that my practice was still sufficient to keep me busy and return me enough income to keep me independent of my father-in-law. There was a settled feeling, too, about living in the Hackett house—for Captain Hackett would not hear of our moving elsewhere—that I had not known before. Meantime I thought no more of the *Essex* for the time being. After all, I told myself, I had no interest in the problems either of the vessel or of her commander. But in that I was mistaken, as I was to learn presently.

There were in Salem a number of associations, though few of them, except the newly formed East India Marine Society, had private quarters. In the main they were informal groups which met at intervals in one or another of the better taverns of the town for purposes of conviviality and discussion. No dues were required, and acceptance by the circle was the only initiation.

It was a pleasant arrangement, and one to which Captain Hackett soon introduced me. His group gathered at the Sun Tavern and devoted itself in the main to political discussion. The leanings of all of the members being outspokenly Federalist, I gathered that there had rarely, in the past, been any acrimony in the debate. Recently, however, the faith of some of the members had been severely shaken, first by the Administration's pusillanimous course in the case of the Illuminati, and second by the President's volte-face in sending envoys to France. After the events of the previous winter, and the stand then taken by the Government, this move seemed, even to Mr. Adams's staunchest supporters, irreconcilable with national honor, and in consequence I gathered that the arguments were inclined to be somewhat sharper than ordinarily was the case.

Affairs of national interest, however, were sometimes overshadowed in argument by matters of local importance. Thus it chanced that one evening the problem of the *Essex's* gun mounts was discussed with some sharpness.

Captain Hackett and I had gone to the tavern somewhat earlier than usual. Thus we were already there when Captain Waters and Billy Gray arrived, bringing with them a spare figure of a man with features so constantly severe as to be set in an almost permanent scowl. We did not need the blue coat and gold epaulets to tell us that here was Captain Preble, of the *Essex*.

Captain Waters did the honors, introducing us, one by one. Preble acknowledged each of us formally, and Eli Hackett sought to draw him into conversation.

"How does it go aboard the *Essex,* Captain?" he asked. "Will you be ready for sea soon?"

Captain Preble turned his head slowly.

"Ready?" he said in a harsh voice. "Ready, Captain Hackett? She's ready for sea on an hour's notice. Ready, that is, except that I haven't a crew on board and no instructions for one; that she lacks provisions and stores; that her guns are not mounted, since the fool who made the carriages made them all too high; that she is but half finished below decks; that——"

There was a bellow from a corner of the room. Deacon Gould reared his massive bulk out of a chair.

"What's that ye say, sir, about the gun carriages?"

Preble's eyes slewed round and fixed the deacon with an incurious stare.

"I said they were all too high," he replied.

"Why, damme, sir, I made those carriages," the deacon bawled, growing red in the face.

"Did you?" said Preble imperturbably. "Then you should learn your trade, sir. The guns could not be brought to bear."

"Igod!" the deacon sputtered. "Man and boy, seventy years I've listened to no such impertinence! I've been building gun carriages since ye were in dresses! I've a mind to lay my cane across your breeches to teach ye manners to your elders!"

Preble's eyebrows raised and something almost resembling a smile twitched at the corners of his mouth, but his dignity did not relax for an instant.

"If I have upset you, Deacon," he said, "I am sorry. No doubt you're an old hand at making them."

"I am! I am!" the deacon admitted. "I built gun mounts for Mugford and Harraden, and I've been buildin' 'em ever since. But I accept your apology, sir. I accept it."

Preble bowed.

"Thank you, Deacon." He paused. The thin smile vanished. "You may have the building of gun mounts, but I have the fighting of them. I say they're too high and the guns could not be used. I've sent 'em ashore to be cut down!"

And there was an end to that. The captain's mouth shut like a steel trap, and the deacon retreated to his corner mumbling. As if to apologize to the rest of us, then, the captain unbent somewhat and, accepting a glass of toddy, gave us a somewhat fuller account of the state of the frigate.

"I ask pardon," he said, "if I gave a mite blacker picture of the state of my ship than is actually the case. The fact is she's in a fair way, but I'll not deny we have our problems. They're mainly bound up in the question of getting to sea before winter sets in. You all know what that would mean."

"You'd be out of action until next summer, Captain," Asahel Clark growled.

"Exactly!" Preble nodded. "However, if the ice will hold off a short while longer, I daresay we'll squeeze by. In the matter of a crew, I've written Secretary Stoddert for recruiting instructions, and I doubt he'll delay his reply. Mr. Beale is already aboard—my first lieutenant—and a number of petty officers. I've found an excellent carpenter, Samuel York Nowell. No doubt you gentlemen know of him. I've been lucky enough, too, to find a young man to go as carpenter's mate—a lad named Price, Nowell's son-in-law, I believe."

A murmur of approval went whispering through the room. Preble went on as if he had not heard it.

"George Stevens has signed as quartermaster, and John Howard for bos'n's mate. These men I have sailed with before. William Mumford, purser, will be with us in a few days, as will Hector Orr, surgeon. Both have been ordered aboard. Mr. Phipps and Mr. Lee, second and third lieutenants, I expect daily. As soon as my instructions arrive I shall open recruiting rendezvous at Cape Ann, Salem, and Boston."

Without blinking an eye he glanced around.

"Would any of you gentlemen care to ship with us for a two months' advance in wages?"

A laugh greeted his jest. The notion of offering these solid merchants two months' advance on a seaman's wage to ship in the frigate apparently tickled their fancy. Someone asked him a question about provisions, but I did not hear his reply, for my attention was wandering. So both Sam and Ben had signed for the cruise! Then what of Patience? Did they mean to leave her adrift?

I went home that evening somewhat perturbed at what I had heard, though why I should have been I could not tell. It was nothing to me, I told myself, what either Ben or Sam did.

It was some time before I saw either Ben or Sam. In the meantime November passed and December came with still no snow and, by good fortune, not enough cold weather to lock the harbor. At home Selina grew more and more irritable, her condition more evident. I had long since learned that Eli Hackett was not an observant man in such matters, but the day came when he drew me aside and spoke of it.

"Is the lass with child?" he demanded.

I told him that she was.

"But," he protested, "is it usual for it to show so soon? Why, it can be scarce two months—or could it be more?"

He fixed me with a quizzical yet dangerous eye.

"It might be twins," I replied evasively.

Whether he was satisfied with this or whether he realized that prying would not mend matters, I have no way of knowing. At any rate, he let it drop and spoke to me no more of it. For my part, I admit the incident set me to thinking, for even to me she appeared further along than, to my knowledge, she had any right to be.

In town there was evidence that the day of departure for the *Essex* was drawing nigh. The painters finished their work and came ashore, leaving her gleaming. The carpenters and joiners put up the last bulkheads and the smiths finished the ironwork. Her batteries were mounted. Meanwhile a steady stream of stores flowed to her: cable and anchors, kentledge, powder and shot, barrels of beef and pork, flour, small arms, butter, cheeses, rum. Not a day went by but some sloop lay alongside discharging its cargo into her.

At the same time her men began to be noticeable about the streets. Like most naval captains, Preble believed a uniform lent distinction and a certain spirit to a ship's crew. Also it made desertion more difficult. Accordingly he dressed his men in keeping with the notion.[1] A wide, tarred canvas hat with streamers, a short blue jacket with yellow buttons over a striped jersey, and wide-bottomed blue trousers set the crew of

[1] Officers' uniforms only were the subject of regulation at this date. The dress of the crew was left to the discretion of the commanding officer of each vessel.

the *Essex* apart from the other seafarers in the town, and it soon became evident that there was a certain pride attached to being so singled out.

The ship's officers began to appear in the local taverns. Mr. Beale, the first lieutenant, was a lanky, quiet man of about my own age, who went soberly about the ship's business ashore. Mr. Lee, the third lieutenant, on the other hand, was no more than seventeen; a mischievous, rollicking towhead, not much older than the midshipmen over whom he lorded it with such severity, though doubtless, in their eyes, he had achieved a world apart. It was Lieutenant Lee who flooded the town with handbills which read:

FRIGATE ESSEX

To all ABLE-BODIED and PATRIOTIC SEAMEN, who are willing to serve their Country, and Support its Cause:

The President of the United States, having ordered the Captain and Commander of the good frigate *ESSEX*, of 32 guns, now riding in the harbor of SALEM, to employ the most VIGOROUS EXERTIONS to put said ship as speedily as possible in a situation to sail at the shortest command.

NOTICE IS HEREBY GIVEN, that a HOUSE OF RENDEZVOUS is opened at the sign of the TURK'S HEAD, kept by Martin Thompson, in DERBY STREET;—where SIXTY able Seamen, SEVENTY-THREE Ordinary Seamen, and THIRTY Boys, will have an Opportunity of entering into the Service of their Country for One Year, unless sooner discharged by the President of the United States. To all Able-Bodied Seamen the sum of SEVENTEEN Dollars; to all Ordinary Seamen the sum of FOURTEEN Dollars; and to all Boys the sum of FIVE to TWELVE Dollars, according to Merit, will be given per month; and two months' advance will be paid by the Recruiting Officer if necessary.

None will be allowed to enter this honorable service, but such as are well organized, healthy and robust; and free from scorbutic and consumptive affections.

A Glorious Opportunity now presents to the BRAVE and HARDY Seamen of New-England to enter into the service of their Country—to avenge its wrongs—and to protect its Rights upon the Ocean. Those brave lads are now invited to repair to the FLAGG of the *ESSEX* now lying at the above Rendezvous; where they shall be kindly received, handsomely entertained, and may enter into immediate Pay.

EDWARD PREBLE
Commander, United States Frigate *Essex*.

It was in passing the Turk's Head one evening that I encountered Ben Price, for the first time since he had signed on board. As I have said, the work of the carpenters and joiners was mainly finished on board the *Essex*. Consequently Ben found himself assigned to assist with recruiting, along with several of his new-found shipmates; something that I was quite unaware of, until one evening, making my way home from a call, I heard my name spoken and, turning, found myself face to face with him.

"Tom Tisdall!" he cried. "Avast there! Would you pass an old shipmate without speaking?"

I laughed aloud at that.

"You've grown mighty nautical, Ben, since you signed aboard a ship that's not yet weighed anchor," I said.

He waved his hand airily.

" 'Tis a habit we fall into. But, come! Have a cup with me, and meet some of my mates. This is a fine life, Tom. I wish you were one of us!"

I glanced up at the sign on the tavern beside us and remembered the handbills.

"I've already refused the post of surgeon," I said. "You're wasting your time with me, Ben."

He stared at me.

"But we have a surgeon."

"I've heard," I said. "His name's Orr, isn't it? No, Ben, save your silver. Besides, I've something to say to you, and I'd rather say it out here."

"To me?" he said, I thought on the defensive.

"Aye, you," I replied shortly. "I'd heard you'd signed on, but I didn't believe it. Now I see 'tis so. You and Sam both?"

He planted his fists on his hips and stared at me.

"What if we have?" he demanded. "Someone has to."

"I'm not questioning that," I said wearily, "but I'll ask you to remember your responsibilities. Who's to look after Pat while you're gone?"

"Pat!" he laughed. "God love you, Tom! She can look after herself. It's not the first time a man's gone off to sea and left a wife behind him. Forget it! Come in and have a drink with me. We've still room for a surgeon's mate!"

"Thanks!" I said. "That's what I'm afraid of. I'll drink with you, Ben, when the *Essex* has shipped its full complement. Until then—I must go home!"

It was a week or so after this that I came home late in the afternoon to an unhappy scene. I entered the house, unaware that anything was amiss, and shook the snow from my great-coat before hanging it up, for we were in the midst of the first heavy snowstorm of the year. After that I passed into the drawing room with no thought other than to take a glass of hot toddy to warm my vitals and toast my breeches before the crackling fire.

I found Selina there before me, looking like a thundercloud in gray silk.

"Oh, there you are!" she exclaimed. "It's about time you came in. That trull of yours was here."

I stared at her in startled amazement.

"Trull?" I demanded. "I know no trulls."

"He knows no trulls!" she mocked mincingly.

"Come to the point, will you?" I rapped out sharply. "Who are you talking about?"

"That Nowell wench," she retorted. "She had the effrontery to come here asking for you! She said she was ill!"

Her voice was harsh with scorn and anger.

"My dear," I protested, "I am a physician. Why shouldn't she come here? Where else would she look for me?"

She laughed scornfully.

"It certainly didn't require a doctor to see what was wrong with her!"

"What are you getting at?" I demanded.

"She's with child, that's what!" she shrilled.

I laughed at that, so relieved that for the moment I did not see the implication of her words.

"And what of it? Does the pot call the kettle black?"

She went white with fury.

"What do you mean by that?" she screamed.

"Good God, woman!" I roared back at her, thoroughly aroused. "You're pregnant yourself, aren't you?"

"Do you speak of me, your wife, in the same breath with that slut?" she demanded, livid.

"Stop it!" I shouted. "She's no slut, I tell you. You forget she's respectably married to Ben Price. I'll take my oath if she's pregnant 'tis but by her husband!"

To my astonishment she fell back as though I had struck her across the face, and every last drop of color drained from her cheeks.

"Oh!" she cried. "Oh! You dare say that to me! This is too much! I'll not bear it another minute!"

Abruptly she turned away, as if to run from the room, but in doing so she tangled her foot in an edge of the rug. The violence of her turn threw her off balance, and with her foot trapped she could not catch herself. One hand she flung out to catch the back of a near-by chair, and missed. At the same instant I leaped forward to catch her.

But I was too late. Even as I reached her, her body slipped from under my hands and she fell, forward, striking the side of her abdomen upon the sharp corner of the chair. A gasping scream of anguish escaped her lips, and with both hands she clutched at her belly. Her knees drew up beneath her chin, and for an instant she writhed in agony. Then, even before I could drop to one knee beside her, she relaxed in a dead faint. As I leaned down to turn her, Eli Hackett's voice came over my shoulder from the doorway.

"What's the matter? What's going on here?

15

IT DID NOT occur to me, at that moment, that he would attach blame to me for what he saw.

"She stumbled over the rug," I said.

Even in my own ears the explanation sounded lame.

"You were quarreling!" It was an indignant accusation.

I was hardly in a mood to listen to abuse from him.

"Aye!" I snarled. "If you will have it so! But this is none of my doing. I would have caught her if I could."

He dropped to his knees beside me and bent over her.

"See!" he cried. "Are you hurt, lass?"

I thrust him aside none too gently.

"You'll do her no good that way," I said roughly, bending

to gather her up in my arms. "Go before me and open the doors. We must get her to bed as quickly as we can."

He gave me a blank look of surprise and went meekly to do as I said.

Selina was no lightweight at best, and in her present condition she was a good two stone over her normal weight. However, I managed the stairs and laid her gently on her bed, still unconscious from the blow. I sent her father below for brandy and spirits of hartshorn. While he was about this I stripped her to her shift and rolled her—none too gently, I fear, for I was still angry—under the covers. On his return I gave her a taste of the brandy and a whiff of the hartshorn, which brought her around slowly. In a moment she opened her eyes and rocked her head from side to side on the pillow, then gave a tremulous gasp and clutched at her side.

"Is she badly hurt, d'you think?" he asked.

"I can't tell without an examination," I replied.

"Well, in God's name, what are you waiting for?" he cried "Examine her!"

"I mean to," I said, and sent him from the room again, promising to recall him as soon as I had finished.

I think even then I had an inkling of the truth. As I closed the door behind him she gazed up at me, white-faced, her great eyes dark with anguish.

"Will I die?" she asked in a small voice.

"I think not," I replied coldly.

She turned her face away, and I fell to my examination. When it was done I knew what I should long since have had the wit to suspect. What I discovered, taken together with half-remembered signs that I had been either too preoccupied or too fatuous to read, told me only too plainly that the child she carried was not mine; could not be mine by a matter of weeks!

Many things were suddenly clear to me now: her haste to marry, her irritability. I even saw with some bitterness the trap she had laid for me. Most clearly of all, however, I saw the reason for her outburst in response to my altogether innocent remark. Her conscience had tricked her where scheming and planning had thus far carried her. Had she controlled her temper and quieted her fears, I would not even then have been aware that I was worse than cuckold. But she had given herself away, and the truth was out.

I rose unsteadily to my feet and went to the door and let the captain in. My expression must have told something of my shock and surprise, though it could hardly have revealed my revulsion. He stared at me with anxious eyes.

"What is it?" he cried. "What did you find?"

I looked at him dully, then let my eyes drop to meet those of the woman on the bed. Somehow she seemed remote to me now; a stranger almost. She was staring up at me wide-eyed over the edge of the sheet, which she clutched tightly on either side of her face so that it was drawn down taut across her mouth. She knows, I thought. She knows!

Captain Hackett shook me by the arm.

"What's wrong?" he cried urgently. "Is she——"

I shook my head.

"She's not hurt beyond a bad bruise."

"The child, then," he persisted. "It will live?"

"I cannot tell," I said.

"What is it, then?" he demanded.

I looked back again at Selina, and this time her eyes fell before my glance. She looked away, turning her head on the pillow, and I saw the tears start.

"It's nothing," I said, "nothing that means anything—only relief that it is no worse."

He stared at me doubtfully, and Selina's head turned again on the pillow, her eyes seeking mine once more with an expression of surprise. I sought refuge in action.

"Here!" I cried. "She'll catch her death in this cold room. Have a fire built for her, while I mix a sedative."

I went to my own room and mixed a draft to ease her pain and let her sleep. When I returned the fire was crackling in the grate and Selina was alone.

"Tom!" she whispered. "Tom, why did you——"

"Madam," I said stiffly, "what lies between us is our secret. I will not tell it first."

I said it coldly, for I was still angry. If I had slapped her she could not have looked more hurt, and I had to steel myself to be harsh. Kneeling beside the bed, I raised her head and held the cup to her lips.

"Drink this," I said.

She would have clung to me, but I turned away.

"Sleep now," I told her. "I'll look in on you later. We'll both be more fit for talking then."

I set the cup on the table by her bedside and went out although she would have called me back. At the foot of the stairs I found Captain Hackett.

"Is she all right?" he asked.

"She should be," I replied. "I have given her medicine to make her sleep. When she wakes I think she'll be no worse for her experience than a little sore."

I reached for my coat and hat.

"You're going out?" he demanded, surprised.

"I have a patient I must see," I told him, seizing upon any excuse to escape the house.

Once outside, however, I bent my head against the storm and walked blindly, caring little what direction I took so long as it was away. I wanted to be alone to think. I wanted to thrash this thing out with myself; to decide upon a course of action, since in my state of shock some course of action seemed necessary. Instead I found my mind wandering in circles, going back and over and around again through the whole course of circumstances that had brought me to this pass.

While my feet, mechanically, carried me out along the Causeway and past Briggs's Yard, I went back over the summer. Sometime in June or early July, I judged, it must have happened. She would have discovered her predicament in August, if she had not suspected it before, and my presence in the house to care for her father in his illness was the opportunity she sought. She had needed a husband, and so she had arranged it. In my hurt pride it seemed to me as simple as that. It did not occur to me to wonder why she should have chosen me before another; why she should not seek the father of her child. Had I thought about it more objectively, I must have seen that there were deeper currents here than met the eye.

Step by step I traced our course from that night. Selina's own illness and the launching of the *Essex;* her behavior on that occasion; our wedding, and her subsequent coolness. I told myself that I was a fool not to have seen the use she was making of me sooner, although candor impels me now to say that her attitude could easily have been explained as I had originally explained it: by her advanced condition. From this my mind turned to our return to Salem and her aloofness since; to this very afternoon when her allusions to Patience had exposed her own guilty conscience.

The thought of Patience brought me up standing. What was it Selina had told me? That Pat had come to the house that afternoon looking for me. I cursed myself for a fool for having forgotten it.

It was growing dark when I turned about, and swiftly as I walked, now that I was spurred on by a purpose, it was full night when I came, at length, to the familiar Nowell door. I rapped, but it was some moments before the light shuffle of footsteps sounded on the other side. In the meantime the snow swirled around me, and I realized suddenly that I was cold.

"Yes?" came Pat's voice from the opposite side of the door, scarce recognizable. "Who is it?"

"It's me, Pat," I called. "Tom."

I heard the bolts slide, and presently the door swung back, casting a shaft of golden light out into the stormy night. She stood before me clad in an old house dress, with a sort of shapeless dressing gown caught about her. Her feet were thrust into sheep's-wool slippers. But her hair was combed and caught with a ribbon so that it reflected the dancing light of the candle, and her face, though tired, was smiling welcome. My first thought as I looked at her was that she was as lovely as ever.

"Why, Tom!" she exclaimed. "What brings you out on such a night as this? Come in!"

I entered the house, and she shut the door behind me.

"I came to see you," I told her.

But she was not listening.

"Tom Tisdall!" she exclaimed. "You've been walking in this storm. You're soaked through!"

I glanced down guiltily. She was right. My boots were soggy with wet and my coat was sopping.

"Here," she cried, "get out of those wet things and come in by the fire!"

Without further talk she led the way into the familiar room in which I had passed so many pleasant evenings it seemed so long ago. With surprise I noticed that the fire was low, no more

than a bed of ashes and red coals. Patience saw my glance
and stooped to the woodbin.

"I'll build up the fire," she said.

"Here!" I cried so loudly that she was startled. "Here!
That's no work for you. Let me do that!"

She blushed furiously but stepped back.

"Where's Ben and Sam?" I asked, perhaps more brusquely
than I thought, as I heaved the big logs over the andirons.

"Gone to the ship," she said half defiantly.

"Gone!" I exclaimed.

"There's been talk of her sailing for a week."

I made no reply but poked at the coals under the fresh-laid
logs, cutting a passage for the draft to take hold. The logs
ceased smoking and burst into flame. I stood the poker in the
corner and went to sit beside Patience.

"And what of you?" I asked, forgetting to pretend. "What
did they expect you to do?"

"Oh, I can manage," she said. "Gaffer went first and then
Ben, and neither told the other until it was too late."

I checked the angry exclamation that rose to my lips. A
stiff little silence fell between us.

"Selina said that you'd been to the house today."

"Yes."

"You came to see me?"

She turned back to face me.

"Yes, Tom, I——"

She broke off abruptly, flushing.

"Look, child," I said, "you came to me as your doctor, didn't
you?"

"I——I don't know any other," she explained in a small voice.

"Of course," I said. "I understand. Why shouldn't you?
That's what I'm here for. Now tell me the trouble, and I'll
see if I can help you."

"I——I don't know just how to begin."

"Well," I said, smiling, "suppose I begin. You're going to
have a baby, aren't you?"

She hid her face in her hands.

"Stop it!" I said. "It's nothing to be ashamed of! It's perfectly decent, honest, and reasonable. I wish——"

I broke off abruptly, realizing that I was letting my personal feelings color my thoughts. She glanced up at me.

"Yes?" she asked.

"Nothing!" I said.

There was a pause.

"You want me to advise you?" I asked.

She looked up at me, her smile bright and eager.

"Oh, would you?" she asked.

"I'd think myself honored by your trust!" I said.

She made a quick little deprecatory gesture.

"It's true!" I exclaimed. "I can think of no one I'd rather serve. But I doubt you need a doctor. It's not usual, you know. In most cases it's left to midwives. Many women don't have even that."

"But I don't know any midwives," she said innocently.

I laughed and patted her reassuringly on the shoulder.

"Leave that to me," I told her.

I got down to cases then, questioning her as to symptoms and feelings: was she ill in the morning, did she feel any pain, was she yet conscious of life, and the like. All of these she answered to my satisfaction.

"You're sound as a nut," I told her. "You've nothing to fear. I'll find a woman to take care of you, and I'll try to find someone to look after the heavy work too." She looked relieved, and I felt rewarded.

It required no more than the first blast of the storm on my face, however, after I had left the house, to shock me back to the realization that, at least insofar as I was concerned, all was not right! I had scarcely passed the gate before it struck me with the impact of a cannon shot. I saw now what I had not before recognized. Patience was the woman I loved, and I had loved her from the day I had moved into her grandfather's house. But I had been too timid. I had not wanted to spoil her. And while I was being timid Ben Price had married her. It was vain to wish that I had had the drive to seize a situation, as he did, and carry it through to the only conclusion possible. Now, because I had lacked the initiative, I found myself so embroiled that I knew not which way to turn. Had I had the courage of my convictions, I would have married Patience first, and though we might be poorer we would certainly be happier. Having lacked that initiative, I had let Ben get before me, and so became fair game for Selina. It was my unrealized adoration for Patience translated to desire for Selina that had worked upon me. Now I stood to be the cuckold of the latter and the physician of the former; the father of neither's children; the tormented slave of both! I could not live with one and I would not live with the other. What was a man in my place to do?

As I asked myself the question a group of short-jacketed, tar-hatted, boisterous figures reeled past me in the swirling dark of Derby Street and disappeared into the yellow maw of a water-front tavern. I stopped and stared after them. My answer struck me of a heap. If Ben Price could go off as he pleased, there was no reason why I should not. Indeed, there was every reason why I should. I could not marry Patience. I had missed my chance at that. But I could see to it that the man who had married her treated her as she deserved. If he went from her, I could follow him and see that he came back to her. If he forgot his obligation, I could see that he was reminded of it. If I could not have that marriage myself, I could guard hers for her and see that no act of his destroyed it.

This, I told myself, was what would serve Patience. As for Selina—what did I owe her? It was as if I had received a sudden revelation! I stood in the midst of the storm and lifted my face.

"Lord God," I said, "grant me to look to her happiness as long as I live!"

Having so prayed, I sought out the Turk's Head.

"Mr. Beale," I said, coming straight to the point, "do you still have a berth for a surgeon's mate?"

He looked up from his table, his lean face blank.

"Why," he said, "why, yes. But I thought——"

"Never mind," I said. "If you'll have me I'll take it."

He grinned as if at some private joke.

"Ah," he said, "will we have you? Indeed, sir, we will, and with pleasure. Will you have a glass with me on it?"

I would and I did, and when I had he swore me.

"Come out to the ship at eight o'clock in the morning," he said with a smile. "It's a pleasure to have you, Doctor!"

I arrived at the house on Derby Street to find the lights out on the ground floor and Eli Hackett sitting in Selina's room talking with her. He looked at me as I entered.

"You were gone a long time," he said.

"I'm sorry if I upset you," I said.

Selina looked at me doubtfully.

"How do you feel?" I asked.

"Much better, thank you," she replied in as pleasant a tone as she had used in months.

I felt a twinge of conscience.

"I'm glad," I said. "I'd not want to leave you in pain."

"What?" said Captain Hackett with a start.

"I thought I'd best tell you I've signed aboard the *Essex*, as surgeon's mate."

"But why?" Captain Hackett asked. "I thought——"

I nodded curtly, interrupting.

"Circumstances change," I said. "If we are not already at war, we will be within a few months. The Navy needs qualified men and is having difficulty finding them——"

He nodded soberly. I felt a fraud, but it was better than to tell him my true reasons, for his own sake.

"Thank you," I said. "Now, if you don't mind, I'd like a word with my wife. I must report on board at eight in the morning."

He tossed a puzzled glance from me to Selina before he rose and held out his hand to me.

"Well, lad," he said, "I doubt you'll regret your decision, now you've made it. 'Tis not as if you were bound to the land."

I shook his hand and saw him to the door. When he was gone I turned to Selina. There was no doubt she was beautiful, and I could see how I might have come under her spell. Her dark hair gleamed black as a crow's wing in the lamplight, and her eyes were liquid with reproach.

"Well, madam!" I said defiantly.

"Tom! Why?" she cried.

"Could I stay here knowing what I know?" I demanded. She shrank back amid the pillows.

"Don't fear," I said. "I shan't reproach you. I don't suppose you could help yourself. I'll keep the secret."

"Tom! Don't!" she gasped in a croaking whisper.

"If the child were mine," I said, beyond pity, "if it could be

mine by any stretch of the imagination—— But you knew
when you married me!"

I paused and she lay still, staring at me. Twice she tried
to speak, without rousing any words. When at length they came
she could say only, "He—he——"

I cut her short.

"I don't want to know about it," I said.

She turned her head away, and in spite of myself I was
touched. I took her hand in mine.

"I'm no fool, Seel," I said, "though you may have thought
so at times. I think we might have been happy together but
for this. But this is something that no man of honor could
ignore. I can forgive you, but I cannot go on. You must forgive me if I seem harsh. Let us say no more, eh?"

She turned to me convulsively and clutched at my hand.

"What am I to do?" she wailed.

"I'll see to everything," I said. "You need have no fear
on that score. You will be well tended."

She stared at me wide-eyed but made no reply.

"I'll say good-by now," I said, and bent over her hand.

16

IT WAS STILL DARK, with the blackness peculiar to winter's pre-
dawn hours, when I left the house the next morning. Early as I
was, Patience was up before me. She had neglected to bolt
the door behind me when I left, and it opened to my touch. I
found her on her knees before the hearth, clad only in her
nightdress, endeavoring to revive the fire from the coals of the
night before.

At the sound of my step she glanced over her shoulder with
a gasp of dismay and clutched her nightdress about her.

"Tom!" she exclaimed. "You shouldn't——"

I went to her and lifted her tenderly by the elbows, acutely
conscious of the way in which her light gown clung to the gentle
curves of her figure and revealed its outlines.

"My dear!" I said. "I told you I would attend to this. Get
back into your bed where 'tis warm, and stay there until I can
get the fires built!"

She obeyed without protest and suffered me to lead her, with an arm about her waist, to the foot of the stairs. When she was gone I built up a good fire on the hearth and put the kettle to boil, fetched water, and tended such chores as I had done before I moved away. This done, I collected an armful of sticks and a handful of shavings and went on upstairs, where I found her abed with the covers drawn up to her chin and clutched tightly.

I gave her a reassuring smile and set about kindling a good blaze in her fireplace. Her gaze followed me while I was about this, but only when I rose at last, with the yellow flames flickering up the chimney, did she speak.

"Tom," she said then. "Tom, I——"

"Wait," I said, and slipped out of the room quickly and downstairs, where I brewed a pot of tea, which I fetched back up again with me. At sight of the tea she looked almost guilty.

"You shouldn't be doing this!" she exclaimed.

"Nonsense!" I said. "I told you I was going to see you looked after. Drink this. 'Twill warm you up."

She sat up, still holding the covers under her chin, and accepted the cup. I rummaged about until I found a dressing gown, which I draped about her shoulders. She thanked me with her eyes as she sipped at the tea.

"Pat," I said, "I've signed on aboard the *Essex* too." She put down the teacup and stared at me in astonishment, forgetting for the moment to clutch the dressing gown closed at her breasts.

"Oh, Tom!" she cried. "Why?"

I was as unprepared to answer that as I had been the night before.

"They need surgeons," I said.

But she did not smile in response. Instead she reached out and took my hand in both of hers.

"That's not the real reason, Tom," she said.

"It's a good enough reason," I replied.

She let go of my hand and looked almost hurt. For an instant it was on the tip of my tongue to tell her that she had played no small part in my decision, but fortunately I had sufficient control not to do so.

"Is it because of Selina?" she asked.

I gave her a startled glance.

"Let's forget it, shall we?" I asked gruffly.

Neither of us spoke for a moment. Then I went on hurriedly, for I felt that time was growing short.

"I tell you," I said, "because I made a promise last night. I did not want you to think I was forgetting it."

I told her then the names of a half a dozen midwives, and she picked one with whom she had a nodding acquaintance. I was pleased that she chose one I considered to be kindly as well as competent.

"I will arrange for her to attend you twice or three times a week and to come and stay when the time comes."

"But, Tom," she protested, "we can't afford——"

"Nonsense!" I scoffed. "Both Ben and Sam will be making good wages at sea. I'll advance the cash, and they can settle with me later—if you must."

"It will make me feel better to know there's someone I can turn to when the time comes," she admitted.

"Of course it will," I said heartily. "You can count on Mrs. Beeman. I'll try to arrange, too, to have someone look in morning and evening and help you with the wood and the fires and the water and such."

"Tom, you shouldn't," she cried.

"Hush!" I said. "You are my patient, even though I may not be here to look after you. I mean to see it done properly."

She said nothing to that but gave me such a look as was all the reward I could have asked. I rose hurriedly.

"I must be going," I said.

I leaned down and allowed myself the small luxury of touching her cheek with my lips.

"Take care of yourself!" I said.

Before I could straighten, however, she caught me about the neck with her left hand, while the fingers of her right brushed my cheek, and lifted her lips to mine.

"Oh, Tom!" she whispered. "You take care!"

For an instant I stood so, almost but not quite yielding to the impulse to crush her in my arms. Then, gently, I took her hands in mine.

"Good-by!" I said huskily, and kissed her finger tips.

With that I turned and fled.

I went over the *Essex's* side at ten minutes to eight with the feeling of entering a strange new world, as indeed I was. I had been aboard many a ship in Portsmouth as a boy, but this was my first visit to a naval vessel. What I expected and what I found were not altogether the same. As I came to the grating at the gangway, the first thing that met my eye was the marine guard, burly and stern and stiff at attention in his short blue coat and blue overalls, edged in red, with a red-belt. He was the most military figure I had yet seen, barring not even Captain Preble himself. A little to one side of him stood a seaman in tarred hat and blue jacket with a glass tucked beneath his arm; and still a little farther distant was a tall, elderly officer in a blue coat and cocked hat. He had an epaulet upon his right shoulder and a sword at his waist and white gloves on his hands, and I took all these as symbols of his authority, in which I was quite correct, for they marked him as the officer of the deck.

All three of them were eying me as if they expected something of me, and I, suddenly abashed, snatched off my hat. They all three seemed relieved, and the elderly officer came forward.

"Good morning," he said courteously. "Can I help you?"

I blinked.

"I'm Dr. Tisdall," I said. "I signed on with Mr. Beale as surgeon's mate last night. He told me to be on board at eight."

I felt awkward as soon as the words were out of my mouth, and was disgusted with myself for not having been more military. But Phipps did not appear to notice.

"Ah yes!" he exclaimed. "Mr. Beale sent word you'd be aboard. He's not arrived yet himself, but he'll be along presently. In the meantime we'll look after you. By the way"—he extended his hand—"I'm Phipps, second lieutenant, and officer of the deck until eight o'clock."

I took his hand gratefully.

"Ah—you may put on your hat, Doctor," he said gravely. "Only petty officers and seamen are required to remain uncovered on the quarter-deck. Commissioned officers remove the hat in coming aboard or going ashore, as a salute to the colors, but may put it back on again immediately."

"Thank you," I said, replacing my headpiece.

He smiled.

"It takes a while to get the hang of it."

I glanced around. The deck on which I stood presented a picture of orderly confusion. Overside a sloop was discharging into us, sling by sling, her cargo of supplies and provisions, and boxes and barrels and bales and casks lay jumbled by the hatchways in seeming disorder but yet with a kind of logical arrangement that might make the stowage of them simpler. Forward, near the galley smoke pipe, lay a great heap of coals, and upon the far side of the deck a great stack of cordwood. Amidships there were crates of chickens and ducks and a pen in which were a foursome of hogs and a half a dozen sheep. Further forward were a pair of bower anchors, evidently newly come aboard, and long loops of cable and rope lying on deck waiting to be stowed. A bucket of tar smoked untended upon a smith's brazier near the foremast. Seamen and marines moved in and out amid this tangle, apparently on aimless errands, and yet one had the feeling that things were being done. Phipps chuckled amiably.

"Looks a mess, doesn't it? You'll be amazed, though, to see how shipshape it's stowed by the time we sail."

"Indeed?" I said politely.

"Yes," he beamed, then scowled suddenly.

He turned to the man with the glass under his arm.

"Have someone fetch up Mr. Tisdall's gear."

I felt somewhat confused.

"I didn't bring any," I said.

The seaman with the glass stopped six paces away and turned to eye me with sardonic amusement. Even the rigid marine gave me a swift, startled look.

"I rather counted on getting ashore for it sometime during the day," I said.

"Ah!" said Phipps, evidently at a loss. "Too bad for you if we sailed at once, eh?"

The seaman—I later learned he was the quartermaster— with the glass broke in abruptly.

"Captain's gig coming, sir!"

Phipps looked excited.

"Where away?"

The seaman pointed. I looked, too, stretching my neck to

see over the bulwarks. The boat was approaching smartly. In the stern sheets, although it was too far yet to make out his features, I could see the stiff, upright figure of Captain Preble and another blue-coated figure beside him.

Phipps was bawling orders when I turned back. He had apparently forgotten me.

"Turn out the guard! Bos'n! Pipe the side!"

A boy I had not previously noticed streaked forward, and within an instant the plaintiff, wailing notes of the bos'n's pipe came drifting back toward us. Four seamen dashed up breathlessly and ranged themselves, two on either side of the gangway, followed by the bos'n himself, who took station a little to one side and behind them. As if by magic, three more marines appeared from nowhere and lined up stiffly against the companionway. Phipps took a position slightly in advance of the bos'n, where he would be placed to welcome the captain the moment he stepped off the gratings and onto the deck between the rigid side boys.

"Er—what shall I do?" I ventured to ask, somewhat disconcerted with all this evident flummery.

Phipps looked at me and gulped.

"Stand behind me and to the left," he said. "Lift your hat when the captain comes aboard."

We heard the low command below as the oars in the boat were tossed. An instant later the ladder creaked and swayed as someone started up.

"Bos'n, hoist him in!" Phipps ordered.

The pipe took up its shrill quavering once more, and a moment later Preble appeared in the gangway.

It seemed smartly done to me, but if Captain Preble thought so, there was no hint of it in his scowling eye. He touched his hat in response to the salute and mumbled a formal acknowledgment, the words of which I did not catch. This done, he glared about him, first at the deck, then up into the rigging, and finally at Phipps.

"You've not yet been relieved, Mr. Phipps?" he demanded.

"No sir! It lacks five minutes of the hour, sir."

"Hmmmph!" Preble grunted. His eye fell upon me and kindled slightly. Phipps spoke quickly.

"Dr. Tisdall reported on board but a moment before you

arrived, sir," he said. "He signed with Mr. Beale last night, as surgeon's mate."

"Ah!" said the captain, his chill gaze raking me from head to foot. "Have we sailed together before, Mr. Tisdall? Your face is familiar."

I put on my best manner, although I was quaking inwardly.

"I've never been to sea before, sir," I said. "But I believe we've met. My father-in-law, Captain Hackett——"

At least on that occasion he had been civil. It did not occur to me that he would be otherwise aboard ship. It was only much later that I was to learn that a captain ashore and a captain on the quarter-deck were like to be different persons.

"I remember!" he interrupted me curtly. "Has Mr. Phipps seen to your gear?"

"I brought no gear, sir," I said. "I——"

"No gear?" he cut in sharply. Among other things that I had not hitherto known, but was rapidly discovering, was that in speaking to a senior officer it is an accomplishment to complete a sentence.

He turned and glared away forward, squinting at the gray horizon and sniffing at the wind, then cast his eyes aloft. But before I could reply he had swung back to me once more.

"You are aware of the conditions of the Service?"

"As a matter of fact, sir," I replied, "I rather looked to Mr. Beale to give me the details. Last night I only——"

"Indeed?" he burst out, and spun about to give a withering glance to Mr. Beale, who had followed him up the gangway. "Hah! Goddamme, Beale, I've told you to have these matters squared away before you fetch your people on board!"

"Aye, sir!" said Beale with a frozen countenance.

Captain Preble glanced back at me.

"You will assist the surgeon," he said, "for which you will be paid thirty dollars per month and two rations per day, two months' wages to be advanced if you wish it. You'll berth in the cockpit and mess with the junior officers there."

I nodded a little uncertainly, for most of this was gibberish to me. I could see the other officers stifling their smiles. And even the seamen and marines appeared to be chuckling inwardly, although there was not the slightest twitch of a facial muscle to betray it.

"Yes sir," I said.

"Mr. Phipps will tell you your duties in more detail," he growled. "I presume you've not provided yourself with uniforms or other necessaries for the voyage?"

"No sir."

He glanced aloft again.

"We'll not be sailing today," he said. "The blow's not over yet. Mr. Phipps!"

Phipps jumped.

"Aye, aye, sir?"

"As soon as you are relieved take charge of Mr. Tisdall and see that he is shown around. When you've made him familiar with the ship and his quarters send him ashore and see him fitted out."

"Aye, aye, sir!"

Preble glanced at me once more and seemed about to say something further, then evidently thought better of it, for he merely nodded curtly and turned away. An instant later he ducked down the companion ladder to the deck below.

17

PREBLE had no more than disappeared down the hatchway when it struck eight bells in rapid couplets. With his departure the rigidness of the moment seemed to relax. I glanced about and noticed a lad in midshipman's uniform, but wearing the epaulet of a lieutenant on his shoulder, talking to Phipps.

"Yes sir," he was saying. "But I couldn't relieve in the midst of piping the side, could I, sir?"

"If you'd been more punctual, Mr. Tew," Phipps rumbled, "you'd been here before we piped the side."

"Aye, sir," said Tew, somewhat crestfallen, I thought.

I wondered if all sea officers adopted this gruff pattern toward their subordinates in matters official.

"Very well!" said Phipps.

Tew raised his hat.

"I relieve you, sir," he said.

"Thank you, Mr. Tew," Phipps responded formally. "You have the deck."

He stripped off his gloves and pushed his hat back on his head and turned to face me with evident relief.

"That's done!" he grinned. "Oh, by the way—Mr. Tew, Dr. Tisdall. Tew's senior midshipman and acting lieutenant when any of us are absent or out of the running. Mr. Lee's in Boston now, recruiting. Tew's taking his watch."

I nodded, I hoped, brightly. To Tew he said:

"Dr. Tisdall's to be surgeon's mate."

I shook hands with Tew. Beale stifled a yawn.

"I'm going below, Phipps," he said. "Take care of the doctor. Show him about. Give him an idea of his duties."

The older man nodded, and Mr. Beale followed the captain down the hatch. Phipps looked at me.

"Ever been on a man-of-war?" he asked.

"No sir," I replied.

He clucked disapprovingly.

"We'll start right here, then," he said resignedly.

I nodded, and he turned and waved an arm in a gesture that took in the entire sweep of the deck.

"This is the spar deck. This part, abaft the mainmast, is known as the quarter-deck and is set aside for officers and the watch on duty. In port the starboard side of the quarter-deck is reserved for the captain. At sea he takes his exercise on the weather side, whichever that may be. Forward of the quarter-deck, amidships, is the waist, and forward of that is the forecastle, which is the crew's country. In the forepeak are the heads——"

"Heads?" I interrupted.

"Er—toilet facilities," he explained. "As you see," he went on hastily, "our secondary battery is mounted on the fo'c'sle and quarter-deck—six-pounders only, ten of 'em, though I can't understand why they didn't give us nines."

As Phipps glanced away forward my eye caught Tew's, and the youngster's eyelid flickered.

"Hammocks are stowed along the bulwarks forward during the day," the elder officer's voice droned on.

Looking where he pointed, I made note of the neat rows of what I had previously taken for canvas bags.

"Airs the bedding," Phipps explained, "and during an action offers some protection from fire from an enemy's tops."

He cleared his throat and spat overside.

"Guards some against flying splinters, too," he added. "Shall we go below?"

At the foot of the ladder he paused and once more waved his arm about him in a sweeping gesture.

"Gun deck," he explained.

I might have guessed that. The deck was open from foremast to mizzen, without transverse bulkheads. Ordinarily the only illumination would come from the midship well, but now, despite the bitterness of the weather, the gun ports were open, and by the light which they admitted I could see the rows of long twelves that made up the ship's heavy batteries on either side.

"The captain's cabin's aft, across the stern, on this deck," he went on. "There are two long twelves in the captain's forward cabin. But during action the partitions are knocked out, making the whole battery one. Midships, there, is the grog tub."

"The grog tub?" I said.

He nodded.

"Twice a day, every day," he said, "a half pint of grog is served out to the men."

He led the way in that direction, and I noticed that as we approached the midships section the slope of the deck above tended to reduce the headroom.

"Mind your head," he warned, ducking his own from force of habit. He halted beside a great round mahogany half barrel bound in shining copper hoops. New as it was, the grog tub was already redolent of its customary contents.

"Most of the men would rather be flogged than have their grog stopped," he said. "They'll go to great lengths to get an extra share. We have to watch 'em like hawks."

He went on a few steps and pointed out a tremendous oaken cask that stood just forward of the grog tub.

"The scuttle butt," he explained.

I must have looked bewildered, for he chuckled.

"The water barrel. At sea it's filled daily and a guard posted to see no man gets more than his share."

We passed on along the deck.

"The spaces between the guns," he said, "are used for different things. Chips—the carpenter—uses one for a shop. The barber another. Yonder, where you see the canvas screen, is the schoolroom, where the schoolmaster instructs the midshipmen."

Forward of the scuttle butt was another hatchway, and beyond that the galley, with its tremendous stove all bricked about for protection.

"This is the only place where the men may smoke," he told me, "and that only when the smoking lamp is lit."

As we turned from the galley a squeal and a raucous but unmistakably feminine laugh came from the gloomy, twilit area forward.

"Are there women aboard?" I asked, startled.

"Some." He smiled sourly.

"Is it permitted?" I demanded, surprised.

"In port," he replied. "Why not? We'll be a long time at sea. We keep a strict log of 'em as they come aboard: their names, whether married or single, who brings 'em and who takes 'em off, and the date and hour of both. We note their behavior, and if they're aught but circumspect or make trouble ashore, they go and no nonsense."

He led me down the forward hatch, yet another deck, to a space still more closely confined than the one above. Between the transverse beams I would take my oath there was not six feet of headroom, and since the beams themselves were a good eight inches thick and thrust down from the ceiling at intervals of four feet or thereabouts, it was impossible even for a fairly small man, let alone a tall one, to move forward or aft without ducking every second step or so. The only light here came from skylights, opening from the already shadowed gun deck, and from a series of small side lights in the infrequent spaces where the deck was open clear from one side of the ship to the other, and which could be opened only in the calmest weather. In consequence this deck was shrouded in an almost constant twilight, and the fact that it was partitioned off with transverse bulkheads at several points robbed it of the spaciousness characteristic of the deck above and made one feel shut in and imprisoned.

"This is the berth deck," Lieutenant Phipps explained. "Most of the ship's people live here."

He turned about the ladder and led me to a compartment, forward of the stout foremast, and in the very bows of the ship. A lantern gave a feeble light, and a scuttle overhead was open, admitting air. A half a dozen hammocks hung on either side of the cabin—not the unstayed sea bags of the seamen, but rather comfortable, stayed hammocks equipped with good pads. Against the bulkhead at the after end on one side was a row of narrow closets. A boy was lying on his back in one of the hammocks, fully dressed, one leg hanging over the side and one hand trailing on the deck beneath him. He was snoring lustily. Phipps prodded him with the tip of his scabbard.

"Ouch!" the lad exclaimed, then, seeing who had disturbed his slumbers, sprang erect and stood stiffly before us, evidently very much confused.

"This is the sick bay," said Phipps, ignoring him. "This is your duty station except during an action. Each morning you or the surgeon or the other surgeon's mate, if we have one, holds sick call here, when anyone with ailments or injuries reports for treatment. If they're seriously ill they go on the sick list and into one of those hammocks. If their trouble's but enough to lay 'em up for the day or put 'em on light duty, their names go on the binnacle list and they're relieved of all heavy work."

"What if they're skulking?" I asked. "It's not always easy to tell if a man's genuinely ill, you know."

He chuckled mirthlessly.

"If a man's on the binnacle list his grog is stopped."

"Does that work?" I asked.

"Ah!" he exclaimed. "It works, I guarantee! Mark my words, Doctor, you'll have to find out most of the ill men for yourself, for they hate to report for fear of missing their grog. Would you believe it, sir, I've seen a man with his ribs caved in from a fall from the maintop stand up and swear he was all right just so he'd not lose his grog!"

I murmured, "Indeed," and glanced at the still-rigid boy. Phipps poked him again with his scabbard.

"This is John Dalton," he said. "He's a loblolly boy. He tends the sick bay and doles out the medicines that you prescribe, and in general acts as assistant to the surgeons, both in action and otherwise. He also looks after your mess, tends your hammock, and so on. There are three more like him, and he knows better than to sleep on the watch."

He rounded on the lad belligerently.

"Don't you, Dalton?" he demanded ferociously.

"Y-yessir!" the boy quavered. He was not a very big boy, and his face was thin, his body spare. I guessed his age at about fourteen.

"Well, see that you don't do it, then," said Phipps. "If I catch you at it again I'll have to have the bos'n touch you up with a rope's end!"

"Aye, sir," said Dalton, "er—I mean, no sir!"

Phipps turned away abruptly with an expression that said he had had enough of this. I followed him, after a reassuring wink for the youngster, back to the great compartment, occupying something more than a third of the deck, in which we had first found ourselves on our descent from the gun deck.

"This we call the fo'c'sle," he said, "though, strictly speaking, the fo'c'sle's above on the spar deck. This is the crew's quarters—you see the hooks where the men sling their hammocks. Each man's allowed a foot and a half by eight feet for his own. You get two hundred men in here at once, and it gets a bit cramped."

Looking about that narrow space, I could well imagine that it might. But Phipps was giving me no time for reflection now. He pointed to a hatchway underneath the ladder from the deck above.

"Down yonder's the orlop deck," he said. "Down there's the brig. Chips has a shop there, too."

He went to the hatchway and peered down. There was a light below. I could hear sounds of someone working.

"Chips!" he called.

Footsteps sounded, and in the next instant I found myself looking down into Sam Nowell's bearded face.

"This is Dr. Tisdall, Chips——" Phipps began.

Nowell did not give him time to finish.

"Tom!" he exclaimed. "What do ye here? How are ye, lad? Ho, Ben! Here's Tom Tisdall!"

Phipps looked startled, glancing owlishly first at me and then down into the hatchway. Ben Price came and stood at Sam's shoulder, staring up at us curiously.

"Hello, Tom!" he said. "What———"

"Dr. Tisdall's come aboard as surgeon's mate," Phipps put in sharply. "Are you done working in the cockpit?"

Nowell swung his eyes from mine to Phipps.

"Oh!" he said. "Uh—yes sir, that's all finished now."

"Good!" Phipps exclaimed, and straightened, beckoning to me to follow.

"See you later, Sam—Ben," I said.

Sam nodded hesitantly, without reply. Ben only stared. I turned away, vaguely disturbed. Phipps was awaiting me where a broad passage led aft, past the mainmast, looking grim.

"Officers do not mingle with the crew or petty officers."

"But they're old friends!" I protested.

"I'm just telling you," he shrugged. "It's ship's regulations, and you'll find it's one Captain Preble insists on. He agrees with Truxtun that it's bad for discipline."

He did not wait for comment on my part, but turned and led the way aft along the passage. As I followed I noticed that there were small cabins on either hand, barely large enough to hold a man. There was a long table in the center.

"Warrant officers' quarters," Phipps explained. "They berth in the cabins and mess here in the passage."

Beyond the warrant officers' mess we passed into a crowded cabin amidships, or slightly aft of it, through which the stout butt of the mainmast passed. On either side of this cabin were still smaller cabins flanking the ship's sides.

"Steerage," Mr. Phipps announced. "This is where the midshipmen berth."

He pointed to a hatchway in passing.

"Cockpit's down there," he said cryptically, and ducked on across the cabin. Beyond the after bulkhead we came into more spacious quarters that filled the entire after end of the ship. On either hand were a series of a half a dozen or more cabins, some eight feet long by perhaps four wide, just large enough for a transom berth, a locker, and a chest of drawers. Each cabin achieved privacy by means of a wooden grilled door which closed it off from the large central cabin, down the center of which, along the keel line, stood a long mahogany table surrounded by securely fixed chairs.

"This is the wardroom," said Phipps. "The officers live

here and mess at this table. Deck officers take the starboard cabins. Larboard cabins go to the sailing master, purser, surgeon, chaplain, and officer in charge of marines."

I had smiled at the beginning of this, thinking that at last I was home, but my face must have fallen as he recited the list of occupants of the cabins, for he grinned at me almost sympathetically.

"You are a junior officer," he said, "so you berth and mess elsewhere; though, of course, you're welcome here at any time outside of sleeping or meal hours."

I stared at him blankly, unable to believe my ears.

"But there are two extra cabins," I protested.

"Oh yes," he grinned. "But you see, the captain's clerk and the purser's assistant and then the schoolmaster take precedence over you. If anyone were moved up here, they'd come first. But, as I told you, the captain's a hard one for ship's discipline. I doubt he'll move any of you in."

"I presume I share quarters with those you mention," I said, somewhat crestfallen.

He nodded.

"Of course," he said, "we in the wardroom can invite you up any time we like."

He chuckled, I thought, almost ghoulishly.

We ducked back out of the comparative spaciousness of the wardroom into the steerage once more, and with a sinking feeling I followed him to the hatchway leading to the cockpit, which he had pointed out to me previously. As I peered down into it I saw that all below was in stygian blackness. Phipps leaned down.

"Ahoy!" he called. "Anyone below there?"

There was a scrabbling sound in the darkness, followed by a voice.

"Hello! I'm here, sir, Howard!"

Phipps glanced over his shoulder at me.

"The schoolmaster," he told me.

"Show a light," he called.

"I can't, sir," came back the mild reply. "The spirit-room door's open."

"Well, close it!" called Phipps impatiently.

"Cap'n's orders, sir! Spirit-room doors must remain open in daylight hours!"

"Oh balls!" yelled my companion. "This is Lieutenant Phipps. Close that goddam door immediately and show a light!"

"Aye, aye, sir!" came back the voice resignedly.

"Goddam sea lawyer!" Phipps growled.

I wondered. When the glow of light showed below, Phipps swung himself over the edge of the hatchway and went down a ladder steeper than any we had yet followed. I came down behind him, still wondering.

I found myself, in the light of a ship's lantern swung from the deck overhead, in a chamber some sixteen feet long, measured as the ship's keel ran, by thirty broad, measuring from one side of the ship to the other. I have never claimed to be a tall man, standing five feet ten in my stockings, but down here I had to stand well hunched over, with knees bent and head drawn down between my shoulders. At the most there was not more than five feet headroom. A long deal table ran transversely of the ship, with benches on either side, and at its ends, in the recesses of the room, I could make out hammock hooks and one hammock still slung far down in the starboard corner. Phipps saw it too and turned savagely to the thin, sparse-haired, round-shouldered man who stood by the table.

"What's that hammock doing slung at this hour?"

The sparse-haired individual shrugged.

"You might ask Ward," he said. "He's in it."

Lieutenant Phipps turned slowly purple.

"Ward!" he roared.

There was no answer beyond a slight stirring of the hammock. Phipps strode over and whacked viciously at the most bulging portion with his scabbard. There was a howl, and a figure that reminded me of nothing so much as a huge, wrinkled, split maggot tumbled to the deck. It required a moment to disentangle the shape from the gloom, but as it rose and came forward into the smoky light I saw that it was an extraordinarily fat young man, dressed simply in long, loose-fitting, flannel winter underwear.

"Damn you, Phipps!" he muttered, rubbing his backside ruefully. "What the devil did you do that for?"

"You know the regulations, Ward," Phipps replied. "All hammocks to be stowed by 0700."

The fat boy looked sullen.

"That's well enough at sea," he replied. "But in port, when the Old Man's kept you ashore until all hours, there ought to be exceptions made!"

"Come off it, Phipps," the sparse-haired individual by the table said. "You know those regulations don't extend to the cockpit. We're privileged characters down here!"

He threw back his head and laughed harshly, while Phipps threw me an I-told-you-so look.

"Uh—Dr. Tisdall," he said, "I'll make you acquainted with Mr. Jason Howard, the schoolmaster, and Mr. Samuel Curwen Ward, captain's clerk; they'll be your messmates for this voyage. Gentlemen, I bring you Dr. Thomas Tisdall, surgeon's mate, who'll share your quarters."

The other two stared at me, I thought, like dwellers in a dungeon and nodded tentatively. No doubt I was equally stiff in return. I did, however, manage to say: "Good morning, gentlemen. Your servant."

Phipps resumed his lecture.

"This is the cockpit," he said. "This is where you will live. You share it with Mr. Howard and Mr. Ward, here, as well as with the purser's assistant, if any, and with any other surgeon's mates that may be brought aboard. For your information, I'll tell you that this is considered the safest part of the ship, and it's certainly the steadiest. That's why it is your post of duty during an action. At such times the surgeon and his assistants meet here. You cover that table with canvas and lay out your instruments at one end, and cover them so as not to frighten the wounded with the sight of them. You'll have tubs of sand to receive limbs and bloody swabs, and the deck will be sanded so that the blood will not make it slippery. All other noncombatants—the chaplain, the purser, the supercargo, as well as the rest of your messmates—will assist you here at such times, and the loblolly boys will fetch the wounded down to you. If I may——"

"You mean we must operate in this light?" I demanded.

He cast a heavy eye upward at the lantern.

"What's wrong with it?" Without waiting for an answer,

he went on: "You are fortunate. Your duties are light. You stand no watches. You have good food, good quarters, good shipmates, and when we're in port you may do as you damned well please! There are some drawbacks, but in the main I envy you."

I glanced about the dismal space and sniffed. Already it was beginning to take on the stench of the bilge, for all the ship had not been launched three months, and I could have sworn I heard the squeak of rats beyond the bulkhead.

"What are the drawbacks?" I asked dryly.

Ward covered his mouth with his hand and appeared convulsed. Howard's eyebrows went up and he looked at me with renewed interest. Phipps took me in all seriousness.

"Forward," he said, "is the bread locker. Aft is the spirit locker. Both have to be broached several times a day, so you've little privacy. Also, there's a rule that when the spirit locker is open there must be no light in the cockpit, owing to the danger of explosion from the fumes. When the weather permits, the spirit-locker door is kept open; consequently you have to get along a good deal in the dark."

"What about mealtime?" I asked. "May we shut the locker if it's open?"

"By no means!" he exclaimed in shocked tones.

"But what——" I began.

"You eat in the dark," he said. "You get used to it."

"I see," I said, "we're by way of being the ship's moles."

"Hah-ha!" laughed Phipps. "I'm glad to see you've a sense of humor, Doctor. We'll get along!"

He put his foot on the bottom rung of the ladder.

"Well, gentlemen," he said, "I'll leave you. Howard and Ward will steer you, Doctor, in anything you want to know. And you two might give the doc a helping hand. He'll need to be fitted out. The captain says we'll not sail today."

He nodded and went on up the ladder, leaving me with my new shipmates, I may say in a far from happy mood.

My first reaction was to go back above decks and say that I would not serve in such conditions, and this thought must have shown in my face, for Howard chuckled.

"Forget it!" he said. "You've signed on, haven't you?"

I nodded.

"Well, then," he said, "they'll not let you go until the voyage is done, and to growl will only get you a bad name. Once you get used to it, it isn't so bad down here. At least it's snug, and warmer than most parts of the ship. And other than meal-times you've the run of the wardroom. The worst of it's having the midshipmen right above!"

Ward listened to Phipps's retreating footsteps.

"The old bastard!" he muttered, then looked at me. "You're in luck, though. You can tie him around your finger."

"I don't follow you," I said.

"Why," said Ward, "the old wart has trouble with his guts —or, anyway, thinks he does. Give him some pills to soothe his stomach, and you'll have him in your pocket, mark my words! I'll be surprised if he doesn't come to you for 'em before we sail."

Howard chuckled.

"We can be glad of one thing, anyway! He forgot to tell us to open the spirit-room door! Gentlemen, we have light!"

Ward eyed me speculatively.

"So you came aboard without gear?" he said.

"Now wait, Ward!" Howard protested.

"Don't be so hasty!" the fat boy replied. "I'm only going to explain matters to him. You can take him ashore. I couldn't go anyway. I've work to do for the Old Man!"

He turned back to me.

"I suppose you've drawn your advance?"

"No," I replied, "but the captain told me I was entitled to it. I presume I can get it by applying to the right place."

Ward's face fell.

"It'll take you forever to get it from Mumford, and I don't suppose your pockets are any fuller than ours."

"I have a little," I said. "If it's not too much, I ought to be able to manage. Who's Mumford?"

"The purser," Howard told me. "He's as fuddy as old Phipps, and twice as weak in the mind. Wait a minute, Ward!"

The fat boy subsided with a gesture of resignation. The schoolmaster turned back to me.

"What he is driving at," he said, "is the mess."

"The mess?" I asked.

"Yes," he replied. "You see, we're each entitled to two rations a day, which is enough to make up bulk if you like salt meat and ship's biscuit and the like. But the extras—wine, preserves, any fresh meat or vegetables, or suchlike—we must provide ourselves. In the wardroom they elect a mess treasurer who takes up a collection. He turns it over to the mess president, who sees it spent to the best advantage. There are so few of us here, however, that we can afford to be less formal. Each man puts up what he feels he can afford—for instance, Ward and I each put up half of our advance, or twenty-five dollars each. Since you must buy uniforms, and all that, perhaps you won't be able to——"

"I think I can manage," I interrupted him, for I was of no mind not to bear my share, "and it may be that I have connections ashore that will give us some advantage. But first, what gear must I get, and what are these uniforms you speak of? Have I time to get them before I sail?"

"Time and a-plenty," he laughed. "But what they are, I'm damned if I know! How about it, Ward? What does a surgeon's mate wear?"

The clerk closed his eyes and began to recite.

" 'Surgeons, coat—long. Dark green, with black velvet lappels, and standing collar, lappels to have nine buttons and one to the standing collar—no lining other than being faced with the same cloth as the coat. Slash sleeves. The cuff same as the facings, with three buttons. Pocket flaps, plain. Vest and breeches—the former red, double-breasted, the latter green, same as the coat. Buttons, same as the officers.' That's for the surgeon. Let's see now. 'Surgeon's mates'—hmmmm. 'The same as the surgeon's with only this difference in the coat, to wit—half lappels, with six buttons and one to the collar; below the lappel, right side, three buttons; left side, three close-worked buttonholes.' "

Howard looked at me triumphantly, as if he were in some way responsible for this amazing performance.

"There!" he said. "That's it. Uniform Regulation of 24 August, 1797! Ward knows them inside out!"

"I'll have to have them made," I said.

"Of course," he nodded. "I know just the man to do it for you. With luck he should have them ready by tomorrow noon, if we go straight ashore now. Will you risk it?"

"Have I a choice?" I grinned.

"None," he assured me.

"Then what are we waiting for?" I asked.

18

As THINGS TURNED OUT, I might have saved myself a good
deal of hurry and scramble, not to mention some anxious moments, had I been better acquainted with navy ways. The
Essex did not sail on the following day, nor the day after, nor
yet the day after that. Indeed, it was better than a week before
she finally weighed anchor and stood out to sea.

Lest I be misunderstood, let me hasten to say here that this
was through no fault of her commander. His estimate of
the weather exceeded his predictions. On the day after I reported, it stormed so fiercely that even at her moorings the
frigate bucked and plunged like a tethered horse with a bee
beneath its tail, and two sloops which arrived belatedly in the
evening from Boston, with supplies for us, were unable to lay
alongside. So rough was the harbor that only two trips to
Derby Wharf were made by the longboat, and none by the
gig. After that we had alternate days of flat calm and northwest gales which effectively kept us at anchor.

This brief respite was a blessing in disguise for me. In the
matter of outfitting it had not the least effect, for Mr. Howard
took me to a shop, owned by a tailor of whom I had never
heard before, where to my amazement I was turned out in
four complete changes of uniform, with all the spare shirts
and kerchiefs and suchlike furnishings I might need by the
following evening.

In other more personal respects, however, I was glad of
the delay. To be sure, I spent most of the daylight hours on
board, but during such times as I was not required to devote
myself to my duties I was free to come and go as I pleased.
This enabled me to confirm the arrangements I had made for
both Pat's and Selina's care.

I was able, too, to pay another visit to Patience and inform
her of what I had done, and this time I arranged that both Ben
and Sam Nowell should be present, for I wanted them to know

what I had done in such a way that it would not be construed
to reflect upon her. I came away from the meeting with the feeling that Ben resented my interference. It was not anything that
he said or did, but only a touch of sullenness in his air, that led
me to suspect this, and it disturbed me lest he take out his
pique on Patience. For his own opinion I did not care two
straws.

Still, I had the feeling that I had done the best I could and
that the rest lay not with me nor with Ben nor with Sam, but
with those I had entrusted with her care. Before I left, more
for the sake of Pat's pride than for any interest I had in it,
I arranged with Ben and Sam to settle the expenses of the
business out of their pay.

Having done so much in behalf of another man's wife, I
could not in conscience neglect my own, whatever the circumstances. I took dinner with Selina and her father several times
before sailing. This I did with a sharp sense of estrangement,
bitter as I was at the injustice I felt she had done me. On each
occasion I tried to be easy and friendly, in an effort to indicate
to her that that was to be our status in the future. But I fear
that I succeeded only in being stiff and formal. Captain Hackett, I feel sure, was puzzled, though he kept his own counsel.
As for Selina, she showed both contrition and an unusual spirit
of patience and thoughtfulness toward me. She made much of
me; or as much as I would permit her to make. Had I not been
blinded by my own hurt and pride, had I been willing to adopt
myself that spirit of Christian humility that I demanded of
others, there might then have been a reconciliation between us.
May God forgive me that I was so blind!

All of this ashore, however, was but the least part of my
activity during that time. On board ship there was plenty to do.
Hitherto, owing to the absence of Dr. Orr in Boston, it had not
been possible to examine the recruits as they came on board.
Now that I was on board, this duty fell to me. I was directed
to examine all hands and to reject any that showed signs of
scurvy, dropsy, the king's evil, weakness of the lungs, or other
incurable ailments, or were not generally sound of wind and
limb.

This was a large task, but I had other duties as well. Every
morning I was required to attend at sick call, to treat those ail-

ments which invariably arise wherever men are gathered in large numbers in close confinement. Sexual distempers and the results of rum occupied a good deal of my attention, but even more prevalent were coughs and tissicks induced by the cold and damp, the results of which it was utterly impossible to expel from the ship. Among those who developed such a cough and caused me much concern was Sam Nowell.

In addition to these duties there were hospital supplies to be checked and supplemented, and I was also informed that it was the duty of the surgeon—and, in his absence, myself—to inspect the provisions that were put on board for the general mess and certify them fit for human consumption. This last required by far the bulk of my time, since such a quantity of stores had already arrived and more were arriving daily.

Toward the end of the week the people from Boston arrived with their recruits. With them came Hector Orr, the ship's surgeon, and John Perkins, the other surgeon's mate, who had been recruited in Cambridge, to lighten my task. Dr. Orr I found to be a gentleman and a scholar. A tall, rawboned Scot, with sandy hair and bushy eyebrows over pale blue eyes, he was a man of more than ordinary intelligence, a surgeon of skill and an able administrator. With it all, too, he had a nice dry sense of humor which frequently served us all in good stead in the months to come. Perkins, on the other hand, I found not so impressive. He was a meek little man, something on the scrawny side, with pale eyes and big ears and a balding head. His clothes never seemed to fit him. His sleeves were too short and he could never seem to find a stock that would fit snugly about his neck. He was of a serious turn of mind, quiet and deeply studious, but I could never see that it did him much good. For all his studies, he never seemed to learn beyond a certain point, and, as for experience, it taught him nothing.

So passed that first week of preparation and waiting. Although we were in many ways far from ready, it was the captain's determination to sail at the first opportunity. Had that opportunity come, we would have had to go shorthanded and underprovisioned, risking the chance of being able to fill our complement and arms chest, our storerooms and our ammunition locker, on arrival in Newport. As it happened, we were able to round out the better part of our crew and take aboard the great bulk of the stores consigned to us, so that, taking it all in all, the delay was in reality nothing like so disastrous as it appeared to our impatient commander.

The twentieth of December dawned cold and raw, with the wind from the north-northeast with snow. As the morning wore on, the wind veered slowly to northwest, the snow changing first to rain and then giving way altogether to clearing skies. At nine the signal for sailing was made, calling all hands on board, and at one in the afternoon we unmoored and prepared to weigh anchor. A great crowd gathered along the shore, between Briggs's Yard and Fort Pickering, as well as on Naugus Head on the opposite shore, to see us off. But at the critical moment, once more, the wind fell off to a mere whisper. By evening the opportunity had passed and we had no choice but to lay the night through to a single anchor, prepared to sail at the first light of day if wind and tide favored. Throughout that night I could hear the captain pacing up and down upon the quarterdeck in a solitary fury of impatience, and through the night only those with urgent ship's business dared approach him. When the morning came, however, it brought bitter cold and flat calm, and there was no choice but to remain as we lay, idly swinging with the tide, while the captain fumed and fretted lest the sudden cold lock the harbor with ice before we could escape.

By midafternoon it was apparent that we would not sail that day, and the captain unbent sufficiently to allow shore leave. I took advantage of this opportunity to pay one last visit and eat one final dinner at the Hacketts', not so much because I wished to see my wife again, which I assured myself I did not, but rather out of regard for appearances and for Eli Hackett. At least that is what I told myself as I walked up from the landing. Looking back upon it now, it comes to me that even then I may have been prodded by the nagging prick of conscience.

I cannot say that it was a merry evening. Selina was even more quiet than had lately been her wont, and I believe the captain was conscious of a certain constraint. Such conversation as there was was made by him, and ran mostly to ships and voyages. In the midst of dinner a bell, somewhere in the town, began to toll mournfully. A moment later another chimed in, and another and another, until it seemed that every steeple in the town was adding its clangor. It is odd how it can be told from the sound of them whether the tidings be good or bad! The church bells of our country ring for victory and for disaster alike, and yet it is always possible to say before it is heard the nature of the news they bear.

It was so at this time. This was no joyous pealing. A servant dispatched to learn the reason returned presently with word of General Washington's death, the day before!

It was a shocking climax to an already somber evening. When the word was brought, Captain Hackett sat as one stunned. When he looked up his eyes were wet with tears.

"I knew him," he said, as if it was a struggle to get the words past the hurt in his throat. "I served with him."

He rose then and excused himself.

I think that both Selina and myself were but little less affected. She stared at me wide-eyed across the table.

"Oh, Tom!" she whispered. "How awful!"

"He was a great man," I nodded, and my own throat was dry and tight and I felt my own eyes smart with tears. "The world may produce others as great, but they will be few, and there will be none like him!"

And this I knew to be true. Of late the general's popularity had waned somewhat, and he had been even hated in some quarters, with that bitterness peculiar to politics which takes no account of the good in a man but sees only his faults. But now I knew that even those that had hated him would mourn him and recognize his greatness, for there was that in his passing that would draw all men together. A death in one's family is cause for personal grief, but the death of such as he stabs at the heart of a nation, and that man must be callous indeed who remains unaffected by it.

Neither Selina nor I had any appetite after that, and we rose and went into the drawing room, where we sat in silence, both of us, staring morosely with our own thoughts into the crackling fire. After a decent interval I rose to go, and she came then to stand before me.

"Tom," she said, and there was pleading and humility in her voice, "can't I—can't we——"

She broke off, staring up into my face with wide, appealing eyes, and in that instant I came near to taking her in my arms

and saying that we should bury the past behind us. But some
devil of perversity prompted me to remember what she had
done, and I steeled myself against her.

"Madam," I said, "you and I have nothing to say to one
another. If we must keep up our pretense in public, let us not de-
ceive ourselves in private."

She went white, and the flicker of pain in her eyes was sharp
and cruel. But she did not turn away. Instead she lifted her chin
a trifle, proudly.

"As you wish," she said simply.

"Good night," I said, and left.

I made my way back to the ship, miserable, I told myself,
because of the news we had received, and yet in the back of my
mind conscious of my own equivocation. When I crept into my
hammock it was to toss and turn and sigh and mutter, until
my messmates cursed me and bade me either lie quiet and let
them sleep or go out on deck, where I might mumble to my
heart's content without disturbing anyone.

The desire to wrestle alone with my problem rather than any
consideration for them drove me to follow their advice, and
wrapping myself in my greatcoat, I went topside, where I paced
and turned and paced again. And ever as I paced and turned I
seemed to find my wife's face before me in the windy night,
with her great dark eyes entreating and a look of hurt about
her mouth like a child that has been suddenly rebuked. In the
end my stubborn will broke and I surrendered to my conscience,
promising that when daylight came I would go ashore and ask
her forgiveness for my brutishness. Whatever might be our
differences, I told myself, there was no excuse for me to play
the knave!

When I went below to my hammock once more, it was to
sleep and rest peacefully. But when I came on deck in the morning it was to find the ship in a vast state of excitement. While I
slept the breeze, which had been light at sundown, from the
southeast, had stiffened and backed around to north-northwest.
The sky was bright and cold and spotted with scattered gray
scudding clouds. When I stepped out of my hammock blue peter
—which is the signal flag for sailing—was already snapping at
the fore, calling all on board; and even as I stepped on deck
the impatient growl of a cannon warned all laggards to hurry.

At the same time the trulls and doxies and sailors' wives who were still aboard were routed unceremoniously from their blankets and, with scarce time to cover themselves, were tumbled over the side into a waiting boat and rowed ashore. A moment later the pawls of the capstan began to clank and the chanty rose as the men laid on the bars and began to heave in the anchor. At a growl of command from the quarter-deck the headsails jerked aloft and the ship came about; courses and topsails fell from their lashings, bellied and thundered. The ship heeled to the wind and gathered way.

It was my impulse to cry, "No!" looking back to see Derby Wharf and the Hackett house, not far from the head of it, splashed warm in the bright early-morning sunlight. I thought, as I looked, that I could see a spot of color waving at one of the upper windows, but my attention was taken in at the moment by the Crowninshield ship *Belisarius,* which had likewise been waiting a fair wind to sail, bearing down past us, to the vast annoyance of Captain Preble. When I glanced back again the house and the town lay behind us, through the passage, looking unreal and distant like painted dwellings pictured on a winter's landscape.

II

The Frigate

IS THERE A MAN BORN who has not at one time or another sat
snug by his fireside and imagined himself off adventuring upon
the high seas; bracing his feet to the pitch of the deck, facing
the gale, running down through tropic latitudes with a soft
moon beaming over the yardarm and the scent of the Spice
Islands coming off on the breeze? When we have troubles from
which we would escape we are like to take refuge in brave
dreams!

I think I have told enough, thus far, to show that it was not
for adventure that I went to sea in the *Essex*. Nevertheless I
cannot deny that for all my reason the hope of it lay deep
within me. It was my grievance with my wife and my determination to hold Ben to his duty; my hopeless, helpless love for
Patience, fundamentally, that drove me to sea. But with all of
that, the fact remains that I looked forward to the excitement
that it might bring in the depths of my heart.

I wish I might report that I found adventure. It would make
easier writing, if I had, and would divert attention from the
dullness of that interval. To be sure, we met storm and calm,
fine weather and foul. We sailed halfway around the world and
back. We were the first American man-of-war to round Africa's
southermost cape. We saw the Spice Isles. We faced pestilence
and near famine and death, and listened to the mutterings of
mutiny. These are the shape and the Jezebel face of Adventure,
that she shows to the fireside sailor. But does such a one ever
see beneath the paint and trappings to the flesh and bones of
which the jade is made? Does such a one envision the terror of
the storm or the despair of the doldrums? Does he imagine the
creeping horror of those mysterious ship-borne plagues and
fevers against which all men's efforts seem helpless? Does he
picture the stinking meat and weevily biscuit, the viscid water
grown thick with age and a-crawl with wiggling life? Does he
consider what is worst of all, the dreary, endless, brain-squeez-
ing monotony of day after day after day at sea?

He does not, and no more did I. Yet I experienced all this

and more. I hope I may be excused if I do not now dwell upon such details but give only a brief account of the highlights of that yearlong voyage and of such events as occurred during it that bear upon my story: I saw Adventure in the privacy of her boudoir, naked and stripped of her paint and trappings. I saw her pendulous breasts and her sunken, evil eyes, her quaking, flatulent belly and her spindling, ill-shaped shanks! Forgive me if I do not describe her in greater detail!

Our departure from Salem was at once a triumph and a disappointment to me. We were away at last. But yet I had not had time to go ashore again and make that apology to my wife that I had promised myself. For this my conscience troubled me, and the only salve I could apply to it was to assure myself that I would write to her from Newport and make some effort to explain my feeling in a letter. Once we were clear of the channel, we shook out our canvas and, under double-reefed topsails and foresail, passed the *Belisarius,* logging twelve and a half knots in doing so. This was a great satisfaction to all, especially to Captain Preble, the *Belisarius* being accounted a fast sailer and she being, at the time we passed her, under all sail, including top and topgallant stuns'les. After that we laid down to southward and proceeded to shake down. By night it was exceeding rough and my cabin mates were all ill of the ship's motion, and I myself had little appetite.

We were six days in our passage to Newport. Throughout, the weather was cold and damp, with no opportunity to prepare hot food because of the high seas, which kept the galley shut down. By the same token the 'tween decks was a place of wet and misery which aggravated colds and tissicks. When the weather moderated slightly, the captain ordered fires built to drive out the damp, but the only result was to irritate the lungs and increase our difficulties. My greatest worry now came from an unexpected source. Sam Nowell, already ill with a cold when we sailed, developed an affection of the lungs which, it was evident, would necessitate his discharge at Newport. I knew that he would take it hard when I broke the news to him. But there was no help for it.

At Newport we found Captain Sever, in the *Congress,* together with several merchantmen, awaiting us. There we discharged those members of the crew, among them Sam Nowell, who had been found unfit for service, and took on board the remainder of our complement, including a number of marines that had been assigned to us. I took advantage of Sam Nowell's return home to entrust him with a letter to Selina, explaining something of what I felt and apologizing for my behavior at our last meeting, and with this I had to be content.

It was not until January that we finally sailed from Newport in company with the *Congress*, with two merchant ships and a brig in convoy for India. Almost immediately we met with foul weather, and for the first time I experienced the helpless terror of a storm at sea. The weather we had encountered in our brief shakedown from Salem had been bad. But the gales that racked us then were nothing in comparison with the fury that beset us now. Whether it was worse by day or by night, I cannot, to this day, tell. By day the vast mountains of green water smashed down at us out of the misty, shredded distance, one after another, visible long before they struck. By night they burst without warning, looming suddenly out of the snow-laced dark, like vast watery avalanches tipped with foam. There were no fires then, and no hot food. Ice formed on the rigging, and it was a wonder to me that the men could cling in the shrouds, let alone work their ways out along the yards to handle the stiffened sails.

I have seen worse weather since, off the Horn and the Cape of Good Hope, but I could not then foresee that. At that time it seemed to me that I had seen the worst fury of the elements, and I will frankly admit to fear. Indeed, I will admit to more than fear. Since the inhabitants of the cockpit were only in the way above decks, we were ordered in no uncertain terms to keep to our quarters save when our business aboard called us out. As a result our stinking little cubby was a shambles long before the month was out, and those of us who lived there had come to feel little better than moles—blind, seasick moles, if a full description be applied.

We were not three days out when the commodore spoke to us and it was agreed to part company with our convoy. They were sluggish sailers, all, and being merely in ballast, it was deemed more important that we drive on as rapidly as we might in order to reach eastern waters in time to protect our laden merchantmen on their return home from those dangerous parts. Thereafter the *Essex* and the *Congress* drove on together several days at a distance of a mile or two apart. On the twelfth, however, late in the afternoon, our green rigging having grown so slack as to make it hazardous to carry sail, we were obliged, for a few moments, to bear away for the sake of the bowsprit, which appeared in danger. In those few moments we lost sight of the *Congress,* nor did we again see her. We drove onward alone, not a little downcast at the fate of our consort, for I think there was not a man of us aboard but was sure she had foundered. It was only six months later, off Java, when we spoke the Derby ship *Columbia,* 109 days out from the Capes of the Delaware, that we learned that she had been dismasted in the storm and had been obliged to put back to Norfolk, where she had arrived in safety with all hands.

This was our introduction to the sea, and except for two or three bright days, so it continued throughout the month. Not until the end of January did we run out of the stormy latitudes and find ourselves in pleasant weather, with the breezes steady and the sun sufficiently warming to shake out our canvas and dry the sails and make repairs upon our masts and rigging. Thereafter we made a steady run of it down across the equator and through the southern ocean to Capetown, where we arrived a little over two months from our departure from Newport.

In those months the landlubbers among us, including myself, became seamen; and all of us became man-of-war's men. When the weather permitted, we stood to quarters and exercised the great guns. On the gun deck they played at war. In the cockpit we laid out the instruments and the sand buckets and simulated our part in an engagement. But lesser experiences bore equally upon the result. The biscuit grew weevily, so that we developed the habit of knocking it upon the table edge to shake the worms out before biting into it. We crossed the line and were duly initiated into the realm of Neptunus Rex. The midshipmen rolled a round shot down the hatchway as a prank on Jason Howard —a prank that might have had disastrous results had it found home! Two of the hands fell to fighting at the gangway when no officer was looking, and both fell overboard and were not seen again. The main trusseltrees broke and had to be temporarily repaired. Salt water destroyed much of our fresh provision and a good part of our medical stores.

All this and more I would describe in detail but it would little advance my story. Of Ben I saw little, save at occasional casual meetings on deck, when the rule of the ship was strictly observed and we said nothing to one another. I thought he seemed disgruntled at first that he had not been appointed carpenter in Sam Nowell's place. But when he saw what a carpenter was called upon to do at sea, I believe, he was secretly pleased at the opportunity to serve his apprenticeship as carpenter's mate; for he was quick to see that there was more to it than the mere handling of tools, and that a man must be a sailor as well before he was fit to meet the emergencies which the sea imposed.

From Capetown, where we replenished our water casks and laid in fresh provisions, we bore on around the southernmost tip of Africa and northeastward across the Indian Ocean, keeping a sharp lookout for French privateers, said to have been operating in these waters. Here was the most tedious part of our voyage out, for while the first part was stormy, the latter part was progressively more somnolent. As we drew near the tropics the wind died and the sun blazed. The pitch started from the seams, and the water in the casks became brown and viscid. Tempers grew short and quarrels frequent, and I was pleased that the gulf of rank separated me from Ben, else I am sure we would have had words between us which would have benefited neither. Not until May did we approach the Strait of Sunda and get the scent of the Spice Islands in our nostrils, and not until almost June did we arrive at Batavia, which was our final destination.

In all this time our nearest thing to a prize was the recapture of an American ship taken by the French from the Isle de France and bound for Batavia, a fact which led to much disappointment on the part of all hands, who had looked forward to a good share of prize money from the cruise. However, there was no help for it.

Batavia we found to be a low and unhealthy spot, though the women who came aboard under the pretext of selling fruit, vegetables, and cloths, which they call "batiks," were handsome in a flat-faced, impassive sort of way, with golden skins and full breasts which they carried quite uncovered and without the least concern. The heat was oppressive, and the insects which the damp shore breeze carried off to us were voracious;

a fact which tended to damp the ardor of the men not a little and, I believe, was largely responsible for the incipient mutiny which we here experienced and which Captain Preble put down with a firm hand and a strong taste of the lash.

As far as the medical staff was concerned, our troubles began here. In a single turn ashore I observed lepers, victims of the yaws and the smallpox, not to mention others bearing all manner of ulcerous sores and growths. The Dutch port doctor warned us against paludal and intermittent fevers, agues and fluxes, cholera, leprosy, and the plague, and while we escaped the devastating effects of the latter, the effects of the former were with us almost from the day we dropped our hook.

Needless to say, we did not lie in port longer than was necessary, but rather weighed and sailed again as soon as we had made our presence known and taken on fresh water and provisions. Thereafter we cruised between Batavia and the Strait until such time as the return convoy was made up and joined. Of this interval only one event is of interest here. This occurred while we were passing down the fairway, through the narrows between the shoals off Point Onting and those of Middleburg Island. There we met a brig standing in which proved to be the *Exchange,* of Salem, inbound for Batavia.

I confess it gave me something of a start to see a Salem ship so far from home, but at the moment it did not occur to me that this was a Hackett ship or that I knew, if only by mere acquaintance, her commander. We had not the opportunity to go aboard her at the time, but all of this was to be driven home to me more roundly and I was to grow more familiar with her in the weeks to come, for she was among those that made up our convoy on our return passage.

In the meantime I was too busy to give much thought to such matters. The fever appeared among us, and one by one our people came down with it: Dr. Orr, the captain, Mr. Perkins— so that the burden of care fell upon me—Mr. Phipps and Mr. Mumford, to say nothing of the men themselves. In the space of two months we lost three men, and no day passed but we had ten men down of the flux and the fever in sick bay. Yet I fairly believe we were the healthiest ship in those waters.

In mid-June we weighed anchor and sailed for home in convoy with fifteen sail, including the *Exchange*.

If we considered trouble our portion thus far, we scarcely knew our luck, for it was here that our worries began. To contend with the well-disciplined crew of a man-of-war was one thing. To deal with the crews of a score of merchantmen, half sick, mutinous, overworked, and independent, to say nothing of their self-willed commanders, was something else again. When we signaled them to fall back or to close up, they would disregard our commands. Yet the least alarm among them in the night would throw them all into a panic and scatter them every which way. Never a day passed but one or more of them reported shorthanded either through mutiny or sickness, and when we were not putting crews aboard to work them we were like to be taking one or more of them in tow. Sometimes we would find that no more than two or three of a ship's people were fit to stand when our men went aboard. Yet when the crews came back we would find them full of the virus of rebellion, for which the only cure was the lash. Full across the Indian Ocean, until we reached the latitude of the Cape and the colder seas that swept around it, this condition plagued us. Yet but one example of the difficulties it fetched need be outlined here. For all it bears upon the generality of the story, it must not be considered untypical.

We were a month and more out from Onrust, and well away for the Cape, when we were spoke by the brig *Exchange,* which was in trouble. Nearly all hands were sick, she informed us, so that she had scarcely enough to work ship, and in the bargain she had sprung her mainmast in a squall the night before and had need of the services of a carpenter as well as a surgeon, her own being laid up with the flux.

Dr. Perkins was sick of the remitting fever and Dr. Orr had but just risen from his bed of the same complaint, and as a consequence it fell to me to go aboard her. I asked for Ben and two others to assist—which I think he resented—and toward midmorning we were laid aboard.

I was first over the side, and as I crossed the rail I was met on deck by Captain Webb, whom I suddenly remembered having met in Salem on that first day I had laid eyes upon my wife. Oddly enough, though I was aware of the name of his vessel, it had not occurred to me that this was that ship or that he was that man before now. He was thinner, I thought, and, for all the weather he had met, paler. He did not recognize me, nor did I have time to remind him of our meeting, for at the sight of Ben, who followed close at my heels, he appeared at first startled and then amused, and burst out laughing.

"So she finally shipped you off, eh?" he demanded.

Ben turned brick red and appeared furious.

"I shipped of my own will aboard the *Essex*," he growled. "I preferred her to a stinking trader."

I thought Captain Webb would strike him, but Ben continued.

"You've met Dr. Tisdall before," he said, "though you don't appear to remember it. He married Selina."

It seemed to me that there was a note of warning in his voice, and certainly Webb seemed taken aback.

"Tisdall!" he exclaimed. "Ah yes! I remember now. Forgive me, Doctor. I didn't know. You see, I've not been back to Salem since we met. My congratulations, sir! She's a fine girl!"

"Thank you, Captain," I said dryly, perceiving that there was more here than met the eye, yet not willing, at this point, to delve into it too deeply. "You've had a long voyage, I take it."

"More than a year now," he nodded. "Into the Mediterranean, a year ago April, and thence to London. From there we crossed to Jamaica and down to the River Plate and around to China, and then down to Batavia. The rest you know."

"Ah," I said noncommittally, "and now you have your troubles, I'm told."

"We have that!" he agreed, seeming suddenly aware that I might one day be his new owner and turning deferential therefore. "This climate—— But there, sir! I need tell you nothing of that. Will you look for yourself?"

I would and did. I found his men down, all but three or four, some with the bloody flux, some with bilious fevers; a few with the Batavian ague and several with the scurvy or combinations of all of them. I did what I could, though I doubted that some would live through the night; suggested that he clean up his ship, prescribed various remedies for the various ailments I had found, and left medicines for his use.

"You're not looking well yourself, Captain," I said as I prepared to go over the side.

"I'm well enough, thank you," he smiled, and that was the last I saw of him.

Two days later the weather thickened and the *Exchange* signaled that her captain was now ill. Since it was impossible to go aboard her in the seas then running, we made shift, as best we could, to signal directions for his care to Mr. Royall, the first mate. For a week thereafter the seas ran high, and it was impossible to put off a boat. Early on the morning of the eleventh of August the *Exchange* signaled once again that her captain was ill and requested a doctor. I asked permission to go aboard, but in the state of the sea Captain Preble did not think it possible. Late in the afternoon a last signal from the brig informed us that Captain Webb had died. Thereafter it may have been my imagination, but it seemed to me that Ben Price avoided me more than ever, and I had no opportunity to talk with him until we were almost come to New York, by which time the incident was driven from my mind.

After the death of Captain Webb we encountered increasingly foul weather as we approached and rounded the Cape. Despite all our efforts to hold them together, the convoy largely broke up, and it was not until we laid over at St. Helena that, limping and one by one, we managed to gather them once again under our protection.

From St. Helena our voyage northward was void of interest other than to reverse the hardships of the passage out. Among others, Ben came down with the scurvy before we came abreast of the Virginia Capes, and I believe we all of us had loose teeth in our heads from the continuous salt diet to which we were subjected during that last long homeward pull. It was a relief to us when we waylaid a schooner northbound from Tortola with a cargo of limes, and I have no doubt but that the lives of some were saved by this chance. It was the end of November when, at last, we raised Sandy Hook lighthouse out of a swirling snowstorm and came to an anchor in seventeen fathoms in New York Harbor. On the following day we weighed anchor at seven in the morning and made sail for the East River, where, at three in the afternoon, we moored ship off Brooklyn Point East, in Wale Bogt Bay, home again at last after nearly a year at sea!

2

I NEED HARDLY DESCRIBE the delight with which all hands welcomed our arrival at New York. No matter what attachment a sailor forms for his ship, there comes a time when the crustiest sea dog yearns to set foot once more on solid ground.

So it was with us. Even Ben, who was more a ship's man than any I have known, was relieved. As for myself, I made no pretense of it, I was overjoyed; and I promised myself that once I was on shore again nothing would ever lure me to set foot upon another deck—which only goes to show how little we can foretell our own future!

For all our impatience, however, we lay a month in Wale Bogt Bay before we were finally paid off.

There was snow on the road and the drifts were piled high on either hand; the new year was a day old and it was already growing dark, although it was yet early in the evening, when Ben and I came at last to our journey's end in Salem. We got down our sea bags from the stage in silence, and I led the way directly to the house in Daniels Street, where the yellow light shone from the windows upon the snow with a cheerful glow. In response to my thundering knock, the door swung open, to reveal Patience upon the threshold, looking not a day older than when I had first laid eyes upon her, and to my mind twice as lovely.

At sight of me she cried out in surprise. In the next instant, to my embarrassment, she was in my arms, clinging to me and saying my name over and over again.

"Pat, child!" I said, gently trying to disengage her arms and stepping back. "I've brought you a husband!"

I pointed to Ben, standing a little to one side of the door, watching with a comical mixture of bewilderment and doubt. For the first time she seemed to catch sight of him, and turned to him, and in the next instant she had gone to him in a way that brought a lump to my throat. It was odd to see the look of doubt vanish from his face as he kissed her. She broke away from him presently.

"Is the *Essex* in port?" she demanded. "When——"

"We came by stage from New York," I told her.

"Oh!" she said, and laughed gaily. "But come inside before we all catch our deaths!"

She led the way to the great kitchen-living room. A bright fire crackled on the hearth, and there was a cradle set at one side where it would catch the warmth yet not blister in the heat. She saw our eyes upon it and beamed proudly.

"Come see your son, Ben!"

"A son!" Ben crowed, and prodded me in the ribs.

Patience reached down and picked up a tiny bundle of blankets and lace, and out of the midst of it came a child's face, as pink and round and rosy as a cherub's and seeming twice as healthy. As his mother lifted him he opened great blue eyes and stared at us in puzzled bewilderment, never once emitting a sound. Then all at once he broke into a smile.

I was startled. The lad had his mother's hair and eyes, but the rest of him was Ben to the life, even to the tilt of his baby eyebrows.

"He's the image of you, Ben!" I cried.

Ben smirked.

"He does favor me, doesn't he?"

She tried to hand him the child, but he shied away like a frightened colt.

Pat laughed and replaced the youngster in his cradle.

"What have you named him?" I asked.

She gave me a look that was almost apologetic.

"I've called him Samuel Eben," she said.

I gave her a delighted smile.

"I see!" I cried. "First for his great-grandfather and then for his father, eh?"

She nodded.

"By the way," I said, "where is Sam?"

Her lip trembled and she turned away.

"He—he's——"

"Pat!" I cried. "You don't mean——"

Ben stared at her, stricken to silence by her grief.

"He's dead," she said.

"Oh, Pat! When?" I cried.

"Three weeks after he returned," she told me. "He died of the lung fever he had on the *Essex*."

I told myself that it might have been better far if I had let him stay with us. It must have been hard indeed, in her condition, to bear the grief of it alone.

"I'm sorry!" I said. "If I'd but known!"

She shook her head.

"It wasn't your fault," she said. "He was old—an old man —and he knew it was coming."

She made a great business of tucking in the baby. Over her head I glanced at Ben, but he gave me only a shrug and a grave shake of the head. When she straightened again, Patience made an evident effort to be brightly gay.

"And how is Selina?" she asked.

"The devil!" I exclaimed. "Do you know that I haven't been home yet? What a husband I am!"

"Oh, Tom!" she cried. "You haven't seen her?"

Something in her tone arrested me.

"Why—no," I said.

"And you haven't heard from her?" she asked.

"No." I shook my head, puzzled.

"Go to her," she said quietly, urgently. "Go to her! She needs you!"

"What——" I began.

But she interrupted me.

"Don't stop to ask questions!" she cried. "Just go! She needs you, Tom! Here! Ben, take a lantern and light his way!"

I protested, taking up my hat.

"I don't need a lantern."

I went to her and took her hands in mine.

"I'm delighted, Pat," I said, "to see you and the boy so well. And I don't need to tell you how sorry I am about Sam!"

She laid her fingers upon my lips.

"Don't speak of it, Tom," she said. "He knows! And it's good to have you two home again, safe and sound!"

3

As I mounted the steps of the Hackett house, on Derby Street, I could not help noting the way in which the light glowed from the windows upon the snow. It had glowed from the Nowell house, too, yellowly, cheerfully, through the little leaded panes. Here it was more diffused, less concentrated, as it streamed through the tall windows. It seemed not so warm. It was more dignified and sedate and less golden. It was the light of rich folk, I thought, as contrasted with the more intimate light of simpler houses. I knocked at the door, and it was opened by an enormous blackamoor whom I had never seen before. He looked askance at my sea bag, but my uniform apparently impressed him.

"Is Captain Hackett in?" I asked. "Or Mrs. Tisdall?"

"They at dinnah, suh," he replied doubtfully.

"Will you tell them, please——" I began, then hesitated and slid in past him. "No! I'll tell them myself."

He opened his huge mouth to protest, but I cut him short with a gesture to silence.

"Don't fear," I said. "You'll not be blamed."

I handed him my sea bag, and he stowed it behind the hall rack. I passed on through the hall to the familiar great dining room. It was just as I remembered it. The long table was still in the center, covered with a snowy cloth and lighted by tall candles in polished candlesticks. In their light the silver on the table gleamed soberly, and the red wine in the glasses held a jeweled reflection of each candle's flame. At the head, somewhat grayer and somewhat older than I remembered him, sat Captain Hackett, while at his right, clad in a gown of warm ivory that set off her dark beauty to perfection, was Selina.

At my entry the captain looked up with a flicker of annoyance which was replaced by a sudden start of amazement.

"By all that's holy!" he exclaimed.

Selina was in the act of lifting her glass to her lips, but at sight of me it slipped from her fingers and crashed against her plate, shattering, and the dark wine spread a wide stain swiftly across the white of the tablecloth. I saw that she was more slender, and more mature, and, if anything, more lovely and desirable than ever.

"Tom!" she gasped in a voice scarce above a whisper.

In the next instant she was up and around the end of the table and in my arms.

To one side I saw the black who had followed me look first astonished and then beam broadly. At the head of the table

Captain Hackett broke into a broad grin and came round to pump my hand behind Selina's back.

"My boy!" he growled, and his voice broke. "My Christ, but 'tis good to see you!"

He turned to the black and bellowed.

"You! Cuffee! Fetch brandy, the best in the cellar! Fetch glasses! And then fetch everyone! Pompey! Caesar! Cato! Cleo! Antonina! Elva! This calls for a drink for all! Tell them Dr. Tisdall's come home! Hurry!"

"Yass suh!" said Cuffee, and hurried away.

Selina clung to me and whispered:

"Oh, Tom! You've come back to me at last!"

She lifted her face to me, and I saw that her eyes were closed and her face was streaked with tears. Her lips were parted, and the kiss they demanded would not be denied. I bent my lips to hers and was conscious of her sweet breath, of her hand upon the back of my neck, clinging, of her body pulsing against my own, and my brain whirled and I asked myself, What am I doing? This can't be!

Yet when we broke apart I was not sorry. That she was happy was apparent, and I myself was so confused by my welcome and so warmed by it that I could not be cool.

She took my hand with a little laugh of almost hysterical gaiety, and the captain slapped me on the back. She led me around the table, laughing and unprotesting, and seized on a chair which she planted close beside her own and between her and her father.

"Here," she cried. "Sit down here, between us. Have you had dinner? You must be starved. When did you get here, and how did you come? Oh, Tom, it's so wonderful to see you! I've missed you so!"

"Give him a chance, lass!" laughed the captain.

I laughed and caught her hand tightly, reckless for the moment.

"I——" I began. "I——"

But I could get no further.

The captain roared with laughter.

"You see, lass, you've robbed him of his tongue!" he cried. "Cuff!"

"Yass suh! I'se comin'!" boomed the blackamoor, appearing from the kitchen with a bottle in each hand, followed by a whole train of servants, all grinning welcome.

One after another I recognized them and called them by name, and they beamed and welcomed me home, so that I felt almost a dog for the way I had felt before. Captain Hackett seized the bottles and called for glasses.

"Everyone drinks to this occasion!" he cried.

Glasses were fetched and lifted and clinked and drained, and welcome was called to me again, and the servants drifted out. Cuffee reappeared bearing a platter, and my plate was heaped with food.

"What sort of a voyage was it?" asked the captain. "Reuben Royall came in with the *Exchange* a week ago and said he had seen you."

"When did you get here?" cried Selina. "And how?"

"I came by stage from New York," I told her, "as soon as we paid off."

"Royall said you were doing the doctoring for the *Essex*," said the captain.

"I went on board the *Exchange*," I replied. "Dr. Orr was ill at the time."

He nodded.

"Poor Webb!"

"We did our best for him," I said. "Perhaps if the weather had permitted seeing him again we might have saved him. He seemed well enough when I saw him last."

"Too bad!" he agreed. "He was a gentleman. Is Jacob Reynst still Sabandaac at Batavia?"

"I believe he is," I replied.

"Father!" exclaimed Selina. "Will you give him a chance to eat his dinner? He must be starved after all those inns and taverns!"

"Not to mention the ship, eh, Tom?" the captain grinned.

I laughed agreement.

Selina's hand found mine under the tablecloth and gave it an emphatic squeeze.

I ate my dinner and answered their questions as best I could, and when I was through we took brandy and cigars in the drawing room. I told them about the voyage, delving in details which I thought myself I had long forgotten. The captain prompted me often, out of his knowledge of the sea, and brought to the surface many things which I had noticed but at the time had been quite unconscious of. It was such an evening as I had never before known, and I was warmed by it and grateful in a way for it. Selina planted herself close to me and fondled my arm or caressed my hand or pressed her cheek against my shoulder in a way that showed plain as day the delight she took in having me back. It was not until I had brought a stop to their questions by exhausting them that I was able to ask a question or two of my own.

"Did you get my letter from Newport?" I asked Selina at last.

"I did," she told me, evidently caring not a bit that her father heard her. "It gave me strength to wait for you!"

"I meant to come ashore and tell you," I said, "but we sailed the next morning."

The look she gave me was eloquent.

"I understood," she said, "when he brought it. Oh, Tom! He was such a fine old man and so sick!"

"Who is that? Who are you two talking about?" the captain demanded.

"Sam Nowell," I told him.

"Ah!" said he, and nodded.

There was a brief silence then, in which each of us, I suppose, considered his own thoughts. For my own part I was puzzled. The mention of the old carpenter had reminded me of Pat's urgency in speeding me here. In the excitement of their welcome I had momentarily forgotten. But now that it came back to me, it seemed to me that there was nothing here that was not very much as I had left it, more than a year ago. There was certainly nothing changed about the house. There were the same tall windows, the same polished wall sconces, the same scowling ancestor above the mantel. Even the fire on the hearth might almost be the same that had burned there on the night of my last visit. There was the captain; a bit grayer, perhaps, but otherwise unchanged. There was Selina herself. She was changed, but, I must say, it seemed for the better.

I glanced up at Selina and found her studying me gravely. As I did so the captain abruptly cleared his throat and rose.

"Hah-hrrmmp! You young people will have things to talk about. I believe I'll just step around to the Sun."

I also rose, protesting.

"Don't let me drive you away, sir."

He chuckled.

"Would you have me be the skeleton at the feast?" he asked, and then seemed suddenly embarrassed. He looked to Selina. "Be gentle with him, my dear," he said, and all but fled with a hasty good night over his shoulder.

When he was gone I turned to Selina.

"What's got into him?" I asked.

She looked at me soberly.

"He thinks you'll be upset about the baby," she replied slowly.

I cursed myself for a heartless fool. The child, of course! This must be what Patience had meant.

"I'd almost forgotten," I confessed. "What of him? I should have asked before."

"I'm glad you didn't," she said in a voice scarcely above a whisper, staring down intently at her hands in her lap. "You see he—he died. He was born dead."

"Oh!" I cried out, shocked. "Seel, I'm sorry!"

"There's no reason why you should be," she replied almost bitterly.

I took her hands in mine, and she let me, neither resisting nor encouraging.

"Don't think me so inhuman," I said. " 'Tis for you I feel sorry."

"You needn't!" she flashed up at me abruptly. "I'm not sorry."

I must have looked shocked, for she bit her lips nervously and fell back again in her seat.

"I know I shouldn't say that," she cried, "and it isn't really true! A woman can't bear her own flesh and feel that way about it, no matter how great her shame. He was my baby, Tom, and I couldn't have helped loving him. He was a part of me!"

"Of course," I said, trying to be sympathetic. "I understand that."

She gazed up at me.

"If you can understand that," she said, "can you understand that that's only a part of what I feel? That it's only one side of me that's sorry?"

I frowned, puzzled.

"I don't see———" I began.

"Of course you don't," she said, interrupting. "If he had lived, though I'd have loved him as dearly as a mother could, he'd always have been a reminder of what lies between us. But he died, and it can't hurt him now to say it: Selfishly—for myself, Tom—I'm glad! With him died a part of my past that I was ashamed of! When I buried him I buried my past and my shame with him. Every last connection with it was gone, and I felt purged and cleansed and was glad."

I shook my head.

"That's what I meant when I said I wasn't sorry," she went on hastily. "I'm afraid it might not have been much of a life for him if he had lived. The truth might have come out someday. This way it's probably best for him. Maybe it will be better for me, too, if———"

"If what?" I asked.

"If only you will believe in me," she replied.

I got up again abruptly and went to stand before the fire, staring down into the flames, trying to collect my wits and sort my thoughts from my impulses. Behind me she went on talking in a low tone.

"I know I wronged you," she said, "cruelly and deliberately and inexcusably. But I was frightened, Tom—afraid. I'd been a fool, a dreadful little fool. I had to have a father for my child, and this seemed the only way—I suppose because I liked you and was attracted to you. You were fine. I could see that. And you could help me. But, you see, I didn't know———"

"What?" I said, turning from the fireplace.

"That I loved you," she said in a voice that was scarcely above a whisper.

I could say nothing, but only stood and stared.

"Oh, I know it seems impossible," she went on. "But it's true! I didn't know it at first. But I think it must always have been true. I think I loved you and wanted you from that first day when we met out here at the gate, and when I found myself in that—that condition, something made me turn to you for help. If only I had had the courage to come out with it and tell you the whole thing from the beginning! But I didn't! I suppose that deep down inside of me, even though I didn't know I loved you, I was afraid that if I told you you would hate me. I suppose that down inside me, too, this seemed like a good way to get you for my own. You see, Tom, I've always been a very selfish little wretch and my first thought has always been for myself."

"Don't!" I said impulsively.

But she went on.

"I'm not saying this very well," she said, "but maybe you can understand me. I loved you, but I didn't know it. At the same time I was going to have a baby, and I was afraid. Then, Tom, that night—you remember?—that night when you came to me. I knew then all at once how much I loved you, and for a little while I was happy, until I began to think about it, and then I saw what a horrible thing I was doing to you."

She glanced up at me quickly, and as quickly looked down again, almost as if she were driving herself on with her story.

"That was when I was really afraid, Tom," she said, "not of what you might do to me, but of what I might do to you! And I was afraid I would lose you. And yet I could do nothing about it. I hadn't the courage. I was afraid—of you and of myself and of everything. I just went on hoping weakly that it would all turn out all right, when I knew in my heart that it couldn't. At the same time my fear made me mean, and I think I turned that spite out on you. Poor Tom, I made you miserable. I know it. I could see it!"

"Nonsense!" I said gruffly and, I am afraid, not too convincingly.

"It's not nonsense," she said quietly. "It's true. Well—you found me out. I knew you must. And you left me, and I could not blame you in my heart."

"I don't——" I began, a little confused.

But she stood up beside me and laid her hand upon my arm, interrupting me.

"Don't say anything now," she said. "I haven't told you this to try to influence you. I'm not going to beg you to come back to me, although that is what I pray for every night. I only wanted you to know how I feel and how I've felt. I want you to know that, whatever you may decide to do, I love you, and I will love you always. If you leave me for good and all, I know it will be no more than I deserve. But I do love you, Tom! I do. I swear I do!"

"Seel——" I said, but she laid her fingers against my lips.

"Please!" she begged. "I want you to think about it before you say anything. I want you to think of you first and me last, and you won't do that if you speak on impulse."

That silenced me, for what I had been about to say, whether on impulse or not, could only have been taken so after that. She smiled gently, and it came to me that she was more beautiful than ever. Her expression was more thoughtful and mature, while having had a child seemed actually to have improved rather than harmed her figure. The childish lines were gone now, and in their place there stood a woman.

"Now," she said, "if you'll excuse me, I'll go off to bed and leave you to think things out alone. Cuffee has put your things in your old room."

She hesitated, as if she had something else that she would say, and then appeared to think better of it, for she touched my arm instead.

"Good night," she said.

"Good night, Seel," I replied.

She turned and ran from the room, while I, standing before the fire, watched her as she went.

I sat a long time after she was gone, turning over and over in my mind all she had said. It did not occur to me to doubt her, for there had been a ring of sincerity about her words as she spoke that could not be denied. And yet I could not decide what course I ought to take, partly because the thought of Patience and my feeling for her kept intruding itself upon my mind, and partly because twice burned is thrice wary. At length, however, I got up and went upstairs to my room, being not anxious that Captain Hackett should find me sitting in the drawing room alone on his return.

Back in my own familiar great room, I felt somewhat more at ease and was suddenly conscious of being very tired from my journey. Whatever I might decide, I told myself, I would be able to think better in the morning, and with this I slipped into bed and blew out the light.

But I was to find that it was not so easy as that. The thoughts that I tried to put out of my mind persisted in slipping back. Sleep would not come, and I turned and rolled fretfully, now coming to one decision, only to work myself into a temper on the opposite tack an instant later. At length I tossed aside the blankets and stood out of bed, agreed with myself at least upon one point: that I must think the matter out tonight if I were to get any sleep.

I went to the window and looked out. There was a lopsided silvery moon, perhaps a third of its journey up in the sky, and its light upon the snow outside turned everything to jet and silver. The gaunt trees stood out like black skeletons against the blue white of the snow, and in the shadow of the warehouses across the way the darkness was like pitch. Out in the harbor a tall ship rode at her moorings, and as I looked at her I tried to picture her with courses and topsails set, standing out to sea. I wondered half idly if a wisp of color waved at this window, where I stood, could be seen from the deck of a ship standing out that far away. The thought took me to the *Essex* on the day we sailed, and this in turn drove me to think of Sam Nowell, and from him my mind turned again to Patience, and to Ben, and to the scene I had only that evening witnessed at his home-coming.

There, I told myself with a touch of bitterness, I had scuttled my best hopes. I had brought her husband back once more to the woman I truly loved. And, so doing, I had cut myself off from any possible connection with her as effectually as if I had entered a monastery. I remembered Ben's own delight and the pride with which she had held up the baby.

No, I told myself savagely, Patience was out of my life as anything other than a friend, and I must make up my mind to it! She had her child and her husband and her home, and she was happy with them. If I loved her, as I told myself I did, I would do nothing to jeopardize her happiness, but would seek such happiness as I might find elsewhere. What pleasure I had from her must lie in her own good enjoyment of the life that I had had a small part in shaping for her. And that I could have only at a distance.

Then, what of Selina? For all her protests, I had been far from kind to her. For all my righteousness, I had flung off from her in a fit of temper and left her to face a bitter and difficult period alone. And in spite of that she said she loved me still. If she loved me—and her attitude seemed to prove that she did—why couldn't I return at least a part of her affection? The feeling that I had for Patience should be no bar to it. That was something on another plane. I remembered that I had once been very fond of Selina. If I had cared once, I asked myself, why should I not again? Certainly she was no less desirable. If anything, she was more so, particularly if she had been sincere in what she had said. And if she loved me, if she truly loved me, as she said she did, was it not my own duty, then, as her husband, to return that love with my own? Wasn't I morally far more responsible for her happiness than I was for Patience's? And wasn't I equally obligated to give her such happiness as I could offer? God knew I needed someone myself! Why not, I asked myself, take today for what it is and build for tomorrow and let the dead past lie buried?

With a sigh I turned away from the window, only half convinced. As I turned I glanced at the door between her room and mine, half remembering how, so long ago it seemed, we had passed freely to one another through it. Without actually intending to open it, I went to it and tried the latch. It was not locked. I opened it and stepped through.

In her room the faint scent of perfume brushed my senses tantalizingly and the bright track of the moon cut a silver slash from the tall windows across the deeply carpeted floor to the bed. In spite of myself I felt drawn to the bedside, so that I stood at the corner, looking down at her from one side, yet not where my shadow came between her and the moon.

She slept in a pool of moonlight, with her black hair spread out upon the pillow and her cheek resting upon one arm. Her eyes were closed and her face at rest; lovely and tender, and yet with such an expression of wistful sadness as to wrench my heart. I started to withdraw, but she stirred at the slight sound of my footstep on the rug.

"Tom?" she asked in a small, sleepy voice, obviously more asleep than awake. "Tom darling?"

I gulped. This more than anything she had said to me earlier in the evening told me she loved me.

"Seel!" I whispered timidly. "Seel!"

She sat up abruptly.

"Seel!" I said again.

"Tom!" she whispered. With an impatient gesture she tossed the covers aside. Impulsively she knelt and held out her arms to me. "Tom! you've come to me!"

I placed my hands on her shoulders, holding her at arm's length, while I drank in her beauty with my eyes.

"There's only one thing, Seel," I said.

She looked almost disappointed.

"Yes?" she asked, kneeling submissively before me.

"My dearest," I said, "you belittled yourself all evening, and told me what a saint I had been. I know better! It isn't so. If what you told me tonight was true, you were wrong. But only on impulse—without thought to harm. But I, on the other hand, behaved from a spirit of vengeance. I wanted to hurt you for what you had done to me, and I was cruel. To my mind that's a worse sin than yours!"

"Darling!" she whispered. "You're too good to me!"

"Nonsense!" I scoffed. "I'm not good enough by half. I'm mean and vindictive and I'm harsh. See! I've even come here to bargain with you."

She lifted her hands to my face, touching either cheek tenderly with her finger tips.

"Yes?" she said.

"Will you forgive me my cruelties," I said, "if I forgive your mistakes? Will you love me always, and cherish me, and kiss and comfort me if I promise to do the same for you? Will you lie in my arms and be a part of me? Will you mother my children——"

"Tom!" she cried, and threw her arms about my neck, stopping my lips with her own. "Oh, Tom! My dearest one!"

"Seel!" I whispered huskily. "Ah, Seel darling, it's been so long!"

4

THE MONTHS immediately following our reconciliation were, for me, among the happiest of my life, and I have reason now to believe that they were for her too. Our new understanding

and the tenderness which it engendered, I think, gave us both
an altogether different outlook upon life, and our energies were
concentrated on the thought of doing for each other that
which would produce the greatest happiness.

Selina made much of me, showering me with presents for my
comfort and for my convenience: a new lounging robe, a case
of fine surgical instruments imported from London, a shiny
new chaise and a little bay mare to carry me on my medical
rounds, for I was quick to slip back into my practice. She insisted that the furnishings in my room were all wrong and
must be all shifted around and made over. I did my best to
dissuade her, but she seemed so hurt and disappointed at my
remonstrances that I quickly gave over and let her have her
own way.

On the other hand, there seemed to me little that I could do
in return, other than give her my unstinting love. For all I
haunted the shops and warehouses and pawed over incoming
merchandise from all the ports of the world, it seemed to me
that the best I could do for her was to make her life such a
round of gaiety as I knew she delighted in. Any occasion which
indicated sociability and a festive hour I seized upon for her
amusement, and for the same reasons I cultivated my own relations with the town's society and threw myself into public
affairs with all the energy at my disposal. Not that I sought
for civic leadership, but I knew that it would please Selina to
have me active.

It was not often that we moved in the same circles with Ben
and Patience. I do not mean by this that we were haughty or
standoffish, but rather that we fell in general among quite
different groups. I saw Ben at this tavern or that, where all
Salem discussed the day's turbulent politics over a pot of ale
or small beer. Patience I saw less frequently, on the street or in
the market or at town meeting or at church.

So the winter passed, or much of it, with little more than
an occasional nod passing between us. On those occasions when
I did see Ben at a distance it seemed to me that he had taken
rather heavily to the cup that cheers. Rarely was he altogether
sober, and on those occasions, when Patience was with him, it
seemed to me that she must be painfully aware of his condition.
My heart went out to her, and I was forced to admire her

bravery in her trying circumstances, for she never, by the least hint, showed the pain that must be in her heart.

As I recall, it was about mid-March that I encountered Ben one evening in the taproom of the Sun Tavern, where I had formed the habit of taking an occasional nip myself. It was a little early for most, and I only chanced to stop in on my way home for a bracer to relieve my fatigue, for it had been a busy day. But for the barman, there was no one in the place but Ben, and he was hanging on his elbows in a way that showed beyond question that he was already well along. At sight of him I would have withdrawn and gone my way, but he saw me and hailed me, and rather than be actively unpleasant I grinned and made the best of it.

"What's got you so well along so early in the day?"

He stared at me owlishly.

"D'you mean you've not heard the news?"

"Nothing to call for such a celebration," I replied.

He slapped a copy of the *Gazette* upon the bar and with a grimy finger pointed out an account of Congress's adoption of the Peace Establishment Act, which reduced the Navy to some 13 frigates and 159 officers.

"I wouldn't think you'd be celebrating that," I said.

"You wouldn't?" he demanded. "Did you read it all? Did you see they've retained the *Essex?* They may do what they like with the rest just so they keep her!"

"Stuff!" I said. "She's but a ship. There are others as fine. Forget the *Essex* and settle down."

He looked scandalized.

"Other ships as fine as the *Essex?*" he demanded. "Hah! Shows what you know of it! I'd as soon drown my wife as hear a word spoken against that ship!"

"No doubt!" I said dryly, and turned to go.

"Hah!" he snarled after me with a drunkard's irrelevance. "And talk of wives, that one of yours is no saint! I've known her longer than you, remember, and——"

I turned about and came back to him, grasping him by the shirt front and slamming him back against the bar.

"Hark, you!" I raged. "I'll hear no mention of my wife! Do you understand that?"

He gaped at me in silence, and I felt a certain satisfaction in having frightened him. But I was too angry to pause at that. I glanced at the barman.

"And that's for you, too," I said. "I'll have no discussion of my family here or anywhere else, d'you hear?"

"Oh yes, sir!" he assured me, popeyed at the sudden turn of events. "We don't approve of anything like that here, sir. You just leave it to me, sir!"

"Be goddamned to your approval or disapproval," I growled. "I'm telling you! See to it!"

I gave Ben a thrust and stalked out. As I passed the doors I heard his voice call out behind me:

"Ask her! Ask her about Captain Webb!"

I heard the barman's furious admonition.

"Here, now! You hush your face!"

It hardly seemed worth while to go back and make an issue of it.

I did, however, speak of it to Selina that night in the privacy of our bed; not because I believed what he had said or thought that it was a thing that could come between us, but because I felt that anything that touched upon our relationship should be discussed freely and openly. In short, I felt that she had a right to know and to have the opportunity to speak in her own defense if she wished to do so. If she did not, I was willing enough to forget it.

She lay a long time in silence after I had spoken, and I could feel the soft warmth of her against me. I saw that she was thinking and did not interrupt her, and presently she spoke.

"Benjamin Webb," she said, "was the nearest to a brother that I have ever known, Tom."

I said nothing.

"But there was never anything between us," she went on. "He had my interests at heart, and he acted once to protect them. That's what Ben means."

"I wish I could have saved him," I said.

The gentle touch of her hand told me that she appreciated my understanding but that she had more to say.

"I can't pretend," she said, "that I have always been what I should be. You know that, and for your understanding I am more grateful than I can tell. But it would do no good to rake over cold ashes. It could only hurt, and it would serve no purpose. Only believe me. I love you and none but you! What went before was folly! Can't we just think of that, Tom, and let the past lie buried?"

I turned to her then and drew her to me.

"My dear," I said, "I had no thought to accuse you, and I don't care what's happened! Our love is all that matters. I only thought that you should know."

Her arms crept about my neck and her lips sought mine, softly and deliciously.

"Tom!" she said presently, in a sleepy, contented voice, when we had kissed and parted.

"What, darling?" I asked.

"I—I do have something to confess."

I stiffened with surprise.

"What?" I said. "What is it?"

She gave a happy little chuckle and snuggled closer to me.

"I—Tom—we're—well—would you rather it were a boy or a girl?"

"Seel!" I cried. "You mean that?"

She nodded, burying her face in my shoulder.

"My sweet!" I said. "What could be more perfect? What could mean more fully the healing of old wounds and our coming together as one? Darling, this is the best of news. You've not told anyone else yet?"

She shook her head.

"Your father must know," I said. "And——"

"Yes, Tom?"

"And we must be careful," I told her. "We must have no accidents this time!"

This was our joy and our delight, and I had double cause to be happy in it and happy that she had told me of it, for it seemed to me that it proved for once and all, and cemented in the bargain, our love for one another.

Captain Hackett, I need hardly say, was as pleased as a baby with it. And there again I was to be doubly thankful at having given him the news, for there is no pleasure in this world, it seems to me, without its concomitant tragedy. Less than a week after this we were taking coffee in the drawing room after dinner, when Captain Hackett suddenly collapsed before our eyes.

He was standing by the fire, stirring his coffee, toasting his breeches, and speaking of one of his ships that but a day or two before had been spoken off Bermuda.

"She'll be in within——" he said, and abruptly his face went gray and the cup and saucer slipped from his fingers and went crashing to the floor before him.

His hands went to his face. With a bound I was beside him. But even before I could touch him his knees gave way beneath him and he went down in a heap on the hearth.

Selina screamed. I dropped quickly beside him and lifted him to the sofa and fell to loosening his cravat and unbuttoning his waistcoat.

"What's happened?" Selina whispered at my shoulder. "What is it?"

From the color of his face I had a notion, but I could not tell her that abruptly.

"Fetch brandy," I commanded.

By the time she had returned I had satisfied myself that my first instinct was right. I took the bottle and glass and set them on the mantel and took her in my arms.

"My dear," I said, "we can do nothing now. He's gone!"

5

I THANKED God then that I was near to console her. The relation between them had been a rare one, for he had been both father and mother to her since her childhood, and although I knew I could never replace him, at least I could offer a measure of understanding and comfort which I think gave her strength to face the emptiness of the days to come. Her grief was heart-rending and real, and if I could only caress her and point out to her that his passing had been quick and without lingering pain, I could at least do that. I could also stand between her and those friends who came to offer her their sympathy. Grateful as she was, their every expression and word was salt upon her wounds, and I was able to take the firm hand and ease the contact with them to some extent. The cerebral apoplexy which carried him off struck suddenly and without warning, and there was nothing that man could do to prevent it. This I explained to the best of my ability, and I think she was satisfied. At least I was there for her to lean upon, and for this I was thankful though I felt inadequate.

In the weeks that followed I sometimes wondered if I were doctor or merchant. The Hackett affairs fell to me, and although I soon found that Selina had a head for business surpassing my own, still, as the man of the household and as the one not bereaved in the sense that she was, the responsibility was mine. It was about mid-April that this division of my activities decided me that I must set up my medical office elsewhere than in the house. If I were to be independent of the Hackett fortune, which I felt was strictly my wife's, I must be separate physically as well as figuratively from the mercantile arrangement. I might sit with Selina on the Hackett interests, but my practice was my own, and must be maintained so for the sake of appearances if nothing else. Accordingly I determined to build an office apart from the house, where I could meet my patients and compound my prescriptions. I bought a plot in Essex Street and engaged Ben to design and raise the structure. Nothing was said of earlier differences, and on the whole our relations, if not cordial, were at least friendly.

So matters stood to the middle of April. As I recall it now, it was on the night of the fifteenth, a drizzly, unpleasant night, when a bit of news that was to set us all off on new paths reached my attention.

I came home fairly early that evening to find that Selina, who was feeling a little out of sorts, had gone to bed and sent word that she would not be down to dine. I went up and looked in on her and found it nothing more serious than a slight indisposition. I offered to have supper served us both upstairs and to keep her company, but she greeted this without enthusiasm, and the truth was that she was neither hungry nor, at the moment, in a mood for sociability. She said, sweetly enough, for there were no differences between us then, that she believed that if she only had a good long rest and a sound sleep she would feel better in the morning. I gave her a kiss and a sedative and left her with my sympathy to go down to my own solitary supper.

I did not dawdle over this, having small taste for a lonely meal. When I was done I picked up my brandy and went on into the drawing room, where I could settle in comfort before the fire and read the *Gazette*. I had not read five minutes, however, when the item caught my eye.

MILLIONS FOR DEFENSE, BUT NOT ONE CENT FOR TRIBUTE.

Salem, 15 April: Word has just been received that Mr. Jefferson and his Republican Friends have at last come to realize what every Federalist has long known, viz: that we cannot properly protect our Shipping in Distant Waters with nothing but Jerry Built Gunboats and insignificant Guarda Costas. It appears also that they have at last recognized that it ill comports with National Honor to accept meekly the Slurs and Aspersions and Outrageous Demands of the Barbarous Turks and Pirates of Tripoli and Tunis who have now added their Voices to those of the Algerines and Moors. So Insistent have these Infidels become in their Cries for Tribute that they plainly show what has all along been evident; that the more they receive the greater and more unreasonable become their Demands. Indeed, both Tunis and Tripoli have *THREATENED WAR* if we will not accede to these Demands, and by this time we may be in an actual State of War with the latter.

Very well! If they wish War, let them have it. Mad Tom and his Republican Cohorts have at last consented to read and heed the Writing which has so long been plain upon the Wall. A Naval Squadron is to be Fitted out and Despatched to the Mediterranean to administer a Lesson in Manners to the Barbarians. In support of this measure, Mad Tom and his Francophiles, unable by themselves to think of anything so telling, have adopted as their slogan those famous words which Mr. Pinckney first applied against their friends, the French, viz: "Millions for Defense, but not one Cent for Tribute!"

In this spirit at last, then, has Mad Tom condescended to move. The Ships which will make up the Squadron are to be the Frigates, *PRESIDENT,* 44, *ESSEX,* 32, and the *PHILADELPHIA,* 36, and the schooner *ENTERPRISE,* 12. Commodore Truxtun is to Command the Squadron. Captain James Barron will have the *PRESIDENT,* and his brother, Captain Samuel Barron, the *PHILADELPHIA* in the place of her present commander, Captain Decatur,[1] who is retiring under the P.E.A. It is not known whether Captain Preble will again command the *ESSEX,* though it is rumored in Washington that he may refuse the Command on the grounds of Health. In this case it is supposed that Captain William Bainbridge, who suffered such indignity at the hands of the Algerines last year, will command her. Lieutenant Sterrett will continue to command the "Lucky Little *ENTERPRISE.*"

[1] This was the elder Decatur, father of the hero of Tripoli.

I read this with considerable interest, since it dealt with the ship on which I had spent a year of my life. However, for the moment I thought little of it beyond that, and continued reading, until I had scanned nearly all the columns. But the recollection of the item stuck in my mind, and I kept turning back to it with my inner eye, trying to seek out in it a significance which some sixth sense seemed to be trying to warn me was there. It was some time before it occurred to me that this intelligence might be of considerable significance to Ben and Patience Price. So sharply did this strike me, however, when at last I thought of it, that I snatched up my hat and coat and went straightaway to the Nowell house. It was dark, of course, when I arrived, and it was plain that I had come behind the news, for Patience was alone with the baby. When she opened the door I could not but observe that she appeared to have been weeping and that there was an ugly bruise beneath one eye.

"What's this?" I said. "Has your husband taken to beating you?"

She made no reply but turned away and went to tend the fire on the hearth, making a great show of fixing it. I tried a different tack.

"Where is Ben?" I asked.

"He's gone out," she replied.

"I could see that much for myself," I said, somewhat tartly, I fear. "I suppose he's read the news?"

She looked round at me with a weary droop at the corners of her mouth.

"Yes, he's read the news," she said.

"I suppose he wanted to go?" I asked.

She nodded, and I saw her eyes fill with tears.

"Did you quarrel?"

She put her hand to her face gingerly.

"Would you believe it if I said 'no'?"

"I would not."

She burst into tears.

"What am I to do?" she cried.

I could not stand to see her weep so and not make some effort to comfort her. I drew her to the settee by the fireplace and sat beside her, holding her in my arms and stroking her hair and telling her: "There, now, it will come out right. If you like I'll talk to him."

But so uncontrollable were her sobs that she was unable to make any reply. Instead she could only cling to me, with her face buried in my shoulder. It seemed to me that the best thing for her would be to cry it out. After that, perhaps, we might sit calmly by the fire and try to work out some solution to her difficulty. However, it never did come to that, for in the midst of this the door opened and in came Ben.

It was evident he had been drinking. It was equally evident that he was in an ugly mood.

"Well," he smirked, "this is merry! May I come in?"

"Don't be a fool, Ben," I retorted angrily. "You know damned well there's nothing of that sort here. Pat's distressed that you think of going off again to the *Essex*. She needs reassurance, affection, a little plain——"

"My God," he cried, "you preach at me like an old woman! What's so dreadful in my going to sea? If some of us weren't willing, how would we man the ships?"

"Let single men go off to sea," I said, "or those who are not happily married."

"You're a fine one to talk of happy marriages," he jeered, "with my wife's kisses fresh on your mouth!"

"Wait a minute!" I cried. "I told you there was nothing of that in this! I'm only trying to do for Pat what you yourself ought to do!"

"So I see!" he sneered, and I hit him.

He caromed backward, falling against the table, cartwheeled over it like an immense pinwheel, and brought up in a heap on the other side, fetching table and benches and dishes and all over after him. He lay quite still. Patience gave a little scream of dismay and flew to him.

"You've killed him!" she flung at me.

I went to her side and bent over him.

"No such luck!" I said dryly. "He's only knocked out. He had that one coming for what he did to you!"

Catching him none too gently under the arms, I lifted him and slung him over my shoulder like a meal sack. Without further words I carried him upstairs, where I flung him on the bed. There I left him and went back downstairs to help Patience pick up the mess I had made.

"I doubt he'll come round again tonight," I told her. "With

all that liquor he'll go straight from unconsciousness to sleep. Don't pay too much attention to him. I have an idea he'll be gentle as a lamb by morning."

Apparently I guessed right about that, though I was wide of the mark as to his motives. The next morning he came around and asked for me. When I came down I found him sheepish and apologetic, which was unlike him.

"I guess I had a bit too much," he said.

"I guess you did," I told him.

"I ought to know better," he went on.

"Yes," I agreed, "you should."

He shrugged.

"Well!" he said. "I'm sorry. Will you accept my apology?"

"You don't need to apologize to me," I said. "It was Pat who was hurt."

"I've made my peace with her," he grinned.

I considered the incident closed.

Two or three days after this he came to me again, looking worried and concerned.

"That office of yours," he said. "I think we ought to use cedar shingles instead of clapboard for siding. It's more expensive, but it looks better and weathers better."

"Well," I said, delighted at what I took to be an indication that he had put all thought of the *Essex* out of his mind, "whatever you advise is right with me."

"The trouble is," he said, "I've looked around and there don't seem to be any to be had in town."

"What do we do about that?" I laughed.

He grinned slightly, crookedly.

"I was thinking, Amos Burch, over at Saugus, has been making 'em, and he has a good supply on hand. If you could just go over there——"

"All right," I said. "I'll go this afternoon."

"That'll be fine," he agreed with enthusiasm.

"You wouldn't want to go with me, would you?"

"I don't think it's necessary," he replied. "I can get more done by staying here."

He grinned sardonically, but I attached no importance to the words.

"If you'll tell me what to order and how much," I said, "I'll see to it."

Ordinarily, to get to Saugus from Salem one would follow the road straight down through Swampscott and Lynn. But I thought this occasion a good opportunity to make a call in Peabody that I had been postponing, and in consequence I set out in that direction. This route led me, about a half a mile outside of town, past Nathan McKittrick's lumber yard, and what was my surprise in passing there to see, stacked in one of his sheds, quantities of what looked to me like cedar shingles. So I turned in and inquired.

Yes, McKittrick told me, he had cedar shingles of the size and grade I wanted—any God's quantity of 'em. Surely, he could let me have as many as I wanted. I gave him my order and thanked him, telling him I was glad I had stopped by, for he had saved me a trip to Saugus.

"Saugus?" he demanded. "What for?"

"Shingles," I told him.

"Why," he exclaimed, "what would ye go way the hell an' gone over there for? There's a half a dozen in town'd have 'em. I know for a fact——"

"That's odd," I said, interrupting him. "Didn't Ben Price ask you anything about them?"

He shook his head.

"He told me he'd asked all over town for them," I said, "and couldn't find any."

"Bah!" he exclaimed, and spat sourly. "That feller may be a good carpenter but he's too damned lazy to get off his arse and look around. Now, what'd he do a thing like that for? Don't he think your time's worth nothin'?"

I thought it strange myself, and I proposed to tax Ben with it on my return. I climbed back in my rig and turned about and drove back into town. When I came where the men were at work laying the foundations of my new office, however, he was nowhere about. Clement Gardner, who was superintending the laying of the foundations, came at my hail and put his foot on the hub and peered up at me over the rim of the wheel.

"Thought you was gone for th' day," he said.

"Where's Price?" I asked.

He hesitated.

"Well, now," he said cautiously, "o' course 'tain't none o' my business, but it seems like to me I heard him say he was goin' over to your place."

"My place?" I exclaimed. "What would he go there for? He knows I'm not there."

"Uuh-huh," he agreed noncommittally.

"What do you mean?" I demanded.

He looked down into the dust at his feet, rubbed a lean cheek with a horny palm, and spat.

"Well, now," he said with maddening deliberation, "as I said, it ain't none o' my business, but I allus thought ye were a pretty good sort, Doc, an' I don't like to be a party——"

"For God's sake, man," I cried, "will you get on with it? What are you driving at?"

"Easy, Doc! Easy!" he protested. "I'm only tryin' to help ye out here."

"What are you trying to say?" I demanded.

"Well, Doc, it's like this," he said. "Ben got a mite likkered up here this forenoon after he come back from seein' you, an' he talked free, mighty free! He allowed he'd been pretty free with your wife at one time there. He said he could have about what he liked of her, seeing he had a kind of a persuasive way where she was concerned. He said she was pretty good an' he thought he'd kind o' step over an' get a piece whilst you was——"

I did not wait to hear more, but whipped up my nag in a fury. Behind me I heard him call out:

"He ain't ben gone long, Doc."

I doubt if the distance from Essex Street to Derby and Daniels was ever covered in so short a time, yet as I approached a certain caution came to me. Instead of driving directly up to the front of the house, as I might ordinarily have done, I approached it the back way and drove straight to the barn.

I entered through the kitchen. It being midafternoon, there was no one there. I went on like a thundercloud through the dining room, where the deep carpet silenced my footsteps, to the double doorway that led into the drawing room beyond. There I came to an abrupt halt.

Until this moment I had not thought it possible that my wife could, in any way, have encouraged Ben's attentions. But what I saw now certainly seemed to indicate that I had taken too much for granted. They were standing by the sofa, locked in one another's arms. That is to say, his left arm was about her, and she was lying back across it at what seemed to me a dangerous angle. His lips were fastened upon hers, savagely almost, and her hands were at either side of his face; from where I stood, it seemed, almost fervently holding his mouth to hers. This was enough, but there was worse. Her dress, in great disarray, was open to the waist. One breast had escaped it shamelessly and Ben's right hand was pawing at it avidly! No words were being spoken. Indeed, they could not have been, such was the closeness of their embrace.

At the instant of my shocked pause in the doorway, they caught sight of me and broke guiltily apart. Selina cried out. But I ignored her and went straight for her companion. He turned agilely, spurred, no doubt, by the purpose he must have read in my expression, and vaulted over the sofa. I went around it, a move that gained him a fleeting instant which was sufficient to allow him to fling himself out through the tall open window. By the time I reached it he was already halfway across the lawn below.

I would have followed him had not Selina at that instant seized my arm and held me, calling my name.

"Tom! Please! Let him go! It doesn't matter!"

I rounded on her.

"It doesn't matter, madam?" I demanded. "Do you tell me when I come home and find you in another man's arms in that condition and state of undress that it doesn't matter?"

She stared at me and shrank back, her hands to her mouth and her dress gaping open before her.

"You don't think——" she gasped.

I might have been disposed to listen had I not been so furious. But in that moment I was beyond all reason. I knew only what I had seen, and that seemed to me sufficiently damning. There were papers scattered on the floor, but I did not take time to see what they were.

"Think?" I said bitterly. "I have no need to think. I have eyes to see!"

"Tom!" she cried. "You must listen to me!"

"Listen to you?" I cried furiously. "Listen to you while you talk yourself out of it again? I've had enough grief from listening to you already, you—you slut! I want no more of it!"

I turned away from her and started from the room. She came after me and clutched at my sleeve.

"Tom, please!" she begged.

But I was far too angry to reason. I was sick at heart, shamed and disgusted. I felt fouled and unclean, and my one thought was to get away. When she caught at me I turned on her savagely and slapped her across the face. She fell back then, as pale as death, and stared at me.

"You struck me!" she whispered, touching the place with trembling fingers.

I think she felt the blow more in her heart than on her face, for her expression showed her utter amazement that I would do such a thing. Then swiftly her pallor faded and gave way to a hot flush as she, in turn, became angry with me. Abruptly she seemed to become aware of her open dress, and she clutched it about her.

"You!" she exclaimed hotly then. "You are so righteous! Who are you to talk to me? You're not the only man to find his wife in another's embrace, I have been told! You and your sweet Patience!"

This last was said in an ugly, sneering way that only fanned my wrath more hotly, as it was doubtless intended. I moved toward her with my hand upraised.

"Don't speak her name in this house!" I commanded. "You're not fit to have it cross your lips!"

"Patience! Patience! Patience!" she spat.

I clenched my fist, and she shrank back, but, thank heaven, I had sufficient control to refrain from striking her again. Instead I gave her a mocking bow.

"Madam," I said, "you and I have nothing more to say to one another. I am leaving."

I went up to my room and began throwing my belongings, willy-nilly, into my two chests and my sea bag. While I was about this Selina came scratching at my door.

"Tom!" she called. "Please, Tom, can't we——"

"Go away!" I shouted savagely.

She evidently took me at my word, for she did not speak again, and presently I could hear her snuffling and sobbing in her own room. In that moment, for one brief instant, my resolution wavered. But then I recalled what I had seen and those other things that had gone before, which, added together, made such a damning picture, and I told myself that I must not weaken. When I had finished packing I went down to the stable and found a horsewhip. I found the blackamoor Cuffee there as well.

"Go up to my room, Cuff," I said curtly, "and fetch down the two trunks and the sea bag you will find there. Bring them up to me at the Eagle Tavern."

He stared at me with round eyes.

"You hear me, boy?" I demanded.

"Yass suh!" he replied.

"Very well," I said. "See to it!"

I turned away and went straight to the Nowell house. Pat answered my knock.

"Where's Ben?" I demanded without any preliminary.

"I—I don't know, Tom," she said. "He—he's gone, I think. He came to the house in a great hurry and packed his sea bag and went away, about a half an hour ago, without saying a word to me!"

"The coward!" I growled. "He knew I'd kill him!"

I turned and walked off. Behind me I heard her gasp and then call my name.

"Tom! Tom, you mustn't! Oh God——"

But I did not pause or turn back. At that instant I felt I would never want to talk to any woman ever again!

6

I PICKED the Eagle Tavern because, though it was one of the town's better hostelries, it was a place I had not been much in the habit of frequenting. I felt that, while they knew me, I would stand a better chance of having my privacy respected there and would not be so apt to be subject to prying and curiosity as I might be at an inn where I was better known. Matt Turner, the landlord, was a gentleman and kept a good table.

Having settled myself there for such time as might be necessary to wind up my personal affairs, I had a little more chance to think of what I was to do now, and the more I thought about it, the more solidly my resolution crystallized. I never once considered the possibility of a return to Selina. I was convinced that I had been twice gulled there, and I meant to have no more of it. I felt that if I were to talk with her she would have some ready explanation, but it seemed to me that there could be no valid explanation for the thing that I had witnessed. That side of my life was over.

I spent the balance of that day and all the following morning squaring my accounts and closing my practice. When this was done I gave the afternoon to repacking my gear, for I had no mind to go heavily burdened. My books and papers and such I packed with my shore clothes in one chest to leave on deposit with Matt Turner, at the Eagle, to call for or have sent to me at such time later as might be convenient. My sea bag and sea chest I packed with such things as I thought I would need, for I did not doubt that Ben had fled again to the *Essex,* and I meant to follow him. What I would do when I found him, I had not yet had time to think, save that I would seek vengeance. I told myself I would probably stay on in the Navy to carve for myself a medical career there. One thing I did not want was to return to Salem. Nor did I desire any part of the Hackett fortune. All that was Selina's, and she was welcome to it!

I was in the midst of packing when Matt Turner came knocking at the door.

"What is it?" I asked.

He opened the door and thrust his head in.

"Here's a letter come for you, Doctor."

"Where did that come from?" I demanded, staring at him. "Who knows I'm here?"

"I couldn't say as to that," he shrugged. "Business, likely. 'Twas fetched up by a lad."

"Mmm!" I agreed absently, trying to decide whether I would need Pringle's *Observations on the Diseases of the Army,* which might have some value in a naval connection. "Throw it over there with those papers on the bed. I'll read it later."

He did so and went away, and I continued with my packing, which took me some time, since I was not always able to decide what I should take or what I should leave behind.

In the end I compromised by gathering up all the remaining books and papers on the bed and dumping them willy-nilly into the chest. Some, I told myself, might be convenient to have, but actually I would miss them very little. This done, I locked the chest and arranged with Turner to keep it safe for me. The next morning I paid my score and boarded the early stage. Not until I reached Boston did I remember the letter and realize that I had forgotten to read it. What, I wondered, had I done with it? It came to me that I must have packed it in the chest I had left at the Eagle.

Well, I assured myself, it was probably not of any great importance. More than likely it had to do with the Hackett shipping, and that was now the least of my worries. Let Selina struggle with it. I was through!

With that I turned once more to the consideration of my plans. In Boston, on impulse, I paused long enough to buy a pair of dueling pistols, but even then I was not certain of the use I would make of them. The Code, I told myself, was reserved for gentlemen, and Ben had certainly exempted himself from consideration under it. I think, had I come face to face with him in those first few days, I might have shot him out of hand, without the least compunction, such was my fury with him.

The journey from Salem to New York, however, is a long one, and I had good opportunity to consider every side of the problem. The more I pondered it, the more doubtful I became. I have never held with dueling, and as my thoughts grew less chaotic I began to wonder how I might justify myself in my own conscience for cold-blooded murder. It was not until we reached Providence that I remembered Patience and abruptly realized that, whatever I might think of the man, for her sake I could not harm him. She had married him. He was the father of her child. I could only assume that she loved him, and since I loved her I could do nothing that might hurt her. However I felt about him, for her sake my hands were tied.

The thought depressed me and left me with a feeling of futility until it occurred to me that, followed to its logical conclusion, it did not mean that there was no longer purpose in my pursuit. On the contrary, there was all the more reason why I should carry it out. The resolve that I had made that night so long ago in Salem, before the *Essex's* first cruise, came back to me. That he had returned once in no way released me from my vow. Nor did any wrong I might have suffered at his hands. It was not he I sought to benefit, but Patience, whom I loved. He had left her again. Therefore it was up to me to fetch him back. And that, I told myself, was exactly what I would do. I would not harm him. But I would stay close behind him, and as soon as the opportunity afforded I would drag him back to Salem and force him to his proper duty. It would be too late to fetch him off the *Essex* when I came up with him, I knew, for he would be already signed aboard, and there would be no question of release. But I could afford to be patient. Where he went, there also would I go. And when the time came we would return—together!

7

As I EXPECTED, I found the *Essex* lying in New York Harbor, much as I had last seen her, save that she was new painted and rigged and making evident preparations for sea. Because of my new resolve in regard to Ben I thought it best not to go straightway aboard her lest my appearance startle him into desertion. For my purposes, it was better to know exactly where he could be found. Accordingly, I waited on shore to waylay some one among the officers, whom I might question discreetly, and presently I was rewarded by the sight of young George Tew, resplendent now in the full uniform of a lieutenant.

He was surprised and pleased, I think, to see me, and I had little difficulty in persuading him to join me in a bottle and a brace of fowl at a near-by tavern in celebration of his promotion. A little judicious questioning over the meal told me what I primarily wished to know: (a) that Ben had, as I guessed, turned up on board, and (b) that young Tom Marshall, one of our former midshipmen, had been assigned as surgeon's mate and was on board, but that, as far as Tew was aware, neither the surgeon nor the other surgeon's mate had yet been appointed. I learned also that few of our old hands were aboard; that great things were expected of the cruise; and that Captain Preble, although he was aboard and would take the ship to Norfolk for her rendezvous with the rest of the squadron, had declined her command for reasons of his health. His place was to be taken by Captain Bainbridge, late of the *Washington*.

This last I accepted as my cue. Bainbridge, if naval custom still held true, would have the appointing of the surgeon and his mate. Therefore I declined Tew's invitation to go on board, and cautioning him to silence on the ground of superstition lest I fail to land the berth if it were noised about that I sought it, I took myself away to Philadelphia, where I sought out Captain Bainbridge and boldly asked him for the appointment.

I found him a large, heavy-set man with a huge leonine head and a cast of feature that might have been intimidating were it not for the lines of humor about the eyes. He appeared somewhat taken aback at the audacity of my request but at the same time seemed somewhat pleased with it. He questioned me as to my reasons for wanting the berth and my qualifications, and I, remembering Ben, replied that I had served aboard the *Essex* on her previous cruise and had formed an attachment for her. As for experience, I referred him to both Dr. Orr and Captain Preble. In the end he clapped me upon the shoulder and told me that the post of surgeon was already gone to Jonathan Wells but that of mate was still open and if I wished I might have it. This I accepted without hesitation, and he ordered me to report to Dr. Wells at the Navy Yard, whence we were to take a draft of seamen and report on board the *Essex* at Norfolk.

Wells proved a dour sort of a man, a lean person of no great sparkle, somewhat disgruntled, I suspected, that I had obtained the post rather than a candidate of his own from the medical school. He was able enough, I suppose, but I had occasion to disagree with him violently more than once, and I cannot say that we got on well together. However, as we were ordered, we gathered together our draft and shortly before the first of June boarded our ship off Hampton Roads. A few days later we weighed anchor, and under Commodore Dale, who had replaced Truxtun in command, the squadron stood out past the Virginia Capes for Gibraltar.

I do not intend to dwell upon this second cruise of the *Essex* any longer than upon the first. In the main there is but one word to describe it. That is, "dull." We left Norfolk with high hopes of adventure. It was even rumored that aboard the *Philadelphia* one of the officers had promised to send his fairest and dearest a lion or an ostrich from the first port we touched and had even gone so far as to have a cage built for the beast! The hopes of the nation also went with us, that we might teach the Turks a needed lesson. But the truth was that when we arrived we did little more than spend endless days blockading empty ports, and still more endless weeks convoying merchantmen from one Mediterranean port to another. For a time we were close spectators to a naval war of some interest, for the British on the one hand and the French and Spanish on the other were active in the neighborhood of the Straits. But even there we missed the most exciting episode, for we were in Tunis when two actions were fought, in plain view of Gibraltar, in which two English line-of-battle ships were lost and two Spanish 120-gun ships were blown up by firing into one another in the darkness.

We had a quick and reasonably pleasant passage to the Straits, in the course of which we shook down into a shipshape crew, able to vie with the smartest units of the British fleet, which we found at Gibraltar. There, too, we found two Tripoline vessels of war, commanded by their Lord High Admiral Murad Rais, a renegado Scot, whose true name was Lysle, whom we proceeded to blockade in port. This was a long-drawn-out business, and in spite of it those of us who were often on shore came to at least nodding acquaintance with Lysle and his officers. Tom Marshall and I were perhaps outstanding in this, for it was we who were sent aboard the Tripolines when, at length, Lysle petitioned the governor to state that because of our activities his crews were in danger of starvation. At the governor's request we made our inspection, and found the situation not far from what it had been stated, for all hands were suffering from malnutrition. We recommended that the ships be detained but that Murad and his crews be permitted to pass over to Morocco, and this was ultimately what was done. Meantime we passed on, to escort the ship *Grand Turk* to Tunis, to patrol the waters between Sicily and Africa, and later to convoy neutral vessels westward to the Straits again. We had a brief flurry in Barcelona, where Lieutenant Decatur, incensed at Spanish arrogance, challenged the captain of a Spanish *guardacostas* and then offered to cut off his ears if they met in the street. We had our share of foul water and short provision and flux and fever, and only once did we seem likely to make a prize, and then it turned out to be a neutral vessel that we had fired into! A year of this found us ready to turn toward home!

On this voyage, however, my relations with Ben deserve something better than passing notice.

Since I was content to do no more than keep watch on his movements for the present, I made no effort to let him know that I was on board, and, such is the complexity of life on a man-of-war, we were well away before he became aware of it. The Capes of Virginia were a blue haze astern of us when we met for the first time.

It happened as I was passing aft through the berth deck, on my way from the sick bay, to my own quarters. Ben was on his knees in the steerage, making some repairs upon the bulkhead, where it had been damaged by the midshipmen in their horse-play. He glanced up at my approach, looking over his shoulder. But at sight of me he went quite gray and scrambled to his feet, with his hammer clutched defensively in his hand. There were a half a dozen or more midshipmen coming and going in the passage at the time, but I doubt if any of them saw anything out of the ordinary. Indeed, if any of them noticed, I doubt they thought it anything but the courtesy due an officer that he should rise and stand when I approached. For my part I said nothing, but passed straight on, only giving him a hard stare which I meant to show my contempt. It seemed apparent to me that he was afraid what vengeance I might be plotting, and since my resolution would allow me no more I was content to let him sweat. In view of events, this may have been a mistake. But I was no more than human, and I saw no reason why he should not roast for a while in the fires of apprehension which his own guilty conscience had kindled.

We were no more than a fortnight at sea, however, before I learned that the game was not to be all one-sided. Toward midafternoon of a blustering, disagreeable day, in hauling up our mainsail, the quarter gunner, in clearing the turns, delayed let fly the sheet, and the sail being wet and it blowing hard, it split considerably. In hauling out, the main-topsail reef tackle tore the sail from the leech rope, and it was necessary to get down the topgallant yard, repair the main-topsail, and bend on another mainsail.

I came on deck while this was about, not aware that anything was amiss, nor knowing that the carpenters had been sent aloft to see to the main-topmast. I was crossing the deck, when Mr. Decatur called to me, causing me to turn about, whereby he unquestionably saved my life, for at that instant a heavy crown block crashed on deck scant inches from me, and exactly in the spot where I would have been had he not diverted me. He had the men down from the maintop and rated them roundly, and I was startled to learn that it was Ben who had dropped the block. It had slipped from his fingers, so he said, though I thought I knew better. After that I went more warily, keeping a weather eye open, so that there were no more "accidents" of that nature. Indeed, nothing untoward happened for so long that I began to wonder if I had not done him an injustice after all. At Barcelona, however, occurred an event which no longer left me any room for doubt.

We had been some days lying at that port, where the trouble between Lieutenant Decatur and the captain of the guarda-costas, already mentioned, fell out. That incident came about in this way: Shortly after our arrival Captain Bainbridge went on shore. He remained several hours and returned to the *Essex* in the evening. Throughout the day his gig had lain unchallenged by the mole, close by where the Spanish xebec lay moored, so that there can be no question that its identity was unknown. Moreover, the *Essex's* boats had been passing and repassing between the ship and the mole all day without question. In spite of this, when the captain attempted to come off toward sunset he was challenged and insolently ordered to lay aboard the Spaniard and identify himself.

This was a scandalous breach of courtesy, for it is not customary to question the commanders of public vessels of war of friendly nations once proper bona fides have been established. Nevertheless Captain Bainbridge kept his temper, supposing it done in ignorance, and explained his identity. But when the command was repeated in still more insulting terms, he became angry in his own turn, indignantly refused, and ordered his men to pull for the *Essex*. Some shots were fired after them, which, fortunately, went wide of their mark, and the captain came on board in a towering rage and immediately made vigorous protest to the governor. Nevertheless, on the next day the incident was repeated, this time upon a ship's boat containing Lieutenant Decatur and several other officers.

Now, where Captain Bainbridge was restrained by the obligations of command, Mr. Decatur suffered no such restriction. He could and did act with more directness to come at the source of the trouble. With several fellow officers he laid aboard the Spaniard the next morning, having already sent word that he would be there at that hour, and demanded to see her commanding officer. On being informed that the Spaniard was ashore, he unhesitatingly declared him a coward and a poltroon and made the threat already described.

As may be imagined, the episode had its repercussions, both on shore and on board, and the result was just such a state of tension as might be turned to the advantage of one who planned mischief. Ben undoubtedly saw his opportunity, while I, by now lulled to a sense of false security, was too fatuous to see how the wind lay.

It happened that a day or two before we were to depart Tom Marshall and I went on shore together for the evening. We visited a number of places along the Rambla, enjoyed a hearty dinner, and after looking in on a place of entertainment, where Spanish gypsies sang and danced to the music of castanets and guitars, we started back, at a late hour, toward the mole, where the ship's boats were waiting. It was quite dark as we approached along the narrow, unlighted streets, and we were hurrying, as we were somewhat later than we should have been, when, almost within sight of the boat, we were set upon.

Our first warning of attack was when someone leaped upon me out of the blackness from behind, and I felt sudden, sharp pain flash into my right side, high and between the ribs, and probe into my vitals. I cried out instinctively, of course, but the knife struck and struck again, three times in all before I could altogether realize what had happened.

Marshall ducked, but I was borne to my knees with everything whirling dizzily about me and fell forward on my hands. It seemed to me that I heard shouts and running feet and felt another wild slash at my back. But I may have these in confused order, for I was already seemingly floating away upon a dark current which I had no power to resist. The next I knew, I opened my eyes in broad daylight in the *Essex's* sick bay, days later, and we were at sea.

The first thing I saw, as my hammock swayed to the movement of the ship, was George Tew, who had been ill for some weeks of a wasting fever. He was staring at me from his own hammock with eyes that seemed as great as his face.

"So you've come round at last?" he said. "We'd begun to give you up for dead."

I tried to turn over to face him, but pain pinned me where I lay and made me cry out.

"What happened?" I managed to gasp.

"They fetched you aboard full of holes," he told me. "Marshall says you were set on by some Spanish wharf rat——"

"Did they catch him?" I asked quickly.

"No," he replied. "He escaped in the alley."

"Strange," I said. "I don't seem to remember much."

"You've been out of your head ever since," he said.

Sometime later Tom Marshall came down and appeared relieved to find me conscious. From him I learned further details. My assailant had made no move toward him. Surprise had thrown Tom off balance, and he had whirled against the wall and drawn his sword, at the same time setting up a shout for the boat's people. At the raising of this hue and cry the man had turned and fled so swiftly that Marshall, in lunging for him, had stumbled over my body.

"Did you see him?" I asked.

"Only a shadow," he replied. "You'll remember 'twas dark."

"You never found him?"

He shook his head.

"The lads from the boat came running, and others in the neighborhood who were coming in to the boat came up. Among 'em was your friend—what's his name? The carpenter's mate."

"Price?"

"Aye," he nodded. "He came out in the boat with you. Of course we sent you on board at once, while most of us stayed and spread out, searching for the dog. Price wanted to hold your head in his lap. He seemed right upset. But Mr. Decatur made him pull an oar—said he'd do you a better service that way than any other."

I shuddered inwardly. Mr. Decatur was unaware how true that was!

It was October before I was able to be up and about. In the meantime, in common with nearly everyone on board, I took the flux, to which my weakened condition made me an easy prey, and for the first time I discovered how it felt to be patient rather than physician. It was a salutary experience!

In this interval also died George Tew, which was a melancholy business to watch, and one that impressed upon me my helplessness. He was an able gentleman, a promising officer, and the best of shipmates, and he was mourned by all.

Nevertheless, and despite its gloom, I was happy to be confined in the sick bay during this time, for there was always a guard posted upon the door and an attendant on duty. There at least I felt I was safe. When I was finally able to be up and about again, I was assigned quarters off the wardroom, in consideration of my convalescent state, and required only to light duty. Thereby it was several weeks before I again encountered Ben on deck. When I did, however, we did not speak, and I will admit that from that day on I went constantly armed.

It was not until near the end of February that a third incident occurred to mark our feud. This time, however, it was an event which I thoroughly believe saved my life and came near to ending Ben's career entirely.

We had been for some time cruising in and about the Straits, keeping a watch upon the Moroccans, who were suspected of sympathy for the Tripolines and not trusted to keep out of mischief were we to leave them alone. On the day I have in mind we had stood across for Tangier for a brief visit and, after satisfying ourselves that all was quiet, had turned about and were beating out of the bay again, under a strong north-northwest wind and a battering sea, on a tack which took us uncomfortably close to Cape Malabaita.

At the time I was forward in the sick bay, attending my duties. Dr. Wells was confined to his cabin with a dysentery, and the burden of the ship's surgery had fallen upon me during two weeks past.

Shortly after we got under way I left the sick bay and with difficulty made my way aft along the berth deck to the cabins off the wardroom, where I looked in upon Dr. Wells. This duty attended to, I started on deck to observe our passage. However, I thought to get a drink of water from the scuttle butt in passing, and for this I went forward to the main hatch and up to the gun deck by the main ladder; no easy task, as at this point the ship was hove well down on the port tack.

I came upon the gun deck and drew my water and drank, after which I passed aft toward the quarter-deck ladder. There was a marine guard on duty at the scuttle butt, as always, but he was out of sight once I had passed the grog tub, and the rest of the deck aft of that point seemed deserted.

It was not, however. As I made my way heavily down the length of the battery, the guns of which were run in and made fast, I came suddenly, between a pair of them, upon Ben Price, crouched down and working at some carpenter's chore.

What he was about I have no way of knowing, but it was a matter that had no connection with me, for he looked up as startled at my appearance as I was at his.

For a fraction of a second we stared at one another. Then his hand moved, perhaps instinctively—although it seemed to me that if I ever saw murder in a man's eye I saw it then—toward a pinch bar that he had been using. Whether he meant to take it up in defense or whether he meant to attack me with it, I do not know. Involuntarily, I ducked.

At the same instant the ship came about on the opposite tack and took a monstrous sea upon her starboard bow. The abrupt shift in the center of gravity, coupled with the sudden lurch as she shouldered the seas aside, threw me off balance, and I found myself sliding down across the sharply heeled deck to fall amid the guns of the larboard battery. At the same instant each gun of the starboard battery, now lifted high above me, lurched back an inch or so into its breechings.

What went wrong at this moment I do not know. Whether the tackles on the gun that Ben was crouched beside had not been sufficiently two-blocked or whether the ringbolt was already weakened, I could not say. At any rate, as I looked up across the cant of the deck I heard the bolt tear loose from its bed with a crack like that of a musket. In the same instant I saw the heavy gun begin to fall toward me.

I confess I cried out in terror, but instead of continuing its fall in my direction, the gun jerked to a sudden stop, brought up short by the lashings on its other side, which held, and then ponderously and inexorably swung, pendulumwise, toward Ben, following the pitch of the ship as she dipped her bows and kicked her stern in the wake of a roaring sea.

I heard Ben scream and saw his face above the breech of the gun, dead white and agonized. His hands clawed at the monster, and the pinch bar that he had seized clattered down, forgotten, beside me. For an instant I could not realize what had happened. Then the ship's bows rose again to an oncoming sea, and the gun swung back in its pendulum course, to reveal Ben, with legs crushed and crumpled, lying between the adjoining gun and the ship's side.

Pain, perhaps, or sheer fright, made him clutch the tackles of the next gun, else the lurch of the ship would have tossed him out of his corner. But he clung like a burr, and it came to me in a flash that the next drop of the ship's bows would bring that deadly pendulum of cannon swinging back once more to squash him like a louse where he lay unless he dropped. I cried out to him to let go. And then, quite without thinking, I clawed my way upward frantically and, seizing him about the neck in a desperate grip, half threw myself, half leaped, about the breech of the adjoining gun.

I was not an instant too soon, for in that moment the bows dipped once more and the awful juggernaut came thundering back. The pitch of the ship made the move difficult. Indeed, it held me down, but fear and desperation lent me strength. The swinging gun brushed Ben's already limp toes and brought up with a crash against the ship's side. In the next moment the bows were lifting again and we were both sliding down across the deck toward the far battery, and I was squalling loudly for help to come and secure the gun.

It must be explained that all this was done without thought on my part. I neither wished to be a hero nor did I have time to consider my oath to return Ben to his family. I acted purely on instinct, as I would have reached out from the safety of a boat and snatched at a drowning man. In response to my cries, men came with bars and tackles and ropes and pinned the dangling monster in place and made it fast. Then, and only then, they came to my assistance and lifted me to my feet and carried Ben off to sick bay.

A hasty examination, as I followed them, revealed that I was little the worse for wear. A few rips in my clothing and a deck burn on my arse, a skinned elbow and a bruised side was the sum of my injuries. Examination in the sick bay, however, showed Ben to be in a more serious state. His left leg had been broken clean between knee and ankle, but his right leg seemed twisted and bent out of recognition from a point perhaps six inches above the knee well down to the ankle, and in the bargain it looked as though the foot had been crushed. Nor was I at all sure that there were no internal injuries, as marks on his belly seemed to indicate a strong possibility of such being the case. Fortunately the pelvis and hip joints had been spared.

He was quite conscious as we laid him out, and he watched me with wide-eyed apprehension and, I knew, excruciating pain as I bent over him. Marshall took one glance over my shoulder and whistled loudly.

"Great God!" he exclaimed, popeyed.

I was too busy to pay much attention to him, and presently he went away, to return a few moments later to pluck at my elbow.

"What do you want?" I demanded impatiently.

"Dr. Wells says both legs must come off," he replied.

I stared at him an instant and then glanced at Ben, who was staring up at me wide-eyed and defiant. Undoubtedly he had heard. In that instant I had a swift vision of Ben returning home to Patience legless, on crutches or worse, and I pictured her horror and abomination of me if she thought that I were the one responsible. After all, I told myself, she loved him. Wasn't that the reason I had made up my mind as I had?

Abruptly I began to curse.

"Dr. Wells says!" I exclaimed. "Dr. Wells is on the sick list and not capable of judging this case. I'm officer in charge here, and I'll rely on my own judgment."

Marshall gulped.

"Aye, aye, sir!" he replied, probably for the first time since he had been a midshipman.

I turned back to the hammock on which Ben lay, bending again to look at that shattered right leg. It was bad, I could see, but aside from lacerations it was actually no worse than the leg I had set for Noahdiah Hethcote that day in the ship-yard at Salem. Perhaps if I had followed Dr. Wells's advice it would have been better, for Ben's seafaring days would have been over. But I felt that I could save his legs, and be it Ben or another, it was a sort of pride in me to try.

I will not go into details. It took four bleedings and Mar-shall and three loblolly boys to hold him down while I set the breaks, one by one, in both legs and the mashed foot and bound them up in splints to hold them in place. Ben screamed and cursed and fought me as I worked, until a bos'n's mate was called to put a wooden plug between his teeth to wedge his jaws wide and hold them. When I was done I knocked the plug out and grinned at him.

"There," I said. "One leg may turn out shorter than the other, but at least they'll be your own."

For answer he cursed me! Well, I did not look for thanks from him!

This was the end of my troubles, at least for the duration of that cruise. I cannot say that Ben ever showed the least sign of gratitude to me for having saved his legs, and Dr. Wells was critical, saying that the greatest mark of skill in a naval surgeon was the neatness and dispatch with which he per-formed an amputation. Nevertheless I was well pleased with myself. I had kept my resolution. I had resisted the temptation to take vengeance upon an enemy whom chance had placed within my reach. I had preserved her man for Patience. And I had given myself a sense of strength which I had not known before.

In addition I had secured for myself the first real moments of peace that I had known in almost a year. It was June be-fore Ben was able to lay aside his crutches, and it was August and we were back again within the Capes of Virginia and stand-ing up Chesapeake Bay toward the Potomac before he was able to walk, without support, albeit with a pronounced limp which he kept from then on. On that day I spoke to him for the first time during the voyage.

"Well, Ben," I said, " 'twill be good to see the streets of Salem again, eh?"

He turned upon me savagely.

"What makes you think I'm going back?" he snarled.

"I mean to take you," I said grimly. "Make no mistake about that."

Nor had he the strength to protest. What he thought I meant to do after fetching him home I neither knew nor cared. I felt confident that he would give me little trouble in the way. We were paid off at Washington on the eleventh of August and started north on the following day. As for the *Essex,* she was laid up in ordinary.

8

We came to Salem by afternoon stage from Boston, quietly and unheralded, and if any noticed our arrival they gave no sign of it. I left my luggage at the stage station and delivered Ben to his own door, determined that nothing should now interfere with these final stages of my self-imposed duty. I did not, however, approach the house, not trusting myself to face Patience.

Now all at once I was faced with my own problem. What should I do now? Where should I go? In my single-minded determination it had not occurred to me to consider my own situation. Now, however, it came to me with full force that my own affairs were scarcely in better shape than Ben's. I was unwilling to remain in Salem, yet it had long since come to me that I owed it to Selina to hear what she might have to say. The edge of my anger having dulled, I was at least ready to concede so much. Accordingly, I now turned my steps in the direction of the Hackett house.

The place seemed oddly quiet as I approached. The tall windows still stared blankly out at the street. The lawns and gardens were, as usual, carefully trimmed and cared for. The veranda was neat and spotless, and the steps had been freshly painted. Yet there was something subtly different. I lifted the great brass knocker and listened to the echoes reverberating through the hall within. Presently I heard steps, and a moment later found myself face to face with Sukey, Selina's maid.

"Good evening, Sukey," I said.

For answer her eyes flew wide and her jaw dropped, quite as if she had seen a grave open and give forth its dead. Instead of replying she turned away suddenly, blubbering, and scurried back into the house.

I followed, puzzled, and went into the drawing room, confident that in due time Selina would learn of my presence and appear. Instead I was shortly aroused by a step on the threshold and turned to find old Jeremy Cotton, who had been Captain Hackett's chief clerk, facing me across the threshold.

"Good evening, Jeremy," I said. "Is Mrs. Tisdall at home?"

He gave me an odd look and cleared his throat.

"Er—welcome home, Doctor," he said. "I'm afraid I've sorry news for you."

"What?" I said, not realizing.

"Why—er," he said, obviously groping. "Why—uh—fact is, Doctor, you mustn't take it hard. Things aren't as you left 'em."

"Come, come, man!" I exclaimed. "Out with it! I'd not expected everything to be exactly the same."

He looked about him wildly and, seeing no escape, came to the point.

"Miss Selina's dead!"

"What?" I gasped, thunderstruck. I think I was prepared for anything but this. He nodded.

"Dead!" he repeated.

"No!" I exclaimed.

"Over a year now," he assured me.

I felt my knees go weak beneath me, and I fumbled for a chair. She had been alive, vital, when I left, and much as I told myself I had resented her behavior, I had not considered this: that she could be gone, cold dead, no more to laugh, to smile, to preen her lovely, voluptuous body.

"Tell me," I gasped.

He gave me a pitying glance, as if he would help me.

" 'Twas but a day or two after you left," he said. "We tried to find you, and only then learned you were gone."

"How?" I demanded fiercely.

"Drowned," he replied. "She went out in the little pinnace that used to be her father's. There was a squall and she drove on the rocks off Baker's. They found her body on the shore of Great Misery the next day."

I felt a chill in my heart.

"But she was a stout swimmer," I protested, "and a better sailor. She'd never go out when weather was making!"

"That's what everyone said," he nodded. "But she did."

I made no reply. Presently he came and put his hand upon my shoulder.

"I'm sorry, Doctor," he said, "to be the one to bring you such news. You have my deepest sympathy!"

I nodded absently, thanking him, and he went away. How long I sat there brooding I do not know, but it was long past dark when I finally went upstairs.

I have seen ships, caught suddenly aback by an abrupt shift of the wind, stagger and lose their rigging and all but founder in the heavy seas. In a sense I found myself in a like predicament.

The regard for personalities; the love of a man for a woman or of a woman for a man; the bond of affectionate friendship, I believe, is never totally obliterated between individuals no matter what quarrels may have come between them. Once established, a vestige of it always remains, so that even though one has come to regard a former friend or lover or close associate with hatred, the sudden news of disaster to such a one comes with a sharp shock.

This was my own reaction to the news of Selina's death. I had not wished her such ill as this! Was I, my conscience demanded, responsible? Even if I could say "no" to that with assurance, I could not forget the life we had led together, the love we had known for one another. She was my wife. We had shared our bed and bodies. If we were not combined in one person, it was not for lack of opportunity. It was merely fortunate in the circumstances.

But I was in no mood to consider the circumstances. I could only think of how sweetly she had lain in my arms, of what she had been to me—not of what I had thought her at our last parting. For all my bitterness, I found, I had still great regard for her, and the thought that she, whom I had once held close to my heart, whose throbbing, pulsing life I had felt beating against my own, was now gone, dead, inaccessible to any human feeling, was one that left me with a sense of self-loathing, a feeling almost of physical illness, at the way we had parted.

Was I wrong? I kept asking myself. Had I done her an injustice? Was there something more in the situation I had discovered that I did not understand?

I tried to assure myself that there could be no explanation for what I had seen and that I had acted only as a sensible man would. Yet the feeling persisted, and the question would raise itself in my mind in the small hours of the night, when I thought myself free of it in sleep, and I could not avoid it. It was long before I was able to force myself to look upon it objectively. Indeed, if truth be told, I was never able to reach that state of mind entirely. But the passage of time helped to deaden the shock, and it was only then that I was able to take stock of matters as they now stood.

Those matters, I may say, needed stocktaking. By virtue of the tragedy I found myself the sole heir to all of the fortune and business that Eli Hackett had amassed. All the ships, the wharves, the warehouses and all the goods stored in them; the great house on Derby Street and everything in it, even the servants, were mine, and I found myself faced suddenly with the tyranny of possessions. There are those, I know, who will envy me what they consider my good fortune, but for my own part I would gladly have given up all claim to any of it if in so doing I could return Selina to life. Since that was impossible, I had no choice but to accept. And in accepting I wound myself more tightly in a web that I was striving desperately to escape.

That web was fundamentally Salem, or so it seemed to me. I felt that Salem was at the root of all that had happened. If I had not gone there in the first place, Patience would never have married Ben Price, for it was I who had brought him into her house. By the same token, if I had not gone to Salem, Selina might yet be living and happy. This was false reasoning, I admit, but in my state of mind then I was unable to recognize its fallacy. The fact was I had come to Salem and met the woman I loved. She had married another, and over the wreckage of that love I had built another. That, too, had crashed, with disastrous results. There was nothing left for me in Salem but memories and wealth. And while the wealth tied me in the town, my memories made it turn to ashes in my mouth. I wanted desperately to shake its dust from my feet. I wanted to get away, to where I might find action and forget all that had happened. I wanted to forget Selina and my feeling of having been responsible for her tragedy. I wanted to forget Patience, whom I still loved but could never possess. I wanted to wash my hands of Ben Price, and of all that he stood for. Yet now that I had my wife's inheritance I seemed as firmly tied to the place as if I had raised a family there.

There was one difference, however. In the situation as it was, I could dispose of my inheritance. And once I had disposed of it I would no longer be bound to remain. I could sell the property and go. Nor need I ever return. This I determined to do before I made any other decision.

I think I had some notion that this might be accomplished in a week, or a fortnight at the latest. I was quickly to discover that it was not nearly so simple as that. There were interruptions to the business of stocktaking and disposal. My neighbors were kindly and called to express their sympathy, none knowing, of course, the things that had passed between us before my last abrupt departure, which to them had merely the look of rejoining my ship. In kindness I could only accept their expressions as they were intended, and thank them. Nor could I hurry their departure. In the first weeks, too, I found that my own state of mind prevented long concentration upon business matters, though this gradually wore away. Then, too, there were my old patients, who, now that "the doctor" had returned, came back to him to treat their ills. Here again, in the name of decency, I found it impossible to turn them away. I treated them, and they returned with friends with other ills to cure. Thus, while with one hand I sought to cut the bonds that linked me to the town, with the other, all against my will, I was forging another quite as powerful!

But it took me less than a week to discover that the actual business of disposal of my inheritance formed the greatest block to my swift departure. For the first time I was brought face to face with the extent of my father-in-law's interests, and the ramifications and far-flung complications amazed me. It was more than a matter of selling a few ships and warehouses in Salem. I discovered that there were properties in England and Italy, in the Low Countries, and in the Indies as well. There were contracts and credits with foreign agents, and bills of exchange on practically every port in Europe.

The task was made lighter by Jeremy Cotton, who had kept things in order in my absence and had carried on the business in the way he felt Captain Hackett would have done had he been there. It was he who showed me what a maze it was, and it was primarily he who carried through the business of disposal, although I felt he disapproved of this solution and kept hoping against hope that I would change my mind. It was midwinter—a good six months—before we had squared away our foreign accounts. And it was April before I managed to sell out the business itself, lock, stock, and barrel, ships, warehouses, and goods, to the Crowninshields, leaving me only the house and its contents yet to dispose of. It was turned June before I was able to strike a bargain on that with Peleg Taylor, who had lately made a successful China cruise and now sought a home to which he might fetch his bride of a month.

It was nearer a year, therefore, than a fortnight, before I was at last free to go my way. In the meantime I avoided all such social contact as I might. I kept myself to myself, as much as it was possible to do. And yet it was not possible to become a hermit altogether. Church was still compulsory in Salem, morally if not by law, and town meeting was likewise not to be neglected. And there were other, similar gatherings, which for one reason or another I felt bound to attend, and my appearance at these, no doubt, kept me from gaining the reputation of a complete recluse. At that, I have no doubt, my fellow townsfolk came to look on me as slightly "odd" since my wife's death, but the great majority were understanding, or, what amounts to the same thing, they thought they were.

Above all I sought to avoid contact with Patience and Ben. In so far as Ben was concerned, I felt that our return to Salem had established a tacit truce between us. Apparently he had accepted it as such, for I saw him, now and again, about town, frequently under the influence of liquor. Yet we never spoke.

I saw no reason why I should either stir up his enmity or pretend to his friendship.

Patience, on the other hand, I avoided for reasons far more difficult to explain. In the first place, the feeling that I had made a fool of myself on our last meeting made me reticent to face her. In the second place, I had no wish to revive my old feeling for her—which I knew underneath everything to be as strong as ever. Added to this was a feeling that my interference at this time might well be misunderstood. During our absence Patience had become a mother again; a daughter this time. Yet, on the occasions on which I saw her, in church and at town meeting, I could not see that it had affected her beauty. She was still as young and as fresh seeming, as firm breasted and as youthfully rounded as ever. And what was more, she held her head as high. I was far from sure that I had been instrumental in bringing her happiness. But at least I had done my best, and I avoided her lest I learn that my efforts had been in vain.

Yet it was impossible to avoid her entirely. On public occasions, as at those mentioned, we must at least meet and nod. And there were other moments, such as when, walking home one day, I fell in with her returning from market. In the circumstances I could not refuse to carry her basket or talk to her as we walked!

"You've been a stranger," she said accusingly.

"I've been busy," I replied shortly.

She eyed me sidelong, under her lashes.

"I'm dreadfully sorry," she said quietly.

I made no reply. I believe we both were thinking of the last time I had seen her.

In time I spoke in desperation.

"How's Ben?" I asked.

"Well, thank you," she replied.

I thought I caught a derisive undertone to her reply.

"Look here," I blurted, "I found Ben aboard the *Essex*. And by the time I'd found him I'd had time to think. I—I changed my mind."

"God hears our prayers," she replied simply.

"Yes," I said curtly, not altogether understanding, "though I don't know who prayed for me!"

She made no reply to that, and we walked on in silence. Out

of the corner of my eye I could not but notice that she seemed to be fighting back tears. I felt some of the old yearning stirring within me, and when we came to her gate I hastily handed her the basket and bade her good-by.

Early in June, as I was preparing to turn over the house to Captain Taylor, I received two official-looking envelopes, one from Washington, bearing the stamp of the Secretary of the Navy, the other from Philadelphia, with the signature of Captain Bainbridge. The first was an order:

You will proceed to Philadelphia [it said] and report to the Frigate *Philadelphia* for duty as surgeon's mate. If for any reason you find yourself unable to comply with these orders, you will communicate with the Secretary of the Navy by the first post, giving your reasons therefor, or submit your resignation from the Naval service without delay.

This was a grim reminder that I was still a naval surgeon. The second letter was less impersonal.

I cannot offer you the post of surgeon [it said], as times have changed, and a captain no longer has the naming of those who sail under him. But I am given to understand you have been designated as surgeon's mate aboard the *Philadelphia,* and remembering your late services aboard the *Essex,* I hasten to assure you that I would rather sail with no man. Should you care to join us again, I will be pleased of your company. Should you wish to decline the service, I would appreciate it if you would let me know at the earliest possible date, in order that I might fill your place with someone, less desirable, perhaps, but equally necessary to our purpose.

It was signed William Bainbridge, Captain, U.S.N.

There was something heart-warming about this, and I set it aside, to answer presently. Since I was quitting Salem, and had no other plan, I saw no reason why I should decline. Indeed it seemed an easy solution to the problem of what to do next.

A day or two later I surrendered the house to Captain Taylor and his bride and, with my money in my pocket and my sea bag on my shoulder, took myself to the Eagle Tavern to find lodging for the night and to lay my plans. There I was greeted by Matt Turner, who assured me that they had room and would be glad to accommodate me. It was when he had seen my fire lit and the rooms warmed that he turned to me.

"I wondered when you'd be calling back for your chest," he said. "Shall I have it fetched up?"

"Chest?" I said. It had slipped my mind.

Then all at once I remembered.

"Oh yes," I said. "By all means, do."

Within a few moments the boy appeared with the dusty, long-forgotten box on his shoulder.

"Put it down," I said, gesturing toward the corner of the room.

He did as I told him, and for some moments after he had gone I paid little attention to it. Presently, however, having a few moments before it was time to go down to supper, I opened it, unable to recall in any detail what I had packed away in it two years and more ago. As a matter of fact, there seemed little in it of interest. I found some shirts, two coats, several pair of pantaloons, a few surgical books and papers and a treatise on bleeding, a set of rusty scalpels, a pair of gloves, and a razor which my wife had given me. Still, I thought, there was no use letting good clothing rot, and I went to work to hang up the coats and pantaloons, which were still quite serviceable. As I took out the top one and shook it out for the hanger, a sheaf of papers fell from it and fluttered to the floor in zigzag swoops. Most of them were receipted bills or penciled notes—once urgent, now dead as yesterday's newsletter. One, however, looked like a sealed letter. It swooped this way and that and then skated across the floor and under the bed.

I got down on my knees and gathered up the papers, retrieving the envelope under the bed last. All were familiar but that one, and as I got to my feet I turned it over and over in my hands, looking at it and wondering what it contained. It was sealed, and addressed to me in a small hand, and I wondered why it had not been opened. Then slowly it came to me. I remembered my host fetching it to me, on the night of my departure; how I had told him to put it on the bed—that I would read it later. I even remembered now packing those papers away in that especial spot. I must have gathered it up with the rest, I told myself, and packed it away. Well, it could not be helped now. I might as well see what was in it. Incuriously, I slit it open and spread it to the light to read.

DEAR TOM [it read],

I dare not address you as beloved for fear you will tear this up unread. I know you would hear the least detail of the least quarrel between the least of your slaves before you would judge them. Then, hear, I beg you, the plea of your adoring wife.

My dearest one! Please read this to the end. If after that you still feel as you now do, then I know what I must do. No blame shall be attached to you for it!

It would be simple for me to say that he forced me; that what you saw was not what it must have seemed to you. I have thought of it from your viewpoint, and I can see how it must be to you. Yet that is the plain truth. But there is more behind it. I will come back to that in time. What else there is to say, I feel you must know. Too long this has lain between us, and I must tell you everything and trust in your mercy and sweet, generous nature to believe in me. If this fails I have but one course left, loving you as I do.

I met Ben Price whilst I was visiting a cousin in Boston. He was then a student at Harvard—and not doing well. I was as giddy then as I have always been. He was handsome. I thought myself attractive. We were attracted to one another; not spiritually, as I have been to you, and I hope you have been to me, you understand, but purely in a physical way.

I managed to resist him during my stay in Boston, and so preserved my chastity—doesn't it seem silly that I ever had any? Oh God, I am an evil woman! But if you will only love me, Tom, I can mend my ways and be yours alone!

But to get back to my story; when he failed at Harvard, but a few weeks later, Ben followed me to Salem. He called on me, secretly, and made advances—not once but several times—which I was still sufficiently virgin to resent. I saw my danger, and I realized his attraction for me. I told him that he would never have me but by marriage, and that he scoffed at. I called on Captain Webb, who was an old friend, and told him that I would never be free of this man until he was removed from my neighborhood. I know what Captain Webb thought, but I did not care. I was afraid.

And so I arranged with Captain Webb to carry him off in his ship— and at that point you stepped in. You found him where Captain Webb's men had dropped him, alarmed at your approach. You saved his life and brought him back to health. And when we met that day upon the street it seemed to me that this was a thing I could not combat. I thought then destiny had singled me out for him—a woman likes to be pursued. It is flattering to her vanity. God forgive me, in you I thought I saw a means to rouse him to the marrying stage! But that was before I knew you, my sweet!

You know something of what followed. I thought to play you against him, hoping to force him to me. Instead he married the Nowell girl, purely out of spite for me, I am still convinced. Then, to show him that it meant nothing to me, I turned to you, flaunting you in his face as much as I could, never thinking, my darling, what I might be doing to you in the process!

I taunted him, little fool that I was, and he rose, as I thought, to the bait. Actually, I was the one that rose. On our picnics he had me. It did not occur to me that I was the victim of our game. I thought, with peculiar conceit, that I was but showing him what he had lost in marrying another. Then I discovered my condition and knew that I, not he, was likely to suffer by it.

It was then that I trapped you, my beloved. I admit it now. You see, my sweet, I did not know you then as I do now. That only came later.

I trapped you, and you found me out and left me, and it was only then, darling, that I suddenly appreciated your worth and all that you meant to me. I saw you as the equal of dozens of Ben Prices, and when you came back to me—darling, my cup was full as only the cup of a woman loving and beloved can be full! I knew that I was not alone in your heart. But I was content with a tiny corner of it, that seemed to me to be growing larger. I was a faithful wife to you, my dearest, from that day, and even before.

I know you may sneer at that. Yet it is but the simple truth. I had not seen Ben, except in your company or Father's, while he was alive, since your return. I did not want to. I love *you,* my darling, no other!

But Thursday he came to the house, after you had gone, all smiles and most gracious, and said that he must see me about this office you are building. He teased me along, saying we must put our heads together to give you a surprise, so that it would be something more than you had expected. Naturally I fell in with this, and he fetched out plans and started to show them to me. I leaned over them, and it was then that he seized me in his arms before I could protest. He had his one arm about me, holding me, and with his other hand he tore my dress down the front. I would have cried out, but he bent me backward and kissed me so that I could not open my mouth. I reached up and caught his ears and cheeks and tried to push his face away—and that was the moment at which you entered!

My dearest one, I am not lying! I do not know upon what I can swear to you that you will believe, and yet it is true!—it *is* true! Ben Price I hate. I would see him hanged and not lift a finger in his defense! But you, my dearest one, I adore, and rather then endure your evil opinion I will do away with myself. I have been far from perfect. In fact I have been deeply blameworthy. If you can find it in your heart to forgive me, then life's cup for me will be filled to overflowing and God's face will shine upon me! If you do not, then I cannot bear to live!

I do not mean this as a threat. I do not seek to force you. If you do not believe what I have written here—which is God's truth—ignore me. I shall not fear to die, having lost you. What is life?

I shall wait three days for your answer. After that, my dearest, you will not have to worry more about me.

Ever your most adoring wife,

SELINA

9

I THINK there is nothing in this world so bitter as the knowledge that we have done an injustice for which we cannot make amends. The impact of Selina's last letter can be imagined! Had I not been careless, had I read the letter, I would certainly have agreed to talk with her; I might even have been convinced. By overlooking it I had condemned her to death!

That, at least, was how I felt. I did not now question her. The facts were too neatly aligned to leave any doubt in my mind. No! I had killed her. Worse! I had killed her and she was innocent of the crime of which I had accused her! As I read the letter a desperate sort of numbness settled upon me, and when I had finished it I sat for God alone knows how long, staring at it between my fingers, with a sense of horror that is indescribable. Presently I turned it over and began to read again, piecing out the phrases and the sentences, slowly, lest I might have misunderstood them. And as the realization of their unequivocal meaning came home to me I began to feel a sensation of self-disgust that was physical in its violence. My gorge rose within me, and I fought against gagging nausea like a man drunk and fighting for breath. Then, when this first wave of retching passed, I sat numbed in mind and body, unable to think, unable to move; able only to stare dully at my hands and the paper in them, thinking her name over and over again.

I have no more idea now than I had then how long I sat so, crushed by the horror of the news and stricken with the enormity of my crime. As I sat the daylight faded and darkness fell, and after a time there came Matt Turner, rapping at my door and asking if I would not be down to sup.

I did not at first hear him. Indeed, I was so absorbed in my misery that I was not aware of him until he became alarmed at my lack of response and rattled at the latch, crying out:

"Are you all right sir? Is aught amiss?"

"Go away!" I replied dully.

But this he would not do until he had satisfied himself about me. He opened the door and thrust his head into the room, eying me curiously through the twilight gloom.

"Do ye not intend to sup, Doctor?" he asked. "If ye wish, I'll have ye served here in your room."

His eyes missed no detail of the scene, dusky though it was, and they raked across me and the open chest and the crumpled letter in my hand.

"Is there aught—can I do anything, Doctor?"

"No! No!" I rasped impatiently. "Go away and leave me be. I've no appetite."

It was rude, I own, but I was not in a state to remember my manners. He opened his mouth as if he would say something, then closed it again with an angry snap and drew back.

"Very good, sir!" he said, and shut the door.

This passage is, in itself, indicative of my state of mind, for in the ordinary course of things, I think, I am rather overly inclined to courtesy than the opposite. However, it served to rouse me. When he was gone I stirred uneasily, and presently, rising, lit a candle and reread the letter. In that rereading, while I lost none of my anger at myself, it seemed to me that if anyone was more to blame than I, it was Ben Price. Through the whole sorry business he had flitted like an evil ghost. Each fresh turn of tragedy had stemmed directly from his spite. His marriage to Patience and his subsequent continuing pursuit of Selina; her shame, her heartbreak, even her death were all the results of his vindictiveness. His endless demand for payment for his injured vanity had caused more misery to more pe_ than he himself could suffer if he lived a thousand ye_ was not right, I told myself, that he should be the c_ this and yet go untouched himself. Let him see_ done! Let him read this letter! Let him know_ ness and vanity had brought about! Sho_ stain he carried now upon his immorta_ or no! After that, if he could still s_

after that I had no plan, only a sort of a dull fury. After that
—— Well, we would see. But first my one thought was to
show him the results of his handiwork. I folded the letter carefully and put it in my pocket. After that I picked up my hat
and went out.

In the dark street I turned in the direction of the Nowell
house. There I found no light outside the door, but I knocked,
and a moment later Patience opened to me.

"Why, Tom!" she exclaimed at sight of me, with what I
thought was somewhat forced gaiety. "You've been such a
stranger, what brings you here tonight?"

I was in no mood for jocularity.

"Where's Ben?" I demanded curtly.

She hesitated, glanced at me, and then stood aside.

"Come in," she said.

I entered, following her into the familiar great room, where
she went to stand with her back to the fireplace, almost defiantly, facing me.

"What do you want?" she asked.

"Where's Ben?" I repeated doggedly.

"What do you want of him?" she demanded firmly.

"I have something here I think he should see," I said.

"What is it?"

It came to me that she too had a right to know. Silently I
handed her the letter. She took it hesitantly and began to read,
then, after scanning the opening lines, shook her head.

"But——" she began.

"Read it!" I commanded her harshly.

In silence then she obeyed. When she was done she glanced
up at me with a sharp little indrawn breath.

"Oh, Tom—no!" she exclaimed.

I nodded toward the letter.

"You see what it says," I replied.

She dropped her eyes to the paper once more, horrified.
Then, all at once, I saw her frown slightly.

"But—but," she said, looking up at me again with a puzzled
stare, "I don't understand. This date——"

As calmly as I could I explained to her what had happened:
how the letter had come for me whilst I was packing; how I
had told Turner to leave it with the other papers upon the

bed; and how, at the last, I had inadvertently packed it without reading it, and only now had come upon it.

As she listened her face drained white. When I had done she gave a little cry.

"Oh, Tom! How horrible!"

"Do you think I don't blame myself?" I replied bitterly. "I should have read it. Even without reading it I should have known—I should at least have listened!"

"It was that night you came looking for him?"

I nodded.

"You frightened me!" she said.

"I didn't kill him on your account," I told her. "It seemed more fitting to fetch him back; to force him to keep the bargain he made with you. I thought you'd want it that way."

She smiled a little bitterly.

"You think life with me a punishment?"

"I didn't mean that!" I cried. "Pat! I didn't! If you only knew!"

She looked at me quickly.

"If I knew what?" she asked.

I reached out and caught her to me roughly.

"I love you!" I exclaimed. "I've always loved you."

She did not resist when I kissed her. Indeed, it seemed to me that for an instant she clung to me. Then, gently, she put her hands upon my breast and thrust me back.

"No, Tom—no!" she whispered.

"Pat," I protested, "don't you see? He had your love. I could not let him throw it away. If I could not have you, he, at least, could not abandon you!"

"But Selina?" she asked soberly. "You loved her."

I made a desperate gesture.

"Can't you see?" I cried. "I came to love her. But that was after you and Ben were married!"

She looked startled, but I hurried on.

"If Ben had made you a good husband, if I had not been such a blinded fool, we might have been happy. But I could never have loved her, Pat, as I have loved you!"

She stared at me dully.

"Can you say that with her letter in your hand?"

I felt suddenly shamed.

"Pat!" I cried. "I mean no harm to her or her memory. Had I known this before I left, it might have made a great difference. But I did not know, Pat! I knew then only what I have told you. That I loved you, and that he was responsible for everything! That hasn't changed! He's still responsible. Where is he, Pat?"

She stared at me as if I were the devil tempting her.

"He—he's gone away," she whispered.

"Then come away with me!" I exclaimed. "Let's forget him! He doesn't deserve your consideration!"

She turned from me abruptly, resting her head upon the mantelpiece.

"Pat!" I cried, reckless.

She waved me away with one hand.

"I—I can't, Tom!" she said. "You should not ask it!"

"Then tell me where he's gone," I persisted. "I'll follow him and we'll have this out—once and for all!"

She turned about on me with such a look of sudden fear that I was startled.

"No—Tom, no!" she cried.

"Yes!" I said. "Tell me—or I will find him for myself!"

She flung herself upon me and clung to me.

"No, Tom!" she cried. "You mustn't!"

But I was not to be put off this time.

"My dear," I said, "I made that mistake once."

Gently I disengaged her arms and turned toward the door. But quick as light she was before me, blocking the way.

"No, Tom!" she begged. "Please! You must not! For my sake!"

I stopped abruptly.

"For your sake?" I demanded, incredulous. "Can you still say that you love him?"

She fell back from me, white as a ghost, and retreated until her back was against the wall, the back of her hand against her mouth, her great blue eyes wide and staring. For an instant I thought she was going to cry out in protest. Then suddenly she seemed to rally and gather strength. She dropped her hand and lifted her head.

"Yes!" she said faintly. "Yes, I love him, and if you kill him you may as well kill me too!"

"You can't mean that!" I cried.

She nodded doggedly.

"I do! Oh, I do!" she repeated.

For a long instant I stared at her, scarcely able to believe my ears. Then at length a sense of unbearable defeat came over me. I turned away.

"Very well," I said. "I shan't kill him. He may go to hell in his own way, for all of me!"

I picked up my hat and went to the door.

"Good-by," I said. "I shan't trouble you again."

I was out the door before she could reply. As I left the house I thought I saw the curtains move at the window. But when I turned about they were hanging motionless, and I turned away and went off in the darkness.

III

Tripoli

NOW IT MAY SEEM in this that I acted with little resolution, but it should be borne in mind that I had suffered a great shock and that I was as little ready to think matters out for myself as a newborn child is prepared to walk. On top of this, Pat's statement that she loved Ben still, despite all that he had done, came as an equally staggering blow. It was somehow as though someone I had always trusted had turned against me. I felt that the last tree in my orchard was blighted, the last structure in the village of my life destroyed, that everything that I had cherished and hoped for and loved now lay in ashes about me. I could think only of getting away. Where, I did not know, except that I no longer had any mind to seek out Ben. I had been honest enough in that. I no longer cared what he did or what became of him. I knew only that I wanted to go. I wanted to run from everything that I had known, and I was fatuous enough to believe it could be done.

In these circumstances it was not strange that I should think of the *Philadelphia*. I already had orders to join her, which I might accept or decline. I had Captain Bainbridge's letter. If I accepted, within a month or two we would sail for the Mediterranean, with the squadron being sent out to relieve Commodore Morris. A year, perhaps even more, at sea would give me opportunity to settle my thoughts, and at the end of it I would be in a better frame of mind to know what I intended to do. Perhaps, even, I might remain in the Navy and make a career for myself there. But I thought little of that yet. For the moment I was satisfied to be away.

I was near three weeks reaching Philadelphia, for I was content to go by easy stages. At New York I purchased fresh uniforms, to conform with the new regulations, as well as new instruments and texts, and, thus equipped, I reported on board the *Philadelphia* early in July.

My first impressions of the ship were favorable. She had been one of the squadron with which I had sailed in the *Essex*, on her last cruise to the Mediterranean, but on that occasion

I had scarcely noticed her, and not once had I availed myself of the opportunity to go on board. Now I found her larger and roomier than the *Essex,* albeit she was rated but four guns more than *Essex's* thirty-two. She was broader of beam and longer of keel, and I looked to find her less crowded, which, so far as I was concerned, she was, since her surgeon's mates— there were three of us—had the entire cockpit to themselves and, wonder of wonders, were able to stand upright. The ward-room, too, was more spacious, and the officers' cabins had a foot or two more space each way. In the berth deck, however, and the steerage, I cannot say that there was less crowding, for, while there was correspondingly more room, the larger complement of the ship filled the space and left each man the same room to sling his hammock and each petty and warrant the same small cubby for his use.

On reporting on board, I was taken directly to Captain Bainbridge, who welcomed me with the utmost informality.

"We'd begun to fear you weren't coming," he told me. "You had my letter?"

"Yes sir," I replied, "only a day or two before I came away. I thought I'd get here as fast, else I would have written."

"That was logical," he nodded. "No doubt some of the others have reasoned similarly."

"The others, sir?"

"Aye," he said, "I wrote to all officers, warrants, and ratings aboard the *Essex*. I couldn't wish a better lot."

My heart sank within me at the words, for I felt a warning premonition. He thrust the ship's articles across the table.

"Just sign there, Doctor," he said.

I signed, not wishing, at this point, to appear hesitant. Nor did I have time to run my eye down the long list of those who had already signed before me.

"Have many returned?" I asked.

He shook his head.

"Not many. There's Mr. Smith and Mr. Henry. And there are a number among the foremast hands."

He did not mention Ben, and so I thought no more of it. But I was no more than settled in and on my way forward to report to Dr. Ridgely for duty, when I came upon him fitting up partitions in the petty officers' mess.

At sight of him I came to an abrupt halt, and he looked up and saw me at almost the same instant. For the space of a minute we must have stared at one another in surprise and disgust. At length it was he who grated:

"What brings you here?"

The words snapped something within me, and I began to curse. I am not one who holds that an officer may behave as he wills to the foremast people. I have always deplored the tendency. But now I had no thought for that. I cursed him with every foul word and name I knew, and when I had done with that I told him that I had no mind to follow him, that I would be as pleased if I never saw him again, and that if he would leave me alone it should be truce between us.

"You may go to hell and be damned to you, for all of me," I remember saying. "I've no interest in anything you do or seek to do. All I ask is to be shut of you! Go your way and I'll go mine, and may you find bad luck in the way of it!"

"And the same to you!" he sneered, and that, for then, was the end of it.

My other shipmates I found, with few exceptions, congenial. Most of them were new to me, but Ben Smith, our third lieutenant, had sailed with us in the *Essex,* as had Bernard Henry, one of the midshipmen. Timothy Winn, who had been purser of the *Essex,* was also expected to join us, but at the last moment we heard he was shifted to the *Argus,* and his place was taken by Keith Spence, a stout, amiable, fair-faced young man who I have no doubt carried out his duties in an equally efficient manner.

For the rest I could find few with whom to quarrel. John S. H. Cox was first lieutenant, a veteran of considerable service, having entered the Navy as midshipman in '98. He was a quiet man—which a first luff should never be—with whom I had little contact. More fiery was our second luff, Mr. Jacob Jones, who also had long service to his credit. Theodore Hunt completed the roster of our deck officers, as fourth lieutenant; a quiet, unassuming young gentleman fresh from the steerage and without outstanding characteristics.

Of closer interest to me were the members of the surgical staff. John Ridgely was our surgeon: a tall, spare man, handsome in a lean way, with humorous brown eyes and chestnut

hair and a manner of listening politely to anything the least of
his subordinates might have to say, as if he valued our judgment. He was a native of Philadelphia and a thoroughly able
physician. He was also an accomplished and cultured gentleman. Unfortunately for us all, his health was poor. Jonathan
Cowdery, surgeon's first mate and my immediate superior, was
a man of different stamp. He was a small, rather pompous
person, exceedingly vain and touchy; fiery with those he could
outface, but rather fawning to his superiors. He had black hair
and eyes, a rather effeminate temper, and fine hands. He was
competent both in physic and surgery, and of all the ship's company he might best feel at home in the *Philadelphia,* for in
several years of service he had never served aboard another
ship.

The third member of our cockpit crew was Nicholas Harwood, surgeon's third mate, a gangling youngster fresh from
the classrooms and operating theater of the Philadelphia
College. He was a protégé of Ridgely's: a shy, retiring, somewhat myopic boy, but one I judged to have great promise once
he had forgotten his book learning and absorbed a little of
practical apprenticeship. With these shipmates I looked forward to a satisfying, if uneventful, cruise. At least the companionship would be reasonably congenial, and if we saw little
in the way of action, that would be no more than past experience had led me to expect. We cleared from Philadelphia on
the eighteenth of July, and within the week were well outside
the Capes of the Delaware, breasting the long Atlantic rollers
with the porpoises playing under our forefoot and the wind
a-hum in the rigging overhead.

Our crossing to Gibraltar was swift since we had, in the
main, fair winds and fine weather. In the course of it ship and
crew shook down a working unit that performed as a single
entity to the brazen lungs of Mr. Jones or the more modulated
commands of Mr. Cox. Scant five weeks after our departure
from Philadelphia found us at the Rock. Our anchor had
scarcely found holding when the consul's boat fetched out to
us news of two Tripoline corsairs, said to be cruising in the
vicinity of the Cape de Gatt.

We lost no time in questions, but cleared with the following dawn, and, after a sidelong glance into Tetuan, stood off

northeastward toward the Andalusian coast and the tawny, snow-capped ridges of the Sierra Nevada.

We did not find our Tripolines. Indeed, I doubt if they ever existed. However, in the dusk of the second evening, rounding the snout of the Cape de Gatt, we fell in with the Moorish cruiser *Mirboka,* twenty-two guns, belonging to the Emperor of Morocco and commanded by Ibrahim Lubarez, of Tangier. A little distance away, and yet clearly in company with the cruiser, was a brig of unmistakably American build.

Although, so far as we knew, we were at peace with the Moors, few of us had any reason to regard them with trust. Accordingly, we rounded to and hailed the cruiser, which, after some effort to ignore us, at length responded in barely understandable English. In the gathering dark, it seemed, Lubarez took us for an English frigate, and we saw no reason to disillusion him. By this ruse we discovered that the brig was the *Celia,* of Boston, which, Lubarez said, had sailed under his protection from Barcelona.

The story had a false ring, and before the Moor could protest we had an armed party on his deck. Ten minutes sufficed to bring to light the captain of the *Celia* and several of his crew from the hold where they had been confined after their capture by the *Mirboka.*

Peace or war, this was enough for Captain Bainbridge. Lubarez and his officers were brought on board the *Philadelphia,* and a prize crew, under Lieutenant Cox, placed on board the Moor, with orders to fetch her into Gibraltar. We then set out in pursuit of the brig, which was making off in the dark, and, coming up with her, seized her also without ceremony.

Lubarez protested at first that he meant no harm to the American vessel but merely sought to protect her. When he perceived that this would not do, he stated that he had taken her on his own cognizance. But when Bainbridge threatened him and all of his men with short shrift at the yardarm as a parcel of scurvy pirates, he produced a license from the Emperor, through the governor of Tangier, to seize and make prize any and all American vessels he might encounter on the seas.

We carried our prizes in to Gibraltar, where I believe the

British were none too pleased to see us. It was hinted that, Britain being at peace with Morocco, we must take our catch elsewhere lest their presence embroil Britain with his Barbaric Majesty. As if to emphasize their point, the commanders of the several British line-of-battle ships in the harbor proceeded to enroll certain deserters from our crew and to impress others from the prize crew of the *Mirboka,* under the pretext that they were, in spite of their sworn records, British subjects. Nor was the atmosphere ashore, between British and American officers, cordial. As a result our visit was marked with tension and ill feeling.

Fortunately we had not long to wait. The other ships of our squadron arrived by ones and twos. On 12 September came Commodore Preble, in the *Constitution,* from Boston, while two days later arrived Commodore Morris, in the *New York,* and Commodore Rodgers, in the *John Adams,* from the eastward. After that we lay in the uncomfortable atmosphere of three broad pendants, while the three commodores eyed one another with veiled jealousy.

In this interval of waiting Lieutenant David Porter came on board from the *New York,* to replace Lieutenant Cox, who was to remain as prize master of the *Mirboka* until some decision should be reached as to the disposition of that vessel. Porter was a man of whom we had already heard more than a little, for despite his youth—he was but twenty-three—he had long since made a name for himself. He proved to be a slight, wiry man, with crinkly, unruly brown hair above a high-domed forehead, large agate-hard black eyes, thin lips, and a nose and chin that seemed to draw down to point in the same, simultaneous direction. He seemed to me to have the strut and temper and the pugnacity of a fighting cock. Some who saw him had misgivings, and the crew was unhappy, for his reputation as a disciplinarian and a fire-eater, they were sure, forecast trouble. But to my way of thinking he was a cut above Mr. Cox, who, though a gentleman to the core, struck me as lacking driving force.

All of this, of course, actually concerned me little. As one of the surgical staff, I was scarcely interested in the shifts and changes of the deck, yet I watched the transposition with aloof amusement. It was diverting to see the way the midshipmen scurried about beneath the eye of this bantam rooster. Lacking second sight, I could not know the part that he was to play in my own life. Yet I must confess that from the moment I laid eyes upon him I was, in some indefinable way, drawn to him.

On the eighteenth of September we sailed, in company with the *Vixen,* to the blockade of Tripoli.

I have no mind here to go into the details of our voyage thither. It was uneventful. On the third of October we reached Malta. On the seventh we arrived off the gray coast of Barbary, where we cruised up and down and on and off and back and forth before the tawny, dun-colored forts and gleaming white cupolas and minarets of Tripoli for what seemed endless days, without so much as a sail venturing out to meet us. On the nineteenth, however, an Imperial brig, bound up for Trieste, informed us that two of the cruisers of the Regency were out in search of prey. At once Captain Bainbridge dispatched the *Vixen* to westward, to Cape Bon, considering that to be the most likely point at which to fall in with them, while the *Philadelphia* continued on her blockading station. Three days later there came up a very heavy gale out of the northwest, which drove us far to the eastward. It was more than a week before we could regain our station and see the terraced walls of Tripoli, rising step by step from the water's edge to the desert behind. By that time the entire Tripoline Navy might have put to sea, for all we knew.

It was a fine bright day as we approached, running in from the east before a brisk wind. The northwesterly gale seemed to have cleared the haze that until a week ago had dimmed the outlines of the coast and softened the rocky barrenness of the land. As we swept along we could make out every rock and gully, every bush and hollow on the steep slope that rose from the coastal shelf to the desert plateau behind. Here and there a cluster of native huts huddled amid a scattering of palms, their color blending with the background of the earth. More conspicuous were the frequent little domed tombs, or marabewts, scattered here and there against the hillside, standing out like white stars in a dusty sky in their gleaming coats of whitewash. There was a tingling freshness and sparkle in the air, not often encountered in those latitudes, that reminded me of late summer weather along our own New England coast. It was the last day of October.

We were within five leagues of the city when the lookout's cry of "Sail ho!" sent a flame of excitement stabbing through the ship. Mr. Porter was on deck. At the cry he came about with feet widespread, bracing himself to the slight roll of the ship, his head thrown back.

"Where away?"

"Broad on the larboard quarter, sir!" came the reply, drifting down in a long-drawn-out wail from aloft.

"What d'you make of her?"

"She's a Turk, from the rig of her, sir, standing close alongshore, making for harbor, I sh'ld say."

From where I had been basking in the sunshine in the lee of the companionway, I joined the rush to the bulwarks to catch a glimpse of the stranger. Mr. Porter leaped for the shrouds and trained his glass upon her. As the frigate rose to a long swell we made her out, long and low and levantine rigged, a ship under full press of sail, scurrying along the shore, apparently in the hope of making port before we should sight her.

Mr. Porter leaped down as lightly as a cat, and even before his feet touched the deck he was bawling orders.

"All hands the watch! Lay aloft! Look alive! Up helm, there—two points to larboard. That's it! Hold her so! Steady as she goes!"

The rigging swarmed with men, scrambling up the ratlines. The topmen were already swarming out upon the yards. Pipes twittered. Commands were caught up from the deck and flung upward and outward. On the gun deck I heard the drum begin to roll. Overhead the reefs shook out of the courses. Topsails and topgallants, and the royals and skysails cascaded from their yards. There was the rumbling thunder of canvas filling with wind. The sails bellied and drew taut. The ship shuddered and then leaped ahead, the foam creaming out to either side from her bows, the spray flying, not wallowing over the rollers now, but knifing sharply through them. Behind me I heard Captain Bainbridge's voice addressing Mr. Porter quietly.

"What do you have, Mr. Porter?"

I had not heard him come on deck, and I scurried for the lee rail, where I belonged. As I went I heard Porter's reply.

"She's a levantine of some sort making up for port, sir. She's well armed. I'd say she was one of their cruisers."

The captain accepted his glass and braced himself for a look. When he lowered the telescope a grim smile of satisfaction wreathed his florid features.

"I think you're right, Mr. Porter," he said. "Can we head her off?"

Mr. Jones put in a doubtful comment.

"She has a good start of us."

"We'll have a try for it, sir," said Porter, ignoring the interruption.

"Do so!" said the captain.

"Aye, aye, sir!"

Captain Bainbridge swung for another look at the enemy, who, having observed that we had seen him, was now crowding on all sail in a desperate effort to slip inside us. After studying him closely he swung his glass along the shore toward the town and then, lowering it, scanned the water between us and the chase and then that between the *Philadelphia* and the port.

"Put leadsmen in the chains, Mr. Porter," he said. "I shouldn't like to go aground at this speed."

"Aye, sir!" Porter agreed. "No fear here. We've deep water now."

In a moment, however, the leads were flashing in the air and splashing far ahead, and the singsong cries of the leadsmen drifted back along the deck.

"By the ma-a-ark ten!—And a half ten!"

"Plenty of water so far," Bainbridge remarked.

"Aye, sir," replied Jones, "but we'll have some dodging to do before we come up with her. Mark how she weaves."

"I wish the *Vixen* were here," Bainbridge said almost querulously. "She has the draft for this sort of work. What does she log, Mr. Jones?"

The chip log was cast and showed a speed of eight and a half knots. I could not help thinking that the *Essex* would show half again as much. Still, in a vessel as large as the *Philadelphia* it seemed as though we were fairly flying. As we came into shoreward waters we too were forced to zigzag and feel our way along the winding channels, but in spite of this we managed to gain slightly.

We were not successful, however, in cutting the Turk off from the harbor. While we were yet better than a half a league from him he slipped inside us, and from that point it became a stern chase. He had the advantage of knowing his water, and made full use of it. Nevertheless, by eleven o'clock we had gained upon him sufficiently to use our bow chasers. He immediately ran up the Tripoline colors, and we fired again. Each time the long twelves thundered it was as if the frigate were struck a blow on the bows, for she seemed to stumble and shudder from the recoil, and the acrid smoke made a dense white cloud, through which we rushed as if impatient to see the results. Each time, too, we had the disappointment of seeing the plume of spray fall short of the mark by long yards.

By noon it became apparent that we would never be able to overtake her before she came under the shelter of the shore batteries. Already we were within a league of the harbor and still she was beyond reach of our fire. Nonetheless, disappointment showed on every face when the order was passed to give over the pursuit and stand off. A murmur of protest, subdued but nevertheless unmistakable, rose from the ship, and I saw men shake their heads in angry disagreement. On the quarterdeck I heard Mr. Porter protest.

"We might cut her out from under their noses, sir."

"Too risky," the captain replied. "We're not here to lose our ship, Mr. Porter. Fetch her about."

"Aye, aye, sir!" Porter replied somberly.

The great yards swung and the canvas slatted. The helm spun and the ship came about and picked up speed toward the open sea. Behind us the wake creamed, and the gap between us and the vessel we had so lately and so relentlessly pursued opened. In the chains the lead flashed and swung. The leadsman's chant came back upon the breeze.

"And a half eight—by the deep eight!" Then all at once, on a sharp, rising note of alarm: "By the mark seven—and a half six a quarter less six!"

Bainbridge's face went ghastly. He swung about.

"Port helm!" he shouted. "Hard a-port!"

The spokes of the wheel flashed in the sunlight, but it seemed an age before the ship answered. In the meantime she seemed fairly to fly across the water.

"A quarter less five!"

I saw men freeze in the rigging. Both Jones and Porter

leaped for the helm, as if to squeeze an extra inch or so of rudder from it. Dead silence fell like a blanket upon the ship, broken only by the hiss of the water overside and the leadsman's next cry:

"By the deep four!"

Only twenty-four feet of water! Less than half again our normal draft! From aloft came the sudden shout of the foretop lookout, high pitched with alarm.

"Shoals! 'Ware shoals!"

But even as he shouted came a sickening, grinding crunch from forward, followed by a crashing, tearing, rending sound. The bow reared skyward. The ship lurched to an abrupt stop. Masts and rigging whipped forward, and bowed as if to tear themselves from the decks. I snatched for a hold but went sprawling. Aloft I could see men clutch at the rigging, the spars, the ratlines. One or two, I saw, lost their footing and dangled dangerously high above the deck, safe only by their handhold. Then I found myself tumbling amid the crew of one of the larboard quarter-deck carronades. Someone fell on top of me, and as I struggled to regain my feet I saw that it was Mr. Porter. Even before I could rise I heard him giving orders.

"Carpenters! Lay below and look for damage! Aloft there! Back your wind! Brace those yards around! Blow her off again! Lively now!"

I came to my feet with my head ringing and found all about me men doing the same. Beneath our feet the deck canted aft and to larboard at an alarming angle.

"We'll never get off!" I told myself, and all about me I could see the same thought in men's eyes. As I began to collect my wits I saw that the captain was one of the few on deck who had not been knocked sprawling by the shock. He apparently had managed to save himself by catching hold of the mizzen shrouds. Yet, though he had not fallen, it was clear that what had happened was as distressing as an actual blow. His face was deathly, and he stared at Jones and Porter in dazed unbelief, unable to speak. He only blinked when Porter addressed him, and the first luff had to repeat his question before he seemed to hear.

"She's six feet out forward, sir," Porter reported, "in twelve feet of water. There's seventeen astern. The carpenters report her making no water in the hold. She'll float, sir, if we can back her off. Shall I have her lightened forward?"

Bainbridge stared at him a long moment before he seemed to understand. Then with a weary gesture he nodded.

"Why," he cried plaintively, "why always to me?"

He shook his head savagely.

"Fetch the guns aft, Mr. Porter," he commanded. "Cut away the anchors. Start the water in the hold and pump her dry. Let's see if that does it."

"Aye, aye, sir!"

The desperate agony of the hours that followed cannot be described. They were hours of toil for officers and men alike. Yet none complained. Indeed we welcomed violent occupation, for only by keeping our hands and backs busy could we drive from our thoughts the consequences of failure. We had no illusions as to the mercy of our captors should we not win free. Like the rest, I turned to and pulled and hauled wherever a hand seemed needed.

Yet we gained nothing. The anchors were cast loose forward, and the water casks emptied, and the hold pumped dry. All guns were run aft to weight the stern, yet we budged not an inch. As a next resource all but the stern guns were thrown overboard. So was everything else heavy and movable. But not so much as a tremor indicated that she was sliding, even a few inches, toward freedom. Nothing appeared to have the least effect. The tide was falling, and for each inch that we gained by lightening her we lost a corresponding amount in depth overside. As minutes turned into an hour, and as other hours came and passed, faces aboard grew longer and more apprehensive, more urgent, more haggard. A dozen times I found myself pulling at Ben's elbow. Yet when he looked at me it was without recognition. As if, indeed, he could not see me. I knew his fear.

We had reason for fear. The enemy was not idle. He was quick to see our predicament, and he swarmed out to add to it. Within an hour there were four gunboats, felucca rigged, lying astern of us like harpies waiting for the feast. They fired on us from a respectful distance, but their shot fell far short. For a time we were able to hold them off with the stern chasers. But after a little the falling tide caused us to heel over still more sharply, and we were unable to bring our guns to bear. Seeing this, a number of other gunboats came out, while those already on station grew bolder and drew closer, choosing to approach upon our lee quarter, where it was obvious that we could but shoot down into the water. On the weather side two or three came within range, but when we tried to depress our guns enough to hit them, we set fire to the side of the ship and only with difficulty, on that sloping deck, managed to put the fire out. Meanwhile the gunboats lay out of harm's way and continued to pour their fire at us.

Fortunately they either shot wild or aimed their fire into our rigging, which took little damage from them. Had they chosen to lie closer and rake our decks they might easily have done so with dreadful slaughter. But either they had too much respect for us or they wished to have us alive and whole, for they did not make the attempt. For my part I own the sound of their shot whining through the rigging overhead was enough to send cold prickles chasing down my back, and each time a gun boomed aboard the gunboats, no matter how far away she might be lying, I would involuntarily hunch my shoulders and draw down my head.

Toward four o'clock Porter confessed his despair to Captain Bainbridge, his expression bitter.

"We've jettisoned everything movable, sir. Shall we——"

He hesitated. I wondered if he meant to touch off the magazine. But evidently Bainbridge was a better mind reader than I. He nodded.

"Cut away the foremast, Mr. Porter, and call all the people aft," he said. "If that doesn't move her——"

The carpenters went to work at the tall mast, their axes flashing in the late sun, while other hands cleared the rigging. It was hard cutting through the seasoned wood—nothing like chopping down a green tree. But at length the mast quivered, swayed, and then, slowly at first but with gathering speed, fell, measuring its length across the larboard bulwarks.

As it crashed we could make out the way the gunboats that ringed us about inched forward, like a pack of wolves, licking their chops. At a command all hands lay aft, to bring such weight as was possible astern, to lift up her bows and, if luck held, to float her off.

But luck was against us that day. She did not budge. Captain Bainbridge looked about at the crowded deck.

"All right, lads," he said, "that's the best we can do. Lay forward now and look to your things. Burn anything you'd not want to fall into their hands."

He turned to the lieutenant of the Marines.

"Mr. Osborne," he said, "keep your men posted to hold them off with muskets! 'Tis all we have now."

The quarter-deck emptied. A chain shot howled through the air overhead. Involuntarily I ducked, and in the same instant I caught the captain's eye. He smiled faintly and, I thought, encouragingly. His face was white, but he did not flinch. After that I did not duck, although it took an effort. I sneaked a quick glance at Porter. He was stiff as a ramrod, waiting. Jones was leaning against the bulwark, examining his fingernails with elaborate unconcern, but even from where I stood I could see that they were black with the day's labor. He did not seem to notice. Cowdery and Harwood stood beside me; the former biting his lips, the latter, like myself, frankly apprehensive. Dr. Ridgely stood close behind the captain. He had been suffering from a fever, but now he seemed calm and cool.

The captain turned to face us, his officers.

"Gentlemen," he said, "it will soon be dark. We can bring no guns to bear. I think you all understand what that means. We have two alternatives: surrender, or blow ourselves and our ship into eternity."

He looked about the circle of white, drawn faces, and his own features held the bitterness of failure.

No one spoke. A gunboat, bolder than the rest, fired at almost point-blank range. I felt, rather than heard, the blam of her guns. New rents appeared in the sails above us. Bainbridge seemed to shake himself.

"Very well, gentlemen," he said, "since you leave it to me to speak. We have three hundred men aboard. Can you or I assume responsibility for those lives?"

Porter's glance swept left and right the faces of us all. No one spoke, but it seemed to me some message passed from each one of us to him. His eyes rested longest upon Jones's. Then he turned away abruptly and faced the captain.

"Surrender, sir?"

Bainbridge nodded almost imperceptibly.

"Very well, sir!" said Porter formally.

A flicker of relief crossed Bainbridge's drawn features. Porter turned.

"Mr. Jones," he said, "will you————"

"Just a moment, Mr. Porter," Bainbridge interrupted him. "We must overlook nothing. Have the carpenters see that she cannot be floated, and make sure the pumps are choked. After that have every man collect that which he would take with him. Then————"

"Aye, aye, sir!" said Porter.

It was quiet in the cockpit, almost too quiet. The deck canted at an uncomfortable angle that made it necessary to pack our sea bags all in a heap in the lower larboard corner. When we tried to walk up the deck to find some particular object that we wished to take with us, we slid back, so that it was necessary to creep on all fours, and even while we packed we felt the ship lurch and settle a little further in her rocky cradle. Cowdery was subdued and quiet. Harwood, on the other hand, seemed to me more excited, livelier than usual—the effect, no doubt, in both cases, of the strain we were under. I wondered if I were similarly affected. Each one of us packed a bag of clothing and a chest of instruments, texts, and such edible delicacies as we could find.

"They'll not let us keep them," Cowdery said, "but we might as well try!"

"I'm going to take my money in a belt about my waist," Harwood put in.

It seemed a good idea. Both Cowdery and I followed suit. We were half packed when a midshipman came with a message from Dr. Ridgely to be sure to take the medicine chest. We were securing this when the ensign came down, and though we could not see it, we could feel the shudder of despair that ran through the ship. Yet when we came on deck the Tripolines had made no move toward us, and Mr. Jones was going off in the jolly boat to assure them that we had actually surrendered. Only then did they sweep toward us, close enough for us to make out the eager, swarthy faces that lined the rails, topped with twisted rags of turbans and greasy *chéchias* and punctuated at intervals with gleaming swords and scimitars. From the skylight of the captain's cabin came the smell of burning papers. Mr. Porter, in full dress, paced the quarter-deck, one eye cocked upon the oncoming flotilla of gunboats, the other turned with occasional restlessness upon the captain's hatchway. But not a word escaped him, and to all intents and purposes he was ready and capable of assuming full command.

Only an instant before the first gunboat hove alongside did Captain Bainbridge appear. When he did Mr. Porter went back to his post by the binnacle, while his eye swept the crowded waist, where the men waited.

"Remember," he said in tones that carried to every corner of the deck. "No resistance! Your lives depend upon it."

Captain Bainbridge seemed to sag. His ordinarily jovial features were set in lines of pain. We knew he blamed himself for our situation, and it would do no good to say that we, at least, held him blameless. He turned to Porter.

"Is she scuttled, Mr. Porter?"

"Yes sir," Porter nodded.

"The pumps choked?"

"Yes sir."

"The magazine flooded?"

"Yes sir. Everything is done."

The captain shrugged heavily.

"Well, then," he sighed, "let them come!"

2

THEY CAME, not more than a minute later, swarming over the side, to larboard first and then upon the weather side, blackening the bulwarks like a horde of insects, crawling and brawling among themselves to be first over. I shall not soon forget that sight, for if I had been uneasy as the shot whined overhead, I knew real fear as I saw those snarling, fighting, ragged pirates pour aboard. They were dirty. They were tattered. Most were stripped to the waist. All were barefooted, and they carried their pistols thrust in the waistbands of their oddly shaped, bag-seated breeches; their wicked-looking, ugly, heavy-bladed, curved scimitars and yataghans were in their hands, or even clenched between their teeth, as they clambered over the side.

Obviously these were the weapons with which they meant to deal with us, if dealing were necessary—and from their expression I judged they hoped it would be. Most of them were ferociously mustachioed. All of them were lean, all of them dark—of a color difficult to distinguish from dockside dirt. And it was clear that our very helplessness roused them to fanatic fury against us. Their eyes rolled wildly and they bared their teeth and yelled or snarled words in their own peculiar babbling tongue whose meaning was unmistakable. As they spewed over our rail I felt my stomach turn within me, and my knees seemed to go flaccid. On my tongue I tasted the bitter, sour taste of fear.

They came aboard first amidships, pouring into the waist, clearly without leaders, for they fell at once upon the men huddled there and began stripping them of belongings, clothes, even snatching rings from their fingers. Several of them fell to fighting among themselves over some particularly choice bit of loot.

On the quarter-deck we were, for a moment at least, somewhat better off. One or two ventured a step or two in our direction but, possibly awed by the captain's black brow and gold braid, stopped and returned to the melee amidships, doubtless fearing the wrath of their own superiors if the officers were touched before they had had their chance. This breathing spell, however, was short-lived. Still another gunboat came up close under our counter and spewed its plundering horde upon the quarter-deck. I saw Porter and the captain whip out their swords and present them—point first—at those who would lay hands upon them. I heard Porter's carrying voice:

"Hands off, you dogs! Where are your officers?"

Then someone seized me by the arms and clutching fingers plucked at the braid and buttons on my coat while still others snatched at my boots.

I struggled. It may have been wrong, but I was not ready to have greasy hands laid upon me. Almost before I knew it I was surrounded, borne down beneath the weight of numbers. I smelled the stench of sweaty, unwashed bodies, strong of mutton tallow and rancid sheep's grease. Fists pummeled me. A knife slashed my cheek—fortunately no more! I felt my coat split up the back, my boots slide from my feet. I struck out indiscriminately, this way and that, and felt the rugged satisfaction that comes with crunching bone and smashing flesh beneath my knuckles.

Then all at once there were others amongst us. I saw the scimitars flash, and the group about me faded and fell back. There was a new group here, as fierce as the rest, but better dressed and fighting as if they knew what they were about.

Whatever they might be at, we were not objects of their attack. It needed an instant to clear my head and regain my feet. When I did I saw these newcomers in among their own people with blades flashing, eyes akindle, shouting, cursing. I saw a Turk slice off another's head, who was throttling our purser, and the blood spurted from the stump of his neck square into Mr. Spence's face in a stream that was like the starting of a barrel's bung. I saw another chop off the hand of a villain that was reaching for our captain's epaulet, as clean and unconcerned as if he had been chopping corn! Closer by, one snatched at me and thrust me behind him, holding me there against the bulwark, while he struck out at his countrymen who surrounded us, driving them back.

For a moment I was confused by all of this. But then, as I shook my head and fetched back some of my wits, it came to me that these were, no doubt, the officers of the gunboats who meant to make us prisoners and hold us—either to plunder themselves or to carry before their own higher authorities, as their orders might dictate. In the instant in which I realized this I glanced about and saw that it was everywhere so. Even in the waist these more disciplined ones were taking charge and driving back the initial wave of murderous looters. Our men down there were scarcely fit for decent exposure. More than half were stripped naked as the day they were born. But they had their lives, and the officers of the gunboats were seeing to it that they were allowed to keep them—more were they using their swords in enforcing the command.

Some semblance of order was brought to our decks by this means, and after this battle amongst themselves was over, we were ordered over the side into the boats to be taken ashore. The officer who had rescued me, a swart-faced young Levantine barely my own age, turned to me and, taking my arm, pointed with his sharp-curved sword.

"Go—*inglesi*—you go!" he said.

I pointed to my loblolly boy, in the waist, and asked if he could not go with me, but he shook his head violently and prodded me toward the side. I reached for my sea bag and medical chest, but he thrust before me and by gestures indicated that I was to take nothing but go at once. I ventured to remonstrate, trying to point out to him that these were only my personal belongings, my clothes and the like, and showing him in pantomime that the tattered shirt and ripped breeches that my struggles had left me were hardly fit for me to wear. Nevertheless he would not let me have them. Instead he patted my shoulder with much nodding, giving me to understand that they would be brought to me on shore, and then, seizing me by the arm, hurried me to the side and helped me over the rail, picking my pocket, as he did so, of what few dollars I had left in it.

He did not find the money that I had rolled in a napkin and strapped about my waist, but this was only a matter of luck. Had he suspected its presence, I have no doubt he would not have hesitated to chop me in half to get at it. In the boat that lay close overside I found a scene of wild confusion. A number of Turks, in the stern sheets, had stripped Harwood naked as he came from his mother and had discovered his money, over which they were quarreling amongst themselves. The carpenter, Mr. Godby, lay unconscious across a thwart, where the milling crowd surged back and forth across his still form without regard for his unresistant figure. Among others, I saw Ben cowering against the gunwale, seeking to protect himself as best his nearly naked condition would permit. Seeing another boat alongside, filled mainly with our officers, I tried to make my way into it. But almost immediately I found myself surrounded by four or five Turks with drawn swords, who threatened me and made as if to strip me, as they had done the others in my boat.

I pretended to submit, and then, as one approached, thrust him violently against the others and leaped up on the gunwale. There one seized me by the leg, but I planted my foot in his face and kicked with all my strength, making him reel backward. Then, seeing my chance, I leaped, and landed safe aboard the other boat, where it seemed to me the Turks were somewhat more civil.

I had not much chance to see who might be my companions in the boat. Mr. Osborne, of the Marines, I noticed, and Mr. Knight, our sailing master, as well as Dr. Cowdery, Mr. Hunt, and three or four of the midshipmen. The rest I had scarcely time to see when I was forced, at sword's point, to seat myself upon a thwart and take an oar. In this condition we were forced to row toward the town. But when we had got near the landing place we were ordered to cease rowing by signs and gestures, and as the boat lost way two of them came to me and, after dealing me a severe blow on the side of the head with the flat of a sword, fell upon me and stripped off the remains of my shirt and bore me to the bottom of the boat.

I need not say that I struggled with all the force at my command. But they were too many for me. Having stripped me down to the waist and found my improvised money belt, they took that from me and extracted from it the gold I had secreted there as well as my case of surgical knives. They then turned their attention to my pockets, taking all that had been left in them by the Turk who had seen me over the side. My watch, my tinder and snuffbox, the key to my chest, even the ring on my finger that Selina had given me long since and that I valued above anything else that I owned; and, indeed, I counted myself fortunate that they did not cut off my finger to come at the ring, as I doubt not they would have done had they found it anyway difficult to remove.

Having finished with me, they turned their attentions to my companions, and not until they had served all alike, and we stood with only our ragged breeches to our name, were they satisfied. This done, they forced us once again to the oars and made us row in to the stone quay, below the bashaw's palace.

By this time it was quite dark. Yet the quay, as we approached it, was ablaze with torches, and what we saw awaiting us did little to allay our apprehensions. In the flickering light it looked as though half the city had turned out to usher us on shore; men, women, and children, some in rags and some in robes; the women swathed to the eyes in white haiks, the children, often as not, stark naked from their filthy little bellies down. All of them stared at us in silence, with black eyes that glittered ominously. As we climbed up the moss-covered steps of the quay I felt myself jostled by Cowdery and heard his hoarse whisper in my ear.

"God help us if they turn us over to that mob!"

That, however, was no part of our captors' intention. As we came out upon the quay and were mustered there by our guards, an angry howling went up from the crowd, and the foremost among them surged forward. But other guards, posted along the water's edge, stepped in to meet them with drawn swords, and after a brief tussle the crowd fell back, muttering, growling, shouting what could only be curses at both us and our guards. In the torchlight I could see the wicked blades flicker; saw one lad who could scarce have been more than eleven split from neck to navel with as little concern as I myself would slit a trout. The act seemed scarcely noticed by the spectators. Indeed, if anything, it seemed to increase their anger toward us. From somewhere in the shadows a stone hurtled to take Mr. Osborne in the cheek and open a gash three inches long. Others followed, and with them a shower of filth and spittle that smeared us from head to foot. In response half of our guards rushed into the throng, driving them still farther back upon the quay, while the rest hurried us forward to a gate in the palace wall.

Only when we were inside the gate did the shower of missiles and curses die out behind us. There we found ourselves in a sort of formal garden, also lighted by torches, and here we were permitted to wait in such comfort as we might make for ourselves while more boatloads of our companions were fetched in to join us. As we waited I looked at Cowdery, and saw that he had not escaped unscathed. A stone had struck him just beneath the eye, and it was puffed half shut, while the cheek below it was blue and bruised. His hair and his body was matted with filth, and he looked as if he had not been shaved in a week. Nevertheless he was able to grin at me.

"You're a sight!" he exclaimed.

"I'll agree with you," I replied, "if I am no more than half as filthy as yourself!"

He held out a piece of a rag to me, evidently clutched from his shirt as they had torn it from his back.

"Here," he said, "wipe the blood from your chin."

For the first time I realized that my own cheek had been cut. I took the rag and mopped at my face.

"What d'you suppose they mean to do with us?" I said.

"We're safe for the moment," he replied. "I doubt they'd have been so solicitous if they'd meant to harm us yet."

I had to admit that there was sense in what he said, and my spirits rose somewhat with the thought. After a time another boatload or two of our fellows joined us, and then just as we began to think we might wait there the rest of the night, an officer appeared and held a consultation with our guards. A moment later we were herded together and driven across the garden and into the great mud-colored building.

We were led in through a small door, keyhole arched and flanked by marble pillars and a pair of tall black mameluke guards in white chéchias and scarlet bournouses and luxurious soft leather boots. At the time I was too miserable to do more than glance at these in passing, but I was later to find them generously sprinkled all about the palace and the palace grounds. I learned then that they formed a special troop—and a particularly privileged class—whose chief function was to guard the bashaw's person wherever he went.

We were driven along a tiled corridor and up a flight of wide steps, to emerge presently in a vast chamber, some fifty feet long by thirty wide, whose ceiling was elaborately worked in carved plaster arabesques and whose walls and floor were lined with exquisite mosaic tile. Tall, narrow windows overlooked the gardens, each window topped with the traditional horse-shoe arch of the East. The side of the room opposite the windows contained a series of doors, similarly arched, which I judged could be thrown open to make the room even larger, while at either end of the chamber triple arched doorways, without closing portals, opened, through short passages, into still other chambers as large as that we were in. Above these doorways balconies of brown latticed woodwork thrust into the chamber, and behind this grillwork we could catch occasional glimpses of movement—the white flicker of cloth or a brief glimpse of a curious eye—and the rustling and whispering and tittering of women's tongues.

All of this we saw at a glance as we entered. After that glance, however, our eyes were drawn to a cluster of men grouped at the upper end of the room, about a large scarlet cushion, the size of a great round bed, topped with numerous smaller cushions of green and yellow and brown and red. No one occupied this evident seat of honor at the moment, though it was apparent that one of two must occupy the place.

These two stood somewhat apart from the rest, and from the deference the others showed them it seemed apparent that they must be persons of considerable importance. One was a mild-seeming man, rather short and inclined to be softly plump. I would have guessed his age at around thirty-five. His pudgy features were cast in a rich olive tint, and his little eyes were coal black. Just now he was smiling, as if very well pleased and even inclined to look upon us with gracious tolerance. He wore a caftan of white silk, over which was a bournous of light gray wool, trimmed in gold thread. On his head was the inevitable chéchia, with its long black tassel, in this case bound round with the long white turban indicating that its wearer was a hadji— that is, he had made the pilgrimage to Mecca.

This was Yusuf Karamauli, bashaw, and supreme ruler, of Tripoli. His companion, whom I found later to be Sidi Mohammed D'Ghies, Minister of Exterior Relations, was a taller, leaner, older man. His face was hawklike in its expression and gave an extraordinary sense of sharp, speculative intelligence, marred only by an ugly cast in one eye. A fringe of beard followed the line of his jaw to his chin, where it was meticulously parted into two well-tended points. His dress was similar to that of the bashaw save in color. His chéchia was plain, unadorned with the turban of a hadji. This man most of us were to come to know better, for it was through him that everything was done.

We were kept several minutes under their critical scrutiny, while they discussed us in much the same way that we would discuss cattle that we had just acquired. Both seemed satisfied and more than a little smug over our capture. Presently, when he had apparently had his fill of examining us, the bashaw made a gesture of dismissal, and we were herded down a corridor to another room, not dissimilar, except in size and luxury of appointments, from that we had just left. Here we found Captain Bainbridge and most of the rest of the officers, who had arrived by a previous boat. Here, also, to our astonishment, was a large table, set in the European fashion, with Neapolitan and Maltese slaves to serve us with an excellent meal of mutton and fish and fowl, and a sort of farinaceous pudding which we were told was "couscous," a number of varieties of fruit, including pomegranates and cherries, and some of the most enormous and delicious grapes I have ever tasted.

Famished as we were—for most of us had not touched food since early morning—we washed ourselves clean of the filth that had been flung at us, in basins held for us by the slaves, and then fell upon the meal without question as to such unexpected generosity. Indeed, if anything, we were encouraged by it, as a sign that they meant to deal fairly with us as prisoners of war. Captain Bainbridge, however, evidently did not share our optimism. In fact, at the moment I doubt he thought of anything save the loss of his ship, and although he must normally have felt as hungry as any of us, he could do no more than toy with his food.

When we had been fed we were all together, once more, herded into the bashaw's presence, where we found the men also mustered. There the bashaw had us formed into a half circle about him and, with obvious relish, counted us, one by one. This done, he looked upon us with evident satisfaction and spoke a few words to Mohammed D'Ghies in guttural, spitting Arabic, at which D'Ghies laughed heartily and nodded violent agreement. We were thereupon dismissed once more. The officers were again separated from the men, and conducted from his presence, by the Foreign Minister himself.

We were led through a labyrinth of passages and ante-chambers and presently were brought to what appeared to be the main palace gate. Here our guard was doubled, the gates were opened, and we were herded out, to find ourselves in the city itself.

It was night, of course, and quite dark, save for the torches carried by our guards, which cast wavering livid shadows against the blank rough walls of the houses on either hand. Here and there we passed a dark, nail-studded doorway. But in all our march, which was perhaps a mile in distance, I saw not a single window. For the most part the streets were deserted, save where we passed through the market. Here the throngs parted to watch our passage in sullen silence, but, possibly because of the large number of guards that surrounded us, we were offered neither hindrance nor insult. Beyond the

market we plunged again into a warren of twisted narrow
streets. On either side the walls rose sharply, seeming almost
to lean out toward one another overhead, and here and there
in places they were joined across the street, so that every now
and again we found ourselves walking through a black tunnel.
Underfoot the streets were haphazardly cobbled, making rough
walking, and several times we came upon tiled fountains set
into the walls. Now and again we encountered strings of asses
driven by ragged drovers in sack-brown djellabas, whose
raucous cries woke echoes in the otherwise silent streets. Once
we passed a train of lordly camels plodding on whispering,
padded feet along the rough way.

It is the smell, or combination of smells, however, which
stays with me to this day. Everywhere the stench of sewage,
from the open gutter, followed us, tinged with the sour-sweet
of rotting garbage. Now strong, now faint, this odor was
everywhere. But more permeating still, and more insistent,
was a dusty, almost earthy smell, which in the long course of
time I finally came to recognize as the peculiar smell of Africa.

We marched thus for some moments, until we came at last to
one of those great nail-studded doors set in the blank wall.
Here we were halted while a ponderous key was produced and
the door opened. Beyond the door a dark, narrow corridor led
to a spacious courtyard, crisscrossed with tiled walks and
planted with palms and orange and lemon trees and other
sweet-smelling shrubbery. Built about this courtyard, in the
form of a hollow square, was the house which we were apparently, at least for the time being, to occupy.

Here Mohammed D'Ghies motioned to the captain and Mr.
Porter and one of the guards to follow him. Together they
entered the house and were gone for some time, leaving the
rest of us to wander about the courtyard under the watchful
eyes of the guards. I cannot speak for the others, but it seemed
to me that in that quiet, almost friendly place a sort of peace
and sense of reassurance came upon me. Overhead the stars
twinkled like flecks of silver in the velvet blanket of the sky,
while the white sheen of the moon gleamed on the edges of the
palms. In that sheltered place the night wind from off the sea
was stilled and the air was mild and balmy. The city of our
enemies lay outside the walls that ringed us, and even the

guards seemed indifferent; wearied, perhaps, of brutality. It came over me then that I was very, very tired, and had I been quite sure that this was where we were to remain, I would have stretched upon the tiles and gone to sleep with only what I wore for covering. The events of the evening, however, and the uncertainty of our position; the possibility that we would again be moved, and the expectancy of something yet to happen, kept me as well as the rest of our company awake. For myself this did not matter, but I could not but feel sympathy for some of the younger midshipmen. As manly as they endeavored to be, most of them were little more than children—the youngest was thirteen—and it was clear that the experience had severely shaken them. I spoke of it to Mr. Jones. He merely snorted.

"Stuff!" he growled. " 'Twill make men of 'em!"

It was half an hour before Captain Bainbridge and the others reappeared at the door. By torchlight, then, Mohammed D'Ghies said a ceremonious farewell, unctuous with salaams, and departed through the black passage to the street. The guards took post at the entrance to the passage, apparently our only avenue of escape, and the captain came down into the courtyard and called us all around him.

"We are fortunate, gentlemen," he said. "This house was formerly occupied by our American consul. It is to be ours— our prison—for the time being. 'Tis better than I dared hope for, and probably we can stay here as long as we behave in a manner pleasing to the bashaw and his minister, or until they can find some pretext for changing our status."

I think none of us were in any doubt as to his meaning. As officers and prisoners of war we were entitled to certain courtesies. But none of us deluded ourselves with the thought that the rules of civilization would hold for an instant with our captors beyond what was to their immediate advantage.

"It won't be like home," Captain Bainbridge continued, "but we'll have to make the best of it. My greatest regret is that we will not be permitted to share it with the men."

He paused and looked sadly about the ring of sober faces surrounding him. His florid, handsome face was apologetic but a little defiant.

"Can you tell us what's to become of the men, Captain?" Jones spoke from the shadow of the palm-lined walk.

The lines in Bainbridge's face deepened. He made a gesture almost of impatience.

"They're being confined in the castle. That's all I know at the moment," he replied.

"Are they being well treated?" Jones persisted.

The captain shook his great shaggy head.

"I don't know," he said miserably. "I'm as anxious to know as yourself, Mr. Jones. I need not add that I have demanded that they be shown every consideration."

There was a brief silence.

"Will we be allowed to communicate with our friends, Captain?" Dr. Ridgely voiced the thought that was in the back of everyone's mind.

Captain Bainbridge shrugged.

"I hope so," he replied. "I hope to find a way. Mr. D'Ghies has agreed to permit the Danish consul, Mr. Nissen, to call upon me. Perhaps he can arrange an exchange of messages for us. He is very highly recommended for his sympathies by Mr. Cathcart, who was our consul here."

He broke off abruptly, as if he had said more than he had meant to say, or as if he were suddenly aware that he had held out to us more hope than he himself held in his heart. He looked about at us blankly from beneath his shaggy brows, his lower lip outthrust slightly, and his lowered, leonine head seemed to sway just the barest perceptible degree from one side to the other. It was easy to see, then, how close to utter exhaustion he was.

"I suggest, gentlemen," he sighed wearily at length, "that you get as much rest as possible now. No one knows what tomorrow will bring."

3

ON THAT FIRST NIGHT of our captivity we slept upon rush mats and a handful of blankets spread upon the bare tiles; hard beds indeed; yet such was our weariness that I doubt there was one of us but found it as welcome as the softest bed. In the morning we were visited by Mr. Nissen, whose house adjoined ours; a tall, spare, flaxen-haired Dane, with deep blue eyes and the

kindliness of a Christ. Officially, he was prepared to act as a
go-between for us in the bashaw's dealings with our own government. Unofficially, he went much further. He arranged that
we should have clothing and bedding, much of it from his own
house. He saw to it that we were fed and supplied. And he
accepted our letters to our friends and families.

These notices of our captivity were the first order of the day
for most of us. For myself, having no family and few friends,
it was finished in a moment. I contented myself with writing
a note to Patience, informing her of what had happened and
assuring her of our present safety and good health, for I had
my doubts that Ben would trouble himself to do so; doubts, I
was to learn later, that were entirely well founded.

Nissen's visit was followed by one from Mohammed
D'Ghies, who came to inform us as to what was expected of us.
We might, he told us, have the run of both our own and Mr.
Nissen's houses and their roof terraces, the Dane having already begged the privilege of his for us. We might go as far
as the gate and bargain with vendors, but we must not attempt
to go beyond. For our part we asked that the clothing and personal belongings, our medicine chests and instruments, that
had been stolen from us, be returned, and he promised glibly
to exert his best efforts to this end, all the while suavely comb-
ing his little forked beard with his long, talonlike fingers. A
request to visit our sick he evaded, promising to take the matter
up with the bashaw.

At his departure Cowdery and I, after seeing to Dr.
Ridgely's comfort, for the treatment of the previous day had
not improved his condition, undertook to explore our new
quarters. We found the house typical of the city. It was plainly
but adequately furnished save for beds, and its rooms were
spacious and ample to accommodate us all. Most interesting
to us was its style, for it abounded in little alcoves and ante-
rooms. Keyhole arches were everywhere, even at the windows.
Floors and walls were of tile to the height of a man's shoulder,
and above this walls and ceilings were of fresh white plaster,
frequently decorated with intricate arabesques.

The best feature, however, was the roof terrace and the
observatory on Mr. Nissen's house. From here we had an excellent view over the city and the sea beyond, of the cupolas

and minarets of the palace and of the oasis and the sear brown countryside. Far to the eastward, upon the reef, we could make out the wreck of the *Philadelphia,* lying as we had left her; a sorry sight, her bows still wrenched high out of the water, her stern deep in the lapping seas, and her flank canted to the empty skies. Her rigging hung in tangled festoons from the two masts that remained standing, and her general air of dejection more than matched our own feelings.

Yet we could not keep our eyes off her. Even at that distance we could make out the figures of her conquerors swarming upon her decks and scrambling in her rigging. A stream of boats passed between her and the shore, and in the streets below we could see quantities of these robbers running about in our uniform coats and breeches or carrying bits of plunder away upon their backs. It was a sight that could not but impress upon us something of the finality of our plight, and we went below wondering if we would ever see home again.

The first two days of our captivity passed uneventfully, but on the third we awoke to find the skies overcast and weather making. Early in the morning our captors took Godby, the carpenter, from amongst us, and later, from the rooftop, we saw boats put out from shore with numbers of our men and make for the wreck.

Obviously they meant to try to float her, and all day we watched and laughed confidently at their efforts, turning every now and again to test the weather.

" 'Twill storm by night," I remember Jones saying.

"If it blows hard enough she'll break up," Mr. Porter replied.

The captain himself came up to see what was passing. He looked worried.

The storm burst about nightfall, and all through the dark hours we lay and listened to the wind whistling through the shutters of our unglazed windows, to the swish of the rain as it fell in torrents, and to the thunder of the surf on the reefs outside the harbor. When we slept it was with confidence that the *Philadelphia* could not last. Yet when we rose in the morning the storm had blown itself out, the sun glinted on the green waters of the harbor and the milky blue of the seas beyond, and the frigate, to our horror and amazement, floated free.

Late that afternoon Godby came back to us, limping gingerly, his already ragged clothing in tatters.

"They made us plug the holes in her," he told us. "They wormed the shot from the pumps and forced us to pump her dry. When it came to blow from the north the seas piled up and she floated free!"

"How could they force you?" the captain burst out angrily.

The old man looked at him steadily.

"Have ye ever felt the bastinado, Captain?"

Bainbridge did not reply. Godby sat down suddenly and, painfully and laboriously, pulled off his boots, then lifted his feet for us to see. They were puffed and bruised, black and blue from heel to toe, with great welts alternating with ragged splits, still oozing blood, across them.

" 'Tis torture, Captain," the old man quavered with tears in his eyes. "We tried to refuse, but they threw us on our backs and histed our feet an' laid on with rods. That's jist one way they had o' forcin' us."

The captain ground out a curse and flung away to his own apartments.

On the following day several of us were on the roof, watching the progress of the work going forward aboard her through Mr. Nissen's glass, when Hamet, the dragoman assigned to us, came to us and told us that by order of the bashaw we were no longer to go there. The next day our new masters came and closed up the passage that led aloft. But we had already seen enough. The guns that we had thrown overboard had been raised, as well as the anchors, and it was already all too plain that our labors on board had gone for nothing.

Shortly after this event Mohammed D'Ghies sent his secretary to us with a parole of honor, written in French, which we were all required to sign. But in spite of this we were not allowed to go out upon the streets. Nor were we allowed to visit the men. Indeed our every inquiry in this direction met only with evasion. A little later still the minister himself waited upon us, his immaculate little forked beard giving him a Machiavellian look and his one cast eye staring off into space, and suavely informed us that he had managed to recover eight of our trunks, which we might have for a payment of twelve hundred dollars, as a token of friendship to himself! Needless to say, none of us availed ourselves of this opportunity.

I tell of these matters in order to show the childish capriciousness of our captors. But we were yet to experience the supreme example of this.

About a fortnight after our capture several Turks paid a formal call upon the captain and informed him that the bashaw had been told that Captain Rodgers, who commanded the *John Adams,* had treated the Tripoline prisoners, taken last summer, very badly, and that they feared we would suffer for it. Captain Bainbridge assured them that he doubted very much any such rumors, saying that that was not our way, and presently, in very friendly fashion, they took their leave.

A day or two later, however, Mohammed D'Ghies sent his dragoman to Captain Bainbridge to say that if he would send an order to Commodore Preble to deliver up those Tripoline prisoners—to the number of about eighty—we might remain where we were; but that if he failed to comply we should certainly fare worse.

Despite its seriousness, the threat was ludicrous. The idea of the captain commanding the commodore was as ridiculous as the thought of the minister sending orders to the bashaw. Endeavoring to maintain a sober face, Captain Bainbridge explained this to the dragoman, who departed growling that he would carry the message to his master. Nevertheless, about nine that evening, when we were all at table, there was a great commotion at the door, and in marched a Tripoline officer, very fierce, with pistols in his belt and a sword in his hand. The captain rose and demanded to know the meaning of this intrusion. The officer glowered and tapped his pistols.

"Tonight nothing," said he. "Tomorrow the castle!"

When morning came we were formed according to rank and marched to the castle, where we were unceremoniously thrown into the common dungeon with the men.

This was undoubtedly intended as a punishment. Yet it was certainly a greater benefit to us than to our captors. For the first time we saw our shipmates, and at first hand we were permitted to see exactly how they had fared. The dungeon was foul and crowded. Poor Ridgely, more than half sick, we laid in a corner and, arrogating authority to ourselves, commanded him to lie there. Cowdery and Harwood and myself then circulated among the men, and what we saw made our blood boil. Striped backs were common. Others had been bastinadoed, and their feet were cracked and swollen. A few had broken toes. There were a number of broken arms and wrists, and several had suffered knife wounds.

There was little we could do for them, lacking either medicines or instruments. When we asked for water from our guards we were laughed at and spat upon. But we tore our shirts and undershirts to shreds and bound up what we could, and spoke of the rest to the captain.

"What would you have me do?" he demanded.

"Whatever you can, sir," we replied. "We know your position. But if anyone can demand attention for the men, 'tis you."

He nodded sadly.

"You see where we are," he replied.

We left him then and continued to do what was possible with the means at hand. Now and again we missed a familiar face.

"Where's Brothers, McKee, Johnson, Adams, Rutherford, McLaughlin, Dowerdisher?" we would ask.

The response was surprise in every case.

"Why, sick!"

"Didn't you know?"

We hadn't known, but we did now. What had been done with our sick was a mystery to us, but we meant to find out, one way or another. If necessary, one of us could feign illness. We were agreed that could be done.

It was not necessary. After a day in the dungeon with our men we were, as suddenly as we had been escorted thither, returned to our former quarters. There we were visited by Mohammed D'Ghies, as unctuous as ever, asking how we did and what might be our wants. Upon being informed of our experience, he expressed great surprise and disclaimed all knowledge of the matter. But we knew he lied.

The event infuriated the captain, and he protested strongly to Mr. Nissen, since it was quite evidently futile to protest to D'Ghies, concerning the treatment of the men and our inability to visit our sick. As a result, a day or two later Cowdery and I were permitted to go to them.

We found them lodged in a small house without a floor, near

the palace. They were without attendants and had had nothing to eat since their removal there but filthy, sour bread. Cowdery and I did what we could, having nothing with which to treat them but our own experience. However, we now had some notion of what was necessary, and with this we returned and reported what we had found.

It was too late that day to make demands of the bashaw, but arrangements were made, through Mr. Nissen, for fresh provisions to be supplied at our expense. Later we managed to obtain leave to use the loblolly boys as hospital attendants. Hitherto these had been confined with the rest of the crew and employed in the backbreaking labor to which all the men were forced. But from this day two of them were always on duty at sick bay under the eye of a guard, returning on completion of their watch to the common prison. Since this duty freed them from harsher work, and since it enabled them to fare somewhat better than most by reason of sharing the better food now provided for the sick, they were delighted with it and frequently came to blows over whose turn it might be.

Proper medicines we could not get at this time, for the bashaw flatly refused to furnish anything. Consul Nissen furnished a few simple remedies, which was all he could spare, and we were forced, for the time being, to make do with these. However, with the assistance of the loblolly boys, we were able to clean out the hospital and to make our patients more comfortable; to see them properly fed and resting upon clean blankets, and since the greater part of their ills consisted in maladies whose principal treatment is rest and bleeding and purging and proper food, they were quick to respond.

A day or two after this one of our men, in a fit of despair, attempted to take his own life by cutting his throat. Fortunately he was observed in the act and prevented by the guards, and he was carried to our sick bay and placed in our care. Cowdery managed to check the flow of blood and to sew up the wound, and the frightened guards—frightened for they would have been held responsible for the death of a ransomable prisoner —were assured that he would recover. A little later I was permitted to call upon a Spanish physician residing in the city for medicines for Dr. Ridgely, whose condition had not improved.

Whether this was reported in higher circles I do not know, but I am certain that what followed was in some way connected with my own and Cowdery's activities at the hospital.

It was during the first week in December, after we had been prisoners for something more than a month, that Mohammed D'Ghies called upon us one day and asked, not for Captain Bainbridge, but for Cowdery and myself. Cowdery, at the time, was giving a lecture on simple anatomy, one of those courses which we officers had organized among ourselves to occupy our time, and accordingly it was I who first responded to the summons. As I entered the room D'Ghies greeted me with far more ceremony than I had been accustomed to and asked:

"Dr. Cowdery, where is he?"

"He's occupied at the moment," I replied.

"Ah!" he nodded, and eyed me gravely.

"May I serve you?" I asked.

"The bashaw would see Dr. Cowdery."

"Oh?" I said, surprised.

"And yourself, too, of course," he added hastily.

I was puzzled, for nothing of this sort had happened before. But before I could comment Cowdery appeared.

"Ah, Doctor!" D'Ghies exclaimed. "If you please, the bashaw would see you and Dr. Tisdall."

Cowdery shot me a quizzical glance, but I could only reply with the most imperceptible shake of the head. He looked back at Mohammed D'Ghies and bowed.

"We are yours to command," he said.

The minister led us to the palace, where we passed, by numerous corridors and passageways, past a score of guards, to a chamber overlooking the sea. There we found the bashaw, lying upon an immense divan, surrounded by pillows, and quite evidently not himself. Mohammed D'Ghies greeted him with the utmost ceremony, and both Cowdery and I followed his example. He waved his hand at us feebly and spoke in Arabic to his minister. D'Ghies turned to Cowdery.

"His Majesty asks that you examine him," he said, "and prescribe for his ailment."

I kept in the background while Cowdery asked a number of simple questions, the answers to which only confirmed what seemed already obvious to me, that the bashaw was suffering from nothing more than biliousness resulting from overindulgence. He was a sick man, but not so sick that a purge and a cupping would not cure him.

I knew that Cowdery must be as aware of this as I, but I kept my own counsel while he gravely took the swarthy potentate's pulse, looked at his tongue, and examined his head, neck, and chest. When he had done this he summoned me, with equal gravity, to confer with him.

"Obviously," he said with a long face, "our man is suffering a severe attack of complexus lassibonibus."

"Indubitably," I agreed.

"I would say that bleeding is indicated, followed by a diacydonium simple."

I nodded as soberly as I could, for a more harmless remedy had never been proposed.

"Yes," I said, "and I would add a decoction of epithimum to be taken at intervals of two hours."

Cowdery nodded sadly.

"If only we had them to give!"

"What do you say, sirs?" D'Ghies asked anxiously. "Is His Majesty's condition serious?"

Cowdery shook his head.

"It is not beyond cure," he replied. "We see a good deal of this among our men. Unfortunately, we have not the means to treat him or them, since everything has been taken from us."

"I have a chest——" the minister began.

"No, no!" Cowdery interrupted him. "I would not stake my reputation on medicines prepared by another. We know the properties of our own. They must be returned to us if we are to accomplish anything here!"

He turned to me seriously.

"Without the Acorus or the Calamus Aromaticus, as I prepared it, we would be lost!"

"Or the Mirabalans, or the Citron and Indian!"

"Aye, or the Emblicks, Belloricks, Polypodium, or Agrick!"

"Or the Thyme, the Calaminth, the Bugloss, and the Stoechas!"

From his couch the bashaw spoke wearily, in Arabic, to D'Ghies. The minister began what appeared to be a long explanation, but the bashaw gave a weary wave of his hand and closed the conversation with a monosyllable. D'Ghies turned to us.

"His Majesty commands that you have whatever you need," he told us, and added meaningly, "but what you prescribe must be effective."

Cowdery nodded.

"You may assure His Majesty," he said, "that, provided our chests are returned to us, with all our instruments, he may be certain of a cure."

The minister nodded and led us from the room. In an outer chamber he bade us wait.

"For what?" Cowdery demanded.

"I will have your chests fetched here."

"Oh no," said Cowdery. "We must have them fetched to our quarters and left with us, for we have not the means here to compound our prescriptions."

I thought it was on the tip of D'Ghies's tongue to refuse. Then all at once he grinned knowingly.

"Very well," he said, and sent us with a guard back to our quarters.

Half an hour later he himself reappeared followed by three slaves bearing the missing chests.

As soon as they were deposited in our rooms we examined them and found them complete. Then, while the minister waited, we prepared a simple purgative and a harmless tonic. We were then returned to the palace, but before we were permitted to revisit the bashaw we were taken to a room in which two officers of the palace guard lay squirming upon threadbare pallets.

"You see," said D'Ghies, "they suffer from the same malady that has attacked His Majesty. Treat them exactly as you propose to treat the bashaw, please."

Cowdery looked at me and winked.

"I doubt it will help them," he said. "But at least it will do them no harm."

He nodded to me, and we set to work, relieving each of a cupful of blood and administering first the purge and then the tonic. When they did not die under our hands and showed no sign of being about to, Mohammed D'Ghies seemed impressed.

* "Very good!" he exclaimed. "Now, if you will treat His Majesty——"

This was quickly done to the satisfaction of all, and the bashaw announced himself better already. When we were finished D'Ghies escorted us to his own apartments. There he turned to us with a hint of embarrassment.

"Sirs," he said, "I hesitate to ask a favor."

I wondered what was coming, but Cowdery was more perceptive.

"If we can serve you in any way, Sidi," he said, "you have only to ask."

"Thank you, Doctor," D'Ghies muttered, toying with his beard and fixing him with his one good eye. "As you have no doubt observed, I have an eye which is of no use to me as it is. I—er——"

"You would like us to treat it, is that it?"

Mohammed D'Ghies bowed.

"That is it," he replied. "It has been so since I was very young. On some days it is very poor and I can see nothing. It gives me pain. On other days it is not so bad and I can see some things."

"I see," Cowdery nodded. "I cannot promise that we will be able to do much for you, Sidi. Indeed, I doubt if anything we can do will help you. But we can try. That is if you are willing to risk yourself in our hands."

In this way our practice of medicine among our captors began. For Mohammed D'Ghies we were unable to do more than to relieve somewhat the pain he felt. His case was too far advanced and the sight of the eye was as good as gone. Nonetheless, he was grateful for our efforts, as was the bashaw, who recovered completely within a day or two. From that day we had as much as we could do prescribing for the people of the palace and other officials scattered about the city, whom we were permitted to visit pretty much at will. By way of reward, in addition to the fees we were permitted to charge, we had, once again, our medicine chests and instruments, our medical texts, and even some of our clothing, which was also returned to us.

Toward the middle of December we were startled one evening at sundown by a sudden great blowing of horns on the roof tops, supplemented by the firing of cannon on the forts and a more than ordinary hullabaloo on the part of the muezzins in the minarets. At first we were apprehensive what all this might mean, fearing some new victory by the Tripolines. But Hamet, who had just finished our daily lesson in Arabic, explained that it only marked the beginning of the month of Ramadan; in which all Moslems are called upon to fast, and no true follower of the Prophet will permit food or drink to pass his lips from sunup until sundown.

As may be imagined, this somewhat complicated our task, for the prohibition against food and drink, it appeared, extended also to medicines. However, we got around this difficulty by sleeping all day and visiting our patients by night, when whatever we ordered was taken with good grace. During this period Cowdery had the good fortune to cement our relations with the bashaw by curing his child of a particularly virulent bout of the intermittent fever; while I solidified our relations with the Porte by attending the ambassador from Constantinople. I was returning from one of my visits to this gentleman's house one evening, when I was called to while passing a coffee stall and requested to enter. Upon responding, I found the Lord High Admiral of Tripoli, no other than our old enemy Peter Lysle, the Scotch runagate, who under the name of Murad Rais had commanded the bashaw's ships which the *Essex* had so long since bottled up in Gibraltar.

He did not recognize me, nor did I refresh his memory, but he was most polite and invited me to be seated beside him among the cushions and offered me coffee in thimble-sized cups. After some polite conversation, in the course of which he inquired after Captain Bainbridge and how we did, he came to the point and stated that he had heard that I had some skill in medicine and surgery. I replied that I did my best in my humble way, whereupon he asked me if I would accept him as a patient. When I told him that I would be glad to do what I could for him, he beamed and pulled up his shirt to show me a great malignant carbuncle upon his belly. He wanted it removed, he told me, not so much because of the pain, which was negligible, but rather because of the effect it had upon his wives, who, he said, could scarcely bear to look upon it without shuddering.

I could not help smiling at the picture, but said that I would have to operate upon it. I thought it could be done without endangering him, however, and he not only was agreeable but even pressed me to perform the surgery on the earliest possible occasion. Accordingly, a day or two later I did so, making a very clean job of it. I will say for him that he scarcely flinched once under the knife, although I was obliged to go quite deep to get at the roots of the growth. He made an excellent recovery, and apparently his domestic difficulties were solved, for he was so delighted that he became a fast friend, after his fashion, and had me often to his house for supper, entertaining me lavishly with both food and drink—for, although he had turned Turk, his conscience remained elastic in the matter of alcohol. On these occasions he would have in the slave girls from his harem and have them dance for us, all the while urging me to turn my coat and settle down in Tripoli, where he vowed I could make a fortune as a physician. I confess I was sometimes tempted! He had a nice taste, quite different from that of the born Moslem, who looks upon mountains of flesh as an attribute of beauty and stupidity as a female virtue. He even went so far as to offer me my pick—barring, of course, his wives, of which he had three. But his price was too high, and I found myself always able, gently but firmly, to refuse.

Our cordiality toward one another was in no way affected by my obdurateness, and later, when he called upon me to treat his wives for various ailments of the country, I came to understand his concern over his former difficulties, for if his dancing girls were lovely, these three made them all look like broomstick witches.

By the end of Ramadan we had settled down to a routine which was not unbearable. Early in February the bashaw appointed Cowdery physician to his family and myself physician to the court. A day or two later he issued an edict permitting the officers to walk out, in groups of six under guard, about the town; and I flatter Cowdery and myself that this sudden burst of generosity was due, at least in part, to our good services.

Apart from the fact that we remained prisoners, we might have found ourselves reasonably content. A forceful reminder, however, remained of our shame. This was the *Philadelphia,*

which now lay close under the guns of the forts and within sight
from our windows. Much had been accomplished upon her.
Her foremast had been replaced and her tattered rigging repaired. Her guns had been raised and remounted; even her
anchors had been brought up and bent to new cables. Murad
Rais gleefully took pains to inform me that he had been appointed to command her and announced that within the month
he expected to put to sea, at the same time playfully jabbing
me in the ribs and bidding me mind what liberties I took with
his harem in his absence.

One afternoon toward mid-February, Cowdery and I were
called to treat the bashaw's eldest daughter, whose husband
was Minister of War. Her case was not complicated, and we
prescribed for her and left the palace a little before sundown.
As we did so Hamet called our attention to two merchantmen,
out beyond the reefs, beating in for the harbor. We looked at
them without much interest: a small brig of somehow rather
familiar lines, and a ketch of Mediterranean rig. Indeed, such
was our disinterest that we forgot to mention them in the
wardroom mess, and in consequence we were as startled as our
companions when, some time after we had rolled up in our
blankets, we were awakened by a cannon shot from one of the
forts below, followed by another and yet another, and then an
entire salvo and a sound of screaming and shouting and hubbub from the lower town.

In a flash we all threw off our blankets and flocked to the
windows, pushing and jostling for a view of what was taking
place below.

At first we could see nothing but the outline of the town
lying curved about the bay and silhouetted against a sky dotted
with small dark clouds. A curved sickle of a moon hung in one
corner, shedding a feeble light upon the roof tops, but the
harbor was black, save for the riding lights of the several
vessels moored there below. Suddenly another cannon boomed
below us, throwing out a fountain of lurid sparks, followed by
several more in ragged unison. The shouting rose to fever pitch,
and the crackle of musketry rattled the bars in our windows
and streaked the night with blades of fire. Then suddenly a
spark of light, intense and white, appeared where the *Philadelphia* lay. In that instant we made out the spars and rigging

of the ship and the masts and cordage of another vessel lying
close aboard. For what seemed a long moment, but which in
reality could have been no more than the merest fraction of a
second, the light glowed brilliantly below us, and then all at
once, with a great whooooosh, a towering blast of flame roared
high in the air from the deck of the frigate, outlining in sharp
relief the smallest rope and halliard of her rigging. For an
instant we could make out the figures of men tumbling from her
bulwarks, and then the harbor and all the ring of forts around
it lay lighted, brighter than by day against the black curtain of
the night.

In all that brilliance the flashing of the cannon on the forts,
all spitting now with venom, seemed almost anemic. We saw
a ketch drawing off from the burning ship, the same ketch that
Cowdery and I had seen earlier in the evening. We capered. We
thumped one another on the back. We cheered, and our cheers
were drowned in the savage roar of the flames as they licked
up through the tarred cordage and burst through the open
ports of the doomed ship. I found myself at one instant shaking hands with Mr. Porter, embracing Midshipman Rinshaw,
and, quite without dignity or regard for rank, dancing a caper
with Captain Bainbridge himself, who, for the first time since
our capture, seemed happy.

"Her guns!" someone cried from the window. "They're
shotted!"

We rushed for the opening and fought for a view. It was
true. As the fire reached them they were exploding, almost
point blank, it seemed, into the ketch, struggling in the airless
night to draw clear. It seemed a wonder to us that she could
continue moving. The toll aboard her must be horrible. Yet
she drew off, slowly, almost painfully, under sweeps. Just as
slowly, just as painfully, we saw the brig heave into sight. Boats
were putting out from shore, boats crammed with musketeers.
They crept toward the two ships. Over against the far shore
we saw the decks of the gunboats black with men. Through the
hysterical, screaming uproar below us we could catch the
ominous clank of their capstans as they warped them about,
bringing their guns to bear. All about the harbor the guns of
the forts were vomiting flame and smoke, and in the center,
just below us, great tongues of fire leaped from the frigate and

licked at the black belly of a cloud of smoke and showering sparks.

It seemed an age as the brig and the ketch drew together. We could not see the hawser pass between them, but pass it must have, for presently they were laid out on a line, the brig leading, the ketch following, sweeps churning and the water foaming. Fountains rose as shot fell on either side of them. But by a miracle not a spar fell, not a rope seemed cut. A boat drew near and fell back before a blasting volley from the ketch, and the screaming and the shouting below us seemed to redouble in force.

It seemed hours that we watched; seemed as if our own wills were pulling with our countrymen at those long sweeps that barely made the two ships creep across the glassy black surface of the sea. Then finally we saw the sails shake out and belly and catch the faint breeze that blew from off the shore; saw them stand away, slowly at first, and then with gathering speed, to disappear in the blackness, beyond the rim of light cast by the burning ship below us. A cannon spoke after them in angry bafflement; another, and then, after a long pause, a final shot. Below us the screaming died, and silence fell, broken only by the crackle and snarl of the fire on the ship. Sharply, as if to punctuate the event, a last stern chaser aboard the frigate boomed and belched a stream of sparks. We could hear the shot crash heavily amid the masonry of the fort at the point. A moment later her cables parted and she began to drift, toward the shore. Half an hour later her magazines, refilled by her captors, exploded with a smashing concussion that for an instant blasted us from the window. Acrid smoke and livid flame balled upward in a roaring inferno of sparks and debris, mounting with a tremendous rush. The ship seemed to open and split at every seam, and to stay so for a visible instant. Then, almost wearily, she seemed to collapse inward upon herself, squattering in the water. Sparks showered down, out of the ball of smoke and flame that hung against the dark velvet of the night, sprinkling the town with fire and ashes. The remnants of the ship, mere burning wreckage now, drifted on toward the shore.

An hour or two later she grounded and settled, but all night long the little flames licked across what was left of her; and as long as a spark remained visible we hung at the windows, watching, cheering, exulting. There was no sleep for any one of us that night. When morning came only a few charred timbers remained.

4

IN THE MORNING it was quickly evident that the Turks were beside themselves with both fear and fury. We officers were placed under a strong guard and were forbidden even to approach the doors or windows of our quarters. Cowdery and I were forbidden to visit our sick, nor were we permitted to treat any of the people of the palace for several weeks. Our dragoman, Hamet, with whom we had grown friendly, appeared sober and thoughtful, and told us that we might all be moved to the castle. When, at length, Cowdery and I were permitted to go under guard to visit our sick, we could not but notice that the town was full of country militia and that, even though several days had passed since the event, the faces of the people were all gloomy and resentful and downcast. We were more than ordinarily snarled at and spat upon that day, and for once I was as well pleased at the presence of our guard, for I would not have cared to venture out alone and unarmed among the people at that time. It was only later that we learned of the brutality with which our men in the castle had been treated. As soon as morning dawned, it was reported, the Turks burst in the doors of their prison and fell among them with clubs and whips until they were exhausted. The men, of course, had been totally unaware of what had happened, having no means to observe the harbor, though they had guessed from the uproar that something much out of the ordinary was taking place. Ben told me, long afterward, that they hoped, from the evident excitement and from all the firing, the roar of which made the walls of the castle shake, that a landing had been effected and that an attempt was being made to rescue them. Throughout the night they had lain half in expectation that the doors would be burst open by a flying squad of Marines, and that they would be armed and permitted to fight their way out.

Their disappointment as the night wore on and no such rescue materialized, and their bitterness when morning brought only more brutal treatment than before, may well be imagined. Their lot had been harsh before. It was made well-nigh unbearable now.

As far as we officers were concerned, the Turks showed a curious vacillation. At one moment we would be told that we would be removed to the castle. In almost the same breath we would be assured that we might remain where we were. We were forbidden to write any letters at all. Then we were accorded the privilege of writing, subject to the scrutiny of the bashaw or his minister. At length, however, on the first of March, we were conducted to the castle, and there lodged in a dank chamber, much like that in which the men were held. In fact, so close were we to their prison that we could hear them quarreling with their guards at night, when their rations were served; and in the morning, when they were herded off to labor, or in the evening, when they were fetched back, we could hear them shuffling along the passageway against which our chamber backed.

In this prison we remained in close confinement. Indeed, the only concession that was made for almost a month was occasional permission to Cowdery or Harwood or myself to visit our sick.

In such circumstances it is not surprising that we looked upon our parole as of no force and began to cast about for means of escape. At first this seemed not impossible. The floor of our cell was of earth and lent itself to digging, and accordingly we had scarcely heard the key turn in the lock upon us before we had chosen a corner and set to work with cups and spoons.

It was slow work to begin with, using such inadequate tools, and we had to take care that we were not discovered. We worked at night, fetching up the earth and spreading it on the floor and treading it down carefully. By day we piled our beds in that corner, in order, we said, to make more room, and in this way we concealed the entrance—a hole about the size of a man's body around—from the eyes of our guards. Later, when we had opportunity to go out to visit our sick, Harwood and Cowdery and I all kept our eyes open for more suitable tools, and in the course of time managed to smuggle in one rusty iron bar, such as is used in prison windows, found in the hospital, two mule shoes, picked up in the street, a camel goad, stolen in the market place, and some odd bits of iron filched casually from here and there. At the same time Mr. Porter managed to persuade our captors to allow us to have two marlinespikes, to help, he said, in teaching our midshipmen the art of seamanship. These instruments, with a couple of baskets, originally containing fruit, considerably facilitated the work, and by the time we had been three weeks in our new prison we had a tunnel extending down and out some distance in what we hoped was the direction of the shore.

This work had been in progress some time when Mr. Jones, picking idly at the wall of our cell with a marlinespike one day, made an important discovery. Like all Turkish buildings of this class, our prison was constructed of large, flat bricks, made of mud, laid flat in a double width and covered by a sort of plaster for smoothness. Mr. Jones discovered that this plaster might easily be chipped away and that underneath it only the flimsiest pretext at mortar held the bricks together.

Having made this discovery, it was but the work of a day or two to open a communicating hole with the passage by which our men were herded to and from their work each morning and evening. The passage itself was dark enough so the hole was not noticed, while on the inside we were able to disguise the opening by slipping the bricks back into place and giving the wall an unbroken appearance.

Having thus established a channel of communication, it was then necessary to devise the means. Responsibility for this fell to the doctors, and on our next visit to the men we managed to whisper to a few, whom we knew to be trustworthy, the location of the hole. From that point it was a simple matter to exchange written messages. At first it was proposed that they attempt a tunnel from their cell which would join that which we were digging. But this was discarded for several reasons: first, because it was feared that there were some among them who would reveal the plan, in order to gain favor for themselves, and second, because, being under more rigid watch than we were, their work might be much more easily discovered. An alternative plan was that we should dig the tunnel in their direction, opening it to their cell when we were ready for the final break, and this was the scheme ultimately adopted.

So fair a beginning deserved a better end. Our first misfortune was the discovery that the presence of guards posted all along the shore would prevent our opening the tunnel in one direction, while in the other we would have to drive another seventy to eighty feet downward and outward, a distance which would fetch the mouth of the tunnel out under water, where digging was impossible. Consequently the project had to be abandoned, at least for the time being, until we could ascertain whether escape were possible in any other direction. We closed up the hole and filled in the first three or four feet of the tunnel, the better to escape detection, and tramped down the earth above the spot. That evening, in his anxiety to pass on the bad word, Midshipman Henry, instead of taking the time to pass along a note in writing, endeavored to whisper the news through the opening in the wall to our men as they passed, and was discovered. The guards thundered into our cell and demanded to know who was responsible. Mr. Porter stepped forward and was hustled off to the bashaw, to whom he, characteristically, protested vehemently regarding our treatment.

Apparently his unexpected attack confused the bashaw, for he was, within an hour or so, returned to us—a thing we had never expected to see—not only unpunished, but with the bashaw's promise of better treatment in the future. Our hole in the wall was stopped up, to be sure, but it was also true that our lot improved considerably for a time.

Shortly afterward another attempt to escape was made that was nearly successful. By the same means by which the hole had been opened in the back wall, the captain and Mr. Jones managed to break a passage through one side wall and found their way into the adjoining apartment, which, though locked, was unoccupied. The ceiling in this room had been broken through, leaving a ragged hole, and through this one of our smaller officers was boosted. He reported the room above also locked, but there was a barred window which overlooked the ramparts of the castle.

This seemed to offer enticing possibilities, and a few nights' work sufficed to loosen the bars sufficiently to remove them, while by day the hole in the wall through which the workers had crept was carefully bricked up to prevent discovery. When all was ready we waited until a small armed sloop entered the harbor and moored not far off the point. A plan was then laid to slip out through the window and lower ourselves to the ground on the beach side from one of the cannon embrasures, and from there swim to the vessel, overpower her small crew, and escape.

When the night agreed upon arrived, we went, one by one, up through the hole in the adjoining room and lowered ourselves to the ramparts by means of a rope made by tying shirts and trousers together. Thence we crept along in the shadows, until we had reached the point of attack upon the guard. We were just preparing our assault, when the relief guards appeared at the far end of the walkway atop the ramparts, and we were obliged to retreat.

Luckily we were able to regain the room through which we had escaped without being detected, and, there being no further opportunity that night to put our plan into effect, we replaced the iron grille in the window and returned to our quarters. On the next day we discovered that the sloop had put to sea early the previous evening, so that it was undoubtedly as well for us that the scheme miscarried, else we might all have drowned swimming about in search of her.

A few days later the loosened bars in the upper chamber were discovered and recemented, this time beyond all hope of loosening again, and that avenue was closed. Not long afterward Captain Bainbridge was removed to private quarters, and I have often wondered if that move had any connection with the loosened bars. If our captors suspected us, that fact was never mentioned in my hearing.

Still later a third attempt to escape by tunneling was made, but this time our passage was pushed beneath a point where the Turks were moving a great forty-two-pounder into a casemate overhead. The weight of the gun caused the tunnel to collapse, and again we were forced to scuttle for safety. For some curious reason the cause of the cave-in was never discovered by our captors. Nevertheless, we tried no more of that.

These adventures carried us through April, and at the outset I was as active as any in them. Toward the end of March, however, the surgeons were called again into service in the palace, and I became too busy to be of much assistance; the more so since, just as April was beginning, Cowdery fell ill and the

entire duty devolved upon me. By the time Cowdery was recovered, I was myself coming down with the bloody flux, and
the wicked syroc, the desert wind which blows sultry at this
season of the year, was beginning. I found myself strangely
apathetic to designs of escape. It was late May before I was
again able to bear my share and take an interest in my surroundings.

In the meantime the blistering sun of the Tripoline summer
licked at us with a flaming tongue. The men, forced to labor in
its blasting heat, grew leaner, blacker. The officers, cooped,
save for an occasional quick march about the city, in the airless,
stinking hole of their prison, grew sickly. They escaped the
physical brutality of the beatings and the labor, but I believe
they carried the marks of their captivity longer than the men,
for the poisons bit deeper. Indeed, there were those who carried them to their graves, for I think poor Ridgely never recovered of his illness, and Captain Bainbridge carried deeper scars
on his soul than any of the men bore upon their backs.

Early in May our squadron appeared off the harbor. The
Turks were at first fearful, while we were hopeful, of an attack. But none came, and gradually our captors began to sneer
at American impotence and swagger at their own strength. The
bashaw even talked of fitting out three frigates with which to
blockade our coast!

In June our ships paraded offshore but took no action. The
bashaw fell ill of an intermittent fever, and Cowdery and myself were summoned to his country palace, in a near-by oasis
overlooking the sea, to attend him. In July he returned, fully
recovered, and Cowdery and I were removed to the palace from
the prison and given a private apartment in order to be more
readily available to the bashaw and his household.

August came in sultry and blazing. I recall that on the second I dined with Murad Rais for the first time since the destruction of the *Philadelphia*. He got very drunk and bragged
that our carpenters' crew had been set to build a vessel to
replace the frigate, which I knew but did not admit. As usual
he tried to persuade me to turn Turk, but this I turned off with
a laugh and returned early to my quarters.

Early the following afternoon Cowdery and I were suddenly aroused by a great hue and cry and bustle of excitement,

a blowing of horns and shouting of commands, that seemed to
burst out simultaneously throughout the palace and the castle
adjoining. We stared at one another across our apartment, for
it was evident that something out of the ordinary was afoot.
At this instant Hamet, who had been assigned to us as our
exclusive dragoman-guard-servant-adviser-and-assistant, burst
in excitedly upon us.

"Ya sidna, sidna!" he cried breathlessly. "Thy fleet, it
comes! There will be a battle!"

We needed no second prompting, but raced for the terrace,
our greater freedom of movement since our removal to the
palace including that privilege, doubtless because it was felt
that there we could scarcely escape the eye of one guard or
another. From that point we would be able to view anything
that might take place in the harbor below and on the sea beyond, and on arrival there our first glance showed us that
Hamet's prediction was likely to be quite true. Our squadron
was moving in close against the reefs to attack the Tripoline
gunboats and galleys in the very shadow of the shore batteries,
while they, in turn, were making hasty preparations to meet the
threat.

The enemy's fleet was already moving in to line of battle,
just within the shelter of the reefs, where our heavy ships
could not approach without running aground or coming under
the fire of the forts. Our own ships stood offshore, making a
cautious approach before an easterly breeze. The day was fine
and hot and bright, and it was warming to the heart to see our
squadron, headed by the *Constitution,* sweep down along the
outer reefs, with white sails spread like fleecy clouds against the
deep blue of the sea. At a distance each movement seemed so
slow and deliberate as to be almost painful, and yet, remembering the way the *Philadelphia* had scudded before just such a
breeze, we were well enough aware of how false was that impression.

"Look!" cried Cowdery. "They're going out to meet them!"

Several gunboats and row galleys were indeed standing out
through the channels through the reefs.

"We'll make mincemeat of them!" I cried.

"They probably only mean to draw the heavy ships in toward

the shoals," Cowdery replied. "Watch! They'll slip back in when the going gets hot."

But a movement in our squadron caught my eye.

"What's Preble doing?" I cried. "Is he going to run from a miserable handful of gunboats and row galleys!"

The *Constitution* had come about and was standing back on a long reach toward the open sea, a string of signals fluttering at her halliards. One by one the other vessels also altered course. From the castle roof the movement appeared confused until, all at once, it became apparent that, ship by ship, each must pass within speaking distance of the *Constitution*. Cowdery chuckled.

"The commodore has a trick up his sleeve!"

The trick developed, slowly, beneath our eyes. Our gunboats and bomb vessels appeared to huddle among the larger ships and for a time disappeared from view. Indeed, the entire squadron seemed to pull together in an aimless mass, and for a time only the *Constitution* stood out.

Nearly an hour passed while they lay thus grouped, apparently ignoring the enemy gunboats and galleys, of which more than a dozen had by now issued through the passes and were outside the reefs. Then with painful deliberation the knot of vessels began, with an almost circular movement, to unravel like a slowly spinning ball. Two bomb ketches stood in toward the batteries on the point, while the gunboats, moving in strings of three, bore down for the passes through the reefs, as if to cut off escape in that direction. Behind them the larger vessels moved in line toward the forts and the enemy craft gathered under their shelter.

"Watch now!" cried Cowdery. But I needed no prompting.

It seemed hours while they crept in, moving like puffs of cloud across the water. With equal slowness the Tripoline gunboats below circled and began to draw back toward the harbor entries. It was like watching a game in miniature from where we stood. I did not see the signal when it came, snapping at the frigate's masthead. My first warning that the action was begun was a great puff of white smoke with a heart of flame that blossomed in the bows of one of the bomb ketches, followed an instant later by a dull boom. The smoke drifted across the vessel, hiding it from view for a moment, all except its tall mast and the corner of its white sail. Then a second booming thud caught my ear, and I glanced away to see that the second ketch had also opened fire. Somewhere in the town below us I heard the shells whistle and crash home. Then, in almost the same breath, the batteries all along the shore front spat their answer in a thunderous roaring crash. Beneath our feet the castle rocked and a cloud of mingled smoke and dust arose, casting a gray haze between us and the ships. Through it I saw the *Constitution* and the *Argus* open fire; saw the spiteful flame lick out from their flanks; saw them reel beneath the recoil and then become shrouded in smoke. Fountains of spray leaped up from the surface of the sea near them and out beyond them. I saw them fire again, and yet again, as they moved majestically along, calmly ignoring the shot that splashed around them. Under my feet I felt the castle tremble and quiver again and again as the batteries belched their salvos. I saw the surface of the harbor plowed suddenly with shot; saw the shells crash home against the forts; heard the dull, snarling whine of the shot as it ricocheted from the fortifications into the town beyond, and was vaguely conscious of the dull wailing of the terror-stricken townspeople. In that instant it crossed my mind that tomorrow would be another sorry day for captives.

The crash of the guns was by this time so continuous that it was almost impossible to make oneself heard above it, while the drifting smoke made it difficult to follow all that happened off the point. But I became aware suddenly that Cowdery was shaking my arm and pointing. I could see that he was shouting, but only when I put my ear close against his mouth could I hear his words.

"The gunboats! They've met!"

Looking away from the heavier ships, I saw that it was so. The gunboats, ours and theirs, were grouped together, and it was evident that one side or the other had boarded, though at that distance it was impossible to see which. I saw a row galley poke its snout through a bank of drifting smoke; saw a gunboat close and grapple. Then another drifting wave of smoke hid both vessels from my view.

It seemed to me the fight had scarcely begun before Cowdery was tugging at my arm again and bawling in my ear:

"They're drawing off!"

It was true. Those Tripolines that could do so had taken shelter behind the reef, while those that remained outside were so battered as to be unmanageable or else they had been boarded and taken. I saw one row galley upon the rocks off the point and several enemy gunboats grounded on the reefs. Three gunboats were being towed off captive, and as they cleared away the *Constitution* crossed briefly astern of them and loosed a last challenging broadside at the castle. Below us the ramparts became shrouded in smoke, and under our feet the whole structure rocked and trembled. I heard the gunners in the battery along the walkway shouting in terror and saw one or two of them scrambling for safety. As the fragments of that salvo whined and whistled about us, it occurred to us that we might do well to follow their example. But that proved to be the last shot of the action.

I was not wrong in my thought that the day's work would mean harsh fare. As at the time of the destruction of the frigate, our men were most brutally set upon and beaten, out of a spirit of pure vengeance, after which they were driven out in groups, loaded with chains, and forced to labor, some in the town, clearing up the debris resulting from the attack, some upon the fortifications, repairing the defenses. There they were kept, laboring until they dropped from sheer exhaustion, when they were allowed to rest only briefly. No rations were served to them during more than twenty-four hours, nor were they protected from the fury of the populace, who were permitted to gather about them and spit upon them and to kick them and throw stones at them.

The officers, as usual, were put upon short rations. Their guard was doubled, and they were denied all communication with their friends, even Consul Nissen being barred from visiting them. Cowdery and myself came off lightest, for by now we were apparently looked upon as indispensable by the bashaw. Nevertheless we were required to keep to the palace. Nor were we permitted to visit either our fellow officers or the men, nor even to attend the sick.

As a result we did not know of the inhuman treatment accorded the men until late the following evening, when Hamet spoke of it in the most casual way as a piece of the news of the town. As soon as he was gone I suggested to Cowdery that we ought to do something. He stared at me.

"Do something?" he said incredulously. "Do I need to remind you that we are prisoners too?"

I leaped to my feet, nearly upsetting the table.

"Aye," I cried, "but privileged prisoners. We may not be able to demand, but we can bargain. And there's no one else who can do anything. We must at least try!"

He was obviously reluctant, for fear our brashness might lose us the privileges we had gained. At the same time, however, he dared not refuse to try. With considerable unwillingness he followed me to the quarters of Mohammed D'Ghies. We were received there with unusual coolness.

"You wish?" the minister demanded curtly, without resorting to any of the customary courtesies. I reflected that he had perhaps learned a lesson in directness from the Americans.

"To see the bashaw," I replied equally curtly.

Mohammed D'Ghies stared at me coldly.

"Why?" he demanded finally.

"The treatment being accorded our men," I told him.

"What about it?"

"It must cease!"

His brief, barking laugh was more like a snarl.

"Because you wish it?"

"Because the bashaw wishes us to serve him as physicians," I replied hotly.

He glared at me, raking his beard with his long fingers.

"Look you, Doctor," he said at length. "You do not know when you are well off. Do you not realize that you can be driven to your work as the men are driven to theirs?"

I laughed at that.

"I never took you for a fool!" I replied. "You must be aware of the damage that could be done by an unwilling physician. Do you think I do not know as well how to increase illness as cure it?"

"You would not dare!" he growled.

"Would I not?" I demanded. "Try me and see!"

"You would not care for your punishment."

"Neither would my patient."

"You would be put to death—horribly," he raged.

"I would have sent one Turk before me!" I replied.

He glowered at me furiously for a long instant. But finally his eye wavered and he looked away. I knew that I had convinced him.

"Moreover," I said, "the bashaw would have to do without our services."

"You will be returned to the prison," he threatened.

I bowed.

"I shall myself insist upon it," I said, "unless this unnecessary cruelty to the men stops and we are permitted to visit them and the sick."

"I'll have you flung into solitary confinement!"

I made no reply to that, but simply shrugged to indicate that it made no difference to me.

"May I point out"—Cowdery spoke for the first time since we had entered the room—"that if you drive these men beyond human endurance, you will only deprive yourselves of their services. You can't work dead men, you know."

"No!" I put in. "Nor will our government ransom them."

Mohammed D'Ghies abruptly stopped his angry pacing and whirled about to face us, and I thought I saw in his eyes the realization of the truth of what we said. Nevertheless, he summoned a pair of guards, whom he commanded to carry us off to the castle and lock us up.

I think Cowdery would have protested, but I took him firmly by the arm and hustled him before me from the room. After that we marched in silence to our new prison, deep down under the castle, with only a grilled doorway for ventilation and without room to stand upright or even to lie out at full length upon the filthy earthen floor.

When the door had slammed behind us and the guards' lantern gone glimmering off along the black passageway, leaving us in the stinking dark, Cowdery began to grumble.

"Now look where you've got us!"

"Did you expect to get off scot free?" I demanded with more confidence than I felt. "After all his threats, Mohammed D'Ghies had to make some such gesture as this. Mark my words, we'll be out by morning and called before the bashaw. If I'm not mistaken, we'll have our way, too!"

My companion merely grunted and fell silent, and I was content to do the same. Nevertheless the morning proved that I had gambled upon a sound guess. We were fetched before the bashaw, who was mildly chiding.

"Sidi Mohammed tells me that you have been threatening all manner of things," he said.

"Not threatening, Your Majesty," I replied quickly, for I was not sure what Cowdery might say, "merely pointing out that with our minds so full of anxiety for our countrymen it would be most difficult to keep them upon our work here. As a result we might make mistakes."

He smiled cynically, and I knew that he understood me perfectly. I think, however, that it was the larger consideration—that in overworking the men he was jeopardizing the ransom—that decided him.

"Very well, my good Tees-dol," he said. "We will show our mercy, but only for your sake. The dogs don't deserve it! The men will return to their quarters this afternoon. You may visit them. You may go to the hospital when you wish."

I bowed.

"Your Majesty is kind," I lied. I knew that no thought of kindness was in his mind. But it did no harm to flatter him.

That evening we visited the men and found them in a miserable state. I, for one, could not blame them for greeting us almost with resentment, not to mention a hint of derision on the part of the hardier ones. Our lot was so obviously so much better than theirs. We did what we could for them, certifying all we could for sick bay and assuring the rest that, at least, they would have rest and rations as before the attack. One or two taunted us with our fortune. Ray, a marine, evidently a man somewhat above the average in educational advantages, was especially bitter; and Ben, whose feet were in ribbons from the bastinado, seemed to take my ministrations as a personal affront, though I had him transferred to the hospital. Later I availed myself of the opportunity to recommend him to Murad Rais as a man whose skill in shipbuilding was worthy of special consideration.

This was the pattern of that entire month and of much of the following. Each succeeding attack—and there were several —resulted in the same display of brutality and vengeance, the same rebellion on ours. The attack of the ninth followed much the same lines as that of the third, except that, if anything, greater damage was wrought upon the town. In the midst of it a hot shot took effect upon one of our gunboats, passing through her magazine, and we had the sickening experience of seeing her blown, in a tremendous flash of fire and smoke, to bits before our eyes. The attacks of the twenty-fourth and twenty-eighth were night affairs, offering a dazzling display of pyrotechnics but resulting in little damage beyond a thirty-six-pounder ball which passed through the captain's apartment, nearly burying him in debris and seriously injuring his leg. Indeed, after passing through the one wall, the ball struck the opposite and rebounded, passing so close above the captain as to snatch the blankets from the bed in which he was lying.

Midmonth Commodore Preble sent a flag of truce ashore and, I later discovered, offered a ransom of $120,000 for us. But this was haughtily refused. Thereafter we were conscious of a gradual tightening of the controls upon us, and we guessed —quite rightly, as it proved—that the bashaw's patience was wearing thin. Once Cowdery and I were taken out to identify some bodies which had washed up on shore, between the town and the bashaw's summer palace. They were undoubtedly those of our countrymen who had lost their lives in the explosion of the gunboat on the ninth, and we begged permission to fetch a squad of men to bury them. This was promised but never carried out, and some time later, when we rode again in that direction, we found them scattered all along the shore, their remains much chewed and eaten by the stray dogs that roam the countryside. Once again we begged that they be buried, but were told that it was against Moslem principles to touch dead Christians.

Early September brought the fifth and final attack of the summer. As usual, Cowdery and I watched it from the roof of the castle, and were impressed with a greater panic than usual on the part of the defenders. We discovered only later that the batteries were nearly out of powder, and had the attack been renewed another day, I truly believe the forts might have been silenced and a landing effected. As it was, many of the townsfolk fled the city, and most of the tribesmen who had flocked in to offer the bashaw the support of their firelocks—

for they owned no modern arms—disappeared as hurriedly as they had come.

On the following day all the usual instances of cruelty to our people took place, but with a mitigating circumstance— the crowds which had formerly spat upon them and flung filth and stones at them were now fled. Among those who considered withdrawal the better part of valor was the bashaw himself, and we were informed that that evening we were to ride out with him and the rest of his household to his country palace. This forestalled our usual protest over the treatment of our men, and indeed, it was evident that this time such a protest would be useless.

We set out from the city sometime after dark and were almost in reach of our objective when we were startled by a sudden blinding flash, which lighted the countryside, and the crash of a tremendous explosion. The ground beneath our horses' hoofs shuddered, and the darkness which closed in after the thunderclap seemed denser than ever.

Our party was at once thrown into a turmoil, and there was a great deal of shouting and argument over the possible cause. Presently we all turned about and rode hell for leather back toward the city. I rode with the hope in my breast that the magazines of the forts had somehow been breached and exploded—forgetting, for the moment, the shortage of powder —and Hamet, sometime later, confided to me that this was the bashaw's fear as well. But on our arrival we found the city intact and learned that the explosion was that of a fire ship sent in to destroy the shipping in the harbor. But, being prematurely touched off, it had done little damage. This was the *Intrepid,* we learned later.

A few days after this the squadron withdrew from the coast to winter quarters, and shortly afterward Cowdery and I were again notified of the bodies of several of our countrymen washed up to the east of the town. Called upon to identify them, we saw that three of them had been officers, by the remnants of their dress that still remained, but the bodies themselves were too horribly mangled to be further recognized. Again, and with faint hope, we petitioned the bashaw to permit us to take a detail of men and bury them, and this once, whether from elation at the withdrawal of our squadron or because he was in an extraordinarily expansive mood, we were permitted to do so.

5

WE NOW ENTERED upon the most difficult period of our captivity, for the bashaw announced to us that he was weary of dickering and that he intended to treat us henceforth with the greatest severity in order to speed acceptance of his terms. For Cowdery and myself this decree had little meaning, for we were become too valuable to him and had obtained too much confidence to be mistreated. Indeed, there were times when I wondered if we would be included in the ransom, so much did he depend upon us. Consequently we came and went about the town in much the same fashion as before. However, we could not but observe the increased harshness toward the men.

All our protests, at this time, were of little avail. The best we could accomplish was the assurance that the men would be worked no longer than from sunup to sundown, and that we would be permitted to visit them and minister to their hurts and to maintain the hospital. Late in September, on one of my visits to the general prison, I noticed that Ben was missing. I inquired after him, but at first encountered only resentment, as much against myself as against him, I gathered, and surly responses. It was the marine, Ray, who finally told me.

"He's played sawbones and kissed the admiral's arse."

"Murad Rais?" I asked, ignoring the uncomplimentary reference to myself.

"Don't mind him, Doc," put in George Urry, our marine corporal. "He'd do the same with half a chance. He's jealous, is all. 'Twas yon Scotch runagate, him they call admiral, that took him. He's to build a new brig for 'em, 'tis said."

As soon as I was back in my own quarters I made discreet inquiries as to Murad's activities, and a day or two later was rewarded with an invitation to sup with him. I had seen little of him of late, and when I presented myself at his door he greeted me boisterously.

"Ye've been a stranger!" said he.

"You've been a stranger yourself," I replied. "I've heard naught from you."

He spread his hands and grinned in jocular apology.

"Your countrymen have kept me busy," he explained, and I laughed because I knew it to be true.

"Come in," said he. "I've a friend of yours a guest in the house."

I knew the friend of whom he spoke, but I did not reveal to him in what our friendship consisted. Instead I followed him in to the long tiled chamber.

As I entered a figure in Turkish dress rose from amid a jumble of cushions and limped to meet me. Although I knew him at once, I had to look twice before I could find a point of semblance to the Ben I had last seen. He was dressed in a bournous of light white wool trimmed in gold braid, thrown over a caftan of mulberry silk. On his head was a long-tasseled tarboosh, and on his feet the yellow heelless slippers of the country. His beard had been combed and trimmed in the Turkish fashion, but the eyes were the same, mocking, derisive. I felt ragged by comparison. We did not shake hands.

"Have you turned Turk?" I demanded.

He flushed, I thought uncomfortably. Murad laughed.

"Gie me time!" he exclaimed. "Gie me time!"

He turned away to give orders for the food and the wine, and I seized the opportunity to question Ben.

"Are you thinking of it?" I demanded, though his dress and my own experience with Murad gave me as much answer as I needed.

"What's it to you?" he replied with a harshness that warned me that questions would only drive him to that end.

I shrugged, thinking of Patience.

"You'll be a fool if you do," I said sharply, unable to restrain myself. "Do you think it serves a man to turn his coat? Look at Cowdery! Look at me! We've not turned. We can go back. Then look at Wilson and Heximer and the others who have. What have they gained that you and I have not? They can't go back. They'll be hanged at the yardarm if they try!"

"Perhaps I don't want to go back," he sneered. " 'Tis an easy life here, and has its advantages."

"Aye," I said, "when you're in favor—but when you're out

—you know what it can be. Do you think you'll be better treated if your luck turns again?"

He laughed.

"You were always a preacher, Tom!" he said.

Murad Rais returned to us at that moment.

"Ye've been trying to persuade him 'tis a dread thing to turn Turk?" he asked. "And what did he say?"

"What would you give for a bit of Scotland and a loving wife of your own?" I countered.

"I ha' three lovin' wives," he replied.

"Aye," I said, "and what about Scotland?"

He did not reply to that, but offered us a drink of stout arrack instead, and I thought it as well not to press the question, considering that I had made my point.

The dinner was excellent. Murad's meals always were. Nor was there any lack of wine to accompany it, but there was an air of restraint. I endeavored to make conversation, asking what manner of ship it was they proposed to build, but neither would give me the satisfaction of an answer. I prodded Murad on the damage done by our attacks, thinking to stir him to argument, but he turned me off with a laugh. After the meal was served there was more arrack and music, the wild squeal of ghaitas and the thump of tambours, while the slave girls danced and I felt my own blood stir within me. How dangerous such a performance was for Ben I well knew, but always and again Patience's face rose before me, and I sat quiet wondering what I could do about this new development.

By degrees our host grew sotted, demanding more and more music and less and less cover for the women, and I, God forgive me, almost forgot that they, too, were captives and forced to this business as our own men had been driven to theirs. If I did not give way and join in the erotic play, it was because of Ben. With him present I could not forget what lay behind us. When Murad rose and staggered away with a voluptuous Spanish wench toward the women's quarters I leaned toward Ben and nudged him.

"Have you written to Pat?" I asked.

He threw me a sharp glance.

"Be damned to you, Tisdall!" he swore. "Must you always be poking your long blue nose in where 'tis not wanted?"

September turned into October. I did not again go to Murad Rais's house, although I was a number of times invited. Since neither he nor anyone in his house had any professional need of me, I preferred to stay away. I took no pleasure in Ben's company, nor did I mean to pretend that I did. Once, in the palace, I chanced to encounter the admiral, and he chided me on my refusal to dine.

"I don't care for the company you keep," I told him bluntly.

He stared at me in amazement.

"Why?" he demanded.

"It's a long story and I don't want to tell it," I said.

"But he's a fine lad," he protested. "Good company an'— an' inteeligent, full o' life an' fun."

"Aye," I agreed grimly. "I know all about that."

"But 'twas yersel' bespoke him," he cried.

"I told you only that he was a carpenter with some skill in shipbuilding," I said.

He glowered at me.

"Is't because he's o' th' foremast crew," he demanded, "an' ye're o' th' afterguard?"

I shrugged, willing enough to let it go at that.

Murad scowled and shook his head.

"Na, na," he growled, "I wouldna hae thocht that o' ye!"

He was not so cordial to me for a long time after.

Time, in the meanwhile, did not come to a stand. Early in the autumn it began to become evident that the drought of the preceding summer, combined with our blockade, would result in a grain famine during the winter. As a result there had been drastic decrees issued by the bashaw, stipulating that no grain should be bought or sold in the open market except to members of his household, and by October all but a favored few were beginning to feel the pinch. The bread which made up so large a portion of our officers' and men's rations had long since been made of sour bean flour, while for meat they had only tough goat or wormy, stringy, half-rotted camel. The townsfolk were little better off, and as their desperation drove them to thievery, so was the harshness of the bashaw's law exaggerated. In a single day, outside the gates, I saw no fewer than three poor devils have their right hands and left feet brutally chopped off at wrist and ankle and the stumps plunged in boiling oil, for no worse offense than that they had tried to steal a little food. On many days the number so dealt with was much greater, and when one considers that the common treatment of runaway slaves in this barbarous country is to cut off both feet, the punishment for theft to have a hand or a foot or both chopped off or a red-hot iron laid to the eyes, and the penalty for heretical speech to have the tongue snatched out with a red-hot pincer, the great number of maimed and crippled or mutilated, blind or dumb beggars encountered in the city is not to be wondered at!

By the end of October even those in more exalted positions were beginning to find themselves on short commons, and this was nowhere better borne out than when Murad Rais was abruptly haled before the bashaw for having dared, in defiance of the royal edict, to bid for grain in the open market.

I was not present at the quarrel, but it must have been worth witnessing. The admiral, I was told, was more than half drunk, and stoutly, with Scotch stubbornness, maintained his right to buy grain when, where, and for what price he would. This the bashaw as stoutly denied, and he having the upper hand, the outcome was inevitable. My friend found himself unceremoniously tossed into solitary confinement, where he was kept on a diet of bread and water and such trifles as his acquaintances might smuggle to him, for better than eight weeks.

Beyond a sense of sympathy, it seemed to me that this event scarcely concerned me, yet it was to affect my future in a way that I could not possibly imagine. Having the privilege of both the prison and the palace, I found it not too difficult, by means of bribery, to visit him in his cell from time to time, and this I did, taking with me whatever I thought would be welcome. He was always pleased to see me, and the coolness that had grown up between us quite evaporated. On one of these occasions, however, he took opportunity to chide me for my unfriendliness toward Ben.

"Ah, these accursed Tripoline swine!" he swore. "Either they fear for their filthy necks or they're sae jealous as tae gloat ower my misfortunes. Were't not for ye an' Ben, God alone knows how I'd manage tae survive this fulthy hole!"

"Ben?" I asked.

"Aye, Ben! Ye were wrong there, lad!"

"Ben?" I said again, scarcely able to credit my ears. "Have you been seeing Ben, then?"

"Seeing him, mon?" he demanded. "Has he no been here nigh eevery theerd day wi' this or thot for me? Has he no stayed in my hoose tae see thot my eenemies dinna ploonder me the whiles I'm here? Has he no looked after my ain so I'll be no th' wurrse when I cam free?"

I saw no point in adding to his worries.

"I did not know that," I said.

Yet when I left him I was troubled vaguely, perhaps because I could not escape the feeling that in some way this might affect Patience. At any rate, I was roused enough to seek Ben out and tax him with it.

"What deviltry are you up to now?"

He put on his air of injured innocence.

"Deviltry? What makes you think I'm up to any deviltry? Can't a man——"

"Belay that! I know you! When you go out of your way to be thoughtful there's foul play somewhere."

"That's a hell of a way to talk to a shipmate!" he protested indignantly. "What would you have me do? Leave the man's house unguarded? Where's the harm if I stay? I'm lucky enough to have been overlooked. So long as I do my work at the yard the overseers don't question me. I eat and sleep well, and I'm free to come and go so long as I don't try to leave the city. Would you have me be fool enough to go back?"

"That's not what I mean," I said. To myself I had to admit that there was logic in what he said, yet my knowledge of the man told me that there was more to it than this.

"What are you talking about, then?" he demanded.

I took a long chance.

"You know what I'm talking about," I said darkly.

"The devil!" he swore, looking at me sharply. "Has that Sicilian bastard been gabbling?"

"He hasn't," I said, "but you may be sure he will."

He laughed.

"I'll deal with him! Leave that to me!"

"Perhaps," I said. "But even so, it doesn't seem to me right to abuse your host's hospitality——"

He broke in upon me angrily.

"Right!" he exclaimed. "There you go preaching again! Why, the old devil's a runagate!"

"That doesn't excuse——" I began, but he interrupted me again.

"What the old cuckold don't know won't hurt him! Kadijah's not a wench to lie long alone. Nor is Azizah nor Habibah! If it were not I, 'twould be Pietro or Mahmud."

I don't know why I should have been shocked, knowing him, but I was, and my face must have shown it. He broke off abruptly, no doubt realizing how much he had told me.

"God damn you, Tisdall!" he swore.

"You've no call to curse me," I replied. "What you do is nothing to me. I'm only trying to warn you."

"I'll look out for myself," he replied.

I shrugged and turned away.

"It's your throat," I said, "not mine."

Murad remained in confinement until past the first of the new year, when we began to hear rumors that the Americans were negotiating with Hamet Karamauli, the present bashaw's deposed brother, and a number of our ships appeared off the city. Yusuf promptly forgot his grudge and, having need of the admiral's talents, with characteristic capriciousness, released him as suddenly as he had imprisoned him, returning to him all his old honors and embracing him as if there had never been any disagreement between them. No doubt the restlessness of the Bedouin tribes of the hinterland, which were beginning to chafe under the costs of the war and the demands made upon them, had something to do with this. Perhaps the bashaw felt that he needed every friend he had.

I looked for an explosion when Murad returned to his house, but apparently I belittled Ben's craftiness. How he managed it I do not know, but it was evident that the admiral remained in ignorance of his horns. Ben continued to live in his house and to eat his food and, for all I know, to sleep with his wives, while the old Scot looked on him with all the favor of an only son. My curiosity got the better of me more than once, and I allowed myself to be persuaded to dine with them, but I never was comfortable. Each time it seemed to me that Ben's eyes were full of mockery, and that inside he was secretly laughing at me, which, no doubt, he was.

Time, meanwhile, dragged wearily on. Through private channels we learned that Commodore Samuel Barron had relieved Preble in command of our squadrons and that Preble had gone home. He carried with him the envy and best wishes of every one of us, and we dared to hope that Barron, in the coming year, would be able to accomplish what Preble had not: namely, our release. One rumor, at least, indicated that our friends were not idle: this was that Hamet Karamauli had been found by the Americans in Egypt and that, together with four thousand men, he had been transported to Sicily with a view to an invasion when the winter was ended. How true this was no one could say, but it was certain that some sort of overtures had been made to Hamet, for it was at this time that Yusuf announced that as our countrymen sought to interfere in the internal management of his realm we were no longer to be regarded as prisoners of war, but rather as members of the rebel party, and that if he were driven to it he would treat us as such.

Toward the end of February there was considerable excitement and military preparation in the city. Presently we were told that certain tribes along the Egyptian frontier of the eastern provinces having shown signs of rebellion, the bashaw was fitting out an expedition to suppress them. Early in March our squadron reappeared in strength, and there was general fear of an attack. The bashaw raged and swore that if one were made he would put every American in his power to death, be the consequences what they may. A day or two after this the Egyptian expedition marched.

As may be imagined, this was a trying time. The men were driven well nigh to the limit of their endurance. The officers were kept under double guard, their communications with the outside world all but blocked off entirely. Even those of us who by our special skills had obtained a measure of confidence among our captors no longer felt easy, although we were still permitted to come and go about the city with comparative freedom, and Cowdery and myself were still accorded the privilege of going as far as the bashaw's summer palace for the purpose of attending his family there. Nevertheless, even we were conscious of an atmosphere of tension, lacking the previous spring.

This was the state of affairs when, one evening, I was making my way back from the general prison—the men having been moved from the castle to an old house on the opposite side of the town, more likely to be struck in the event of an attack. I had passed the former consulate, in which we had first been lodged, and was turning up toward the palace, when in the dusk a figure came at me out of a doorway and said, "Hist!"

I recoiled against the opposite wall and turned about to take to my heels, for I was totally unarmed and there had been sinister occurrences in the city of late. But even as I turned the figure spoke again.

"Hist! Tom! Wait!"

I recognized Ben's voice and turned back, feeling slightly ridiculous.

"Oh, it's you!" I said. "What the devil d'you mean, jumping out at me like that?"

"I couldn't help it," he said in a hoarse whisper. "Wait. Listen. I need your help!"

"My help?" I cried, amazed that he should have the effrontery. "What's wrong? Have your sins come home?"

He clutched at me and held tightly to my bournous, for I had put on the Tripoline garb. My own clothes had long since worn out.

"Wait!" he gasped again. "I know I haven't the right to come to you, but I've nowhere else to turn. You were right. I own it! He caught me. I was with Kadijah and I thought him at the shipyard. She had her slippers at the door,[1] but he came in anyway! I think he was suspicious! I knocked him down and came away! But he'll be after me. Please, Tom, you've got to help me!"

"Why?" I asked. "I warned you."

"Yes, yes!" he cried. "But you know what it means!"

"Of course," I said. "He'll be within his rights, too!"

"Oh, I own it! I own it!" he cried. "But we've been shipmates, Tom!"

"You come to me," I demanded, "to me, whom you have used as you have?"

[1]In Moslem countries when a wife puts her slippers at the door of her room not even her husband may enter until she removes them.

"Tom!" he exclaimed. "I know I wronged you. But I swear to you, I've never regretted anything as I've regretted that! What I did to you——"

" 'Tis not what you did to me," I interrupted him harshly. " 'Tis what you did to Selina. You killed her!"

"No!" he cried. "No, I didn't!"

"Yes you did," I told him. "It was no accident."

"But—but——" he began.

I wrenched myself free, and he fell back.

"All right," he said. "All right. I suppose you're right. I shouldn't have asked you. But I hoped—being on the *Essex* together and all—— I had nowhere else to go."

He fell back across the narrow street and leaned for an instant against the wall, then turned slowly away. I had a quick sudden vivid recollection of Patience as she and I had faced one another on that last night in Salem.

"Wait!" I said. "Wait!"

He turned back toward me.

"What did you expect of me?" I demanded.

Hope sprang alive in him.

"Get me out of the city," he said eagerly. "If you can let me have some money—not much but a little. If you can get me a horse, even an ass—at least I'll be free. I'll go east and join Hamet Karamauli."

"Hamet?" I said. "But he's in Sicily."

"Don't you believe it!" he cried. "What do you think the bashaw is sending an expedition eastward for? Hamet has raised an army in Egypt. That's why!"

"No!" I exclaimed, for I had heard nothing like this before. "You know why the expedition was sent."

"Aye," he cried, "I know why they said it was sent. But this I have from Murad himself, who surely must know. General Eaton has landed at Alexandria with a force of marines and joined Hamet. They're marching on Derne now!"

It could be true. I thought of the evasions and tensions of the past two months. It probably was true.

But what of that? I felt confused. I thought of Selina, and of Patience. I had vengeance within my grasp, but could I carry it out? If I denied him now, would not his blood be on my head? Would I not place myself in the position of having

let him go to his death only so that I might one day claim
Patience for my own? If I did so, could I honorably ask Patience to—— My own heart told me that I could not.

"Wait!" I said again.

He had not moved.

How could I help him? I had money. I had not treated any
but the bashaw without fee. I might even pass him out through
the gates. After that, what? He would be on his own. It was
a long journey to Libya and the Egyptian frontier. There were
tribes living between, Bedouins, whom even the bashaw feared.
It was possible, it was even probable, that he would not win
through. Yet would I not have done my part? Could I not
then go to Patience with a clear conscience?

I thought then that I could. But what to do first? Where
could I hide him until I could make the necessary arrangements
to smuggle him from the city? To the palace? Obviously not!
He would be observed, and Murad would probably ask after
us both. To the prison? To the hospital? They would be the
first places he would look.

"I can't take you to my quarters," I said.

"Your quarters?" he asked, surprised.

"You'll have to hide somewhere until I can get things together."

"You'll help me, then?" he cried. "You'll do it? Ah, God
love you, Tom! I knew I could count on you!"

" 'Tis not for any regard I have for you," I said curtly.

He was discreet enough to make no reply to that.

"I've got to think where to hide you first," I went on. "What
about the shipyard?"

"He'll look there," he replied.

"Probably," I agreed.

I thought desperately, and suddenly remembered a small
coffeehouse in the bazaar, kept by a runagate Irishman whom
I had cured once of a pox. It was a tiny place, and the man
was my friend. I often went there when I wished a few moments' quiet alone.

"I have it," I said. "Come along!"

He followed me, and I led the way by a roundabout, darkened route to the place I had chosen. It was a small open shop,
where the customers squatted upon cushions and sipped at their

tiny cups, but I felt certain that behind its one small room there were other accommodations. Fortunately the place was empty, as I was sure it would be at that hour. I took Ben in and made him sit with his back to the street and, after ordering coffee, beckoned the proprietor to come and sit with us.

In a low voice I explained some of the circumstances to him: that my comrade was a fugitive and that I meant to help him escape; that I needed some place to hide him momentarily and that it was unlikely that any search for him would extend this far, it being a private matter for which he was wanted— this last with a wink, so that he might understand the nature of the offense. He took me, though he was for a moment doubtful. But presently he fell in with the idea, having long entertained the hope of escape himself, and finally he agreed to hide Ben in the single room behind his shop, on condition that it would not be for more than a day or two.

At the palace, in our own apartments, I ate a silent meal with Cowdery, who was moody over a fancied slight which the bey—the eldest son of the bashaw—had put upon him, turning over and over in my mind the possibilities of Ben's escape. It came to me, as I ate, that it was possible that Ben might win through to safety. It was possible that he might wander for years in the deserts, to turn up later when I had claimed Patience for my own, and upset all that we might by then have built. Such cases were not unheard of. Many a captive had returned from Barbary long after he was given up for dead, to haunt or delight those he had left behind. If he did not, how could I ever be sure that he would not? My thoughts turned again to Patience and our last parting, and I knew that I could not, in conscience, ask her to love me and be mine unless I knew for a certainty that Ben were dead. Neither could I have a hand in his death.

In those circumstances it seemed to me that only one course was possible. Where he went there must I also go!

Cowdery finished his meal and went out to play chess with the Minister of Exterior Relations, a pastime I knew he did not relish but followed to ingratiate himself. For my part I went to my room and counted my money, while Hamet cleared away the remains of our evening meal.

While I had not stinted myself in my living, neither had I

belittled my services to the members of the bashaw's court. I had demanded fees in proportion to what I considered my patients' means, and as a consequence I was not short of money. My own experience told me that in this land of the extended palm I could buy a dozen average men for as much as I held in my hands. So I began to wonder if Hamet, our dragoman, might not be amenable to the persuasion of gold. A little judicious inquiry, I thought, would not be out of order. I put away my money and went out to talk to him, offering as a pretext that I wished to practice my Arabic, in which he had been tutoring us since our arrival.

"How long hast thou served the bashaw, Hamet?" I asked, using the familiar pronoun as is done in that tongue.

"Three—four years," he replied. "Before that I worked two years for the Amrikani Consul Cascar (Cathcart), and before that six years for the Inglesi Mokdono (MacDonough)."

"Thou wert young, then," I said.

"I had eleven summers, ya sidi," he replied. "It was Sidi Mokdono who found me in the market place and bought me from the Bedaween."

"Eh?" I said, at once interested. "Thou art not of Tripoli, then?"

He shook his head.

"I am of Beni Isguen, in the country of the Mzab, southward of the Bled es Chebka."

"Where is that?" I asked.

He waved a hand vaguely across the city.

"To the west, below the mountains, at the edge of the desert. A month's journey by camel if one does not fall in with robbers."

"Eh, that is a long way," I nodded. "But not as long as to America. How came ye here?"

"The Beni Mzab are traders," he said. "I came in a caravan with my father, from Ghardaia, for Homs, where we planned to take ship and continue the pilgrimage to Mecca. But near Jefren we were set upon by the Bedaween, who killed my father and carried me slave to Tripoli."

I was not surprised, for I knew the tribes of the back country to be lawless.

"And will ye spend all thy days in Tripoli?"

"What would ye?" he shrugged. "One day, perhaps, if I find the means, I will continue to Mecca. There is naught to hold me here. Nor have I anything to return to in the Mzab."

"If thou hadst money," I said, "thou mightest complete thy pilgrimage and then return to the Mzab. Thou wouldst be a personage."

He looked at me sharply.

"Why do ye say that?"

"How much would it take, Hamet?" I countered. "Two hundred sequins in gold?"

That was the equivalent of about one hundred dollars of our money, yet I knew it to be a vast sum here.

Hamet put down the cloth with which he was polishing our couscous bowl and eyed me thoughtfully.

"Art offering me this money?"

"Would ye accept it if I did?" I said.

He hesitated.

"Suppose," I suggested, "it were not two hundred but four hundred sequins?"

His black eyes gleamed, then suddenly turned wary once again. He shrugged and picked up the cloth.

"Why make such talk?" he asked carelessly. "Such things do not happen. Ye make sport of me!"

"I do not make sport of thee, Hamet," I retorted. "Thy story interests me."

He gave me a sidelong glance and continued polishing, waiting.

"If I were to give thee such a sum," I said, "would ye leave Tripoli?"

"Yes," he said shortly.

"Very well," I replied, "I will give it to thee."

He dropped both cloth and bowl and turned to me.

"Ya, Sidi Doctor!" he cried. "Dost mean this?"

"Ssssh!" I cautioned him. "This is not to be cried aloud from the roof tops. I will give it to thee——"

A look of unbelievable joy overspread his face.

"—but on two conditions only," I concluded.

His expression of happiness was abruptly wiped away and as suddenly replaced by a scowl of suspicion.

"Ah!" he growled. "The gift camel is usually lame!"

"There is nothing without its price," I retorted.

He nodded gravely.

"That is true," he said at length. "What is it ye wish?"

"First," I said, "that ye start as soon as may be, and second, that I and one other go with thee."

He looked at me in astonishment.

"Thou!" he exclaimed. "But ye do well here!"

"I would return to my own people," I replied.

"Ye will be ransomed," he said.

"I have been here a year and a half," I answered him. "I am not as sure of that as I once was."

He stared at me for a long time, no doubt turning over in his mind my sincerity, weighing the risk.

"It will be difficult."

"Leaving the city will be the most difficult," I said. "I think it can be managed."

"It will be dangerous."

"That is why I need thy help," I replied. "We will be many days on the road, and we are strangers."

He nodded.

"I see," he said, and fell into thought while I sat with my stomach tied in a tight knot, for I had risked everything. Presently he looked up.

"And this other?" he asked.

"A friend," I told him. "One of the other Amrikani."

"Not Sidi Cowdery?"

"No," I said.

He half smiled.

"That is good. What do ye propose?"

I knew what he meant. It was time to speak plainly.

"I will give thee fifty sequins in gold now," I said. "Once free of the city and safely on the road, I will pay thee fifty more. When we reach Egypt, or any other place where we are able to rejoin our people, I will pay thee the balance—three hundred sequins! In fact," I added, " if ye will place me on board an American man-of-war, I will give thee five hundred sequins!"

His eyes gleamed briefly, but he did not answer at once. Instead he sat cross-legged in silence, evidently considering my proposal from every side, while I, literally, held my breath. If he were loyal to the bashaw he might denounce me and end the matter, though this I thought hardly likely, for it could only result in my imprisonment and would offer no gain for him. I was well enough acquainted with the Moslem character to know that in matters of money our notions of honesty did not meet. It was more likely that he would obtain what he could from me and then turn about and sell his information for a reward to our enemies.

I had one horrible instant of doubt, and then he glanced up, smiling, and held out his hand.

"I am thy man," he said.

I was conscious of a wave of relief. Had he contemplated treachery, I felt, he would have bargained for a greater advance in order to have from me as much as possible before going to the bashaw or Mohammed D'Ghies. His willingness to accept my offer at its face value I considered an earnest of his good faith, and I gave him my hand upon it.

I took him into my confidence then, outlining the situation to him as it stood, though without going into the basis of Murad's quarrel with Ben, letting it stand simply that he was in hiding and that we had agreed together upon escape. Hamet nodded understanding.

"First," he said, "we must pass the gates."

I knew what he meant. Although Cowdery and I had a certain latitude which permitted us to come and go between the city and the summer palace, this was allowed only when we were armed with proper passes and accompanied by guards. True, of late such guard had consisted of Hamet and a single mameluke, but even that one had been assigned to us upon application at the mameluke's barrack, where we also received our mounts, and passage beyond the walls without him was impossible. By custom the city gates were closed at sundown and reopened only at sunrise, and between those hours it was difficult even for the bashaw himself to pass in or out. Our passes were never written to include this privilege. If we were benighted at the summer palace we must wait there until morning before we could return to the city. And only the most urgent necessity would permit us to pass out at night. By day there was a constant stream of traffic: farmers and inhabitants of the surrounding countryside passing to and from the market, traders with caravans from or for the hinterland, all the in-and-out passage of a sizable center passing through the gates. These people were seldom questioned or examined. Yet it would be impossible for one of our people, without either a permit or an excellent disguise, to slip through.

"He might pass over the walls," I suggested.

Hamet shook his head.

"They are well guarded, and will be even better watched when he is missed."

"Thou couldst take him through," I said, "as a drover of asses."

"They will be on the watch for him," he objected, "and if he has not had practice in pretending, the best of disguises might not serve him. Has he experience with animals? Does he know the cries of a drover?"

I had to admit that it was unlikely. He smiled.

"Then," he said, "it is best to be bold."

"Thou hast something in mind?" I asked.

He nodded.

"Suppose thy friend were the mameluke?" he demanded.

"Why!" I exclaimed, for this had not occurred to me. "I suppose he might pass for one, with his beard trimmed and his face blacked, and if he were not questioned."

"Has the guard ever yet been questioned?" he asked.

I thought. It was true. It was invariably Hamet who presented our passes and answered questions.

"But the uniform," I said, "and the guard assigned?"

"I have a plan," he grinned. "Hark ye!"

For an hour we talked, and when we were finished our scheme was laid. I paid him the money I had promised and an additional sum besides, for bribes and to make certain purchases to provide for our journey. Later I went out to the coffeeshop where I had hidden Ben. There we were joined presently by Hamet. After a cup or two, to the relief of our host, we left and went to the home of a friend of Hamet's who kept a tea stall near the Babelpasha, the gate through which it would be necessary to leave the city. After receiving assurance that Ben would be safe hidden there, I returned to my quarters in the palace. I had not been half an hour there before Murad called upon me in a state of fury.

"Where is he?" he demanded. "The dog! The ungrateful spawn of hell!"

I did not pretend I did not know of whom he spoke.

"So the devil has come home to roost?" I laughed.

"D'ye mock at me, ye yankee dog?" he bawled.

"Mock at you?" I demanded. "Did I not try to warn you?" He stared at me.

"You seem to know a great deal!"

"Eh!" I exclaimed. "You came here, didn't you?"

"Aye!" he cried. "I came here because I know——"

"Because you know what?" I demanded. "Because you knew that I knew Ben! But I warned you. Didn't I tell you that he was a good carpenter—no more? Did you not tell me that I misjudged him? Now you come crying to me that 'the dog' is an 'ungrateful spawn of hell.' D'you think I cannot guess whom you mean? I have had my own experience of him!"

He stared, half trying to fathom what I knew.

"I don't know what he has done to you," I said, striking while I had the advantage, "but I know the man, and I can add two and two! What has happened?"

"Happened?" he cried, wilting all at once. "Lad, ye were right!"

And he went on to tell me all that Ben had already told me, and a little more. I was half tempted to go back on my promise to Ben, remembering my own case. But then, thinking sharply of Patience, I caught myself.

"Has he been to ye?" he demanded abruptly.

"He knows what I think of him," I countered.

He nodded.

"He has no better opinion o' yersel'," he grumbled.

"Have you looked at the yard for him?" I asked.

"At the yard, at the preeson!" he exclaimed. "Everywhere! He's hid i' th' town somewhere, I'll warrant."

"Unless he's tried to swim out to the squadron."

He stared at me incredulously.

"D'ye think he'd risk it?"

"He's a fine swimmer."

"He'd never make it!"

I shook my head.

"Never in this world," I agreed, "but I'll stake my life 'tis what he's tried!"

He looked sober.

"I'll nae believe it!" he exclaimed. "Th' fool! I'll nae believe it!"

He went away at length, not at all convinced that Ben was not hiding somewhere in the town, but apparently satisfied as to my own innocence.

There followed, then, a period of waiting which was harder to support than all the months of captivity that had gone before. Ben fretted and fumed. He was for making a dash for it at once, and devil take the consequences. I must admit that I was not much behind him in impatience. But Hamet maintained a firm hand and a steady head, stoutly asserting that unless the ordering of our escape were left to him he would have none of it. Such a journey, he pointed out, could not be lightly undertaken. We would need supplies of food and drink, and beasts to carry them. We would need disguises, for once in the country, we must make ourselves as inconspicuous as possible. And, having done all this, we must lay a plan of action, so carefully considered and so familiar to each one of us that we might be prepared for any slip in its execution. Moreover, he pointed out, at the moment the town was in a state of excitement over Ben's disappearance. All of the prisoners' guards had been doubled. Searching parties continued to scour the streets—although by the end of the third day it was pretty well accepted that he had attempted to swim off to the squadron. All passers by the gates were carefully examined, and even Cowdery and myself were more carefully watched. Until this vigilance was somewhat relaxed there could be no hope of escape, and we had no choice but to wait.

In the meantime Hamet prepared for the journey. Since it was impossible to obtain provisions in the city, he made several excursions to near-by hamlets where, a little here and a little there, he gradually secured what we would need and brought them together at the house of a friend in Ain Zara, a little distance south of the great oasis which surrounds the city. At the same time he secured disguises and instructed us in the roles we were to play, for he had decided that once clear of the city, we should pass as Moors, of Morocco; myself to be a learned tabib, or doctor, making the pilgrimage, accompanied by my servant, Hamet, and Ben, my runagate slave. This would account both for my accent and for Ben's almost total lack of Arabic, while at the same time my skill as a physician might be used to our advantage to pacify such as might be suspicious of us. For this purpose, however, he was careful to instruct me to take only the simplest of instruments and remedies: a cup, three or four lancets and a scalpel or two, and anything that might serve as a burning iron, a pot or two of healing ointment, and a handful of simple herbs or drugs, he said, would be sufficient, for if I appeared too elaborately equipped, such was the primitive state of medicine in that country, it might excite suspicion!

In this way we sweated and fretted away nearly a fortnight until, one morning, Hamet quietly let me know that everything was ready and that I might now set about my part, which involved our actual departure from the town.

My plan for this was fairly simple. The bashaw's eldest son, the bey, and his family were that month at the summer palace. Before his departure I had had occasion to treat the bey for a mild indisposition of the kidneys; as a result nothing had been simpler than to hint a time or two, during our wait, that it might be well to examine him and inquire as to his progress. Since I had thus quietly indicated my intent, it came as no surprise to Mohammed D'Ghies when I applied to him for permission to ride out that afternoon to see the bey. Without other comment than a jest at continuing business with pleasure, he sat down and wrote out the necessary permit which would pass me and my dragoman and a guard through the gates, and at the same time prepared an order to the captain at the mameluke barracks to provide me with a guard and the necessary mounts.

Now came the most trying time of all, for we had decided that it was best to pass the gates as late as possible in the day in order to have a night's journey behind us before any pursuit might start. In view of the ride ahead of us, it would have been sensible to have slept at least a part of the day, but, though I tried, I soon found this to be out of the question. I started up at each sound, fearful lest, by some mischance, our scheme had been discovered, while at midday, when our dinner was served, I ate so little that Cowdery remarked upon it.

"What's the matter with you?" he asked.

"I'm not hungry," I said, trying to appear offhand.

He eyed me seriously.

"If you're coming down with anything," he said, "you'd better let me see the bey in your place."

"There's nothing the matter with me," I growled, for I had said nothing to him of our plans. "I'm liverish, that's all. The ride and a physic will do me good."

"As you will!" he shrugged.

The hours crept by after that at snail's pace, but I have observed of time that it never quite stands wholly still. A little past midafternoon Hamet looked in.

"Are you ready, ya sidi?" he asked me.

I nodded and rose, gathering up my equipment.

Cowdery glanced up from the book he was reading.

"You're off?" he asked.

"We're away," I replied, trying to appear casual.

"My respects to the bey," he remarked. "Will you be back tomorrow?"

"Unless I can find some excuse to stay longer!"

He grinned and winked.

"Well, don't hurry on my account," he said dryly.

As we went out I heard Hamet's chuckle of approval.

At the mameluke barracks we were given mounts and assigned our guard, a stout, pleasant-natured black, who had accompanied me on previous occasions. A moment later we were riding slowly toward the Babelpasha.

It was now my turn to show that I could be as good a mountebank as physician. I took my place at the head of our little procession and sat my horse listlessly, allowing him to amble along dispiritedly and from time to time passing my hand across my face and drooping as if ill. Twice I took the wrong turning and had to be reminded of our direction. Hamet pretended to eye me with concern. All of this was not lost upon our guard, and presently he began to look serious, as if he were aware that all was not well with me, and to question Hamet. The latter called ahead to me to know if I were all right. At that I reined in.

"I am a bit faint," I said. "Perhaps it would be well to rest before we set out."

Hamet glanced at the sun, as if calculating the time we might spend, then spoke to the guard.

"The doctor is unwell," he said. "He would like to take some refreshment before starting his journey."

The mameluke looked doubtful.

"A mere glass of tea," I put in. "I can add to it a powder which will revive me. Perhaps thou wouldst join us?"

"I have a friend who keeps a teashop not far from here," Hamet suggested.

The guard shrugged.

"Ai, well!" he sighed. "Where is the harm? I would feel better for a glass myself."

Hamet led the way to the place where we had Ben hidden, I all the way maintaining my play-acting. There we dismounted and entered, and our host fetched cushions for us to sit upon, a brazier and a small brass kettle, tea, mint, and a loaf of sugar. Hamet brewed the drink, mixing the mint and the tea together, adding two lumps of sugar the size of my fist, and pouring hot water over the whole and fetching it to a boil. The pitcher of hot water he passed to me to put down, while he stirred the brew, and I, with seeming indifference, set it upon the floor near my knee, between me and the guard. When the tea was ready Hamet served it out in small glasses, whereupon I picked up my pouch and rummaged in it for a small paper containing a few grains of belladonna, previously prepared. This I mixed carefully with my tea, the while Hamet and the guard sat politely watching. But when I turned to put my pouch upon the floor beside me, as if by accident I tipped over the pitcher of water in the direction of the guard.

Hamet leaped and caught at the pitcher. The guard scrambled aside, snatching his bournous out of the way. Hamet bellowed for our host to fetch a swab, while I moved out of my seat and over into Hamet's with the dignity befitting my position, at the same time picking up Hamet's glass and holding it, as if it were my own, waiting for them to resume their places. When the flurry of excitement had died down Hamet took the place lately vacated by the guard, leaving the mameluke that in which I had been sitting. As the black took his seat he glanced at the glass in front of him.

"I exchanged glasses," I said, "when I moved. That is the one that was here."

I indicated the empty space before me. He nodded, and I felt the trick had worked. Though he had not seen me move it, he was aware that his attention had been distracted, and he was willing to accept my assurance that the exchange had been made. Nevertheless, I did not breathe easily until, with much polite smacking of his lips to show his appreciation, he had drained his glass. Thereafter I refilled the glasses around and engaged him in conversation. Within a matter of minutes I saw that the drug was beginning to take effect, and within a quarter of an hour more he was gibbering and shaking and making desperate efforts to remain awake, evidently aware that something was amiss, yet not having the power to call out for help.

This was the point, I felt, at which we were in the greatest danger, for the shop was open to the street, and a chance passer-by might easily observe that something was wrong within. Accordingly, I now signaled to Hamet, and while our host kept watch at the entrance we raised the unfortunate man between us and carried him off into the room at the back where we found Ben awaiting us in a frenzy of impatience, his hands and feet already blacked and his beard trimmed in preparation for the role he was to assume.

Our mameluke was by now totally unconscious, and I began to have some qualms lest I might have given him an overdose. But there was no time to consider that now. Without further delay we stripped him of his uniform and helped Ben into it.

"Couldn't you have picked a guard more my size?" he complained. "'Tis miles too big!"

"Nonsense!" I growled. "'Tis not so bad a fit but the bournous will cover it. Be thankful that it's rather too large than too small!"

As we passed from the teashop I gave the owner a gold piece and would have stopped to give directions for reviving our victim. But this Hamet would not allow.

"Come, sidi!" he cried. "The gates will be closed!"

They were, indeed, already unhooked and ajar when we came up at a smart hand trot. As we had previously arranged, Ben did not pause as we came to them, but continued on through, reining up a dozen yards beyond to wait for us, while Hamet and I stopped to present our pass.

As we had expected, in Ben's case, the bournous and chéchia of the mameluke were sufficient. But the officer in charge took our pass and read it carefully, giving us a searching look before handing it back. Then, with a careless glance toward Ben, he waved us on, and we rode off at an ambling walk.

6

WE RODE for an hour or more until we were come, by my reckoning, about a quarter of the distance to the summer palace. There, just as we were overtaken by the swift African dusk, we left the main highway abruptly, striking off along a winding, hard-beaten little footpath. This we followed for a mile or more and then turned off again, along an even more obscure trail that slithered through the thick undergrowth beneath the towering palms of the oasis and came, after another hour or so of silent riding, into a little clearing, at one side of which stood one of those little domed, whitewashed tombs, or marabewts, with which this countryside is dotted. It was full night by now, but there was a lopsided moon, and in its light the white tomb stood out ghostly sharp in the shadows, while its single arched doorway gaped in its front like the eaten-away hole in a leper's face. All around us we could hear the chirp and chatter of nocturnal life, while overhead the fronds of the palms caught the silver sheen of the moonlight and stirred and clattered gently, whispering in the hot wind that blew from the south.

Here Hamet reined in and slid to the ground. Ben and I followed suit. Without a word Hamet handed me the reins of his mount and disappeared inside the tomb. An instant later he reappeared carrying a bulky bundle.

"Here ye become Moors," he grinned. "These are the clothes I have procured for ye."

Piece by piece he held them up, naming each and explaining its use and mode of wear: the serwal, or baggy pantaloons, full in the seat but tapering about the calves; the tshamir, a brief shirt, shaped like a sack, with holes for the head and arms, and worn as an undershirt; the gandoura, a longer shirt, reaching slightly below the knees, embroidered, and shaped to fit at the neck and shoulders and having short sleeves; the caftan, or outer shirt, which is colored and the same as that in use in

Tripoli; the hzam, a wide, brightly decorated girdle; and the
whole topped by a short-sleeved, hooded, sacklike garment of
rough wool, called a djellaba, which replaced the bournous, or
outer cloak, worn by the Tripolines. For headgear we were
introduced to the fez, a somewhat higher, more conical form
of the Tripoline chéchia; while for footgear Hamet had provided soft leather stocking boots called t'mag, over which were
worn the yellow slippers common in Tripoli.

Having gone over these costumes piece by piece, he helped
us put them on and then changed his own clothing. Our discarded garments he gathered up in a bundle and, disappearing
in the underbrush, returned presently without it. Ben and I
prepared to mount. But Hamet stopped us.

"No, no!" he said. "Wait here. If anyone comes, hide in the
tomb."

He turned away and, leading all three mounts, disappeared
in the darkness, following a barely discernible pathway.

"Hey!" Ben exclaimed as he watched him go. "What the
devil's he up to now?"

"Your guess is as good as mine," I replied.

"I don't like this," he grumbled. "What if he doesn't come
back?"

"He'll be back," I said. "I don't know what he's doing, but
he has some reason for it. You've got to trust him."

"I don't trust any of these people," he growled.

Nevertheless he waited. There was nothing else to do.

I will confess that my own faith was wavering when, at the
end of several hours, he had not returned. The moon climbed
higher, and Ben growled his dissatisfaction.

"A pretty mess you've got us into!" he complained. "Like as
not he plans to help them find us and claim a reward!"

"Nonsense!" I scoffed. "He's trustworthy, and if he's not,
he's well bought!"

However, I thought my own voice lacked conviction.

"If he isn't here in another half hour I'm off on my own,"
Ben growled. "You may do as you please!"

"Have patience!" I told him.

"Patience!" he scoffed. "What the hell d'ye think I've had
all these days? We'll never get there at this rate!"

I did not trouble to reply, but held my breath and listened,

The only sound that came to my ear was the chirping of insects in the night, the rattle of the palms above.

It was nearly an hour before we heard the patter of small hoofs and a low, gruff voice saying: "Errrd!"

We drew back into the shadows, for neither of us had any stomach for entering the tomb. But a moment later Hamet, mounted upon a burro and driving three other shaggy little asses before him, rode into the clearing.

Ben exploded.

"Donkeys!" he cried. "Does he expect us to ride those?"

Hamet slid off his mount beside us, and even in the moonlight I could see his grin.

"What's this?" I demanded, for I felt much as Ben.

"Thy mounts, ya sidna," he replied, "for our journey."

"But asses!" I protested. "A beggar's mount! When we had horses!"

"No Moorish tabib would be able to afford a horse," he explained, "especially such as those. In Morocco they might ride a mule. But here there are few mules."

"But the pursuit?" I cried. "They will overtake us!"

"If they do," he replied, "ye will look like what ye are supposed to be, and perhaps they will overlook ye. If ye rode horses ye would be conspicuous, and they would see through thy disguise. But there will be no pursuit."

"No pursuit?" I demanded. "What of the mameluke? Think ye he will not stir them up?"

"Nay!" he replied with a cryptic smile.

"What mean ye?" I cried.

He made a significant gesture across his throat.

"Think ye my friend will risk punishment?"

I gulped. I had not contemplated anything quite as cold-blooded as this. Yet I should not have been surprised.

"But they will discover it," I said, "when we do not arrive at the palace."

"Thou'rt not expected there," he replied, "and thyself ye hinted that thou mightest stay longer than a single day. It may be two, even three days ere thou'rt missed. By then we will be well on the road. They will not seek far for us, thou mayest be sure. There is no love for the bashaw and his soldiers where we go."

"That's all very well," I said, "but can we be sure it will happen so? What if they miss us by morning?"

"Then they will search for us," he agreed, "and thou mayest be sure that three rich Moors on fine horses would be remembered. But who will take heed of three poor Moors passing upon their asses? What's more, my friends, it is not wise to make a display of wealth in the bled—neither wise nor safe!"

"But we are not wealthy," I protested. "I wouldn't call this making a display!"

Hamet shrugged.

"This—no," he agreed. "But poverty to a townsman is riches to a beldi—a man of the back country. Who rides a horse will be thought rich, and him the Larbi will rob. If they think thee poor as they, they will take pity on thee and feed thee. Believe me, ya sidna, I know."

I saw that he was arguing to some purpose. I said so to Ben, who only snorted. Hamet chuckled.

"Later, when we are better on the road," he said, "and where it will be less noticed, we may change to camels. But for now, O gentlemen, it is better so."

I explained this to Ben, who shrugged impatiently.

"All right!" he growled. "Whatever you say. Let's get on with it!"

Hamet glanced with some concern at the musket we had taken from our guard, and which Ben had not turned over with the rest of the uniform.

"There is one thing," he said.

"What is that?" I asked.

"The gun," he said. "It should be left behind."

I told Ben. He laughed without humor.

"If he thinks I'm going to leave it, he's crazy," he said.

Hamet shrugged.

"We will not need it except," he said, "for defense. And if that need comes, of what use will one gun be?"

I explained this to Ben. He snorted.

"Stuff!" he exclaimed. "I'm keeping it. Hamet can have the horses, but I want the gun."

I explained to Hamet, who seemed resigned.

"It may not be important," he said. "Perhaps we can hide it

if matters look bad, and it may be the means of finding some
food. Come! We cannot lose more time here!"

He picked up the rest of our gear and stowed it in the flat
cone-shaped panniers that each of the shaggy animals carried.
After this he showed us how to sit our small steeds: either
midships, with both legs draped over one of the animal's shoulders, forward of the pannier; or aft, sidewise upon the
animal's rump, with both heels hanging down together upon
the same side so that they might, if occasion demanded, keep
up a constant tattoo against his flank to keep him jogging along
at his normal short-footed trot. A quarter of an hour later we
were on our way, pattering along the winding trail through
the nodding palms, and I for one was glad that we had chosen
the night for our flight, for there was a trick to keeping one's
balance upon these diminutive beasts. An hour or two, however, sufficed to give us the hang of it, and long before dawn
we were riding as if we had been accustomed to it all our lives.

Our way lay to the south and slightly west, cutting back behind the city walls, threading between the low walls of the
gardens, and keeping always beside one of the little shallow
irrigation ditches. Every now and again we would pass another
empty marabewt, or a silent well, the gaunt arms of its pulley
rests standing like ghostly sentinels in the moonlight. Frequently the garden walls were topped with a dense hedge of
Barbary fig, causing us to ride along silently in shadow. But
the scents of lotus and hibiscus and gardenias and dung were
as strong there as in the open light. As we came near the edge
of the oasis the palms thinned out, and the gardens gave way
to sandy scrub, and out beyond the trees we could begin to
make out the sweeping outlines of the great dunes; dun colored
by daylight, but dull gold now in the shine of the moon, looking like arrested waves in a storm-tossed sea.

Here we turned and followed a dusty roadway, in which our
burros' feet made not a sound, westward, between the oasis and
the towering sands. After a bit we came to a village, nestling
at the edge of the palms, among the dunes; here we turned
again and bore to the south, outside the village walls. Hamet
rode quietly back beside us to whisper, "Ain Zara."

At the end of the village, leading away to the southeast, between the dunes, we found a beaten track. This we followed

among the sand hills, now sharp against the brilliance of the moonlit sands, now flitting like black ghosts through the only slightly blacker shadow of a dune. Underfoot our beasts made heavy going of the sand, but though we never climbed the crest of one of them, the way between the dunes seemed always to rise, until all at once we were through them, on solid ground once more, our donkeys' hoofbeats pattering loudly in the silent night along the bottom of a stony, brush-grown, dry wadi.

This gully we followed for a mile or more, to come suddenly out upon a vast upland which rolled away before us, rising imperceptibly into the distance, with never a sign of habitation; an immense stretch of almost level, stony, ground, broken only here and there by a patch of low-growing brush or stunted shrubbery, bleak and cold in the wash of the moon. Only the little thin wisp of a trail broke it, winding away as far as we could see to lose itself in the distant hazy shadows.

"The Jefara—the tableland," Hamet told us.

I turned and looked behind us, expecting to see the roofs and minarets of Tripoli. But they were hidden. Instead there was only the edge of the plain, and beyond that the tops of the palms reaching into the darkened distance, waving and tossing gently in the soft night breeze, like a black-and-silver sea in the moonlight. Somewhere to the south a jackal yelped, to be answered in the distance by the eerie, screaming laugh of a hyena. I shivered slightly and rode hastily after my companions.

By dawn we had been on the road close to seven hours, by my best calculation, and had come something more than nine leagues. As the darkness which had followed the setting of the moon first turned pale and gray, and then fled before the advancing day, we found ourselves fairly adrift on the vast, almost level upland. On all sides of us it stretched without a break, stony and harsh, bleak gray and sear brown, for the most part, with here and there a thin patch of green or dusty yellow. Only in the south was there any break in the monotony. There, far ahead, like a vast, uptilted knife blade, the misty-blue, flat-topped ridge of the Jebel, the mountain, rose athwart our track against the pale sheen of the morning sky. Sparse brush, in patches as high as a man on horseback, but in the main no more than knee deep, studded the plain here and there like tufts of wool upon a sickly sheep. In between, brown grass, and low-growing clumps of cactus, and numbers of little desert flowers managed what seemed to me a precarious foothold on the barren soil. To me it seemed desolate. I was not yet sufficiently acquainted with Africa to appreciate how rich it was!

A few moments after it became light Hamet turned abruptly off the meandering track into a slight brush-grown depression, threading through the undergrowth until, in the center of the hollow, well hidden from the trail above, he halted in the shelter of a low, spreading argan bush and slipped from his mount. Both Ben and I were happy to follow his example. I for one felt as if every bone in my body had been ground under a millstone and all the splinters then replaced. It was evident that Ben was no better off.

"Rest," Hamet announced briefly.

Ben and I sank to the ground, while Hamet fell to stripping the burros. Presently I found the strength to rise and help him. When the beasts were tethered Hamet produced a handful of dates and a cold shoulder of mutton. But before we could eat he spread his rug and knelt upon it facing the east.

"Do as I do," he commanded, "and repeat after me."

Ben roused himself from his weary lethargy momentarily. "What for?" he demanded.

Hamet eyed him, I thought, with some distaste.

"Ye are not Mussulmen, sirs," he explained, "but before we come to the end of this journey it will be necessary for ye to act as such many times. It is well then, now while we are not observed, to learn our morning and evening ritual."

Ben grumbled, but I silenced him, for it was evident that of all his bargain this was what Hamet regretted most. There followed our daily prayers to the east, and after a time, and some prompting and repetition, Hamet announced himself satisfied.

"That is enough," he said. "Remember! If aught happens to me, this must be done morning and evening without fail, and at intervals through the day. If thou canst not remember the words, thou mayest mumble them. But the movements must be followed exactly. Do not forget them! Thy lives may depend upon it."

He served out our breakfast then and instructed us in the

way we must eat, using only our right hands, for this, also, was the common custom. As we ate he told us something of the route we were to follow, which was south through the mountains and then bearing east, keeping always back from the coast.

"Why don't we follow the coast road?" Ben asked when I explained this to him. "Isn't that the usual way?"

Hamet nodded.

"Aye, that is the usual way, and for that reason we do not follow it. That way will be searched. Moreover, it is the route of the army that has but lately marched. It will be traveled by couriers, passing to and from the army and the city, and we might be recognized. This route is longer, but it is also safer."

I saw the point and agreed. Ben was too weary to argue.

"We sleep now," Hamet announced, and wrapped himself in his blanket. Nor did Ben and I need any second hint.

I awoke when the sun was high and the flies were thick upon my face. Hamet was already before me, replacing the panniers upon our animals, who showed less fatigue than any of us. Ben was difficult to arouse, but came, grumbling, at last from his blanket and stood up with an almost audible creaking. He groaned, and I knew how he felt. Hamet grinned.

"It will soon work out," he said.

Ben only spat. We ate another handful of dates and an orange with difficulty, for the flies were so thick that it was all but impossible to keep them clear of the food for the instant necessary to convey it to our mouths. I fear I showed my disgust. Hamet laughed.

"It is the bled—the country. Make thyself accustomed to it and ignore them, else wilt thou mark thyself a stranger!"

It was about midmorning when we resumed our march, and now the track, which the night before had been deserted, had a fairly frequent passage of travel. About once in the hour we would meet a family or a party of beldi, or countryfolk, their belongings packed upon camels and asses, their old folk riding and their younger ones running barefoot, driving their sheep and their goats across the countryside, without regard to the trail. Now and again we met a smaller party, passing from group to group, riding upon asses or walking; ragged folk, in the simplest homespun bournouses, and without a slipper to their name, yet seemingly happy. Unlike the townsfolk, the women were unveiled and bold, meeting glance for glance and exchanging banter for banter; tattooed forehead, nose, and chin, but for the most part far from handsome. Here and there we passed black tents, out of which ran a swarm of children, half naked, and idlers, to run at our flanks and pass with us the time of day, and I wondered how we had chanced to miss these groups during our passage of the night until I realized that their camp sites were so chosen that in darkness they would not be evident.

With all of these we passed greetings, and though I had had small confidence in my command of Arabic at our departure, I was amazed at the speed with which I fell into the habit of it. Nevertheless, Hamet was careful to halt at midday at a spot where we might take our food and our brief rest in private. At that time he chose to compliment me.

"Ye do well," he said. "Thou wilt have no difficulty."

By dusk we had reached the long wadis of the Jebel and had begun to climb between barren, rock-scarred slopes with a stream gurgling at our left amid a scattering of gnarled trees. Here Hamet turned again from the trail and, crossing the little splashing river, led the way to some caves in the face of the mountain, where he announced we would pass the night. As darkness fell we could hear the hyenas laughing in the ravine above us, and the chatter of the apes upon the upper slopes kept company with the gurgle of the stream at our feet. But, though our bed was a ledge of rock and the musty smell of Africa lay like a hand upon us, I will confess that I, for one, slept as soundly as ever I did in a bed at home. In the morning we rose with the sun and pushed onward, climbing into the mountains, until, topping the ridge, we came upon the village of Tarhunah, a cluster of flat-roofed mud houses huddled together about an open market place in the midst of a scattering of date palms and olive trees.

We rested here only long enough to replenish our supplies of dates and figs, fearful lest we might be recognized. But nothing untoward happened, although I noticed that several of the villagers eyed Ben's musket with a touch of envy. Toward noon we pushed on, and by nightfall found ourselves, after traversing a rugged, barren, up-and-down country, at Gasr ed Tenshuiah, a walled outpost composed of a mud castle and a cluster of hovels enclosed in a high, thick, mud-daubed wall in the midst of jagged mountain country.

Until this point I had not been called upon to act my role of tabib. Now, however, being for the night among others, at the small fondouk where man and beast lay down together, it was necessary to account for my presence in one way or another. Consequently Hamet spread my fame about and fetched me several patients, with ailments extending from running sores to afflictions of the eyes. For these I prescribed various remedies: salves for both eyes and sores in the main, but now and again ordering burning for the sores and sheep's, ass's, or goat's urine for the eyes—which Hamet informed me was often the custom of the country quacks. Here and there I applied some remedy which I knew to be efficacious for a malady which I recognized. Each treatment, whether sound or for effect, was accompanied by a pious incantation, and I must admit that both Hamet and Ben—the former by his vociferousness, and the latter by his evident awed silence—added much to the performance. The upshot was that we left the caravanserai the next morning at dawn, in company with some folk bound for Bir el Uar, with something of a reputation, although I observed that there were here again a few who eyed Ben's musket with some covetous-ness.

Nevertheless we were not molested that day, during which we got some leagues to the south and eastward of Gasr ed Tenshuiah, over rugged, precipitous country, before we camped in a gorge of the Oued Maader. The next morning, bidding farewell to our companions, who turned off to the west, we con-tinued to Graret Darbuc, another small walled village and mud castle, where we spent another night. From here it was still another long day's journey to Beni Ulid, in the country of the Beni Orfella, a bright valley spotted with oases of date palms and green with new fields of barley and young corn be-tween the rock-crested hills.

Here at last Hamet breathed easily.

"From here," he announced, "we need not fear pursuit. These people are not friendly to the bashaw's deputies, and they will not follow us here. Only the dangers of the road lie before us."

He did not enlarge upon this, but it seemed to me that the

people we encountered here were little different from those we
had met in the mountains. They were a little better fed and less
wary, but they had the same difficulties. Three men came to me
with carbuncles, which I burned, having learned by now that
the harsher the treatment the surer the cure in their simple
eyes, actual cautery being regarded as the sovereign remedy for
all external ills save those of the eye.

Despite Hamet's optimism, however, our difficulties increased from this point onward; though, as he predicted, they
were the difficulties of the road. From Beni Ulid to Bu Njem
was a five days' journey under the best conditions. We needed
eight. Our first day led us across flat uplands and over the
green gullies of three sizable wadis. But not long before dusk
we encountered a cloudburst which so swelled the Wadi Soffe-
ghin that it was questionable whether we should attempt to
cross. Since we had not long before passed a party of Bedaween,
Hamet was determined, if possible, to put the river between
us and them, and accordingly we drove into it, Hamet leading
the spare animal, carrying our food and blankets, while Ben
and I followed close behind.

All might have been well had we been able to keep to the
ford, but the swift current and high water had washed it away
in one spot, and all at once we found ourselves floundering in
the current and, all three of us, being swept swiftly down-
stream. Ben managed to save himself by clinging to his ass's
tail, as Hamet shouted to us to do. I struck out for the shore
with all my strength, half dragging my beast by its lead rope
and half clinging to it for support. Hamet clung to a pannier
upon his own beast and so came safely to the far shore, but
not without losing his hold on the lead rope of the pack burro,
which, heavily laden, was swept down in the turgid yellow
stream and lost. Nor did all our search along the bank reveal
the least sign of him.

We spent a cold, supperless night by the river; Hamet be-
wailed his fortune, while I, in my naïveté, counted our bless-
ings. To be sure, we had lost our provisions and our blankets,
and the earthen jug of water that the spare beast had carried.
But we still had a small kettle and all our personal belongings.
My medicines and instruments were still in the pannier on my
own burro, and Ben still had his musket and a hornful of dry

powder, the stopper of which had remained tight during his ducking, not to mention a reasonable supply of shot. Thus far small game had not been scarce, nor had water, and since I still retained the bulk of my money in my belt about my waist I felt we would have no trouble getting on to Bu Njem, where we should be able to re-equip.

Long before morning, however, my empty stomach was crying out in protest, and when, in the dark hour before dawn, Hamet rolled over and woke me, bidding me rise and follow him, I was glad enough to do so without question. In the darkness I did not see him take the musket and powder horn and shot pouch from Ben—who never once stirred—until he had straightened and I saw the tip of the piece against the blueblack of the sky.

"Where are we going?" I asked.

"To get food before we starve," he replied.

He led me upstream in the gradually graying dawn, evidently searching for something upon the ground. Presently he grunted and showed me a well-beaten path that came down to the water's edge.

"Stay back," he commanded, "a small way from the river, and below the track. If anything comes to drink, do not show yourself until they break. Then, if they run toward you, rise and fling these clubs among them. Throw for their legs."

He armed me with three or four clubs cut from a thornwood tree, each about three or four feet in length.

"What shall I expect?" I asked. But he was already gone, climbing the escarpment above the riverbank.

I did as he told me, lying close hidden amid the brush for what seemed to me hours before a small herd of gazelles appeared upon the runway and came down toward the river to drink.

The sight of them excited me, and I was about to rise and rush toward them, when a shot from above startled the animals. One of them tumbled in the pathway, and the rest turned sharply away from the sound and came leaping and bounding toward me in such prodigious jumps that for an instant I was too startled to act. By the time I had gathered my wits they were upon me, and I rose up, scattering them in all directions and twirling my clubs, let fly where they were thickest.

One of my weapons caught one of the graceful little beasts in the ribs and tumbled him momentarily to the ground, where I flung myself upon him. Another club apparently cut squarely across the legs of a third, for Hamet presently appeared holding up that one and the one he had shot, and assisted me in subduing the one that I had fallen upon—no small task, for his horns and his hoofs were sharp as razors and I had rents in both myself and my clothing by the time I was relieved.

By this means we had meat for this day and the next, as well as the day following, for the animals were about the size of a large hound, with meat of a texture similar to venison, only more delicate. On the third night, however, we woke just as an overbold jackal slipped into camp and made off with what remained of the last carcass, so that we were left with neither meat nor water, the river in which we had lost our ass being the last we had crossed, and our lone remaining water bag being now empty.

Thus we were in sorry straits throughout our fourth day, and we began to know something of the torment of thirst on the land, which is different from thirst at sea in that it is not possible there even to wet one's hands and face. To add to our difficulties, the character of the country had changed almost mockingly, and we now found ourselves in a region where the tawny sand of the dunes was only briefly interspersed with rocky, treeless barrens in which the only living things we saw were snakes and scorpions and lizards and an occasional vulture.

About midmorning of the fifth day we came to a tiny oasis, a mere cluster of palms, in the midst of the rocks, with a spring of water bubbling up in the middle of it. Imagine my disgust, however, when we found the place aswarm with locusts and the spring's surface a good six inches deep under their squirming bodies.

Ben, too, was repelled. But Hamet gave out a whoop of delight. I stared at him in amazement.

"Jeraada!" he cried. "We will not starve, at least!"

Taking up Ben's musket, he directed us to gather sticks for a fire. When we returned he had shredded a few rags and, with powder from Ben's horn, had made of them squills to serve as tinder. He placed a handful of sticks over these and, flashing the lock of the gun into them, set a quick little fire. Then he took our remaining small kettle and scooped up a kettleful of the squirming locusts from the spring and put them on to boil. After they had steamed for a few moments he lifted the pot from the fire and offered it to us.

I thought Ben would be ill.

"I'm not hungry enough for that!" I said.

"Try!" he grinned. "Try! This is an old dish in the desert. Thou'lt find it not bad."

"No, thank you!" I replied.

He shrugged and pulled the pot toward himself and, dipping in gingerly, selected a large insect. Carefully he stripped away legs and wings and popped the creature in his mouth, chewing with an almost offensive crackling and a grin that said we were plain fools if we did not follow his example.

I rose and walked away, unable to watch, but after a moment my hunger and loneliness drew me back, and as I approached I saw Ben reach out for the pot. As I sat down, quietly, not far from him, he glanced at me and drew back, hesitating; then, almost defiantly, he reached out again and selected a good-sized locust, peeled it as he had seen Hamet do, and thrust it into his mouth.

I expected to see him spit it out instantly, but instead a look of ludicrous amazement spread across his face. He gave me a startled glance, swallowed, and reached again quickly for the pot and took another of the creatures, followed by another and another. For a few moments I watched him in utter wonder, and then, unable longer to deny either my curiosity or my hunger, I too reached out and picked up an insect as big as a mouse. With the greatest distaste I peeled away legs and wings and took a bite of it. To my intense surprise it was meaty and crisp and had somewhat the flavor of a prawn. Hastily I gulped the rest of it and reached for another. Within half an hour we had emptied the pot and Hamet had put a second on to boil.

"I'm damned!" exclaimed Ben. "I'm damned! If anyone had told me a while ago that I would eat grasshoppers and like 'em, I'd have called 'em crazy! But d'ye know," he added, turning to me, "they're most as good as a trout!"

"They're better fried in olive oil with a pinch of salt and a drop of vinegar," Hamet chuckled. "A pity we have none!"

"How did it happen ye knew this?" I asked.

"In my country, which is at the edge of the desert," he shrugged, "when the jeraada come there is nothing else to eat."

We rested the balance of that day and night in the tiny oasis and felt that our troubles were over when we managed to snare a half dozen rabbits. A porridge of locusts and stewed rabbit gave us strength for the next day's journey, while the palms of the oasis yielded us a near half pannierful of dates. Using the hides of the two gazelles, which we still had left after the jackal's thievery, Hamet fashioned a rude water bottle, so that with that and the goatskin we felt prepared to push on.

On the seventh day, in the evening, as luck would have it, we came at dusk to an encampment of Bedaween in the single oasis which we encountered. It was too late to avoid them, and Hamet advised us to ride boldly in and bid them a proper good night.

We followed him down from the high dunes, feeling not at all certain of our reception, and rode among the black goatskin tents, giving greetings here and there to silently staring folk as we passed in the direction of the wells.

Once among them, I confess I also had doubts, for these were none of the half-farmer-half-nomad people that we had thus far encountered. I saw, too, that Hamet was also afraid. These were what he called Laurbi—desert folk—lean, warlike men with sharp, alert eyes, who masked their faces in blue cloth against the sun and wore little but breeches and a haik for clothing. They eyed us with ill-concealed suspicion.

At the wells, obeying Hamet to the letter, we halted and, after making our obeisances to Mecca, we set about quietly to make camp. A few of our neighbors gathered about, no move of ours escaping their sharp eyes; yet we strove to pay them no attention, and presently a tall one, better clothed than the rest, appeared from among them and squatted before our fireside.

This was the moment, I felt, for which I needed all my wits, for Hamet had warned me that I would be expected to take the lead.

"The blessing of Allah on thee," I said.

"And on thy people," he responded punctiliously.

He glanced about our camp, and I offered him a bit of the stew we were eating, apologizing that we had no better.

He dipped in his hand politely and ate, asking at the same time if I had no tea. I told him what had happened.

He grunted and dipped again into our pot.

"Thou'rt strange to these parts?" he asked.

"I am a tabib of Morocco, bound on the hadj," I replied. "These are my slave and my servant, whom I have from Tafilet."

This was what Hamet had told me to say, and I was relieved to see that our guest nodded acceptance.

"Ye travel in poor circumstances," he said. "Have ye come all the way so?"

I thanked God then that we had rehearsed every possible situation as we rode across the empty desert.

"We were robbed in el Jefren," I replied. "Only by grace of the kaid of el Garian did we escape with our lives!"

"They are thieves, el Jefreni," he agreed. "Ye have done well to come so far, blessed is the name of Allah!"

"Bismillah!—in the name of God!" I replied piously.

His eye fell upon Ben's musket.

"A handsome gun!"

I reached over and picked it up.

"It is thine!" I replied.

He took it in his hands and bowed ceremoniously.

"God's peace be on thee!" he said.

"And on thy people peace," I replied.

He rose, holding the weapon in his hand.

"My house is at thy command."

"In God's mercy will I call upon thee," I answered.

Hamet gave me a quick nod as he disappeared in the darkness.

"Go to his tent," he said, "and eat what he puts before thee. We will be taken care of."

"What about my gun?" Ben growled.

"It would be taken from thee in any case," Hamet told him. "But I think ye will find its equal returned."

I confess to a sense of misgiving as I went, but I was surprised to find the sand of the oasis, under the rough goatskin tent, laden with rich carpets and lighted with lamps of argan oil. My host was seated upon the rug, much more richly dressed than when I last saw him.

"My house be thine," he remarked as I entered.

"Daif Allah—the guest of God," I replied, which bound him to our protection as long as we were within his domain.

The meal he produced then was such as I had not had since leaving Tripoli. Indeed, it was such as I had seldom eaten before. Gazelle and mutton, couscous and barley formed the principal course, followed by corn and honey, and a paste of sweetened gum afterward, which was entirely new to me. We ate with ceremony, served, not by male slaves, but by women unveiled, who were no beauties but who met the eye steadily and who smelled rankly of rancid sheep's grease.

I was careful to behave as Hamet had taught me, and apparently I passed muster, for the kaid, my host, asked me if I could cure his son of boils. When I replied that I could, he brought in a youth whose face was marked with the usual eruptions of his age. These I touched lightly with the hot iron, more for the appearance than for any actual effect, and thereafter anointed them with a salve of euphorbium resiniferum, which is native to the desert, and assured him that if he repeated the treatment, touching not too deeply with the iron, all trace of the eruption would be gone in a matter of time.

In the morning our host came to bid us farewell, and as a parting present gave us twenty ducats in gold and two firelocks, guns to be sure, requiring the touch of a match to set them off, but nonetheless firearms, and by that token twice what we had surrendered to him. For my own part I thought the exchange well worth making, although Ben grumbled at the antiquity of the pieces. These were above suspicion, while the other bore the bashaw's stamp and, had we met any of his people, might have led us into difficulties. In addition the kaid himself supplied us with directions to Bu Njem and enjoined us to notify him if we met with any molestation, swearing that he would avenge us if he could not rescue us. Upon this promise of friendship we parted.

I left that place much cheered, for it seemed to me that the people of the desert were not so savage as Hamet made out. However, we were not three hours from Bu Njem when we fell in with a different sort. In the course of following up a rocky wadi to the plain upon which the city stood, we found ourselves suddenly confronted, seemingly from out of the barren rocks themselves, by a half a score of Arabs in ragged caftans, who barred our road before and behind and to the flanks, with clubs in hand, and demanded who we were, whence we came, and whither we went.

Hamet turned gray and appeared to lose all power of speech at sight of them, whereat I, to the best of my ability, answered that we were pilgrims from Morocco, under the protection of the kaid of Er Recha, our late host, and bound for Bu Njem. At this they seemed unimpressed, and one of them reached suddenly for the musket which Ben carried slung across his shoulder. Ben drew back and struck out with his fist, whereupon they fell on us in a body, beating us with their cudgels, wresting our weapons from us, and all but stripping the clothing from our bodies.

Their onslaught was not altogether unexpected. I was surprised to see Hamet tumble from his mount and cover his head with his arms, whilst three of the ruffians whacked the dust from his back with their staves. But more than this I had little chance to observe, for their spokesman came at me, and I was obliged to put my foot in his stomach. Then, tumbling off my ass, I bounced up with a handful of stones, which I flung in his face. As I did so I saw Ben whip out his knife and bury it in the throat of his assailant, while simultaneously it seemed to me the man's staff caught him alongside the head, opening his cheek from mouth to ear.

My own opponent came back at me at this instant, and I saw no more of what my companions were doing for a moment. But there is no question but that, despite our resistance, they must ultimately have overpowered us and stripped us, if not murdered us, had not a party of our late host's, sent to see that we came safely to Bu Njem, arrived and sent them packing.

They left one of their number—the one that had felt Ben's knife in his throat—dead upon the field. But we, on our side, were not without losses. In fleeing they took both of the muskets that we had been given, as well as Hamet's burro with all of his belongings. Ben had the ragged cut I had seen him receive and a rapidly closing eye, and I was myself conscious of a spreading nose and a couple of loose teeth. But Hamet appeared the worst sufferer of us all, for he lay face down upon the pathway, kicking his toes in the dust and scrabbling in the

gravel with his fingers. Alarmed, I endeavored to turn him
over and knelt beside him, while our rescuers gathered about us.

"Aieee!" he wailed, and I feared his ribs were broken,
wherefore I handled him with the greatest tenderness.

"Where is it worst, Hamet?" I asked.

"Aieee!" he groaned again. "Give me thy knife that I may
end my misery!"

"No, man!" I cried. "It cannot be so bad as that. Tell me
where it hurts worst, and I will tell thee what I can do."

He rolled over and sat up abruptly.

"Can I tell thee that?" he cried. "Am I not ground to little
pieces within my guts?"

I grew alarmed at that, thinking that he had sustained some
inward injury, and tried to press him back. But he would have
none of this. Instead he seized a handful of dust and poured
it upon his head.

"Woe is my lot!" he cried. "Allah has visited this upon me!"

"What is it, man?" I cried.

"Can ye ask?" he cried. "Am I not destitute once more?
Have I not been robbed of my all—of my ass and my robes and
my money? What is left to me but the clothes I stand in?"

I could not help myself, I began to laugh. He glared at me
resentfully.

"Ye think it a matter for laughing?"

I sobered instantly.

"I laugh," I told him, "for relief. I thought it so much
worse! Come, man! We have our lives and two asses, and I
have yet all that I brought from Tripoli. Bu Njem is no great
distance. There we will find other mounts and I will make up
to thee all that thou hast lost!"

What our friends of the Ouled Recha thought I am not prepared to say, but it was all the tonic Hamet needed. He
scrambled to his feet and wrung my hand and then fell to dust-
ing himself off gingerly.

"Every bone in my body is broken!" he complained.

"If thou hast more than bruises I will trade skins with thee,"
I told him dryly.

I turned my attention to Ben then, stanching the flow of his
blood and binding his cut. Thereafter we resumed our journey,
taking turns upon our two remaining burros and escorted by

our rescuers, whom I took care to reward, to Bu Njem, which we reached a full hour before sundown.

We lay four days at Bu Njem, a desert city at the northernmost edge of the Fezzan, considering our next step. Hamet was for striking northeastward to the coast, there to follow the road into Cyrenaica, whence we might again strike toward the east and pass around the bashaw's expedition, which was rallying at Derne. He gave as reason for this a tribe called the Senussi, which he apparently held in great fear.

For my part, I preferred the Senussi to the bashaw's people. It was my plan to go directly east a prudent distance, keeping away from the coast, then to turn northward to the sea somewhere east of Derne, where we might either join General Eaton or continue eastward into Egypt as might best suit our case. Since I controlled the purse strings, it was I who had the last word, and we proceeded to dispose of our burros and undertook to hire camels for the rest of the way.

This was easier planned than done. The cameleers of the city seemed as frightened by the Senussi as Hamet. Had I been wise, I suppose, I should have settled the matter by buying the animals and proceeding independently. But a good camel is not cheap, and this seemed to me an unnecessary expense. Moreover, I knew nothing of the beasts, and it seemed to me that advantage would easily be taken. Nevertheless I was determined that we should have them. I was done with traveling in poverty. On camels we would ride in comparative luxury, covering as much distance in a single day as we would on asses in three. We could carry enough provisions to see us to the end of our journey. And if we were set upon by thieves, we would have at least a chance of outrunning them.

I was emphatically supported in this by Ben, who rarely had occasion to agree with me but who had also had his fill of dawdling. I had almost come to the decision to buy the animals if need be when, on our third evening in the town, a villainous-looking Arab presented himself at our fondouk and asked for el Tabib Moghrebbin, by which he meant me.

Hamet was absent at the moment, seeking camels, so I could not call upon him; accordingly, I greeted my caller after the Moslem fashion, at which I was by now fairly adept, and invited him in. After the customary coffee and the usual flowery compliments, I gradually found means to ask him his business, thinking that no doubt it had to do with my profession. Instead he said that he had heard that we were contemplating continuing our journey to the east and were in search of transport.

His name, he told me, was Ahmed Ben Khali Ibn Abd er Rahman, and he had lately arrived in the city and learned that a wealthy tabib of the west—on whom be peace—was bound upon the hadj and sought camels into Egypt.

I let the question of wealth pass for the moment and assured him that I was indeed in search of the means of continuing my journey, but that, for reasons of my own, I wished to avoid the usual route through Benghazi and Derne. When I asked if he thought this were possible and what it would cost, he cast up his eyes to the ceiling and calculated and finally named a price that, as I had expected, was out of all reason.

We descended then to the haggling, without which no bargain is ever struck in those parts, and over innumerable cups of coffee and a quantity of sweetmeats we dickered backward and forward, exchanging the vilest of insults, as is also customary, until, in the end, I made him a price beyond which I would not go. At this point Hamet appeared, and my guest rose to take his leave, saying he would bring me his answer in the morning.

When he was gone Hamet turned to me.

"What is this?" he asked. "Who is this man?"

I explained to him the circumstances and he spat.

"Arbi!" he exclaimed. "He is a thief. I do not trust him!"

"Aye!" I cried. "He is an Arab, and undoubtedly a thief. But he offers what we need and must have."

"But the price," Hamet protested. "It is too high!"

"It is high," I agreed, "but have we a choice? We must get on! I am willing to pay!"

"It is too much!" he argued.

"I agree," I replied. "But I do not mean to spend my days in Bu Njem!"

"I do not trust him," he growled, falling back upon his first argument.

"No more do I," I said, "but what can he do? No doubt he knows I am no more Moorish doctor than he, but there is honor among thieves!"

"Not among such as he," he replied.

"Nonsense!" I scoffed. "He is as afraid of the Senussi as thyself. Our common dread will drive us together. What if I pay him something more than he is worth? Once he is on the road he will go through with it, if only because he must!"

"Didst tell him that thou hast thy gold on thee?"

"I said nothing of where I carried my wealth," I replied, adding with a laugh, "If ye call it wealth! A thief he may be, but he is at least astute enough to know that his reward will be greater for bringing us through safely than for leaving us in the desert."

"Thou'rt more confident than I," he said lugubriously.

"Ye start at shadows!" I laughed.

"May it not be the shadow of death!" he said piously.

With that we left it. In the morning Ahmed Ben Khali called upon me again and, after a short argument, agreed to the terms I had set. Ben was jubilant.

"Now we're getting on!" he cried. "I thought you'd never make sense!"

"If I make sense now," I told him coldly, "as far as you are concerned, it is only because I am in this as deep as you."

"If it weren't for me you'd be still a prisoner," he retorted, "and God knows when you'd be free, if ever!"

"We're not free yet," I reminded him.

"Sidna! Sidna!" Hamet protested uneasily. "If we quarrel amongst ourselves, how can we meet our enemies?"

Even Ben was shamed to silence by that.

We left Bu Njem, not that day, but upon the morning following, after trying, in vain, to obtain arms of some description. Muskets in that region commanded a higher price than camels. As for pistols, they were not to be had.

Our company consisted of Hamet and Ben and myself, Ahmed Ben Khali, and four "cousins" who were his assistants. Hamet protested, but Ahmed swore they were necessary.

"We must return by the same route," he said, "and a small party is not safe."

I was inclined to agree with Hamet but saw no worse in it than that they meant to make as much advantage of a good thing as possible, and certainly, I felt, there was safety in numbers. And so I did not protest more than halfheartedly, although a more villainous-seeming crew I hope I may never see again.

Despite their evident villainy, however, we made excellent going at first. Our route followed the line of the black rock mountains, the Jebel Welad Hasan, the Jebel Es Suda, and the Jebel Morai Yeh, whose successive ridges towered upon our right flank and shut us off from the endless steppes of the Fezzan. The road we followed lay through barren, rocky country, in which, oftentimes, there was not so much as a low bush or a hummock of grass to break the hot expanse of stone and shale. In such country even a sand dune was a welcome diversion, and the intensity with which the sun beat down upon the bare rocks soon taught me why the people of this region rode with faces veiled. On the second night we stopped at el Khadder, a cluster of scrawny palms grouped about a stinking puddle of water scooped in the rocks and by courtesy called a well. On the next we were at Mrada, a more extensive oasis at the end of the rock country. Beyond this we entered the region of seemingly eternal sand, where we rode as if through a petrified sea, over wave after wave of wind-whipped dune, only now and again coming upon a tiny pocket of palms in the hollow of the sand hills, where a little water oozed up about the roots and the dung of all manner of desert beasts strewed the edges of the pools.

At first it was weary riding, so different was it from the short little jog of the burros. Even when they walked, which was seldom, the camels had a sort of racking pitch which threatened to snap our necks where they joined our spines. When they ran, which was much of the time, at a long swinging trot, it was like being tossed about on a bouncing pole. But one grew accustomed to it, learned to swing with the movement, and while I could never learn to love it, or even to pretend that I enjoyed it, I at least learned to endure it in silence.

On the fifth day, after a dry camp, we pressed on across an endless sea of sand, with the hot breath of the syroc upon our necks and the last vestiges of the mountains left far behind. About midday we passed a long caravan, escorted by blue-veiled riders, who eyed us with hostile suspicion. I noticed that they wore neither the bournous of the Tripolines nor the djellab, such as we, as Moors, wore, but rather had on a sort of fine woolen, striped, capeless cloak, which I came to know later as an aba. On their heads, above the blue veils which covered their faces except for their eyes, they wore what looked like a species of low turban, bound round with cords of black goat's hair, and the eyes they turned upon us, following us as we passed, were bright black and sharply unfriendly. My companions seemed nervous and apprehensive as we passed among them, and for some time afterward I noticed Ben Khali casting quick glances backward and around the southern horizon.

When I asked him what troubled him, however, he only gave me a sheepish glance and a mumbled answer, of which the only word I could understand was, "Senussi."

That night we continued our journey until almost dusk, stopping at last at a tiny oasis called Bir el Ghodran, where, when the hour for supper arrived, our companions drew a little apart from us with their meal and presently fell to arguing violently among themselves in tones so low that we could not catch a word of it. When the meal was ended Ben Khali rejoined us, sitting down cross-legged before our small fire, and sipped the coffee we offered him; a man with something on his mind.

At last I could bear this no longer, so I wrung the tail of the devil, as the saying is, and asked what troubled him.

He shook his head ominously.

"This is a bad journey," he said. "We—my cousins and I—now wish that we had not undertaken it."

"Nonsense!" I exclaimed. "What do ye fear?"

"Fear?" he cried angrily, and I saw his hand move beneath his bournous. "Who dares to call Ben Khali afraid?"

I spat into the fire, though my throat felt suddenly dry, and Ben and Hamet sat across from me like statues.

"Take thy hand from thy dagger, Ben Khali," I managed to growl. "Ye gain nothing with bluster. What is it ye want?"

I thought he relaxed slightly.

"We draw nigh to the country of the Senussi," he growled.

"Aye," I agreed noncommittally.

"We should have passed further north—by the coast road."

"Ye knew the road we were to follow before we started," I replied abruptly. "If ye were afraid or unwilling to take it, then was the time to say so—not now, when we are half over it."

"We did not think then of the Senussi," he said.

This was such an obvious lie that I did not even deign to answer it, but merely grunted in derision. He scowled.

"My cousins wish to turn back."

I shrugged.

"The jackal starts at his own shadow," I said, "and not even Allah can stop him!"

He cast his eyes toward the heavens, as if calling upon the stars to witness that he was an honest, patient man, trying to advise me to my own good, but that I was too stubborn to listen.

"It is not that they are afraid," he explained carefully. "It is only that they see no profit in it."

"Their profit," I replied, "is a matter to be agreed upon between ye. Our agreement was between thee and me."

"That is true," he nodded. "But it is this which troubles them: What if we are set upon by the Senussi and aught happens to thee? Then, do ye not see it, they have all their trouble and danger for naught."

"Not," I prompted him, "unless the same fate befalls thee."

"If I could but show them some gold," he sighed, "I might persuade them to go on."

"I paid thee a third of thy hire before we left," I replied. "Why not give them their share of that?"

He stared at me.

"That!" he exclaimed. "That was all spent for supplies. I have none of it now!"

"I am sorry for that," I said.

He pursed his lips, as if he found it hard to bear with my obtuseness.

"If thou wouldst pay us now what ye owe us," he said, "I will answer for my cousins that they will complete the journey."

I stared at him.

"I owe thee?" I cried. "Ben Khali, thou knowest our agreement! One third to be paid in advance, and the rest on arrival at our destination! I owe thee naught until that day!"

"Pay us half," he countered.

"I will pay thee naught," I cried, "until the appointed time!"

He rose with a shrug.

"I cannot answer, then, for what my cousins will do."

"Tell thy cousins," I replied, "that if they ever expect aught of me they will continue their journey to its end!"

It was Ben who burst out when he had gone. In the course of our journey he had picked up enough of the language to be able to understand some of what had been said.

"The dirty swine!" he cried. "I knew they were up to some deviltry. By God, you did not encourage him, Tom?"

"Did it look to you that I had?" I demanded.

Hamet only shook his head.

"Did I not warn thee?" he said.

"What's to do?" Ben demanded.

"Do?" I cried. "Why, nothing but stand firm!"

Hamet leaned forward abruptly.

"If we are wise, this is what we will do," he said in a low tone. "Wait until they sleep. Then slit their throats."

I stared at him aghast. As much as I learned about these people, I was never able to accept their complaisant attitude toward treachery.

"That's murder!" I protested.

He looked at me as if I were half-witted.

"We will never see the coast if we do not!"

"Nonsense!" I cried. "They're merely trying to bluff us. If we stand firm they will carry out their bargain."

Hamet sighed and turned away, offering no further argument, and presently we retired to our blankets.

I slept but fitfully that night, something of Hamet's unease sticking in my mind. From time to time I started awake and roused up, glancing to see that all was quiet. But each time all was serene. In the morning we breakfasted and the packs were filled and made fast, quite as if nothing had happened. When we mounted and set out, however, instead of turning toward the east, in the direction we had been traveling, Ahmed Ben Khali calmly turned his beast's head back along the trail we had but just followed and started back the way we had come.

"Where are you going?" I cried. "This is the way!"

Ben Khali halted and turned about to eye me gravely.

"This is the way we go, my cousins and I," he replied.

It was at this point that I made my gravest blunder.

"Wait!" I cried, feeling helpless. "Come back! Let us not be too hasty! Let us discuss the matter further."

Without going into the interminable haggling that followed, the long and short of it was that I agreed to pay them, then and there, half the sum remaining, and to allow an additional sum for each "cousin" upon arrival at the coast. With this they appeared satisfied, and I, in all innocence, counted out the gold upon a blanket and paid it over. When we were once again upon our road Hamet, with a grave face, found occasion to draw back alongside of me, imperceptibly shaking his head.

"It were better if ye had not done that," he said.

"Why?" I said. "We are upon the way again, and they are happy. It is nothing to me if they have their money now or later, and a small bite was no more than I expected."

He shrugged.

"Aye," he said, "but the thief who steals a little will steal more if he sees the opportunity, and they know now that ye carry gold with ye. It will be wise to keep a close watch from here on. Let thy hand be never far from thy knife!"

I told myself that this was nonsense, yet at the midday halt they drew apart again and put their heads together. Though they said nothing further at that time, I knew then that Hamet was right and that we had not heard the end of the business. Yet when we resumed our journey I was almost persuaded that I was starting at shadows, so cheerful and friendly were they.

We pushed on, making excellent time despite the sharp up-and-down nature of the going, until late afternoon, when our shadows leaped before us from the western crests of the dunes, like those of beasts on stilts, and the chill which accompanies the desert night began to be felt in the air. It was near dusk, and we were yet far from any oasis, when Ahmed Ben Khali halted in a deep hollow between two dunes and forced his mount to kneel.

"What are we stopping for?" I demanded, suddenly alert.

He shrugged as he slid to the ground.

"It is yet far to Bir es Zitoun," he replied. "It is well to take here some refreshment."

There was nothing in this suggestion to arouse my suspicions, for it was often our practice to take tea and to eat a few dates in the afternoon when it was likely that we would be traveling late into the night. Nothing untoward happened until the tea had been brewed and served and we were lifting our glasses to our lips, when Ahmed Ben Khali spoke.

"Give us the gold ye carry," he said, "and we will bring ye safe to the coast."

Even then, I think, I might have bargained, or at least gained us a respite. But Hamet was before me.

"Oh, thief!" he cried, dashing his glass of hot tea in El Khali's face, and started to his feet with knife half drawn.

Out of the corner of my eye I saw Mustapha and Idris fling themselves upon him, their blades flashing in the last rays of the sun, and I, too, started up, fumbling for my weapon. But I had not gained my knees when the sky seemed to fall upon my neck. The dunes and the camels and my companions all seemed to merge in a vast whirling explosion, turning to bright lights and flashes and then into darkness. I felt myself plunge forward with a great weight upon me. For an instant I struggled, and then a second blow fell and everything seemed to draw away, leaving me floating in a vast vacuum as black as the night of hell.

It seemed to me no more than an instant that I lay so, floating in the darkness. Yet when I opened my eyes it was night and I lay with my face in the cold sand, with a sound of diabolical laughter ringing in my ears. When I moved, raising myself upon my hands, a wave of nausea and pain sent me spinning back into oblivion, and I collapsed once more upon the sand, where I lay weakly, half between living and dying, until gradually, over what time I had no conception, I came slowly back and became fleetingly conscious of stealthy patterings about me.

For a long time, it seemed to me, I lay, overcome by a great lassitude. But after a time I opened my eyes and cautiously raised up on hands and knees, and then wearily turned over and sat.

It was dark. The skies overhead were like a purple blanket studded with jewels. But there was no moon. I glanced about, though each movement of my head set it to spinning, and abruptly encountered a warm, slavering breath and was conscious of a sound as of panting. Almost in my ear the screaming laughter rang out again, and instinctively I clutched a handful of sand and flung it indiscriminately toward the sound. There was again a noise of pattering flight, and the scream was repeated from a greater distance. I shook my head and struggled to my knees.

"Ben!" I cried. "Ben! Hamet!"

I was answered by a groan, which seemed to come from my left. Gingerly I felt my way in that direction and presently came upon a body which stirred under my touch.

"Who's that?" I cried, and recoiled abruptly.

I was answered only by another groan.

Gradually something of my position crept in upon my consciousness. I ran trembling hands across my body and found myself naked as the day I was born. For a moment I crouched where I was, until I heard a faint stirring before me, and, my eyes growing a little accustomed to the night, I made out the dark figure of a man against the lighter background of the sand. Gingerly I turned him over. He stirred and fought feebly.

"Ben!" I whispered. "Ben! Is it you?"

The response was no more than a half-grunted moan.

"Unh—aaahhh!"

"Ben!" I cried again. "Ben! 'Tis me, Tom!"

He sighed heavily.

"Tooommm!"

Behind me I heard the scrabbling sound once more and turned and flung another handful of sand. When I turned back Ben was sitting up.

"Tom?" he said.

"Here!" I replied.

"What happened?"

I sat back and pondered that for a moment, for my own head was still spinning.

"They attacked us," I said. "Have they left you aught?"

There was a moment's silence, then his reply.

"I'm naked as a babe!"

"And I," I said.

"Where's Hamet?" he asked.

I raised up on my knees and stared about, trying to penetrate the night with my eyes, and abruptly was conscious of a dark huddle of forms against the sand, some distance away, and of an ominous sound of slobbering and champing. With a

cry I rose to my feet and stumbled toward it, flinging sand as
I went, and the dark mass parted with angry snarls and gray
shapes slunk off into the dark, leaving one only behind them.
Beside this I fell on my knees and thrust out my hands, to
encounter a mass of cold viscera from which I recoiled in
shock.

"Ben!" I cried. "Ben! He's here! He—he's dead!"

Laboriously Ben struggled to his feet and stumbled over
beside me.

"Dead!" he whispered. "Dead?"

"Dead!" I replied with emphasis.

There was a long silence.

"What are we to do?" he whispered finally. "What, Tom?"

"I don't know!" I answered. "I don't know!"

7

I HAVE NO IDEA how long we squatted there facing one another
across that still, shapeless form, while our thoughts gradually
gathered themselves and bore home to us the situation in
which we found ourselves. From time to time we would snatch
up a handful of sand and, turning, fling it at the hyenas that
skulked in the background, lacking the courage to come in so
long as we defied them. Presently the moon rose and cast a
thin white light over the desert, so that we were able to see
one another and the thing—it was now little else—that lay
between.

"Are we to die here in the desert?" Ben whispered finally.

Something within me rebelled at the thought.

"No!" I cried.

"What then?" he sobbed.

His evident despair acted somehow like a tonic on me.

"I don't know," I said. "But I'll not stay here to die! I'm
going on!"

"Don't leave me!" he begged.

"Come with me, then!" I cried.

"Where?" he asked.

"I don't know that either," I told him, "but I've no mind to
rest here and wait!"

He staggered upright.

"You lead," he said. "I'll follow."

"We'll bury him first," I replied.

"What's the use of that?" he demanded.

I shrugged.

" 'Tis the least we can do."

We scooped out a hollow in the sand, as deep as we could make it, and turned in the shapeless mess that had been our friend and companion.

"Should we say a prayer?" Ben asked. I was surprised he would think of it.

"I don't know how Moslems bury their dead," I replied thoughtfully. "But I'll do my best!"

"Please!" he muttered.

"Allah befriend this friend of the friendless!" I whispered in Arabic. "Lend him thine hand to Paradise and to the rest of good men. May his soul never weary; may he dwell in the arms of thy houris and escape the fires of Gehenna, for his heart was that of the lion and his goodness that of the dove. May thy face not turn from him, and may thy hand guide him through the life that is to follow!"

"Amen!" said Ben in English. "May he rest happy!"

He settled back upon his heels and looked at me.

"Which way?" he asked.

"East!" I replied promptly. "The way we were going!"

He shrugged.

"If we are to die, it may as well be on the road!"

"Yes!" I said, and stood up.

I was glad, then, that I had attended Mr. Porter's lectures on navigation in the prison, not that I knew enough to find our position upon a chart, but at least I knew east from west and was able to tell from the stars in which direction to go. At the top of the first dune I made Ben sit down, while I went over him in the moonlight in an effort to learn the extent of his wounds, fearing a knife stab that might fester and weaken him beyond such help as I might give. Fortunately, however, he, like myself, appeared to be more bruised and battered than wounded. Apparently our assailants had struck with sufficient swiftness to put us out of the fighting before we could arm ourselves, and so we had been left to die where we lay without further trouble on their part. Whether this was a curse or a blessing I had yet to decide.

All that night we stumbled eastward, through the deep sands, up the back of each round-shouldered dune, sliding and scrambling and then slipping down the face of it. Exercise kept us warm, and determination kept us moving. Yet when the dawn came we might simply have walked a treadmill. From horizon to horizon the desert stretched, dune upon rolling dune, with never a splash of green to break the monotony. Nevertheless, although I was fully aware of the desperation of our position, I could not but laugh at Ben, whose face and neck and arms and legs were still stained with the juice of his disguise, but whose body was as lily white as my own. As day came up over the edge of the sand we stood and roared at one another with uncontrolled mirth.

"You're the picture of shining virtue!" Ben grinned.

"You're little better," I chuckled.

He sobered suddenly.

"We'll not be so long, once the sun reaches us. What now?"

"Keep going," I said. "We get nowhere sitting here."

We plodded on, through the cool of the morning. Presently the sun came up, first warming then burning us. Ben spoke.

"Are you thirsty?" he asked, croaking the words.

"Shut up!" I replied roughly.

He followed me in silence, stumbling now and again.

"Tom," he gasped at length, "we've got to get out of the sun somehow. 'Twill kill us else!"

"What d'you suggest?" I demanded harshly.

"There's shadow in the crest of the dunes."

He was right. We found an overhang that faced slightly westward and lay down in the shade of it until the march of the sun brought its rays stabbing at us once more. By then my throat was as dry as the sand we lay upon, and I could feel my lips beginning to puff and crack. Ben's back was red, and my own was hot and smarting to the touch.

"Well?" said Ben harshly. "What now?"

There was no more shadow. But a thought struck me.

"Dig in," I said. "Bury ourselves until the sun has gone far enough over to offer shade from the other side."

This we did, burrowing into the sand and leaving only our

eyes and noses uncovered, which we protected as best we might with our hands. There we lay and baked while the sun slowly marched toward the west. By midafternoon I was faint and dizzy, and my throat felt as if stuffed with cotton. I could bear it no longer, and I squirmed from my sandy cover and stood up, feeling the comparative coolness of the air about me. On the eastward face of the dunes there was a length of shadow that was growing momentarily, and toward this I stumbled, throwing myself full length in it. There Ben joined me, and we lay without speaking until dusk brought respite from the blinding glare of the sun.

That night we stumbled onward. Mile after mile, dune after dune, we alternated between sudden chills and burning heat, while our bodies cried out in agony whenever we stopped to let them down upon the sand, for we were covered from head to foot with blisters. Toward morning, when the dune turned gray, Ben flung himself down.

"I can't go on!" he croaked. "It's better to die here! I won't go on!"

For some reason I was furious. I snatched him by the hair and tugged with all my strength.

"Get up!" I snarled, and my voice was a mere harsh breath whistling in my throat. "Get up! Keep moving! Pat expects me to bring you home. I'll not disappoint her!"

Almost humbly he struggled to his knees and then rose and tottered on ahead of me, while I staggered behind with fists clenched and anger driving me.

That day we had not the sense to take shelter in the sand. Rather we kept struggling on, walking, stumbling, falling, crawling, fighting to rise and stagger on again. Our throats turned to mere pipes of molten sand, it seemed, and I noticed that Ben's lips were cracked and gaping and his tongue hung out and turned black, and I supposed that my own must be the same, though I could not tell from the feel of it.

Several times that day we mistook the shimmer of the heat rising from off the sand for water in the distance, and once we were sure we saw trees, and staggered toward them, only to find on arriving at the spot where we supposed them to be that there was nothing but sand and more sand. I cannot remember when night came, or the next dawn, or how we kept going, or in what direction, though it is apparent that we did move in some way forward. I do not recall the day, save that the heat was there again. I cannot remember falling and lying, nor can I recall just when the camels appeared upon the great dune. These things I remember only in brief flashes. Then I seem to recall men clustering about me, men in striped abas, bending down, hands upon me; the grateful touch of water upon my lips, forcing a trickling way down my throat, and the soothing feel of oil upon my body; then motion, as of being lifted and carried, a musty smell as of a camel's hide. And then nothing until I opened my eyes in the night and found myself lying upon a pile of sheepskins in a tent that was open to the night, and hearing the wind whispering in the palms overhead.

I must have cried out in the darkness, for almost instantly hands were fumbling for me, passing across my body. A woman's voice whispered: "Fear not! Fear not!"

I rose up on my elbow, wondering at my stiffness, trying to remember how I might have come where I was. In almost the same instant tinder flared and a light bloomed in the dark, flickering in the gloomy confines of the great tent. I looked about me. A number of figures, wrapped like cocoons in blankets, lay on pallets similar to my own. Close by me I saw Ben, upon another mound of sheepskins, stark naked as when I had last seen him and glistening with oil and apparently asleep or unconscious, for he stirred not, neither did he seem to breathe.

Between us squatted an Arab woman whose age I could not determine in that light, though she appeared to be young. Her face was full and tattooed across chin and forehead, and her eyes were large and dark. She was clothed in a shapeless garment of some rough-textured cloth. In one hand she held a flickering rushlight. Her other hand rested upon my chest.

"Where am I?" I whispered.

Across the tent one of the cocoonlike figures stirred restlessly, and abruptly she blew out the light, at the same time forcing me gently back upon my bed, while her lips came close and I heard her whisper:

"Be still! Thou art safe here!"

In the darkness I heard a low liquid gurgle and felt warm oil spread across my belly. The hand on my chest moved down-

ward and was joined by another, and both of them began to
rub me, spreading the oil about, up onto my chest and down
across my loins, and I felt myself go suddenly hot with embarrassment, for all at once I realized that I, too, was as
naked as the day my mother bore me. I felt life stir within
me, but when the greasy tendrils of her hair brushed my face
and I smelled the stench of rancid mutton tallow, I was forced
to turn my face away.

"Where am I?" I repeated in a low whisper.

She answered in a strange accent.

"In the tent of Yakoub Ben Ali es Senussi," she whispered.
"He found ye in the desert and fetched ye in to die, giving ye
to me if I might save ye."

"Who are you?" I demanded.

"I am Jorah, the concubine, favorite of Yakoub," she replied, I thought, with more than a hint of pride. "Ye are my
slave, by right of gift, as is this other, if I can save him. Who
are ye?"

"I am Ibrahim et Tahir," I told her, "a tabib of Moghreb.
This one is my slave."

"Ye lie!" she whispered. *"He* says ye are Roumis."

I sighed, for it seemed to me useless to argue.

"It matters not to me," she said softly. "Ye are mine. I
have not owned slaves before!"

"We are Roumis, then," I admitted wearily, "but lately
escaped from the bashaw in Tripoli."

The admission could make little difference now.

"What place is this?" I asked.

"Aujila," she told me.

I seemed to remember hearing the name mentioned as a
place somewhat south of our route, which we must avoid at
all costs. I sighed again.

"Rest now!" she whispered, and her hands again passed
over me, I thought, caressing as much as anointing. But I had
not the strength to care.

When I woke it was morning and I was covered by a thin
blanket of wool that scratched my sunburn. The woman was
nowhere to be seen, but a tall man in a black-and-white-striped
aba stood by my side looking down at me.

When he saw that I was awake he smiled wolfishly, his yellow teeth gleaming through his black beard.

"Who are ye?" I demanded weakly, although I thought that I could already guess.

"I am Yakoub Ben Ali es Senussi," he replied. "I found ye in the desert. And who are ye?"

I hesitated, of two minds whether to try to continue my masquerade despite my confession of the previous night.

He saved me the trouble, raising one eyebrow knowingly and saying but a single word.

"Roumi!"

I sighed.

"I am Thomas Tisdall, Tabib Rais of the Amrikani," I said, "but lately escaped from Tripoli. This other is my assistant Ben Price."

"Ye speak the Moslem tongue well for a Roumi."

"I was nigh two years in captivity," I replied.

He nodded as if he understood.

"Return me to my people," I said, "and I will guarantee ye will be well rewarded."

He laughed.

"I have other plans for ye!" he said. "How came ye where I found ye?"

As briefly as I could, with many halts and pauses, for I was still weaker than I cared to admit, I told him our story. He spat at the mention of Ahmed Ben Khali, but gave no other sign. Instead he rose and stalked from the tent.

When he was gone I heard a weak "hist" from the other pallet and rolled my head to see Ben grinning at me.

"Who was your friend?" he whispered.

"Be still!" I warned him, and, turning on my side, cautiously whispered to him as much as I knew of our situation.

When I was through he grinned weakly.

"God surely looks after fools and drunkards!"

"We are not out of this by a long shot," I warned.

"At least we are alive!" he said.

"Aye," I replied, "and if you want to stay that way, pretend to be weaker than you are."

I did not see Yakoub Ben Ali for three days after that,

though every day we were brought food, and every night the woman, Jorah, came and anointed us with oil. This I found more than embarrassing, as, though she attended to each of us equally, it was over me that she lingered longest, and there was no doubt as to what was in her mind. Ben seemed amused, and I cursed him. But I was yet too blistered to move, and presently my skin began to fall away in great rents and I itched furiously all over.

On the third day Yakoub returned, followed by two blacks bearing between them a bloody blanket, which at his command they flung open at our feet. To my horror I recognized the gory heads of Ahmed Ben Khali and his "cousins," Hassan and Idris. They rolled crazily across the rug and came to a stop against my couch, gaping up at me slackly with lolling tongues and uprolled eyes.

"The two other rogues escaped us," Yakoub explained apologetically with a shrug.

I waved my hand feebly, thinking some gesture should be made but not caring to show I was capable of more.

"Spare your gratitude," he growled. "I need none for such as these! Besides, I am well rewarded."

He slapped his belt soundly, with a knowing leer, and I guessed he had pocketed our gold. Then all at once he aimed a hearty kick at my side.

"Arise, dog, when thy master speaks!" he roared.

The cry that I gave then was unfeigned, for pain stabbed into my vitals and made my head swim. But I retained presence of mind enough to struggle and fall back, and struggle again and ultimately to stand swaying before him.

"Stand!" he began. But at the word I collapsed again upon the couch, making such a realistic fist of it that I rolled off upon the loathsome heads that still lay by the side of it. Without a word he dealt me another kick and turned and strode out, only pausing at the entrance to order the slaves to gather up the heads and feed them to the jackals.

An hour or two later, when it was dark, Jorah came to me and bathed me in fragrant oil of argan, crooning over me the while, with many a sympathetic cluck, so that when she was gone Ben was doubled upon his couch in silent laughter.

"Thy woman," he chortled, mocking their speech, "will be the death of me! Hast done thy duty by her?"

"My woman," I growled in reply, "will be the saving of us both if you, poor fool, will only be silent! Would God it was you he kicked! I believe he split my rib!"

We remained two days more in the large tent, each day undergoing a similar brutal testing, and each day letting it be thought that we had not the strength to stand, although our blood was beginning to course again with more force than even Jorah knew. During the day she would come from time to time to wait upon us, bringing us food and drink and seeing to our comfort, and in the daylight I saw that she was not unhandsome in her wild way. Her body, which she was at little pains to hide from us, was small and well formed, of a dull, rosy-copperish tint; her breasts large and full, but not sagging or disproportioned, her waist small and her stomach flat. Her features were regular in a wild, Arab sort of fashion, with a sharp, straight nose and thin, high-arching eyebrows. Her eyes were large and black, and she was much addicted to the use of kohl in them, which had the effect of making them seem even larger and darker and brighter. Her hands and feet she tinted a sort of burnt-orange color with henna, and her hair she wore bound in long braids, strongly greased with rancid mutton tallow and wrapped tightly around her head.

She was a wild creature, apparently caring no more than a snap of her fingers for her master's commands, for she came and went as she pleased, paying not the slightest heed to his orders, and quarreling with him as loudly and brashly as if she were a man and his equal; a circumstance that appeared to amuse rather than irritate him. With her he had the attitude of a man who has tamed a young wildcat and who knew exactly how much leeway to allow in giving her native spitting tendencies play. He would hark to her railing and laugh, and often as not allow her her way. But often he would suddenly grow tired of her venom and would then cuff her, not too gently, arse over end, whereupon she would pick herself up sulkily and go out to mope in another part of the encampment, to return only at mealtime, when she would serve him exactly as if nothing had happened—although never, in keeping with Moslem custom, overstepping herself to the point of touching food in his presence. Unlike the women of the towns, and like all her sisters of the desert, she never wore a veil.

On the third day after Yakoub's return, about midday, when Jorah was cleaning up the remnants of our breakfast, he came striding into the tent and threw a glance of almost venomous amusement at the girl.

"Ho, now, little she-cat!" he greeted her. " 'Tis come time to part with thy playthings."

She turned about on him, spitting.

"What talk is this? Hast forgotten thy word?"

He laughed uproariously.

"Wouldst take a jest to heart?" he demanded.

" 'Twas no jest when thou gave it!" she retorted

He flung up his hands eloquently.

"What would ye, woman?" he demanded. "The caravan is reported on the road from the Fezzan. I must ride, and the others with me, to intercept it! There will be none here but women and old men. Wouldst have me leave them?"

"What else would ye do with them?" she asked.

"What else?" he cried, and laughed again, immoderately, I thought, though all the time I was pretending to be so feeble as not to care what was said one way or the other.

"Why, chop off their heads, as I did the other three rogues, and set them on stakes for the birds to pick! What else?"

"I would have ye keep your pledge to me," she cried. "Ye promised, and now ye would deny it!"

He gave her an exasperated glare and started to roar. "But——"

"But—but—but!" she mocked at him. "Always thou art filled with excuses. Look at them, how weak they are! What harm can they do? Set Khalil to guard them while thou art gone! Surely thou canst trust him!"

"But why?" he cried. "Why art thou so set upon it?"

She lowered her head and looked about at me.

"Because I would have a Roumi slave, and thou promised!" she retorted. "Especially that one!" She flung up her hand with her finger pointing at me. "The white one is a Roumi tabib. Would it not be an honor for Jorah to say that she had a Roumi tabib for a slave? Look how he will be! When he has flung off the desert fever thine own tabib can geld him then and make him like Khalil, and he will grow sleek and fat. Only he will be white, not black like Khalil, and he will serve me! The other can be served likewise!"

The idea seemed a new one to Yakoub, and he eyed us almost with surprise for an instant and then broke into a sudden grin, as if the thought pleased him. Almost in wonder he patted the girl on the head.

"Aiee!" he exclaimed. "That is a good thought. Surely they will be more useful alive than dead! Sometimes, little she-cat, I think thou hast more in thy head than most men!"

She simpered, obviously pleased with his praise, and I felt my stomach turn over.

He turned abruptly stern, glowering at us.

"But they shall be moved to another tent," he growled, "where Khalil may watch over them."

"So be it!" she agreed with apparent indifference.

An hour or two later we were moved, not gently carried to our new quarters, as you might imagine, but kicked to our feet and driven staggering—more than might actually have been necessary, it is true, but nonetheless staggering—through the village of black goatskin tents, until, upon the far side, we came to a smaller one that stood a little off to itself. Here we were flung within, with nothing more to cover us than the skins we were born in, while a great blubbery mountain of a black man—Khalil—was set to guard us at the door.

After the men that had brought us were gone we lay for a long time silent. At last it was Ben who spoke.

"What do they mean to do with us?" he asked in a fearful voice, for it had been a dismal experience. Every step of the way we had been spat upon and befouled with muck and kicked and beaten by the villagers, and I did not wonder that he was frightened, but it did not occur to me, until he asked, that he had not understood what had been said. I began to laugh, for it struck me in a sense as grimly humorous.

He cursed me.

"God damn you, Tisdall!" he raged. "What are you laughing at? What is it they mean to do?"

"Do?" I gasped. "Why, Ben, I'm laughing because I never thought of it myself. It took an Arab wench!"

"What are you gabbling about?" he cried.

"They mean to make an honest man of you," I told him, "and put a stop to your prowling about in other men's gardens like an old tomcat! They're going to castrate us, Ben. That will take care of you!"

"No!" he gasped.

"Aye!" I assured him. "Would you ever have thought to go to sea for that?"

We were scarcely in a talkative mood during the rest of that day. What may have been the tenor of Ben's thoughts I cannot say, but my own were not such as I cared to discuss with him.

Toward evening we became gradually conscious of a growing sound of clamor and hubbub from the direction of the main side of the encampment; the polyphonous mutter of many people gathered together; the sound of shouts and laughter, the singing chanting of storytellers, now and again a whoop and a shot or the brief thump of tambours, the tuning squeal of a ghaita, with over all the steady rising-falling murmur of many folk talking all at once. At first it was so slight as to be scarcely noticeable, but it swelled and grew louder, until all at once we were conscious of it, and though neither of us spoke, we both wondered what was afoot. I, for one, will admit to apprehension lest our capricious captor had again changed his mind. About dusk the music broke out in earnest: booming drums and clashing cymbals, accompanied by the weird squealing of the reed pipes and the wild minor chant of Arab songs. But as far as we could tell, it drew no nearer. Rather it seemed to be centered about the main tent and seemed in the nature of a celebration.

Our tent was in complete darkness when a slight figure etched against the dusk of the door and spoke to the guard. Khalil answered, high protest. Then we heard him heave up his great bulk and lumber slowly away. The figure stooped and lifted a small jug and entered.

"Ya, Tabib Sidi!" she whispered.

"Go away!" I growled.

Her laugh had the harsh, unmusical quality of the Moslem woman's voice, yet it was not cruel or gloating. Rather it conveyed amusement and a certain affection.

"Art angry with Jorah?"

I did not answer. She came and crouched beside me.

"Art not still alive?" she said.

"Alive!" I growled. "Aye! Though I prefer death!"

"Then thou art a greater fool than I thought thee!"

"Oh, then," I demanded bitterly, "is the life thou hast offered worth living?"

"Pah!" she snarled angrily. "Thou'rt a stupid Roumi! What good wouldst thou be to Jorah or any woman gelded and cut like Khalil?"

I was both shocked and startled.

"What do ye mean?" I demanded. "It was thine own thought!"

"Aye!" she replied. "Had I not had it, thy head would be on a post now, fit bait for vultures! Nay, Teesdel Tabib, think not hardly of me. Saving is done by steps, and the first was to keep thy head on thy shoulders!"

My heart bounced within me and my breath caught in my throat. Sudden hope fetched me up on my elbow.

"Jorah!" I cried.

She put her hand quickly to my lips.

"Hush!" she said softly. "I have sent Khalil for water that ye may wash. He will be back. Canst stand and run?"

"Aye!" I assured her, starting up.

But she pressed me back.

"That is as I thought," she said. "It is well. Tonight I cannot tarry, for they make a great feast, and in the morning they will ride. But here is oil to rub thee, and Khalil will fetch water for washing. Tonight I will send thee food, and tomorrow I will make shift to visit thee again. Make the best of these things, for by then I may have found a way."

"Jorah!" I said. "Why do ye do this?"

"Hush!" she whispered. "Khalil comes!"

Her ears were sharper than mine. I did not hear him approach, but it was but a moment later that he entered, momentarily blocking out even the dim dusk with his bulk. By that time Jorah was standing, as if waiting his return.

"That is well, Khalil," she said harshly in commendation. "Guard these dogs with thy life, for they are mine!"

"Aiee, Lalla!" he agreed in his high, singsong voice. "Place thy faith in me."

She left us, and the mountainous black set down the two water jugs and returned to his post at the door. When he was settled Ben turned his head cautiously in my direction.

"What——" he started to whisper.

I placed my hand quickly over his mouth. It was unlikely that the slave understood English, but it was worth while not to take chances.

"Here's water," I said in my normal voice, "for washing, and oil for our blisters. Can you manage?"

As I spoke I smoothed a spot in the sand where the faint light from the doorway struck it and traced the word "tomorrow." Ben looked at it and then glanced at me eagerly.

"I can do for myself," he mumbled, nodding understanding, and adding, for Khalil's benefit, "God, I'm sore!"

"Let's get rid of this filth," I said. "She told the guard she'd send food for us later."

We washed then, in silence, each too full of hope to risk talking. Later a bowl of couscous was brought to us and we ate. The feast in the main encampment continued far into the night, and as long as it could be heard our guardian maintained his post at the door. When, at length, it began to diminish, however, he came inside and bound us wrist to ankle. Then, wrapping himself in his cloak, he went back outside and lay down across the doorway, falling presently into a snoring sleep, from which he did not waken until morning.

Ben and I passed the night in fitful dozing, for our position could scarcely be accounted comfortable. Yet such was my own hope that I was well satisfied, and I took advantage of our guard's obvious slumber to whisper to Ben the burden of what she had told me. He lacked my own optimism.

"Bah!" he growled. "She plays with you!"

"That's as may be," I retorted. " 'Tis that or nothing!"

Toward morning, sometime before dawn, we heard the trample of hoofs and the plopping shuffle of camels' feet, the clink of accouterments, as the expedition against the Fezzan caravan got under way. A long time afterward, it seemed, the day broke and the sun rose. Khalil awoke and removed our bonds and fetched us the remnants of last night's couscous.

All through the day we waited. It grew stifling in the tent, and though I urged Khalil to raise the sides, permitting the air to flow through, he stoutly refused. Food came, at midday and again in the evening, by whose hand we could not tell. At nightfall we were again secured as on the evening previous, and again the mountainous black took to his bed and slept sonorously. Ben laughed without mirth.

"What did I tell you?" he demanded.

By midnight, I confess, my own optimism was fled. I cursed Jorah and all women. I cursed Africa and the Navy and all that had brought me here. I cursed myself for a fool, which was undoubtedly most apt. I struggled with my bonds. But Khalil apparently knew his business, and at length, exhausted, I gave over and lay panting in the sultry darkness.

In the doorway the huge Negro snored rhythmically. Beyond, and in the intervals between his sonorous breaths, I could hear the small noises of the oasis, the rustle of the palms in the wind, the chirping of insects, and the occasional scurrying of some animal in the brush. I envied them their freedom.

All at once Khalil's snoring ended in a gasping gurgle. I stiffened. A dark figure momentarily blackened the deeper darkness of the doorway. A rustle sounded close at hand. A voice whispered: "Teesdel Tabib?"

"Jorah?" I ventured.

"Art safe, Aziz?"

"I'm tied," I replied gruffly.

She was beside me then, fumbling. Her knife touched the ropes that bound me, and I sat up and rubbed my arms.

"Art ready?" she asked.

"As ready as I will ever be," I told her.

Her hand found my arm in the darkness and, almost caressing, felt down to my hand. I felt the hilt of a knife.

"Free him!" she whispered. "I will return!"

And she was gone. Quickly I turned and felt for Ben.

"By God!" he whispered as I found him. "You were right! Where is she?"

"Gone for a moment," I replied. "She'll be back."

Quickly I cut his bonds that held him.

"What now?" he asked.

"Your guess is as good as mine," I replied.

"For Christ's sake," he said, "don't bungle it!"

"What do you mean?" I demanded.

"Don't be an ass!" he replied.

Jorah returned. We could see her figure darken the door momentarily, and we fell silent. In the dark I could hear her fumbling at something, and then abruptly the tent flap fell and we were plunged in still deeper blackness. There followed an interval of silence, and then the abrupt scratch-scratch of flint upon steel, and an instant later a rushlight flared, flinging the cavelike interior of the tent into flickering, smoky-orange light. In that instant I observed that she wore no more than a single garment of thin gray silk, caught at the waist with a cord of black goat's hair and fastened with a silver buckle. Her hair was dressed as carefully, if as repugnantly, as for a feast. She stood before us almost triumphantly.

"I told ye I would come," she said.

"I never doubted thee," I replied.

She bent and caught up two bundles. One she opened and passed to Ben—an aba of thin wool, striped gray and black, a caftan of green silk, yellow slippers, baggy breeches.

"Put them on," she commanded.

He obeyed and stood up before us.

"That is good!" she nodded finally. "Now, go!"

He glanced at me. I translated.

"The guard?" he protested.

"Khalil?" I asked, glancing at her.

"Khalil!" she exclaimed contemptuously. "He will trouble no one—ever. Go thou and sit in his place. If any approach, give warning!"

I repeated this order to Ben, who gave me a sardonic lift of the eyebrow and obeyed. Jorah turned to me.

"And now, Teesdel Tabib," she said, drawing the second bundle toward her, "see what I have for thee!"

She opened it, revealing a rich, pearl-gray aba, a mulberry caftan and fresh drawers and a shirt, a headdress, such as worn by the Senussi, two pistols, a shot pouch and powder horn, a gold-hilted dagger, and slippers.

"For thee," she whispered, "I have stolen the best!"

I reached for them, but she caught my hand.

"Wait!" she exclaimed.

I looked round at her inquiringly.

"Let me once more anoint thy hurts."

For a long instant we gazed at one another, and there was no mistaking the look in her eyes.

"Jorah!" I said. "Why do ye do this?"

She unbuckled the clasp at her waist and slipped the silken gown from her shoulders, standing before me naked.

"I have called thee beloved," she said.

I rose abruptly.

To my astonishment, she reached for the jug of oil and decanted some in the palms of her hands, running them across my sides, seeking out the remaining blisters of my sunburn.

"Oh, thy poor body!" she cried.

"Jorah!" I whispered in desperation. "Jorah! Is this wise? What if we are discovered?"

It was selfish, I own. She recoiled from me.

"Dost think of danger?" she demanded. "I swear thou'rt no more worth saving than Khalil, with all thy parts!"

I caught her and drew her to me, trying not to smell the rancid sheep's smell of her hair. The touch of her body against mine was like a fluttering finger, and in spite of me desire swept over me.

"No, no!" I cried. "Thou dost not understand! If we are to go, it must be now. There will be time for love later!"

She clung to me.

"Teesdel Tabib!" she whispered. "Aziz—beloved! I have nursed thee and loved thee and brought thee back to health. Is it much that I ask? Let me know that which I have saved!"

She drew me down and pressed herself against me. I sought her lips and we strained together, she clinging fiercely in bliss and I with my elbows in the shaggy wool beneath her, for the instant believing that the earth stood still. Her thighs were strong against my flanks, and her nails dug at my shoulders; her mouth was hot and demanding, and for the instant there was no earth, no heaven, no hell, but only the two of us!

When, presently, we broke apart her fingers sought my brow and passed over it, caressingly.

"Ah, Teesdel Tabib," she sighed, "thou'rt a man!"

For an instant, I own, I pictured her with hair washed and perfumed and dressed in silks; exotic, commanding.

"Jorah!" I whispered. "We must fly now! Thou wilt come with me and be my woman!"

She laughed, abruptly, almost harshly, and lay back in my arms, her breasts gleaming like new copper in the rushlight yet with a tenderness in her great eyes.

"To the land of the Roumi, Teesdel Tabib?" she demanded. "What would I do there, alone of my kind, but thirst for freedom as thou dost here?"

"But what of thee," I cried, "when Yakoub returns?"

"Yakoub!" she exclaimed, laughing. "He is a great fool! I wind him about my finger!"

"Then I will stay!" I cried recklessly.

She laughed again.

"And for what?" she demanded. "To be like Khalil?"

She put out her hand and caressed my brow.

"No, Teesdel Tabib!" she whispered. "This we have had together! I will remember thee! Do thou remember me!"

I could have wept in that moment, feeling a dog to know that she was right and that I must leave her.

"Come!" she said gently after a moment. "Come! Put on thy clothes, and I will show thee!"

We left the tent presently, stepping over the great prostrate form of Khalil, who, I saw, was quite dead.

Ben was sitting a little distance away, among the trees, where he could at once watch the tent and still be unobserved in the darkness. Jorah took my hand and led me along the edge of the oasis, away from the encampment, holding to me with a grip that was eloquent of my own heart's reluctance at parting. Ben followed us at a little distance, keeping, I thank God, silent for once. After a time we came to a little hollow between the dunes and the palm trees.

"Wait here!" Jorah whispered, and we sat while she disappeared in the darkness.

Fortunately Ben said nothing. Nor was I inclined to talk. Presently she returned, leading two horses, saddled and bridled and with full goatskins hanging at the saddlebows.

"They are 'drinkers-of-wind,'" she said, naming the breed which the Arabs prize most highly. "They will cover three days' journey in one, but ye must feed them on camel's milk, which ye will find in the goatskins, else they will lose their speed. Ye will find what else ye need in the saddlebags, and if ye ride north, thou wilt come to El Maghar in one day's journey and a half. Beyond that go to Khedir Laguas and Shafa and Kasr Bou Hasan, and thus ye will come finally to Derne and the sea."

"When will Yakoub return?" Ben asked abruptly.

I translated, and she laughed.

"Not for a fortnight at best," she replied. "By then thou wilt be at Bou Hasan, or Shafa, at worst. He will not follow—or will not find ye, if he does!"

I felt a stirring of conscience and turned over the reins of my mount to Ben, drawing her aside into the thicket.

"I am afraid for thee, Jorah," I whispered. "Come with us. I will fend for thee!"

She held me at arm's length for an instant and laughed.

"And have thy women laugh at me and be a stranger among strangers?" she asked. "Ah, Teesdel Tabib, thou'rt but a man for all thou'rt blessed and canst not see what sorrow 'twould be for me to share thee!"

"But who talks of sharing?" I demanded.

She hesitated, then evidently stiffened.

"No!" she cried. "No! Thou'rt like all men, no different! I would be amongst thy wives and amongst Roumis, and could I be happy but in thee?"

"I have no other wives," I told her.

"More fool thou!" she replied. "And if thou hast not, then would we both be unhappy, for thy Roumi friends would point the finger of scorn at both of us! No, Teesdel Aziz, it cannot be. We must remember this night, and no other!"

I saw that it was no use arguing with her, and, indeed, I knew in my heart that, for all my gratitude and for all my quick fondness, she was right. What, for instance, would Salem say of her, or how would I find her a place aboard one of our vessels? I kissed her almost belligerently yet lingeringly, and she clung to me.

"Remember me, Jorah!" I whispered, unconscious now of the scent of rancid mutton. "I will remember thee!"

"And I will remember thee, my Teesdel," she said, "all the days of my life!"

She embraced me swiftly and thrust me away, and a moment later we had mounted and were riding northward toward the sea. Neither Ben nor I spoke, while the hoofs of our mounts padded soft in the sand beneath and the stars hung like brilliants in the sky above. Only when we had turned the oasis and headed well to the north did Ben speak.

"Old Tom," he exclaimed then, "the ladies' man!"

"Shut your filthy mouth!" I told him, and then cursed him as I have cursed no man before or since.

He said nothing more, and we rode in silence from that time onward through the rest of the night.

8

THE NAME which the Arabs had given the horses we rode, "drinkers-of-wind," was no misnomer. They kept up a steady pace, despite the deep sand. Dawn came while we were still among the dunes, but not long afterward we climbed to rocky ground and rode at a steady trot, following a crisscrossed track through rising country much like that we had traversed before passing Bu Njem. Argan trees grew in the hollows, and the ground beneath gave way to flinty desert in which low shrubs and brush struggled for a foothold and cactus and long-spiked hemp, Barbary fig and Dergamuse, or gum euphorbium plant flourished. Ahead of us loomed a region of dark mountains that at a distance appeared green with the first forest we had seen since coming to Africa. At midday we halted in the shadow of an argan tree and drank some of the camel's milk and ate some of the dates that Jorah had furnished for us. This we did in silence, Ben, in some apprehension, glancing always furtively back at the trail we had just ridden; I with my thoughts upon the girl, feeling somehow like a cheat at having taken so much from her, leaving her nothing in return nor even fetching her with me. Only when we were somewhat rested and refreshed and ready to ride again did either of us speak.

"I keep thinking of how they looked rolling out there on the rug," Ben said.

"What?" I asked, startled, for a moment unable to think what it was he was speaking of.

"The heads," he said. "You know, that's what they'll do to us if they catch us. There'll be no escape next time."

"Aye," I replied soberly. "We must keep going until we are beyond their reach."

"They must have gone a long way to catch Ben Khali."

"True," I agreed, "though we were able to tell them something of the direction he took."

"They can track us easily enough."

"Aye," I said, "if they return in time."

"Well," he said, "I hope their raid is a long one."

"I am more concerned about Jorah," I said. "What will happen to her? Yakoub would think nothing of torturing her to force her to tell what became of us."

Ben laughed.

"Set your mind at rest!" he cried. "The wench can look out for herself! It makes my hair stand on end, the story she'll have cooked up for him when he returns—how we were stronger than we let on; how we murdered poor Khalil with his own knife and then slipped out and stole what we needed in the dead of night and made our escape! I'll wager she'll even have it in that you stole into her tent and looted his wardrobe and chests and forced her to serve you——"

"Shut up!" I growled, angered although I knew it was no doubt true.

But he did not appear to have heard me. Instead a thought appeared to have struck him. He stared at the horses.

"I say! Have you looked in the saddlebags?"

"Only that one, where I found the dates," I replied.

"She was a thorough wench," he replied, "who left little to chance. Did she speak to you of money?"

"No," I said. "I never thought of it."

"Money's important in this country," he said. "I'll warrant our Jorah thought of it if you did not!"

He rose and went to my mount.

"Forgive me if I search your saddlebags first," he said mockingly. "'Tis there she'd be most like to put it!"

"Oh, give over," I said. "What difference does it make? If it's there we'll find it when we need it."

"Stuff!" he retorted. "There's nothing like knowing. Let's see. Here's a razor, and—I say! Didn't I tell you she thought of everything? Here are your knives and your burning irons and such! Yakoub must have pinched 'em from Ben Khali! Here's a—little something for you."

He turned and tossed me a glittering something. I caught it

in mid-air and found it to be a golden chain, fine as a thread almost, to which was attached a little golden hand, a common charm among Moslem women, known as the hand of Fatima, which is supposed to bring its wearer good luck. I recognized it as one that Jorah had worn, and a curious tightness came in my throat, for I understood why she had put it there. I was tempted to turn about and ride back for her.

"Aha!" cried Ben suddenly. "What did I tell you?"

I glanced up from the little golden hand and saw that he had turned about and was holding up my money belt. From the way its pockets bulged, there was more in it now than there had been.

"All right!" I growled. "All right! She thought of everything. Put it back and let's be on our way. 'Twill be no good to us if we lose our heads!"

By late afternoon we had reached the beginning of the foothills, where the plain broke into rocky gullies, sparsely covered with scrub oaks and acacia and tamarisks and here and there a scrawny species of pine. Here we rested again for a brief period and then pushed on into the mountains, riding as long as there was light to see the way and then stopping only until the moon rose and cast sufficient light for us to see where we were going. Sometime after midnight exhaustion overtook us and we were forced to stop in the shelter of a towering cliff and sleep. When morning came we found ourselves in heavily forested country, rugged and rocky, with deep gullies and winding gorges between ridges thickly covered with pines, with streams of pure mountain water—real water—gurgling through their hollows.

We pressed on and presently came into a valley which showed signs of cultivation.

"What's the name of that first place?" Ben asked.

"El Maghar," I told him.

"D'ye think we're on the right road?"

"It goes north," I replied. "We can ask yonder shepherd."

I nodded toward a spot some distance ahead where a flock of sheep dotted the hillside, tended by a ragged Arab who was drowsing in the morning sunlight with his back against a rock. Apparently he had not yet become conscious of our approach, but as we drew near evidently the sound of our horses' hoofs upon the rocky path caught his ear and he looked up. In the next instant he had leaped to his feet and was flying up the mountainside away from the road.

"Is this the road to El Maghar?" I called after him.

But, though he must have heard, he paid not the slightest heed, but plunged into the brush above and disappeared.

"What the devil's the matter with him?" Ben demanded.

"Damned if I know," I replied, utterly mystified.

"We certainly scared him!" he said.

"He was frightened of something," I replied, and we both laughed and thought no more of it than that the fellow was a timid hillman who was not used to seeing strangers.

We pushed on, and at the next turn opened a broader vista of valley, with a small river flowing through the middle and an expanse of tilled fields about a cluster of huts.

"Well!" cried Ben. "Civilization! Now we should learn where we are!"

We rode toward the village, and I noticed a group at work in the fields. They did not at first seem to notice us, but presently I saw one of them straighten and stare in our direction. Evidently he spoke to his fellows, for instantly they all stood erect and looked toward us. In the next moment they, too, had turned tail and were flying for the village.

I shouted and gave spur to my mount, Ben following, but they only fled the faster and a moment later disappeared among the huts. At almost the same instant a musket rang out, and I heard the ball whine uncomfortably close. Instinctively I reined in my mount, then snatched off the white headdress I wore and waved it in the air in token of peace.

Undoubtedly it was foolhardy, and had I had my wits about me I would never have done it. Yet it was all that occurred to me at the moment, and evidently it had the proper effect, for there were no more shots. Presently two men came out of one of the huts with muskets in their hands and stood staring at us, fingering their locks. I waved the headdress again and, with my hands in the air to show that I held no weapons, rode toward them. Ben followed my example and rode at my heels. When we came within speaking distance they moved to raise their muskets, and I halted abruptly.

"Hold thy fire!" I called. "Why do ye shoot?"

The two men glanced at one another. We were close enough to see their expression of surprise.

"Ye are not Senussi!" one of them said flatly.

It was a statement, not a question. The reason for their hostility struck me. The raiders from the desert were feared and hated here, and we might well be mistaken for them.

"We are not Senussi," I cried, "but captives who have escaped from them!"

"Ye wear the dress and ride their horses," the man replied suspiciously. "If ye are not Senussi, how come ye by these?"

"We stole them," I replied, taking a long chance.

They glanced at one another again, then spoke quickly over their shoulders, into the hut behind them.

"Dismount," commanded the bolder of them, "and advance with thy hands in the air."

He made a threatening motion with his musket. We obeyed, and one brought the muzzle of his weapon around to point at my breast, while the other covered Ben.

"Speak!" commanded the man who confronted me.

"I have already told ye the weight of our tale."

He shouted something in a tongue that was strange to me, though I later learned it was Berber. Immediately the huts erupted their human contents. A crowd gathered about us, hemming us in upon all sides. Presently an old man in a white bournous thrust through them and confronted us. I guessed that he was their cadi, or head magistrate, and in this I was not mistaken.

"Who are ye?" he demanded.

I told him our story, saying that I was a pilgrim, a tabib from Moghreb, and that Ben was my assistant; that we had been peacefully upon our journey when we had been set upon by the Senussi; that the men of the tribe had gone to intercept another caravan, and that we had seized the opportunity to escape. When I finished there were some who appeared to believe me. The old man appeared thoughtful.

"They will follow ye," he said at length.

I shook my head.

"It will be some time before they discover our absence," I replied. "There were none left at Aujila to follow us or carry the news of our escape."

"Aujila!" a dozen throats echoed the name. The old cadi, however, looked sober.

"If ye are, as ye say ye are, a tabib," he said presently, "then ye can cure my wife!"

I saw that it was at once a test and a hope. I was cautious.

"As to that," I replied, "I cannot say. But if I may see her, it may be that I can help."

He turned away abruptly.

"Come with me," he said. "Leave thy companion."

Even had I wished otherwise, it was plain that I had no choice. I followed him with a warning glance at Ben.

He led me to a hut in the middle of the village, where I found an old woman lying on a musty pallet, in the clutch of delirium. I examined her but found no symptoms that I recognized. Even if I had, I would not have known how to prescribe for her, since I had no medicaments with me. All that was evident was that she had a raging fever.

Presently I settled back upon my heels in thought, and abruptly I remembered that I had seen vast numbers of poppies in bloom in the fields about the village.

"Send thou," I said, "and have thy people gather me poppies, as many as they can gather."

He went to the door and gave the command, at the same time ordering that Ben be brought to this hut and that our horses be tethered outside. In an hour or so the doorway was heaped with blossoms, and I called for a kettle and fire and water, and in these I made an infusion by steeping the blossoms. When this had cooled I gave it to the woman to drink and then ordered that she be covered with as many robes as possible to induce a sweat. After that we sat in silence, watching, while the life of the village stood still and a few of the menfolk kept watch upon the trail we had ridden. Once in the course of the day Ben spoke.

"Why are we waiting here? What do they mean to do with us?"

"The woman is ill," I replied. "I have treated her. If she recovers, I think we may go on. If she dies, I think you and I may die also."

I did not mention my doubts of the treatment I had suggested. The old man looked at me sharply.

"What is the tongue ye speak?" he asked.

"It is a dialect of Morocco," I replied.

He appeared satisfied. No doubt he knew naught of the lands beyond the seas.

By nightfall the woman was worse. She raved, and it was necessary to hold her down. By midnight, however, the fever reached its peak and she broke into a soaking sweat. By morning, though she was weak, it was evident that the worst was past. Our host was pitifully grateful.

"Allah forgive me that I doubted ye!" he cried.

"I could not be sure myself," I told him, "but God is good. Thy woman's recovery is witness of the truth."

He bowed his head.

"Thou speakest wisely," he said. "I am a poor man, but whatever thou shalt ask, if it is in my power, shall be given thee!"

An idea suddenly occurred to me.

"I ask no pay," I replied, "but only a fair exchange."

"What is that?" he demanded.

"Give us clothes of the sort thy people wear, to replace these Senussi garments," I replied, "and give us two asses in exchange for the horses we rode!"

His eyes gleamed.

"The 'drinkers-of-wind'?" he demanded. "But such mounts are not to be found every day!"

"Aye," I agreed, "and when we appear on them we are thought to be either Senussi or rich men, the one of which is as dangerous as the other!"

"Thou sayest true," he chuckled, "though it looks a one-sided bargain."

"Take them and welcome," I told him. "I have no wish but to go my way in peace. On these that is not possible."

"I understand thee." He nodded. "So shall it be!"

We left the village the next morning, having completed the circle of transport available in this part of the world. Once more we were a poor tabib and his assistant, clad in well-worn rags and mounted upon great-eared, patch-coated donkeys. Though we kept our gold and weapons, they were well hid beneath our shabby exterior, and I will confess that I felt far more comfortable that it was so. We said farewell to our new friends and pushed on to El Maghar, to which they directed us. There we spent the night in a dismal little fondouk, and the following day joined a caravan for Benghazi.

By this means we got, in a few more days without further adventures, through Kedir Laguas to Shafa, where we parted with the caravan, which bore away to the west. We turned up into the mountains, following a rugged trail, and came by late afternoon to the northern slope, where the short rivers fall away toward the sea, and there was a blueness to the air once more that told us that the coast could not be far away. Here, in the little village of Kasr Bou Hasan, we found the market place in an uproar, for there had just arrived a messenger from the north.

"—their numbers," he was saying as we joined the crowd, "are as the locusts in the seventh year. With my own eyes I have seen their five thousand foot soldiers, and their horsemen are beyond counting!"

A sigh of pious unbelief rose from the throng of villagers. I wormed my way closer, risking a few hard looks for the sake of hearing better what was afoot.

"They are encamped now on the heights above Derne."

I risked an interruption.

"Thine indulgence, friend," I said. "I came late. Who is encamped above Derne?"

He broke off and glanced at me.

"The bashaw's army," he replied.

My heart within me went bucketing to my belly.

"Oh," I said.

"Aye," he continued. "They marched in yesterday in multitudes, as I have explained."

"There has been a battle, then?" I asked, and at once could have bitten out my tongue.

He did not, however, appear to notice my slip.

"Not yet," he said, "but there will be one, perhaps tomorrow. A message was sent to Mustapha Bey, calling for surrender of the city, to which he only replied: 'My head or thine!'"

This left me more confused than ever, for I reasoned that if the bashaw's troops lay outside the city, demanding its surrender, either the city was in rebellion or had previously capitulated to our people.

"The ships of the Roumi hover off the city," he went on, "but dare not approach too near."

I could make little of this, but I had made one slip of the tongue, and I did not intend to make another. I gave Ben a discreet signal and withdrew.

I led Ben away to where our burros stood, mounted, and rode on. The less we lingered in this vicinity, I reckoned, the better. As we rode I told Ben what I had heard.

"What do you make of it?" he asked.

"I don't know," I replied, "but as nearly as I can judge, our people have taken Derne and are now bottled up inside by the bashaw's army."

We rode as late that night as it was possible to see, and stopped then only because the track had become steep and rocky and dangerous. Nevertheless we were up again and on our way before the break of dawn, for the scent of the sea was strong on the wind that swept up the mountainside into our faces, and we knew that we could not have much farther to go. When the day broke it was to find the mountain dropping away at our feet to a distant shelf of level plain, and beyond that, bluer than the sky and more welcome, the sea. I have known times when I thought there was too much water in the world. But at that moment, after all those weeks in the desert, I thought I had never seen anything so beautiful.

At the same instant both Ben and I saw the ships. Almost directly before us, looking like toys at that distance, were a schooner and a brig, of a rig such as never was spawned in the Mediterranean. A little to the east cruised a small sloop.

"Isn't that the *Argus?*" Ben demanded.

"She has a familiar look," I agreed.

He whooped.

"Easy!" I warned. "Remember, we could see the entire squadron from Tripoli, for all the good it did us. How are we to get off to them if the bashaw's army is encamped 'twixt them and us?"

He gave me a glance of irritation.

"That's it!" he sneered. "Always seek an obstacle!"

"We'd not be here," I retorted, "if one of us did not."

"All right!" he growled. "At least we're our own masters here. We stand some chance of getting out to the ships. There we had none."

"Exactly!" I replied. "That's why I say let's take care! I've no mind to be fetched back to Tripoli."

He grunted agreement with that, at least, and we began to search the distant line of the shore for the town. It was some time before we managed to find a scattering of roofs and the tip of a single minaret, barely showing above the rim of the escarpment that rose abruptly from the narrow coastal shelf on which the city stands. Neither was it easy to locate the vast camp of the bashaw's troops, such as our informant had described. But presently, as we continued our way downward, swinging slightly to the left, we began to see a scattering of tents under the side of a low hillock that had hitherto stood between us and the escarpment's edge. As we moved farther to the west, still more tents came into view, and although it was apparent that the numbers encamped there had been exaggerated, still there was no doubt that it was a considerable force. I began to feel more than ever depressed. Clearly our difficulties were not yet ended. All at once Ben seized my arm.

"Tom!" he cried. "Look there!"

He pointed toward the town, which, as we approached, had come somewhat more in view, down the rugged vista of the ravine. Now we could see, not only a scattering of roofs, but here and there a few buildings, and at one point, where the notch of the gully cut deep and a tongue of land thrust out into the blue waters of the sea, a fortlike cluster of whitewashed walls and battlements. It was toward this that he drew my attention.

"What is it?" I said blankly.

"On the staff!" he told me impatiently. "Can't ye see?"

My eye followed the white ramparts until I found the flagstaff at one corner. Even as I found it a breeze stirred the flag at its head and set it streaming. Against the blue of the sea it stood out so that there could be no mistaking it—fifteen red and white bars about a field of blue, studded with fifteen white stars!

"Ben!" I cried. "Ben! It's——"

"Aye!" he shouted excitedly. "It is! It's our flag!"

With that we both slipped from our mounts and began to caper up and down, whooping and laughing and pounding one another on the bank, all enmity between us for the moment forgot.

I think I am not an unduly sentimental man, but in that instant the tears came to my eyes and a lump burned in my throat. I could see that Ben was affected in much the same way, and I think that we both had a sudden realization then of all that that flag stood for. When I could speak at last I shook Ben to make him listen.

"Ben!" I cried. "You know what it means?"

"Aye!" he roared back at me. "D'ye take me for a fool? It means they're there! Our people are in the town!"

"And all we need do now," I replied excitedly, "is get in to them."

He sobered abruptly.

"Aye!" he said quietly. "Aye! That's all."

I caught his meaning before the words were out of his mouth. It was true. Actually we were little better off. If we had correctly interpreted what we had heard at Kasr Bou Hasan, though our people were in the town, the bashaw's troops were still outside, and we would have to pass their lines.

"Well," he said, "how are we going to do it?"

I thought a moment.

"There's one way," I said finally.

"How's that?" he asked.

"Are you game to risk it?" I countered.

"Name it!" he retorted. "I'll try anything you will."

"Make a dash for it," I replied, ignoring the taunt. "Look you! The camp is on the east, above the town. The bashaw's troops will be concentrated there, for it overlooks the fort as well. We know there is a road along the coast from the west. Suppose we slip around to that side and get on the road, and then ride in toward the town like ordinary innocent travelers? If they have patrols out, I'll try to talk our way through. If they recognize us or try to stop us—well, you have your pistol and I have mine. We'll try to shoot our way through and run for it into the town. The main thing is to get as close as we can first."

Ben looked at me, then turned about and stared hard at his sleepy-looking little burro. He began to laugh.

"What's wrong?" I demanded tartly, for I thought myself it was not a bad suggestion and by its very brazenness had a fair chance of success.

He pointed to his mount.

"Can you imagine that making a dash?" he demanded.

I shrugged.

"They're all we have, and I'll wager they'll run like scared rabbits if any shooting starts!"

We mounted and struck across country, making a circuit of the town and trying carefully to avoid being seen from the camp. This was not so easy as it might seem, for although the countryside afforded fair cover, it was rugged and gullied, and often we were forced to take long detours upon the mountain or down toward the plain.

There is no path so long, however, that it has no ending, and at length we came down through a last deep-cleft rocky gully and came out upon the coast road, about a league westward of the town. It was early afternoon by then, and the sun was high and hot, a circumstance for which I was thankful, for the road was deserted. Neither Ben nor I had eaten since before dawn, but we were scarcely aware of hunger such was our anxiety to reach the town and our friends. Ben suggested that we drop our panniers and proceed without them, holding that this would give us greater speed if we were forced to run for it. But this I vetoed, for I felt that the panniers, which were by now nearly empty, were but little added burden to our beasts and would help support our account of ourselves, while their absence would of itself give it the lie.

Having settled this, we resumed our journey with the languid air of weary travelers upon a long and lonesome road, yet inwardly a-tremble with apprehension. Although the road was quiet and deserted, it seemed to us that it was an ominous quiet, and we were ready to start at the least sudden sound. To our left we could hear the noise of the sea, gently breaking on the rocky shore, and we strained our ears and sat rigid on our mounts in an effort to hear anything that might be accounted the least unusual above its constant minor thunder. We had not gone halfway to the town before I was acutely conscious of a painful cramp in my neck, so stiffly did I hold myself.

But the town itself was well within reach, no more than a quarter of a mile distant, before I heard Ben, behind me, hiss: "Here it comes!"

I looked up abruptly and saw what he meant. Out of a little gully, to our right, a score of horsemen were riding at a trot. They wore abas and desert headgear, which struck me as strange, but they were heavily armed. Evidently they had seen us and were coming to investigate, for they rode directly toward us. I had not a doubt that they were the bashaw's men, perhaps recruited along the coast. I called back warily to Ben:

"Ride up alongside me, and keep your hand on your pistol, but don't let them see it. And don't look so scared!"

He pulled a wry grin.

"Speak for yourself!" he replied. "You ought to have a mirror!"

The foremost rider, a lean fellow with a wicked mouth and a crooked nose, was drawing almost within hailing distance.

"You might have your knife handy for a spur, too," I said quickly. "I think we'll need it."

"I thought of that ten minutes ago," Ben sneered.

"Hola there! Ye on the road!" the horseman called to us in Arabic. "Hold where ye are!"

I stared at him, feigning blank stupidity.

"Halt!" he bellowed, rattling his saber ominously.

When we did not immediately stop he leaped his mount into the road and barred our way, so that we were forced to a stop. The others came up and clustered around us, not quite jostling us, yet close enough so that we were hemmed in.

"Who are ye," the leader demanded, "and whence come ye? Why did ye not halt when I commanded ye?"

"Because we thought ye robbers, ya sidi!" I whined. "We are but poor travelers, bound into Derne. We have naught of value to such as ye!"

"A likely tale!" he sneered. "Poor travelers, indeed, coming into the city at this time!"

He nodded to two of his men.

"Search them!" he commanded.

I waited until they had started to dismount. Then I shouted, "Now!" and whipped out my pistol, at the same time clapping heels to my diminutive mount.

The fellow ducked involuntarily. My pistol roared and kicked almost out of my hand. I felt my beast surge forward and at the same instant heard Ben's pistol bang and saw the man's horse rear. His forefeet missed my head by no more than a hair as we shot beneath them. Someone made a grab at me, and I turned and flung my pistol in his face, in the next movement whipping out my dagger and giving my animal a jab with the point.

The little beast flattened out and skimmed at a frantic gallop over the ground while I clung with all my strength to the strap which held the panniers in place. Behind me I could hear Ben's mount laboring.

"Keep going!" I heard Ben shout above the clatter. "We surprised 'em! Did you hit him?"

"No, damn it!" I yelled back. "Did you?"

"Not I!" he bellowed. "These beasts make damned poor shooting platforms!"

We kept our distance for a hundred yards or more, by virtue of surprise, but a jackass is no match for a good horse, and presently they began to draw up on us swiftly, riding furiously, bent low over their saddles. For all that, we were almost within reach of the gates when they overtook us.

As if by prearrangement, the first of them swept past Ben, overriding him, and came on for me. As he swept up behind I turned and struck at him wildly with my knife, but he only laughed and ducked easily under my lashing arm and caught a handful of my streaming bournous. In the next moment he was past, pulling the bournous up and over my head, so that my arms and shoulders were caught in its folds, and before I could slip myself free I felt myself ignominiously plucked up, like a trussed turkey, and flung over my burro's head.

As I felt myself take to the air I lost my knife and made a frantic grab for the pannier strap, missed, and a second later was plowing the flinty gravel of the roadway with the side of my face. I had a momentary, fleeting vision of what seemed like a regiment of hoofs, felt the ground tremble and heard a crashing as of thunder, and then I tumblesaulted and must have struck my head, for I remember nothing else until I opened my eyes to find myself lying flat upon the ground, surrounded by now dismounted Arabs.

"Ah!" said a voice. "He wakes!"

I screwed my head around and saw the one who had questioned me. His savage black eyes met mine as I looked up, and narrowed almost with humor. He held up my money belt.

"A considerable sum for a 'poor traveler,'" he remarked. "Perhaps thou canst explain this to the bashaw."

I felt my stomach sag within me, and such faint hope as I dared permit myself fled. Well, we had tried! I rolled my head away so that this Arab might not see the helpless, impotent fury and despair in my eyes. He turned to his followers.

"Raise him upon his feet," he commanded. "Bind his arms and place halters about their necks. We'll fetch them in."

"Where to, ya sidi?" one of them asked, and he turned upon the man contemptuously.

"Eh, to the castle, of course, fool! Where else?" he demanded. "They must be brought before the bashaw at once!"

I puzzled an instant at that, even as they were jerking me to my feet and roughly binding me. The castle would be in the town, of course, and if the town were in our hands, how could the bashaw be there? But I could beat out no possible answer, which was scarcely strange, for my head was spinning sickeningly from my fall, and I was in no condition for clear thought upon anything. As I stood swaying, shoulder to shoulder with Ben, our captors remounted their horses and, seizing the ropes that had been fastened about our necks, set out at a brisk, curvetting canter, into the town.

What followed was one of the most horrible and humiliating experiences of my life, and I think I may say the same for Ben. It is not easy to run for one's life with a rope about one's neck and with arms bound tightly behind one's back, over a stony roadway in bare feet—for our yellow slippers had gone flying when we were snatched from our racing mounts, and our feet had no other coverings. Yet this is what we did, for it was a case of run or be dragged!

Our captors apparently counted it rare sport to ride at such pace as must force us to stretch our legs like ostriches. They rode without regard for the road over which we must race, and before we had gone halfway—something over a mile—my feet were cut to ribbons by the sharp flints and pain like that of red-hot knife blades seared my legs from angle to groin, and lungs were like to burst. My heart felt smothered by their weight and my throat was like a river of flame.

Yet somehow I managed to keep my feet under me and keep them racing, just sufficiently to keep myself from falling, forward momentum being furnished by the rope that yanked at my neck. Had we lost our balance and fallen, either to one side or the other, the ensuing jerk upon our necks must certainly have broken them. But such was the fiendish skill of our tormentors at this bestial game that we did not, for whenever we showed a sign of wavering they would check the speed of their mounts just sufficiently to allow them to catch us up and set us on our feet again, when they would clap spurs to their horses' flanks and be off again.

Once within the town, although the ground underfoot was somewhat smoother, the way was more winding and narrow, and we whipped about corners and thundered through narrow alleys, caroming from wall to wall, until our already threadbare clothing was in tatters and our faces, necks, and shoulders were scraped raw. As we flew thus, our captors rode like very devils, paying not the least heed to the crowds of people in the streets, sending them flying, screaming, this way and that before them, while those behind screamed curses after us and flung rocks or offal at our heads.

We were more dead than alive when we were fetched to a crashing stop before a building whose façade I remember only vaguely as an area of steps and whitewashed horseshoe arches. Both Ben and I sank, fainting, to the ground. But before we had opportunity to catch our wind we were snatched up again, each between two burly captors, and hustled up the steps and into the building, our feet more than half dragging and leaving a bloody trail where we went. I have a vague recollection of crossing a courtyard and coming to a stand before a flight of stairs, where our chief captor spoke sharply to a pair of white-robed guards, who barred the way. As he talked a dignified Turk in a gray bournous came out of a small antechamber, and our Arab turned to him with a flood of words that I was still too far exhausted to catch. The Turk gave us an impassive look and spoke sharply to the Arab, telling him to wait, then turned away and climbed the stairs. Our captors relaxed imperceptibly, and Ben and I were permitted to sink to the cool tiles of the floor and rest, and gradually I became somewhat more aware of our surroundings. We were in a sort of an arcaded cloister that ran along one side of the courtyard through which we had entered. Across the court was a similar cloister, giving upon the great entrance doors, while at each end were doors evidently leading into long corridors. In the center of the court was a tiled fountain in which cool water tinkled tantalizingly. There were a good many people passing back and forth, coming and going through the great main doors, or diving off into the blackness of the corridors at either end of the court, but these I scarcely saw until one came out of the farthest corridor and started across the courtyard.

Even in my half-dazed state I jerked erect at the sight of him. It was not that I recognized him in that fleeting instant, for I was still, myself, half conscious of a need for avoiding recognition, and consequently had been inclined to look away from the curious stares of those who passed by us. But this man was different. Instead of the robes and drapings of the Eastern world he wore the coat and trousers and waistcoat, stock and cravat of civilization. In themselves these would have been sufficient to set him apart, but it was not this alone that fetched me gasping to my knees in trembling excitement. Rather it was the cut and color of the things he wore; for the blue trousers and the red waistcoat, the blue coat with its red facings, its gilt buttons and its epaulet worn upon the right shoulder, the leather stock, and the high polished hat with its bright cockade, all proclaimed him a lieutenant of United States Marines.

I gasped and all but rubbed my eyes, and as I did so he turned out of the shadow and into the sunlight that flooded the mid-court, by the fountain. Instantly I recognized the officer who had been in command of marines on board the *Adams* during our last stay at Gibraltar. Often we had met and toasted one another on shore there. Involuntarily memory put his name in my mouth and I cried out:

"O'Bannon!"

My guard stepped forward and dealt me a cuff to the side of the head that sent me sprawling. But my cry had done its work.

The marine stopped, almost in mid-stride, it seemed, and then turned in our direction.

"Who called?" he demanded, staring about at us all. "Who spoke my name?"

I thrust upon the tiled floor to lift myself up.

"O'Bannon!" I gasped.

The guard moved again to strike me, but O'Bannon's voice rang out harsh and hard.

"Let be!" he cried. "Ye bloody devils!"

He moved forward with his hand upraised, and the man drew back defensively.

"O'Bannon!" I gasped again, for I could do no more in my present state.

He stopped abruptly and stared down at me.

"Who are ye?" he said. "Ye know my name!"

"O'Bannon," I said once more. "Don't you know me?"

He stared at me as if reaching back in his memory.

"I——" he said, frowning. "No, I can't say I do."

I felt suddenly aware of how I must look. Even before we had been taken he could scarcely have seen in me more than another Turk, bearded and blackened by the sun and dressed in the costume of the country. Now, with my face half blood and mangled flesh, where I had plowed the roadway with it, and the other half hidden beneath layers of dust and filth, with my native rags in tatters and my legs and feet all bloody and cut to ribbons, it was small wonder he did not recognize me.

"I am Tisdall!" I said. "We met—remember? At Gibraltar. I was surgeon's mate of the *Philadelphia*."

"Good God!" he exclaimed.

He leaned closer, examining me closely.

"Good God!" he repeated. "I know ye now. Yes, by the Lord, I remember!"

He straightened abruptly and turned upon our captor.

"What's the meaning of this, Tayeb?" he demanded. "What have ye done with these men? By the Great Jesus, I've longed for an excuse to get my fingers on your cowardly neck——"

The Arab who had taken us stared at him, obviously not comprehending the words, yet recognizing his fury and being taken aback by it; not so much that O'Bannon felt it, for it was clear that they were old enemies, but that we should be the cause of it. He glanced at us blankly.

"How now?" he demanded of me in Arabic. "What have ye said to this Roumi dog?"

But before we could answer, another voice cut sharply in upon us in English.

"What's this, Mr. O'Bannon? Have I not asked you to keep clear of the sheikh?"

I turned my head and saw that another evident American had come up. He was a short man, stocky and rather stout, with a square face and a straight, rather prominent nose and his hair done in the old fashion, caught behind in a small queue tied in a bow of black ribbon. I noticed that he wore his left arm in a black sling. O'Bannon straightened before him, saluting.

"I'm sorry, General," he said, "but the dog has taken these two Americans. Ye may see the condition——"

The newcomer stared at us.

"Americans?" he said blankly.

I struggled to my feet, though the pain when I brought my weight upon them was excruciating.

"Aye, sir," I managed to gasp. "Americans! Thomas Tisdall, sir, late surgeon's mate of the *Philadelphia,* and Benjamin Price, carpenter's mate, of the same vessel. We escaped from Tripoli, sir, and made our way hence——"

"Of the *Philadelphia?*" he cried in amazement.

"I'll vouch for that, sir," O'Bannon put in quickly. "Ye see, General, I knew the doctor in Gibraltar."

The older man gaped at him.

"Do you say so?" he demanded. "Why, then it must be!"

"Aye, sir!" O'Bannon nodded. He turned to us. "Gentlemen, I present ye General Eaton, who's had command of our expedition from Egypt."

We bowed as best we could in response, while our captors looked on in undisguised amazement. But before I could respond in any other fashion the dignified Turk who had spoken first with the Arab, El Tayeb, reappeared.

"He waits," he said, and then, all at once, caught sight of the general and O'Bannon.

"Your pardon, Excellency!" he exclaimed obsequiously. "The

Sheikh el Tayeb has fetched in these two prisoners, whom he caught upon the road from Benghazi. Forgive me that I did not notice that you had arrived——"

He spoke in Arabic, and it was clear that the general understood him, for he answered fluently in the same tongue.

"But these men are Americans," he objected, "lately escaped from Tripoli!"

The Turk stared at us.

"Amrikani?" he demanded, and then smiled indulgently. "Ah, but, Excellency, that is impossible! Your Excellency has only to look at them——"

"I say they are Americans!" Eaton growled. "O'Bannon Sidi has identified them, and I myself have spoken with them!"

The Turk turned to El Tayeb.

"What is this?" he demanded. "Eaton Sidi says these men are Amrikani!"

The sheikh sneered.

"Amrikani! How can that be? Why, then, did they shoot at us? Why did they try to escape? Why did they hide this and pretend to be poor travelers?"

He jerked out my money belt and presented it dramatically. The Turk looked at the general, who stared at me.

"You shot at them?" he asked. "You resisted?"

"We did not know who they might be," I explained. "They sought to stop us. We have been robbed, beaten, tortured, taken prisoner by Arab tribes and escaped again. We have wandered half across Africa, and come within sight of our flag. Were we to surrender meekly at that point?"

The general looked sympathetic. The Turk stirred uneasily.

"The bashaw waits, Excellency," he suggested.

Eaton started.

"I'd forgot. Well, come, you might as well tell it all to him at once, as have it to go over again. I'll go with you. You too, Mr. O'Bannon. We may need your support."

"With all my heart!" O'Bannon exclaimed, with a glance at me. "Come, Doctor, ye've no need to be alarmed. He's none so bad a one, this bashaw!"

In the name of God, I asked myself, could this be a nightmare? How could these two be concerned with the bashaw?

O'Bannon saw my hesitancy and, attributing it to weakness,

sprang to my aid, supporting me with an arm about my waist
and drawing my own arm up and across his neck. At the same
time he ordered Ben's guards to do the same for him, so that
we were conducted up the stairs and along a tile corridor to a
large chamber with a good deal more tenderness than we had
been haled into the building. The Sheikh el Tayeb followed behind us, the very picture of disgust and bafflement.

Upon entering the chamber we came face to face with a
chubby, effeminate-seeming little man, who had about him a
vaguely familiar air, although I was certain I had never before
clapped eyes upon him. He was dressed in a rich caftan and
bournous, and he wore the turban of a hadji. His fat fingers
were covered with rings, and his chubby jowls were sparsely
adorned with a struggling beard, though I would have guessed
his age to be somewhere in his late thirties. He smiled, and
looked in owlish surprise at Eaton and O'Bannon.

"Ah, General, I had not expected you," he said in Arabic.
"Well, El Tayeb, where are thy prisoners?"

General Eaton cut in abruptly.

"These are they, ya sidi," he said, indicating Ben and myself.
"But there has been a grave mistake. They are Americans, escaped from Tripoli."

The little man was as taken aback as had been the rest. "Amrikani?" he cried. "Impossible!"

Then, turning to Eaton, he added chidingly:

"What joke is this, General? Do ye claim my subjects now
as thy people?"

Eaton shook his head, smiling.

"I found it impossible to credit myself, Your Highness, until
they were identified to me. I give you my word it is so!"

He turned to us.

"Doctor—er—gentlemen! His Royal Highness, Sidi Hamet
Karamauli, bashaw of Tripoli, who was deposed by his brother
Yusuf several years ago, and whom we have undertaken to
restore to his throne. Your Highness, these are Dr. Tisdall, late
of the *Phila*——"

In my amazement I forgot my manners.

"Hamet!" I exclaimed. "Sir! Did you say Hamet Karamauli? Bashaw?

All at once it came to me what had happened, and all the

tensions and anxieties, the hopes and fears and disappointments and miseries of weeks burst upon me, emphasizing the ridiculousness of our final mistake. I began to laugh hysterically, at the same time breaking into tears, so that together my sobs and laughter were mixed in a hysterical gibbering, beyond my power to control.

For an instant they all stared at me, aghast and astonished. Then the bashaw's face screwed up in an insulted snarl. His eyes bulged and his jowls purpled.

"He laughs! He dares to laugh! At me! Hamet Karamauli! Bashaw of Tripoli! He dares! He——"

"No!" I sobbed, yet only dimly aware of the havoc I wrought. "No, ya sidi! Not at you! At myself!"

I turned to Eaton and fought to control myself.

"Tell him!" I cried. "This was the way of it! Everyone said 'bashaw,' and I thought it was Yusuf! It was he we heard called bashaw in Tripoli. That is why I laugh! That was why we shot! It was to escape that bashaw; the one we thought he served!"

"Easy, lad!" O'Bannon said. "Give us the story!"

Eaton turned to Hamet Bashaw placatingly.

"He feared he was to be brought before your brother, Your Highness," he explained. "He has suffered much. Perhaps, if ye will let him explain——"

Hamet scowled at me but waved his hand in assent. I caught my breath shakily and spoke to him directly in Arabic. Eaton's jaw dropped.

"Ye speak their tongue?"

"I could not have escaped otherwise," I replied, and went on speaking to Hamet Bashaw.

I explained how, at Kasr Bou Hasan, we had first heard that 'the bashaw's' army was encamped outside the city and that a battle was expected; how I had leaped to the conclusion that it was Yusuf's army that had been meant; how we had discovered the camp, still above the town, and our flag upon the fort, and what our feelings had been to think we had come so far to such a chance; how we had endeavored to win through into the town, and how we had been taken and tried to fight for our freedom; how I had been confused when El Tayeb had brought us into the city instead of to the camp above, and how I had but just now realized the mistake I had made.

Eaton translated my story for O'Bannon as I spoke, and the marine's jaw hung slack. As I went along, too, the bashaw began to see the humor of it, and by the time I had finished he was laughing uproariously. I thought it less funny than that myself, for my feet ached and I was bone weary. But I laughed with him politely and sobbed too. O'Bannon slapped me heartily on the shoulder.

"And this," he demanded, "was after ye'd crossed the desert, and—did ye say—been retaken, and what all?"

"By the Lord, yes!" Eaton exclaimed. "How did you manage it?"

I started to reply in English, but he stopped me.

"Tell it to the bashaw in his own tongue," he said. "I will translate for O'Bannon."

I started, and as I talked Hamet Bashaw, while listening, silently gestured for cushions to be brought, that we might all sit. I told the story much as I have told it here, leaving out only certain details which could have little interest for my listeners there.

When I had finished they exclaimed at length, while I felt myself growing hot and cold by turns, and my head took to whirling in an alarming fashion. I answered their questions as best I could, at times having difficulty concentrating upon them, and asking one or two in my turn.

"What has become of Yusuf's expedition?" I said. "They left Tripoli two weeks before us."

O'Bannon chuckled.

"It seems they were not in the hurry that ye were. They're yet forty miles west, and have not moved for several days. They say they number no more than two or three hundred."

"And you've taken Derne?" I asked stupidly.

He nodded proudly.

"Aye, yesterday, with the help of the Navy and eight marines!"

I felt the room beginning to go a long way off. It seemed to grow very hot and stifling, and I felt as if I were soaring, upon my cushion, high above them all.

" 'Twas more——" I began, then tried again to say that it was more than the entire squadron had been able to accomplish before Tripoli. " 'Twas more——"

"Catch him!" I heard Eaton cry out, and I giggled foolishly, for it seemed impossible that anyone could reach me at the vast distance to which I had floated. Then, gently, I drifted off beyond them into comfortable oblivion.

9

WHEN I opened my eyes, sometime later, I was laid out upon a couch in a small room with a high, small horseshoe window letting in a spatter of sunlight. Someone had evidently gone to some trouble with me, for even without looking I could tell that my hands and feet and arms and legs and body had been washed, and my face felt clean and fairly comfortable. Ben lay, perhaps ten feet from me, across the narrow room, upon a similar couch, and looking at him, I had some sort of an idea of my own condition, for his wounds had been washed and dressed, comfortingly if crudely, and the dust and filth and stains of travel had been washed away.

As I rolled my head I heard a chuckle and glanced down to see O'Bannon lounging in the doorway.

"Good morning," he said.

"Morning?" I cried, surprised. "But 'twas afternoon but a few minutes ago."

He laughed outright at that.

"Do ye think so?" he demanded.

"What—what happened?" I asked.

He grinned broadly.

"Ye fainted," he replied, "before ye were much more than just done ye'r story. That was yesterday. Ye've been asleep since. How d'ye feel?"

I stretched, to test the answer for myself before I gave it, and found myself not much more than one large bruise.

"Stiff," I replied.

"Well ye might," he chuckled, "from what I hear of the way ye were fetched into town! I'll tell ye the bashaw lit into El Tayeb for that! But ye've no more to worry ye. The general has sent for a boat to carry ye out to the *Argus*."

"What's the matter with this?" I asked.

"Have ye come this far to rest in Derne?" he grinned.

"There'll be one of the ships returning to Malta in a day or two, and the general has it in mind the commodore may be interested to hear what ye have to say."

We fell to talking then, and I learned from him something of the expedition from Alexandria.

At the outset they had numbered some three hundred; himself and a sergeant and a detachment of six marines from the *Argus*, Midshipman Peck, the general and his immediate staff, some sixty mixed Greek and Levantine Christians, cannoneers and foot, and all the rest Arabs, including Hamet Bashaw, whom he pictured as a weak individual, blowing now hot, now cold over the undertaking. Their hardships in the desert—he said that betwixt Alexandria and Bomba they had not passed one flowing spring of water, a distance of near six hundred miles—I could sympathize with; and their troubles with the Arabs—shifty, grasping, capricious as I knew them to be—I could well understand. Nevertheless, he told me, by the time they had reached Derne they numbered more than a thousand, through reinforcements gained along the way.

It was here that he waxed most bitter and displayed his contempt for the Arab fighting man. Despite their numbers, he swore, they had lain back, leaving the handful of Christians and the few marines to bear the brunt of the attack.

"The ships came in close alongshore and threw their metal in among the batteries, making it hot for them," he said. "But there was a time when I thought we'd had it all for nothing; when our one piece was disabled and they seemed well lodged behind their mud walls. It would have been, too, but for the general and the way he led our charge! I tell ye, Tom, he's got guts! He rallied the Greeks and Levantines and led 'em in. We marines managed to get up on the fort and dowse their colors. The ships had made it hot for 'em there, and when they saw us coming over the edge I suppose the gunners thought there were more of us than there were, for, anyway, they flung down their matches and fled. We found the guns shotted and ready—no attempt to spike 'em. So we hauled 'em about and turned 'em on the town, and after that our Arabs came on in and the rest was easy!"

I found out later there was a good deal more to it than that. To all intents and purposes O'Bannon and seven marines carried the fort defended by several hundred. But he was too modest to make capital of that.

While he was talking a detachment came with litters from the *Argus,* and he saw us taken up and walked with us through the streets, narrow and hot and smelling and buzzing with flies, to the quay. Before we were embarked he bent over me and tucked my money belt in beside me.

"Hamet Bashaw made El Tayeb give it up," he said with a wink. "I thought ye might want it. There's more in it than I'd care to lose!"

It was good to feel the lift and roll of a ship beneath me once again. Although there had been a time when I believed that if I could but get ashore I would never go to sea again, now I found myself only too happy to be leaving.

The *Argus* being a brig, and smaller than a frigate, I was assigned quarters in the main cabin, while Ben was sent forward to the diminutive sick bay, which he shared with the wounded members of the expedition. Here, in our respective quarters, we were attended by Larkin Griffin, surgeon of the *Argus,* who made a great point of displaying our hurts to our new shipmates, as an evidence of Tripoline brutality, and, indeed, succeeded in stirring up so much indignation that I felt embarrassed.

We spent two days on board the *Argus,* when we were transferred to the sloop *Hornet,* twelve, Lieutenant Evans commanding, which was to be dispatched that afternoon, with word of the victory and requests for supplies, to Malta.

The voyage westward which followed, I think, I shall always remember as one of the pleasantest sea journeys of my life. The weather was fine, as it is apt to be in those parts at this time of the year. We were a small ship with nothing to do but go where we were bound, and with a much greater sense of comradeship and equality among all hands than is customarily found aboard larger vessels. We drove as fast as the winds that we met would take us, yet there was no sense of urgency. And best of all, those of us who had come on board at Derne, the wounded, a courier from General Eaton to Commodore Barron, and Ben and myself, to whom such a life of leisure at sea was all but unheard of, had nothing to do and were required to do no duty. We were sixteen days in passing, and by the time we came within sight of the narrow gullet, with its washing tides, and the all but perpendicular slopes of Valetta, both Ben and I were as fully recovered, save for a few slightly stiff scars, as we would ever be.

We reached the harbor mouth an hour or two before daybreak and cruised offshore, mindful of the regulation which permits no ship to enter between sunrise and sundown. As the dawn came up I found myself in the eyes of the vessel, for, belonging to no watch, I might come and go as I pleased, and, to me, at least, there is no sight comparable to raising a harbor with the day. I found Ben there before me, and we nodded as we met and recognized one another, but beyond that exchanged no greeting.

Gradually the cleft of the gullet opened and cleared and we were able to look down it. There were several British ships, frigates and ships of the line, at anchor in the pool, their black sides and yellow stripes gleaming through the misty dawn, while over on the shadowed side, in the Great Port, lying close against the town, where the mists had not yet risen, lay several other vessels, as nearly as I could make out a brig or two, two ships, a schooner, and a mixture of smaller craft. Yet even before we had turned into the harbor, before I could make out the detailed outline of these vessels, Ben grabbed my arm in a flash of excitement.

"Igod!" he cried. "Look there!"

"What? Where?" I said, for I saw nothing unusual.

"There!" he cried, pointing emphatically. "D'ye not make her out? D'ye not recognize the figurehead—say naught the sweep of her lines?"

I looked again, harder, straining my eyes through the morning mist at the ship he indicated and saw a frigate, neat and trim. It was almost a minute—a long minute, while he stared at me in unbelief—before I recognized her.

"Why!" I cried. "Why, 'tis——"

"'Tis she! 'Tis the *Essex!*" he cried. "The sweetest ship afloat! They've fetched her out again! She's back in commission! Look at her, man! Have ye ever seen anything so lovely? Have ye ever seen such lines, such sheer? There's not a vessel afloat can touch her. I'd know her anywhere!"

"You talk as if she were a woman!" I gibed.

"What woman ever had that beauty?" he demanded.

I thought of Patience.

"It strikes me," I said, "you're drawing a comparison between things that you can't compare."

He rolled his eyes at me significantly and grinned.

" 'Twas your comparison," he said, and looked back at the anchored ship. "But I'm not sure but what you're right. Have ye ever seen aught to compare with her?"

Our pilot came on board, and we entered the harbor and came to anchor not far from where she lay. The other ships proved to be the *Constellation,* thirty-eight, Captain Campbell, and the *Vixen,* twelve, John Smith, Master Commandant commanding. Captain James Barron, in the *Essex,* proved senior officer present afloat and, as such, flew the pendant, which required Mr. Evans to report aboard. Since I was in a sense a part of the dispatches, I accompanied him in the jolly boat.

Captain Barron received us in the great cabin, and we stood at attention until he gave us "at ease." We were joined there by Captain Campbell of the *Constellation* and Mr. Smith of the *Vixen,* and there Mr. Evans made his report, thrusting me forward as his primary exhibit. Captain Barron questioned me sourly, with the severity of the good-natured man turned by the consciousness of his responsibility, and it may be that I took a liberty in attempting to break through his reserve, for he heard me out with a scowl upon his round face and ordered me to report in the morning, with Ben, for duty aboard the *Essex.* I suggested that perhaps the commodore would like to hear our stories. But his pink-nosed, blue-jowled face purpled at the thought that I would question his command, and he bawled at me furiously:

"What you may think has little weight with me, Sirrah! I carry my brother's resignation in favor of Captain Rodgers', and 'tis to him I am obliged to carry all my reports!"

"Aye, aye, Captain," I replied. I did not know that he had advised his brother not to resign and was disgruntled at his refusal. How could I? Yet we were all to know it presently, for it resulted in bad blood between him and Rodgers.

"Harrrummmph!" he grunted. "Well and good! Well and good! See you report aboard first thing in the morning, and fetch that carpenter with you. We can use him!"

"He's been a prisoner, sir!" I ventured to remonstrate.

"What difference does that make?" he demanded. "He's a carpenter, isn't he? He's an American? He signed on the *Philadelphia?* His sea time is not up, is it? Goddammit! We need a carpenter. Bring him here!"

"Aye, Captain," I said, and let it stand at that, knowing it useless to do otherwise.

To my surprise, when I told him the news Ben was far from reluctant.

"We go aboard the *Essex?*" he cried. "Now there's good news! I had not thought ye such a friend of mine!"

"Hold on!" I replied. "Don't thank me. 'Twas none of my doing, and I doubt you'll be so pleased with it when you stop and think what it means."

"What does it mean?" he snorted.

"Why, that Captain Barron means to sign you on," I replied, "and seeing the ship is but new come into these waters, it may be a long cruise. It may delay your return home."

"Home!" he laughed. "Who wants to go home? Here's the *Essex* just come out, and you prate of going home!"

I looked at him in amazement. I had never heard a foremast hand speak so. Nor, from what I had seen of the life, was there any reason why one should. It was harsh and cruel and exacting, often unjust, and though Jack soon develops an affection for this ship or that, he is usually a born growler and always ready for a turn ashore. As a rule there's never a one of them but would give his right hand to be free. Yet here was Ben—a man, I thought, of some intelligence—turning about and flying in the face of all reason.

"Well," I said, "you may not want to go home, but I do, and I'll admit it freely."

"And what's to stop you?" he demanded with a mocking glint in his eye. "You're welcome to the first opportunity!"

I wondered how he could be so callously indifferent.

"What of Pat?" I said.

His eyes narrowed angrily.

"Look!" he exclaimed. "Why don't you go back to Pat? You're so solicitous about her! Why don't you go back and tell her what kind of a swine I am? Poison her against me! Take her away from me! Why don't you?"

"I would," I said coldly, "but she'd not have me. She married you, Ben, and she loves you. She told me so. Even if she did not, she's an honest, honorable woman who's made a contract and will stand by it."

He threw back his head and laughed.

" 'Honest, honorable woman!' " he quoted me. "Ah-hah-ha-hah! That's good, Tom! You put it so concisely—your foolish little morals! D'you think I can't see through you? D'you think I don't know you both? Honest, honorable are the words—synonyms for simple! So long as I know ye both honest and honorable—or even one of ye—I have nothing to worry about!"

In that moment I would have happily smashed my fist in his face, but we stood upon the deck of a naval vessel and I would not have even him think that I would take advantage of my rank. I turned upon my heel, but he caught me.

"Wait!" he said. "I'd not have you think me the complete villain."

"You couldn't be as complete a villain as I think you!" I said stiffly.

He chuckled thereby infuriating me the more. He was so completely the master of the situation. It irritated me.

"If it were any other ship," he said, "I give you my word, Tom, I'd refuse it. But the *Essex!* Tom, she's always been a lucky ship for me. I can't help feeling it, my life and hers are someway bound together."

"That's nonsense!" I snorted. "Plain superstition! Besides, if you can feel that way about an inanimate hulk, why can't you recognize the greater claim of living flesh?"

"Inanimate hulk?" he roared indignantly, and for an instant I thought it was he who would strike me. "Can you say that about the *Essex?* Why, you—you—you turd-stinking mud puppy! If ever a ship lived, 'tis she!"

"Just a minute, Price!" I cried, shaking with rage now. "Hold on! If you were an officer, I'd have you out for that insult. You take advantage of your inferiority in rate to bait me."

"I'm sorry!" he sneered petulantly. "Never let it be said I took an unfair advantage of you!"

I left him then, knowing that if I stayed longer I would have murder on my hands. In fact I wondered why I had not seized the thousand-and-one opportunities that had been mine during our escape. He called me fool for my honesty, and I felt now that he was right.

This was our declaration of a renewal of hostilities, our notice to one another that the truce was ended and that henceforth we were to return to our former relationship.

We transferred from the *Hornet* the next day, and, as I suspected, Ben was signed on as carpenter's mate with no assurance that if another ship left for home before the *Essex* he might go in her. Nevertheless I made up my mind to put in a word to that effect, if the opportunity arrived.

For my part I was treated as a passenger. The captain remained peevish—which is the only word I can find to describe his attitude, for he seemed to resent me.

With the other officers I got on well. With my fellow passenger, however, Colonel Lear, our consul to Algiers, who had been empowered to treat with Yusuf Bashaw for peace, and who was en route to Tripoli for that purpose, I was at odds, for we disagreed as to the merits of General Eaton's expedition, he maintaining that we had no right to interfere in the internal affairs of the country, while I held that we might properly avail ourselves of what means came to hand to win our point.

The *Essex* sailed from Malta on the twenty-fifth of May, coming the following evening before Tripoli, where we found the *Constitution* and the *President* cruising offshore. The sight of the city in which I had spent so much time as a prisoner, and in which so many of my comrades were still confined, was profoundly moving to me, even though it was a great satisfaction to view it once more from an American man-of-war.

Immediately upon our arrival Captain Barron boarded the *Constitution,* taking Colonel Lear and myself with him, to deliver the orders which formally turned over command to Commodore Rodgers. I was amused at the meeting of these two, for if Barron was a martinet, the new commodore was an even more uncompromising disciplinarian. Stern and tight-lipped to the point of disagreeableness, he received us in the great cabin, and, after accepting the dispatch which formally named him commodore—and which seemed to make him even more sensible of his own importance—he received the letters which General Eaton had sent and heard my account of our captivity and escape. When I was done he eyed me balefully.

"You say you left Tripoli on your own impulse, Doctor," he asked, "without Captain Bainbridge's consent?"

"Sir," I replied, not a little hotly, for I saw which way the wind blew, "there is not an officer there would not have done the same, and with the captain's blessing. Indeed, it has been planned and tried a number of times."

"Humph!" he grunted. "Had you been aboard ship 'twould have been called desertion. Under the circumstances, I don't suppose we can bring charges; certainly not until we've had opportunity to learn Captain Bainbridge's views. Meantime, sir, consider yourself in a state of informal arrest!"

He bent bushy brows upon Captain Barron.

"What about the other man, Captain?" he asked.

'Oh, I've put him to work, Commodore," Barron replied unctuously. "Signed him on. He'll give us no trouble."

"Good! Good!" Rodgers nodded his approval.

I found myself seething.

"Sir," I said, "neither Price nor myself had any intention of deserting. We sought only to escape, and that we are here now, I think, is evidence of our honorable purpose. As a matter of fact, Price has expressed a wish to remain in the *Essex,* and I would like to ask the same privilege."

He blinked at me owlishly, obviously taken aback.

"Damme!" he rumbled.

He swung round and addressed himself to Barron.

"There, Captain! D'ye see how a man may be mistaken in his first impressions? Here are two young lads, separated by many degrees of rank, yet shipmates through thick and thin! There's the stuff that makes a fighting crew, mark my words!"

He spun back to me and offered his hand in apology.

"Forgive me, sirrah!" he said. "I misjudged you. Of course you may stay aboard the *Essex*. I shall see to it! You may forget that tarradiddle about arrest!"

"Thank you, Commodore," I said, I fear without enthusiasm.

He did not appear to notice. He turned to Barron.

"You've a surgeon aboard, haven't you, Captain?"

"Why, yes, of course, sir!" Barron replied. "Mr. Dorsey."

"Well, put him aboard the *President*," the commodore ordered. "Put Mr. Tiddle, here, in his place. That's all right with you, isn't it?"

"Oh yes, certainly, sir!" Barron said hastily.

Rodgers turned back to me, beaming mellowly.

"There you are, Tiddle, my lad!" he said. "That's all! That's all! You may go."

"Thank you, sir," I said dryly. "I thought, perhaps—well, sir, you see, I have a pretty thorough knowledge of the city. I might be able to help if you've planned any attack."

"Ah, harummph!" he coughed. "Yes, yes, I see! A creditable thought, too. 'Tis unfortunate you were not here with us last summer. Now—well, frankly, I don't know. Here's Mr. Lear come to talk peace. Ah—did ye say you'd been in fairly close contact with the bashaw?"

"I think I may say I'm fairly acquainted with him, sir," I replied.

"Hah?" he grunted politely. "And what, say, would you judge was his attitude toward us—er—that is, when you last saw him, which I understand was several months ago?"

"In March, sir," I replied. "That is true. These people are very childish, sir, very capricious, and what they swear to today they will pretend ignorance of tomorrow. When I left, sir, the bashaw was very much in fear of an attack by your squadron and enraged at our seeking out his brother in Egypt. He was then swearing that if an attack were attempted he would put every prisoner in his hands to the sword."

"There, you see?" he nodded. "If that's the case, we must rely on Mr. Lear to negotiate a peace and rescue your shipmates. It would hardly do, would it, to have their blood upon our heads? Certainly not until we had tried every means to release them peaceably!"

"Sir," I said, "I think you need worry very little on that score. It would be my guess that General Eaton's success in the east, in taking Derne, combined with the good sense of his minister, Sidi Mohammed D'Ghies, who is nobody's fool, would prevent him from making any such fatal move. Alive, the prisoners are a weapon in his hand, for through them he may obtain better terms of us. Dead, they no longer have any value to him. I might point out to you too, sir, that because of his persistence in this war, and its consequent heavy taxes, he is now fairly surrounded, on all sides, by a dissident population. This I can testify by my personal experience. Without it we would never have been able to cross his country unsuspected."

He nodded pontifically.

"Interesting! Interesting! But all the more reason why we must leave matters to Mr. Lear. I thank you, Tiddle, but I think we'll have no further need of you. You may go now. I'll send for you if I want you."

His dismissal was unmistakable and left no room for argument, and I bowed myself out of my only attempt at international diplomacy with more profuse thanks than I felt.

As he had half predicted, however, Colonel Lear was able, by bribery and negotiation, to accomplish in a few days by peaceful means what all our frigates and gunboats had been unable to do in three years. On the third of June the bashaw accepted the terms offered him and signed the treaty bringing peace to our two nations, not to mention freedom to all of my countrymen still held prisoner in his castle. I know there are some who feel that the price, sixty thousand dollars, was too high, and that it smacked of the tribute we had sworn never to pay. But for my own part I say one does not put a price upon men's suffering. Had we paid a like sum to each man still in captivity for what he had undergone, it would not be too much.

However, that was a matter over which I had no control. On the last day of May, Captain Barron assumed command of the frigate *President*, while Master Commandant George Cox, lately commanding officer of that ship, assumed command of the *Essex*.

So ended, to all intents and purposes, the Mediterranean phase of our adventures, for, although the *Essex* remained yet a full year in those waters, it was, for me at least, a period of dull routine and waiting. Our comrades in captivity were released and fetched aboard the various vessels of the squadron. Lieutenant Porter remained upon the Mediterranean station, first as commanding officer of the *Constitution*, under the paternal eye of the commodore, and later in command of the *Enterprise*, in which he had served once before. Most of the other officers of the *Philadelphia*, however, returned home either in the *President*, in July, or in the *Constellation*, which sailed not long afterward. A few of the men were lucky enough to find berths aboard those ships and so went home. But for the most they were distributed through the squadron and required to serve until such time as their particular ship went home. This was done without regard to their condition, which in the main was pitiful, and quite without consideration for the fact that they had been more than a year and a half in captivity and so might be thought to have earned the right to return. It was an injustice which made my blood boil, though I was powerless to do anything about it, other than to see that life was made as easy as possible for those that were assigned to the *Essex*.

In July, Master Commandant Charles Stewart relieved Captain Cox in command of the *Essex*, and I, for one, was sorry to see the change, for although Captain Stewart was an able officer, he was also a stern disciplinarian. For two months thereafter, while we cruised off Tunis, the greater part of my duty lay in treating lacerated backs which had felt the discipline of the cat.

In August the bey of Tunis signed a treaty of peace. Shortly afterward Captain Hugh Campbell relieved Captain Stewart in the *Essex*. From then on, through the winter, we cruised back and forth between Gibraltar and the central Mediterranean, for the most part convoying American merchantmen up and down. In these months almost our only excitement came when we put into Gibraltar or Malta or Syracuse or Port Mahon, all ports in which we could expect to find British vessels and look for a good fight or a duel or some similar unpleasantry, for our British cousins, even then, grew daily more arrogant and condescending toward us, and in plain self-defense we were forced to put the chip upon our shoulder.

Early in June, more than a year after our release, it was announced that we would shortly sail for home. For several days we were kept busy in preparation, until finally Commodore Rodgers came aboard, hoisting his broad pendant in the *Essex*, for he was to return with us. The next day we weighed anchor and stood out to sea, dipping our colors punctiliously to the *Constitution*, the only ship of the squadron remaining in this station. Running westward through the Mediterranean, we were occasionally baffled by contrary winds, but once through the Straits and in the open ocean, we soon picked up the trades and bowled merrily along. On the twenty-second of July, after what must have been close to a record run for a ship of our class, we raised the white beaches and piny flats of the Virginia Capes, and six days later we warped into our berth at the Washington Navy Yard. When we signed our pay accounts and went ashore a few days later, it was for Ben and me and for some of the rest of us the first time in more than three years that we had set foot upon American soil. At that it was sooner than some of us had expected.

IV

Free Trade and Sailors' Rights

THE *Essex* paid off early in August, foremast hands, as was customary, including Ben, being released entirely from the service; those who wished to "ship over" being required to sign new articles. The officers, on the other hand, including myself and excepting only those who were immediately ordered to new ships or stations, were granted leave.

There was no real reason why I should have insisted on accompanying Ben to Salem. With the *Essex* in ordinary and most of the other frigates being laid up as well; with the experiences of three years behind us, I could be reasonably certain that he would not delay his return. I told myself that it was because I could not trust him, but even then, I think, I knew in my secret heart that it was only for the sake of a glimpse of Patience, however hopeless that might be, that I did it.

We traveled by stage, through Baltimore, Philadelphia, and Trenton to Amboy, where we took a ferry for New York. After pausing there a day, we continued through New Haven, and Providence to Boston, and thence, through the long, warm summer's afternoon, to Salem. It was a journey which, before we reached home, gave us both an opportunity to renew acquaintance with our native land. In Washington, no doubt because so many Western folk came there, much of the conversation centered about Western affairs, events on the Ohio and the Mississippi, and the activities of the Spaniards in the South and West. One heard the names of Burr and Blennerhassett, Wilkinson, de Yrujo frequently mentioned, and only less frequently was mention made of Clark and Lewis and General Pike, who had gone to explore the West. There was agitation for the National Road, and Congress was still arguing the merits of gunboats versus frigates for the protection of our coasts. Farther north, however, we found men's eyes fixed more distantly outward, most likely because that way lay the seaports and the focus of our trade. In the main there was popular indignation at the arrogant insolence of the British in presuming to claim control over the entire Atlantic, even to our very shores. There was disapproval likewise of the highhanded methods of the Corsican bandit toward our commerce. It is my own feeling that the French, in those next few years to come, did our trade as much harm as the British. But even as early as that the British ships, ranging far across the ocean in a way the French never dared to do, and, to all intents and purposes, blockading our very ports, brought themselves and their attitude just so much more within our ken, so that we were unable to ignore them, as we did the French. The case of the *Essex*— not the frigate, but a merchant vessel belonging to the Derbys out of Salem—a ship that had made a voyage from Barcelona to Havana and been seized and condemned in a British Court of Admiralty upon the principle of continuous passage—had set not only Salem, but all New England, by the ears. The unwarranted attack upon an American coasting vessel by the British frigate *Leander,* within sight of Sandy Hook, resulting in the death of one of the American's crew, was scarcely calculated to increase American affection for our haughty cousins. Even the most dyed-in-the-wool Federalist resented such acts, and the Orders in Council which attempted to close continental ports to our ships were hotly resented. Nor were Bonaparte's retaliatory decrees much consolation to the anti-Republicans. They, being traders in the main, were as much hurt as helped by them.

All of this and more we heard in our northward journey, the bitterness of the expressions attending it depending upon the political coloration of our informant of the moment. For me it was scarcely a comfortable journey, for the uniform of the Navy, which I wore, was a constant signal to some hanger-on to demand what we meant to do about all this, and why we were not at sea ready to fight and defend our trade as we were paid to do. Explanation that we had but just returned from three years in Barbary had some mollifying effect, but led to questioning on that score, and at the next stop the whole proceeding would have to be gone through again.

Throughout the trip Ben was quiet, almost inattentive, and to my mind almost suspiciously tractable. I had not seen him in this mood in many a year, and I could only suspect some roguery developing in his mind. I kept a sharp watch upon him. It was not until we were between New London and Providence, however, that he opened his thoughts to me and showed me what had been in his mind.

Travel was light, and we had the coach to ourselves when he turned to me abruptly with an almost pleading look. So sudden was his move that I almost ducked involuntarily.

"I've been a fool, Tom!" he burst out.

I gaped at him in astonishment.

"Well!" I said, completely taken aback. "Well——"

"Don't try to deny it," he cried. "You've said so yourself. You've been years trying to show it to me!"

"Well!" I said again, still not quite knowing what to make of this. "I'm pleased that you see it. I hope you won't forget it!"

"You don't believe me!" he exclaimed. "You don't believe I mean to behave differently from now on!"

"I'll believe it when you prove it," I replied dryly.

"I'll prove it!" he cried. "See if I don't!"

"I don't doubt you have it in you," I said. "You've ability enough, I know. But I wonder if you have the will?"

"Wait and see," he replied shortly.

"What brings this on?" I said caustically. "It isn't like you."

He turned to me.

"Don't plague me!" he cried. "I tell you I'm ashamed of the way I've acted. I've had time to think since we got back to the *Essex,* and it's been pretty plain I've played the fool. I know I can't square everything."

I thought of Selina.

"No," I said harshly, "you can't."

"But I can make some reparation," he went on. "I can do something to repay Pat for the hell I've given her. I'm done with the sea! Sam Nowell always said I had the makings of a master builder. I'll set myself to that!"

"It will be a great day for all your friends when you do, Ben," I said.

"I will!" he promised. "You watch!"

In spite of myself I was almost convinced. Rather, let me say that I felt his conviction of the moment but was still not sure of his sticking qualities.

"I'll be watching," I said. "But I'm not the one that must be shown."

"But you are," he retorted. "Pat will know it and will have the benefit of it. But you—twice I owe you my life, and what have I done to repay it?"

"I never wanted pay for it," I said.

"No, no!" he cried. "But what have I done? I've cheated you and hated your guts and———"

"Must we go into it?" I asked sharply.

"No," he said humbly. "But any time you'd the right to shoot me. Instead you've stood by. You didn't need to. You could have stood aside and let things take their course, with no blame to yourself. But you didn't! And I—I don't know—what can I do to show I'm sensible of it?"

I stared at him curiously. He really did mean it, I thought. It meant an end to all my hopes, but it would mean happiness for Pat, and I was ready to settle for that.

"Stick to it, Ben!" I said. "Not for me, for I've naught to do with it, but for Pat. She's yours and she loves you. She's worthy of your attention."

"I will," he said. "I will!"

"Then here's my hand on it," I replied. "And if I can help you, call on me. Let what's over and done with be forgot!"

We came to Salem in the warm dusk of a summer's evening when the smell of the tide flats beyond the town hung like an intimate memory upon the air and the trees in leaf cast sheltering arms across the streets. At the stage stop at the tavern we gathered our sea bags and went quickly into the dark, up Derby Street, before any might recognize us and delay our homecoming, for in a sense I looked upon it as mine as well as Ben's. There were lights in the Hackett house as we passed, and I wondered somberly what the lives of its new owners might be like. A ship and a brig were moored at Derby Wharf, and by the light of the thin moon we could make out the faint outline of other vessels anchored in the harbor. When we left the water front and turned up Daniels Street the white fronts of the houses and the white fences, and the scent of the phlox, heavy on the night air, tugged nostalgically at my heart and fetched a lump in my throat and made my eyes wet. As we approached the house the golden light gleamed out of the narrow windows. The old gate creaked as we entered, and my own steps sounded in my ears like thunder on the walk.

Ben lifted the knocker, and we heard the echoes of it ring within. A moment we waited, and then footsteps sounded on the other side of the door. The bolt clattered and the latch lifted. The door swung wide, sending a shaft of mellow light licking out into the darkness.

Pat stood before us, in a gown of some simple gray stuff, and for an instant my heart stood still within me. Time had not dulled the radiance of her loveliness nor wrought havoc with her figure. She was a woman grown, no longer eighteen, but none the less desirable for that! The light behind her gleamed through the golden mist of her hair, and her figure was firm and rounded in its outline.

For an instant she stood, transfixed with surprise, unable to speak.

"I've brought him back," I said lamely.

She nodded, almost as though she had been expecting us.

"I—I knew you would, Tom!" she said.

Ben laughed suddenly, more heartily than was necessary.

"Ah!" he cried. "So you sent him after me?"

Patience looked startled, almost frightened, but Ben went on chuckling, apparently oblivious of it.

"Well you might!" he exclaimed. "I've needed looking after!"

"Ben!" I said.

He cut me short with an abrupt gesture and drew her forward until we were standing face to face.

"Ask him!" he said. "I've already confessed my faults to him. I'm a reformed character. I've given my word, and you are the two that have done it: my wife and my best friend—though I wonder how I dare call him that!"

She looked up at me quickly, questioningly.

"Stuff!" I growled, embarrassed. "She did not send me. I came because I was ordered. If aught's reformed you, 'tis your own conscience. God knows, I could not do it!"

He threw back his head and laughed, while Patience looked at me strangely.

"You're too modest!" he cried, and turned to her, sobering abruptly. "He's right, though! I've been too pigheaded to see the friends I've had! I've not appreciated you! But all that is over!"

She glanced from me to him and back again.

"Wait!" she said, looking more than a little dazed. "It's been a long time. I—I had a letter from Tom saying you'd both been taken, but—but——"

Ben stared at her, for once startled.

"You've not—you've not——" he stumbled.

She laughed, and even though it was not for me, I thought I had never heard anything lovelier.

"Of course not!" she cried. "Come in! I was not expecting callers. Have you had supper? I've a few things in the house."

"Ah! Food!" he cried. "Bless you, Pat! We've not et since Boston!"

We entered, and at once she was away, into the larder, returning presently with a ham and a roast of mutton, cold, and a bowl of eggs. While she prepared a late supper Ben paced up and down the room.

"I give you my word, Pat!" he cried. "I've turned the corner! I've treated you shabbily, my dear, and I would apologize! But apologies won't do. It takes more than that. Tom has convinced me. I'm for shore now!"

She glanced at him oddly but turned to me.

"When did you get back? Most of the *Philadelphia's* people were long since home. I'd almost given you up for lost."

Ben laughed and replied before I had opportunity.

"Aye," he cried, "first away, last home! We escaped."

"Escaped?" She stared at him.

"Aye, escaped! The only ones that did. And we'd the bad luck to end aboard the only ship, bar one, to stay behind."

"The *Essex?*"

I gave him a startled look and met his warning glance.

"The *Essex!*" he nodded.

Evidently, though he claimed himself reformed, he was not yet ready to go the full road to confession. When the food was on the table and we were seated he must tell the whole story of our escape, barring only the reasons that made it necessary, and of our adventures in the desert, giving me more than enough credit and, to my embarrassment, leaving out no detail. I thought he smacked his lips somewhat over Jorah, and ventured to protest, but succeeded only in emphasizing the episode. There was no stopping him.

When he was finished I was ready to pick up my sea bag and escape to the nearest tavern.

"And you did this because—because——" Pat said.

"Because I was as anxious as he to be free," I said roughly.

"He did it because he'd sworn to fetch me back to you!" Ben laughed. "And for that, my dear, God knows, we both owe him a debt of friendship!"

She looked from one to the other of us, I thought, in some confusion. Ben sobered abruptly.

"I've said it to Tom," he said seriously. "I may as well say it to you, too, for you deserve it as well as he. I've seen the error of my ways, Pat, and I mean to mend them. You and Tom have stood by me in these years, and it's your fidelity that's brought it home to me. To you I promise, I mean to be a better man in the future!"

Pat glanced at me sharply, and I gave her an almost imperceptible nod. She rose and placed her hand upon his arm.

"Ben—Ben dear," she said, almost with an effort.

He caught her to him.

"I mean it!" he cried.

I rose.

"I must be going," I said.

He released her and stared at me.

"Going?" he cried. "Where?"

"To the tavern," I told him, "before they close."

"The tavern?" he exclaimed. "My royal arse! You stay right here, my friend! Doesn't he, Pat? Tavern, indeed!"

"I don't want to put Pat out," I protested.

"Be damned to that!" he snorted. "We have room, haven't we, lass? Here! Sit on that bag, and don't ye let him leave!"

The upshot of it was, of course, that I stayed, though I had little stomach for it. The thought of them together kept me awake long after we had retired, and I made up my mind that as soon as I gracefully could I would go!

But resolution was not enough. Ben swore that if I did not stay he would not know how to go about his program of reform, and Patience added her voice to his. I found myself as much a prisoner to their hospitality as ever I had been in Tripoli, and since they were both so earnest I had not the heart to refuse.

There were compensations. Young Sam Eben and little Elizabeth delighted in my shiny buttons and spent such hours of the day as they were allowed to, climbing on my lap and demanding one yarn after another. I told them what I knew of the Navy—that is to say, what I knew of it that would delight their young ears. Again and again I described the burning of the *Philadelphia*. I told them all the anecdotes I could remember of sea service and pumped their father for more. Young Sam, I delighted in, for he had the handsomeness of his father combined with the sweetness of his mother. But Elizabeth was my especial love, for she was all her mother, and she would eye me with lowered glance and then run to me with arms outstretched in such a way that I could almost think her my own.

Patience herself was unchanged. She carried herself with a pride and loveliness that was a treat to watch, and motherhood had seemed only to emphasize her womanliness and make her more desirable, so that I found myself glancing away, almost self-consciously, when she entered the room. Whether Ben was aware of this I do not know. I feel sure that she was, for once, when we were alone in the house, while Ben was out looking for work, she turned upon me abruptly.

"I'm a married woman, Tom!" she said.

"Worse luck!" I managed to reply, although she had caught me quite aback.

"And an honest one," she went on.

"I'd be happy to kill the man that implied otherwise," I said, "and you know why!"

"Tom!" she cried reproachfully. "I owe you so much!"

"You owe me nothing," I told her. "You told me you loved him, didn't you?"

She turned away sharply and did not answer for so long that I thought I had offended her in some way. When she turned back to me her jaw was set, her face composed.

"I owe you thanks, Tom," she said, "and the children more so. You brought him back safe, and you seem to have influenced him for the better."

In justice to Ben, I thought I should explain.

"He comes to his own decisions," I replied. "I take no credit for the course he's following."

"You wouldn't!" she exclaimed.

"What d'you mean by that?" I demanded.

"Oh, nothing!" she cried. "Nothing! You wouldn't understand a woman's thoughts!"

"Tell me a woman's thoughts!" I growled.

"Jorah seemed to have had some," she retorted.

I flushed hotly, desperately embarrassed.

"Pat!" I cried.

"You don't deny it!" she replied.

"I don't deny it!" I said stiffly. "She did a great deal for us both. 'Twas little enough I could do for her!"

She looked around at me almost softly.

"Was she pretty, Tom?" she asked.

"She had a wild sort of beauty," I replied curtly.

"And did you love her?" she asked, persisting.

"She had a rancid Arab smell," I said, thinking to shock her, "and she sweated abominably. Yes, I liked her. She was good to me in a place where friends were few."

She turned and stared at me, then returned to her work.

"I see!" she said harshly.

"You needn't be so high and mighty!" I told her. "She risked her life for us, and I would be an ungrateful dog not to do all that she asked!"

"I don't suppose you wanted to!" she replied tartly.

"Oh God!" I cried. "We're here, aren't we?"

She nodded.

"We wouldn't be, but for her!" I said.

She did not answer.

Ben came in not long after that.

"Good evening, my turtledoves!" he said gaily.

I looked up at him sharply, but he returned my look with a bland, innocent stare.

"Turtledoves!" I snorted, trying somewhat to cover my confusion. "You should have been here five minutes ago."

He glanced from me to Pat and back again.

"Oh?" he said. "Have you been quarreling?"

"I wouldn't call it quarreling," I grinned. "Just disagreeing. Pat doesn't approve of my—my affair with Jorah."

"Tom Tisdall!" she exclaimed, outraged.

Ben cocked an amused eyebrow at her.

"What's the matter?" he demanded. "Do you think Tom

should have defended his virtue? You know what Yakoub planned!"

She faced him furiously.

"I—I don't care what he did!" she cried. "But if either of you were gentlemen you'd not discuss it in my presence!"

Ben laughed and turned to me, dryly.

"Don't mind her. She's just jealous, that's all."

He was within hand's reach of her when he said it, and her next move astounded us both, for she turned and slapped him across the face with all the strength of her arm—which, for all her small size, was not inconsiderable. Then without further words she turned and fled away up the stairs.

Ben clapped a hand to his face and turned to stare after her in amazement.

"Now what the devil ails her?" he demanded.

"I'm damned if I know!" I replied, as startled as he.

"Ah well," he said, grinning, "she'll get over it. I'll not let that spoil the news I've got!"

"I thought you'd something on your mind," I said.

"Wait till you hear!" he chuckled. "You know Ballard's ship-yard, out on North Point?"

I nodded.

"It's for sale," he announced.

I looked at him blankly.

"Don't you see?" he demanded. "It's my chance! It's a good yard, well found and well located. If I can get it, Tom, I'll be able to show you that I mean what I say."

"Can you swing it?" I asked.

He evaded my eyes.

"I—I don't know," he said. "It's not being given away. Ballard wants seven thousand with no ships in the stocks. I've got about seventeen hundred of my own, counting back pay these three years past. I've talked to Ballard, and I think he might be persuaded to accept that much cash and give me a mortgage on the rest."

"A pretty heavy mortgage," I replied.

"Yes," he said shortly.

I stood up and began to pace about the room. It came to me that here was an opportunity to do something substantial for Patience. If he was sincere, and I felt that he was, a helping hand now might insure her future. I turned to him.

"I might be able to help you," I said. "Would you accept a loan from me?"

He glanced up eagerly, then appeared to think.

"Would you come into it with me?"

"Make it a simple loan," I replied.

He shook his head.

"I'll swing it alone first."

"All right," I told him. "I'll match your stake as a partner. That will cut the mortgage down to reasonable limits. But, mind you, I know nothing about shipbuilding. I'm only a silent partner. It's in your hands from start to finish, and I want you to have the right to buy me out at any time."

He leaped to his feet and bounded across the room to me, seizing me in his arms and pounding me on the back, and at the same time attempting to dance a wild hornpipe.

"By the Lord!" he cried. "I knew you'd do it! Ah, man, if ever there was an honest gentleman, Tom, 'tis you!"

"Stuff!" I protested. "I know a good investment when I see it!"

"Like hell!" he cried. "But I promise you'll not regret it!"

He bounded to the foot of the stairs and bellowed up them. "Pat! Pat! Come here! I've great news!"

She came down slowly, sulky but curious.

"Darling!" Ben cried, and I felt a sharp stab of jealousy. "We're going to buy Ballard's yard. Tom's agreed to come in with me. We're going to be partners!"

She shot me a quick, startled glance.

"I'm only a silent partner," I put in hastily.

Pat stared at us.

"You—you think it's wise?" she asked. "With things as they are?"

"What's wrong with it?" Ben demanded hotly. "Trade's risky, to be sure, what with foreign seizures and all. But that's all the better for shipbuilders. There were never such profits to be made in shipping. For every ship seized there are four that reach home. And every ship that makes port pays for the loss of two ships! Owners are not going out of business with such profits to be made. For every ship they lose they're going to build two to replace it. How can a shipbuilder lose?"

Patience looked doubtful.

"Can you—can you build them well enough?" she asked.

He put on a hurt expression.

"Your grandfather had no doubt of it," he replied. "And if that were not enough, I've had experience with Briggs and at sea, and I was more than a year in charge of the bashaw's shipyard in Tripoli. I have no fear of it, if you have!"

She turned to him.

"Oh, Ben, I haven't!" she cried. "I haven't, but it seems a lot to ask of Tom."

He snorted impatiently.

"Do you think I haven't considered it—from every side? I tell you I know what I'm doing, and Tom has agreed."

He looked to me for confirmation, and I nodded.

"It's all right, Pat," I said. "I'd not ask a better risk for my money."

Ben turned toward her triumphantly.

"There!" he exclaimed. "You see?"

She smiled at me then.

"It's sweet of you, Tom," she said. "I hope Ben appreciates it and lives up to your expectations."

"I like that!" he cried indignantly. "Of course I appreciate it! And as for living up to Tom's expectations, you watch! We'll make our fortunes. You'll see!"

"I hope so!" was all she said.

I remained in Salem another six weeks after that while Ben negotiated the purchase of the yard and sought for contracts. Before I left he had agreed to build a ship for the Derbys, a brig for the Crowninshields, and three gunboats for the Navy. He hired a crew, and before I left three keels were laid.

When I announced my intention to leave both Ben and Patience protested.

"Why?" they cried.

I shrugged and shook my head.

"I—we hoped you'd stay longer," Pat said.

"I don't want to wear out my welcome," I replied.

"That's nonsense!" she retorted. "You know you're always welcome here. Isn't he, Ben?"

"Of course!" Ben nodded.

"Besides," I said, "I have orders, you know. I'm still in the Navy, and it's time I began to think about getting back."

Ben stared at me.

"But I thought——" he began. Then: "You're not going to stay in the Navy, are you?"

"Why not?" I smiled, not yet caring to admit that I had not been able to make up my own mind.

"Why, it's all right in wartime," Ben replied. "But what kind of a career is it for a man in peace? What thanks do you get? People have already forgotten about us and what we did in Barbary! Look what Jefferson is doing to our fleet. All the best ships being laid up to rot and building preference given to little puny two-by-four gunboats! It's scandalous! What kind of thankless work is that to spend your life in?"

"I never thought I'd hear that from you," I chuckled. "You're getting to be a regular Tory since you went into business. As for the Navy, if everyone leaves it we'll have none when we need it."

"Let those who can do no better stay in it," he retorted. "If you must go to sea, sign on with Derby or Crowninshield, or even this Boston fellow Perkins. They're crack ships, and George Derby was telling me the other day that they'd found it paid to have a surgeon aboard these long China voyages. It's clean work and easy work, and none of your bloody hacksaw-bone messes that you have in the Navy. You'd be well lodged and well found like a gentleman. What's more, you'd have the privilege of a private venture. A man can make a fortune that way."

I laughed.

"Oh, I'm not especially anxious to go to sea," I said, "and as for making a fortune, I don't need that. I've already more than enough for all my needs."

Ben flung up his hands in despair.

"If you don't want to go to sea," he demanded, "why rest in the Navy?"

I shrugged.

"Someone has to stay in it, and I seem to be one who can afford it."

He shook his head impatiently. It occurred to me we had argued this once before, from opposite sides of the fence.

"What's the use of arguing with you?" he growled. "You don't want to go to sea, but you're going to stay in the Navy!

Why don't you just settle down here? You could pick up your practice again in no time, I'd guarantee!"

I shook my head, carefully not glancing Pat's way.

"It doesn't appeal to me, Ben," I said. There was a long moment of silence. Then, abruptly, Pat rose and fled from the room. Ben scarcely noticed her going, but I saw that she had her face in her hands.

"Well," he said sulkily when she was gone, "I don't suppose there's any changing your mind, but I still think you ought to stay here."

"No," I said, "I don't mean to change my mind."

We made our arrangements in the next few days for the proper disposition of my share of the yard's proceeds. Ben was to deposit them with the Derbys for reinvestment to my account and was to report to me three or four times a year the state of the business.

"Don't forget you have the privilege of buying out my share at any time," I reminded him.

"Don't worry!" he replied. "I shan't forget. In fact I mean to take advantage of the privilege before a year is out!"

I raised my eyebrows at that, thinking him overoptimistic, but he misunderstood me.

" 'Tis not that I do not like you for a partner," he said hastily. " 'Tis only that I want the business for myself. I want it to be all my own. You can understand that, can't you?"

"I do," I replied. "More power to you!"

"I'll buy your share before next August," he boasted.

And he did, repaying me my investment and a handsome slice of the profits the following May.

Pat was very quiet those last few days and had little to say to either of us. Ben was so engrossed in his business that I doubt he noticed it, but I, having time on my hands, could not fail to observe it. Only once, however, did she give me any inkling of what was in her mind. I was going through my letter case by the great fireplace, burning all such papers as were worthless —for I had made a point now of keeping up to the minute with my correspondence. Pat was busy about her household chores. But presently she put her work aside and came to stand before me.

"Tom!" she said.

I looked up at her and saw that she was very much in earnest about something.

"Yes, Pat," I said, pushing my papers aside.

"Why have you done all this for Ben?"

I stared at her.

"You know well enough," I told her. "I told you a long time ago that I loved you."

She stiffened and pursed her lips.

"I'm a married woman, Tom," she said coldly. "I don't think you ought to talk like that to me!"

"Is it insulting to be told you are loved?" I asked.

I thought she relented somewhat.

"You—I—we haven't the right," she protested.

"I ask no return," I said. "Sit down, Pat. Let me explain."

She did as I asked, keeping her eyes fixed on my face.

"I won't pretend to love Ben too," I said. "I look on him still as the cause of every bitter thing that's happened to me. He killed my wife. He cost me three years of my life, half in a Tripoline prison, half in a man-of-war. He——"

"Don't, Tom!" she said.

I waved her to silence.

"But that's not all!" I went on. "I hate him because of you, Pat. I loved you. He took you from me before I could realize it. Maybe you would never have had me anyway. That I don't know. But I can't help feeling it."

She turned from me abruptly. I scarcely noticed it.

"But that's not altogether it, either," I said. "That's happened to better men than I. What I have hated him for most has been for what he has done to you. He hasn't been a good husband or provider, Pat, and it hasn't been because he hadn't the opportunity."

"Don't!" she cried.

I shook my head at her.

"Wait till you've heard me out," I told her. "That's how I've felt—how I still feel—about Ben. I've told you how I feel about you. And you have told me how you feel about him! You love him! Naturally, even if you had not told me, I should suppose that you would, since you married him—since you've stuck to him through all he's done."

"Tom!" she cried again. But I silenced her.

"Very well!" I said. "Perhaps I have been wrong. Perhaps I have let myself be blinded by my own resentment for the things he has done to me and to you! He has come back to you sincerely convinced that he wants to turn over a new leaf. I think he means it. But how long he could maintain his determination in the face of difficulty, I don't know. His plan to take on the shipyard with a tremendous mortgage was praiseworthy but quixotic. He could never have carried it, and the burden would have dragged him down and thrown him back into the old ways before he was done."

She ran her finger thoughtfully along the edge of the table beside her and avoided my eyes.

"Perhaps," she said.

"Oh, I wouldn't expect you to agree with that," I said, "knowing how you feel about him."

She looked up quickly and, for an instant, seemed about to say something. When she did not I went on.

"But that's how I felt about it," I said. "All right, then! What should I do? Here am I, a lonely man with more money than I need. I love you. If I can use some of what I have to help Ben to get his feet under him, why not? Success may steady him. Certainly success is a greater stimulus than failure. If he succeeds at this you will be happy—and that's all I want!"

She rose and stood looking down at me.

"Do you understand now?" I asked. "I don't want anything except your happiness. It's a small price to pay for that!"

"I——" she began, and faltered. "I wish you hadn't told me!"

With that she turned away and ran out of the room, leaving me to stare after her in stupefied bewilderment.

I had no opportunity to reopen the subject with her before my departure, a day or two later. Nor am I sure I would have done so had I found it. Actually I was anxious to be away because I could not trust myself to be near her and not make love to her. Had I felt that she loved me rather than Ben, I might not have been so moral. But to be near her in those circumstances seemed no more to me than the most exquisite torture. On the first day of October I said good-by to them and took up my journey for Washington.

2

I WAS BY NO MEANS in so great a hurry to return as I had
intimated. My orders did not require me to report at Washington for nearly a month, but the truth was that I took little joy
in being their guest, under the circumstances, and, moreover, I
found the town, with its memories, more and more depressing
and unsettling to my peace of mind. As a consequence, once
clear of Salem and alone in Boston, I dropped to a footling
pace and made a leisurely journey of it, pausing in Providence,
New London, New York, and Philadelphia, both to visit with
old shipmates and to inquire into the most recent developments
of the medical world. Among my colleagues in medicine I discovered that the past three years had brought progress which
rendered much of my own knowledge old-fashioned, and I acquired a number of new texts and instruments, which I hoped
would help to bring me more currently abreast of my profession. Among my shipmates I found the greatest excitement—
besides the perennial fury at the insolence of the British and
the French—the introduction of steam to navigation, as Mr.
Fulton and some others were about experimenting. Wherever
seamen gathered, I found, it was possible to stir up a lively
discussion with the mere mention of this subject. Naval folk
were divided in two schools: that which held that the use of
steam in place of sails would revolutionize not only navigation
but naval warfare, and that which declared the whole idea
fantastic and impractical and a positive danger to the existence
of the country should the hotheads who wished to see it introduced to the Navy have their way.

With this latter view, I must say, I found myself in agreement. The use of steam for the navigation of rivers and bays,
where the water is quiet and a shore always handy from which
to obtain a supply of fuel, may be practicable if expensive. But
to think of the infernal contraptions going out into the ocean,
out of sight of land, is quite ridiculous. Even if an engine of
sufficient size and power to drive a vessel across the sea in the
face of storms and winds could be built, where could one find
a vessel large enough to support the machinery and also carry a

sufficient supply of fuel for the journey? Such a vessel would have to be built, and, once built, it would be too large for the original engine to move. Thus it would be necessary to build a still larger engine, and then a still larger vessel to accommodate it—and so it would go, in ever-increasing but never-ending circles! But even supposing the application of steam to ocean navigation to be practicable, I cannot concede that it would have any advantage for a vessel of war. When warships engage it is necessary to dowse all fires, even those in the galley, because of the danger of fire and explosion. Thus, in an action, it would be equally necessary to draw the fires under the boilers. Without fire there could be no steam, and without steam where would be the advantage? The truth is that such a vessel would find her maneuverability seriously hampered by the weight of her useless machinery, while vital space now occupied by food and ammunition lockers, magazines, armory, and cockpit would be sacrificed to make room for her dead engines!

At New York I had opportunity to observe the operation of steam upon the water for myself, for I crossed to Hoboken on one of Mr. Livingston's new ferries, a wondrous affair that vomited sparks and smoke and soot and seemed to me at each wheezing lift of the walking beam to be about to explode. However, I will admit that it made the crossing in safety and in a remarkably short time. From there my journey was uneventful. I crossed Jersey by the new Flying Machine Stage which made the journey from Hoboken to Burlington in a single day's span. From there, emboldened by my experience on the Hudson, I took the steam ferry for Philadelphia, where I spent several days. Beyond there it was a matter of plodding, by slow stage, over miserable, rutted roads, through Chester and Baltimore to Washington, where I found the *Essex* in ordinary, lying much as I had left her, though with all her top hamper sent down and her decks shrouded in a protective covering of boards and canvas. Upon arrival I was assigned to duty at the Navy Yard.

That assignment was the beginning of some four years of shore duty, in the course of which my experiences were in the main but remotely related to either Ben Price or the *Essex*. Ben and Patience were in Salem, while I was either too remote or too occupied to keep closely in touch with them; and the *Essex* lay in ordinary, useless as a forgotten hat in a dusty attic. If I give no more than a bare outline of those years, it is because there is little in them to advance my tale.

I spent a dismal winter in Washington, which I may say has as foul and unpleasant a climate as any place on earth, to my way of thinking. There was little or nothing for me to do, since there were but a handful attached to the station, and these were rarely ill save for such minor ailments as colds and the results of overindulgence. Most of our patients were venereal sufferers, yet even they were relatively few. The answer, no doubt, was that not even a prostitute would remain in that gloomy, mud-caked, Godforsaken little metropolis of the wilderness any longer than necessary.

I passed my time, in good part, sitting in the drafty galleries of the great, barnlike Capitol, listening to the vituperative debates of Congress. It seemed to me they were always haranguing about something. The senators and representatives from New England railed against the Republicans, and the French and Mr. Jefferson in particular. Those from the South and Middle States hurled defiance at the British and the New England Federalists, while the men from the West called down curses upon France and Britain and Spain to boot, and sneered at and reviled the merchants of the Eastern cities. There was a good deal of excitement over Colonel Burr's conspiracy, and charges of treason and complicity were flung about with reckless abandon. The most marvelous thing about Congress, to my way of thinking, was the accuracy with which the Westerners could hit a brass spittoon at almost any distance and from any angle, without appearing to hesitate for the least fraction of an instant in their debate!

Apart from visits to Congress, I paid my respects at the White House, as Naval Etiquette demanded, and attended several entertainments there. But these proved too Frenchified for my taste, and I presently gave them up. In December and again in March I heard from Ben, each letter bearing a brief postscript from Patience wishing me good health. According to Ben our business was excellent.

The Decree issued by Boney in November, from Berlin, closing the ports of Britain [he wrote], seems not to be enforced. More than likely the Corsican has realized he has bit off more than he could chew. Still I won't say the frog eaters leave us entirely alone. The British Order in Council of January, which we just now have news of, forbidding neutral trade from port to port with France or her allies, seems more formidable. We are like to lose ships if that's enforced, and if Boney ever gets around to backing up his bombast with action, we'll be prettily pinched between two millstones. However, let 'em seize, say I. The profits in trade are immense, and the more ships they take the more the owners will come to me to build! We are doing very well indeed, my lad, and I believe that by the time I write my next I shall be able to redeem my promise.

He was as good as his word in this. Early in May he wrote that he had made enough to repay me, as well as to give me my share of the profits, and that he had deposited the money with George Derby for my account. At the same time I had a note from Derby confirming this, and, according to our contract, I sent Ben my receipt, which turned my end of the business over to him.

It was about this time that I received orders to join the *Chesapeake*, in the capacity of surgeon. She was destined to relieve the *Constitution* on the Mediterranean station, and I, having but barely returned from that service, had little heart for so prompt a return. Moreover, I felt that in the years of my absence I had fallen somewhat behind in my profession. Accordingly, I appealed to the Secretary of the Navy for relief from these orders and appointment to a station in which I might have opportunity to regain my lost ground. Whether it was this petition or protest on the part of Commodore Barron, with whom I had never made my peace and who was to command the ship, I never knew. But at the eleventh hour I found myself suddenly relieved and ordered to Philadelphia, for duty in the naval hospital there. By such a hairsbreadth did I escape involvement in the most unparalleled example of British arrogance and effrontery of our time.

The attack by HM frigate *Leopard* upon the *Chesapeake*, almost within sight of the Capes of Virginia, on June twenty-second of that young summer, is too well remembered to need description here by me at second hand. When the news reached us in Philadelphia, there was not one among us but felt that the event meant war, and I think few who read this will forget the bonfires and speeches and mass meetings, the vast public indignation of the time. For weeks, it will be recalled, it was touch and go. Like my comrades, I held myself in readiness for immediate orders to sea duty, the while I determinedly pursued my studies at the Philadelphia College of Medicine, which I had been permitted to attend in my off-duty hours. But no such orders came. On the one hand, I think, we must commend Mr. Jefferson and his administration for not immediately plunging us into a war for which we were so patently unprepared. On the other, however, they cannot be too harshly condemned for neglecting to take instant steps to prepare us for what, on that day, became so obviously inevitable.

Meanwhile, as I say, in Philadelphia we waited, but nothing happened, and little by little the furor subsided and the usual interminable investigations and courts-martial began. The summer passed and gave way to fall.

In November the British issued new Orders in Council to stir up our ire, and these were followed in December by Bonaparte's Milan Decree, declaring that neutral ships which submitted to the British Orders would be considered denationalized and fair game for the French. In retaliation the Administration produced an equally highhanded measure in the Embargo, which closed our ports to all overseas commerce, foreign or domestic, and ordered home all our ships abroad.

If this was not cutting off the leg to save the foot, then I know not how to describe it; for, though the leg of our commerce was pinched, yet our trade, the foot, was not wholly lost. But by this act we chopped it off without a thought for how we were to get it back, and the results were instantly visible. Shipping piled up in Philadelphia, which was where I was best able to observe it, until the hulks lay three and four deep along the quays, and the river was so thick with them that they had scarce room to swing with the tide. When one looked out from the town toward the river it was as if a forest of dead sticks and crossed spars, too poor ever to burst into leaf, had sprung up overnight. At Boston and Salem and Newport and New York, at Norfolk and Baltimore, I was told, the conditions were the same, while at Charleston and Savannah, they said, Spanish moss grew upon the spars. The shipping of the nation was tied up and rotting. Vessels that had been valued in thousands of dollars would have sold for mere hundreds had it been possible to find anyone fool enough to bid for them. The trouble was that no one could give them away!

Watching it pile up under my nose through that dank Pennsylvania winter, I could not help wondering how all this might be affecting Ben. I hoped, how desperately I hoped, that he had not had too heavy an investment upon the stocks when the blow fell. I wrote to him to ask how he did, and offer help if he needed it, but I never had any reply to that.

As far as my own fortunes were concerned, I was not so badly off as one who depended entirely upon sea-borne trade. Whether it was foresight or mere luck, I would hesitate to say, but sometime before, on the advice of friends, I had taken a portion of my capital and invested in woolen mills being set up in Rhode Island, and these, now free of foreign competition, were beginning to pay me well. Apart from this, my investments were in the hands of large shipowners, like the Derbys, who could afford to sit back and hope to weather the storm. To be sure, these would pay no return in such times, but when the Embargo was lifted and the European quarrels were ended, as eventually they must be, there should once more be profits to be made in trade.

In those days, in spite of my other means, I came to realize my good judgment in having remained in the Navy. A seafaring man that knew where his next meal was coming from was a rarity. As the ships came into port and tied up and paid off, their crews would come ashore and spend their money. For the first few days there would be food and drink and fun for all. After that it would begin to grow a little more difficult, and then still worse. At the outset it was not too hard, for not many ships were yet laid up, and as new ships arrived and new crews were paid off there were always some lucky sailors with money to spend. Jack is a freehanded fellow, for all his faults, and when he finds a comrade on a lee shore he is usually ready to spare a dollar or so to ease his suffering.

Presently, however, there were more men on the beach than were entering the port, and the competition for Jack's idle dollar grew keener. Ultimately the day dawned when no more tall ships came in, and all the deep-sea men were beached. From that point it was sad to watch. Some men just sat and rotted, like the ships they had sailed. Some begged. Some stole. Some took to the coastal trade, which was still carried on under license, and if some of these vessels were blown offshore—say to some West Indian port—by storms or contrary winds, and were forced there to sell their cargo for the means to return, who could penalize them for that? The result was a good deal of smuggling, and this absorbed some but it could not take all. There were still others who tried their hands at fishing, and some made it pay their way. A few, when spring came, even tried to scratch a living from the land. But these were very few.

It was about mid-March, as I recall, when I received sudden orders to report to Washington for further assignment. I cannot say that I was overjoyed, for I would have preferred to remain in Philadelphia a month or two longer, to complete my studies, when I had it in mind to ask for leave to visit Salem and reassure myself as to Ben and Patience, not having heard from them for some time. However, I had no choice but to comply, and upon my arrival in the capital I was commanded to report to my former shipmate, Lieutenant, now Master Commandant, Porter, for instructions. I found him at the Navy Yard, a little older and somewhat more matured, I thought, but otherwise unchanged. He welcomed me with more enthusiasm than I had any reason to expect.

"Tisdall, by the Lord!" he exclaimed. "You're a sight for sore eyes! How are you? You look well enough."

I assured him that my health was good, and that he, too, appeared to be thriving. I learned then that he had been sitting as a member of the court-martial appointed to try Commodore Barron; that he was sick of the duty and delighted that it was ended; and that he expected shortly to be married. I offered him my congratulations and said that I had been ordered to report to him.

"Ummm!" he said, cocking a quizzical eye at me. "Have you ever been to New Orleans?"

"No," I said.

"Have you ever wanted to go?"

"I can't say that I have," I replied.

"No more have I," he said dryly. "But that's what I've drawn. I'm ordered there as commandant, and I've been allowed the privilege of choosing my own officers. I'll need a good man in charge of the hospital, and as I recall it, you've had some experience with the sort of thing we're most likely to find there. I can't think of anyone I'd rather have. Will you take the post?"

"Have I any choice in the matter?" I asked.

"You have," he assured me. "If you'd prefer not to take it, I'll see that your orders are changed."

I hesitated. It was a tempting offer. I would have a hospital of my own and a post of some responsibility. It would mean that I would have to forego my trip to Salem, but it came to me that I could probably accomplish as much in that direction by letter. Porter fidgeted.

"Well?" he demanded. "Is it aye or nay?"

"Aye," I said. "I'll take you!"

He thrust out his hand impulsively.

"Good!" he exclaimed. "I thought I could count on you! Report here in the morning with a list of all you'll need. We start in two weeks' time."

That night I sat down and wrote to Ben and Patience, asking how they did and telling of my new assignment, closing with an offer of any assistance in my power if it were needed. But to this, like my last, I received no reply. Two weeks later, not long after the first of April, we set out upon our journey to New Orleans.

We went by wagon and horseback to Pittsburgh, some thirty of us, officers and servants. There we were under orders to take up three gunboats which were supposed to be building and near completion, and float them down the river to our new station. However, the gunboats, though building indeed, were, as we had already suspected, far from finished, and accordingly Commandant Porter chartered a flatboat, upon which we hoisted his pendant and set sail upon the tawny bosom of the Ohio.

In our passage we saw nothing of the vaunted river pirates, of whom we had heard such lusty tales. Indeed, we wished we had, for we were well armed and would have given them a hearty surprise. As it was, there was little for us to do to pass the time but shoot squirrels along the bank or troll a line over the stern in the faint hope of catching some whiskered river monster. My companions were set by the commandant to chart the rivers, from Pittsburgh to New Orleans, and to prepare particular descriptions of it, giving especial attention, in his own words, to "Geographical, Historical, Philosophical, Topographical, Nautical, Thermometrical, Aquatical, Botanical, Mineralogical and Astronomical Subjects."

Being a mere surgeon, and unacquainted with any of these, I was left to my fowling piece and fishing line, and I daresay I enjoyed the trip as much as any.

I have often wondered if our commander would have been in such a hurry had he had the least inkling of what was in store for him. To me New Orleans was a pleasant place in many ways; for him it must have been, at times, plain hell. At no time before our arrival, and still less afterward, was the Navy popular. Politics were malicious. Official support, even from Washington, was nonexistent. His entire tour of duty was marked with bickering and threats and litigation and expense. If he seized a pirate, he was haled into court and forced to give bond for his appearance as if he were the accused! The lawlessness of the place was appalling, and the condition of the naval establishment was worse. Yet he struggled alone against a populace and an officialdom accustomed to make their profits from the proceeds of smuggling and piracy. And he dug into his own pocket, to an extent that nigh ruined him, to see his men better housed and fed and shipped.

I had my own official troubles. The naval hospital was quartered in a group of buildings in the Faubourg de la Course, dilapidated, tumble-down, and in every way inadequate to the purpose. I did what I could to put them to rights. But appeals to their owner—for they were rented—were of no avail, and seeing my chief's difficulty in procuring payment for what he had advanced from his private funds, I had little stomach for following his example. I made the best of what I had and came out of it whole.

Apart from the official side of it, I found the city interesting. In time I was to find it pleasant. For all my travels, it was something that I had never before encountered. Cadiz, Malaga, Barcelona were Spanish cities that I had seen. Marseilles, Toulon, were French. Our own Eastern seaboard cities were American. Yet New Orleans was something of all of these, with an additional indefinable quality added. The fact that it was a frontier city, a meeting point of savagery and civilization, undoubtedly had much to do with this. Yet this could not entirely explain the difference. There were buildings of imposing architecture; the cathedral and the convent and the old Spanish barracks. The houses of the city, frequently of two or even three stories, of brick, and with iron balconies, were the equal of any in Charleston or Norfolk or Boston, while those on the plantations of the surrounding country were as gracious as any in Virginia. But these were the fingers of civilization thrusting through the mud of the streets and the swampy lowlands roundabout. The people were as diversified. Boatmen from the river, pirates and smugglers from the bayous, Negroes of the town and back country, Indians, half-castes, Cajuns, Kentuckians, Creoles, refugees from the French islands, malcontents from all the Spanish colonies about; ladies, gentlemen, prostitutes, sailors, adventurers, traders rubbed shoulders in the streets together, trod the same dust, the same muck, stumbled in the same sewage, washed their feet of the same slime before entering bar or ball or brothel as the case might be. The Creole women were haughty and beautiful. The men were handsome and sensitive on the minutest points of honor, as I had occasion to learn. The quadroon women were lovely and warm and breath-taking, with breasts that were firm as fists beneath their dresses and bright as russet apples when uncovered, as I was privileged to find.

Only much later, when I visited certain Spanish colonial cities, did I understand the basis for such a world. Then I saw how the imposition of a wild American frontier society upon an Old World civilization; a combination of new and old politics and policies, could produce such a city. At the time I was not concerned with causes. I sought only my way in it.

It is not my intention, however, to describe all that took place in the two years of my duty there. It is enough to say that despite all our problems they were pleasant years. Life, when we were not quarreling officially with the local authorities, was easy and gracious. We of the naval establishment, of necessity, formed a small clique and were happy enough in one another's company. Not long after our arrival Commandant Porter was joined by his wife, and it was I who delivered their first child, a son so tiny that he would fit easily into a cigar box, though he was later to grow into a man of more than two hundred pounds. It was Porter's delight to pass the lad around the dinner table for the inspection of his guests, upon a platter lined with cotton.

But, pleasant though it was, our life in New Orleans was not without its tragedies. Outstanding was the death of Commandant Porter's father, a fine old gentleman who had held the rank of sailing master under Washington. He was taken suddenly with a stroke of the sun while fishing on Lake Pontchartrain, where he was found by a Mr. Farragut, a resident of the neighborhood, and taken to his home. Porter and I at once rushed to the old man's bedside, but he was beyond human aid by the time we arrived, and all I could do was endeavor to ease the grief of the son. Not long afterward, since the Farraguts were in somewhat straitened circumstances, the commandant, in recognition of their kindness, adopted their second son, David, a bright-eyed lad of seven, for whom he later procured an appointment as midshipman and with whom I was one day to become shipmates.

From this it will be evident that I came to know Porter in a much different role from that in which we had formerly been acquainted. I will expand that, indeed, and say that it was during this period that I came to have a great admiration for him as a man and to look upon him as a firm friend. I think he chafed beneath the duty, as well he might, being so often placed in a position of embarrassment by lack of support. For my part, however, I enjoyed it immensely, in general, and I think I would have been content to stay indefinitely could I have been sure that all was well with Ben and Patience.

That I did not hear from them I found disturbing, and several times I contemplated requesting leave, but I had not the heart to approach Porter at a time when I knew his own troubles would allow him no escape. In consequence I kept postponing it, and in the end it became unnecessary. It was in October 1810, more than two years after my arrival in the city, that the commandant's orderly sought me out in the surgery and requested me to come as soon as possible to Porter's office. There I was greeted with a barely concealed hint of exultation.

"Well, Tom!" he said, for we had long since dropped the

formality of "sir" and "Mr." "We're bound for new adventures."

"How so?" I asked.

"I'm being relieved, thank heaven!" he replied. "And so are you. Here are your orders."

He passed them across to me, and I, reading them, saw: "When relieved by Dr. Heerman you will proceed without delay to Washington and report to the Secretary of the Navy."

I looked up at him and saw that there was something else on his mind.

"Well?" I said.

"Well?" he cried. "I thought you'd be pleased!"

"Oh, I haven't minded it." I shrugged. "I wouldn't mind staying if you were going to be here. But then I didn't expect it to last forever."

He seemed pleased.

"They're giving me the *Essex,* Tom," he said.

"No!" I exclaimed, for this was a surprise.

"Yes!" He nodded emphatically. "How about it? Will you come aboard as surgeon?"

I thought of Ben and Patience. Once before I had fallen in with his suggestion and neglected them. My conscience pricked me.

"There's something else I ought to do," I said.

He looked startled, almost insulted.

"Don't misunderstand me," I cried. "There's no ship I'd rather serve in and no skipper I'd rather serve under. It's just that this is something I've been putting off a long time. I feel that I ought to do it now."

"Do you want to resign?" he asked. "I'll give you my endorsement if you would."

I stared at him.

"Would you like to see that?" I asked. "I've always thought I did my duties well."

"Great God!" he cried. "I never meant to imply that you didn't. I was only thinking of your personal preferences."

"Thank you, Dave," I said, not a little pleased, for I knew that from him this was praise. "Thanks! But I don't mean to turn in my commission. I only mean to ask for leave. I've had none in four years, you know, and there's this I must be doing."

He rose and held out his hand.

"I understand," he said. "I'll recommend you for leave. But don't forget, whenever you want it, the surgeon's berth on my ship is yours!"

"Thank you, Dave. I'll remember," I said, though it never occurred to me then that I might someday be taking him at his word.

3

IT WAS December before I reached Washington, mid-January of the new year before I came to Salem. The snow was deep on the ground, and in the town it was piled in miniature mountains on either side of the road and walks. It lay heavy along the bare limbs of the trees and glistened upon the roof tops. Blue smoke rose from the chimneys of the houses, etched sharp against the background of snowy hills and slaty skies, and the sea was a leaden green when viewed from the rises in the road. Salem harbor contained a few more ships than usual, iced in at this season, but most had put to sea again following the lifting of the embargo. New England, I found, was as bitter against Mr. Madison as it had been against Jefferson. There was some talk of secession.

On my arrival I was torn between my desire to see Patience again and prudence occasioned by my fear of what I might find. In the end prudence won out and I made my way to the Eagle Tavern, where Matt Turner greeted me amiably, if with surprise, and found me comfortable quarters. There I began a series of discreet inquiries the answers to which left me feeling sick at heart. From him I did learn that my fears had been founded. Ben had been worse than ruined by the embargo.

"He was too big for his britches," he told me. "Got too much on his books an' then couldn't get rid of it when the embargo came. His creditors took over the yard."

"What's he doing now?" I asked.

He gave me an odd look.

"Not much of anything," he replied. "Odd jobs mostly, I guess. What he can pick up roundabout, here and there. From what I hear, most of what he makes goes for liquor. He borried on the house when it first begun to look bad, an' I hear Grunsell's had to foreclose on him. Let's 'em stay on there, though, out o' regard for the missus and her grandsir that died, I'm told."

"Great God!" I exclaimed. "How do they live?"

He gave me that queer look again and shrugged.

"Oh, the missus takes in wash and helps out here and there. I daresay they'd go hungry but for her. He's just plain no good."

"Why didn't he go to sea again?" I demanded, seething inside, though I endeavored to hide it.

"God knows!" he replied. "Just hasn't the ambition, I guess."

I turned the subject and asked him about other local matters with what patience I could for a half an hour or so, until I felt that I could leave him with good grace. Once clear of the inn, however, I made my way at once through the early winter's dusk to the house in Daniels Street, my blood boiling.

Ben opened to my knock, and, prepared as I was, I was shocked at his appearance. His feet were thrust into run-over ancient carpet slippers. His trousers were well-worn, much-patched blue duffels, and his shirt was threadbare from many washings. His chin was hidden under a week's growth of stubble, and it was plain that he was even now more than half drunk. He stared at me boozily.

"Oh, it's you," he snarled. "I might have known you'd turn up sooner or later."

"I always seek out my friends," I snapped. "Where's Pat?"

He jerked his head back over his shoulder and stood aside. I pushed in. He shut the door and followed me, calling past me:

"Here's company."

If I had been shocked at Ben's appearance, I was heartsick at sight of Patience. She had been bending over the fire in the great fireplace, preparing a frugal supper, when I entered, and she straightened with a little gasp of mingled surprise and dismay. Her dress, if anything, was more ragged than Ben's, but it was the lines of care and fatigue and worry in her face that wrung my heart.

"Tom!" she cried after her first spasm of surprise. "Why, Tom! Where did you drop from?"

"New Orleans," I replied shortly. "How are you, Pat?"

I tried to put into the question all of the compassion I felt. She smiled, and some of the old sweetness came back into her careworn features. She came forward with hands outstretched.

"Why, I'm fine, thank you, Tom," she said.

I wanted to say that she did not look it. Instead I said: "You're looking well."

She knew I lied and turned from me.

"Children," she said, "here's Uncle Tom, come to visit. Haven't you a word for him?"

For the first time, then, I noticed the children, who had been sitting quietly, almost subdued, at the table, awaiting their supper. From their neatness it was plain that their mother, at least, had not neglected them. But their eyes were large in their faces, and their cheeks seemed hollow to me. Young Sam, grown tall now and spindling, came forward with great poise and gave me his hand with a grave "Hello." Little Elizabeth gave me a quick curtsy and a smile as radiant as ever her mother's had been and then ran to hide behind Pat's skirts. Out from under the table, then, scrambled a third little toddler, with tawny hair and wide, inquisitive eyes; a new addition since my last visit. Patience leaned down and scooped him up.

"And this is young Tom," she said. "I named him for the best friend we ever had."

She looked at Ben with something like defiance as she said it. Something lodged in my throat, and I rounded on Ben.

"Did you get my letters?" I demanded harshly.

"Yes," he growled.

"Why didn't you write?" I said angrily. "Why didn't you tell me how it was? I offered to help."

"What was the use?" he said harshly.

"I wouldn't have rubbed it in," I replied. "What was it? The embargo?"

"Aye!" he exclaimed. "The cursed 'O-Grab-Me'! It grabbed me, all right!"

"Why didn't you go to sea?" I demanded. "If you didn't want help from me, you were assured of a good berth there as soon as trade began once more."

"Why the devil should I?" he flung back. "The only ship I'd serve in is laid up in ordinary."

Something clicked within me.

"The *Essex?*" I said.

"What else?" he demanded scornfully.

"Go up and shave and put on your best," I ordered him. "The *Essex* has been recommissioned and is lying now at New York, making ready for sea. If you hurry you can catch her."

His eyes flew wide with astonishment and joy.

"The *Essex* recommissioned?" he blurted.

"Tom!" Patience gasped in such a tone of dismay that I almost relented. But I steeled myself.

"Aye!" I said. "If you catch the late stage for Boston you can take the through mail coach that leaves tomorrow morning. You'll be in New York by Wednesday at the latest, and she'll not clear for a fortnight yet."

"Tom!" cried Patience again.

"You hush!" Ben told her fiercely. Then, abruptly, he wilted. "It's no use," he mumbled.

"Why not?" I demanded, fired now with excitement.

"I haven't the fare," he admitted glumly.

"I'll stake you," I told him.

"Besides," he went on, determinedly pessimistic, "how do I know they'll have room for me?"

"Captain Porter's to command her," I replied. "He owes me a thing or two from New Orleans. While you make ready I'll write him a letter that will guarantee you a berth."

"And you?" he demanded.

"I'm not leaving yet awhile," I said. "Do you want it or don't you?"

"D'ye think me a fool?" he snarled, and, turning, raced from the room and up the stairs.

When he was gone Patience eyed me bitterly.

"And I thought you my friend, Tom Tisdall!" she said.

"Pat!" I cried. "Don't you see it? Would you have him stay here to rot like an embargoed vessel? He's not happy here, nor are you! What good is he to you or to anyone like this? Isn't it better for him to be away with the ship he loves, making a respectable living for himself and you, than—than this?"

She swallowed hard.

"But what will we do?" she demanded. "It's hard enough now, God knows. But with him gone———"

"Will you have faith in me?" I asked. "You know why I am here."

She stared at me strangely.

"What do you mean to do?" she demanded.

"I'll talk about that with you after he has gone," I replied. "Only trust me, Pat. That's all I ask."

She pursed her lips and turned away toward the fire.

"You'll stay for supper?" she asked.

"I will," I told her.

Ben reappeared in a matter of minutes, washed and shaved and dressed as I have no doubt his children had not seen him in many a week. He fetched with him also his box of tools and a sea bag packed. While Pat set the table I sat down and wrote a quick letter to Porter reminding him of Ben's service in the *Philadelphia* and asking him in the name of our friendship to make a place for him in his carpenter's crew. This I gave into Ben's hand, and he insisted that we have a drink upon it.

It was not the happiest of suppers that we ate. Ben wanted more to drink, but I was adamant on that point, fearing lest he so befuddle himself as to be unable to get beyond Boston. As a last resort I threatened not to advance him the money for his passage, and at that he subsided into grumpy silence. Patience, I could see, was nervous and not at all certain that I was right, while at the same time, I think, she was shamed at the frugality of the meal, remembering well how once we had fared in that house. I did my best to ease the situation, keeping them entertained to the best of my ability with tales of New Orleans and my adventures since I had seen them last. Nevertheless I was relieved when it came time to go.

Ben went with scarce a good-by for Patience or the children, so anxious was he to be off, and I went with him, shouldering his sea bag while he carried his kit of tools, as far as the stage station. There I bought him his passage to Boston and gave him more than enough to see him from there on to New York. Not until the driver had whipped up his nags and gone whirling off into the night, however, did I turn my face about and make my way, through the snowy streets once more, to the house in Daniels Street. There I found Patience waiting by the fireside.

"How long has it been like this, Pat?" I asked.

She looked down at her hands in her lap.

"It seems as though it's always been like this," she said in a low voice. "Oh, there was a time, just after we saw you last, when things were better. I was fool enough then to believe they always would be—and I guess you did too. But they weren't!"

Abruptly then she put her head down in her arms and burst into tears.

"Oh, Tom! Tom!" she sobbed. "What am I to do?"

Knowing myself what I had in mind to do for her, I misunderstood.

"Pat!" I cried. "Pat dear! Don't worry for him. He's better off this way. Oh, don't think I don't know how hard it is to see the one you love——"

She raised her head abruptly and stared at me wildly.

"The one I love!" she exclaimed. "Will you stop talking about that? I hate him! I think I have always hated him! I don't know why I ever married him!"

I gaped at her rudely.

"But you told me!" I protested. "You told me you loved him!"

"Aye!" she sobbed bitterly. "Would I not? I was afraid for you. I was afraid you'd kill him. Do you think I wanted to see the hands of the one I truly love stained with his blood?"

She stopped abruptly, suddenly aware of what she had said, and rose and would have fled from the room had I not, with my own heart leaping within me, jumped up and caught her and turned her to me.

"Pat!" I cried. "Pat!"

In the next instant she was in my arms, sobbing hysterically on my shoulder, while I held her, trying to soothe her, the while my own heart was pounding furiously, triumphantly.

"Pat dear!" I said. "There, child! It's all over now!"

Presently she calmed enough to be coherent.

"I—I—I've loved you for so long, Tom!" she whispered.

"Why, then," I said as cheerfully as I could, "why do we keep up this fanfaronade? Come with me, and bring the children! I swear I will make you happy!"

She drew back from me quickly.

"Oh, Tom!" she cried. "I couldn't!"

I stared at her.

"Why not?" I demanded. "You have just told me you loved me. I told you long since that I loved you. We have both said that we hate him. Why should we let him ruin our lives? Come with me, Pat! What difference does it make that we can't marry? I can make you happy. I will make you happy. That I promise!"

She turned away and shook her head.

"I can't!" she cried. "Don't ask me!"

"In God's name," I cried, "why not!"

She turned to me proudly.

"I gave my word, Tom!" she said softly. "I said before the altar, 'for richer for poorer, for better or for worse, in sickness and in health,' and I cannot go back on that!"

I felt all at once very small.

"You shame me, Pat!" I said.

"I do not mean to," she replied. "I have meant all that I said!"

"Why did you marry him?" I cried. "Didn't you know that I would ask you sooner or later?"

She stared at me almost panic-stricken.

"You told me—you told me that you loved me like a sister! Could I hope for more after that?"

"Ah, Christ!" I cried. "What a fool I have been!"

"No!" she said. "You have been honest, and for that I love you the more!"

"Pat," I cried, "there are things that are stronger among humans than mere beliefs! There is self-respect, Pat, and decency! Come with me, Pat! Leave him, and let me take care of you. For the children's sake I beg of you!"

She shook her head somberly.

"If I accepted," she said, "where would my self-respect be? Where would your respect be?"

"I could never respect you less!" I protested.

"That's easy to say," she replied. "'Tis not so easy to accomplish. No, Tom! I can't! So long as he lives I am his wife, and no man must interfere."

"Pat!" I cried.

"I made my bed," she said with the bitterest expression I hope I shall ever see man or woman wear, "and I must lie in it!"

I stared at her, miserable yet at the same time unaccountably proud. I saw now why I had not been able to kill him when it was in my power and in my mind. Her strength had been my strength. We may have been fools, but at least we were honest fools; honest with the world and with one another.

"I love you, Pat!" I said. "Never forget that!"

"And I love you, Tom! Always remember it," she replied.

We did not embrace. We did not even touch one another.

"At least let me help you," I said. "Let me put something aside for you to draw upon in times of need."

"No, Tom!" she said. "I would not feel right to accept from you what he cannot give me."

"Nonsense!" I cried. "That you will not come away with me—that I can understand, after what you have told me, and I honor you and love you the more for it. But this is a practical matter! Don't let your pride stand in the way! I can afford it."

She continued to protest and I to insist, but in the end I wore her down, and she agreed that I might deposit a sum with Mr. Bentley, whom we both knew to be discreet, that she might draw against as the need arose. But even so she made this concession only because of the children, and stated emphatically that she would not accept it but for them.

However, I also insisted that she accept, in addition, an immediate advance in cash sufficient to clothe and feed both her and the children and maintain them for some time, until Ben's pay could begin to arrive. When I had accomplished this I felt that I had done well enough. Nor did I tell her that it was my intention to see Crowninshield in the morning and, if possible, purchase the house from him, in order that she might be secure in the roof over her head.

I said good night then and went back to the tavern. In the morning I made the arrangements that I had planned, finding both Mr. Bentley and Mr. Crowninshield willing and eager to abet me. In the afternoon I went to the house and explained what had been done, and thereupon, not trusting myself to remain longer in her presence, I left her and returned to Washington, long before my leave was up, to find orders ready for me to report, as surgeon, to the frigate *President*.

4

IT WAS NOW getting on toward the end of February, and the situation within the country was even then growing daily more tense. There seemed little doubt that we should soon have war, but the question was—with whom? Approximately the state of affairs was that England and France might rather have been allies than enemies, in so far as their dealings with us were concerned. Since the Administration had discovered that Embargo and Non-Intercourse was ruinous to none but ourselves if applied indiscriminately, it had delivered a double-edged suggestion to each of the belligerents. If, said Mr. Madison and his friends, the British would repeal their Orders in Council, the United States would then remove its restrictions upon trade with Britain and would enforce certain articles of the Non-Intercourse Acts against France. On the other hand, if France would rescind the Berlin and Milan decrees, then we would remove the bars to French trade and enforce the Non-Intercourse articles against Britain. What we should do if both accepted was not indicated, and fortunately for us, perhaps, the problem did not arise. France accepted, and notified us that on the first of November—that is, of 1810, the year but just ended—the obnoxious decrees would be suspended. To be sure, this assurance was not unconditional, yet Mr. Madison chose to regard it so, and his proclamation was issued, on the second of November, to serve notice upon Britain that she must now either abandon her Orders in Council or face the application of our proposal.

How naïve were we to think that we might thus coerce either of these old hands at international chicanery! Of course there was no honesty either in France or in Britain. The French decrees were not repealed upon the first of November, despite every assurance. Indeed, toward the middle of the month several of our vessels that had presumed to take advantage of the resumption of trade were seized in French ports. At the same time the British sent their ships back across the Atlantic, to resume, once more, their arbitrary practice of search and seizure beneath our very noses, and to impress our seamen within sight of our shores.

The New England merchants in the main, with an eye for the purse of trade, growled that was unnecessary, but that if we must fight, then let it be with France, who had broken faith. No doubt there was reason behind this. On the other hand, Everyman, standing upon our shores, could see the British cruisers lying arrogantly in wait. It was Everyman whose friends and relatives were snatched from our ships and forced to serve the British. Everyman had tasted British insolence in dealing with the boat crews and officers sent ashore to purchase supplies; and Everyman along the coast lived in fear of possible landing parties, sent on shore by some highhanded commanding officer, to raid livestock and garden and cellar, to rob and insult and perhaps worse. So that it was Everyman's choice that we fight Britain; and Britain did nothing to discourage us.

The *President,* on which I now found myself, remained in port at Norfolk, refitting, painting, rigging, and recruiting, until such time as we were shipshape, after which she sailed upon the bay, exercising the crew at every possible emergency in sham, and I will say that I then learned the true meaning of the expression "a taut ship." Commodore Rodgers was strict, even harsh, and the crack of the lash was an almost daily sound at the gangway. Yet the ship was manned as smartly and precisely as clockwork, and I never heard the complaints aboard her that I had on less tyrannically ruled vessels—the *Chesapeake,* for example, on her cruise to the Mediterranean under Commodore Morris, when even the warrants were permitted to ship their women, and all was bedlam aboard!

For my part I had long since discovered that in the pursuance of strict military routine much that is ordinarily the subject of discussion and indecision is automatically carried out. Either it is right, according to the rule, or it is wrong; and in the main adherence to the rule serves and simplifies life. The danger, I have found, comes when a commander relies too long and too heavily upon the rule, losing initiative and the proper sense of when the rule must be broken. This was the pitfall of the Barrons, of Morris, and even to some extent of Bainbridge. It was the glory of Truxtun and Hull and Decatur.

Which way Rodgers would bend when the crisis arose, for me remained to be proved. But the indication seemed to be that he would stand among the latter.

In the meantime, however, it was good to feel the deck of a ship beneath my feet once more, for I was fed to the teeth with the politicking and pipe clay and involved practices of shore billets.

Thus we passed the early spring, and in the first week in May came to anchor in the Severn mouth, off Annapolis, where all hands were granted shore leave by watches by way of a well-earned rest.

For my part, having no place I particularly desired to go for so short a time as our leave allowed, I was content to stay in Annapolis, close aboard, and after the third day I returned in order that my alternate might also have a turn ashore. We were something better than half staffed at that moment, some of the officers having gone to Baltimore, others to Washington to visit friends. The commodore himself was at Havre de Grace, at his home, and the outlook was quiet and peaceful. Yet that evening brought news of the interception by the British frigate *Guerrière,* off Sandy Hook, of the American brig *Spitfire,* and the impressment of a passenger, John Deguyo, a native-born citizen of the United States.

Excitement and indignation ran high on board and was coupled with speculation as to how the news would be taken in official circles. Early the next afternoon, only shortly after dinner, we made out a gig coming down from the north, pulled at a furious rate, and hasty examination through the glass revealed the commodore's pendant fluttering at her staff. Instantly the drums rolled and everything was put in readiness to receive him. He came on board with scarcely a glance for the side boys and guard of honor, and immediately ordered the recall run up to the main and a gun fired to command attention. Within two hours we were standing down the bay under all sail, although we were but little better than three fourths manned, while riders dashed posthaste to Washington and Baltimore with orders for the rest of our people to join us at Norfolk. We learned then that we were ordered out in search of the *Guerrière.* Then, too, we heard the latest British gasconade. In order that his ship might not be mistaken, the Englishman had had the name of his vessel painted, in large letters, across the entire width of his foretopsail. Not to be outdone, Commodore Rodgers had the name of the *President* painted upon each of her three topsails, as an indication that we were prepared to accept the challenge.

We lay for several days at Norfolk, taking on supplies, and at length, on the sixteenth, we put to sea, passing out between the Capes and reaching to the northeastward, in a condition of readiness such as I had not experienced on any other ship in which I had sailed at any time. Although the season was well advanced, the full warmth of summer had not yet arrived, and the wind was chill, the sky high and bright, and the sea leaden and coming in long swells. Sea and weather meant business, exactly as did we. The mood of man and nature were identical. Both were reckless, and both were hungry for action.

Toward midday the masthead lookout sent down the cry of "Sail ho!" and presently, from the deck, we were able to make out a ship upon the eastern horizon, standing toward us under full sail. From the cut of her canvas and the reach of her yards it was evident that she was a man-of-war, and since we knew of no other such vessel upon our coast, except the *Guerrière,* the *President* immediately cleared for action, and we stood to meet her. Toward midafternoon, however, when we were close enough to see the bone in her teeth and the lift of her bows, she ran up a string of signals, which, being strange to us, went unanswered. Thereupon she sheered off and resumed her course to the southward which would take her ultimately around Cape Hatteras. At once we too came about and stood down through the graying seas in pursuit of her.

It was night before we were close enough to speak her, at which time she rounded to and hoisted her colors. However, it was too dark to distinguish them, and after some jockeying for position we obtained the weather gauge and ran down for her, at the same time beating to quarters.

Of the rest of what occurred I can give little information at first hand, for I was at my post in the cockpit. Down there the battle lanterns swung, casting long wavering shadows, this way and that, while my mates and I waited, listening to the gurgle of the seas only a few inches beyond the wooden walls of our workroom and above our heads. What was taking place upon the decks above was a complete mystery to us, but all at once we heard a shot, but felt no tremor of our own ship, such as would indicate that it came from us. Almost immediately this was followed by a return from us. Beneath my feet I could feel the lurch of our own vessel under the recoil.

" 'Tis the *Chesapeake* over again!" I heard Spriggs, third surgeon's mate, say.

He was answered by three shots in quick succession from the enemy. We could feel them hit somewhere above us, but there were no cries in answer. Hours seemed to pass. Then all at once our own ship staggered under the recoil of a full broadside, followed almost instantly by another. There was a brief lull, then the crash of gunfire from our adversary, and again instant response from us. Yet no one appeared at the head of our ladder. It was thirty minutes before a single casualty was brought down to us. This was one of our boys, a mere child, with part of his cheek shot away. We were cleaning and dressing the boy's wound, when a midshipman came clattering down our ladder.

"Dr. Tisdall, sir!" he cried. "The commodore asks that you come up on deck, sir!"

"Very good," I replied. "Coming!"

As I snatched up my deck kit and leaped for the ladder I noticed that the firing had ceased.

"Stand by!" I ordered my assistants, and hurried up through the hatchway.

As I passed through the gun deck each crew stood to its gun, ready and waiting to fire. There was some smoke, some tinge of burned powder hanging in the narrow space, and this added to the faint glimmer of the battle lanterns made a grim scene. But there was no confusion, no indecision, no shouting, no cursing, no hint that this was anything more than an exercise of the great guns. Officers stood to their divisions smartly. Gunners and gun crews, stripped to the waist despite the bite of the weather, waited, matches, swabs, sponges, and rammers in hand. The tackles were manned and the powder monkeys stood by, having, for the moment at least, completed their task. I had a sense of pride and power as I set foot upon the ladder. If it was to be a fight, the *President* would give a good account of itself.

When I came on deck it was to find the captain and the first lieutenant and the commodore in conference. There were no wounded in sight, and very little battle damage. Overside the seas swished quietly, yet there was an air of tension and readiness on deck. I presented myself to the commodore.

"You sent for me, sir?"

He turned.

"Yes, Doctor. I think she's finished. She lies yonder, end on, and I think she's out of control. But we'll stand by in case she wants to renew or needs assistance. Hold yourself ready to go on board in the latter event."

"Aye, aye, sir!" I responded. His matter-of-factness, his readiness for what might come, impressed me strongly.

The hours crept by as we stood on and off to windward, yet there was no sound through the night save an occasional faint cry and the soughing of the wind. Dawn revealed a ship much cut and battered, smaller than ourselves, wallowing in the trough of the waves. We ran down close upon her and hailed, and now, being on deck, I was able to see what happened.

"What ship is that?" our sailing master called.

"His Majesty's twenty-two-gun ship *Little Belt!*" came the response, "Captain Arthur Batt Bingham!"

"Why did you not answer our hail last night?"

"We did! Why did you fire on us? Are we at war?"

"No! We heard no response to our hail save a shot and fired in return. Are you hurt?"

"I have eleven killed and twenty-one wounded!"

"I am sending an officer aboard you," the commodore hailed. "Do you wish other assistance? My surgeon is standing by."

There was no response. We lowered away a boat and Mr. Creighton went on board, to return presently with the report that no assistance was desired, whereupon we came about and stood up for Sandy Hook, leaving our late assailant to make the best of his way to a friendly port.

We did not put in to port immediately. We had not found our objective. We cruised off the coast, running up to Sandy Hook and out to Cape Cod and back in search of her, finally putting in to New York without having found her. In that time it did not occur to anyone aboard that we had stirred up a national clamor. Only when we dropped anchor in New York Harbor and sent a boat ashore did we learn that all the country had been talking of us, speculating on what had happened, wondering if the affair of the *Chesapeake* and the *Leopard* had been repeated. It seemed that two vessels, standing in for the Virginia Capes upon the night of our action, had heard our fire and had reported it, so that it was known that something of the sort had taken place. But when the *President* did not immediately return to port to report the incident, it was feared that she had been taken by the *Guerrière* and carried off, a prize, to Halifax.

The excitement which our appearance in the harbor caused was considerable, and our report of the affair prompted more than a little impromptu celebrating among the city's hotheads. Few of us on board, however, had opportunity to participate, for we lay no more than forty-eight hours there and then put to sea once more. Throughout the length of that summer and fall and into the winter we cruised up and down and back and forth along the coast, patrolling without incident. Now and again we would slip quickly into one port or another for water and fresh provisions and a quick turn ashore. But those turns were brief indeed, and always unheralded, so that although I might write letters to various friends, there was little chance of receiving a reply. As a result I was not aware of how matters stood in Salem, nor was I now greatly disturbed. During our fitting-out period in the bay there had been time for an exchange of letters, and I had heard once from Patience that she was well and the children thriving, and that she had received a draft allotment against his pay from the Navy, so that, although she had not heard directly from Ben, she felt safe in assuming that he had found the *Essex,* as I had promised, and had shipped on board. By my own channels I confirmed this and wrote to her that it was so. Further than this, however, we did not attempt to correspond. It was as though, having to this extent insured security, there could be no more pass between us. By tacit consent for the future no news must be good news; and without either of us saying it in as many words, we were agreed that so long as matters stood as they did we must each go our way alone.

Toward mid-March the *President* put into New York once more to refit, and there, one by one, the other ships of our Atlantic Squadron joined us. Last to drop anchor in Wale Bogt Bay, late in May, when the hills of Brooklyn were all green with new leaves and the tiles of the roof tops gleamed brick red in the sunlight, was the *Essex,* whom we had spoken but once, in February, off Cape Hatteras. As may be imagined, I did not long delay a visit aboard her.

Captain Porter greeted me with open arms.

"Tom!" he cried. "It's good to see you! I hear you're in the *President.* You couldn't have a better berth."

"I like her well enough," I grinned, "but there are others I'd like better. What are the chances of war, do you think?"

" 'Tis unavoidable!" he declared. "Mark my words."

"I'm inclined to agree," I told him.

We passed the time of day then, pleasantly enough, he giving me news of his family and how they did, while for my part I described to him our meeting with the *Little Belt.* Before I took my leave, however, I managed to bring the conversation around to Ben. He gave me a strange look when I mentioned him.

"Aye," he said in response to my question, "he came aboard —half seas over. But for your letter, I'd have had him pitched overside. Instead I signed him on and sent him to the brig for a fortnight. We've had no trouble with him since. In fact he's one of our best. He's a curious lad, Tom."

"Aye," I agreed somberly, "he's all of that. I'm glad you found him a berth. It was the saving of him. Sometimes I think he nailed his heart to the keel of the *Essex* when he helped build her. He has thought for little else."

"So I've observed," he said dryly. "Would you like to see him? I'll have him fetched aft."

"No, no," I said hastily. "Let well enough be. We'll meet ashore or on deck."

At that we left it, and I took my leave of him. Yet when I was back once more aboard the *President* I fell to thinking. Porter felt there would be war, and in that he no more than echoed the general feeling in the fleet. If it should come to that, I asked myself, was not my logical place in the *Essex?* Since my last talk with Patience I was no longer deluded by quixotic notions of fetching Ben back to her sound of wind and limb. But war meant battle, and battle meant death, and if we were in different ships the end might come for either of us and the other be none the wiser for months—even, perhaps, for years. Patience, too, might be kept long in ignorance. It seemed to me that this was something in the nature of duel for survival and that I must play out my part in it.

I turned this over in my mind for several days, worrying it as a dog will a bone, and the more I considered it the more the notion took me. Twice I saw Ben ashore, and both times he was more than a little drunk. On neither occasion did he see me, however, for I took care to keep out of his way. I had no desire to deal with him, especially in that condition. It made me brood to think that such as he could stand between me and Patience. Yet there was naught I could do about it. But if I could not help that, I could at least stay near him, so that if aught happened to him I would be the first to know it. Strangely, it did not occur to me that anything might happen to me.

In the end I called again upon Captain Porter.

"This is a surprise, Tom," he said. "What's on your mind?"

"Do you mind you once told me I could have the surgeon's berth aboard the *Essex?*" I asked bluntly.

He blinked at me in surprise.

"Yes," he said guardedly.

"I'm asking for it," I said.

He stared.

"But—but," he protested, " 'tis a comedown for you, Tom! From the *President* to the *Essex!* From a forty-four to a thirty-two! From the commodore's flagship to the smallest frigate in the fleet! Why?"

"Well," I said slowly, "I've a number of reasons. First, I like a smaller ship. Second, the *Essex* was the first ship I served in. Third, if it's to be war, I prefer to serve with you."

He did not even blink at that.

"And fourth?" he said.

"That's purely personal," I replied.

He nodded.

"I thought so," he said dryly. "Part of that unfinished matter you mentioned in New Orleans, no doubt?"

"It is," I said.

He grinned suddenly.

"I guessed as much. Are you sure you want it so?"

"Certain!" I assured him.

"Very well!" he said. "I'll see what I can do. The commodore's an old friend and he might do me the favor. We served together under Truxtun, you know. Fortunately I've a good man of my own to offer in trade."

"I don't ask to be surgeon," I said. "I'll be satisfied to be mate, just so I sail in the *Essex*."

"I take that as a compliment," he said.

"I mean it so," I replied.

"Thank you, Tom," he grinned. "And I'll tell you I want none better with me."

A fortnight later I received orders to transfer to the *Essex*, to the amazement and almost the indignation of my shipmates in the *President*, who regarded the exchange as a rebuff to me. For my part I felt more fortunate than I would admit, for I boarded the *Essex* as senior surgeon, and not as surgeon's mate, as I had expected.

I found the *Essex* not much changed save for her people, who, with one or two exceptions, were entirely new; and for her battery, which had been converted to one of forty thirty-two-pound carronades and six long twelves—although she was still officially rated a thirty-two. This change was not to Porter's taste. He had had bitter experience with carronades in the *New York*, and he considered them scarcely worth the powder to blow them overboard. At close quarters, he agreed, they were capable of heavy damage. However, he pointed out, it was not always possible to fight at close quarters. If, for instance, the *Essex* were damaged, even temporarily, in her top hamper, so that her sailing was impaired, she would be virtually helpless against even a lighter vessel armed with long guns, for, the carronades lacking both range and accuracy, the enemy might lie just out of reach and cut her to ribbons at his pleasure. This was to say nothing of what might be done by a frigate of comparable weight but carrying, say, long eighteens, as most of the British did. This was a favorite plaint of our commander's, and he bombarded Washington with demands for a change. But he might as well have tried to blow down the walls of Jericho at a breath for all the response he ever had of it.

Within a fortnight of my reporting on board, we were at war, and all the squadron except the *Essex* put to sea in search of such British ships as they might be able to find. The *Essex* alone, which had not yet completed her repairs, was forced to remain behind, until this could be done. Nevertheless, we were at sea within two weeks after the squadron's departure, despite the fact that when the commodore sailed we were stripped almost to a girtline.

In spite of our late start we had the luck to take the first prize of war. Indeed, in a brief cruise, actually no more than a shakedown, we had the good fortune to take seven brigs and two ships, one of which was H.M. Corvette *Alert,* twenty, which struck to us after no more than eight minutes of action. By mid-September we were back at Philadelphia, with $300,-000 in prizes sent in to port.

In this interval—indeed throughout the duration of our service together in the *Essex* at this time—I had little contact with Ben. He was on board on the day I reported, setting up gratings over the midship well against the day of our next sailing, and his face at sight of me was a study in mingled emotions. Surprise, irritation, disgust, combined with an expression of almost hangdog shame. We exchanged no words then, in deference to the ship's regulations. Later, however, as I was passing him in the steerage on my way forward to sick bay, I stopped and greeted him coolly.

"Well, you made it, I see," I said.

"Aye," he growled. "I made it. I suppose you want to be repaid?"

"Not at all," I told him. "It was worth it. I'm satisfied if you are."

"Oh, aye," he grumbled sulkily. "I'm satisfied. Thanks."

"Don't mention it," I said, and turned away.

Beyond that we exchanged no word with one another beyond what was required of our various duties for several months. On the twenty-eighth of October we weighed once again from Philadelphia, for a cruise that was to be longer and more fraught with adventure than I think any on board anticipated.

5

IT IS one of the mysteries of life aboard ship how the import of presumably sealed orders can become so universally known before they are opened. Yet it is a fact that this is often the case. Those who have the word, so it is said, impart it to the scuttle butt as they draw their rations of water. And the scuttle butt, in turn, passes it on to those more ignorant, as they come up for their share. However it goes, as often as not, it proves astonishingly accurate.

The *Essex* was no exception. Before our cables had been hosed clear of the Delaware mud and the anchors catted home, the lowliest waister knew that we were bound to a rendezvous at sea with the *Constitution* and the *Hornet,* after which we were to round the Cape of Good Hope for a cruise in the Indian Ocean, to prey upon the rich British-India trade.

Cape May was not hull down behind us when I went forward to attend my duties. As I passed through the midshipmen's country I met with the usual chaffering to which I was subject here, I being the only inhabitant of the wardroom who did not inspire the little devils with awe and terror.

"Hello, Uncle Pullguts!" cried Mr. Midshipman Farragut, now just past eleven and undoubtedly put up to this by his lordly elders. "We're off to fight Tippoo Sahib in the South Seas and twist the tail of the John Company into a Chinese knot!"

"Mr. Farragut," I grinned, "your sense of history and of geography are appalling. Tippoo Sahib died nearly fifteen years ago, and we are not bound to the South Seas. I shall mention this to Sam Slate (Mr. Adams, our chaplain and schoolmaster), who will doubtless teach you better! In the meantime, young sirs, I don't pull guts, as you may learn, I cut 'em!"

"On my soul!" cried Mr. Tittermary, one of our elder midshipmen. "I'd rather Chips would work on me with a draw-knife! I swear I would!"

"I hope you have no occasion to remember that, Mr. Tittermary," I replied stiffly, for the reference to Ben, who, as carpenter, was traditionally known as Chips, irritated me.

"Why, Tits!" chided Mr. Odenheimer. "Didn't you know? There's professional jealousy 'twixt Chips and Pullguts?"

His remark was quite innocent, and had I not been so touchy I would no doubt have passed it off.

"Gentlemen!" I barked at them. "Must I remind you that when you have reached your present positions you are expected to *be* gentlemen?"

They gaped at me, startled and somewhat taken aback, for I was still their superior, were I inclined to apply it.

"No offense, Doctor!" Mr. Feltus said.

"Then let's have no more of this," I replied curtly, and went on my way, leaving them staring at one another in blank amazement the while my own ears burned and my face was crimson, not so much for having taken them to task as for being so sensitive. What if anyone suspected? I must be more careful in future, I told myself, and keep a check upon my temper. A ship is a small world in itself, and gossip, via scuttle butt, moves through it like wildfire.

We had scarcely left the Capes when we fell in with heavy weather and gales which caused the ship to labor, and, being very deep, opened her waterways, so that much of the provision we had aboard was spoiled. However, once we had crossed to the northward of the Bermudas and come into comparatively calm seas, we were able to break out the rest and dry them and rescue them from a similar fate.

A month after our departure from Philadelphia we stood into Porto Praya, in the Cape de Verds, and sent Lieutenant Downes ashore to communicate with the authorities, who, for all they were nominally allies of the British, made us extraordinarily welcome. Here we replenished our stores and took on board a number of hogs and kids, which gave us the appearance of a latter-day Noah's ark.

We had here half expected to find the *Constitution,* but as there was neither word nor sign of her we presently put to sea again and sought her at another rendezvous, standing off first to the southeastward, as if heading for the coast of Africa, so that our late hosts might not suspect our true intentions, and then, when safely out of sight, coming about south-southwest and standing across toward the Brazils.

Up to this time we had had no luck in encountering prizes

and, somewhat spoiled by our first cruise, were conscious of a sense of disgruntlement. However, there was an end to this when, on the twelfth of December, we overtook and captured H.B.M. packet *Nocton,* from Rio de Janeiro bound for Falmouth, in England, with fifty-five thousand dollars in specie aboard. The money was taken out of her, and Mr. Finch, our fourth lieutenant, with a prize crew, was sent aboard, with instructions to carry her in to the nearest available American port.

Not long after this we hove to off Fernhao do Noronha, where we learned that the *Constitution* and the *Hornet* had lately called but had sailed again for the coast of Brazil. We promptly set out after them and, on Christmas Day, came up off Cabo Frio, where we stood on and off in search of them.

Being unsuccessful here, and the possibility of British cruisers being strong in the vicinity, we moved first up and then down the coast to St. Catherine's, where we put in briefly for provisions, but with the luck to find neither a proper engagement nor a decent prize, other than a couple of Portuguese packets, which we halted but did not detain. From these we learned that a convoy had gone north some time before our arrival; that the British ship of the line *Montagu,* seventy-four, was lying in Rio, in company with at least one frigate; that there had been an engagement off the coast between an American and a British frigate, and that the latter had been sunk while the former had gone north to refit; that an American sloop of war, twenty-two guns, had been brought in to Rio as a prize; and that several more British frigates and a sixty-gun ship were daily expected upon the coast. Since we knew of no other American ships of war in these waters, we were left to assume that the frigate which had gone north after its victory was the *Constitution,* while the captured sloop must be the *Hornet.*

This, if it were true, left us, not only without support in a hostile sea, but also in a fair way to be surrounded and forced into port by a strong blockading force. Since we could by no means feel certain that such a force would respect the neutrality of the ports in which we might take refuge—indeed, we had every reason to doubt it—a change of plan, or at least one of scene, seemed indicated. Consequently few were surprised when a council of the officers was called. There was an air of expectant tension as we came together in the captain's great cabin, with its polished fittings and smooth rubbed panels and the bluish reflection of the sunlight dancing in from the following seas through the open stern ports. The shadows played fleetingly across Porter's sharp features, accentuating the high dome of his forehead, as he faced us at the head of the long table. Behind him, on the bulkhead, a pair of brass lamps swung silently in their gimbals, and in the overhead, so placed that it could be seen from all parts of the cabin, especially the captain's berth, the telltale compass wavered gently and came back again to course as the ship's stern heaved to the running sea. For a long moment, after we were all assembled, there was a complete silence, in which only the creak of the ship's timbers could be heard. Then abruptly Porter fixed the purser with a sharp eye.

"Now, Mr. Shaw," he said, "what's the state of our provisions?"

"Why, sir," Shaw replied thoughtfully, making a particular effort to return an accurate answer, "we've enough beef for thirty-six weeks. We're short bread and pork, having but twenty-two weeks' supply. We've but two weeks' molasses. Flour is short. So is meal. We've plenty of raisins. We have onions and potatoes for as long as they'll last, and the same for eggs. Those we got at St. Catherine's were none too good, sir."

"Umm!" agreed the captain, with a wry face. "I know! And the rest? Water and grog?"

"Close to a full supply of water," Shaw said, "but rum's mighty scarce. We could only pick up a few puncheons in St. Catherine's. The men will have to go on short rations if we're to remain long at sea."

"Thank you, Mr. Shaw," was Porter's only comment.

Of Mr. Cowell, the sailing master, he asked the condition of the provisions enumerated, it being the master's and my duty to inspect them at intervals, seeing that those most likely to spoil first were so stowed as to be first used. Mr. Cowell assured him that they were in as good condition as could be expected after so long at sea, and that he thought we might count upon them lasting as much as four or five months at need. The captain then looked at me.

"And the men, Doctor? What of their health?"

At least I could return him an encouraging report.

"The health of all hands is excellent, Captain," I said. "No signs of scurvy nor of dysentery, though we had a small fright a few days since, after leaving St. Catherine's."

"So I hear," Porter said dryly, unable to resist a grin. "As I recall, Doctor, you said 'twas bad rum the Portygees sent off to us that did it. Have you changed your mind?"

I flushed in embarrassment.

"I have, Captain," I smiled. "The men are fit and have been returned to duty. The symptoms resembled painter's colic and I was convinced that the rum was leaded. I think, now, it was no more than too sudden a shift from salt to fresh provision."

"That's as may be," he said. "How do you stand now?"

"We've but one man on the sick list this morning, sir," I said. "That's the carpenter (Ben), who slashed his foot with the drawknife, three days since."

"I heard that," Porter chuckled. "I understand you made it a point to call Mr. Tittermary's attention to the accident."

"I did, sir," I replied. "I could not resist pointing out to him that, even in the hands of an expert, a drawknife is not a proper surgical instrument!"

A shout of laughter rose at that. Apparently some report of my exchange with the midshipmen on our first day out had gotten around the wardroom, at least.

"And you think the men can stand a long voyage, Doctor?" said the captain, breaking into the merriment.

Abrupt silence fell about the table. It was the first time the least hint had been offered as to the meaning of this conference —although we all suspected it.

"Captain," I replied, "the endurance of human beings is extraordinary. The men's health is sufficient to allow them to last as long as our provisions—and how much longer than that, I cannot say. At present they are healthy and hearty and cheerful, though I could wish we had more rum. Cold water is no diet to maintain health!"

He nodded again, soberly, and looked at the first luff.

"And the ship, Mr. Downes?"

"She's as sound as a ship ever was after three months at

sea, sir," Downes replied. He glanced down the table at me. "I could wish for a few things, too, in the way of new spars and rigging. But those we have will do till we find better."

"Will they last a year?" Porter demanded.

We all sat up sharply and stared at him, but he signaled us to silence.

"Provisions will be found before that," he said, "and men live by provisions. But it may be longer before we can find fresh cordage and canvas and suchlike ship's stores."

We remained tense.

"She'll be a patchwork quilt by the end of a year, Captain," Downes said, "but she'll last if the rest of it's looked after."

Captain Porter slapped his hand upon the table and leaned forward.

"Very well, gentlemen!" he barked. "You have told me what I wish to know. Now listen to me! There is no longer any need for secrecy. As you undoubtedly know, our original plan was for the Indian Ocean, for a strike at the John Company, with Bainbridge, in the *Constitution* and Lawrence in the *Hornet!*"

He glanced around at us, and we each nodded.

"Good enough!" he snapped. "No need then for explanations. You know the strength of the John Company's ships, and we may be sure that trade will be well convoyed. With two frigates and a sloop we might achieve some damage. But with a frigate alone—gentlemen, we wouldn't even get near them."

Lieutenant Downes nodded soberly.

"More than likely," he said.

"There you have it," Porter continued. "The original plan must go by the board, since it seems unlikely that either the *Hornet* or the *Constitution* can join us now. What are the alternatives? If we stay here we choose between starvation at sea or capture in a neutral port—for you know as well as I that the British will respect that neutrality no longer than it suits their purpose. If we sail north we run the risk of capture before we can reach a home port or, supposing we reach one, of being blockaded there and sitting the war out in harbor."

He glared round at us all once again.

"Now, then, gentlemen," he went on, "you've been with me

long enough to know that is not what I came to sea for; and I think I know you all well enough to believe that you, too, came here to do as much damage as possible to the British."

"That's right, sir!" someone said, and there was a general growl of approval about the table.

It was Downes, however, who touched the important point.

"I daresay, sir," he remarked, "that you've another scheme up your sleeve."

Captain Porter glared at him.

"I have, sir!" he replied. "I'm going to take you round the Horn!"

There was a gasp of astonishment and almost dismay from everyone, for there was not one of us but had heard tales of the hardships of that passage or knew that no other American man-of-war had yet made the attempt.

"In this season, sir?" asked Downes coolly.

The captain shrugged.

"Why not? The season will do as well as any other, I misdoubt, and if we are in luck we may yet find good weather. You know the risks. You have all heard the reports. We are provisioned for a little more than three months. With a fair break in the weather, we should be able to reach Chile within that time."

"What about sea stores, Captain?" Downes asked. "They'll be scarce on that coast. They tell me the whalers carry a four years' supply when they go out. We'll stand in need of them before we can return."

"I'm coming to that!" Porter snapped. "The fact that the whalers carry such stores is in my mind."

He turned to the rest of us.

"Are you aware, gentlemen," he said, "of the benefits of such a cruise?"

"We should have no trouble from the British," said Mr. Cowell. "They might have a ship or two in those waters, but they'll not be expecting us."

"That's only a part of it, Mr. Cowell," Porter retorted. "I don't mean to run from anything but ridiculous odds. But the fact remains that here we have little chance of prizes, while the enemy has overwhelming strength. If we can't fight his cruisers, gentlemen, we must, at least, do as much damage to him as may be. Have any of you any concept of the enemy's investment in the Pacific whale fisheries?"

We stared at one another. Here was an example of Porter's energy and thirst for knowledge. Although we all knew that British whalers, as well as our own—stinking ships, whalers, and properly despised by all true men-of-war's men —operated in the Pacific, it had occurred to none of us to calculate the importance of the trade.

"Gentlemen," he went on, "Britain derives eighty-five per cent of her light from the whale fisheries, and of this seventy-six per cent is drawn from the Pacific! Think of that, gentlemen! If we can cut off that trade, we can deal her a heavier blow than if we shut off the John Company twice over!"

Someone whistled in amazement.

"Those are the figures, gentlemen," Porter said. "You see what an opportunity we have?"

"Why, a single frigate in those waters could play hob with the trade!" cried Mr. McKnight. "She'd have the ocean to herself!"

The captain nodded.

"Exactly, Mr. McKnight! And better than that! Think of the prize value! I'll put it conservatively and say that there are now in the Pacific at least twenty British whalers, with their cargoes valued at more than four millions of dollars! I'll warrant the John Company would not offer such pickings, and I, for one, say 'tis time this ship earned something for us in that direction!"

"Four million dollars!" It was almost a shout that arose. He could not have offered greater incentive, for prize money is a sailor's dream, and in the case of most officers it is an absolute necessity.

"What about sea stores, Captain?" Downes put in in a mild voice as soon as he could make himself heard.

"Confound you, Downes!" Porter exclaimed. "You're a persistent beggar!"

An abrupt silence fell about the table.

"But I'll answer your question, just the same," the captain went on, with a sharp grin, for he undoubtedly saw that we thought him evading the issue. "Didn't you just tell me that whalers carried four years of sea stores when they sailed?"

"I did, sir," Downes nodded.

"Well, then!" exclaimed Porter. "Each ship that we take will render us sea stores to continue a little longer! In fact, if they carry as much as four years' stores we might continue our cruise indefinitely!"

There was a shout of approval, which must have made the helmsman over our heads start in astonishment. I noticed that the telltale yawed sharply and then came back, bit by bit, to the original course. Something of the captain's enthusiasm caught the conference, and we beamed and nodded at one another and all began talking at once.

"I hope you are right, sir!" Downes said quietly. But I doubt more than one or two others besides myself heard him.

We stood off, now, to the southeastward, and for all the captain had ordered us to secrecy for the moment, the voice of scuttle butt soon began to sound among the men. Those who are superstitious might think that the water cask and the rum barrel spoke, but more practical indications, I think, warned the men of what was afoot. When the skysails and stunsails and royals were fetched in and stowed away; when the loftier spars were sent down and made fast; when extra shrouds and preventer stays were sent up to the standing rigging and the yards, and the ship took on a clumsy look, even the dullest of foremast hands must have known that we were in for dirty going. And what weather is dirtier, in those parts, than that around the Horn?

Within six days there was an eclipse of the sun, and with it came the wickedest weather and heaviest cross seas we had encountered. The long swells of the South Atlantic were chopped by the fury of the gale, which seemed to come from all directions at once, and we fought it beneath bare poles with only the jib to maintain steerageway upon her. The heavy seas smashed in the rudder coat and tumbled a deluge of icy water into the wardroom, and we should have put in to port to make repairs had one been handy. But there was none such, and we had to make the best we could of the situation at sea. Volunteers did their best and the rudder was rehung. In the meantime the gun ports were battened down and the guns run in amidships, to reduce her rolling, while the upper-deck guns were dismounted and stowed below, where there was no chance of their breaking loose and creating havoc on deck.

Then, on a gray, grim day, under a slaty sky, the captain called all hands aft to the break of the quarter-deck and spoke to them, much as he had spoken to us in the cabin, and it spoke well of the magnetism of the man that his appeal was greeted with cheers and enthusiasm in the main, despite the fact that the time of many of the hands was expiring and that they could not hope to return to a home port until long after they were due! Slops and small stores were broken out, and each man was issued what he needed, without regard to his account, but considering only what was available. Some men needed shoes for such a passage as we proposed. But there were not enough for all, and those who could not have shoes drew an extra pair of woolen stockings and went cheerfully aloft to cling with their toes to shroud and ratline as determinedly as if no more were necessary.

The passage of the Horn has been described by hundreds before me. I can add nothing to what they have told. Our escape from the rocks in the Straits of LeMaire and on Cape San Diego; our fine luck in having good weather abruptly off the shore of Staten Land; the green, indented, precipitous shores of Tierra del Fuego; and then the island of Diego Ramirez and all the fury of the Horn! All these we fought and passed and welcomed and fought again. As surgeon I lay below. What passed on deck was none of my affair. I could mend bones—if the table on which I worked would stand still long enough. I could not mend the ship. But my table would not stand still, nor did we have, officers and men, usually more than cold salt provisions to sustain us through the worst of the passage. At one point seas that seemed to me to have all the height of the precipitous shores we had not long since passed smashed over us and crashed in the fore and after hatches and series of gun ports, and panic was born aboard. Yet the men I had looked upon as cheerful good fellows, with little more than a sense of the joy of life, turned now and rallied the rest and, with quips and with prodding which elsewhere might have given offense, inspired their fellows to rescue the ship—not to mention me, who had long since given up hope!

Other seas tore down upon us; green walls with whitecapped

crowns, which threatened to overturn us in complete somer-
sets. Yet at the most breathless moment, each time, it seemed,
we knifed through them and slid down the opposite flank, yet
unscathed but dreading the next to come. I cannot laugh, even
now, but there was something ludicrous about the anxiety I
saw then upon each man's face—save those who were injured—
as if each one's sins were come home to roost and each thought
himself in a watery hell already, from which there was no
escape.

There was no escape, had the Lord willed it so. We might
yet have been tossing, all dead souls off the Cape, like Flying
Dutchmen, but in due time, after we had learned what fools
we had been to think that we might win unharmed round the
Horn, we came into calmer weather and, having gained our
westing, stood north along the west coast of South America
for such landfall as we might find.

For the first time in three months we were able to open
the gun ports and knock out the deadlights and let air, not
water, into the 'tween decks. Two weeks later we put in to the
island of Mocha; not upon a port but on a sandy bay, well
supplied with water and backed with green-clad, snowcapped
peaks, where there was an abundance of wild hogs and horses
to provide us with fresh meat.

From Mocha, after filling our water casks and replenishing
our larder, we stood on northward. Fog and a heavy gale prevented our looking in at Concepción, and a few days later
found us off Valparaiso, where we put in, offering, as a ruse,
that we were an American frigate which had lost her storeship
in the passage of the Horn; it being Captain Porter's con-
tention that the Spaniards could not refuse assistance if they
thought us in distress. Accordingly, we followed in after Mr.
Downes in the jolly boat, with the flag at our masthead bearing the painted motto—adopted by Porter for the occasion of
this cruise—FREE TRADE AND SAILORS' RIGHTS!

To our amazement we were welcomed with open arms, Mr.
Downes coming off with word that the Chileans had declared
themselves independent of Spain and that they looked upon
our arrival as a gesture of friendship and support from the
Republic of the North.

For the captain this was something of an embarrassment.

Nevertheless, we saluted the new republic as we entered the harbor, which is all open to the north and largely so toward the west, and let go our anchors in six fathom just off the town. There we were promptly greeted by all manner of boats from the shore, including one that bore word from our consular agent that Mr. Poinsett, the consul, had been summoned from Santiago and would undoubtedly be down within the next day or two.

The next few days were full of the business of taking on water and provisions, of which our new friends could not seem to find enough for us. Although the country appeared bare from seaward, the hills and valleys above the coast were extremely lush, judging from the quantities of vegetables and fruits and beef and wine that were brought down to us.

In addition we were feted at a grand ball, given by the governor, which more than two hundred of the outstanding ladies of the country attended. I must say that I enjoyed it, as I think did most of my fellow officers—the men, Ben among them, were attending their own celebration in the cribs of the lower town. The ladies were handsome, after the Spanish fashion, with great dark eyes and high breasts, a good deal of paint and a wanton manner, though perhaps this judgment may have been the result of having been too long out of sight of land. It was four and a half months since we had seen a woman long enough to greet her civilly upon the streets, and we were by no means particular.

Entertainment ashore had its polite corollary aboard. Arrangements were made to hold a return ball on board the *Essex,* and every detail was prepared and the officers were at the landing, welcoming their fair guests and escorting dignitaries, when the jolly boat dashed madly up to the landing steps with an excited Midshipman Odenheimer in the stern sheets.

"Sssirrrs!" he cried. "There's a large frigate sssstanding into the harbor! She fetched up her course, sir, when she seemed to sssee th-the *Essex!*"

As may be imagined, all was instant excitement. The ladies and most of their escorts were left waiting at the dock, although Don Luis Carrera and Mr. Poinsett, the consul, as well as the governor, insisted on accompanying us, in order, as they put it, "to view a naval engagement," while the fair ones and their duennas that we had left behind crowded along the hills, quite frankly more anxious to watch a battle than a dance.

We slipped our cables and stood out for sea, within a few moments at quarters and cleared for action. But the wind fell, as we later discovered it often does on those shores, and we were forced to get out our boats ahead and tow out of the harbor. This in itself would not have been humiliating had we not, upon reaching the open sea, discovered the stranger to be a Portuguese frigate, out of Lisbon, coming in search of flour! How Don Luis gnashed his teeth! How the captain turned purple with confusion! How even Mr. Poinsett seemed dashed, not to mention all hands who thought that here at last was a prize worth taking! How disappointed were our female *aficionadas* upon the hillsides, who had foregone a reception for this fiasco! But all was well. We enjoyed another banquet the following evening, and had the advantage of being in port when the arrival of an American whaler brought news that three American ships had been taken to northward.

Hasty interrogation of her captain revealed that the *Charles,* the *Barclay,* and the *Walker,* of Nantucket and New Bedford, had fallen in with a British letter-of-marque whaler, the *Nimrod,* twenty, and a Peruvian privateer, the *Neyreda,* and been taken in to Coquimbo. The enemy, apparently, had much the same idea as ourselves, knowing the Americans to have an equal stake in the Pacific whale fisheries. But, feeling safe from molestation, they were content to arm their own whalers and issue letters of marque, authorizing them to deal, as privateers, with such Americans as they might meet. This, as we saw it, was to our advantage, for it told us that we were not looked for and that we could expect to cope with everything that we might meet. However, we learned also that the British ship of the line *Standard,* seventy-four, was at Callao, which might be an embarrassment. We were fast enough to elude such a ship in a chase, and we might even cope with her in a single combat. But it was unlikely that her commander would risk such an affair. Rather he would lie in port, once he learned of our presence, and send a message overland, through Buenos Aires, summoning faster ships to his assistance; meantime lending the weight of his prestige, rather than that of his metal, to our opposition on the coast.

Having received this information, and being by now well stocked with provisions and water and brandy in lieu of rum, we set sail in pursuit of the *Nimrod* and the *Neyreda,* looking in first at Coquimbo, whose open roadstead we found empty of any vessels of interest to us. For several days we stood up the coast, and presently fell in with the *Neyreda* which we took and disarmed, without much difficulty, and sent on in to Callao with a note of warning to the authorities there that we cared not whether we fought British, Spanish, or Peruvian. If it was war they wanted, they should have it from us, unless they observed the neutral rights of Americans!

We now stood up for Callao ourselves, taking every pain to disguise the ship as much as possible and make her look like a Spanish merchantman by building a false poop upon her and giving her a new coat of paint—a trick we employed a dozen times during our cruise in those waters. Off Callao we had the luck to seize the *Barclay,* one of the prizes of the *Neyreda,* and whose captain we had taken off the *Neyreda.* Randall, her skipper, was so delighted with her recapture that he offered to sail in company with us and go wherever we pleased, but Porter, better aware of the laws of war than he, chose to keep him aboard and sent the *Barclay,* under Mr. Midshipman Cowan, with a prize crew, up for Galapagos, to intercept whatever he might meet with in the way and to lie there and wait for us until we, too, appeared.

Next, on the advice of the captain of a Spanish brig, who thought us English, we bore up into the Gulf of Payta, in search of British ships to "protect," being at last sorely in need of sea stores, the breechings on the guns being discovered rotted and only with difficulty patched so that we dared hope they might hold. Upon the one hand, as we stood northward, the tawny coast rose abruptly from the sea, with the mighty peaks of the mountains lying against the sky's background like purple clouds against the blue, while the clouds themselves hung etched above them in gold filigree, as garish as a bishop's robes. The sea beneath us and all around was as smooth and blue and unruffled as the sky, purple by night, cerulean by day. Now and again a vast school of fish broke its stillness beneath our forefoot, but as for ships, the only vessels we saw were crude catamarans from the mainland; rough vessels made of two logs and a scrap of sail, which often make voyages of hundreds of miles, mute testimony to the gentleness of these seas.

However, it was not the gentleness of the seas that interested us. A word or two of grumbling began to be heard among the men—"Prizes, 'twas those we came for! Where are the prizes?" Never such as an officer could lay his finger upon, yet unmistakably there. And who could blame them? We were now nigh six months at sea, and the only legitimate prize that we had taken—for the *Barclay* and the *Neyreda* could not be regarded as such, in returns of prize money—had been the *Nocton*. Yet we carried on with promises. The lookout's cry of "Land ho!" some days after we had dropped the coast of Peru behind fetched all hands tumbling on deck. If there were prizes in the Pacific, we all felt it was here they would be found. But they were not found this day, nor yet the next. The Galapagos, green but arid, beset with bewildering currents and still more bewildering calms, were the center of whaling in these waters. Whales were everywhere about us, but nowhere was there a whaler to be seen!

6

THE DISAPPOINTMENT which all hands felt at not finding prizes at the islands was tempered somewhat by the prospect of a turn ashore. After scouring the surrounding waters and finding no trace of our game, we came to anchor in the harbor of Charles Island. There I recommended that as many of the crew as could be spared for it should be put ashore, for we were beginning to see signs of scurvy as a result of the constant diet of salt provision, and I know of no better anti-scorbutic than the smell of green trees. Moreover, by taking turn and turn about on shore, we could maintain a constant supply of fresh provisions, for, if water was scarce upon these islands, at least food was abundant. Among the rocks alongshore there were sea lions to be had for the clubbing, and great green turtles abounded in the surrounding waters, coming out upon the beaches at night to lay their eggs. There it was rare sport to trap them and flip them over upon their backs before they could race clumsily back into the water. These were excellent, and the turtle especially was a great delicacy. But other meats were equally tasty and of far greater importance. Foremost among the former were the iguanas, huge lizards which were so common as often to lie, in a sunny place, heaped over an area of an acre or more, and so closely intermingled that there was scarce room for another to touch the ground. Their flesh, as nearly as I can describe it, was something like the tenderest chicken. Good as these were, better for our purposes were the huge tortoises which abounded on all the islands. Often six feet long by four across and three deep, they weighed as much as a fat hog, tipping the beam not infrequently at as much as three hundred pounds. Their meat was tender and delicate yet with a substance lacking in the lizards, being much like fine young veal. But what was of even greater significance to us, they were ideal seafaring livestock, for they could go for days, even months, without water or food, and fifty of them dumped without ceremony in the hold of a vessel would assure a supply of fresh meat for weeks.

In addition to these, the waters around the islands, clear and green, abounded in many different varieties of fish, and there was sport to be had in catching them. As with all tropical species, however, care had to be taken in selecting those which were edible, and in the main, other food being so superior and abundant, we contented ourselves with admiring their vivid colors and returned them to the sea.

During the first days of our stay in these islands Captain Porter did everything to encourage the men in the pursuit of these sports—so useful and at the same time so diverting. I had no doubt, however, that a strong factor in his so doing was to distract the men from the unpleasant truth that, having come so far for prizes, we now saw none, nor any prospect of them. I know this worried him, for he asked me often for sedatives and sleeping potions to help him sleep of nights, while on deck during the day he would pat his fist restlessly with his open palm and at the same time let his eye wander constantly out over the empty horizon.

For a time their fun ashore put thought of complaint out of the men's heads. But such pastimes do not retain their power to divert for long, and before a fortnight was out the old grumblings began to be heard again. It was time to be out and about! The "Post Office," as a box nailed to a tree upon Charles

Island to serve as a depositing place for messages between the captains of whaling vessels in these waters was called, had yielded nothing. The most recent letter in it, although there had been many, was nearly a year old. The men growled that no one was getting rich here, and the relations between them and our officers became almost strained. Each day, however, we searched another sector of the adjacent sea, and at last, near the end of April, we were aroused at dawn by the excited cry of the masthead lookout:

"Sail ho!"

Had a fleet action been promised, I doubt our people would have tumbled to their stations more swiftly!

That first prize proved to be the British whaler *Montezuma,* a wallowing, unhandy vessel, but carrying fourteen hundred barrels of whale oil in her hold. The chase proved a long and tedious one, due to the light airs and curious currents with which the islands are surrounded. During it we raised two more sail, and Lieutenant Downes and Mr. Farragut were sent off in the boats to intercept them. They, too, proved to be whalers, and, having no guns mounted, surrendered at command and were brought back under the lee of the *Essex.* They were the *Georgiana* and the *Policy,* both with full cargoes of oil and plenty of sea stores. Considering that in the course of the morning we had taken prizes worth something more than a half a million dollars, and had at the same time supplied ourselves with all necessary stores, including water, it is not remarkable that all hands felt cheerful once more and that as I passed through the berth deck forward to the sick bay I was greeted with grins instead of scowls, and even Ben had a cheerful word.

This was the first of a series of successes. The *Georgiana* was a stout ship, built originally for the John Company. To her we transshipped the *Policy's* guns, giving her a total of sixteen. She was then placed under the command of Lieutenant—now Master-Commandant—Downes, with a prize crew of forty-one, and became the *Essex's* consort.

To some extent this depleted our complement, particularly in the way of officers, for though we found a number of foremast hands aboard our prizes who claimed to have been pressed and were willing to volunteer for our service, officers were not come by in that fashion. A month to the day after this we took the *Atlantic* and the *Greenwich,* which gave us a squadron of eighty guns and four hundred and twenty men.

By this time, however, Captain Porter found that he had an embarrassment of prisoners, and it became necessary to call at the mainland, where it was hoped that some of our spoils might be disposed of. We turned up for Tumbes, but on arrival there found our welcome only lukewarm, to say the most. Some days were spent dickering with the avaricious governors of this province—who had never the least intention of dealing with us in a fair way—and presently Mr. Downes fetched in three more prizes: the *Catherine,* the *Rose,* and the *Hector,* all well loaded and equipped.

Now the situation became well-nigh desperate, for, although we had taken eight prizes and the *Barclay,* the number of prisoners was not far from equaling our own complement and our men were scattered throughout the fleet! Accordingly the *Rose* was made a cartel and sent off with seventy-three of the prisoners on parole, and directions to make for St. Helena. Thereafter the rest of our little squadron put back to the Galapagos, where the guns and crew of the *Georgiana* were transferred to the *Atlantic,* which was a faster sailer and in all a smarter ship. Though she was pierced for only six guns originally, Ben and his mates made her over for a battery of twenty. She was renamed the *Essex Junior,* and command of her given to Mr. Downes. At the same time the stores taken in all the prizes were transferred to the *Greenwich,* which became our storeship and part of our train.

In spite of all this shifting and transshifting, however, it was apparent that more would have to be done if we were to maintain our fighting efficiency aboard the *Essex* and at the same time realize the profits of our captures. Our fleet now consisted of the *Essex* and eight other vessels, and by this our strength was so diffused by prize crews that we had scarcely enough men to man the frigate, let alone fight her. Officers, as I have hinted, were especially short, and nearly all of the midshipmen had been advanced to acting lieutenants. To add to our difficulties, Mr. Wilson, originally our third lieutenant, took to drink at Tumbes and tried to shoot himself and had to be put in irons, while Mr. Cowan, one of the most promising of our midshipmen, was killed in a duel.

This produced some oddities in command. All of the midshipmen had opportunity at one time or another to serve as prize master, even little Mr. Farragut, but just turned twelve, who was put in command of the *Barclay.* Yet this was not as astonishing, I think, as it may sound, for these boys were being trained to sea command. Their every waking moment was directed toward that end, and that their opportunities came soon rather than late was no more than the working of chance. On the other hand, the fact that the lieutenant of marines, the purser, and even the chaplain were also pressed into command of captured vessels seems to me truly to indicate an unusual situation! Of all the ship's commissioned officers, the surgeon alone was not called upon; a circumstance perfectly acceptable to me, for I doubt I would have known what to do had I been given one of the ships!

We had by now taken prizes whose total value was something over a million dollars, and since this represented a substantial cut of prize money—at least the equivalent of three years of sea pay for even the meanest boy—there were few who complained. But by July it became evident that we were in somewhat the same position as a man who has a bag of gold to spend but must needs swim a wide river with it before he can reach a town. We were embarrassed by an abundance of riches which gave us more and more difficulty in the carrying, yet which we could not spend.

In this situation Captain Porter decided to send Downes and Farragut to Valparaiso in the *Essex Junior* and the *Barclay,* accompanied by the *Montezuma,* the *Hector,* the *Catherine,* and the *Policy,* in order that these prizes might there be sold and a supply of spirits and other necessities fetched back in the *Essex Junior.*

The *Essex* was now left with the *Greenwich* and the *Georgiana* as consorts, and Captain Porter had no mind to lie idle. We stood up for Charles Island and, putting in there to harbor, found the "Post Office" empty and every evidence of the place having been lately visited by whalers. Immediately we set out in search of them, and presently, in the vicinity of Banks' Bay, three strange sail were raised and chased. After an exciting scramble in which the *Greenwich,* under Mr. Gamble of the marines, and the *Georgiana,* under our fighting parson, Mr.

Adams, fought it out gun to gun with their respective quarries, while the *Essex* took advantage of her superior speed to prevent them from escaping, we succeeded in capturing all three. They proved to be the *Seringapatam,* fourteen, the *New Zealander,* eight, and the *Charlton,* ten, all British whalers. Indeed, the *Seringapatam* was one of the best ships of her kind in these waters, having been built originally as a man-of-war for Tippoo Sahib.

The guns were promptly removed from the *Charlton,* which was made a cartel and sent off for Rio de Janeiro under two of the captured captains, carrying about half our prisoners. At the same time Porter pardoned Lieutenant Wilson and, placing him in command of the *Georgiana,* sent him off, with the rest of the prisoners and such men as had served their time and wished to return home, for the nearest possible American port with a report of our activities. Some seventy-five of the prisoners chose to remain, declaring that they were Americans and preferred to serve with us.

We now spent several weeks patrolling about the islands in search of further game or lying hove down in the harbor, painting and refitting so as to disguise the vessels of our little squadron. Toward the end of July we chased a large vessel, but lost her through the capriciousness of the wind and the trickiness of the currents. On the fifteenth of September, however, we overhauled the same vessel, made fast to a whale and cutting out blubber, and such was the change that we had wrought in our own appearance that we were close aboard and had her well under our guns before she realized that we were the same ship. She proved to be the *Sir Andrew Hammond,* another fine ship, a letter of marque, carrying a full cargo of whale oil in her hold.

Better than this, however, from the standpoint of our immediate needs, she also carried nearly a full supply of fine Jamaica spirits. The men had been long on short rations without complaint, and because he expected the *Essex Junior* back shortly from Valparaiso with still more spirits, the captain now ordered all hands back upon full rations of grog immediately, saying that a little inebriety would do them no harm. The results were curious. So long had the men been accustomed to their weakened ration that when their grog was once again

served out to them full strength, their reaction was all but
instantaneous, and within twenty minutes of grog call there
was scarcely a man aboard ship but was drunk as David's sow.
Yet there was but one who gave us any trouble, and he was
long known as a malcontent and a malingerer. I was curiously
relieved that it was not Ben.

Downes and Farragut now returned from Valparaiso in the
Essex Junior, bringing with them not only a fresh supply of
spirits but also news of a world so long since left behind that it
seemed almost to be another planet. At home Mr. Madison had
been re-elected in spite of the Federalists. We had a new Secretary of the Navy. On land the war seemed not to be going as
well as we might hope, although nothing conclusive seemed yet
to have occurred. But at sea we appeared to be giving a good
account of ourselves. Jacob Jones, in the *Wasp,* had beaten the
Frolic. Decatur, in the *United States,* had captured the *Mace-
donian.* And the *Constitution* had whipped the *Java* in the
battle of which we had heard rumors. The *Hornet,* it appeared, had not been taken after all, and the latest word of
her was that she had sunk the *Peacock* in an engagement off
Demerara.

Of more immediate import to us, however, was word that
the British frigate *Phoebe* and the sloops of war *Raccoon* and
Cherub had been sent round the Horn with orders to hunt us
down. If they did not succeed at once, it was rumored, other
ships of war would follow and join in the chase.

Captain Porter chuckled when he heard this.

"They begin to hear of us, then!" he exclaimed. "Good! It
means that they have been hurt!"

He looked round the table at us, for he had called us all to
dine with him to hear the news.

"Well, gentlemen," he said, "according to the best information I have, there is but one more whaling vessel left in this
part of the Pacific, and she has disappeared, God knows where!
I suggest that we forget her and move on. We shall need speed
when we meet these three gentlemen who have been sent out
after us."

"Aye, sir," Mr. McKnight put in. He had been serving as
first lieutenant while Downes was in the *Essex Junior.* "But we
ought to refit, too, before we risk a real engagement."

Porter nodded.

"I was thinking of that too."

"And the rats have become so numerous, sir, 'tis as much as your life's worth to go down in the hold or the cockpit," Cowell said.

"If we hope to reach home in health," I could not resist adding, "we should have new casks and fresh water."

The captain threw up his hands in self-defense.

"Gentlemen! Gentlemen!" he cried. "All of this has been in my mind, and I was coming to it, if you will but have a moment's patience with me!"

He paused, but no one spoke. It was evident that he had some plan.

"I suggest," he said, "that we run down to the Marquesas, west and south of here, where I understand there is a good harbor and water and natives that are not unfriendly." This last with more than a hint of a twinkle in his eye. "I think that there we can accomplish everything that is necessary, and perhaps when that is done go on a hunt of our own."

There was a general mutter of approval. Six months of the Galapagos are sufficient for any man, and the proposed change was welcome to us all. Two days later we weighed and stood southwest by west for these new islands. Toward the end of October, almost a year to the day from the time we had sailed from Philadelphia, we dropped anchor in the harbor of Nukuhiva, the largest of the Marquesas.

How can I describe those islands and do justice to them? They start up abruptly, green and lush, out of a sea of the richest blue which breaks in a girdle of snowy white about their shores. Their outline, against a sky only slightly less blue than the sea, is rugged, peaked, and craggy, yet the flanks of the mountains are clothed in the velvet green of a tropic jungle, for they are well watered. In cruising along their shores one can see the white wisps of many waterfalls that tumble from the mountains at the heads of deep, baylike valleys which everywhere run back from the shore between precipitous ridges and which, in their turn, thrust their butting headlands out into the sea to end in black, jagged cliffs of basalt and sharp volcanic rock. Where the valleys meet the shore, a crescent beach of dazzling sand curves about the bayhead, overhung with palms

and sea grape and manchineel, while the villages of the island-
ers stand back a little from the shore, overlooking the bays. So
steep and rugged are the mountains which ring these valleys
that their inhabitants form single tribes to themselves, having
little intercourse with their neighbors, indeed being frequently
hostile to the folk on either hand and behind. They have always
the sea before.

The people of Nukuhiva appeared, at first, somewhat suspicious of us, but when we produced for them such treasures as
whales' teeth and iron hoops, to say nothing of knives and
scissors, kettles, axes, saws, and similar tools, offering them in
trade for such, to them, valueless things as coconuts and hogs,
breadfruit and bananas, or a woman's virtue, they turned immediately friendly and welcomed us with open arms. Beads and
similar trinkets they spurned, taking no interest in them whatever. Apparently they had been visited before, although not
with sufficient frequency to make them hostile.

The men we found to be generally handsome and well made,
and of a curious golden-copper color save where they were covered with intricate tattooing. This was sometimes so extensive
and so elaborate as almost completely to cover their entire
body with fine, closely interlaced lines and scrolls, so that at a
distance they would seem almost black. At the same time there
were varying shades of skin, so that while some were definitely
of a rusty hue, others were as light, if not lighter, than many
of our own people who work much in the sun.

Among the women there appeared to be a distinct line of
separation, based definitely upon class and age. On the one
hand there was the common race: rather small, wizened, apparently aged before their time, stooped not merely from care
and labor but from a sort of cringing habit of growth. On the
other were the daughters of the chiefs and petty chiefs and
aristocracy of the island. These were straight and smooth and
lusciously golden; handsome, high-breasted, proud and well-
formed, and withal flirtatious and willing to a degree that well
nigh frightened our hornyhanded seamen. By island custom, it
appeared, the white man's regard for female virtue as a com-
modity to be guarded was unknown here. Girls from twelve to
eighteen roved at will, confining their hearts and attention
during this period to the pursuit of pleasure and offering their

favors where, for the instant, they willed. Nothing restrained their actions, nor were they bound down by domestic occupations. They had naught to do to spend their time but to dissipate it in dancing and singing and swimming and bathing and ornamenting themselves, so as to become more attractive to the man who for the moment had their fancy or whom they would snatch from a rival. These swam out to us as soon as it was established that we were friends and meant no harm—for it was forbidden to women under pain of death to enter a canoe —and, swarming aboard and overrunning the ships, made us free gift of that flower of comfort which is a woman's finest possession. Indeed, so friendly were they that it was almost impossible to step out of one's quarters and move about the ship without falling over couples shagging in the scuppers, playing at pully-hauly in the passages, or making the beast with two backs in the shadowy corners of the ship. All of this was for the love of it, or if a man saw a wench he especially desired the merest trifle would procure her for him, while for a whale's tooth, which was considered a treasure of the highest value among these people, he might have the favors of the best among them and she would boast of her bargain afterward. One thing may be said for such a state of affairs: our men formed few permanent attachments among the island women. I noticed that Ben was not backward.

We were six weeks lying at Nukuhiva, during which time we careened all six of our ships, caulked, scraped, painted, and refloated them. In addition we rigged and refitted throughout; made and filled new water casks and built a fort out of our old casks filled with earth; put down a store of fresh salt pork and loaded a supply of native fruits and vegetables—taro, coconuts, breadfruit, plantains, and bananas; claimed the islands in the name of the United States; fought two wars with neighboring tribes—the Happahs and the Typees—for the benefit of those who were our friends, as well as for our own; and at the same time in this tropical paradise we feasted and sang, swam and danced with and made love to the loveliest golden savages in the world. Even after we began to have reason to suspect them to be cannibals we were reluctant to leave!

In November the *New Zealander* was dispatched for the

States with a shipload of prisoners, the captain having discovered a plot among them to poison their guards on board the *Essex Junior* and make off with that vessel. However, scarcely a wistful eye followed her. Men so long deprived of the company of women were in no hurry to give up the charms of such as these!

Long before this we had fought our first battle on the island. A neighboring tribe, the Happahs, had been at war with our friends, the Taeehs, at the time of our arrival, and although the island wars consist of hurling stones and spears in the thickets and cracking one another's skulls with carved and polished war clubs, so that the casualties were few, yet our friends begged us to take a hand in it and help bring their enemies into subjection. This put us in an awkward position, for while we had nothing against the Happahs, if we wished to maintain the good will of our friends, the Taeehs—not to mention enjoy their favors and continue to receive provisions —we must accede. And so we did, sending off a six-pounder and a small party into the mountains, where the crash of the muskets and the boom of the cannon soon brought the Happahs to their senses and they sued for peace.

This led to a treaty with all the tribes of the island, save four or five, most of which were at too great a distance to be reached but one of which, the Typees, held back from sheer stubbornness. A part of our treaty was that each tribe should furnish us with certain supplies, and this the Typees refused to do. They had managed well, they said, without ever having had a treaty with us before, and they presumed that they would continue to do so in the future. If this was not the case, they dared us to come and prove it to them, calling us white lizards who could not climb the mountains, and declaring that we were not worth their notice.

Now, we hardly cared what their opinion of us might be, but their defiance had a disturbing effect upon the other tribes. Our flow of supplies began to dwindle, and it soon became evident that unless we took up the challenge of the Typees, our position would be no longer tenable.

Accordingly, an expedition was fitted out and sent against them. But this time we found ourselves brought up against a different sort from the timorous Happahs, and our first landing was all but repulsed with a shower of stones and spears. Downes was brought down with a broken leg, and several others suffered greater or lesser injuries. Our men were forced to withdraw and await another day, and the effect of the defeat upon the other tribes was evident. It was plain that what we had started we must finish, else we would confirm, in their simple minds, the taunts of the Typees and they would abandon us. A second attempt to raid the valley over the ridge of mountains was foiled by a deluge of rain, which damaged much of our company's powder. But at last a third and final invasion overland was accomplished, and in a day's hard fighting throughout the length of the Typees valley most of their villages were laid to waste and their warriors routed. After that the Typees sued for peace and agreed to the customary exchange of meat and fruit and water for whales' teeth and iron hoops. But the four-day war brought me and my mates more work than we liked to contemplate.

It was now drawing nigh time for us to be on our way again, and after fumigating the *Essex*—thereby murdering some fifteen hundred innocent rats and an infinite quantity of cockroaches—she was once again floated and made ready for sea. This done, a division of the men was made. Mr. Gamble, of the marines, was to remain at Nukuhiva with the *Greenwich,* the *Seringapatam,* and the *Hammond,* and Midshipmen Feltus and Clapp and enough men to man the fort or all three ships as need might be. They were to wait there for further orders, or until our return, should we find the way to the southeast too stoutly barred by enemy men-of-war. If we did not return within a specified time, Gamble was to take such vessels as he might, destroying the others, and make his best way home.

This preparation filled the air with a sense of impending events, and it was easy to see that some of our shipmates viewed the approach of the day of departure without much enthusiasm. For this no one could much blame them. It is not often that a sailor finds a landfall where life is so easy and restraints so few; where the sun shines warm all day and the moon and stars are bright by night; where food is plenty and the women are playful and warm and willing and wear by habit no more clothes than their mother Eve in the Garden before she tasted the apple! Grumbling and dark looks were to be expected, even allowed; for, as the captain said, how else were they to work off their disappointment? But threats of mutiny, and hints that certain men would refuse to work when the time came, were not to be tolerated. Consequently it came as no surprise to some of us when one morning, early in December, the captain had all hands mustered in the waist.

"Now, lads," he said bluntly, "this is a ship of war, and you all know what that means. It means we're at sea for a purpose: to wage war upon our country's enemies. You know, too, what chance we have of carrying out that purpose if every man Jack doesn't jump to obey orders when they are given!"

He glared at them for an instant, and they stood in tense, embarrassed silence waiting what he might say next.

"I have heard some rumors," he continued finally, "to the effect that some of you intend to refuse duty when it comes time to sail. Now—I'll agree with you that this is a pleasant place and these are fine people. But this isn't our country, and these folk are not our folk. Staying here's well and good for a time. But if the rest of you are like me, or like the men I think you are, you'll be wanting to get home one of these days, and that's a thing we'll never do unless we stand together and work ship like men."

He paused again, and I thought one or two of the men shifted uncomfortably, but as far as I could see, Ben was unmoved. He stood leaning against the bulwark with a little sneering smile on his lips, as if this were all an old story that he had heard often before. He had no comment to make, but I knew he had as much attraction ashore as any of them. I almost hoped that he might make up his mind to stay behind.

He was not to be given the choice, however.

"Now then!" roared the captain suddenly, picking up his cutlass and standing with feet widespread. "Every man who favors weighing when I give the order, and who will submit to my command, lay to starboard! Those of you who have any doubts line the larboard rail!"

As one man the entire crew leaped, even Ben, for all his complacency, and moved to starboard.

"White!" the captain barked. "Robert White! Stand forward!"

A seaman stepped out and stood twisting his hat nervously in his hands. I recognized one of the men we had taken in the *Montezuma* and recalled that I had no very high opinion of him. He claimed to be a native of Rhode Island.

"White, did you say yesterday, on board the *Essex Junior,* that some of the men of this ship would mutiny when called to weigh anchor?"

"Nooo sir!" White replied, swallowing convulsively.

"You lie!" Porter roared. Then, pointing his cutlass at first one and then another and calling them by name, he summoned them to witness the accusation. "Harker! Stryker! Collins! O'Connell! Did you hear this man say that the men would mutiny?"

"Aye, sir! Yes, sir! I did, sir! And that ain't all, sir!" came their various replies.

Porter turned and lunged toward the terrified White.

"Run, you scoundrel!" he shouted, and the frightened man had no choice but to obey. He turned about and fled for the larboard rail, plunging over it, head foremost, and landing with a splash in the water below, where he was picked up by a native canoe and carried ashore. We never saw him again.

Porter turned again to face the crew.

"I'd have cut his heart out if I could have caught him," he declared, although it had been clear enough that he had made no very great effort to seize him. "Now then, the rest of you! You're all good men, and I'm proud of you! Proud of everything you've done, and I'll not have you lose your senses. At the first sign that you have done so, I will not hesitate to touch off this ship's magazines and blow us all to hell together. Do you understand me? That's all! Secure! Bos'n, pipe all hands to weigh anchor!"

The pipes shrilled. The drum rolled. The men jumped; some aloft, others to man the capstan or take their various stations on deck. To the clanking of the cable the anchors heaved up and the ship's head payed round. The white sails cascaded down and shook out and bellied in the wind. Out of the corner of my eye I saw that the *Essex Junior* was following our example, while from the beach, not far away, rose a wailing chorus from the crowds of women who had somehow known that this day we would leave them and had come down to the waterside to make an effort to hold us. In pathetic pantomime they pretended to cut their throats with shells or waded out waist deep into the water and held out their arms to us, all the while weeping and keening as if in deep misery.

Slowly at first, and then with gathering speed, we swept past them and stood out through the break in the reefs. By midday the island was only a misty-blue shape hanging hull down upon the horizon behind us. By dusk it was gone and we were two ships alone on the sea, dipping and plunging, lifting and rolling slowly as we thrust forward through the long swells. The wailing and the sobbing of the women and the crying of the sea birds were left far astern; and the only sounds that now remained to break the silence were the gentle, almost tired creaking of the timbers as the ship swayed, the steady hum of the wind in the rigging, and the soft hiss and swish of the seas overside as we knifed through them, running down our course, southeastward, for Valparaiso and the Horn and home.

7

We spent Christmas at sea again that year, for it was six weeks before we raised, once more, the high, tawny desert coast of Chile and saw piled against the sky above it, like a ragged, threatening cloud bank, the snowy spine of towering mountains that pins this land against the sea. A day or two later we crept through the wispy mist of a golden-shadowed dawn to cast anchor once again in the broad, bright-blue roadstead of that little green pocket in the yellow hills which the folk who live there call the Vale of Paradise.

Outwardly, we found Valparaiso little changed. There was the same long, single street curving about the bay, hugging the line of the cliffs, from the Port around to the Almendral, the suburban residential section which takes its name from the almond groves which flourish there. To all appearances the people were as friendly and hospitable as ever, but there had been changes in the politics of the country of which we could not be aware. The Republic still existed, but it was fighting for its life; Spanish troops, sent by the viceroy of Peru, had landed to the southward, and the struggle was, by all accounts, a hot one. Valparaiso, being a seaport and especially vulnerable, tended to caution. It was not that the Republican spirit was dead, but rather that some inhabitants in high places felt caution the better part of friendship and were less inclined to choose sides in our quarrel than they had been. Indeed, when it came to a final test, we were to discover, their sympathies were all for that side which seemed stronger!

As I say, however, this was not immediately apparent. We were greeted with the same courtesy that we had before enjoyed, and not forgetting the precipitate way in which our reception had been postponed, Captain Porter promptly announced his determination to make amends to our previously disappointed guests. Invitations to a reception on board the *Essex* were issued and accepted with eagerness, for it was not every day that a foreign man-of-war entertained here.

On board refreshments were prepared and the punch bowl filled. The ship was dressed in all her flags and lanterns. The awnings were stretched and the brightwork polished till it glistened like the sun at noon. On the appointed evening the officers broke out their full dress and received their company at the gangway, while half the crew enjoyed liberty ashore and the *Essex Junior* came in to the harbor and anchored in order that her people, too, might enjoy the festivities.

The affair was an unqualified success. Little more need be said of it than that. The ladies were lovely and coquettish and duly dazzled with the splendor of our uniforms and our arrangements. The gentlemen—those from shore, that is to say—were handsome and gratifyingly jealous and in consolation did full honor to the punch. The ladies were impressed with the luxury and spaciousness of our quarters, the gentlemen with the size and evident power of the ship. The ladies danced and flirted, and the men danced and sulked, like so many children. At midnight Mr. Downes went unobtrusively back to the *Essex Junior* in order to be prepared to take her out on patrol in the morning. The rest of us danced the night through and only took our guests ashore again in the dark hour that comes before the break of dawn. But the blackness had been dissipated by the time we turned about and put back for the ship. The misty shores were turning gray with approaching light and the purple shadows were racing fast and faster up the gulchlike canyons that cut down through the flanking cliffs toward the sea. At the harbor's mouth the *Essex Junior,* her anchors up and her courses set, was standing out to sea, and over beyond her the jolly boat from a British merchantman lying snug in the protective neutrality of the port was also pulling out toward the open ocean. On the *Essex's* deck the crew on watch were undressing ship. Flags were coming down slowly, awnings being furled.

As we approached the *Essex* we watched the Englishman's jolly boat with sleepy curiosity. The tiny craft danced dangerously upon the waves that rolled up from beyond the point, and there was some speculation in our boat as to what might take it out in such a direction at such an hour. Most of us were only interested in getting to our beds and paid little attention to it. But a lively discussion of it sprang up between Mr. McKnight and Mr. Farragut, who seemed to disagree.

"Some of her officers are going fishing," was McKnight's theory.

"Balderdash!" Farragut snorted. "At this hour? Not they!"

"Why not?" McKnight wanted to know.

"Because," Farragut retorted, "they're too lazy, for one thing. For another, they've seen something beyond the point."

"A couple of British frigates, I suppose?" McKnight scoffed.

"I don't know," the youngster said seriously. "But I'll wager I'm right! Look at the ship they came from. They've a lookout at the masthead, and what's that for in harbor?"

McKnight looked.

"By God!" he cried. "You're right! You've keen eyes!"

"There goes a string of signals!" someone else exclaimed.

We all turned to look. There was no question about it. Something had excited the Englishman.

"Can you read 'em?" Farragut demanded.

"Not I, lad!" McKnight replied. "They're code of some sort."

"Then that shows——" cried Farragut.

"Look there! Look at the *Junior!*" someone else broke in.

All eyes swung around to see a new string of signal flags blossom and snap at our consort's halliards.

"Hold hard!" cried McKnight. "What's he say? 'Two enemy'—what's that next?—'frigates'—I'm damned!"

He gave young Farragut a stare of amazement.

"Standing in!" that youngster added. "Look alive there, men! There's no time to waste if that's true! Smartly now! Extra grog to the first boat's crew aboard!"

The rest of us laughed at that, for the boy overstepped his authority in making such a promise. Nevertheless the men bent to their oars and we fairly sang over the water.

As we swept in toward the ship the last of the dress flags came down in a run and a responding set of signals bloomed at our own halliards. At the same time the recall gun boomed, summoning aboard all hands ashore. As we came alongside we scrambled for the ladder and swarmed up it, while the boats we had just left, in answer to the orders of the officer of the deck, spun about and put back to pick up the shore parties.

As we reached the quarter-deck the captain appeared with a glint in his eye and a word for Mr. Wilmer, who had the deck.

"Is the gig ready?"

"Yes sir!"

"Very well!" Porter snapped. "I shall be back in a few moments, as soon as I've had a look from the *Junior*. Meantime, get this mess cleaned up and strip for action!"

"But—but it's a neutral port, sir! Surely they wouldn't——" Wilmer managed to gasp.

"Don't question my orders, sir!" the captain bellowed.

"No sir!" Wilmer gulped.

"Then see to them!" Porter snapped.

"Aye, aye, sir!" said Wilmer smartly.

The captain turned and went through the gangway, but as he put foot upon the top rung he looked back somewhat more kindly.

"Have you forgotten the *Chesapeake* and the *Leopard*, Mr. Wilmer?" he asked.

"No sir!" Wilmer replied.

Porter only nodded meaningly and passed on down to the waiting gig. In another moment his men were pulling him out across the water, now choppy with the dawn breeze, toward where the *Essex Junior* lay with backed mainsail, waiting.

A moment later the men from ashore began to swarm aboard, not a few of them slightly the worse for liquor, not a few of them showing signs of hasty dressing, but all of them ready and spoiling for a fight. As swiftly as they came they were directed at the double to this or that task, and almost as if they melted with the coming day the final remnants of the night's confusion disappeared. By the time the *Essex Junior* had made a quick turn outside the harbor and put back again, to anchor a short distance off our starboard quarter, the decks were cleared. By the time Captain Porter returned aboard, the guns stood loaded and manned and ready to be run out. His eye, as he came over the side, ran over the scene with quick approval.

"Very good, Mr. Wilmer! Have the guns run out and the ammunition placed ready, then turn all hands to for breakfast."

"Aye, aye, sir!" Wilmer replied, beaming at the praise.

"And have an extra tot of grog served out."

He turned and plunged down the hatchway. A few moments later, when we were at breakfast in the wardroom, he reappeared amongst us, an unusual proceeding, and told us what he had discovered.

"They're two British men-of-war," he said. "Doubtless the *Phoebe* is one, and the other may be the *Raccoon* or the *Cherub*, though my first guess is she's another frigate. They're yet too far off to say. But they're bearing up. Evidently they know we're here, and unless I miss my guess yonder lime-juicer has informed 'em that we'll be unprepared after last night's doings! If you gentlemen can keep your eyes open long enough, I daresay we'll give 'em a surprise!"

"Will we fight, sir, here?" McKnight asked.

Porter gazed at him blandly.

"We'll fight wherever we're attacked, Mr. McKnight," he replied. "If they seek it they'll get it. But we'll not be first to violate the neutrality of the port."

He nodded briefly and turned on his heel.

"Finish your breakfasts, gentlemen," he said.

When we went on deck a few moments later we found him braced in the gangway watching through his glass the approach of two tall ships, impressive under a towering cloud of snowy canvas.

"One's a frigate," he called over his shoulder. "Tother's a sloop. They make no secret of their nationality."

He watched them a long moment in silence, while the rest of us maintained the respectful distance required by custom.

"See how they come!" he exclaimed presently with a chuckle. "And every man aboard at quarters, I'll warrant!"

He lowered his glass and turned about, running his eye once more along the deck.

"Damn these carronades!" he muttered. "If they'd allowed me long guns, as I asked, I'd be out to meet 'em both now!"

He turned to Wilmer.

"Have the kedge anchors ready to run up to the yardarms," he ordered.

"They're ready, Captain," Wilmer replied.

"Good!" Porter nodded. "Very well! Send the men to quarters. They'll be up with us in a few moments!"

"Aye, aye, sir!" Wilmer responded, and instantly the drums began to roll and the decks trembled and thundered to the tread of running men, racing to take their stations. I waited, until the first rush had passed, since my own station was not immediately urgent. Then I passed below to the grim black hole of the cockpit, where with my mates I sat and waited.

From this point I can report only the few small snatches of what I heard passing on the decks above me and what I was told later, for in the gloom of my battle station in the belly of the ship I could see nothing of what went on.

I have often wondered if it is more difficult to stand at an open gun port and watch an enemy bear down upon you than it is to sit surrounded by darkness and wonder how near he may be. I can understand readily how it might be to see the moment drawing toward you when the guns will open their throats to hurl a storm of sleeting shot upon you. Yet I wonder if it is not almost worse to sit in the creaking half gloom, waiting, waiting for that sudden rending crash which, be it never so expected, never fails to make you start in fright and shock, and which tells you that at last the battle has begun.

It was so as I sat now, upon the lowest round of the cockpit ladder, and waited. Around me, some squatting on the floor, some leaning on the long table, some drawing back in the deepest gloom, so that we might not see their nervousness and showing little more than the whites of their eyes in the darkness, some standing directly under the swinging lanterns, as if defying us to find their fear—for every man who goes to battle has it!—stood and sprawled and sat my assistants, the mates and the loblolly boys. There was no conversation, for I was a stickler upon that point of the regulations, as had been Dr. Orr. So far as the cockpit went, it was not so much a matter of having a rule to obey and insisting upon it, as demanding the utmost silence in order to catch the slightest sound of what might be taking place on deck.

At the moment there was not the slightest murmur from above. Only the slight creak of the ship as she swung to her mooring and the occasional squeak and scurry of a rat in the bilge below emphasized a silence so absolute as to be foreboding. Even the breathing of my comrades was muffled. Seconds dragged by like minutes. Minutes became hours.

"In God's name," whispered Hoffman abruptly, desperately, "what are they doing up there?"

"Quiet!" I growled. It seemed to me that I had heard a faint hail, a murmur of voices, somewhere far above. Then all at once came the captain's voice, angry, belligerent, truculent, carrying down through three decks even to the cockpit.

"What the devil d'ye mean to do, sir? Foul me?"

More murmurs from above. That would be the British captain replying. Then abruptly again that voice that drove through layers of stout New England oak!

"I don't care a damn, sir, for your intentions! You have no business where you are! If a stick of yours brushes a rope yarn of this ship I shall board you instantly!" And then, louder still: "Stand by, boarders! Keep fast the starboard battery! Mr. Downes, there! Let me see your boarders on deck!"

After that a silence even more intense settled over the ship that seemed to last for hours. Only once was it broken when a jeering voice, somewhere over our heads, cried:

"Laugh, will yer? I'll bloody soon teach——"

This was cut off by a smack, as of fist on flesh, and a thud. Then silence once again, while we below in the darkness sat grinding our fingernails into the wood beneath us and waiting for the cry of "Boarders away!" that all we had heard thus far had led us to anticipate.

Instead, at the long end, came the pipe down, the bos'n's signal to secure all hands and resume the day's routine.

I went on deck torn between relief and disappointment; relief that nothing had happened, and disappointment that what I felt must come had merely been postponed. The British were here. We were face to face with them at last, and sooner or later we must meet them. To delay could only put off the evil day.

At the same time I was filled with curiosity as to just what had occurred. In the wardroom I was not long finding out.

The *Phoebe,* for it was she, with the *Cherub* close at her heels, had swept into the harbor, evidently expecting to find us fair prey and easy game. There could be no doubt that her captain, Hillyar—whose family Porter had once transported from Malta to Gibraltar in the *Enterprise* as a gesture of courtesy— had looked to find us in confusion after the night's festivities.

However she came by her information, there was little question of her intent. Straight down upon us she bore, with her gun ports up and her guns run out, and all her crew at quarters, doubling our quarter, where she ran up between us and the *Junior* and, putting down her helm, luffed so as to fall aboard us.

Up to this point no word or signal had passed between the two ships. But now Captain Hillyar leaped upon his rail.

"Captain Hillyar's compliments to Captain Porter," he hailed, "and hopes he is well!"

The ships were no more than fifteen feet apart, I was told, and it must have been suddenly obvious to Captain Hillyar that he had not the unprepared vessel to deal with that he had anticipated, for those who were on deck say that he suddenly looked very much like a small boy caught stealing apples.

Captain Porter returned his compliments dryly and followed this up with the furious demand which we had first heard below. Hillyar suddenly found himself in an even worse position than he had believed possible, for he was hung in irons with his jib boom across the *Essex's* forecastle, so that without being able to bring a gun to bear he might be raked from end to end by both the *Essex's* and the *Junior's* broadsides. He made haste to protest his good intentions, which had fetched from Porter the next remarks we had heard, together with the visual signal, unseen of course by us in the cockpit, to hoist away grapnels to the yardarms.

For an instant, so my shipmates told me, it was difficult to see how Hillyar could extricate himself, and, if truth be told, there was little hope aboard the *Essex* that he would. There was no question that had we taken that moment to attack, the *Phoebe* would have been ours, for her decks would have been a shambles in a flash of gunfire. Indeed, one youngster on the gun deck, still feeling the effects of the vino he had consumed the night before, and thinking that he could see a British gunner leering at him through the ports of the *Phoebe,* not thirty feet from his own face, had cursed and reached his match for the touchhole of his piece. But Mr. McKnight had knocked him down. This accounted for the scuffle we had heard.

In due time, after a display of seamanship which even our people were forced to admire, the *Phoebe* drew clear of the *Essex* without touching so much as a hair and crossed the harbor, to anchor where the *Essex* lay within range of her long eighteens but beyond the reach of our cursed carronades. At the same time the *Cherub* came to anchor within pistol shot of our quarter, whereupon Porter gave orders to the *Junior* to moor so as to fetch the *Cherub* between our fires—a move which seemed to give Captain Tucker, of the *Cherub,* great offense.

So ended the first brush. In our wardroom, opinion was about evenly divided as to whether Porter had played his cards wisely. One side maintained that we had enjoyed the hospitality of the port and had no alternative. Since Hillyar had not chosen to make the first hostile move, they maintained, Captain Porter was correct in withholding his fire. To have attacked under the circumstances would have been to have taken an unfair advantage. On the other side, it was held that war is war and the enemy's intentions were obvious. That he had found us better prepared than he had expected was his misfortune. Had we attacked when we had the opportunity, we might have saved ourselves much. To the devil with sportsmanship and the rules of neutrality! Had Hillyar been prepared to observe either?

Although I recognized the elevated plane of the former argument, I must confess I was in agreement with the latter. If men must kill one another, I wondered, why should they be squeamish about the means of it?

The three weeks that followed, while the *Essex* and the *Phoebe* and their consorts lay gun to gun, were almost ludicrous for bowing and scraping and hostile gentility for the sake of our hosts. The governor gave a reception to which the officers of both forces were invited. At this it was my privilege to over-hear the conversation between Captain Hillyar and Captain Porter, since neither was at pains to keep it private.

" 'Tis a pleasure to find you, Captain," Hillyar greeted. "It's been a long cruise! Do you mind the time we met at Syracuse?"

"Yes, yes," Porter replied, "but we were at peace then. Do you mean to respect the neutrality of this port? Or must I keep my men constantly at quarters?"

It seemed to me that Captain Hillyar showed a great deal of restraint.

"Why, Captain," he replied, "you have paid so much honor to it already that I feel in honor bound to do so myself!"

"Good!" exclaimed Porter, not one whit loath to insult as he felt himself insulted. "Then I may give my men shore leave. Since mine is the lighter ship my government would not approve my sending you a challenge. However, if I were to re-ceive a challenge from you, I could not, in honor, refuse. Of course the *Cherub* and the *Junior* would stay at anchor, and we would make it a contest between our own ships. Eh, Captain Hillyar?"

The Englishman was noncommittal.

"Well," he said, "we'll see! We'll see!"

Whereupon they bowed to one another with all the formality of the representatives of nations at peace.

Both officers and men took their cues from their command-ers, and for a time such peace and harmony reigned between them as never was seen! But this could not long exist in the face of natural hostility. Presently the *Phoebe* hoisted a flag bearing the motto: GOD AND COUNTRY, BRITISH SAILORS' BEST RIGHTS, TRAITORS OFFEND BOTH!

At first this was ignored, Captain Porter feeling that he had already offered his challenge. But when it reappeared for the second day, the captain called the sailmakers and the painters aft and instructed them to prepare an answering signal, to read: GOD OUR COUNTRY AND LIBERTY, TYRANTS OFFEND THEM!

"We'll keep our best for the day we meet them!" he re-marked.

Astonishingly enough, when this was run up to the masthead

of the *Essex,* the *Phœbe* responded with three cheers, and, naturally, these were returned by the *Essex,* which was not to be outdone in any courtesy or quarrel. Thereafter, however, a coolness developed, which gradually grew more and more bitter, until the men were breaking bottles over one another's heads and brawling in the streets whenever they met ashore, while the officers were approaching the point of exchanging challenges as they already had insults.

Twenty days, exactly, passed before the next move of definite hostility. In the meantime wags between decks took advantage of the still nights of these latitudes to sing taunts at one another in that peculiarly insulting fashion which only the foredeck imagination can produce. A lively correspondence passed between the two captains on the subject of the treatment of prisoners and their disposal; Captain Porter offering to send what remained of ours in a cartel to England, to be exchanged for an equal number of Americans. But this was refused by Captain Hillyar, who countered with the proposal that the prisoners in question be released where they were, on parole. Though this was finally acceded to, some of the innuendoes expressed in Hillyar's letters led to considerable resentment on Porter's part, and no doubt he responded in kind.

But all of this was mere preparation. After taking on supplies, the *Phœbe* and the *Cherub* stood out to sea, to cruise off the port, blockading the *Essex* there. In this they were successful to the degree we did not seek to escape. For one thing, Captain Porter was reluctant to run without first crossing swords with the *Phœbe;* for another, he had no intention of abandoning the *Essex Junior,* and until the wind held right there was no chance to get to sea together.

During the next weeks, then, we continued to lie in the harbor, one or the other of us every now and again making a short dash out to make sure that no further reinforcements had yet arrived to support the enemy. On one of these sorties the *Essex Junior* almost succeeded in capturing a storeship carrying supplies to our blockaders, and in turn was nearly cut off herself by the approach of both the *Phœbe* and the *Cherub.* Fortunately for Mr. Downes, however, the wind fell calm and he was able to tow the *Junior* to safety with his own boats and the help of several from the *Essex.* On another occasion the

Essex towed the *Hector*—which had been lying in port since September, awaiting disposal as a prize—to sea and burned her under Hillyar's very nose. A few days after this we were thrown into great excitement when the *Phoebe,* after sending the *Cherub* off to the southwestward, stood down toward the harbor and hove up just outside, firing a single gun to leeward.

Perhaps I should explain that this is known the seas over as a challenge to come out and fight. Since Captain Porter had already indicated that he was ready to match the *Essex* with the *Phoebe* alone at any time, he took this for the Englishman's meaning, and instantly the *Essex* slipped her cables and stood out of the harbor, while the people of Valparaiso, who had been awaiting this occasion as eagerly as if it were a high-grade bullfight, flocked to the hills to watch. Imagine our astonishment, then, when the *Phoebe* turned about and took to her heels and scurried down to join her consort. Two shots were thrown ahead of her, but she paid not the slightest heed to these. Obviously Hillyar had no intention of meeting the *Essex* without the support of the *Cherub,* and since the *Essex Junior* was so lightly armed as to be virtually useless in an engagement of this sort, Captain Porter did not feel justified in attempting to meet both the *Phoebe* and the *Cherub* alone.

Porter was beside himself with exasperation and contempt. He stormed down into the wardroom, as we drove back into the harbor, and glared about at all of us.

"The man's a coward and a poltroon!" he fumed. "I've offered him every opportunity to prove otherwise, but he leaves me no choice!"

He found none among us to defend Hillyar, and so stumped away to the great cabin to sulk in silence. Later, on shore, he was not less vehement, and this, coming to Hillyar's ears, led to a further coolness between them.

So we returned and lay for the better part of yet another month, sneering at one another—I cannot help but say it— like boys who put chips upon their shoulders and dare one another to knock them off. Toward the end of March, however, we heard that the British frigate *Tagus* and the sloop *Raccoon* were daily expected to reinforce the *Phoebe* and the *Cherub.*

This put us in desperate straits indeed, for none of us doubted that with such strength at their command the frigates would hesitate to lay us alongside, even in the harbor; and it was equally apparent that once these ships arrived all chance of single combat would be gone. Not only was that true, but even if the neutrality of the port were respected we would be so tightly blockaded that it would be impossible for us to move. Accordingly, at a council of officers in the great cabin, Captain Porter told us his plans.

"We cannot stay," he said glumly, "nor can we fight, since that cowardly dog refuses to meet us! So we must run."

Even to say it was gall to his soul.

"At first opportunity," he went on, "when the wind favors, the *Essex* will put to sea. I'll take most of your crew, Downes, but I'll leave you enough to work ship. I will endeavor to draw off both the *Phoebe* and the *Cherub* in chase. Give me a fair wind, I can outrun them both. Maybe, since the *Cherub's* a dull sailer, I can draw the *Phoebe* far enough ahead to be able to turn and engage her, who knows."

He smiled at us, evidently cheered by the thought.

"In any event, Downes," he went on, "as soon as I have drawn them clear, make your escape. We will plan to meet at Nukuhiva and, if Gamble is still there, fetch him off—perhaps strike for home by way of the Indian Ocean, leaving our hornets buzzing about the Pacific in search of us!"

"That's a long way home, sir," McKnight ventured.

Porter turned on him.

"That's true, Mr. McKnight," he said, "but will you tell me, with the British pouring frigates around the Horn in search of us, how much chance have we of getting home that way?"

We all saw his point and laughed.

The captain beamed.

"We'll not likely be sought off Cape Town," he explained, "and it may be we'll have opportunity to do more damage to them!"

So it was left, and each of us was cautioned to secrecy. Yet as an instance of the way in which word passes aboard ship, I have this to tell: less than an hour after the meeting I chanced to meet Ben in the passage forward of the steerage. He looked at me with that taunting grin of his.

"I hear we're taking the old lady to sea again," he said, "to go home the long way round."

"Who told you that?" I countered sharply.

"Oh," he shrugged, " 'tis all about ship. For me, I'm as well pleased. But I'm sorry we'll not have a go at that limey coal barge yonder. I warrant the old girl'd show her a stout fight, if we did!"

"Your old girl," I could not resist taunting him, "will be lucky to come free of this, let alone show fight!"

"You think so, do you?" He bristled. "Let me tell you the *Essex* can show her heels to anything in these waters if she's a mind to. Or if it comes to that, she'll stand up to the best they have to offer in a fair fight!"

"I shan't argue with that," I retorted, and went on my way.

The next day came up with a fresh wind blowing, and there was no question but that if ever we were to make a run for it, it should be now. Yet there was much to be done before we could sail. Last-minute supplies for the long voyage must be taken on board: meat and fresh vegetables, spirits and water. These had been supposed to be ready to be brought off the night before, but daybreak found them not yet all at the landing, and the morning dragged away as they were being brought down and fetched out. In the meantime we improved the hour by making last-minute repairs to our weathered rigging and spars, for once we were at sea we must put our trust in them, and they must not fail us. As the morning wore on, the wind increased to gale force, and the enemy, observing signs of unusual activity, worked in against the western side of the bay, so as to be in a position to intercept us if we ran. Captain Porter grinned.

"He looks for us to run northwest," he remarked dryly. "He's due for a surprise."

By early afternoon all was ready and the ship was laboring at her moorings under the lash of the gale. Mr. Wilmer reported the fact to the captain. All who could with propriety be there were upon the quarter-deck and heard the report and the captain's answer. Under our waiting glance he looked off to sea and then turned to stare at the two British ships, standing across the harbor mouth, a little distance beyond the Point of Angels.

"We'll wait, Mr. Wilmer," he said, "a little longer, until they get further down and give us more room to windward.

We'll take the weather gauge of 'em yet. Pipe all hands to stand by!"

"Aye, aye, sir!" said Wilmer. But the words were scarcely out of his mouth and the order given, when the ship gave an unusually severe plunge at her moorings, staggered an instant, and then seemed to lurch back upon her stern. From forward came the sound of a report, almost as loud as a gunshot, and a splintering crash.

Most of us were too startled for an instant even to wonder what had happened. But the captain remained calm.

"That does it!" he exclaimed.

By the time he had said it even I could see what he meant. The larboard cable had parted, and the single anchor to starboard was not enough to hold us. Already we were beginning to drag on shore. Porter turned back to Wilmer.

"Mr. Wilmer," he said, "I think we shall not wait, after all. Heave up the starboard anchor and get the men aloft to make sail. Keep her under close-reefed tops'ls and t'gall'nts and bear across for the point! We can still run to windward of 'em if we try!"

"Aye, aye, sir!" Wilmer replied. The drums began to rumble and the capstan pawls to clank. Men scrambled into the rigging, and the white bellies of the sails bulged suddenly in the wind. The ship quivered like a live thing as the sails caught and drove her and she split a long green comber with her bows, sending a fountain of spray squirting along the weather rail, to fall with a drenching crash upon the deck and the men below. In the next instant she was heeled over and flying like a frightened deer, straight across the bay toward the Point of Angels, and the *Phoebe* and the *Cherub* were scrambling to come about to intercept us.

But they were too late. They were still far out of gun range as we breasted the Point. Out beyond it we could see the great seas running, and it was plain that we must take care. Yet once we had reached them and cleared the land, the ocean would be ours and our enemies left behind. It would be a long chase after that, but we would have the advantage of them by having passed them to windward. At this moment, when tension was highest as we clawed our way about the Point, Porter's eye fell upon me.

"Better go below, Tom!" he called with a grim smile. " 'Twill be wet here in a moment or two."

I had no mind to miss any part of the race.

"If you please——" I began.

But he had already turned away.

"In the t'gall'nts! Brace up!"

The waisters hauled in unison and the yardmen clung to their perches. A great sea lifted our bows, and the masts whipped like straws in the wind. We cleared the Point and were square in the gale. Green seas scudded across our decks and ran foaming out the scuppers. For an instant it seemed as if we were free and clear, and then it happened: a white squall struck us, with all the sudden fury of an explosion. The ship cringed and lay over on its beam ends, rolling gunwale under. A great sea washed at me, and I saved myself by catching at a stay and clinging for dear life. In the thunder of the gale I could hear voices shouting.

"Let go the halliards by the run! Let go, I say! Damn you! Let go!" And then a different voice crying: "Great God! 'Tis jammed!"

This was followed—all in the same instant, so it seemed to me, struggling to maintain my foothold on the deck—by a tremendous rending crash, a snapping and tearing sound, and a whole chorus of shouts and screams, no one of which alone would have made sense to me in that moment. A loose rope end slapped me wetly across the face and then dragged away, and something hard and heavy seemed to strike the rail not far from where I stood. There came a last, long, gurgling scream, and then abrupt, comparative silence, as the ship seemed to right herself of her own accord.

"That does it! That does it!" I heard someone shout. "She's lost her maintop! She'll never make it now!"

I looked up, as best I could for the water in my eyes, and saw that it was true. A little more than halfway up the mainmast the tapering stick, once so tall and straight, now ended in a jagged, splintered stump that trailed a mess of tangled rope and spar and canvas down across the mainyard and over the side to the sea, not a dozen feet from where I clung. As I stared at it it came to me, in a hazy sort of way, that it was odd that there were no men clinging to it. There had been men there before—before it had crashed. Where were they now? As if in answer, a great sea hissed alongside, close at my feet, and I remembered that last wailing scream I had heard and shuddered.

Behind me, by the weather rail, Porter was giving orders again.

"Pay her away, there! Fetch her head down for the harbor. We'll have to try to beat back to the anchorage! Mr. Wilmer! Get some men aloft there and clear away that wreckage. Doctor! I thought I told you to get below?"

I started. He seemed to have time to see everything.

"Aye, aye, sir," I mumbled. "I was just starting when we caught it."

He nodded but said no more, and I found my feet and made my way to the hatch. As I went I heard him speak to Wilmer, quite conversationally.

"Here they come," he said. "They don't mean to let us escape this time if they can help it!"

I took the time to throw a swift glance in the direction of the enemy and saw them standing for us under all the sail it was safe to carry. It was almost possible to make out their jubilation in the way they sailed.

"If we can get back to the anchorage they won't dare attack, sir," I heard Wilmer say.

"I wouldn't be too sure of that," Porter replied.

I heard no more, for I went below then and got into other clothes. If we were going to be called upon to work, I preferred to be dry. The ship was still laboring heavily, kicking her stern high to the onrushing gale, as we fought for the harbor, and I made slow work of it, for I had to hold on with one hand while I dressed with the other. By the time I had my wet clothes off, however, and my dry breeches on, we were come into smoother water, and though we still rolled and pitched, yet I was able to stand on my own feet without bracing myself and to use both hands freely. By the time I was fully dressed and ready once more, I heard the anchor cable thunder out and felt the ship's head come round to a steadier position. By this I judged that we had come back to our old anchorage in the harbor and that it was now probably safe enough to go on deck once more. Accordingly, I scrambled up the ladder again and pushed through the hatchway. To my surprise, we were not at our former anchorage. In fact, we were nowhere near it, but had come to anchor in a small cove, about a pistol shot from shore, about three quarters of a mile to leeward of one of the shore batteries on the eastern side of the harbor and at least three miles outside our former position. Apparently we had not been able to beat back to our old place in our damaged state. Yet we were still within neutral waters and, indeed, still within the limits of the bay. Under the guns of the battery, I was fatuous enough to believe we would be safe from molestation, at least until we could complete repairs and get to sea again.

Some of this must have shown in my face as I came on deck, for Porter's eye was sardonic as it caught mine.

"Well, Tom," he said, "I hope you're ready for a day's work. You'll have enough if I'm not mistaken."

I blinked at him.

"But——"

"Humph!" he snorted. "You don't think they'll attack here either, eh?"

I could find no answer, but I must have looked my doubt, for he pointed out to sea and to windward.

"Look there!" he said.

I looked. The *Phoebe* and the *Cherub* were standing down toward us, not over a mile away, with gun ports open and little doubt showing of their intent.

Even as I looked I heard Wilmer speak to the captain.

"I can hear their drums, sir! They're beating to quarters!"

Porter glanced up at the sky, as if to estimate the time. I judged it to be about four in the afternoon. Then his eyes swung toward the shore.

"It seems we'll have an audience, gentlemen," he remarked dryly.

All eyes came about and followed the direction of his glance. The heights inshore were crowded with spectators.

"Very well, Mr. Wilmer," Porter said, "never mind that top hamper now. Get the men down from aloft and send them to quarters. Get a spring on that cable, if you can, so as to bring our broadside to bear. We'll give them a fight at least— if we can get them in range!"

"Aye, aye, sir!" Wilmer responded.

"Oh God, for a battery of long eighteens!" I heard Porter grumble beneath his breath as the first turned to execute his commands. "I warned 'em, Lord! Didn't I warn 'em? Yet they insisted on carronades!"

The pipes were shrilling now, and in another instant the drums began to rattle. As if by magic, every loose and movable piece of equipment that might constitute a hazard if struck by a shot disappeared into the hold, if it could be stowed there, over the side if it could not. Gun tubs, displaced when the squall struck, were replaced, sand buckets fetched and matches lighted. Loggerheads found their way to waiting braziers, and the powder monkeys scampered for the magazines.

"Get those flags up!" Porter roared.

Ensigns broke on the breeze at the gaff and mizzentruck, while FREE TRADE AND SAILORS' RIGHTS whipped defiantly from the fore. A puff of white smoke bloomed at the *Phoebe's* bow in response, and the boom of her gun came down the wind to us as the ball splashed close aboard. I suddenly remembered my own duties and scuttled below.

8

THE GLOOM that hung over the cockpit as I came down to it was more than the gloom of the dim battle lanterns. The stench held in it something more than just that of the gurgling bilge under our feet. I think there was not a one of us there below but had a grim premonition that this day was to be like no other we had known. I had no need to enforce the rule of silence. We were each busy with his own thoughts, and mine, oddly enough, were not for Patience nor for the home I might never see, but rather for the ship—this ship that I had known so long and so bitterly and whose career had paced mine so closely during these last years. My prayer for her now was that she might not be too sorely hurt, but that, at the same time, she might make a brave showing!

Above us we heard the thud of a shot, fired by the *Phoebe,* and braced ourself for the crash of a hit. But it did not come. More thuds followed, but this time there were hits—crashes on the deck above, and a cry, and a sort of a long, shivering sigh.

"All right, gentlemen!" I said. "Get ready!"

As if in answer, there were more thuds and almost instantaneous crashes above in response.

"Why don't we answer?" someone cried in the cockpit's gloom.

"Because we doubtless can't fetch our guns to bear," I replied tartly. "Mind your work, gentlemen. Those aloft will tend to theirs!"

Steps sounded on the deck above and a gunner's mate was passed down to us with a mangled forearm.

"Hoffman!" I snapped.

My first mate leaped forward, as the boys passed the man to the table and strapped him down. The man screamed desperately as someone brushed his raw flesh.

"Gently, lad," I told him. "You're lucky! First down and only an arm to lose. There'll be others worse, and you'll have extra grog. We'll have it off you in no time, and then you'll have naught to do but lie snug and listen."

It was part of the surgeon's small talk, intended to encourage a man, though I confess when I thought about it I wondered how it could do more than frighten him. He rolled his eyes at me.

Another thud and a crash punctuated his reply.

"Cut!" I said.

Hoffman spit in the palm of his hand to wet the blade of his scalpel, so that it would not draw against the dry skin, and expertly sliced the arm, through muscle and ligament, round and about above the elbow to the bone. The man gasped, and one of the boys thrust the bit between his teeth and held it tight. I snatched up the saw and began to cut through the great bone between shoulder and elbow. The man rolled his head and screamed slobberingly, spitting out the bit. Blood spurted in a pumping stream across Hoffman's apron.

"Damn you, boy!" I cried. "Get that bit back! D'you want the whole ship afraid of us? You, Jack! Hold still now! 'Twill be over in a moment!"

The only reply was a strangled groan. An instant later the mangled limb fell and was caught by one of the boys and tossed into the sand bucket. At the same instant the ship rolled to the crash of our own broadside, shying skittishly sidewise like a nervous colt.

"Iron!" I snapped, and the hot loggerhead was placed in my hand. The smell of burned powder drifted down from the deck above and mingled with the stench of burned flesh as I applied the cautery. Overhead I heard more cries and more crashes, the rumble of something heavy being dragged over the deck, then the steps that warned of more wounded coming.

"Pitch!" I snapped, and the brush was laid in my grasp. I tarred the bloody stump, and at the same time the boy at the man's head removed the wooden bit from between his teeth. The fellow screamed.

"Quiet!" I growled. "We'll have worse than you here before the day's done! Give him a tot of rum."

"Let me up!" the man sobbed. "Let me up where I can help!"

"Put him in the corner!" I ordered, and turned to meet the next man coming down. Above we were firing now in earnest, though all the sound seemed to come from astern. The ship jerked and trembled, so that it was impossible to distinguish our own shot from the enemy's. The boys helped the passers hand down a man pierced with a splinter as large around as my wrist that passed in at his right abdomen and came out through the fleshy part of his left buttock. I passed him across to the surgeon's mates and admonished them.

"Cut that billet off short, so he can rest easy. Don't try to remove it. Give him a drink of rum if he'll take it. Poor devil! 'Tis all he'll ever have use for!"

I turned back to the passers. I was growing accustomed to the continual thunder and rolling, so that I scarcely noticed it. The smoke, too, that drifted down from above, sharp and acrid, seemed natural.

"Don't fetch us men like that," I cried up through the thunder. "We can do nothing for them! We'll have little enough room here for the living before much longer!"

"Aye, sir," one of them mumbled in response, handing down a lad with half his face shot away. The boys put him on the table and I whipped out needle and gut from under my collar, where I carried them, but found difficulty handling them, for my fingers were slippery with blood.

"How goes it aloft?" I asked over my shoulder.

The passer behind me helped another man down through the scuttle and lifted him onto the table. His leg, from groin to knee, was torn, but yet not wholly without shape.

"It's bad!" cried the passer. "They've the range on us, and we can't get our broadside to bear but once. Then we couldn't reach 'em. They've shot three springs off the cable. Now we're shootin' the long twelves through the stern ports."

Hoffman glanced up from the lad with the mangled leg.

"We'll save this one," he said.

"Good!" I mumbled, and drew the jagged edges of the face under my hand together and stitched them roughly.

"We're hittin' 'em now, though," the passer added grimly.

"Aye, and they're hitting us," I replied as I heard a crash on the deck above and listened dully to the thud of the ball smashing through the bulkhead.

"Aye!" he agreed grimly.

I finished the lad with the face.

"There you are," I said. " 'Twill do for now. Here, give him some rum and show him room to lie."

The boy tried to say something but could only mumble unintelligibly. I had time neither to answer nor to feel sick, though I wanted to do both. Wounded were coming in fast. Another and another and another was passed down. The narrow quarters filled with smoke and the stench of blood and burned flesh. I kicked at the overflowing bucket of limbs.

"Boy!" I bawled. "Take that up and empty it over the side! Let's have some sand here on the deck."

The sand was spread. The bucket was emptied and returned. I felt like a butcher as I hacked and sawed and sewed and cauterized. My arms were bloody to the shoulders and I felt my face was black. My breeches were wet and my boots soggy with blood, and my shirt was soaked and I tore it off.

Casualties came in a steady stream, some walking, finding their own way, some carried, some fighting still, trying to keep from being brought, until I wondered that there was a man left standing. Those we could we patched up and returned to the fight. Time seemed to stand still around me as I worked.

A new smell crept in with the smoke that poured down the hatchway. Over my shoulder I remarked upon it to the passer.

"Isn't the galley out?" I asked. "That's wood burning."

"We've been three times afire," he snorted. "That's the fourth."

I was no longer conscious of where the shots were striking or of when we fired. Above me all seemed bedlam. No sound could be identified above another. Under my feet the deck seemed more slippery than ever, and once when the ship seemed to roll more heavily than usual I felt liquid course over my instep.

"Sand, here! Sand!" I bawled. "And scoop up some of that blood. We'll be swimming in a moment if it keeps on like this."

"That ain't blood," said a voice in my ear. "That's water. We've been hulled. Can't you hear it running in the hold?"

There was an instant's silence, an instant's lull in the battle above. The ship seemed to be moving, and all hands in the cockpit turned their eyes to me. I laid down my knife and moved to the forward bulkhead and listened.

I could hear it, plain enough, the unmistakable gurgle of water flowing. But above it I could hear, too, the clank of the pumps. I went back to the table and picked up my knife.

"Get these men up into the steerage," I commanded. "They can't lie on the deck here. When the cockpit's cleared let me know, and we'll come up and do our work there."

I cannot say that I was not afraid—only numb. The ship could sink and we would all be caught like rats in a trap down here, and drowned, for all we could do about it. But I was too hoarse and tired to be able to raise my voice or to think of other than that this work must be done. Evidently the fact that I spoke quietly was taken for courage, for the others seemed to take heart, and the surgeons bent once more to their work, while the boys and the passers began lifting the men out.

A man came down for every two that went up, however, and we carried on our bloody work as the water beneath our feet rose to cover our shoes and sloshed about our ankles.

Above decks, too, the battle resumed once more, after its seeming lull, though now it seemed to me that our guns spoke less often, and the rending shock of the enemy's fire came more and more often against us. A hand snatched at my elbow and a voice sounded once more in my ear.

"That's the last here, sir. We're holding 'em in the steerage now, like you said to."

I looked about me and saw that save for myself and the man before me on the table, upon whom I had just finished working, and the passer at my side, the cockpit was empty. Another passer skidded down the ladder, and the two of them laid hold upon the wounded man and boosted him up through the hatchway. I took a last look around. Even the instruments had been taken up without my being aware of it. I snatched down the lantern from its hook and scrambled up after them.

In the steerage there was more light, but, looking at it, I was not sure but what I preferred the cockpit. The place was a shambles. The bulkheads stood splintered in several places where shot had crashed through them, and here and there in the side of the vessel, near the upper deck line above, were other great, jagged, splintered gashes, where other shot had torn through her sides, ripping the stout oak timbers as if they had been mere paper. Through these it was possible, now and again, to catch a glimpse of daylight and clear blue water, even to smell a draft of cool air, but the smoke hung in the 'tween decks like a fog, and when I turned back to see once more to my task I had to grope my way across the rows of the wounded to the long table at which the midshipmen regularly messed, to find my work. I had barely begun again when a shot came crashing through the side and smashed through the bulkhead between me and the wardroom aft. At the same time it seemed to me the smoke grew thicker than ever, and Mr. McKnight came lurching through the gloom, black with powder stains and reeling with exhaustion.

"All hands lay up to the gun deck to fight fire!" he bawled.

Seeing me standing near him in the murk, he seized at my arm.

"Here, you! Up you go! Lay up there!" he shouted.

He stopped abruptly and peered into my face, then laughed almost foolishly.

"Oh, it's you, Doc?" he said. "Well, lay up there, man!

It's all hands that can stand to this work if we don't want to be crisped as well as shot! Up with ye!"

I laid down my knife and followed the rest. The scene that my eyes met there was worse than that in the steerage. Great guns lay uprooted from their carriages and careened upon their sides. There were dead men and the remnants of dead men hanging across their breeches and across their muzzles. Those guns which still stood untouched, however, were not manned, for forward, toward the galley, the deck from side to side was an inferno of flame, a bright orange hell from which the tongues licked, to flick out at us and draw back in a trail of smoke and then lick out once more.

Already two lines of men had formed, passing buckets from hand to hand, up one side full and down the other empty. Even as I took my place in a line, two shots crashed through the sides and tore the stomach out of a man three places ahead of me. A huge splinter off a beam whined the length of the deck, and I heard a man scream in agony as it crashed to a halt.

But there was not time to look around. The buckets kept moving, up one side full and down the other empty.

"We're getting it!" someone forward shouted. "Keep those buckets coming! Christ, wouldn't you think they'd let up long enough for us to put a fire out?"

As if in answer, the ship reeled again under the impact of shot, and again there was the sound of splintering wood in the air all about us.

"Sonsabitches!" I heard someone growl.

It seemed an hour before I heard the shout from forward. "That's got it!"

"It's out, lads! Back to your stations! We're not finished yet!"

Where the flames had been was a blackened and charred mass of burned timber, still smoking, giving off the acrid stench of dead fire to mingle with the sickish odor of blood on the deck underfoot and the smell of burned powder. I longed to climb to the spar deck for a breath of fresh air, but instead I dropped down through the main hatch to the steerage to find a new batch of wounded waiting. Almost reluctantly I picked up my knife and bent over the nearest.

"Mr. Cowell!" I cried.

His leg was splintered at the knee, hanging in shreds below that, and two men sat upon his arms in an effort to hold him down. But his strength was equal to theirs combined. As I bent over him again he wrenched free and struck out at me.

"Damn you!" he sobbed. "I'm not hurt! Look to these others first. They need you more!"

"Get him on the table!" I commanded. "Strap him down. I'll look to each in his turn."

I turned away to attend the next man, lying beside Cowell. As I did so a shot crashed through the side and killed him under my hands.

"Throw him over!" I ordered, straightening, but there was none to carry out the command. The same ball had taken one of the men who had been lifting Cowell, and I could not see another dozen men standing throughout the length of the deck. Seeing nothing better to do, I turned, slipping in the red muck underfoot, and helped the surviving passer get Cowell upon the table and strap him down. After that I moved automatically down and performed the necessary amputation and cautery without assistance. Fortunately he fainted, for I could not have lifted him otherwise. Hoffman and Adner and Montgomery were occupied elsewhere, and half of our boys had been killed. I lifted him from the table and laid him on the deck and turned to lift another when a midshipman slid, sobbing, down the remnant of a ladder.

"We've struck!" he cried. "We've struck, and the bastards won't stop firing!"

I had to look twice before I recognized Mr. Farragut.

"Go away!" I growled. "Can't you see I'm busy?"

"But we've struck!" he moaned. "We've struck!"

I caught him by the arm and snatched up a pannikin of rum. "Drink this!" I ordered.

Without question he tossed it off and gasped.

"There!" I told him. "That will fix you up, mister."

He gulped through his tears, caused half by the rum and half by his emotion.

"I'm sorry, sir!" he squeaked. "I guess I was upset."

I almost smiled at that. Upset indeed!

There came another bellow of gunfire from across the

water, and another splintering crash from above, followed by the whine of iron on metal and a shuddering scream.

The child's lip before me trembled again suddenly.

"But, sir! But, sir! We did strike! And they——"

I reached out and patted his arm.

"Steady!" I said. "Steady, Davie!"

He caught his breath and looked up at me.

"Aye, aye, sir!" he said.

Involuntarily we both braced ourselves for another shot, so regular had the interval between them been these last few moments, but none came.

"They seem to have ceased firing at last," I said.

He stared at me and then cocked his head, as if listening. Along the length of the deck I saw first one and then another, Adner, then Hoffman, then Montgomery, then one by one the boys, stop their work and straighten to stand listening. At the same instant it seemed as if the wounded stopped moaning, held their breaths, waiting. A silence fell upon the ship. From somewhere came a faint drip-drip-dripping sound, whether of blood or of water I could not tell, though I doubted it was the latter. Abruptly a wounded man screamed shrilly, accentuating the silence; making it deeper when he stopped.

Young Farragut stared at me suddenly, as if he had seen me for the first time.

"They've stopped!" he said.

"Aye," I said wearily. "It's ended."

His eyes ran over me.

"You—you're hit, sir!" he said.

I glanced down and saw myself smeared from chest to toe with blood and soot, some fresh and bright, some old and dried. I shook my head.

"What about yourself?" I asked, for there was nearly as much blood on him. "Are you hurt?"

He eyed me evenly.

"No. I was fetching primers when a shell hit and blew someone on top of me."

I gripped his shoulder encouragingly.

"What of the captain?"

"He's not touched," he replied, "except for a splinter that grazed his head. He——"

He stopped abruptly as if he just remembered something.

"He sent me to fetch you," he said. "I forgot for the moment. What will he do to me?"

Now that he had thought of it, I could see that he was more afraid of Porter's wrath than ever he had been during the battle, such was the discipline in which he had been trained. At the same time I realized that the hours we had seemed to stand facing one another had, in reality, been no more than moments.

"Have you not seen me attend to the wounded?" I demanded.

"Wounded?" he said blankly. "But you didn't—you haven't, since I came here—you've talked with me."

"Ah, but yourself, Mr. Farragut," I said. "Don't you recall? A wound of the spirit is as much to be feared as wound of the flesh. Have you forgotten the treatment I offered you?"

He stared at me, completely at a loss, and a sailor who had lost a hand beside us and had been listening chuckled.

"He's right, Davie!" he exclaimed. "God knows your treatment was more healin' than mine!"

Young Farragut glanced from me to the sailor and back again with a look of horror.

"You frighten the lad, man!" I said. "Davie, fetch him a pan of rum, and mind you have a care to his arm!"

"Aye, aye, sir!" the youngster replied, and caught up the pannikin he had but just drunk out of and filled it at the cask. I helped him hold the man's head, so that he might drink it down, and he gave us a smile in gratitude.

"They'll never press me aboard a British man-o'-war again," he managed to grin.

I let him lie back gently as I could, for the drive was now over and a man had time to think.

"You've done your share today," I said, "for the rest of us for the rest of time. I'll do my best for you."

"You've done your best for me, Doc," he said, smiling faintly. "Go look to the others, and if you've a minute to spare later, come back and give me another taste o' that rum."

"I'll do my best," I repeated, and rose to my feet. "Mr. Hoffman, Mr. Adner, Mr. Montgomery! Carry on, gentlemen. I'm summoned aloft. No doubt we'll have help presently."

I nodded and turned to Farragut.

"Very well, Mr. Farragut," I said. "You may lead the way. What is it the captain wants? Or do you know?"

"'Tis Chips," Farragut called back as he scuttled up the ladder. "He—he's wounded, sir."

"Chips!" I exclaimed. That would be Ben.

"Aye, sir," Farragut replied breathlessly. "I'd have said so before, but I—I'm afraid it slipped my mind."

"You mean I took your mind off it, Mr. Farragut," I retorted, determined that he should not blame himself.

"Oh yes, sir!" he exclaimed. "But Chips—well, sir, you know, he went overside to stop the holes, and they shot him away then, right off the scaffold, sir, but only cut the ropes, and we fetched him aboard again. Now he's—he's stopped a bad one, sir, and the captain—sir, the captain—he said, sir —he said that you should be there, sir——"

"Steady, Davie!" I said. "We're almost there! Leave it to me, lad!"

But I knew what he meant. For all our hostility, I think there were few aboard that knew of it. The legend had gone down that Chips and the doctor were old shipmates, and it had been accepted.

"What's happened to him?" I asked as I struggled up the ladder behind him.

"A splinter, sir," he replied over his shoulder.

We came on deck before I could ask further questions, and the captain met us at the head of the ladder.

"You were long enough," he said.

"I have other wounded to attend to!" I put in abruptly, before young Farragut could have a chance to take blame to himself, as I saw he was about to do. "Where is he?"

Porter gave me no more than a startled glance and then nodded toward the wreck of the bulwarks. I turned from them both abruptly and strode to the tangle of gear and cordage that lay huddled against the larboard gangway.

There was a body on it. There was a body on almost every heap of wrecked gear on the ship. But this one moved and clutched at the tangle under it, and heaved up at my approach and lifted a strained face to greet me.

"Well!" he gasped. It was Ben, no mistake about that. "You got here, did you?"

"Easy," I said, "easy!" and dropped to my knees beside him. Out of the corner of my eye I was aware of the *Phoebe* standing by and of two boats dancing across the water toward us. But my main glance was not for that. It was for Ben's wound, for, friend or enemy now, I could have only a surgeon's eye, and what I saw was not encouraging. Farragut had said he had stopped a splinter, but he had not told me what a splinter. The chip of the starboard bulwark was no mere splinter. It was a length of timber as large around as my fist that had pierced him straight across, halfway between hips and shoulder blades, driving from one side to the other. As he lay now, it looked to enter one side and extend from the other, and there was no question of removing it. Everything that had lain in its way was smashed, and when he forced himself up on his fists to look at me it was only the upper part of him that moved. Yet his eyes were bright and clear and intelligent, for all they were full of pain. They were full of mockery as well.

"So you came, Tom?" he demanded. "You came to see if you could save old Ben once again, eh?"

I was aware of the captain close behind me.

"I came because I was sent for," I said. "Let's have a look at you."

"Ahhh!" he whispered, dropping his face to the pile of rubble beneath him. "You came to gloat and to jeer. You——"

"I never!" I cried. "Ben, I never——"

I forgot that the captain was standing at my shoulder. It would have made no difference had I remembered. I leaned toward him. He screamed harshly.

"Don't touch me! Don't touch me!"

I looked over my shoulder at Captain Porter.

"I can do nothing for him," I said.

The captain nodded toward him.

"He wants to speak to you," he said quietly.

I turned back. Ben's cheek was pressed against the ropes. His eyes were open and fixed on me. His lips moved. I put my ear close to them and caught their faint whisper.

"I loved her, Tom," he said. "I loved her before you loved her, and she was mine before she was yours."

I stared at him.

"You mean Patience?"

"I mean Selina," he whispered. "I loved her, Tom, and she loved me—once! But we quarreled and—and you know the rest of it! I've been wrong ever since, it seems. C-couldn't get back to going the way I sh-should. Don—don't hold it against me. I—I shouldn've done what I did, but—but—— Pat's a good girl, Tom—you—you——"

He broke off abruptly, as if he had gone to sleep, and I bent down toward him. But he opened his eyes once more and stared up at me.

"Look out for her, Tom!" he said. "She loves you. I've known that always!"

"Ben!" I cried. "Ben!"

He turned me a wan grin.

"Can't save me this time, Tom!" he whispered. "Water's too cold—too far to go! Can't save me, Tom, can't—can't—ca——"

"Ben!" I cried again. "Ben!"

But I knew it was too late. He was gone.

Captain Porter touched me on the shoulder.

"The *Phoebe's* boat is alongside," he said gravely. "Hillyar's sent his surgeon. Will you need help?"

"I'll take all the help I can get, Captain," I said.

His eyes slid past me to the still body.

"He was a good man!" he tried to comfort me.

"He was a scoundrel, sir," I replied. "But he might have been a good man but for me. Where he's gone now it won't matter!"

He gave me a startled glance but gave me no opportunity to explain, even had I a mind to.

"Very well!" he exclaimed. "Will you come with me to meet the *Phoebe's* people?"

9

I SHALL NOT go into the details of the surrender, nor of the events and negotiations that followed. As if he had not tried to blast us out of a neutral harbor and succeeded in the most dastardly British fashion—I must be pardoned if I am bitter, for I have seen my comrades slain—Captain Hillyar offered us every aid which humanity could devise.

Our dead—Ben among them—were given a decent burial. Our wounded were placed aboard the *Essex Junior.* Our prisoners, except myself and my mates, were held aboard the hulk of the *Essex,* which was towed into port. As surgeon, I held perhaps the most privileged position among the captives, and it was doubtless on this account that I was called upon to sit in upon the conferences between Captain Hillyar and Captain Porter concerning the disposal of the *Essex* and her people.

These took place in the governor's palace ashore, and left no doubt as to which side that gentleman favored. Perhaps he looked to Britain for greater aid against the Spanish Crown. As to that I could not say. However, he was not friendly to us. He could not understand why Hillyar did not throw us all in chains and drag us off to England. But this was not the end that had been envisioned for us. Ultimately we were, prisoners and wounded alike, sent aboard the *Essex Junior,* under our own Captain Porter, for passage as cartel to the United States. It was my fortune to be in the cabin of the *Junior* when Captain Hillyar came aboard to give his instructions to Captain Porter. As the officer charged with the health of all on board, it was required that I be on hand. Captain Porter greeted Captain Hillyar smartly as he was piped over the side.

"Happy to have you aboard, Captain," he said grimly. "As you see, we are all ready."

Hillyar nodded, not missing the innuendo.

"Thank you, Captain," he replied. "But believe me, you do not understand the situation. I wish I could make you see it!"

"Understand it?" cried Porter. "I would God that I could! I must say that I feel your humanity to us since our surrender, but there is much that I cannot find compatible with honor in our capture. You may be sure that I shall lose no chance to speak of your kindness to us. At the same time I shall make sure that my report carries all the details of our action, including your attack upon me in neutral waters, sir!"

Hillyar looked pained.

"My dear Porter," he exclaimed, "you have no idea of the orders under which I was sent in search of you!"

"They might have been Byng's," Porter replied, "or the penalty the same. It would not excuse the breach of honor!"

After that I was surprised that we were permitted to sail, but we were. Nor was any provision for our safe passage withheld.

We left Valparaiso late in April and came off Sandy Hook in July, which was as quick a passage as anyone could wish. To this point our letter of cartel had been honored by all whom we had met, but now, with home in sight, it seemed, there was to be a different story to tell. Off the Hook we fell in with H.B.M. Frigate *Saturn,* one of the ships blockading New York.

At her signal we hove to while she put a boat aboard us. Our credentials were handed over to the boarding officer, a jaunty, almost effeminately gentlemanly young lieutenant, who accepted them and carried them back to the *Saturn* for Captain Nash's inspection. Within half an hour he was back with a bundle of late newspapers—significantly enough, printed in New York and Boston—a basket of fruit, and the captain's compliments. We might, he told us, proceed upon our course at will.

Thereafter the *Saturn* and the *Essex Junior* stood together upon the same tack, reaching northeast, in order to be able to come about and run down the wind into the channel. About dusk, however, the *Saturn* fired a gun and again broke out the signal to heave to, which we did, wondering, but at worst supposing, that Captain Nash had some message for us to carry in. Within a few moments the same young lieutenant came over the side, and at his heels swarmed an armed boat's crew. Captain Porter, who had been prepared to meet him courteously at the gangway, stared at them in furious amazement.

"What is the meaning of this, sir?" he demanded hotly.

The lieutenant flushed in some confusion.

"Your pardon, sir," he apologized. "Captain Nash has ordered me to search your holds—a matter not clearly covered in Captain Hillyar's letter."

Captain Porter turned purple.

"Preposterous!" he cried. "This ship is a cartel, sir, proceeding under agreement between officers and gentlemen, and in accordance with the rules of war! There is nothing in our holds for which we might be detained."

The lieutenant looked even more uncomfortable.

"I can't help that, sir," he replied abjectly. "I have my orders and must carry them out." And then, as if to excuse himself and soothe our captain's ruffled feelings, he added: "To tell you the truth, sir, Captain Nash is inclined to doubt Captain Hillyar's authority to make such an arrangement."

"What?" roared Porter. "Does Captain Nash hope that by searching my holds he may find something he may use as an excuse for breaking the agreement?"

The lieutenant shook his head bewilderedly.

"As to that, sir," he replied, "I cannot say. But I have my orders. May I search your holds?"

"I cannot stop you!" Porter replied coldly, and the lieutenant turned about and ordered his men below.

Throughout the search Captain Porter paced the quarterdeck in a black rage. When at length the lieutenant came back on deck, having found nothing, Porter turned on him.

"Tell your captain, sir," he ordered, "that I am now thoroughly convinced that British officers have no regard for one another's honor! Tell him that his act cancels my parole. Tell him that either I proceed at once, without further hindrance, or that I consider myself an ordinary prisoner privileged to escape at my first opportunity. Take my sword, sir!"

With a gesture almost of defiance he jerked off the belt upon which the weapon was hung and held it out to the officer. The lieutenant started back.

"Oh no, sir!" he cried. "I couldn't think of that. I'm sure, sir, that Captain Nash——"

"Be damned to Captain Nash!" roared Porter. "Carry my message to him, and leave none of it out, since you are too much craven to carry my sword! Tell him what I have said and get to hell off my ship!"

The lieutenant went while our own men on our deck hid their smiles behind their hands and silently applauded. In a few moments the boat was back with a different officer. He did not trouble to board.

"Captain Nash's regrets," he hailed. "You will lie to dur-

ing the night. He will decide what action to take with regard
to you in the morning."

"Tell your commanding officer," Porter replied, coldly furious, "that he has been informed of my intentions and may act
accordingly."

Since this was all the answer he got, the officer presently returned to the *Saturn,* which a moment later opened her gun
ports and ran out her guns and ran down to windward of us,
so close that had she wished she might have blown us out of
the water with a single broadside. There she lay throughout
the night.

As soon as it was dark, Porter summoned all of the remaining officers—Downes, McKnight, Cowell—with but one leg
—Shaw, Haddiway, Farragut, Bashiell, Hoffman, Montgomery, Adner, Tittermary, Odenheimer, and myself—to his
cabin. There he faced us with a sober countenance.

"Gentlemen," he said, "we lie thirty miles off Long Island.
I mean to leave the ship in the longboat, taking with me as
many of you as I can, and row that distance."

We stared at him, startled.

"That's risky, isn't it, Captain?" Downes asked quietly.

Porter smiled at him without humor.

"Have you ever known me to shrink from risk?" he asked.

Downes shook his head but made no other answer.

"Before I announce my selection, and before I go, however,"
Porter continued, speaking to the rest of us, "I want you all
to know my reason for attempting this—so that those who
must be left behind will not think themselves willfully abandoned."

A murmur of protest arose.

"No, no, gentlemen!" he cried. "I have every reason to
know that I can count upon your loyalty. But I insist that you
understand mine! As you know, we have made a rapid passage from Valparaiso. We have made that passage at that
speed for a reason. If word of our loss can be carried swiftly
to Washington, there may yet be time to fit out an expedition
to intercept the *Phoebe* on her way home and perhaps to recapture the *Essex.* Had our cartel been honored, it would have
been simple to carry this word immediately. Even now we
would have been entering New York. But now there is no

knowing what delays we may encounter. The news must reach Washington without loss of time, and I am convinced that those dunderheads in the department will only be convinced of the loss of our ship and the urgency of this opportunity by my own appearance. Do you understand that, gentlemen?"

"Of course, sir!"

"It goes without saying!"

"Who else should go?"

"It is your duty, sir!"

Our replies were flung at him in a chorus, protesting not that he should choose himself to go, but rather than he should doubt our approval of his decision.

He smiled at us gratefully.

"Thank you, gentlemen! Since that is understood, I will pick certain of you to accompany me. The rest of you will draw lots to fill in the places left vacant in the boat."

John Cowell glanced bitterly at his empty trouser leg.

"You'd better count me out, Captain," he said. "I'd be no good to you in an adventure of this kind."

Porter glanced at him proudly.

"I planned to leave you in command, John," he replied.

Cowell's head came up sharply.

"I hope I shall merit your trust in me, sir!" he said.

"You will, John!" Porter said. "You will! Now then, the rest of you. Mr. Downes, Mr. Shaw, and Dr. Tisdall will come with me. I will need you to substantiate my report. There will be room for three more. If you will draw, gentlemen——"

"Leave me out of the draw," cried Farragut abruptly.

"And me!" put in Odenheimer.

"And——" Tittermary started to say.

But Porter's bellow cut him short.

"No one will be left out of the draw," he barked, "except Mr. Cowell, who will command. The rest of you will all take your chance with the rest of us."

Put so—even had it not had the ring of an order—there could be no denying it. McKnight, Hoffman, and Tittermary drew the lucky straws, and the rest were almost happily congratulatory. Captain Porter turned to Cowell.

"Very well, John," he said. "I hope the dog doesn't hold you, but if he does, you may be sure I'll turn heaven and hell to see you all free! Will you see to a boat's crew for us? Let the men volunteer or draw lots—any way you see fit—but emphasize that this is not without danger. If we are caught it will go hard with us."

"Aye, aye, sir!" said Cowell, and started to swing away upon his crutches, but Porter stopped him.

"One moment, John!" he said. "While these others are present, I want you to give this message to Captain Nash in the morning: Tell him that now that I understand a British gentleman's honor, I know it to be worthless as between one another; that my boat is armed, and that if he overtakes me he must be prepared to fight! If we meet, it must be as enemies!"

"Aye, aye, sir!" replied Cowell impassively. As for the rest of us, we cheered.

We got away in the dawn, while the wind was yet light, and we were nearly a gunshot from the *Saturn* before our escape was noticed. Immediately upon sighting us she fired three shots at us. But we were a poor target, bobbing and dancing as we were, and the first two shots were short, while the third was wide by a matter of feet. Thereafter she cracked on sail and bore down for us, but before she could come up to us we ran into fog, and for a long time afterward we could hear her driving this way and that, the leadsmen in her chains singing out the soundings, and the occasional cry of her lookout as he thought he had discovered us. But gradually these sounds dropped farther and farther astern, until they died out entirely, and we rowed in silence, through the soft gray mist. We dared to hope that while the *Saturn* sought us in the mists the *Junior* had found opportunity to escape, and so, indeed, it proved.

All day we rowed, and toward dusk reached Fire Island Inlet. Two hours later we landed at Babylon, on Long Island, where we were first seized and roughly handled until the captain produced his commission to prove that he was not a British officer, when the local inhabitants loaded our boat upon a wagon and escorted us in triumph, through the night, to Brooklyn. Thence we were carried across the river, like heroes instead of the bedraggled, escaped prisoners that we were, to New York.

I cannot dip too deeply into the events of the weeks that followed. I accompanied Captain Porter to Washington, though every instinct within me tugged in the opposite direction. There our reports were heard gravely and courteously forgotten. Soon afterward the captain was placed in command of a battery on the Potomac, for the British were cruising Chesapeake Bay as they pleased and there were fears for the capital.

I had my own fears, it must be admitted, lest this threat force a delay in my northward journey. But either I was regarded as dispensable or my earnestness softened the secretary's heart, for just as I thought it most unlikely, I was granted leave, with orders to report at the Navy Yard in Boston at the expiration of it. It was in consequence of this that I missed the attack upon Washington, for I was on the road at the time. But I must confess that I did not let the news delay me. Rather I rode the faster, fearing lest orders to return should overtake me. I reached Boston in six days from Washington, and paused there only long enough to sup. It was long past dark when I finally came to Salem.

It did not occur to me to stop at the tavern and wait until morning before calling on Patience. I was here. I had news—not happy news, perhaps, but nonetheless word which must be carried. I left my mount at the posting stable and borrowed the stableboy's brush to remove some of the stains of travel from my coat, and set out.

The night was warm and the stars were bright, though there was no moon. The trees that overhung the streets were in full leaf and quiet, for there was no air stirring from the sea, and war seemed far away. The lights that shone from the windows of the houses that I passed gleamed yellow upon green lawns, and the few folk that I met nodded to me in respectable fashion, though I could see, where it was light enough to see, that they were wondering who I might be. In those few rods that I walked I could not help remembering the smell of the desert, the sound of the wind in the palms, the light of the moon on the snowy peaks of the Andes, the crash of gunfire at sea, and the roar of the storm off the Horn. Salem was a far cry from Tripoli or the Galápagos, from Nukuhiva, from Batavia, from Valparaiso, yet it held something of each of them, for its ships had been in all of them, and there was scarcely a home here but had some memory of these and other places. Under my heels the cobbles of Derby Street rang sharp in the night air and the Hackett house bulked white in the darkness. Up from the harbor came the tang of the mud flats at low tide, and the loom of the warehouses and the spider masts and yards of the ships at anchor beyond were outlined dimly against the sky.

I turned the corner and climbed the hill, and the white fence of the Nowell house showed ghostly in the shadow of the tall trees. My steps made no sound here, for there were no cobbles on the street, no bricks on the walk. There was a light in the window, golden and warm and welcoming. I pushed in at the gate and went through the garden, fragrant with the scent of the late summer stock. I felt a sense of peace and contentment. I'm home, I thought, home at last! At the door I paused, only an instant, and then knocked.